I0730426

PLANE GEOMETRY
WITH ANSWER KEY

This edition published 2024
by Living Book Press

Copyright © Living Book Press, 2024

ISBN: 978-1-76153-842-1 (hardcover)
          978-1-76153-804-9 (softcover)

Based on the 1917 edition with answer key
published by Charles E, Merrill Company.

All rights reserved. No part of this publication may be reproduced, stored in a retrieval system, or transmitted in any other form or means – electronic, mechanical, photocopying, recording or otherwise, without the prior permission of the copyright owner and the publisher or as provided by Australian law.

A catalogue record for this book is available from the National Library of Australia

PLANE GEOMETERY

WITH ANSWER KEY

BY

FLETCHER DURRELL, P.D.

HEAD OF MATHEMATICAL DEPARTMENT,
THE LAWRENCEVILLE SCHOOL

AND

E. E. ARNOLD, M.A.

SUPERINTENDENT, THE PUBLIC SCHOOLS OF
THE PELHAMS, NEW YORK,
FORMERLY SPECIALIST IN MATHEMATICS, THE
UNIVERSITY OF THE STATE OF NEW YORK

PREFACE

THE main object in writing the present book has been to produce a text in plane geometry which the average high school class can be fairly asked to cover in one year; which omits none of the essential theorems and, at the same time, embodies certain important improvements in the teaching of the subject; and which initiates the student into the subject in a natural manner, and arouses and sustains his interest in the facts and applications of geometry.

The outstanding features of the book are as follows:

I. *A reduction in subject matter.* The list of propositions used corresponds closely to the Harvard Syllabus, and the number of propositions has been reduced by about one fourth, as compared with those customarily included. The book, moreover, taken as a whole, covers the recommendations of the Committee of Fifteen of the National Education Association and hence exactly meets the requirements of the College Entrance Examination Board.

II. *Improvements in the organization of material.* In this respect, special attention is called to

1. The introduction, which furnishes a natural approach to geometry by informal treatment and by use of facts known to the student.

2. The construction work in exercise groups 1–6. These exercises familiarize the pupil with the use and value of the straightedge, compasses, and protractor, and give him a self-active interest in the subject.

3. The simplified, pedagogical order of arrangement of the first fifteen propositions of Book One, which have special value as an introduction to demonstrative work in geometry. No

one of these propositions should prove a stumbling block to
the average pupil. The authors are confident that the arrangement of propositions in the remainder of the book will be
found equally satisfactory.

4. The arrangement of the proofs as steps and reasons in
parallel columns. This is a help in cultivating the logical
faculty in the pupil and is an important aid to the teacher
in inspecting and correcting written work.

5. The steps in proofs for which pupils must supply reasons.
This aims to make the pupil independent of the book, fosters a
spirit of original thinking, and develops mathematical intuition.

6. The theory of limits has been used only in informal ways
in accordance with the recommendations of the Committee of
Fifteen.

7. Every construction figure contains all the necessary construction lines.

III. *Improvements in the methods of teaching pupils to solve
original exercises.*

1. The most valuable of these is the improved method of
analysis, presented in § 173 (p. 90). This method is so stated
that it may be utilized much earlier if the teacher wishes.

2. The group method of solving originals, which formed so
successful a feature of Dr. Durell's earlier Geometry, has been
retained and improved, as by the insertion of introductory and
simpler groups throughout the text.

IV. *The development of practical applications and of efficiency
values of geometry.*

1. The treatment of the practical applications has been simplified. Whenever the correlation is close and when these
applications clarify or promote interest, they have been inserted
in the text in such a way as to give them the maximum effect.

2. Emphasis is placed on the efficiency values of theorems
and principles.

As a whole, the object of the book has been to make the
teaching, study, and later use of geometry as efficient as possible in relation to present conditions.

CONTENTS

SYMBOLS AND ABBREVIATIONS

\+ *plus*, or *increased by*.

\− *minus*, or *diminished by*.

× *multiplied by*.

÷ *divided by*.

= *equals; is* (or *are*) *equal to*.

$\stackrel{m}{=}$ *is measured by*.

> *is* (or *are*) *greater than*.

< *is* (or *are*) *less than*.

~ *is* (or *are*) *similar to*.

∴ *therefore*.

⊥ *perpendicular, perpendicular to,* or *is perpendicular to*.

⊥s *perpendiculars*.

‖ *parallel*, or *is parallel to*.

∠, ∠s *angle, angles*.

△, △s *triangle, triangles*.

▱, ▱s *parallelogram, parallelograms*.

⊙, ⊙s *circle, circles*.

⌒ (as in $\overset{\frown}{AB}$) *arc*.

Adj., *adjacent*.

Alt., *alternate*.

Ax., *axiom*.

Comp., *complement*.

Constr., *construction*.

Cor., *corollary*.

Corr., *corresponding*.

Def., *definition*.

Ex., *exercise*, or *example*.

Ext., *exterior*.

Fig., *figure*.

Geom., *geometry*.

Hyp., *hypothesis*.

Ident., *identity*.

Ineq., *inequality*.

Int., *interior*.

Opp., *opposite*.

Post., *postulate*.

Prop., *proposition*.

Rt., *right*.

St., *straight*.

Sug., *suggestion*.

Sup., *supplement*.

Q.E.D. *quod erat demonstrandum;* that is, which was to be proved.

Q.E.F. *quod erat faciendum;* that is, which was to be made.

A few other abbreviations and symbols will be introduced and explained later.

PLANE GEOMETRY

DEFINITIONS AND FIRST PRINCIPLES

1. Some geometry which you already know. — From your study of arithmetic, and in other ways, you have already learned some of the most important properties of the straight line, circle, triangle, cube, sphere, and some other similar objects.

You know that a solid has three dimensions, viz.: length, breadth, and thickness. How many dimensions has a surface? A line? A point?

2. Efficient methods of treating geometric objects. — In dealing with objects like those just named in § 1, you have learned that often it is an advantage to use certain methods rather than others.

EXERCISES: GROUP 1

Ex. 1. Obtain the area of the triangle *ABC* by counting the small squares in the triangle (piecing together parts of squares). Also obtain the same area by multiplying the number of linear spaces in the base by the number in the altitude, and taking one half the product. Estimate how many times as much work you did in the first process as in the second.

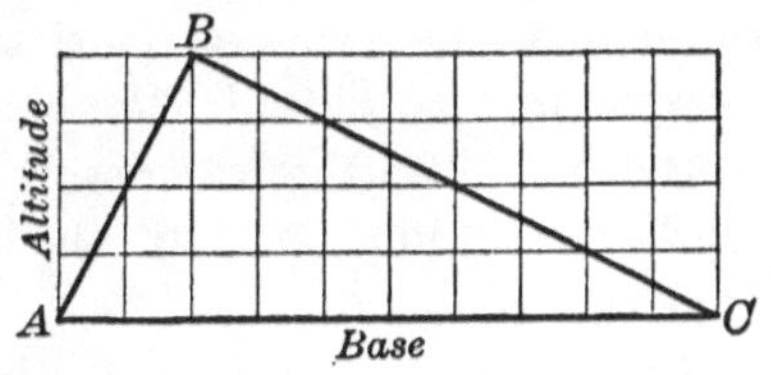

Ex. 2. The number of bushels of wheat in a given bin might be determined by filling a bushel measure with wheat from the bin, time after time, till the wheat is exhausted, and counting the number of times the bushel measure is used. The number of bushels might be determined also by measuring (in feet) the three dimensions of the

7

bin and dividing their product by the number of cubic feet in a bushel ($1\frac{1}{4}$ cu. ft. approx. = 1 bu.). Compare the amount of work in the two processes, assuming that the bin is a large one.

Ex. 3. A given ladder AB is 5 yd. long, and its foot A is 3 yd. distant from the wall BC. In order to determine BC, which is easier: to measure BC, or to use the following computation?

No. yd. in $BC = \sqrt{5^2 - 3^2} = \sqrt{25 - 9} = 4$.

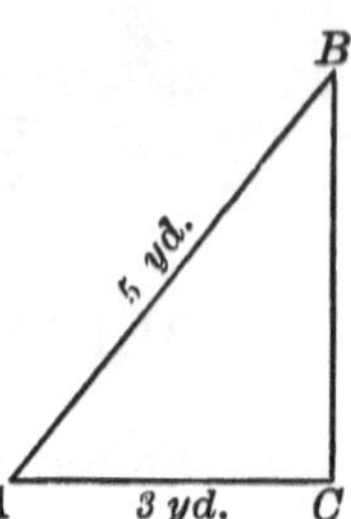

For the following exercises the student should have a ruler with an edge divided into inches and eighths of an inch.

Ex. 4. By folding a piece of paper, form a straight edge. With the aid of this straight edge, draw four lines of unequal length. Estimate the length of each of these lines and then measure the length of each to the nearest $\frac{1}{8}$ inch. Tabulate your results as follows:

LINE	ESTIMATED LENGTH	MEASURED LENGTH	ERROR
1			
2			
3			
4			

Ex. 5. With the paper straight edge, draw a line which you estimate to be twice as long as line 1. Check your estimate by measuring with the ruler the length of the line drawn.

Ex. 6. With the paper straight edge, draw a line and by estimate mark the middle point of the line. Test your estimate by use of your ruler.

Ex. 7. With the straight edge, draw a line which you estimate to be equal to the sum of lines 1 and 2. Check your estimate by use of the ruler.

Ex. 8. With the straight edge, draw a line which you estimate to be equal to the difference between lines 2 and 3. Check by use of the ruler.

Ex. 9. With the straight edge, draw a line and by estimate mark points which divide the line into three equal parts. Check with the ruler.

Ex. 10. In each of the following figures estimate whether the line a is longer or shorter than the line b. Check your estimate with the ruler.

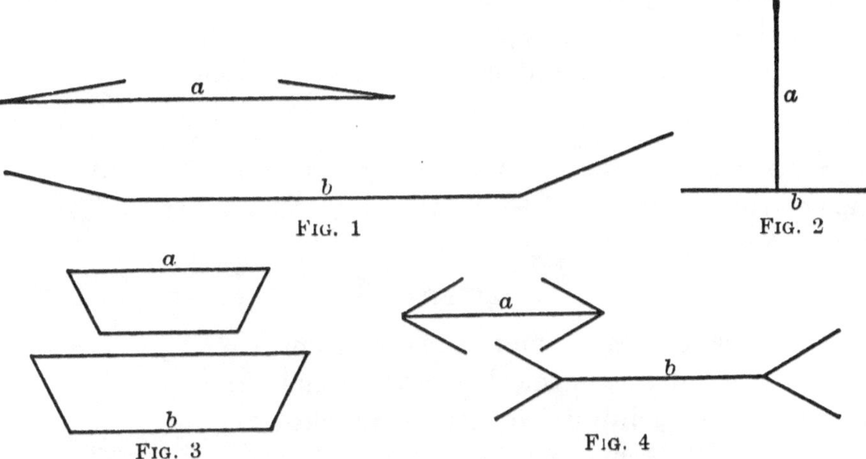

FIG. 1   FIG. 2

FIG. 3   FIG. 4

Ex. 11. Of the geometric objects — the solid, surface, line, and point — which is the boundary of a solid? Of a surface? Of a line?

3. Geometry is the study of the most efficient methods of dealing with the shape, size, and position of objects.

4. The **fundamental geometric objects** are the point, line, surface, and solid. For the present, you understand sufficiently well what these are without studying formal definitions of them.

5. A **geometric figure** is a point, line, surface, or solid, or any combination of these.

Thus, in arithmetic you have already used geometric figures like the following:

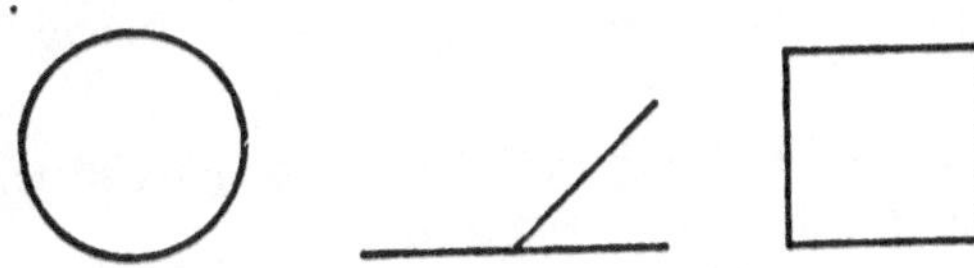

6. The **form** or **shape** of a figure is determined by the relative position of the various parts of the figure.

7. Similar geometric figures are those which have the same *shape*.

Equivalent figures are those which have the same *size*.

Equal or **congruent figures** are those which have the same *shape* and *size*, and can, therefore, be made to coincide.

8. A **point** is represented to the eye by a dot and is named by a letter affixed to the dot; as ·A, called the point A.

LINES

9. Straight line. — You already know that a straight line is the shortest line that can be drawn joining two points, and are familiar with some of the other useful properties of a straight line.

The word "line" is often used instead of "straight line."

10. A **curved line** is a line no portion of which is straight.

The word "curve" is often used for "curved line."

11. A **broken line** is a line made up of different straight lines.

EXERCISES: GROUP 2

Ex. 1. On a sheet of paper or on the blackboard, locate a point and draw two lines through this point.

Ex. 2. Can the lines drawn in Ex. 1 meet at another point?

Ex. 3. Can more than two lines be drawn through the given point? How many?

Ex. 4. On a flat surface can you draw two lines which would not meet, however far the lines are produced?

Ex. 5.   On a flat surface, if you can, draw three lines, no two of which will meet on being produced.

Ex. 6.   On a flat surface, how many lines can be drawn so that they will not meet?

Ex. 7.   If a line is drawn on the given surface and meeting one of the lines in Ex. 6, how many of the other lines will it meet if it is extended?

Ex. 8.   On a sheet of paper or on the blackboard, locate two points and draw a line passing through both of these points.

Ex. 9.   Can another line be drawn passing through the two points of Ex. 8?

Ex. 10.   Can more than one curved line be drawn passing through these two points?

Ex. 11.   How many points are required to fix the position of a line?

Ex. 12.   On a piece of paper or on the blackboard, draw a line along the edge of your ruler; then turn the ruler over and fit the same edge to the line.   Will this test the edge of the ruler for straightness?

Ex. 13.   Fold a sheet of paper.   Test the edge of the fold in the same way that you tested the edge of the ruler in Ex. 12.

Ex. 14.   Fit the edge of your ruler to the edge made by the fold of the paper (Ex. 13).   How many points in the two edges must be made to coincide, in order that the two edges shall coincide throughout?

Ex. 15.   Why are two sights necessary for a gun?

Ex. 16.   In order to hold a straight iron rod in a given position, at how many points is it necessary to fasten the rod rigidly?

Ex. 17.   When a farmer wishes to set out three or more apple trees in a straight row, how does he proceed?

Ex. 18.   From a point on a line which is not an end point (as the point O), how many directions are indicated by a line?

Ex. 19.   If one of these directions is east, what is the other direction?

Ex. 20.   Point out two intersecting lines in the room.

Ex. 21.   Point out two lines which would not meet on being produced.

Ex. 22.   Which of the capital letters of the alphabet are formed by straight lines?   Curved lines?   Broken lines?   Curved and straight lines combined?

12. A **rectilinear figure** is a figure composed only of straight lines. A **curvilinear figure** is a figure composed only of curved lines. A **mixtilinear figure** is a figure containing both straight and curved lines.

13. Kinds of straight line. — A straight line may be definite or indefinite in length.

The line of definite length is sometimes termed a **segment** or **sect**.

14. Naming a straight line. — A straight line is named by naming two of its points; as the line AB (a sect), or the line CD (indefinite in length). A segment or sect may also be denoted by a single letter, usually small; as the line a.

15. Parallel lines are lines in a flat surface which will not meet however far they are produced; as the lines PQ and RS.

16. A **circle** is a closed curve all points of which lie in the same flat surface and are equidistant from a point called the **center.**

An **arc** is any portion of a circle; as AB.

A **radius** of a circle is a line drawn from the center to any point on the circle.

17. Compasses are used to draw circles, and also to mark off and compare segments of lines.

EXERCISES: GROUP 3

Ex. 1. Draw a line and denote it by l. Also draw two much shorter lines and denote them by m and p, respectively.

Ex. 2. By use of the compasses, on l mark off a part equal to m

Ex. 3. Construct a line equal to $l - 2p$. To $l - m - p$.

Ex. 4.   Construct a line equal to $l + m - p$.   To $l + p - 2m$.

Ex. 5.   Draw a line and on it mark off three equal segments in succession.

Ex. 6.   Draw a line three times as long as a given line.

Ex. 7.   Draw a circle with a radius of three fourths of an inch.

Ex. 8.   Draw two circles having the same center but different radii.

Ex. 9.   Draw two circles which intersect.

Ex. 10.   Draw two circles which do not intersect.

Ex. 11.   Draw a line, and with each end of the line as a center draw circles which will intersect.

Ex. 12.   In Fig. 1, does one of the circles a, b, c, appear to you to

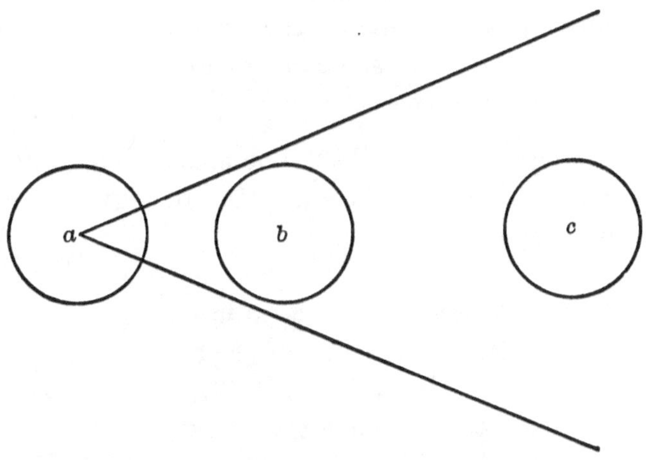

Fig. 1

be larger than the other two? Does one of them appear to be smaller than the others? Determine the relative size of the three circles by use of the compasses.

Ex. 13.   In Fig. 2, which half circle has the greater apparent radius? Determine the relative size of the two half circles by use of the compasses.

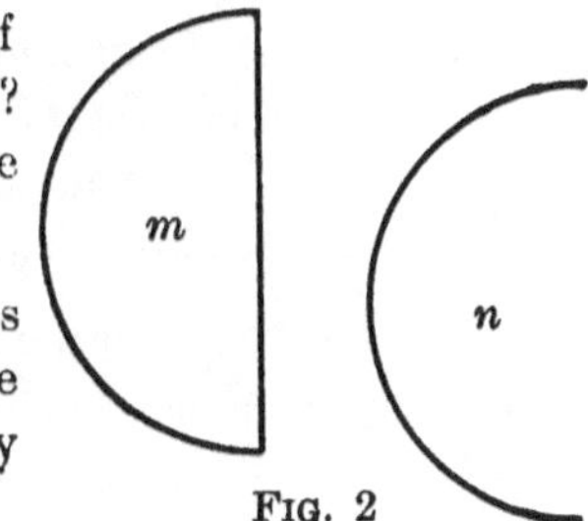

Fig. 2

Ex. 14. By use of the ruler and compasses, copy the following figures:

FIG. 3

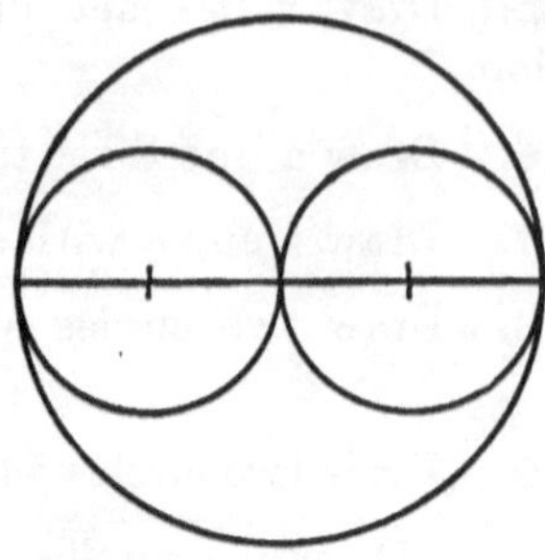

FIG. 4

ANGLES

18. An **angle** is the amount of opening between two straight lines which meet at a point.

The **sides** of an angle are the lines whose intersection forms the angle. The **vertex** of an angle is the point in which the sides intersect.

19. Naming an angle. — (1) The most convenient way of naming an angle is to place a letter or figure inside the angle and near the vertex; as the angle a.

(2) The most precise way is to use three letters: one for a point on each side of the angle, with the letter at the vertex between these two letters; as the angle ABC.

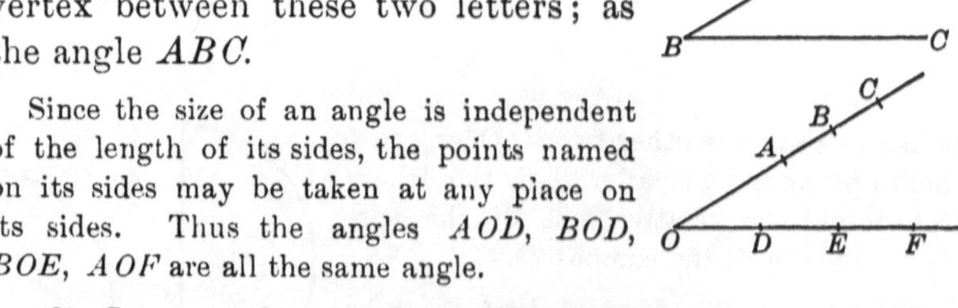

Since the size of an angle is independent of the length of its sides, the points named on its sides may be taken at any place on its sides. Thus the angles AOD, BOD, BOE, AOF are all the same angle.

(3) In case there is but one angle at a given vertex, the letter at the vertex alone may be used to denote the angle; as the angle O in the last figure.

20. Unit of angle. — The customary unit of angle is the **degree** (°). If a circle is divided into 360 equal parts, and the ends of one of these parts are joined with the center by two straight lines, the angle formed at the center is 1°.

21. A **protractor** is a convenient instrument for measuring angles. It is a half circle with its rim divided into 180 equal parts, called **degrees of arc**. The center of the half circle is indicated by a dot or dash (see the mark at *B*).

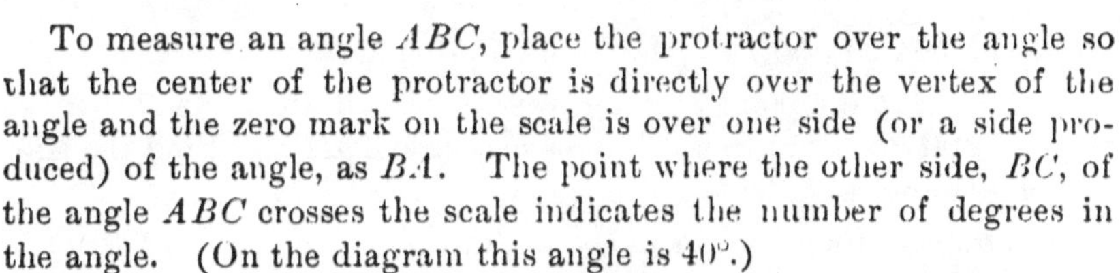

To measure an angle *ABC*, place the protractor over the angle so that the center of the protractor is directly over the vertex of the angle and the zero mark on the scale is over one side (or a side produced) of the angle, as *BA*. The point where the other side, *BC*, of the angle *ABC* crosses the scale indicates the number of degrees in the angle. (On the diagram this angle is 40°.)

22. A **straight angle** is an angle whose sides lie in the same straight line and extend in opposite directions from the vertex; as the angle *AOB*.

23. A **right angle** is one of two equal angles made by one straight line meeting another straight line. Thus, if the line *PQ* meets line *AB* so as to make angle *PQA* equal to angle *PQB*, each of these angles is a right angle. A right angle is half of a straight angle.

24. A **perpendicular** is a line that makes a right angle with a given line. Thus PQ in the figure is perpendicular to BA.

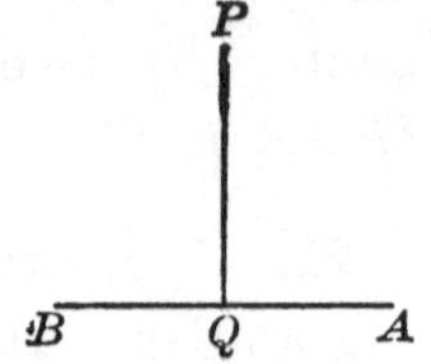

The **foot** of a perpendicular is the point in which the perpendicular meets the line to which it is drawn. Thus Q is the foot of the perpendicular PQ.

EXERCISES: GROUP 4

Ex. 1. Draw two lines that intersect. Measure the four angles formed by the lines. Find the sum of any two of the angles which are adjacent. Find the sum of all four of the angles.

Ex. 2. Draw a figure similar to the adjoining one, but having longer sides to the angles. Measure each of the angles a, b, c, d, and e.

Ex. 3. Compute the number of degrees in $\angle AOD$. In $\angle COF$. In $\angle AOE$.

Ex. 4. Verify your answers to Ex. 3 by measuring the angles named in it.

Ex. 5. By use of the protractor, construct angles of 30°, 60°, 90°, 15°, 45°, 120°, 135°, 180°.

Ex. 6. From a point P in a given line RS, draw a line PM making the $\angle MPS$ equal to 50°. Also measure $\angle MPR$. Find the sum of the two angles.

Ex. 7. On the diagram of Ex. 6, draw PN making $\angle NPR$ equal to 90°. Measure $\angle NPS$.

Ex. 8. Draw an angle of 60°. How many points on the scale of the protractor between the sides of this angle are marked 30°? Hence, how many bisectors can an angle of 60° have?

Ex. 9. How many lines can be drawn which will bisect any given angle?

Ex. 10. Bisect the angles MPS and MPR in Ex. 6. Measure the angle formed by the two lines which bisect these angles.

Ex. 11. Draw any two angles and then construct an angle equal to their sum.

Ex. 12. Draw two unequal angles and then construct an angle equal to their difference.

Ex. 13. How many points on the scale of the protractor are marked 90°?

Ex. 14. How many lines can be drawn perpendicular to a given line at the same point?

25. An **acute angle** is an angle less than a right angle; as the angle AOC.

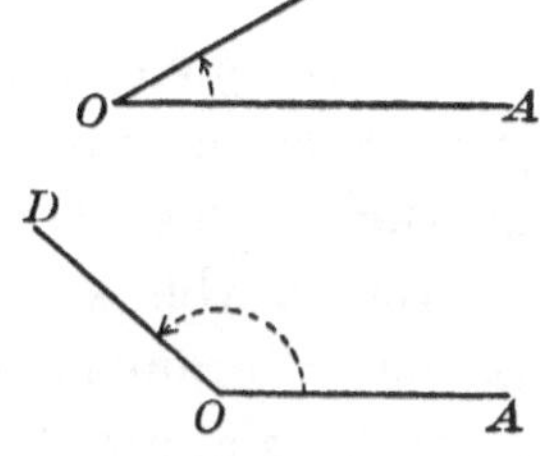

26. An **obtuse angle** is an angle greater than a right angle but less than a straight angle; as angle AOD.

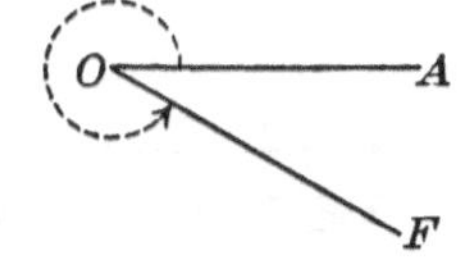

27. A **reflex angle** is an angle greater than a straight angle, but less than two straight angles; as angle AOF.

In this book, angles larger than a straight angle are not considered unless special mention is made of them.

28. An **oblique angle** is an angle which is neither a right angle nor a straight angle. Hence, "oblique angle" is a general term for acute, obtuse, and reflex angles.

An **oblique line** is a line which makes an oblique angle with another given line.

29. Adjacent angles are angles which have a common vertex and a common side between them; as angles AOB and BOC.

30. Vertical angles are angles which have a common vertex and the sides of one angle the prolongations of the sides of the other angle; as the angles AOC and BOD.

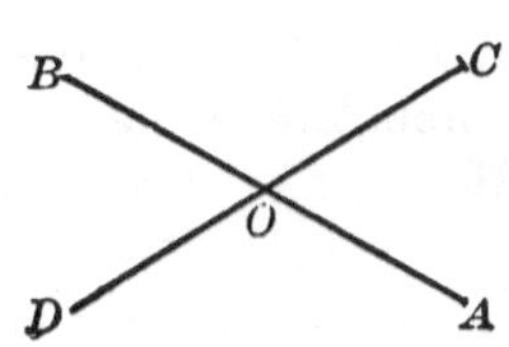

31. Complementary angles are two angles which together equal a right angle ; as the angles *A OP* and *POQ*.

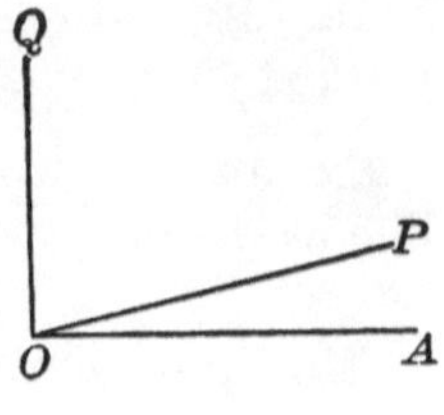

Hence, the **complement of an angle** is the difference between that angle and one right angle.

32. Supplementary angles are two angles which together equal two right angles (or a straight angle), as the angles *A OP* and *POR*.

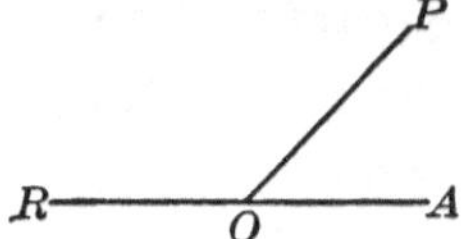

Hence, the **supplement of an angle** is the difference between that angle and a straight angle.

EXERCISES: GROUP 5

Ex. 1. Draw an acute angle. An obtuse angle. A reflex angle.

Ex. 2. Draw two adjacent angles. Two vertical angles.

Ex. 3. How many degrees are there in the complement of an angle of 43°? In its supplement?

Ex. 4. Find the complement of 57° 19′. Of 62° 23′ 43″. Find the supplement of each of these angles.

Ex. 5. Draw an angle of 25°. What is the simplest way to construct the complement of this angle? The supplement?

Ex. 6. Is $\frac{5}{9}$ of a straight angle acute or obtuse?

Ex. 7. The dial of a clock is divided into sixty equal parts. On such a dial, how many degrees are there between two successive points of division?

Ex. 8. Find the number of degrees in the angle made by the hour hand and the minute hand of a clock at two o'clock. At three o'clock. At five o'clock.

Ex. 9. Find the number of degrees in the angle made by the hands of a clock at 1 : 30 o'clock. At 2 : 15. At 8 : 45.

Ex. 10. How long does it take the minute hand of a clock to turn through an angle of 60°? Of 50°? Of 240°? How long does it take the hour hand to turn through these angles?

Ex. 11. When a wheel makes $2\frac{1}{4}$ revolutions, through how many degrees does one of the spokes turn?

Ex. 12. If a spoke of a wheel turns through an angle of 144°, what fraction of a revolution does the wheel make?

Ex. 13. A pair of scales for weighing mail has a pointer moving over one half of a circular dial. If the capacity of the scales is six pounds, through how many degrees would the pointer move to indicate a weight of one pound? Three pounds? Twelve ounces? Eight ounces? One ounce?

Ex. 14. What weight will cause the pointer on the scales to move through an angle of 30°? $11\frac{1}{4}$°? 45°? 70°? 3°? 180°?

Ex. 15. What kind of angle is the supplement of an obtuse angle? Of an acute angle? Of a right angle?

Ex. 16. Draw two angles which have a common side but which are not adjacent.

Ex. 17. Draw two supplementary adjacent angles. Also two supplementary angles that are not adjacent. Also two adjacent angles that are not supplementary.

Ex. 18. The sum of a right angle and an acute angle is what kind of angle? Their difference is what kind of angle?

Ex. 19. The sum of an obtuse angle and a right angle is what kind of angle? Their difference is what kind?

Ex. 20. What kind of angle is equal to its supplement? Greater than its supplement? Less than its supplement?

Ex. 21. The difference between the supplement and the complement of any given angle is what kind of angle?

Ex. 22. What inference can you make in regard to the relative size of the angles r and t from each of the following statements?

(a) $\angle r$ is the comp. of $\angle s$; also $\angle s$ is the comp. of $\angle t$.

(b) $\angle r$ is the sup. of $\angle s$; $\angle s$ is the sup. of $\angle t$.

(c) $\angle r$ is the comp. of $\angle s$; $\angle s$ is the sup. of $\angle t$.

(d) $\angle r$ is the sup. of $\angle s$; $\angle s$ is the comp. of $\angle t$.

Ex. 23. State the inference which can be made in regard to the comparative size of angles m and p in each of the following statements:

(a) The comp. of $\angle m$ is less than the comp. of $\angle p$.

(b) The sup. of $\angle m$ equals the sup. of $\angle p$.

(c) The sup. of $\angle m$ is greater than the sup. of $\angle p$.

(d) The comp. of $\angle m$ equals the sup. of $\angle p$.

Ex. 24. How many degrees are there in an angle which equals twice its complement?

[SUG. Let $\angle AOB$ be a right angle and $\angle AOC$ the required angle.

Let $\qquad\qquad \angle AOC = x.$

Then $\qquad\qquad \angle COB = 90° - x.$

Also $\qquad\qquad x = 2(90° - x), \text{ etc.}]$

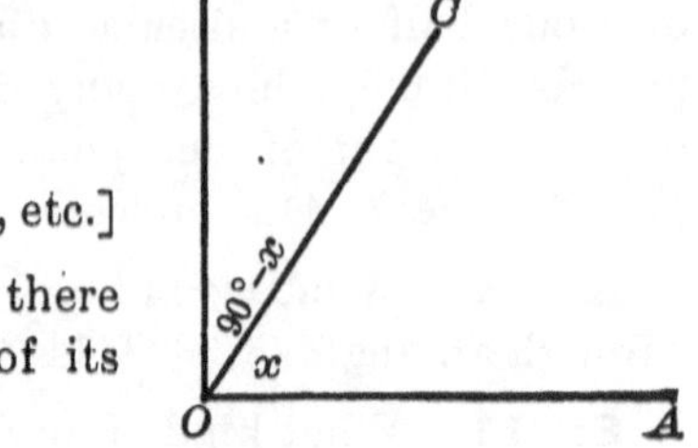

Ex. 25. How many degrees are there in an angle which equals one third of its supplement?

Ex. 26. How many degrees are there in an angle which equals four fifths of its supplement?

Ex. 27. How many degrees are there in an angle which exceeds its complement by 12°? Its supplement by 15° 30′?

Ex. 28. How many degrees are there in the angle whose complement and supplement. are together equal to 126°?

Ex. 29. How many degrees are there in an angle whose supplement equals four times its complement?

Ex. 30. Make up and solve an example similar to Ex. 26. To Ex. 27.

SURFACES

33. A **plane** or **flat surface** is a surface on which a straight edge will fit in any position.

34. A **plane figure** is a figure such that all its points lie in the same plane.

35. A **curved surface** is a surface no part of which is plane.

36. **Plane geometry** is that branch of geometry which treats of plane figures.

37. **Solid geometry** is that branch of geometry which treats of figures in which all points are not in the same plane.

EXERCISES: GROUP 6

Ex. 1. What kind of surface is the floor of a room? The surface of a baseball? The surface of an egg? The surface of a hemisphere?

Ex. 2. Can you apply your ruler to a stovepipe in such a way that every point of the edge will be in contact with the pipe? Will the ruler be in contact throughout its length when applied to the pipe in any direction?

Ex. 3. Can you apply your ruler to a ball in such a way that the entire edge of the ruler will be in contact with the surface of the ball?

Ex. 4. If you should make a tennis court, how could you, by use of a plank with a straight edge, test the surface of the court so as to make sure that it was flat?

Ex. 5. If two points of a straight line are on a flat surface, will the whole line lie on the surface?

Ex. 6. Mention four flat surfaces.

Ex. 7. Mention four surfaces which are not flat.

PRIMARY RELATIONS OF GEOMETRIC MAGNITUDES; AXIOMS

38. Certain **primary relations of geometric objects** have already been given in the definitions used for geometric objects. We now proceed to investigate the relations of geometric magnitudes more generally and systematically.

39. An **axiom** is a truth accepted as requiring no demonstration.

40. Two kinds of axioms are used in geometry:

1. **General axioms,** or axioms which apply to other kinds of quantity as well as to geometric magnitudes; for instance, to numbers, forces, masses.

2. **Geometric axioms,** or axioms which apply to geometric magnitudes alone.

41. The **general axioms** may be stated as follows:

AXIOM 1. *Things which are equal to the same thing, or to equal things, are equal to each other.*

Axiom 2. *If equals are added to equals, the sums are equal.*

Axiom 3. *If equals are subtracted from equals, the remainders are equal.*

Axiom 4. *Doubles of equals are equal; or, in general, if equals are multiplied by equals, the products are equal.*

Axiom 5. *Halves of equals are equal; or, in general, if equals are divided by equals, the quotients are equal.*

Axiom 6. *Like powers or like roots of equals are equal.*

Axiom 7. *The whole is equal to the sum of its parts.*

Axiom 8. *The whole is greater than any of its parts.*

Axiom 9. *A quantity may be substituted for its equal in any process.*

42. Axioms as fundamental instruments of efficiency. — The axioms given above seem so obvious that the student at first is not likely to realize their value. This value may be illustrated as follows:

If the distance from Washington to Philadelphia is known, and also the distance from Philadelphia to New York, the distance from Washington to New York may be obtained by adding together the two distances named; for, by Axiom 7, the whole is equal to the sum of its parts. Thus the labor of actually measuring the distance from Washington to New York is saved.

Again, if the height of a boy in Paris is measured, and the height of a boy in New York is also measured, and the result of the two measurements is the same, we know that the boys are of the same height, without the labor and cost of bringing the boys together and comparing their heights directly; for, by Axiom 1, things which are equal to the same thing are equal to each other.

Thus the general axioms are to be considered not merely as fundamental equivalences, but also as fundamental instruments of efficiency. For many purposes, the latter point of view is more important than the former.

43. The **geometric axioms** may be stated as follows:

GEOMETRIC AXIOM 1. *Through two given points only one straight line can be passed.*

GEOMETRIC AXIOM 2. *A geometric figure may be freely moved in space without any change in form or size.*

This axiom is equivalent to regarding space as *uniform;* that is, as having the same properties in all its parts.

GEOMETRIC AXIOM 3. *Through a given point one straight line and only one can be drawn parallel to another given straight line.*

GEOMETRIC AXIOM 4.   By § 7, *geometric figures which coincide are equal.*

44. Efficiency value of the geometric axioms. — The efficiency value of the first geometric axiom is illustrated by the fact that it enables us to shrink to two points a straight line that is unlimited in length.   By the second axiom, the knowledge which we have of one geometric object may be transferred to another like object, however widely separated in space.   The value of the third axiom lies partly in the inclusion or limitation which it gives, and partly in the power of transfer.

45. A **postulate** in geometry is a construction of a geometric figure which, without proof, is admitted as possible.

46. The **postulates of geometry** may be stated as follows:

POSTULATE 1. *Through or between any two points, a straight line may be drawn.*

POSTULATE 2. *A straight line may be extended indefinitely, or it may be limited at any point.*

POSTULATE 3. *A circle may be described about any given point as center, and with any given radius.*

These postulates limit the student to the use of the straight-edged ruler and the compasses in constructing figures in geometry. One of the objects of the study of geometry is to discover what geometric figures can be constructed by a combination of the elementary constructions allowed in the postulates; that is, by the use of the two simplest drawing instruments.

47. Logical postulates. — Besides the postulates which are used in the actual construction of figures, there are certain other postulates which are used only in the processes of reasoning. Thus, for purposes of reasoning, a given angle may be regarded as divided into any convenient number of equal parts. Whether it is possible actually thus to divide this angle on paper by use of the ruler and compasses, is another question.

EXERCISES: GROUP 7

Ex. 1. In the figure measure AB; then measure BC. Now find AC without measuring it. What axiom have you used?

Ex. 2. If $\angle AOB = 60°$, $\angle BOC = 80°$, and $\angle COD = 130°$, find $\triangle AOC$ and BOD (reflex) without measuring them. What axiom have you used?

Ex. 3. The following is a numerical illustration of the meaning of Ax. 2:

$$\begin{array}{r} 7 = 7 \\ +\,2 = +\,2 \\ \hline 9 = 9 \end{array}$$

Give a similar illustration of the meaning of Ax. 3.

Ex. 4. Give an illustration of the meaning of Ax. 4. Of Ax. 5.

Ex. 5. Illustrate the meaning of Ax. 6.

Ex. 6. If $AB = EF$,
$AD = 3\,AB$,
and $EH = 3\,EF$,
what axiom justifies us in saying that $AD = EH$?

Ex. 7. If $LM = NO$, what axiom justifies us in saying that $LN = MO$?

Ex. 8. By use of a diagram similiar to that used in Ex. 7, give an illustration of Ax. 3.

Ex. 9. Give an illustration of the utility of Ax. 1 similar to that given in § 42.

Ex. 10. Give an illustration of the utility of Ax. 7.

State the axiom used in making each of the following inferences:

Ex. 11. If $a = b$ and $b = c$, then $a = c$.

Ex. 12. If $a = b$ and $c = d$, then $a + c = b + d$.

Ex. 13. If $a + b = c$ and $b = d$, then $a + d = c$.

Ex. 14. Fold a piece of paper of irregular outline so as to form a right angle by the creases. What geometric principles have you used?

DEMONSTRATION OF GEOMETRIC RELATIONS

48. **A geometric proof,** or **demonstration,** is a course of reasoning by which a relation between geometric objects is established.

49. **A geometric theorem** is a statement of a truth concerning geometric objects which requires demonstration.

Ex. The sum of the angles of a triangle equals two right angles.

50. **A geometric problem** is a statement of the construction of a geometric figure, which is required to be made.

Ex. On a given line, to construct a triangle containing three equal angles.

51. **A proposition** is a general term for either a theorem or a problem. Thus, propositions are subdivided into two classes: (1) Theorems; (2) Problems.

52. **Immediate inference** is of two kinds:

1. Changing the point of view in a given statement.

Thus the statement, "Two straight lines drawn through two given points must coincide," may be changed to "Two straight lines cannot inclose a space."

2. Reasoning which involves but a single step.

Ex. All straight angles are equal;
∴ All right angles are equal. (Ax. 5.)

53. A **corollary** is a truth obtained by immediate inference from another truth just stated or proved, or one whose proof may be stated briefly and informally.

54. Hypothesis and conclusion. — A proposition consists of two parts :

(1) The **hypothesis,** or that which is known or granted.

(2) The **conclusion,** or that which is to be proved or constructed.

Thus, in the proposition, "If two straight lines are perpendicular to the same line, they are parallel," the hypothesis is, that two given lines are perpendicular to another given line. The conclusion is, that the two given lines are parallel.

PROPERTIES OF LINES INFERRED IMMEDIATELY

55. *If two straight lines have two points in common, the lines coincide throughout their whole extent.* (§ 5, Geom. Ax. 1.)

Hence, *two straight lines can intersect in but one point.*

56. *If two straight lines coincide in part, they coincide throughout.*

57. *Only one straight line can be drawn connecting two given points.*

58. *Two straight lines cannot inclose a surface.*

59. *A given straight line (sect) can be divided into two equal parts at but one point.*

For (by Ax. 5) halves of equals (or of the same thing) are equal.

PROPERTIES OF ANGLES INFERRED IMMEDIATELY

60. *All straight angles are equal.*

61. *A given angle can be divided into two equal angles by but one line.*

For (by Ax. 5) halves of the same magnitude are equal.

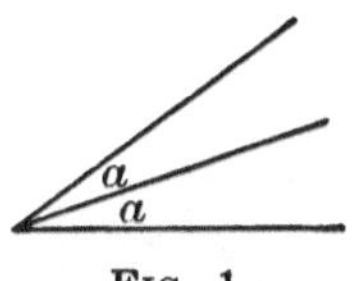

FIG. 1

62. Hence, *at a given point in a straight line but one perpendicular can be erected to the line.*

63. *All right angles are equal.*

For all straight angles are equal (§ 60) and halves of equals are equal. (Ax. 5.)

64. *The sum of the two adjacent angles formed by one straight line meeting another straight line equals two right angles.*

For the angles formed are supplementary adjacent angles. (§§ 29, 32.)

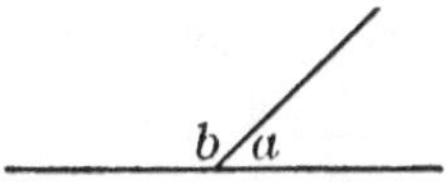

FIG. 2

65. *If two adjacent angles are together equal to a straight angle (or two right angles), their exterior sides form a straight line.*

For their exterior sides form a straight angle, and hence must lie in a straight line. (§ 22.)

66. *The complements of the same angle or of two equal angles are equal.* (§ 63 and Ax. 3.) *The supplements of the same angle or of two equal angles are equal.* (§ 60, Ax. 3.)

67. *The sum of all the angles about a point equals four right angles.*

Thus,

$$\angle a + \angle b + \angle c + \angle d + \angle e = 4 \text{ rt. } \angle\text{s.}$$

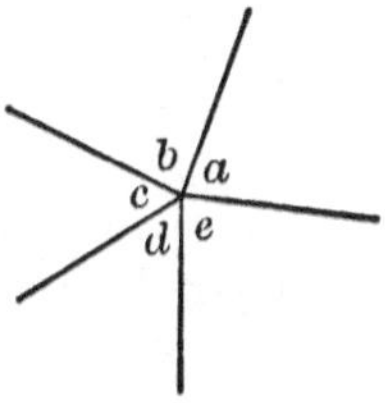

FIG. 3

68. *The sum of all the angles about a point on the same side of a straight line passing through the point equals two right angles.*

Thus, $\angle p + \angle q + \angle r = 2$ rt. $\angle$s.

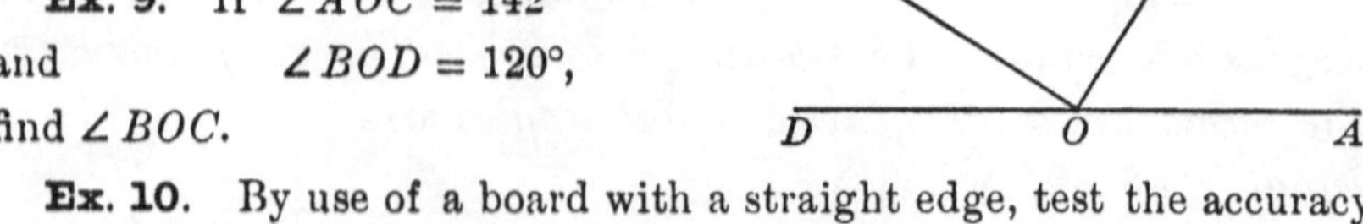

Fig. 4

EXERCISES: GROUP 8

Ex. 1. How many different straight lines are determined by three points not in the same straight line?

Ex. 2. How many straight lines are determined by four points in a plane, no three of the points being in the same straight line?

Ex. 3. How many times more efficient is a point in Ex. 2 than in Ex. 1? That is, what is the ratio of the number of lines that a point helps us to locate in the two examples?

Ex. 4. How many curved lines may be drawn through two given points? How many broken lines? How many straight lines?

Ex. 5. If, in Fig. 3, p. 27, $\angle$s a, b, c, $d = 40°$, $50°$, $60°$, $70°$, respectively, find $\angle e$.

Ex. 6. If, in Fig. 4 above, the lines forming $\angle q$ are perpendicular to each other and $\angle p = 47°$, find the other angles of the figure.

Ex. 7. By use of a protractor, find the number of degrees in $\angle a$ of Fig. 2 on page 27. Find $\angle b$ without measuring it. Now measure $\angle b$ and compare the two results.

Ex. 8. Given $QB \perp AB$, $PB \perp BC$, and $\angle ABC = 130°$; find the other angles of the figure.

Ex. 9. If $\angle AOC = 142°$ and $\angle BOD = 120°$, find $\angle BOC$.

Ex. 10. By use of a board with a straight edge, test the accuracy of the outside angle of a carpenter's square by the method indicated in the diagram. How, then, would you test the accuracy of the inside angle of the square? What geometric principle have you used in each case?

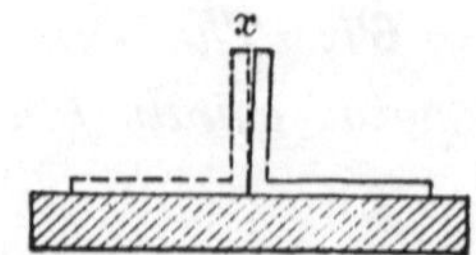

BOOK ONE

RECTILINEAR FIGURES

PROPOSITION I. THEOREM

69. *If two straight lines intersect each other, the vertical angles are equal.*

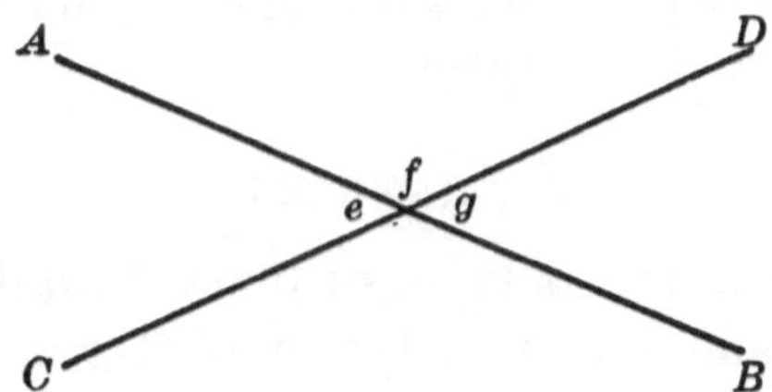

Given the straight lines AB and CD intersecting and forming the vertical $\angle$s e and g.

To prove $\angle e = \angle g$.

STEPS	REASONS
Proof. 1. $\angle e$ is the supplement of $\angle f$.	1. The supplement of an $\angle$ is the difference between the $\angle$ and a straight $\angle$. (§ 32.)
2. $\angle g$ is the supplement of $\angle f$.	2. Same reason as 1.
3. $\therefore \angle e = \angle g$.	3. The supplements of equal $\angle$s are equal. (§ 66.)　Q E D.

Ex. 1. If one of the angles formed by two intersecting lines is 70°, find the other three angles of intersection without measuring them.

Ex. 2. If three straight lines intersect at a point, how many of the angles formed must be measured in order to determine all the angles?

Three straight lines intersect at a point O and form the angles p, q, r, s, t, x, as indicated on the diagram.

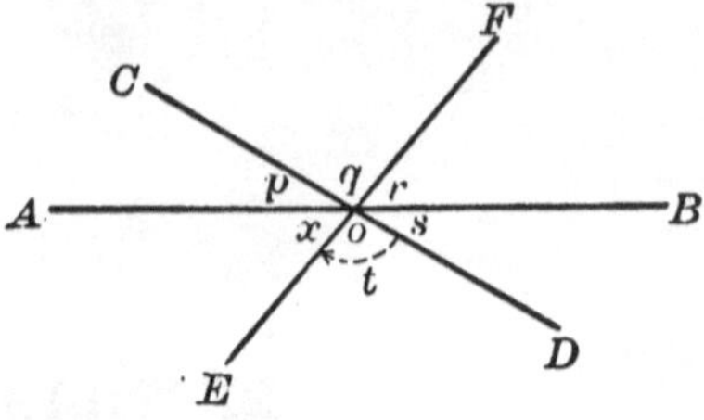

Ex. 3. If $\angle q = 110°$ and $\angle r = 47°$, find $\angle AOD$.

Ex. 4. If $\angle AOF = 153°$ and $\angle t = 107°$, find $\angle s$.

Ex. 5. If $\angle AOF = 153°$ and $\angle COB = 165°$, find $\angle t$.

Ex. 6. If $\angle p = 24°$ and $\angle q = 3 \angle r$, find $\angle x$.

Ex. 7. Construct a diagram in which four straight lines intersect at a point, and make up and solve three examples concerning the diagram, similar to Exs. 3–6 above.

TRIANGLES

70. A **polygon** is a portion of plane bounded by straight lines. A **triangle** is a polygon of three sides; as the triangle ABC.

71. The **sides** of a triangle are the lines which bound it. The **perimeter** of a triangle is the sum of the sides. The **angles** of a triangle are the angles formed by the sides; as the angles A, B, and

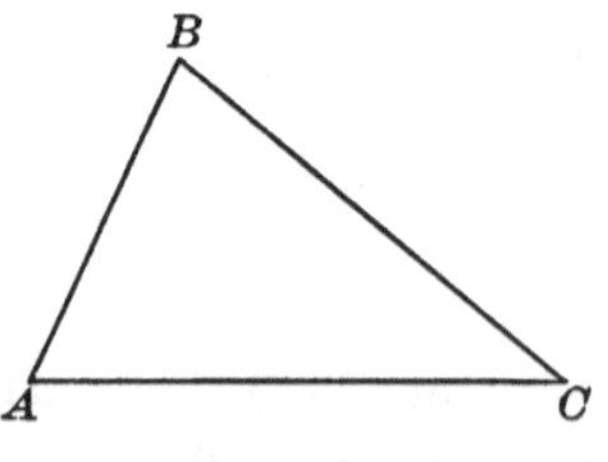

C. The **vertices** of a triangle are the vertices of the angles of the triangle.

72. An **exterior angle** of a triangle is an angle formed by one side and by another side produced; as the angle BCD. With reference to the angle BCD, the angles A and B are termed the **opposite interior angles**.

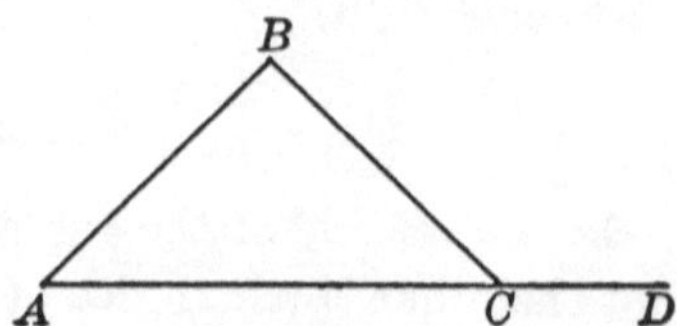

73. Classification of triangles according to relative length of the sides. — A **scalene triangle** is a triangle in which no two sides are equal. An **isosceles triangle** is one in which two sides are equal. An **equilateral triangle** is one in which all three sides are equal.

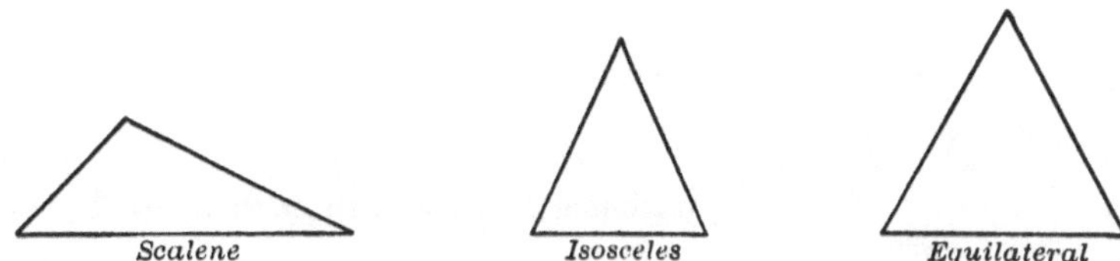

74. Classification of triangles as to their angles. — A **right triangle** is a triangle *one* of whose angles is a right angle. An **obtuse triangle** is a triangle *one* of whose angles is an obtuse angle. An **acute triangle** is a triangle *all* of whose angles are acute angles. An **equiangular triangle** is one in which all the angles are equal.

75. The **base** of a triangle is the side upon which the triangle is supposed to stand; as AB. The angle opposite the base is called the **vertex angle**; as angle ACB. The **vertex** of a triangle is the vertex of the vertex angle of the triangle.

The **altitude of a triangle** is the perpendicular from the vertex to the base or to the base extended; as CD.

76. In an **isosceles** triangle, the **legs** are the equal sides, and the **base** is the remaining side.

77. In a **right** triangle, the **hypotenuse** is the side opposite the right angle, and the **legs** are the sides adjacent to the right angle.

78. Property of a triangle immediately inferred. *The sum of any two sides of a triangle is greater than the third side.* For a straight line is the shortest line joining two points. (§ 9.)

Ex. 1. Point out the hypothesis and conclusion in Prop. I (p. 29).

Ex. 2. Find the angle whose complement is 18°. The angle whose supplement is 76°.

Ex. 3. If the complement of an angle is known, what is the shortest way of finding the supplement of the angle? If the supplement is known, what is the shortest way of finding the complement?

Ex. 4. In 25 minutes, how many degrees does the minute hand of a clock travel? The hour hand?

Ex. 5. Draw three straight lines so that they shall intersect in three points. In two points. In one point.

Ex. 6. If one side of an equilateral triangle is 4 inches, what is its perimeter?

Ex. 7. Is it possible to form a triangle whose sides are 6, 9, and 17 inches? Try to do this with the compasses and ruler.

Ex. 8. Is it possible to form a triangle in which one side is 10 inches and the difference of the other two sides is 12 inches?

Ex. 9. On a given line as base, by exact use of ruler and compasses, construct an equilateral triangle.

Ex. 10. In Ex. 10 on p. 28, prove that the error in the outside angle of the carpenter's square, if there is any, equals one half the angle (x) between the outside lines of the square as shown in the diagram. (Denote the error by e and show that $e + e = x$.)

This principle is important because it is essentially the method used in correcting the axis of a telescope, and hence in correcting instruments of which the telescope is a part, such as various surveying and astronomical instruments.

PROPOSITION II. THEOREM

79. *If two triangles have two sides and the included angle of one respectively equal to two sides and the included angle of the other, the triangles are equal.*

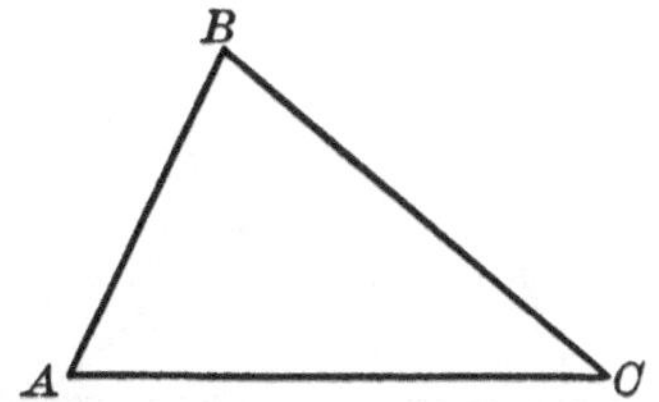 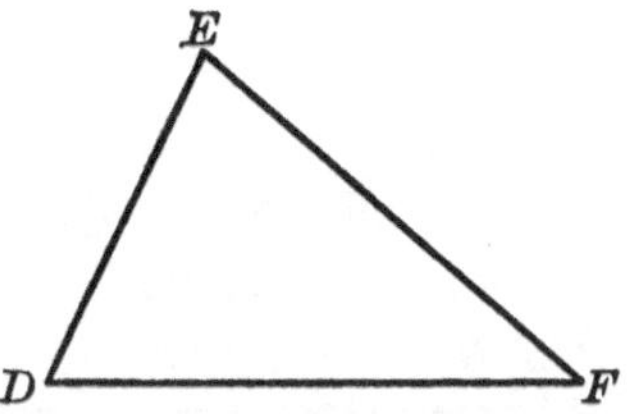

Given the $\triangle\ ABC$ and DEF in which $AB = DE$, $AC = DF$, and $\angle A = \angle D$.

To prove $\triangle\ ABC = \triangle\ DEF$.

STEPS	REASONS
Proof. 1. Place the $\triangle ABC$ upon the $\triangle DEF$ so that line AC coincides with its equal DF, and AB falls on the same side of DF as DE.	1. A geometric object may be freely moved in space without any change in size or form. (Geom. Ax. 2, § 43.)
2. Then the line AB will take the direction of DE.	2. $\angle A = \angle D$ by hypothesis.
3. The point B will fall on E.	3. $AB = DE$ by hypothesis.
4. Line BC will coincide with EF.	4. Only one straight line can be drawn connecting two points. (§ 57.)
5. $\triangle ABC = \triangle DEF$.	5. Geometric figures which coincide are equal. (Geom. Ax. 4, § 43.) Q.E.D.

Ex. If $\angle A$, B, and $C = 60°, 70°, 50°$, $AB = 16$, $AC = 19$, $BC = 18$; also $\angle D = 60°$, $DE = 16$, $DF = 19$: find $\angle E$ and F and side EF without measuring them.

PROPOSITION III. THEOREM

80. *If two triangles have a side and the two adjoining angles of one respectively equal to a side and the two adjoining angles of the other, the triangles are equal.*

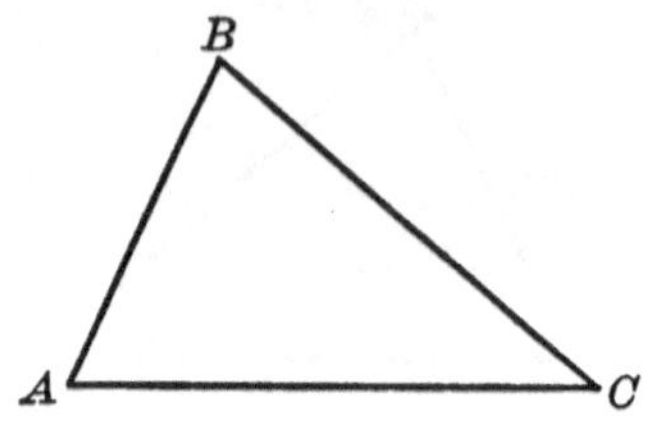 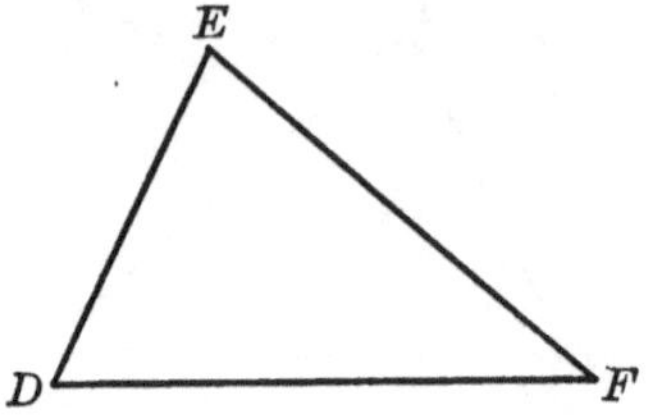

Given the △ *ABC* and *DEF* in which ∠ *A* = ∠ *D*, ∠ *C* = ∠ *F*, and *AC* = *DF*.

To prove   △ *ABC* = △ *DEF*.

STEPS	REASONS
Proof. 1. Place the △ *ABC* upon the △ *DEF* so that *AC* coincides with its equal *DF*, and the point *B* falls on the same side of *DF* as *E*.	1. A geometric object may be freely moved in space without any change in size or form. (Geom. Ax. 2, § 43.)
2. Then *AB* will take the direction of *DE*.	2. ∠ *A* = ∠ *D* by hypothesis.
3. Also *CB* will take the direction of *FE*.	3. ∠ *C* = ∠ *F* by hypothesis.
4. Point *B* will fall on *E*.	4. Two straight lines can intersect in but one point. (§ 55.)
5. △ *ABC* = △ *DEF*.	5. Geometric figures which coincide are equal. (Geom. Ax. 4, § 43.) Q.E.D.

81. Abbreviations. — In quoting § 79, to save time and labor. the abbreviation *s. ∠ s.* may be used as a substitute for the theorem. Similarly, the abbreviation $\angle$ s. $\angle$ may be used as a substitute for the theorem of § 80.

Ex. 1. If $\angle\!\!\!\angle\ A, B, C = 65°, 55°, 60°, AB = 24, AC = 18, BC = 27$; also $\angle\!\!\!\angle\ D, F = 65°, 60°$, and $DF = 18$; find DE, EF, and $\angle E$.

Ex. 2. By exact use of ruler and compasses, construct a scalene triangle whose sides are 2, 3, and 4 times a given line.

EXERCISES: GROUP 9

Ex. 1. **Given** lines AB and CD bisecting each other at O. **Prove** $\triangle ACO = \triangle OBD$.

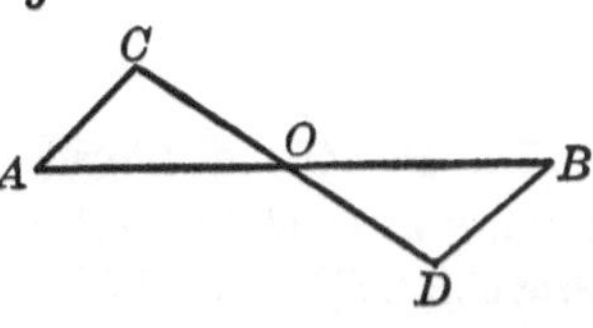

Ex. 2. **Given** $\angle ABC$ bisected by BD, P any point in BD, $BQ = BR$. **Prove** $\triangle BPQ = \triangle BRP$.

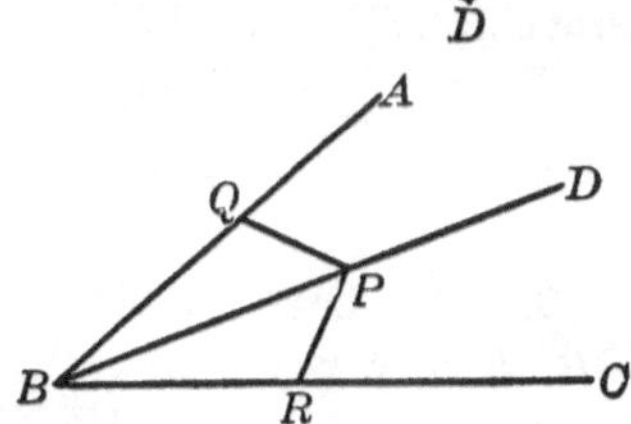

Ex. 3. **Given** O the midpoint of the line AB, $CO \perp AB$, P any point in CO. **Prove** $\triangle APO = \triangle OPB$.

Ex. 4. Construct a figure and give proof for the following:

Given $\triangle ABC$ with side $AB =$ side BC; AB produced through B to Q, and CB produced through B to P; also $PB = BQ$. Prove $\triangle APB = \triangle BQC$.

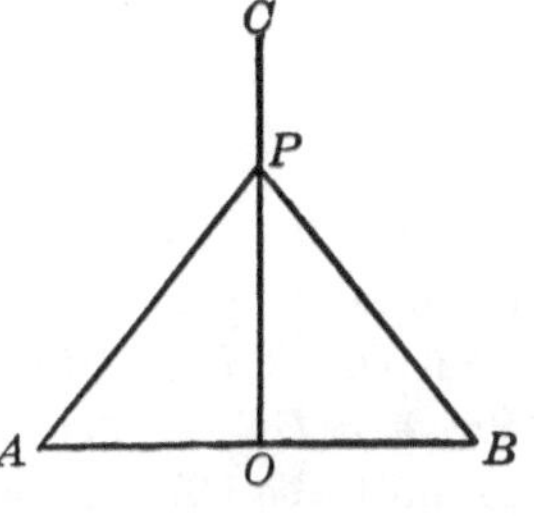

Ex. 5. To determine the distance AB, take a convenient position C, measure AC, and produce AC to F making $CF = AC$. Also measure BC and produce BC to D making $CD = BC$. Prove $\triangle DCF = \triangle ACB$. If we now measure DF and find it to be 217 yd., how long is AB?

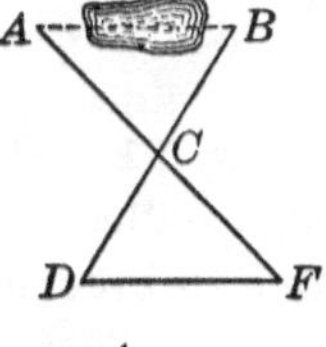

Ex. 6. **Given** $\angle AOB$ bisected by OC, P any point in OC, line $QPR \perp OC$. **Prove** $\triangle QOP = \triangle POR$.

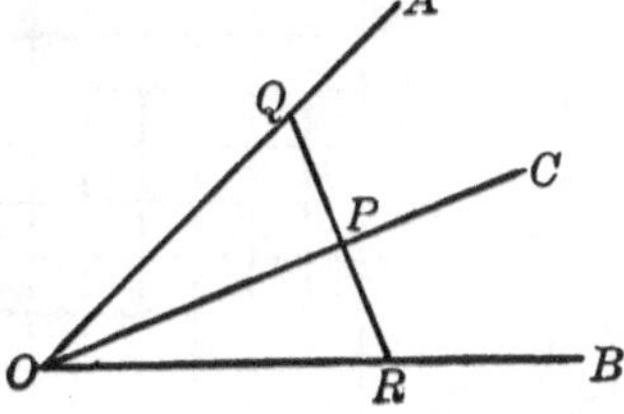

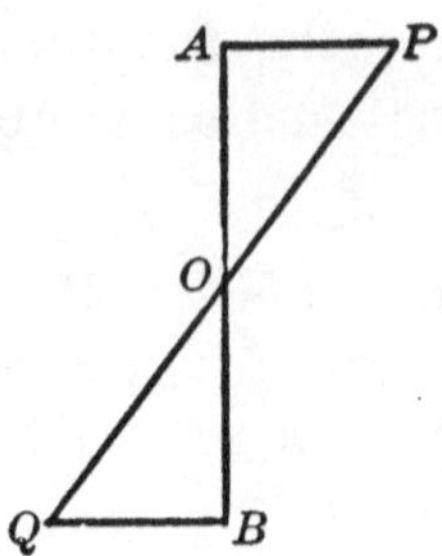

Ex. 7. Given O the midpoint of line AB, POQ any straight line through point O, AP and $QB \perp AB$. **Prove** $\triangle OAP = \triangle OQB$.

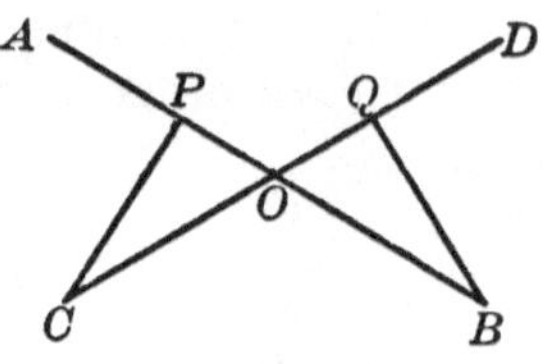

Ex. 8. Given lines AB and CD intersecting at O, $OP = OQ$, $PC \perp AB$, $QB \perp CD$. **Prove** $\triangle CPO = \triangle OQB$.

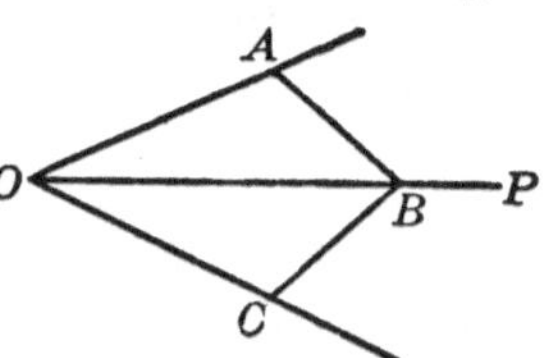

Ex. 9. Given $\angle AOC$ bisected by line OP, B any point in OP, $\angle ABP = \angle CBP$. **Prove** $\triangle OAB = \triangle OCB$.

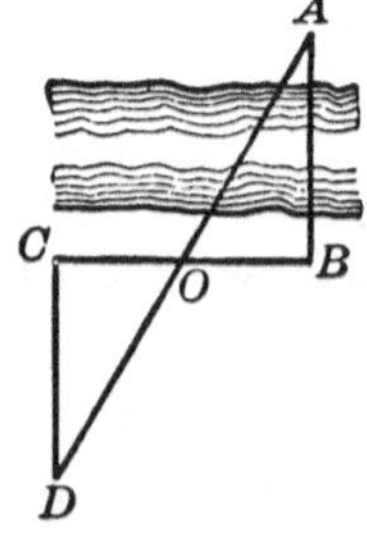

Ex. 10. To measure the distance AB, construct the line BC perpendicular to AB, making $CO = OB$. Construct $CD \perp CB$ and meeting AO produced at D. Prove $\triangle DCO = \triangle OAB$. If CD is measured and found to be 137 yd., how long is AB?

Ex. 11. By the aid of squared paper, construct the following design, called a meander line. (It is an advantage to draw the meander line in blue or red pencil or in red ink.)

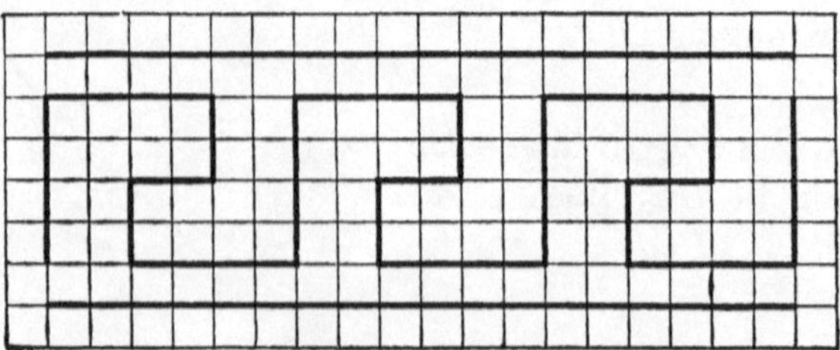

Proposition IV. Theorem

82. *In an isosceles triangle, the angles opposite the equal sides are equal.*

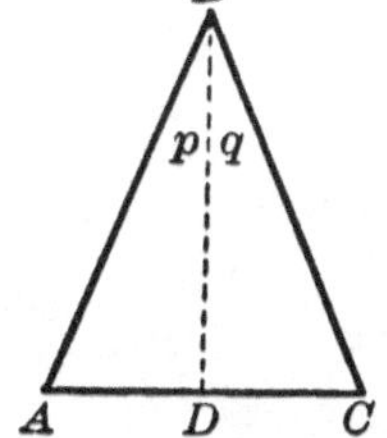

Given the isosceles $\triangle ABC$ in which $AB = BC$.

To prove $\angle A = \angle C$.

STEPS	REASONS
Proof. 1. Let BD be drawn so as to bisect $\angle ABC$ and meet AC in D.	1. A given $\angle$ can be divided into two equal parts by but one line. (§§ 61, 47.)
2. Then in the $\triangle ABD$ and DBC, $\qquad AB = BC$.	2. Hypothesis.
3. $\qquad BD = BD$.	3. Identity.
4. $\qquad \angle p = \angle q$.	4. Construction.
5. $\therefore \triangle ABD = \triangle CBD$.	5. If two $\triangle$ have two sides and the included $\angle$ of one respectively equal to two sides and the included $\angle$ of the other, the $\triangle$ are equal (or s. $\angle$ s.). (§ 79.)
6. $\qquad \angle A = \angle C$.	6. Corr. $\angle$s of equal $\triangle$.

Q.E.D.

Ex. 1. In the diagram of Prop. IV, if $AB = 10$ in., $BC = 10$ in., and $\angle A = 67°$, how do we find the number of degrees in $\angle C$ without measuring the angle?

Ex. 2. Draw a triangle the foot of whose altitude is on the base produced.

Ex. 3. Draw a triangle whose altitude coincides with one side.

Proposition V. Theorem

83. *If two triangles have three sides of one respectively equal to the three sides of the other, the triangles are equal.*

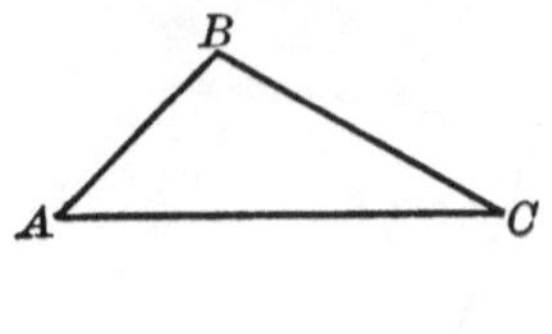
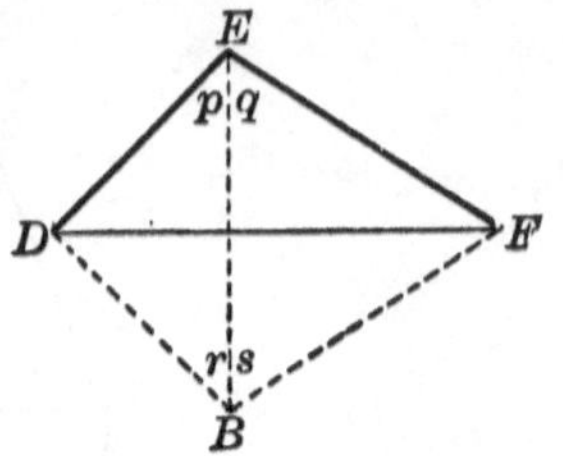

Given the △ *ABC* and *DEF* in which *AB = DE*, *BC = EF*, and *AC = DF*.

To prove   △ *ABC* = △ *DEF*.

Steps	Reasons
Proof. 1. Place △ *ABC* so that the longest side *AC* coincides with its equal *DF* in the △ *DEF*, and the vertex *B* falls on the opposite side of *DF* from *E*.	1. Geom. Ax. 2. (Where only the reference is thus given, the student is to quote in full the principle referred to.)
2. Draw the line *EB*.	2. Postulate 1, § 46.
3. *DE = DB*.	3. Hypothesis.
4. $\angle p = \angle r$.	4. In an isosceles △, the ▵ opposite the equal sides are equal. (§ 82.)
5. In like manner, in the △ *BEF*, $\angle q = \angle s$.	5. Same reasons as for steps 3 and 4.
6. Hence, $\angle p + \angle q = \angle r + \angle s$.	6. If equals are added to equals, the sums are equal. (Ax. 2, § 41.)
7. Or, $\angle DEF = \angle DBF$.	7. The whole is equal to the sum of its parts. (Ax. 7, § 41.)
8. ∴ △ *DBF* or △ *ABC* = △ *DEF*.	8. S.∠s. (§ 79.) Q.E.D.

The abbreviation *s. s. s.* may be used in quoting the theorem of § 83.

EXERCISES: GROUP 10

Ex. 1. Given $\triangle ABC$ with $AB = BC$, and AC produced so that $AD = CF$. Prove $\angle p = \angle r$; also $\triangle DBA = \triangle CBF$.

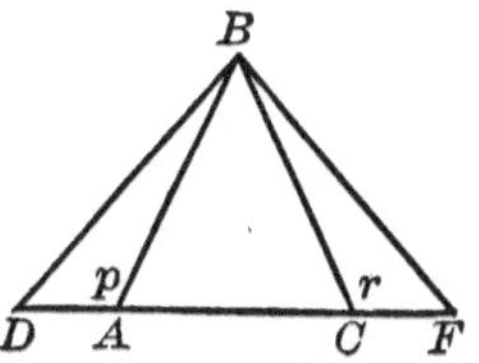

Ex. 2.

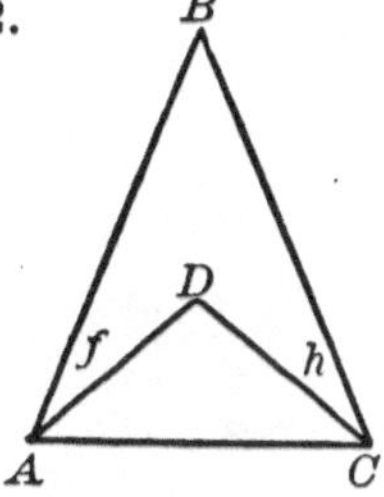

Given $\triangle ABC$ and ADC on the same base AC, with $AB = BC$, and $AD = DC$.

Prove $\angle f = \angle h$.

Ex. 3.

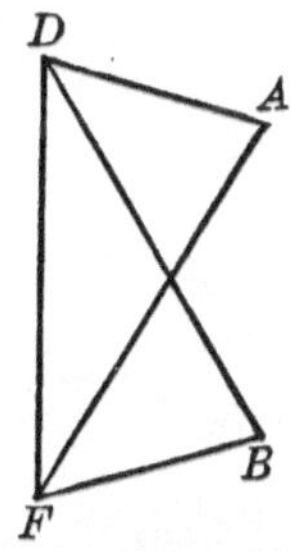

Given $DA = FB$, $DB = AF$.
Prove $\triangle DAF = \triangle DBF$.

Ex. 4.

Given $\triangle ABC$ in which $AB = AC$ and D is the midpoint of BC. Prove $\triangle ABD = \triangle ADC$.

Ex. 5.

Given the four-sided figure $ABCD$ in which $AB = AD$ and $BC = CD$. Draw a line connecting two of the vertices, which shall divide the figure into two equal triangles. Give proof that the triangles formed are equal.

Ex. 6. By the aid of squared paper, construct the following design :

Proposition VI. Problem

84. *To bisect a given angle.*

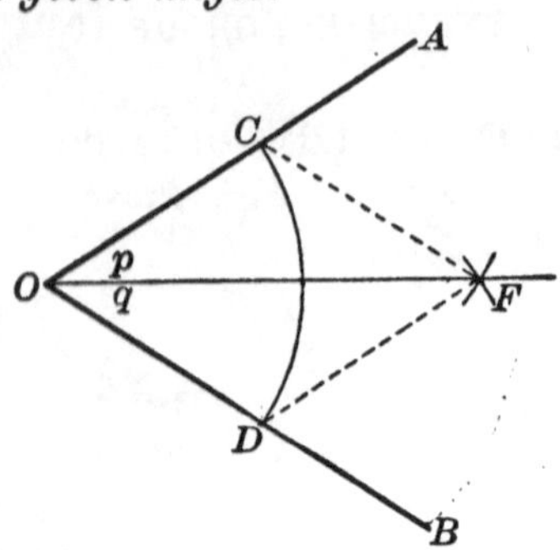

Given angle *AOB*.

To bisect angle *AOB*.

Construction. 1. With *O* as a center and with a radius *OC*, draw an arc meeting *OA* at *C* and *OB* at *D*.

1. A circle may be described about any given point as center, and with any given radius. (Post. 3, § 46.)

2. With *C* and *D* as centers and with convenient equal radii greater than $\frac{1}{2}$ the distance from *C* to *D*, describe arcs intersecting at *F*.

2. Post. 3.

3. Draw *OF*.

3. Post. 1.

Then *OF* bisects ∠ *AOB*.

Proof. 1. In the △ *OCF* and *ODF*,   *OF* = *OF*.

1. Ident.

2.   *OC* = *OD*.

2. Constr.

3.   *CF* = *DF*.

3. Constr.

4. ∴ △ *OCF* = △ *ODF*.

4. If two △ have three sides of one respectively equal to three sides of the other, the △ are equal (or s. s. s.). (§ 83.)

5. ∠ *p* = ∠ *q*, or ∠ *AOB* is bisected by *OF*.

5. Corr. △ of equal △.

Q.E.D.

Proposition VII. Problem

85. *At a given point in a straight line, to erect a perpendicular to that line.*

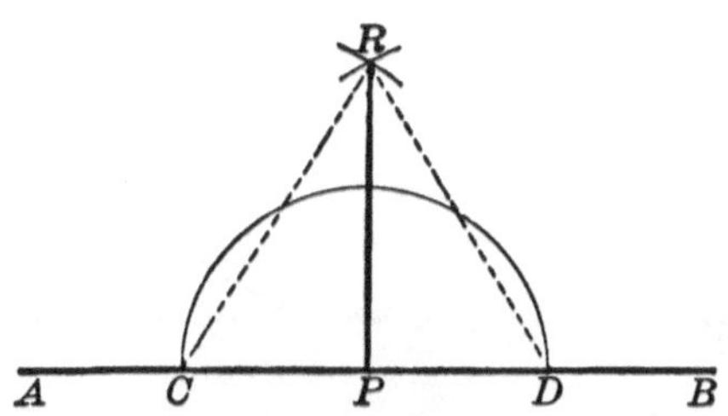

Given the point P in the line AB.

To construct a perpendicular to the line AB at the point P.

Construction. 1. From P as a center, with a convenient radius, describe an arc cutting off equal segments PC and PD on the line AB.   1. Post. 3.

2. From C and D as centers with equal radii greater than PD, describe arcs intersecting at R.   2. Post. 3.

3. Draw PR.   3. Post. 1.

Then PR is the perpendicular required.

Proof. 1. Draw the lines CR and DR.   1. Post. 1.

2. Then in the $\triangle$ CRP and PRD,   2. Ident.

$$RP = RP.$$

3. $CP = PD.$ 3. Constr.

4. $CR = RD.$ 4. Constr.

5. $\therefore \triangle CRP = \triangle PRD.$ 5. Why?

6. $\therefore \angle CPR = \angle DPR.$ 6. Why?

7. $\therefore \angle CPR = $ rt. $\angle$, $RP \perp AB.$ 7. §§ 23, 24.

Q.E.F

Ex. 1. Construct an equilateral triangle and bisect its angles.

Ex. 2. Construct an angle of 45°. An angle of 135°.

Ex. 3. Construct a right triangle whose legs are 1 in. and $1\frac{1}{2}$ in.

PROPOSITION VIII. PROBLEM

86. *Through a given point on a straight line, to draw a line making a given angle with the given line.*

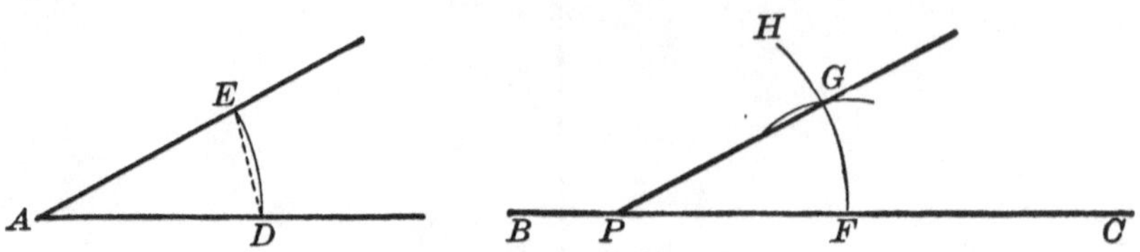

Given the $\angle A$ and the point P on the line BC.

To construct through P a line which shall make an angle with BC equal to $\angle A$.

Construction. 1. With A as a center and with any convenient radius, describe an arc meeting the sides of $\angle A$ at D and E.	1. Post. 3.
2. Draw DE.	2. Post. 1.
3. With P as a center and with a radius equal to AD, describe an arc cutting PC at F.	3. Post. 3.
4. From F as a center and with a radius equal to DE, describe an arc intersecting the arc HF at G.	4. Post. 3.
5. Draw PG.	5. Post. 1.
Then $\angle FPG$ is the angle required.	
Proof. Let the student supply the proof by drawing FG and proving the $\triangle AED$ and PGF equal.	
	Q.E.F.

Ex. 1. At a given point in a given line, construct an angle of 45°, one of whose sides shall be the given line.

Ex. 2. Construct a triangle, given two sides and the included angle.

Ex. 3. Construct a triangle, given two angles and the side included between them.

Proposition IX. Theorem

87. *An exterior angle of a triangle is greater than either opposite interior angle.*

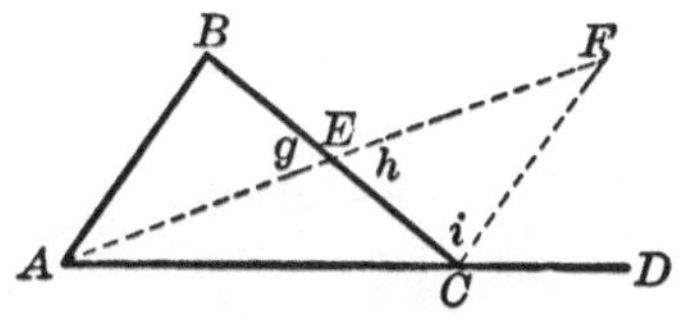

Given $\angle BCD$ an exterior $\angle$ of the $\triangle ABC$.

To prove $\angle BCD$ greater than $\angle B$ or $\angle BAC$.

Proof. 1. Let E be the midpoint of the line BC.

1. A given straight line (sect) can be divided into two equal parts at but one point. (§§ 59, 47.)

2. Draw AE and produce it to F, making $FE = AE$. Draw FC.

2. Posts. 1 and 2.

3. Then in the $\triangle AEB$ and FEC, $BE = EC$, $AE = EF$.

3. Constr.

4. $\angle g = \angle h$.

4. Why?

5. $\therefore \triangle ABE = \triangle EFC$.

5. Why?

6. $\therefore \angle B = \angle i$.

6. Why?

7. But $\angle BCD$ is greater than $\angle i$.

7. The whole is greater than any of its parts. (Ax. 8.)

8. Substitute $\angle B$ for its equal $\angle i$. Then $\angle BCD$ is greater than $\angle B$.

8. A quantity may be substituted for its equal in any process. (Ax. 9.)

By a similar construction and proof, it may be shown that $\angle BCD$ is greater than $\angle BAC$.   Q. E. D.

Ex. On a given line as base, construct exactly an isosceles triangle each of whose legs equals another given line.

88. A **transversal** is a line that intersects two or more other lines.

Thus EF is a transversal of the lines AB and CD.

If two lines are cut by a transversal, it is convenient to give special names to the eight angles of intersection.

a, b, g, h are called **exterior** angles.

c, d, e, f are called **interior** angles.

c, f form a pair of **alternate interior** angles.

b, f form a pair of **corresponding** angles.

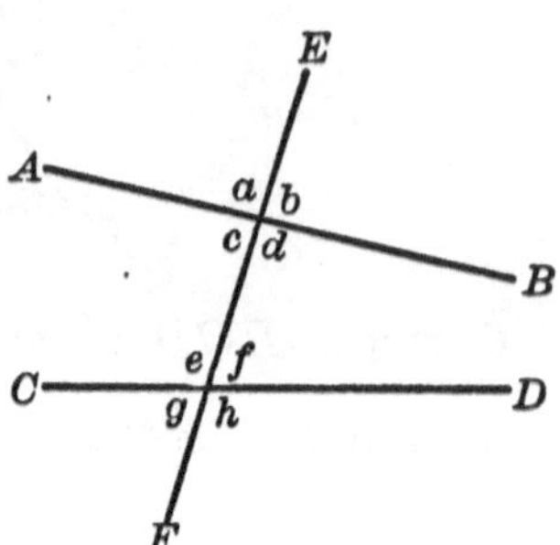

Let the student name another pair of alternate interior angles. Also name another pair of corresponding angles. Also a pair of interior angles on the same side of the transversal.

PROPOSITION X. THEOREM

89. *When two straight lines are cut by a third, if the alternate interior angles are equal, the two straight lines are parallel.*

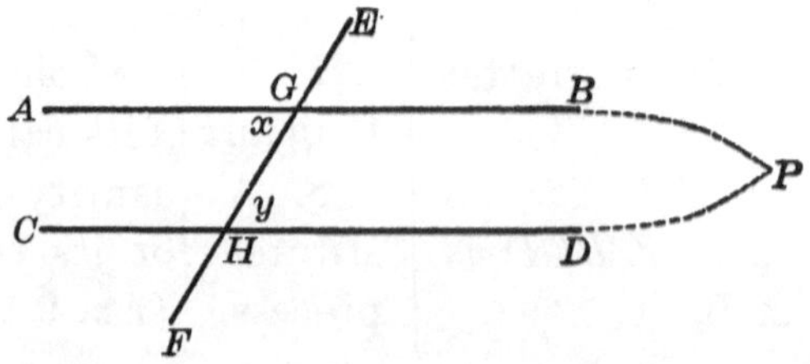

Given AB and CD, two straight lines cut by the transversal EF at the points G and H, respectively, making $\angle x = \angle y$.

To prove $AB \parallel CD$.

Proof. 1. If AB and CD are not ‖, they must meet at some point P and thus with GH form the $\triangle GPH$.	1. Def. of ‖ lines. (§ 15.)
2. $\angle x$ would then be greater than $\angle y$.	2. An exterior $\angle$ of a $\triangle$ is greater than either opp. interior $\angle$. (§ 87.)
3. But $\angle x$ cannot be greater than $\angle y$.	3. $\angle x = \angle y$ by hyp.
4. $\therefore AB \parallel CD$.	4. § 15. For it has been proved that AB and CD cannot meet.

Q.E.D.

90. Methods of geometric proof.—An examination of the demonstrations used in propositions thus far shows that several different kinds of proof are used in geometry. Of these the principal kinds are as follows :

1. **Direct demonstration.** — Examples of this kind of proof are given on pp. 29 and 37.

2. **Proof by superposition**, in which two figures are proved equal by placing one of the figures upon the other and showing that the two figures must coincide. See the proofs on pp. 33 and 34.

3. **Indirect demonstration**, which consists essentially in showing that a given statement is true by showing that its negative cannot be true. An illustration of this kind of proof is the demonstration which has just been given in § 89.

Ex. 1. By aid of the protractor, construct a triangle in which one side is $1\frac{1}{4}$ inches long and the angles adjoining this side are 40° and 55°.

Ex. 2. By aid of the protractor, construct also a triangle in which the sides are 1 inch and $1\frac{1}{2}$ inches long and the angle included by these sides is 63°.

Proposition XI. Theorem

91. *When two straight lines are cut by a third, if a pair of corresponding angles are equal, the two lines are parallel.*

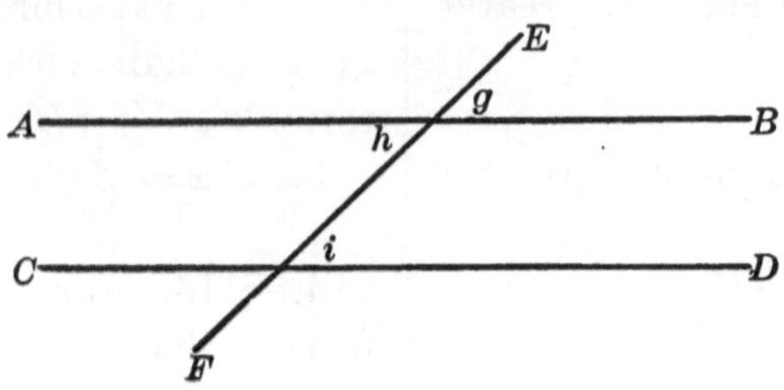

Given the lines AB and CD cut by the transversal EF, making the corresponding $\angle$s g and i equal.

To prove $AB \parallel CD$.

Proof. 1. $\angle h = \angle g$.	1. Why ?
2. $\angle i = \angle g$.	2. Hyp.
3. $\therefore \angle h = \angle i$.	3. Why ?
4. $\therefore AB \parallel CD$.	4. When two straight lines are cut by a third, if the alternate interior angles are equal, the two straight lines are parallel. (§ 89.) Q.E.D.

92. Cor. 1. *Two lines perpendicular to the same line are parallel.*

93. Cor. 2. *From a given point outside an unlimited straight line, only one perpendicular can be drawn to the line.*

For if AB and AC were both perpendicular to BC, then AB and AC would be parallel (§ 92); or we should have two parallel lines meeting at a point A, which is impossible. (§ 15.)

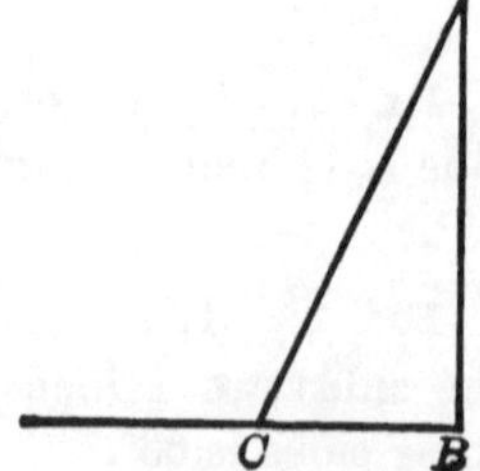

Proposition XII. Theorem

94. *When two straight lines are cut by a third, if the sum of two interior angles on the same side of the transversal is equal to two right angles, the two lines are parallel.*

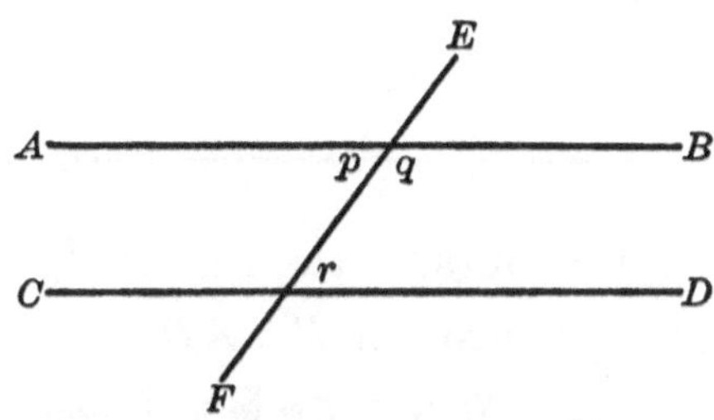

Given the lines AB and CD cut by the transversal EF, q and r int. $\measuredangle$ on the same side of EF, and $\angle q + \angle r = 180°$.

To prove $AB \parallel CD$.

Proof. 1. $\angle p$ is the sup. of $\angle q$.

    2. $\angle r$ is the sup. of $\angle q$.

    3. $\therefore \angle p = \angle r$.

    4. $\therefore AB \parallel CD$.

1. § 32.

2. Hyp.

3. The supplements of equal angles are equal. (§ 66.)

4. When two straight lines are cut by a third, if the alternate interior angles are equal, the two straight lines are parallel. (§ 89.)   Q.E.D.

Ex. 1. Draw a line AB and on it take a point C. By use of the protractor, through C draw a line DH making the $\angle DCB = 42°$. On CD mark off $CF = \frac{3}{4}$ in. By use of the protractor, through F draw a line $PQ \parallel$ to AB.

Ex. 2. On the diagram on p. 43, name two pairs of alternate interior angles. Also name one pair of corresponding angles. Also one pair of interior angles on the same side of a transversal.

Proposition XIII. Problem

95. *Through a given point, to draw a line parallel to a given straight line.*

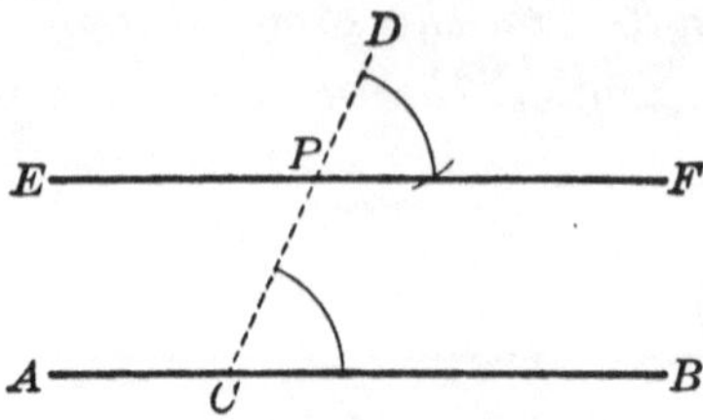

Given any point P outside the line AB.

To construct a line through $P \parallel AB$.

Construction. 1. Through P draw any convenient line CD meeting AB in C.

2. At P, and on the same side of CD with B, construct $\angle DPF$ equal to $\angle PCB$. Then EF is the line required.

  1. Post. 1.

  2. § 86.

Proof. 1. $\angle DPF = \angle PCB$.   1. Constr.

2. $\therefore EF \parallel AB$.   2. § 91.

Q.E.F.

Ex. Through each vertex of a $\triangle$, construct a line $\parallel$ opposite side.

Proposition XIV. Theorem

96. *If two parallel lines are cut by a third straight line, the alternate interior angles are equal.*

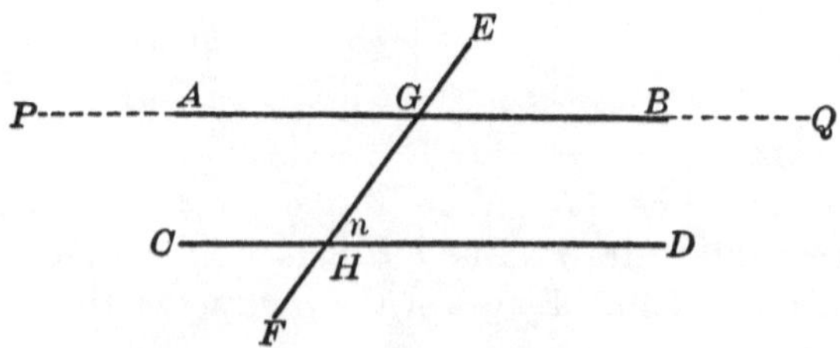

Given the $\parallel$ lines AB and CD cut by EF at the points G and H, respectively.

To prove $\angle AGH = \angle n.$

Proof.   1. Through the point G draw the line PQ, making $\angle PGH = \angle n.$

2. $\therefore PQ \parallel CD.$

3. But $AB \parallel CD.$

4. $\therefore PQ$ and AB coincide in direction.

5. $\therefore \angle AGH = \angle n.$

1. § 86.

2. § 89.

3. Hyp.

4. Through a given point one st. line and only one can be drawn parallel to another given st. line. (Geom. Ax. 3, § 43.)

5. $\angle AGH$ coincides with $\angle PGH$ which $= \angle n.$ Q.E.D.

97. Cor. 1. *If two parallel lines are cut by a third straight line, any two corresponding angles are equal.*

Thus, if $PQ \parallel RS$, $\angle b = \angle f$, since each of them $= \angle c.$

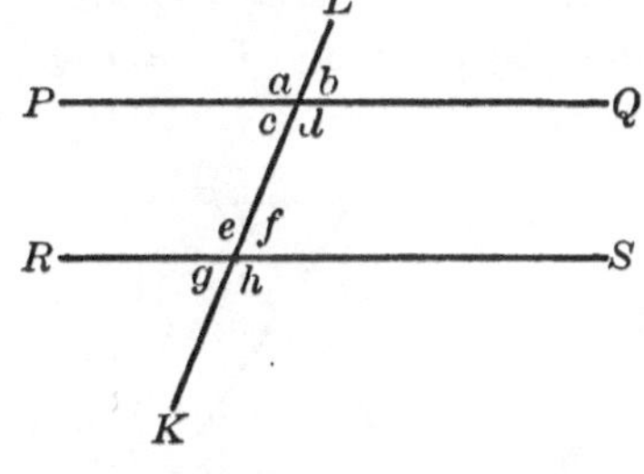

98. Cor. 2. *If two parallel lines are cut by a third straight line, the sum of the two interior angles on the same side of the transversal is equal to two right angles.*

Thus, $\angle f$ is the sup. of $\angle d$, since $\angle f = \angle c$ (§ 96) which is the sup. of $\angle d$ (§ 32).

99. Cor. 3. *If, when two lines are cut by a transversal, the interior angles on the same side of the transversal are not supplementary, the two lines are not parallel.*

100. Cor. 4. *If a straight line is perpendicular to one of two parallel lines, it is perpendicular to the other also.*

101. Cor. 5. *Two straight lines parallel to a third straight line are parallel to each other;*

Lines parallel to parallel lines are parallel;

Lines perpendicular to parallel lines are parallel;

Lines perpendicular to non-parallel lines are not parallel.

Ex. 1. If, in the diagram of § 97, $\angle b$ equals 67°, find the other seven angles in the figure without measuring them.

Ex. 2. If $\angle a = 110°$, and $\angle f = 60°$, are PQ and RS parallel?

EXERCISES: GROUP 11

Ex. 1.

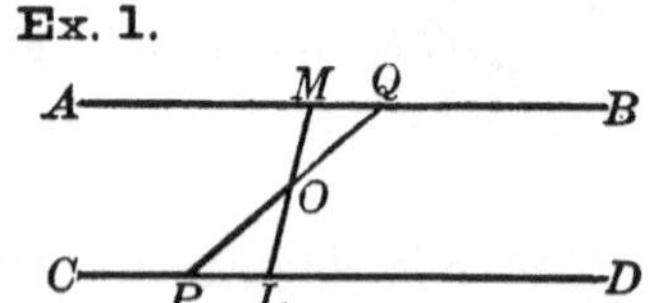

Given $AB \parallel CD$, PQ and ML straight lines, and $PO = OQ$.

Prove $\triangle POL = \triangle OMQ$.

Ex. 2.

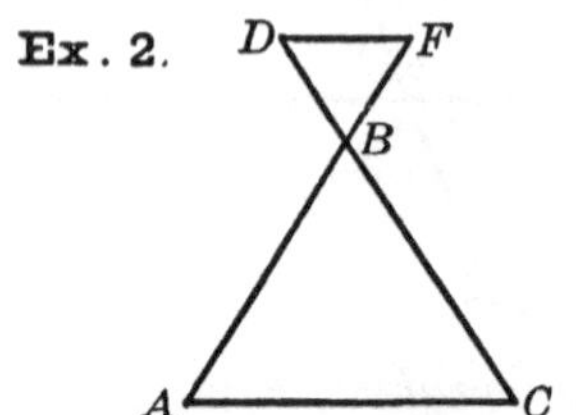

Given $\triangle ABC$ in which $AB = BC$; AB produced to F; CB to D; $DF \parallel AC$.

Prove $\angle D = \angle F$.

Ex. 3.

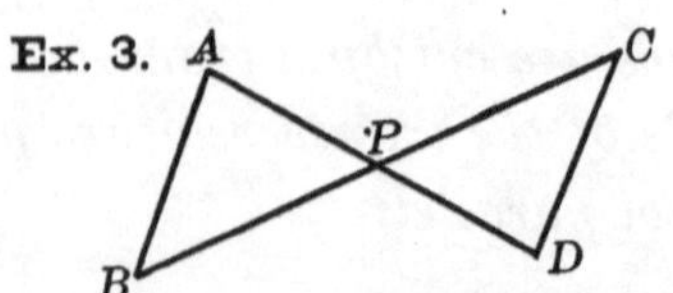

Given AB and CD = and $\parallel$.

Prove that lines AD and BC bisect each other.

Ex. 4.

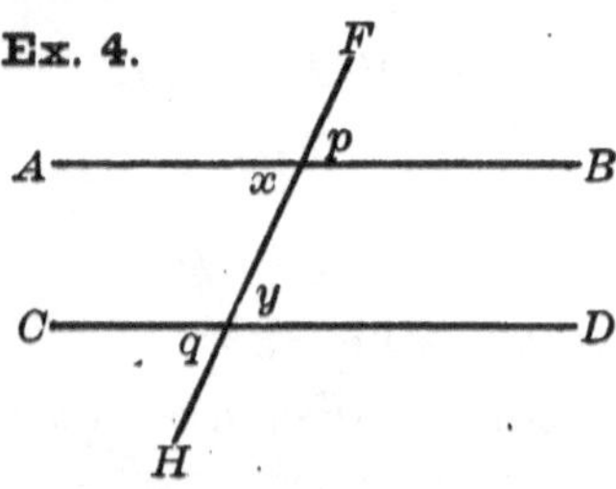

Given AB and CD intersected by transversal FH, $\angle p = \angle q$.

Prove $AB \parallel CD$.

Ex. 5.

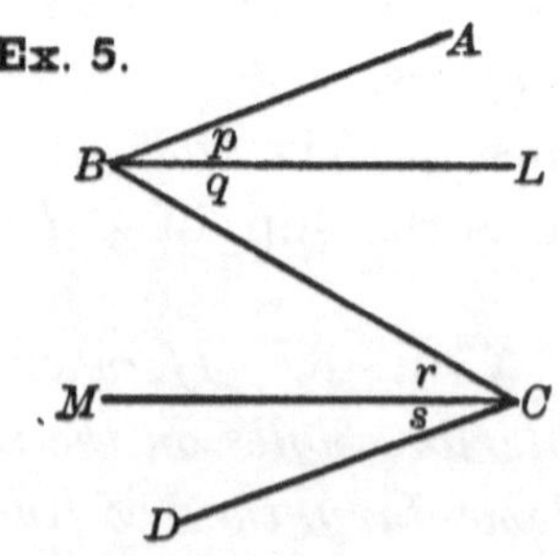

Given lines meeting at B and C so that $\angle p = \angle s$ and $\angle q = \angle r$.

Prove $AB \parallel CD$.

Ex. 6.

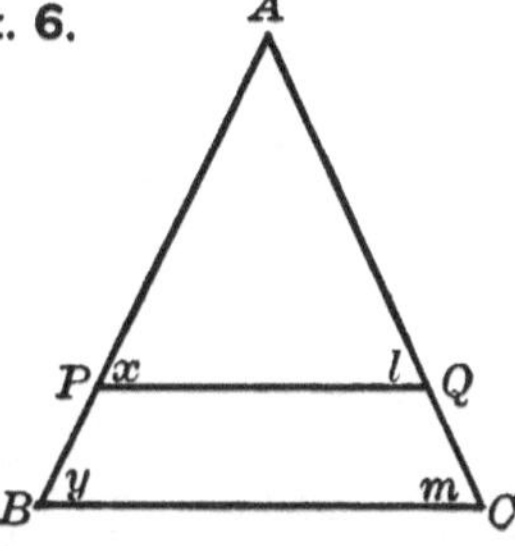

Given $\triangle ABC$ in which $AB = AC$, and $PQ \parallel BC$.
Prove $\angle x = \angle l$.

Ex. 8.

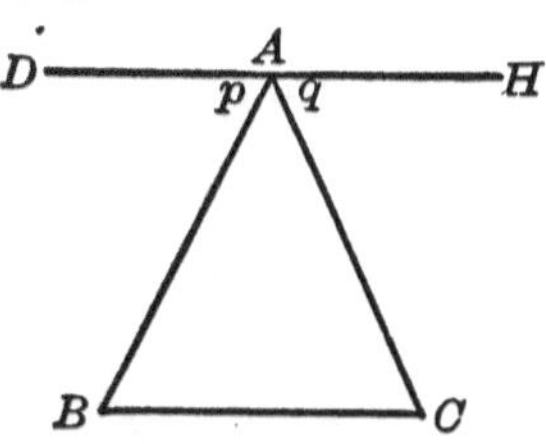

Given $\triangle ABC$ in which $AB = AC$, line $DAH \parallel BC$.
Prove $\angle p = \angle q$.

Ex. 7.

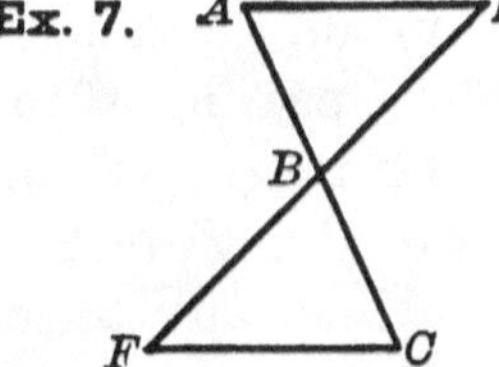

Given lines AC and DF bisecting each other at B.
Prove $AD \parallel FC$.

Ex. 9.

Given $\triangle BCD$ with exterior $\angle ABD$, $\angle C = 65°$, $\angle CBD = 40°$, $\angle DBE = 75°$.
Prove $BE \parallel CD$.

Ex. 10. On the diagram of Prop. IX (p. 43) prove that CF is parallel to AB.

Ex. 11. By the aid of squared paper, construct the following design:

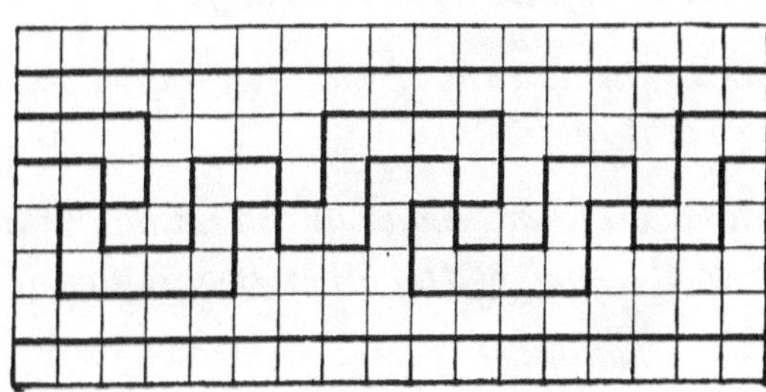

Proposition XV. Theorem

102. *The sum of the angles of any triangle is equal to two right angles.*

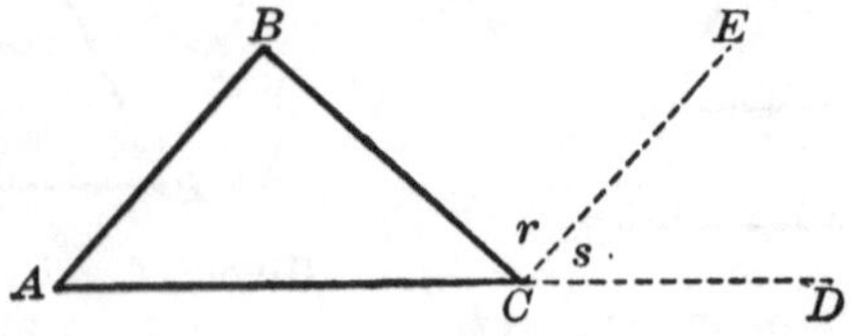

Given the $\triangle ABC$.

To prove $\angle A + \angle B + \angle BCA = 2$ rt. $\angle$s.

Proof. 1. Produce AC through C to D.	1. Post. 2.
2. From C draw $CE \parallel AB$.	2. § 95.
3. $\angle s + \angle r + \angle BCA = 2$ rt. $\angle$s.	3. The sum of all the $\angle$s about a point on the same side of a st. line passing through the point $= 2$ rt. $\angle$s. (§ 68.)
4. $\angle s = \angle A$.	4. If two $\parallel$ lines are cut by a third st. line, any 2 corresponding $\angle$s are equal. (§ 97.)
5. Also $\angle r = \angle B$.	5. Why?
6. Substituting for $\angle s$ its equal, $\angle A$, and for $\angle r$ its equal, $\angle B$,	6. Ax. 9.
$\angle A + \angle B + \angle BCA = 2$ rt. $\angle$s.	**Q.E.D.**

103. Cor. 1. *An exterior angle of a triangle is equal to the sum of the two opposite interior angles.*

104. Cor. 2. *The sum of any two angles of a triangle is less than two right angles.*

105. Cor. 3. *If one angle of a triangle is a right angle or an obtuse angle, each of the other two angles of the triangle must be acute.*

106. COR. 4. *In a right triangle, the sum of the two acute angles equals one right angle;*
Each angle of an equilateral triangle contains 60°.

107. COR. 5. *If two angles of one triangle equal two angles of another triangle, the third angle of the first triangle equals the third angle of the second.*

108. COR. 6. *If an acute angle of one right triangle equals an acute angle of another right triangle, the remaining acute angles of the triangles are equal.*

109. COR. 7. *If two triangles have two angles and a side of one equal to two angles and a corresponding side of the other, the triangles are equal.*

For this statement, the following abbreviation may be used : *s. ∠∠.*

110. COR. 8. *If two right triangles have the hypotenuse and an acute angle of one respectively equal to the hypotenuse and an acute angle of the other, the triangles are equal.*

The abbreviation *h. a.* may be used in quoting this principle.

111. COR. 9. *If two right triangles have a leg and an acute angle of one respectively equal to a leg and the corresponding acute angle of the other, the triangles are equal.*

Ex. 1. If two angles of a triangle are 56° and 62°, find the remaining angle.

Ex. 2. If one acute angle of a right triangle is 36° 15′, find the other acute angle.

Ex. 3. How many degrees are there in each angle of an equiangular triangle?

Ex. 4. How many degrees are there in each acute angle of an isosceles right triangle?

Ex. 5. Is it possible to have a triangle whose angles are 45°, 62°, 72°?

Ex. 6.   If one angle of a triangle is 42°, find the sum of the other two angles.

Ex. 7.   If two angles of a triangle are 38° and 65°, find all the exterior angles of the triangle.

Ex. 8.   If the vertex angle of an isosceles triangle is 38°, find each angle at the base.

Ex. 9.   If an angle at the base of an isosceles triangle is 50°, find the vertex angle.

Ex. 10.   An exterior angle at the base of an isosceles triangle is 102°.   Find all the angles of the triangle.

Ex. 11.   Construct an angle of 60°.   Of 30°.   Of 15°.

Ex. 12.   Construct an angle of 120°.   Of 75°.

Ex. 13.   Construct an angle of 150°.   Of 195°.

Ex. 14.   Construct a triangle in which two of the sides are 1 in. and $1\frac{1}{2}$ in., with an angle of 135° included between them.

Ex. 15.   Construct a right angle and divide it into three equal parts.

Ex. 16.   Construct an isosceles triangle in which the vertex angle is 120°.

Ex. 17.   Construct an isosceles right triangle in which the hypotenuse is 2 inches.

Ex. 18.   Construct a square whose side is $1\frac{1}{4}$ inches.

Ex. 19.   Draw a line, AB, 2 inches long.   Then, by aid of the protractor, construct a triangle in which $\angle A = 65°$ and $\angle B = 50°$. Also on another base $DE = \frac{3}{4}$ in., construct a triangle DEF in which $\angle D = 65°$, and $\angle E = 50°$.   Are each of the three angles of the triangle ABC equal to the corresponding angle in the triangle DEF? Are the triangles equal?

Ex. 20.   Draw any acute angle and in the shortest way construct its complement.

Ex. 21.   Draw any acute angle and in the shortest way construct its supplement.

Ex. 22.   Make up and solve an example similar to Ex. 5.

Ex. 23.   To Ex. 14.   To Ex. 19.

Ex. 24.   Make up and solve two examples entirely your own concerning the numerical properties of the angles of a triangle.

Proposition XVI. Theorem

112. *If the sides of one angle are parallel, respectively, to the sides of another and extending in the same direction from the vertices, the angles are equal.*

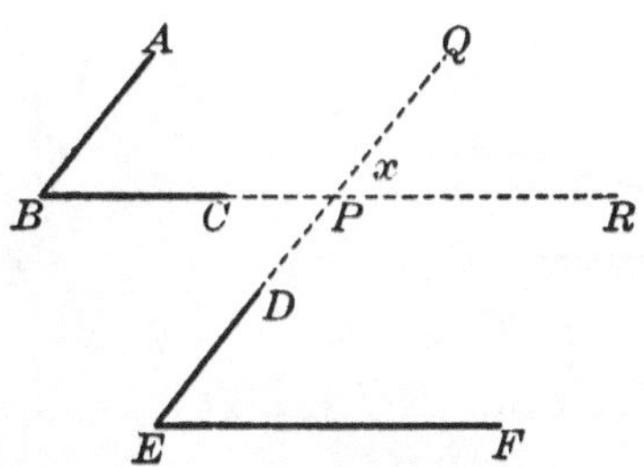

Given $AB \parallel ED$ and extending in the same direction from B and E; and $BC \parallel EF$ and extending in the same direction from B and E.

To prove $\angle B = \angle E$.

Proof. 1. Produce the lines BC and ED to intersect in P.	1. Post. 2.
2. Then $\angle B = \angle x$.	2. § 97.
3. $\angle x = \angle E$.	3. Why?
4. $\therefore \angle B = \angle E$.	4. Why?

Q.E.D.

113. Cor. *If two angles have their corresponding sides parallel, but with one pair extending in the same direction and the other pair in opposite directions from their vertices, the angles are supplementary.*

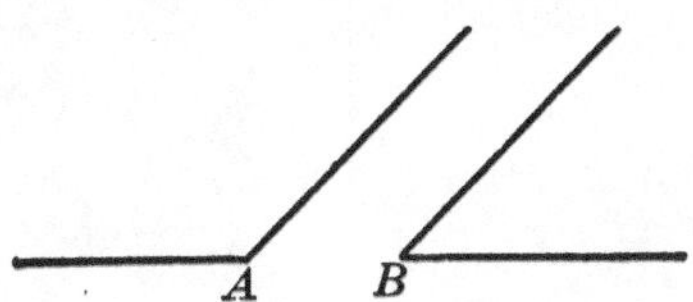

Thus $\angle\!\!\!\angle$ A and B are supplementary.

Proposition XVII. Theorem

114. *If the sides of one angle are perpendicular, respec-tively, to the sides of another, the angles are either equal or supplementary.*

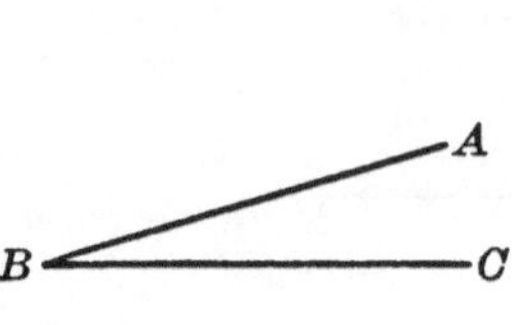

Given $BA \perp EF$, and $BC \perp DD'$.

To prove $\angle B = \angle FED$, and $\angle\!\!\!\angle\, B$ and FED' supplementary.

Proof. 1. At E construct $EK \perp EF$ and in the same direction with BA; also construct $EG \perp DD'$ and in the same direction with BC.

1. At a given point in a straight line, to erect a perpendicular to that line. (§ 85.)

2. Then $BA \parallel EK$, and $BC \parallel EG$.

2. Two lines $\perp$ the same line are $\parallel$. (§ 92.)

3. $\therefore \angle B = \angle r$.

3. If the sides of one $\angle$ are $\parallel$, respectively, to the sides of another and extending in the same direction from their vertices, the $\angle\!\!\!\angle$ are equal. (§ 112.)

4. But $\angle r$ is comp. of $\angle DEK$.

4. § 31.

5. Also $\angle s$ is comp. of $\angle DEK$.

5. Why?

6. $\therefore \angle r = \angle s$.

6. Why?

7. $\therefore \angle B = \angle s$ or $\angle FED$.

7. Ax. 1.

8. But $\angle FED'$ is sup. of $\angle s$.

8. § 32.

9. $\therefore \angle FED'$ is sup. of $\angle B$.

9. Ax. 9.

Q.E.D

EXERCISES : GROUP 12

Ex. 1.

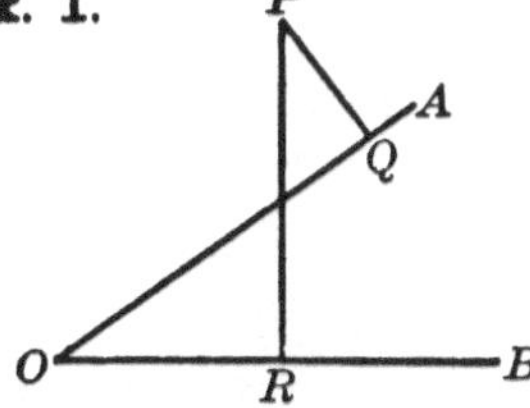

Given $\angle AOB$, $PQ \perp OA$, $PR \perp OB$.

Prove $\angle P = \angle O$.

Ex. 2.

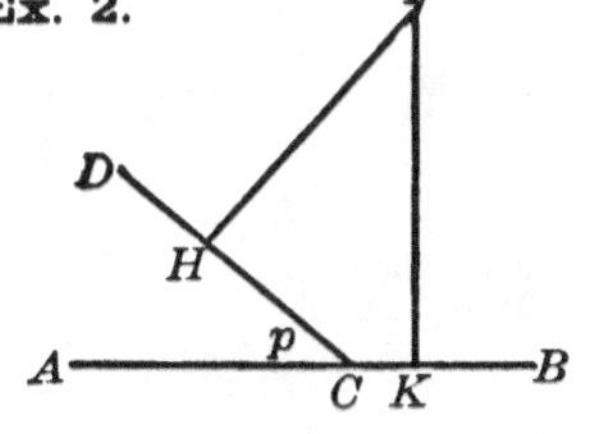

Given $FK \perp$ line ACB; $FH \perp$ line DHC.

Prove $\angle F = \angle p$.

Ex. 3.

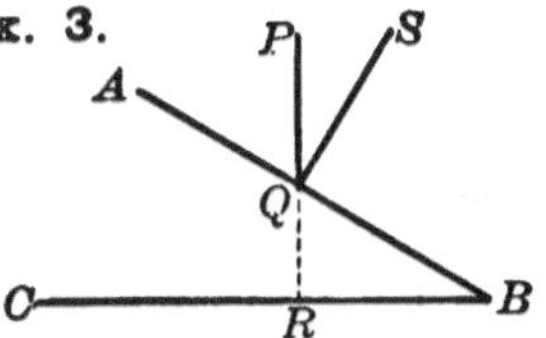

Given line $PQR \perp BC$, $SQ \perp AB$. What $\angle$ on the diagram $= \angle PQS$?

Prove your statement.

Ex. 4.

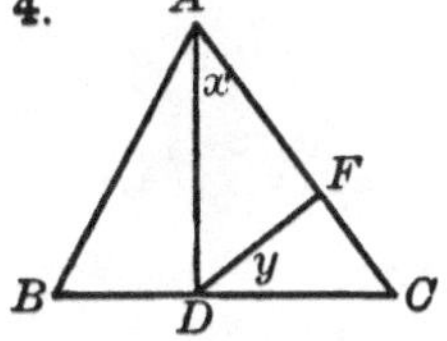

Given $\triangle ABC$, $AD \perp BC$, $DF \perp AC$.

Prove $\angle x = \angle y$.

Ex. 5.

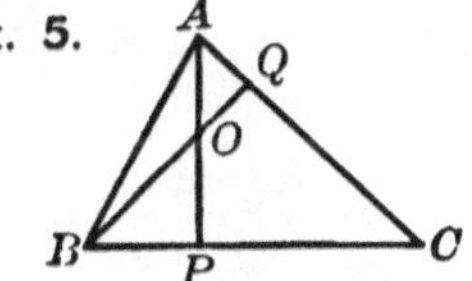

Given AP and BQ, altitudes of the $\triangle ABC$. Name the pairs of equal $\angle$ on the diagram.

Ex. 6. Given $\triangle BFC$, $ABCD$ a straight line, $BF = FC$. **Prove** $\angle x = \angle y$. Also, make $AB = CD$, draw AF and FD, and prove $AF = FD$.

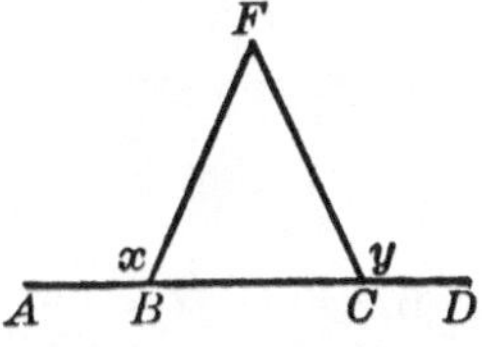

Ex. 7. By the aid of squared paper, construct the following designs :

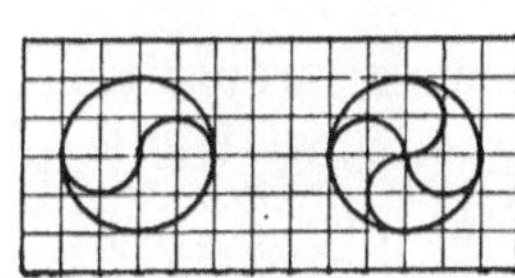

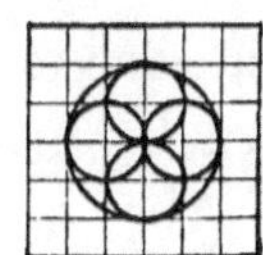

Proposition XVIII.　Theorem

115. *If two angles of a triangle are equal, the triangle ·is isosceles.*

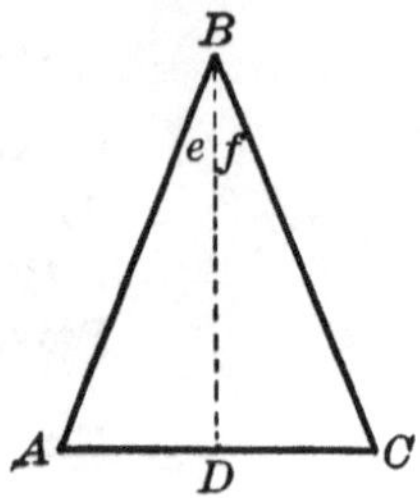

Given $\triangle\,ABC$ in which $\angle\,A = \angle\,C$.

To prove $BA = BC$.

Proof. 1. Draw BD bisecting $\angle\,ABC$ and meeting AC in D.	1. To bisect a given angle. (§ 84.)
2. Then in $\triangle\,ABD$ and DBC,	2. Why?
$\qquad BD = BD.$	
3. $\qquad \angle\,A = \angle\,C.$	3. Why?
4. $\qquad \angle\,e = \angle\,f.$	4. Why?
5. $\therefore \triangle\,ABD = \triangle\,DBC.$	5. If two $\triangle$ have two angles and a side of one equal to two angles and a corresponding side of the other, the $\triangle$ are equal (or s. $\angle\angle$). (§ 109.)
6. $\qquad \therefore BA = BC.$	6. Corr. sides of equal $\triangle$.

Q.E.D.

116. The **converse of a proposition** is another proposition formed by interchanging the hypothesis and the conclusion of the original proposition. Thus § 115 is the converse of § 82.

Proposition XIX.   Theorem

117. *If two right triangles have the hypotenuse and a leg of one respectively equal to the hypotenuse and a leg of the other, the triangles are equal.*

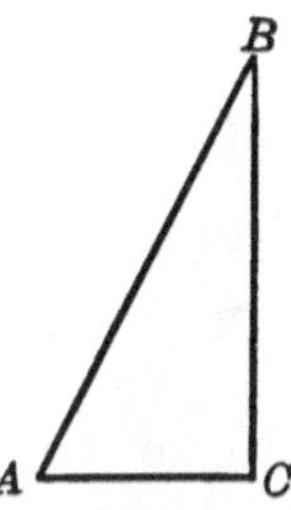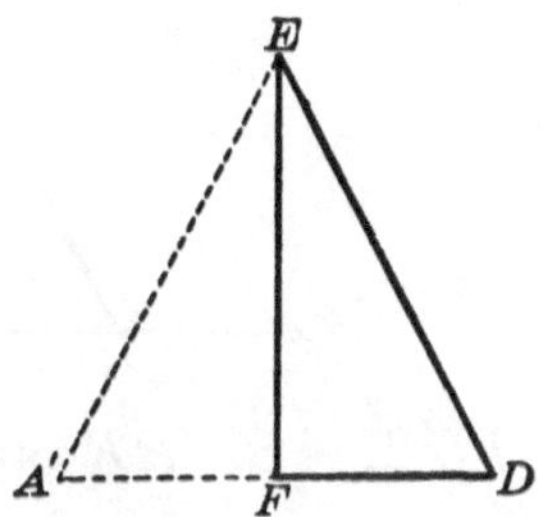

Given two right $\triangle$ ABC and DEF having the hypotenuse $AB =$ hypotenuse DE, and $BC = EF$.

To prove $\triangle ABC = \triangle DEF$.

Proof. 1. Place the $\triangle ABC$ so that BC coincides with its equal, EF, and A falls on the opposite side of EF from D, at A'.

1. Geom. Ax. 2.

2. Then $A'F$ and FD will form a straight line, $A'FD$.

2. If two adj. $\angle$ are together equal to a st. $\angle$, their ext. sides form a st. line. (§ 65.)

3. But $A'E = ED$.

3. Hyp.

4. $\therefore \angle A' = \angle D$.

4. In an isosceles $\triangle$, the $\angle$ opposite the equal sides are equal. (§ 82.)

5. $\therefore \triangle A'EF$ or $\triangle ABC = \triangle DEF$.

5. If two rt. $\triangle$ have the hypotenuse and an acute $\angle$ of one respectively equal to the hypotenuse and an acute $\angle$ of the other, the $\triangle$ are equal. (§ 110.)   **Q.E.D.**

Proposition XX. Theorem

118. *If equal lines are drawn from a point in a perpendicular to a given line, they cut off equal segments of the line from the foot of the perpendicular.*

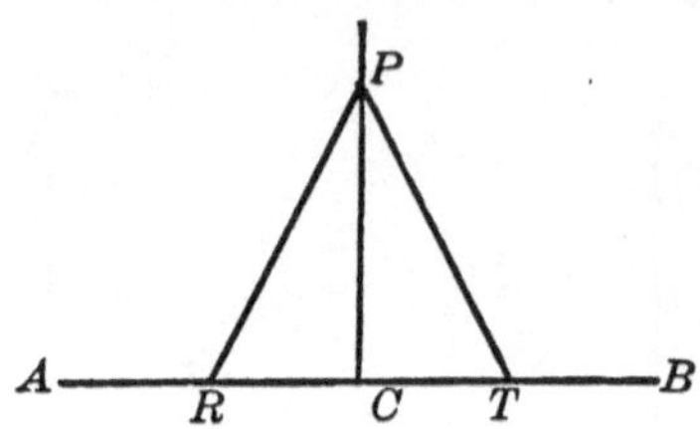

Given $PC \perp AB$, PR and PT oblique to AB, and $PR = PT$.

To prove $CR = CT$.

Proof. 1. In the right $\triangle$ RPC and CPT, $\qquad PC = PC.$	1. Why?
2. $\qquad PR = PT.$	2. Why?
3. $\therefore \triangle RPC = \triangle CPT.$	3. If two rt. $\triangle$ have the hypotenuse and a leg of one respectively equal to the hypotenuse and a leg of the other, the $\triangle$ are equal. (§ 117.)
4. $\qquad \therefore RC = CT.$	4. Why? Q.E.D.

119. Cor. *If two oblique straight lines drawn from a point to a straight line meet the line at equal distances from the foot of the perpendicular drawn from the point to the line, they are equal.*

Of what theorem is this statement the converse?

Ex. Given $\angle AOB$ with $OR = OQ, PQ \perp AO$, $PR \perp BO$. **Prove** $\triangle PQO = \triangle PRO$. Does $PQ = PR$? Why?

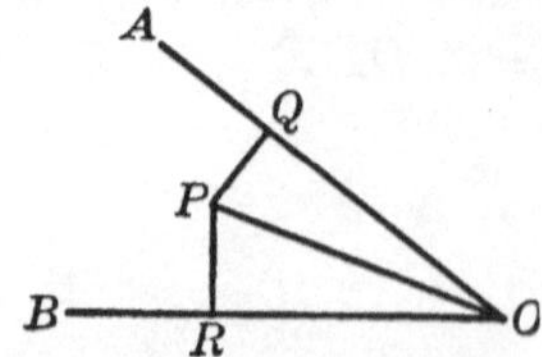

PROPOSITION XXI. THEOREM

120. I. *Every point in the perpendicular bisector of a line is equally distant from the extremities of the line;* and

II. CONVERSELY, *every point equidistant from the extremities of a line lies in the perpendicular bisector of the line.*

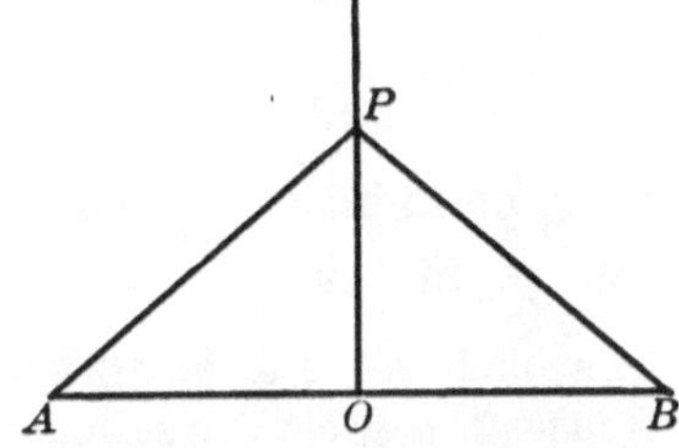

I. **Given** O the midpoint of the line AB, $OC \perp AB$, P any point in OC.

To prove $AP = PB$.

Proof. 1. $AP = PB$.   1. § 119.

II. **Given** O the midpoint of AB, and $AP = PB$.

To prove $PO \perp AB$.

Proof. 1. In the △ APO and OPB, $\quad PA = PB$.	1. Why?
2. $\quad\quad PO = PO$.	2. Why?
3. $\quad\quad AO = OB$.	3. Why?
4. ∴ $\triangle APO = \triangle OPB$.	4. Why?
5. ∴ $\angle AOP = \angle POB$.	5. Why?
6. ∴ $\angle AOP$ is a rt. $\angle$.	6. Def. (§ 23.)
7. ∴ $PO \perp AB$.	7. Def. (§ 24.) Q.E.D.

Ex. **Given** $\angle AOC$ bisected by the line OB, P any point in OB, $PQ \perp OC$, and $PR \perp OA$. **Prove** $\triangle OPQ = \triangle OPR$.

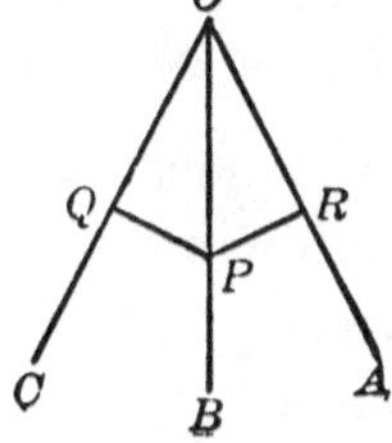

121. Cor. *Two points each equidistant from the extremities of a line determine the perpendicular bisector of the line.*

This corollary gives a useful method of determining the perpendicular bisector of a given straight line, since by this method we need find only two easily located points on the required line.

LOCI

122. The **locus of a point** is the path of a point moving according to a given geometric law.

If a point moves in a plane so as to be always two inches distant from a given point, its locus is a circle whose center is the given point, and whose radius is a line two inches in length.

The locus of a point moving so as to be equidistant from two given parallel lines is a straight line lying midway between the two given lines.

The locus of a point may consist of two or more separate lines or parts.

The locus of a point moving so as to be always at a given distance from a given line is two lines, one on either side of the given line, at the given distance from it and parallel to it.

123. Demonstration of loci. — In order to prove that a given line is the locus of a given point moving according to a given geometric law, it is necessary to prove :

1. *That every point in the given line satisfies the given law or condition.*

2. *That every point which satisfies the given condition lies in the given line.*

Hence, the theorem of Prop. XXI may be stated in the following form: *The locus of points equidistant from two given points is the perpendicular bisector of the line joining these two points.*

124. To **describe a locus,** state what kind of line, surface, or other geometric object the locus is; then state where it is situated, and, if possible, give its dimensions.

The locus of a point moving so as always to be two inches from a given point is a circle whose center is the given point and whose radius is two inches.

125. Efficiency value of loci.—Loci are useful in determining a point (or points) which shall satisfy two or more geometrical conditions. For, by finding the locus of all points which satisfy one of the given conditions, and also finding the locus of all points which satisfy a second condition, and then finding the intersection of these two loci, we obtain the point (or points) which satisfy both conditions at the same time.

Thus, if it is required to find the points which are 2 in. from one given point and 3 in. from another given point, the two given points being 4 in. apart, the required points are the intersections of two circles.

Let the student make a construction and obtain the required points.

Ex. 1. Draw exactly the locus of a point moving at the distance of 1 in. from a given point.

Ex. 2. Draw exactly the locus of a point moving at a distance of 1 in. from a given line.

Ex. 3. Draw exactly the locus of a point moving so as to be equidistant from the extremities of a given line one inch long.

Describe the following loci:

Ex. 4. The locus of the center of a carwheel 2 ft. in diameter, as the wheel rolls on a straight level track.

Ex. 5. The locus of a point which moves so as to be equidistant from two fixed points which are 1 ft. apart.

Ex. 6. Draw three isosceles triangles on the same base and connect their vertices. What truth is illustrated by this figure?

Ex. 7. Draw a straight line and locate a point 2 in. from it. By the use of loci, locate the points which are $1\frac{1}{2}$ in. from the given line and at the same distance from the given point.

PROPOSITION XXII. THEOREM

126. I. *Every point in the bisector of an angle is equidistant from the sides of the angle ; and*

II. CONVERSELY, *every point equidistant from the sides of an angle lies in the bisector of the angle.*

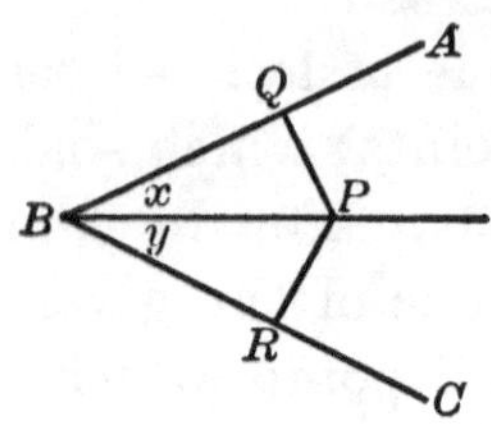

I. **Given** PB the bisector of the angle ABC, P any point in PB, $PQ \perp BA$, and $PR \perp BC$.

To prove $PQ = PR$.

Proof. 1. In the rt. $\triangle$ PBQ and PBR, $\qquad PB = PB$.	1. Why ?
2. $\qquad\qquad \angle x = \angle y$.	2. Why ?
3. $\qquad \therefore \triangle PBQ = \triangle PBR$.	3. Why ?
4. $\qquad\qquad \therefore PQ = PR$.	4. Why ?

II. **Given** $\angle ABC$, $PQ \perp AB$, $PR \perp BC$, and $PQ = PR$

To prove that PB is the bisector of $\angle ABC$.

Proof. 1. In the rt. $\triangle$ PBQ and PBR, $\qquad PB = PB$.	1. Why ?
2. $\qquad\qquad PQ = PR$.	2. Why ?
3. $\qquad \therefore \triangle PBQ = \triangle PBR$.	3. Why ?
4. $\qquad\qquad \therefore \angle x = \angle y$.	4. Why ?
Or BP is the bisector of $\angle ABC$.	Q.E.D.

127. COR. The theorem of Prop. XXII may also be stated in the following form: *The locus of points within an angle and equally distant from the sides of the angle is the bisector of the angle.*

For it has been proved that every point in the given line satisfies the given law or condition, and that every point which satisfies the given condition lies in the given line.   (See § 123.)

Proposition XXIII.   Problem

128. *To bisect a given straight line.*

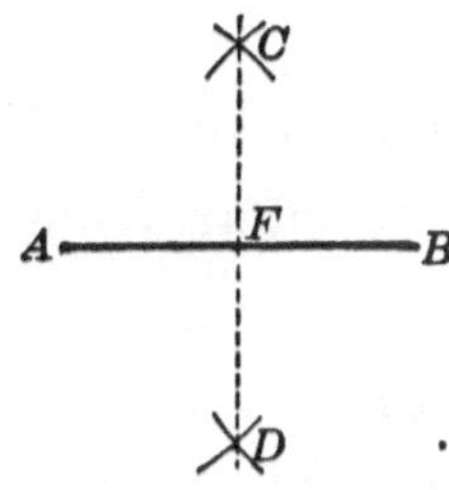

Given the line AB.

To bisect AB.

Construction. 1. With A and B as centers and with equal radii, greater than $\frac{1}{2} AB$, describe arcs intersecting in the points C and D.

1. Post. 3.

2. Draw CD intersecting AB in F.

2. Post. 1.

Then AB is bisected at F.

Proof. 1. C is equidistant from A and B.

1. Constr.

2. D is equidistant from A and B.

2. Constr.

3. CD is $\perp$ bisector of AB.

3. Two points each equidistant from the extremities of a line determine the $\perp$ bisector of the line. (§ 121.)   Q E.F.

Proposition XXIV. Problem

129. *From a given point to let fall a perpendicular upon a given straight line.*

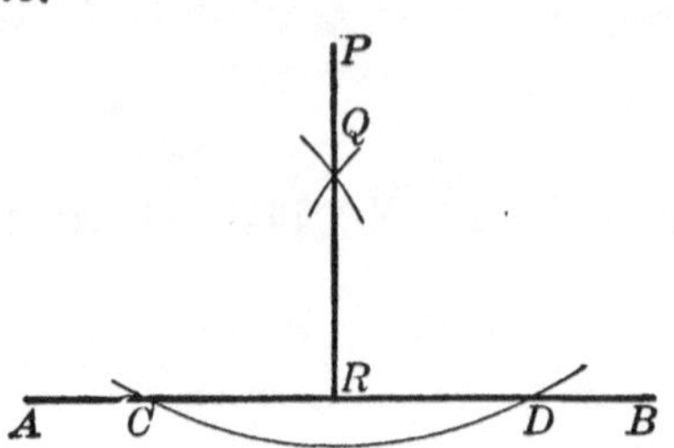

Given the line AB and the point P outside AB.

To construct a perpendicular from the point P to the line AB.

Construction. 1. With P as a center and with any convenient radius, describe an arc intersecting AB in two points, as C and D.   1. Post. 3.

2. From C and D as centers, with convenient equal radii greater than $\frac{1}{2} CD$, describe arcs intersecting at Q.   2. Post. 3.

3. Draw the line PQ and produce it to meet AB at R.   3. Posts. 1 and 2.

Then PR is the $\perp$ required.

Proof. 1. P and Q are each equidistant from C and D.   1. Why?

2. PR is the $\perp$ bisector of CD and $\therefore \perp AB$.   2. § 121.   Q.E.F.

130. Altitudes of a triangle. — The altitude of a triangle has been defined in § 75 (p. 31). In any triangle, any side may be taken as the base. Hence, the **altitudes** of a triangle are the three perpendiculars drawn one

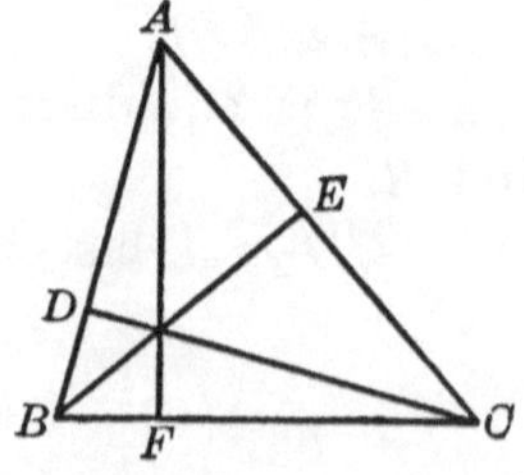

from each vertex to the side opposite (or this side produced). Thus, in △ *ABC*, the three altitudes are *AF*, *BE*, and *CD*.

131. A **median** of a triangle is a line drawn from a vertex of the triangle to the middle point of the opposite side. How many medians has a triangle? Draw a triangle and then construct its medians.

132. An **angle-bisector** of a triangle is a line which bisects an angle of the triangle. An angle-bisector is usually regarded as produced to meet that side of the triangle which is opposite the bisected angle. Thus *BD* is an angle-bisector of the triangle *ABC*. How many angle-bisectors has a triangle?

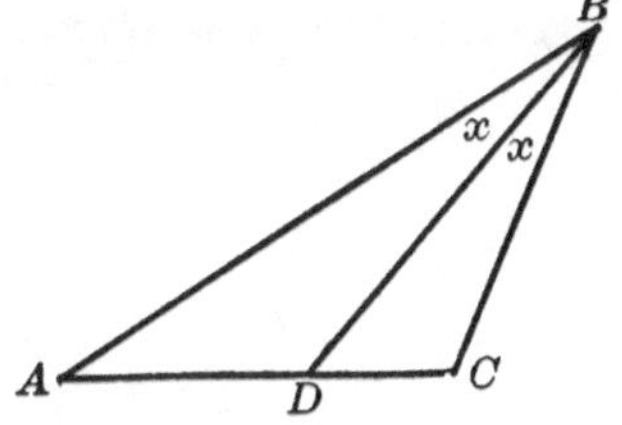

Ex. 1. Construct an equilateral triangle in which each side is half of a given line.

Ex. 2. Draw an obtuse triangle and construct its three medians.

Ex. 3. Draw an obtuse triangle and construct its three altitudes.

Ex. 4. Draw an isosceles triangle and construct its three angle-bisectors.

133. Inequality axioms. — To the list of GENERAL AXIOMS (p. 21), the following axioms, relating to unequal magnitudes, are to be added:

INEQUALITY AXIOM 1. *If equals are added to, or subtracted from, unequals, the results are unequal in the same order. If unequals are added to unequals in the same order, the results are unequal in that order.*

INEQUALITY AXIOM 2. *Doubles, or halves, of unequals are unequal in the same order.*

INEQUALITY AXIOM 3. *If unequals are subtracted from equals, the remainders are unequal in the reverse order.*

INEQUALITY AXIOM 4.   *If, of three quantities, the first is greater than the second, and the second is greater than the third, then the first is greater than the third.*

INEQUALITY AXIOM 5.   *A given magnitude, when compared with another magnitude of the same kind, must be either equal to, less than, or greater than the other magnitude.*

PROPOSITION XXV.   THEOREM

134. *If one side of a triangle is greater than a second side, the angle opposite the first side is greater than the angle opposite the second side.*

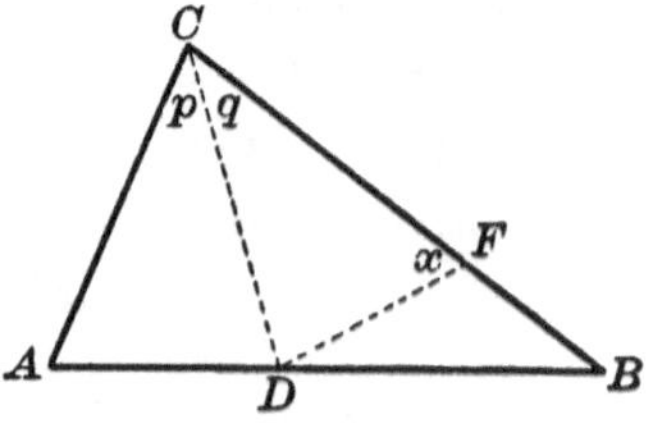

Given $\triangle ABC$ with side $BC >$ side AC.

To prove $\angle A > \angle B$.

Proof.   1. Draw CD bisecting $\angle ACB$ and meeting AB in D.

2. On CB lay off $CF = AC$. Draw DF.

3. In $\triangle ADC$ and DFC, $AC = CF$.

4. Also $\qquad\qquad CD = CD$.

5. $\qquad\qquad\qquad \angle p = \angle q$.

6. $\qquad\qquad \therefore \triangle ADC = \triangle DFC$.

7. Hence, $\qquad \angle A = \angle x$.

8. But $\angle x$, being an ext. $\angle$ of $\triangle DFB$, is greater than $\angle B$.

9. $\qquad\qquad\qquad \therefore \angle A > \angle B$.

1.	§ 84.
2.	Posts. 2, 1.
3.	Why ?
4.	Why ?
5.	Why ?
6.	Why ?
7.	Why ?
8.	§ 87.
9.	Ax. 9.

Q.E.D.

Ex. Which is the longest side of a right triangle? Of an obtuse triangle?

Proposition XXVI. Theorem

135. *If one angle of a triangle is greater than a second angle, the side opposite the first angle is greater than the side opposite the second angle.*

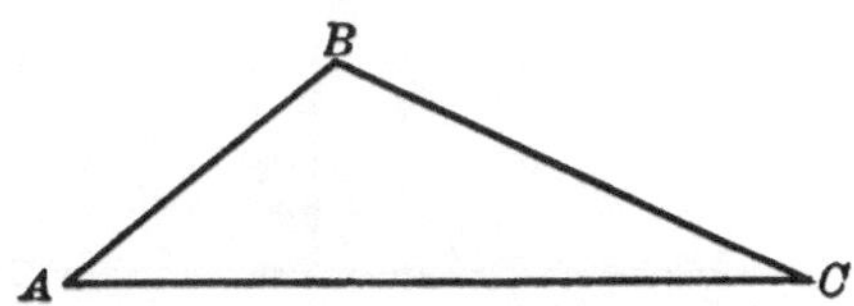

Given $\angle A$ greater than $\angle C$ in the $\triangle ABC$.

To prove $BC > AB$.

Proof. 1. BC equals AB, or is less than AB, or is greater than AB.

1. A given magnitude, when compared with another magnitude of the same kind, must be either $=$, $<$, or $>$ the other magnitude. (Ineq. Ax. 5, § 133.)

2. But BC cannot equal AB.

2. If it did, $\angle A$ would equal $\angle C$ (§ 82), which is contrary to the hypothesis.

3. Also BC cannot be less than AB.

3. If it were, $\angle A$ would be less than $\angle C$ (§ 134), which is contrary to the hypothesis.

4. $\therefore BC > AB$.

4. Since it neither $= AB$ nor is less than AB. Q.E.D.

Ex. 1. State the inequality axiom which is illustrated in the following statement: If $7 > 5$, then $14 > 10$.

Ex. 2. Give a numerical illustration of each of the different statements in Ineq. Ax. 1.

Ex. 3. Give numerical illustrations of Ineq. Ax. 2. Ineq. Ax. 3.

Ex. 4. Give numerical illustrations of Ineq. Ax. 4.

Ex. 5. The theorem of § 135 is the converse of what theorem?

Proposition XXVII. Theorem

136. *The perpendicular is the shortest line that can be drawn from a given point to a given straight line.*

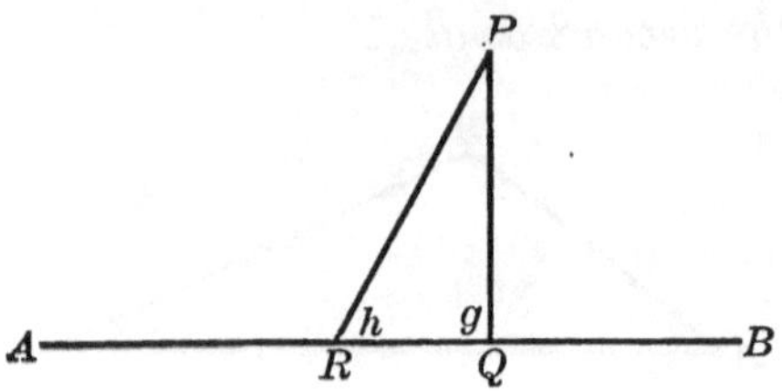

Given the point P and the line AB, $PQ \perp AB$, and PR oblique to AB.

To prove $PQ < PR$.

Proof. 1. $\angle g$ is a rt. $\angle$.	1. Hyp.
2. $\angle h$ is an acute $\angle$.	2. If one angle of a $\triangle$ is a rt. $\angle$ or an obtuse $\angle$, each of the other two angles of the $\triangle$ must be acute. (§ 105.)
3. $\angle h$ is less than $\angle g$.	3. An acute $\angle$ is an angle less than a rt. $\angle$. (§ 25.)
4. $\therefore PQ < PR$.	4. If one angle of a $\triangle$ is greater than a second angle, the side opposite the first angle is greater than the side opposite the second angle (§ 135.) Q.E.D.

137. Cor. (Converse of Prop. XXVII). *If a line is the shortest line that can be drawn from a given point to a given line, it is the perpendicular from the point to the given line.*

Thus, given PQ the shortest line from P to AB, then $PQ \perp AB$.

Proposition XXVIII. Theorem

138. *If two triangles have two sides of one respectively equal to two sides of the other, and the included angles unequal, the triangle which has the greater included angle has the greater third side.*

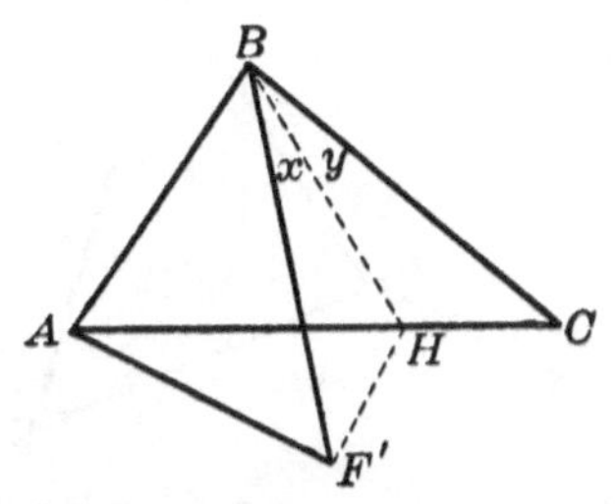 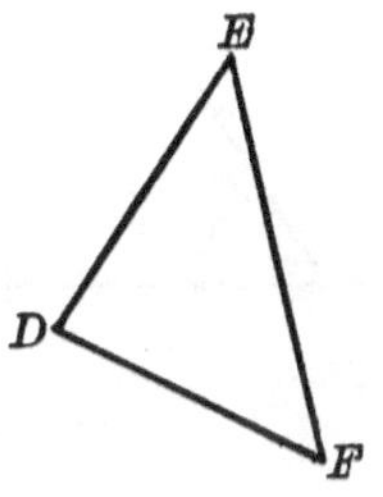

Given the $\triangle$ ABC and DEF in which $AB = DE$, $BC = EF$, and $\angle ABC$ is greater than $\angle E$.

To prove $AC > DF$.

Proof. 1. Place the $\triangle$ DEF so that DE coincides with its equal, AB, and F falls on the same side of AB as C, at F''.	1. Geom. Ax. 2.
2. Construct the line BH bisecting $\angle F'BC$ and meeting the line AC at H. Draw $F'H$.	2. § 84, Post. 1.
3. Then in the $\triangle$ $F'BH$ and BHC, $F'B = BC$.	3. Hyp.
4. $\qquad BH = BH.$	4. Why?
5. $\qquad \angle x = \angle y.$	5. Why?
6. $\therefore \triangle F'BH = \triangle BHC.$	6. Why?
7. $\therefore F'H = CH.$	7. Why?
8. But $AH + HF' > AF'$.	8. Why?
9. Substituting for HF' its equal, HC, $AH + HC$, or $AC > AF'$.	9. Why?
10. $\therefore AC > DF.$	10. Why? Q.E.D

Proposition XXIX. Theorem

139. *If two triangles have two sides of one respectively equal to two sides of the other, and the third sides are unequal, the triangle which has the greater third side has the greater included angle.*

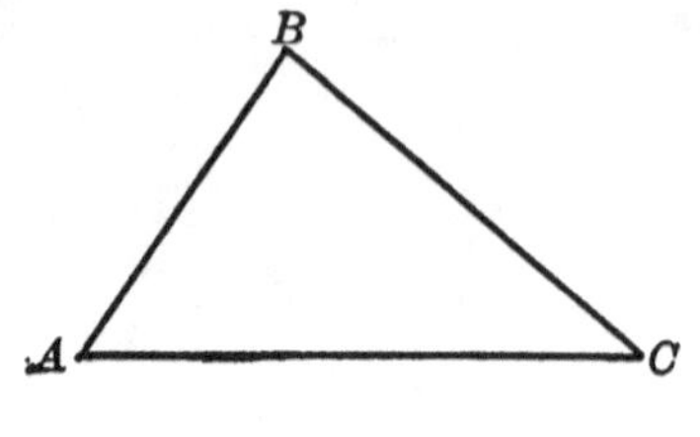 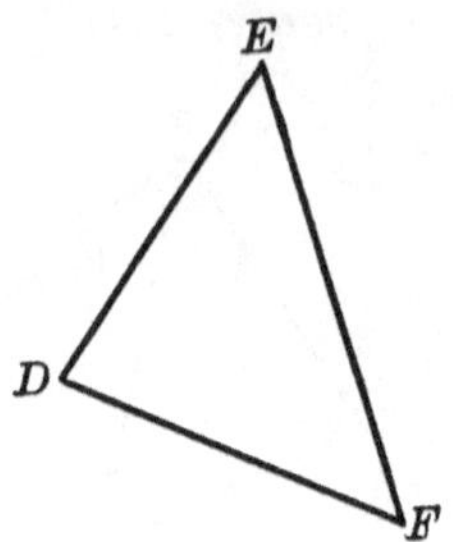

Given the △ *ABC* and *DEF* having *AB* = *DE*, *BC* = *EF*, but *AC* > *DF*.

To prove ∠ *B* greater than ∠ *E*.

Proof. 1. ∠ *B* either = ∠ *E*, or is less than ∠ *E*, or is greater than ∠ *E*.

1. Ineq. Ax. 5.   (§ 133.)

2. But ∠ *B* does not = ∠ *E*.

2. If it did, △ *ABC* would equal △ *DEF* (§ 79) and *AC* would equal *DF*, which is contrary to the hypothesis.

3. Also ∠ *B* cannot be less than ∠ *E*.

3. If it were, the side *AC* would be less than the side *DF* (§ 138), which is contrary to the hypothesis.

4. Hence, ∠ *B* is greater than ∠ *E*.

4. It neither equals ∠ *E*, nor is less than ∠ *E*.   Q.E.D.

Ex. 1. How many points in a plane are necessary to determine two parallel lines? Three parallel lines?

Ex. 2. Are two triangles necessarily equal if three angles of one equal the corresponding three angles of the other? Illustrate by drawing a figure.

Proposition XXX. Theorem

140. *If two oblique straight lines drawn from a point to a straight line meet the line at unequal distances from the foot of the perpendicular drawn from the point to the line, the more remote is the greater.*

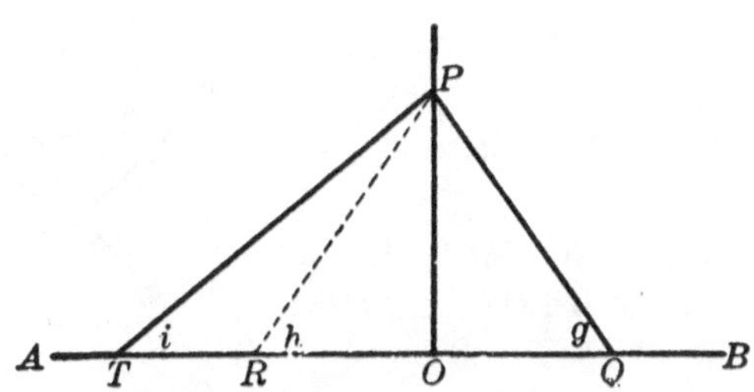

Given $PO \perp AB$, and T and Q points on AB such that $OT > OQ$.

To prove $PT > PQ$.

Proof. 1. On OA mark off $OR = OQ$.	1. Post. 2.
2. Draw PR.	2. Post. 1.
3. Then $PR = PQ$.	3. § 119.
4. $\angle h = \angle g$.	4. § 82.
5. But $\angle h$ is greater than $\angle i$.	5. § 87.
6. Substituting $\angle g$ for its equal, $\angle h$, $\angle g$ is greater than $\angle i$.	6. Ax. 9.
7. Then in $\triangle TPQ$, $PT > PQ$.	7. § 135. Q.E.D.

141. Cor. *Of two unequal lines drawn to a given line from a point in a perpendicular to that line, the greater line cuts off the greater segment from the foot of the perpendicular.*

Thus, if $PT > PQ$ (Fig. of Prop. XXX), OT cannot $= OQ$ (§ 119); nor is $OT < OQ$ (§ 140). $\therefore OT > OQ$.

Hence, also, *from a given point only two equal straight lines can be drawn to a given line.*

EXERCISES: GROUP 13

Ex. 1. Given $\triangle ABC$, $AP = PC$, $\angle r$ acute. Prove $AB > BC$.

Ex. 2. Draw any four-sided figure $ABCD$; let F be any point in the side BC. Prove perimeter of $ABCD >$ perimeter of AFD.

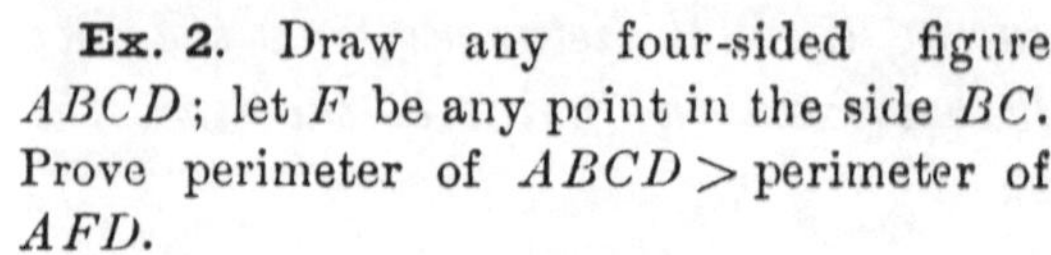

Ex. 3. Draw a triangle ABC; let D be any point in AB and F any point in BC. Prove $AB + BC > AD + DF + FC$.

Ex. 4. Given a four-sided figure $ABCD$, $AB = CD$, $\angle BAD > \angle ADC$. Prove $BD > AC$.

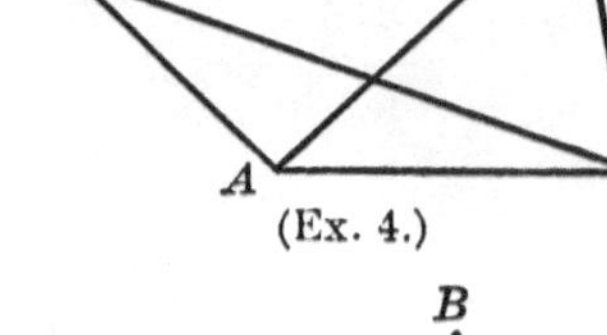

(Ex. 4.)

Ex. 5. Given $\triangle ABC$, $AB = BC$, $AD > DC$. Prove $\angle p > \angle q$.

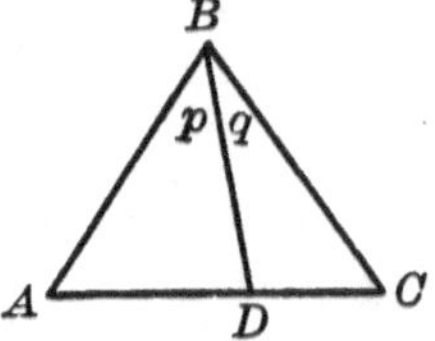

Ex. 6. By the aid of squared paper, construct the following designs:

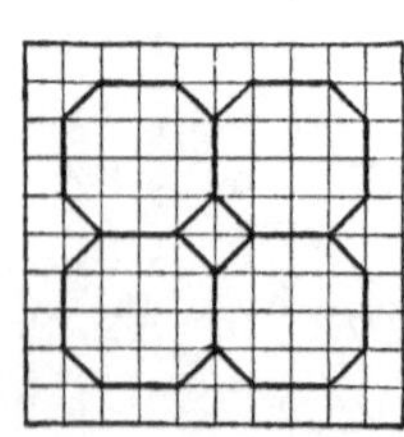 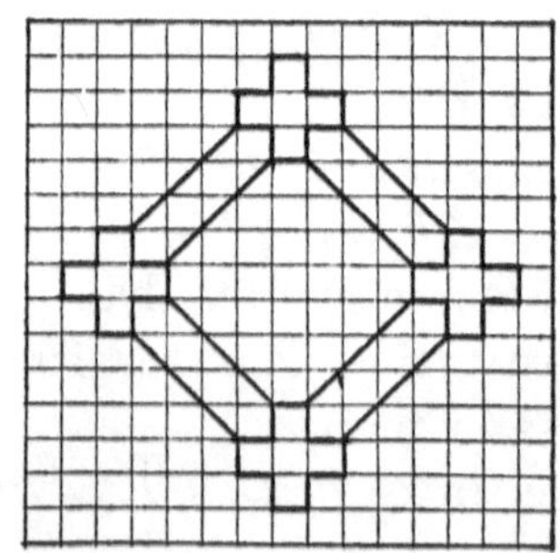

QUADRILATERALS

142. A **quadrilateral** is a polygon of four sides.

The **sides** of a quadrilateral are the bounding lines. The **angles** are the angles made by the bounding lines. The **vertices** are the vertices of the angles of the quadrilateral.

The **perimeter** of a quadrilateral is the sum of the sides.

143. A **diagonal** of a quadrilateral is a straight line joining two of its vertices that are not adjacent.

144. A **trapezium** is a quadrilateral in which no two sides are parallel.

145. A **trapezoid** is a quadrilateral which has two, and only two, of its sides parallel.

146. A **parallelogram** is a quadrilateral whose opposite sides are parallel.

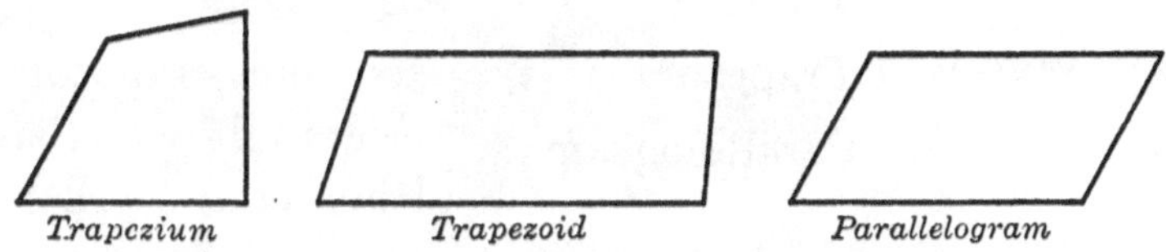

147. A **rhomboid** is a parallelogram whose angles are oblique angles.

148. A **rhombus** is a rhomboid whose sides are equal.

149. A **rectangle** is a parallelogram whose angles are right angles.

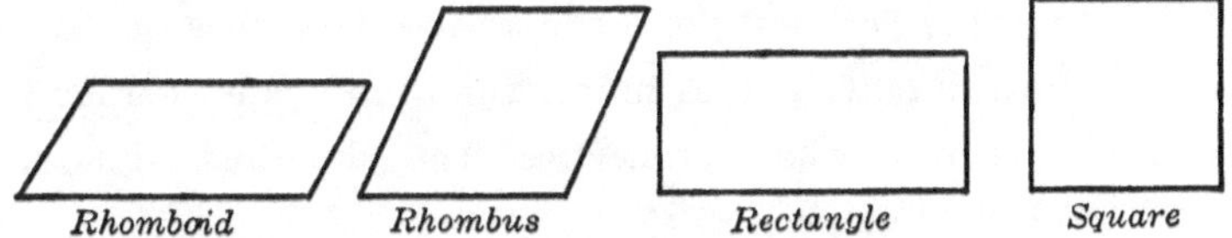

150. A **square** is a rectangle whose sides are equal.

151. The **base of a parallelogram** is the side upon which the parallelogram is supposed to stand; as AB. The opposite side is called the upper base (CD).

The **altitude** of a parallelogram is the perpendicular distance between the bases; as EF.

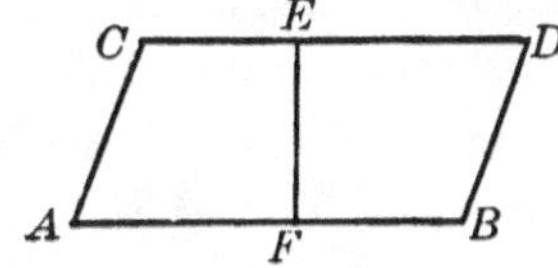

152. The **bases of a trapezoid** are its two parallel sides. The **legs** of a trapezoid are the sides which are not parallel. The **altitude** of a trapezoid is the perpendicular distance between the bases.   The **median** of a trapezoid is the line joining the midpoints of the legs.

153. An **isosceles trapezoid** is a trapezoid whose legs are equal.

154. Classification of quadrilaterals.

$$\text{Quadrilateral} \begin{cases} \text{Trapezium} \\ \text{Trapezoid} \ . \ . \ . \ . \ \ \text{Isosceles trapezoid} \\ \text{Parallelogram} \ . \ . \begin{cases} \text{Rectangle} \ . \ . \ \text{square} \\ \text{Rhomboid} \ . \ . \ \text{rhombus} \end{cases} \end{cases}$$

Ex. 1.   Draw a quadrilateral with three acute angles and one obtuse angle.

Ex. 2.   Is every rhombus a rhomboid? Is every rhomboid a rhombus?

Ex. 3.   What is the difference between a square and a rhombus? What properties do they have in common?

Ex. 4.   Find the perimeter of a square foot in inches.

Ex. 5.   Determine what four names the rhombus is entitled to.

Ex. 6.   Determine what properties the rhombus, square, and rectangle have in common.

Ex. 7.   A diagonal of a rhombus divides the rhombus into how many triangles?   What kind of triangles are these?

Ex. 8.   Construct a parallelogram $ABCD$. Let P be the midpoint of the side BC and Q the midpoint of AD. Draw AC, BQ, and DP. Denote the angles of the figure by small letters like a, b, c, etc. On the figure thus constructed point out 8 pairs of alternate interior angles.   Also 6 pairs of corresponding angles.   Also 4 pairs of interior angles on the same side of a transversal.

Ex. 9.   Construct two parallelograms whose corresponding sides are equal, but whose corresponding angles are unequal.

Proposition XXXI. Theorem

155. *The opposite sides of a parallelogram are equal, and its opposite angles are also equal.*

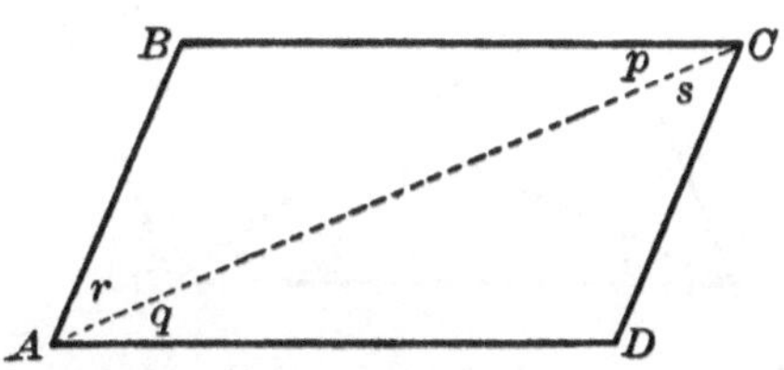

Given the parallelogram $ABCD$.

To prove $AD = BC$, $AB = DC$, $\angle B = \angle D$, and $\angle BAD = \angle BCD$.

Proof. 1. Draw the diagonal AC.	1. Post. 1.
2. Then in the $\triangle ABC$ and ADC, $\quad AC = AC$.	2. Why?
3. Also $\quad \angle p = \angle q$.	3. § 96.
4. $\quad\quad \angle r = \angle s$.	4. Why?
5. $\quad \therefore \triangle ABC = \triangle ACD$.	5. Why?
6. $\therefore AD = BC$, $AB = DC$, $\angle B = \angle D$.	6. Corr. parts of equal $\triangle$.
7. In like manner, by drawing the diagonal BD, it may be proved that $\quad \angle BAD = \angle BCD$.	7. Reasons 1–6. Q.E.D.

156. Cor. 1. *A diagonal divides a parallelogram into two equal triangles.*

157. Cor. 2. *Parallel lines comprehended between parallel lines are equal.*

158. Cor. 3. *Two parallel lines are everywhere equidistant.*

Ex. 1. In the above figure, prove $\angle BAD = \angle BCD$ by use of Ax. 2.

Ex. 2. In the above diagram, produce BC and DC through C and prove $\angle BAD = \angle BCD$ by use of §§ 112 and 69.

PROPOSITION XXXII. THEOREM

159. *The diagonals of a parallelogram bisect each other.*

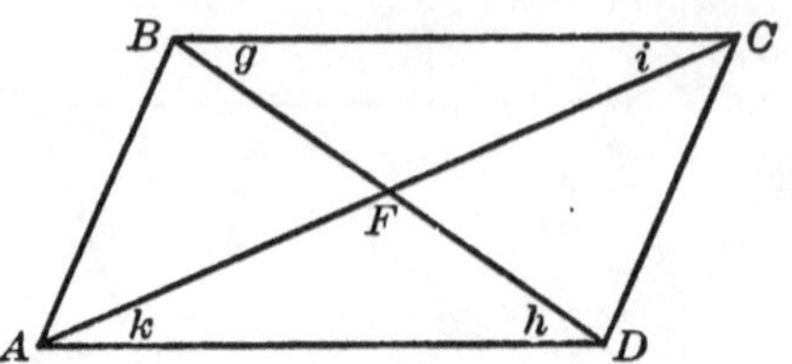

Given the diagonals AC and BD of the $\square\,ABCD$, intersecting at F.

To prove $AF = FC$, and $BF = FD$.

Proof. Let the student supply the proof.

[SUG. In the $\triangle\,BFC$ and AFD, what sides are equal, and why? What $\angle$ are equal, and why? etc.]

Ex. 1. How many pairs of equal triangles are there in the above figure?

Ex. 2. If two angles of a triangle are $p°$ and $q°$, find the third angle.

Ex. 3. If two angles of a triangle are $x°$ and $90° + x°$, find the third angle in terms of x.

Ex. 4. Draw the figure and letter it for the following theorem: "The diagonals of a rectangle are equal." Then, in terms of the figure drawn, state the hypothesis and conclusion (but do not give proof).

Ex. 5. By use of the ruler and compasses construct an angle of 105°. (Observe that $105° = 60° + 45°$.)

Ex. 6. Construct a parallelogram two of whose sides are 2 in. and 1 in. and one of whose angles is 60°.

Ex. 7. Construct two triangles which have two sides of one triangle equal to two sides of the other, and the angles opposite one pair of corresponding sides equal, but having the equal parts so arranged that the triangles themselves are not equal.

Proposition XXXIII. Theorem

160. *If the opposite sides of a quadrilateral are equal, the figure is a parallelogram.*

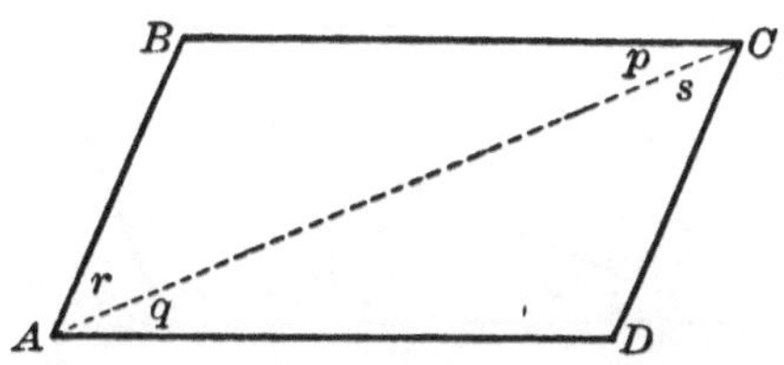

Given the quadrilateral $ABCD$ in which $AB = CD$ and $BC = AD$.

To prove $ABCD$ a $\square$.

Proof. 1. Draw the diagonal AC.	1. Post. 1.
2. In $\triangle ABC$ and ADC, $AC = AC$.	2. Why?
3. $BC = AD$.	3. Why?
4. $AB = CD$.	4. Why?
5. $\therefore \triangle ABC = \triangle ADC$.	5. Why?
6. $\therefore \angle r = \angle s$.	6. Why?
7. $\therefore AB \parallel CD$.	7. When two straight lines are cut by a third, if the alt. int. $\angle$ are equal, the two straight lines are parallel. (§ 89.)
8. Also $\angle p = \angle q$.	8. Why?
9. $\therefore BC \parallel AD$.	9. Why?
10. $\therefore ABCD$ is a $\square$.	10. § 146. Q.E.D.

Ex. State in order the theorems and other geometric principles used in proving that if two triangles have the three sides of one respectively equal to the three sides of the other, the triangles are equal.

PROPOSITION XXXIV. THEOREM

161. *If two sides of a quadrilateral are equal and parallel, the figure is a parallelogram.*

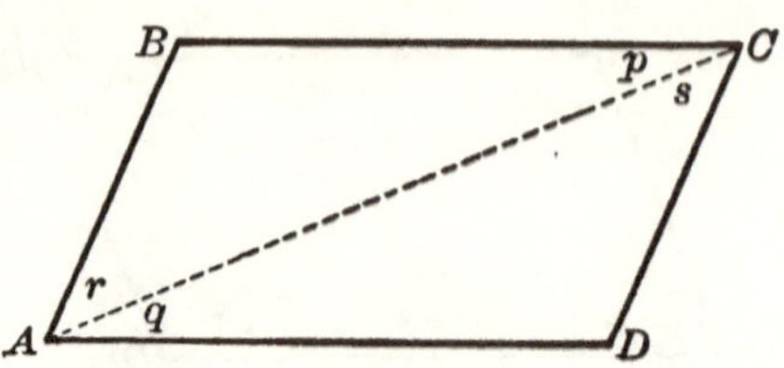

Given the quadrilateral *ABCD* in which *BC =* and ‖ *AD*.

To prove *ABCD* a □.

Proof. 1. Draw the diagonal *AC*.	1. Post. 1.
2. In the △ *ABC* and *ADC*, *AC = AC*.	2. Why?
3. $\qquad$ *BC = AD*.	3. Why?
4. $\qquad$, $\angle p = \angle q$.	4. Why?
5. ∴ △ *ABC* = △ *ADC*.	5. Why?
6. $\qquad$ ∴ $\angle r = \angle s$.	6. Why?
7. $\qquad$ ∴ *AB* ‖ *CD*.	7. Why?
8. ∴ *ABCD* is a □.	8. § 146.

Q.E.D.

Ex. 1. Show that in a □ each pair of adjacent angles is supplementary.

Ex. 2. One angle of a parallelogram is 43°; find the other angles.

Ex. 3. If one angle of a parallelogram is three times another angle, find all the angles of the parallelogram.

Ex. 4. If one angle of a parallelogram is $a°$, find the other angles.

Ex. 5. If, in the triangle *ABC*, $\angle A = 60°$, $\angle B = 70°$, which is the longest side in the triangle? Which the shortest side?

Ex. 6. In the diagram on p. 87 point out 6 pairs of corresponding angles. Also 6 pairs of alternate interior angles.

Ex. 7. Make up and solve an example similar to Ex. 5.

Proposition XXXV. Theorem

162. *If the diagonals of a quadrilateral bisect each other, the figure is a parallelogram.*

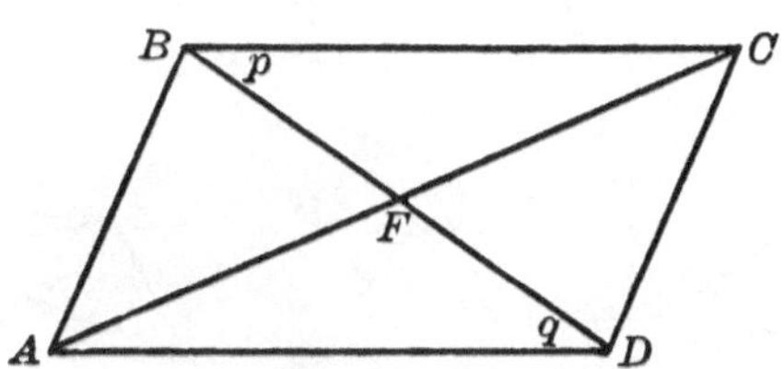

Given the quadrilateral $ABCD$ in which the diagonals AC and BD bisect each other at F.

To prove $ABCD$ a parallelogram.

Proof. 1. In the $\triangle\ BFC$ and AFD, $BF = FD$.
  2. $CF = AF$.
  3. $\angle BFC = \angle AFD$.
  4. $\therefore\ \triangle BFC = \triangle AFD$.
  5. $BC = AD$.
  6. $\angle p = \angle q$.
  7. $\therefore\ BC \parallel AD$.
  8. $\therefore\ ABCD$ is a $\square$.

1. Why?
2. Why?
3. Why?
4. Why?
5. Why?
6. Why?
7. Why?
8. If two opposite sides of a quadrilateral are equal and parallel, the figure is a parallelogram. (§ 161.) Q.E.D.

Ex. 1. Prop. XXXV is the converse of what theorem?

Ex. 2. Is the converse of a proposition always true? Give two propositions which illustrate your statement.

Ex. 3. The efficiency value of § 160 is that it enables us to ascertain that the opposite sides of a given quadrilateral are parallel by measuring the length of the sides of the quadrilateral. State the efficiency value of § 162.

EXERCISES: GROUP 14

Ex. 1. To determine the distance AB, construct AD and $BC \perp AB$, making $AD = BC$. Prove $ABCD$ a parallelogram.

If we measure DC and find it to be 312 yd., how long is AB? Why?

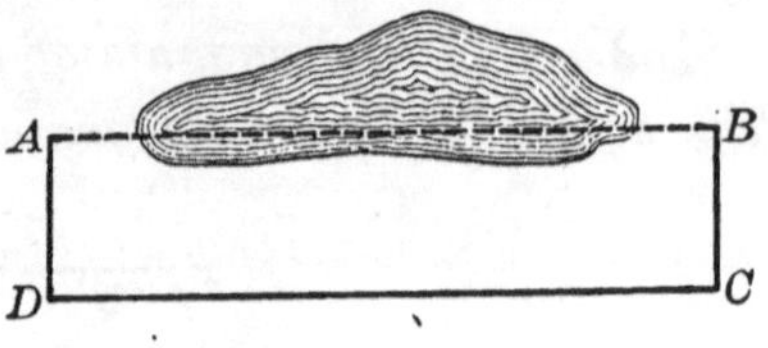

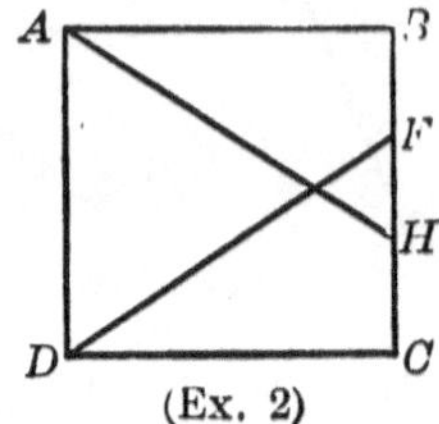

(Ex. 2)

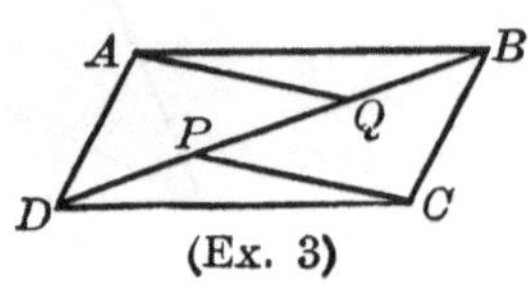

(Ex. 3)

Ex. 2. Given $ABCD$ a square, and $BF = HC$. Prove $AH = DF$.

Ex. 3. Given $ABCD$ a parallelogram; on the diagonal DB, $DP = BQ$. Prove $AQ = CP$.

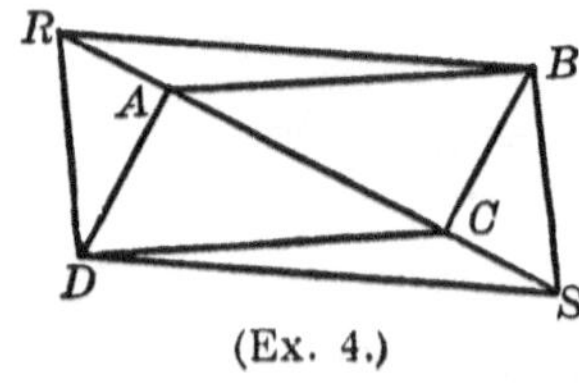

(Ex. 4.)

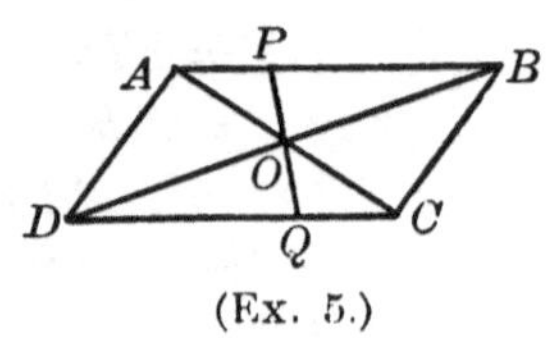

(Ex. 5.)

Ex. 4. Given $ABCD$ a parallelogram. The diagonal AC is produced so that $AR = CS$. Prove $RBSD$ a parallelogram.

Ex. 5. Given $ABCD$ a $\square$ with its diagonals intersecting at O; PQ any line through O terminated by the sides of the $\square$. Prove $OP = OQ$.

Ex. 6. Prove that the diagonals of a rhombus are perpendicular to each other, by the use of § 121.

Ex. 7. By the aid of squared paper, construct and complete the following design:

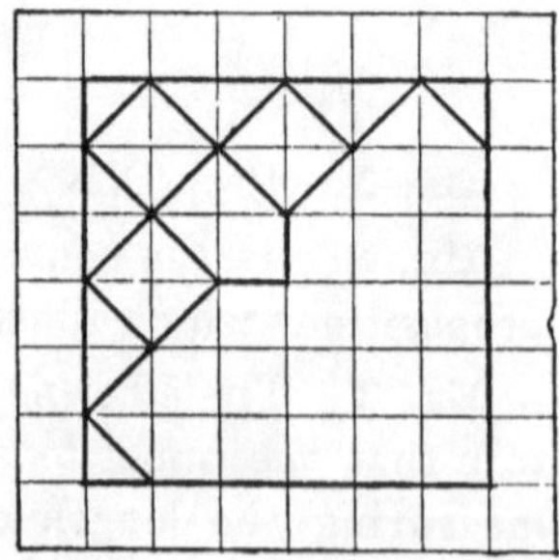

Ex. 8. Given *ABCD* and *FBCH*, parallelograms with the side *BC* in common. **Prove** the line *AD* = and ∥ *FH*.

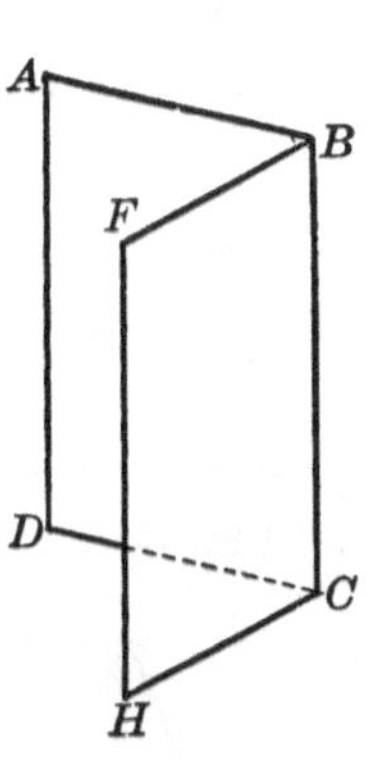

Ex. 9. Prove that the sum of the four sides of a quadrilateral is greater than the sum of the diagonals.

Ex. 10. Upon a given straight line as a side, construct a square.

Ex. 11. Construct a rectangle whose base is 2 in. and whose altitude is 1 in.

Ex. 12. Upon a given line as a diagonal, construct a square.

Ex. 13. Construct a rhombus, given the two diagonals.

POLYGONS

163. A **polygon,** as already defined, is a portion of a plane bounded by straight lines; as *ABCDE.*

The **sides** of a polygon are its bounding lines. The **perimeter** of a polygon is the sum of its sides. The **angles** of a polygon are the angles formed by its sides. The **vertices** of a polygon are the vertices of its angles.

A **diagonal** of a polygon is a straight line joining two vertices which are not adjacent; as *BD* in Fig. 1.

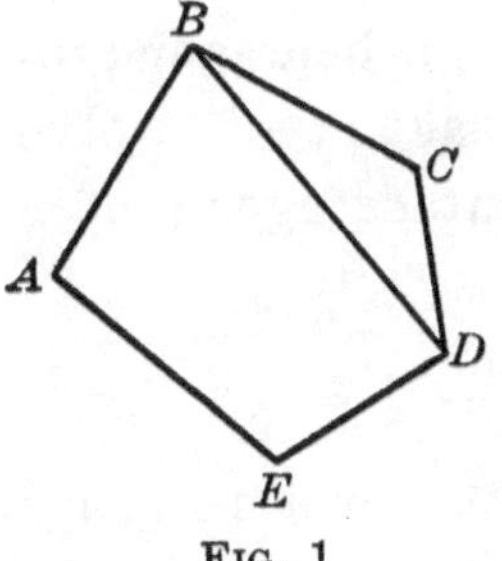

FIG. 1

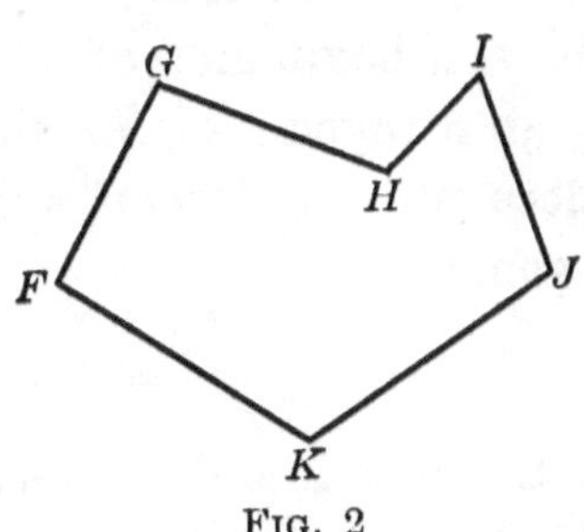

FIG. 2

164. An **equilateral polygon** is a polygon in which all the sides are equal.

An **equiangular polygon** is a polygon in which all the angles are equal.

What four-sided polygon is equilateral but not equiangular? What four-sided polygon is both equilateral and equiangular?

165. Two mutually equiangular polygons are polygons whose corresponding angles are equal; as Figs. 3 and 4.

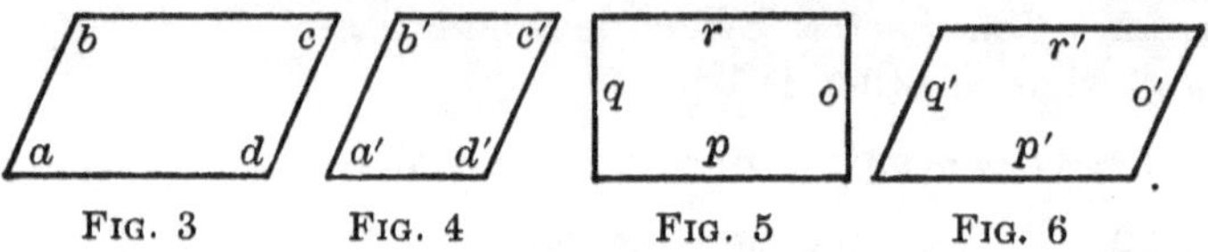

FIG. 3   FIG. 4   FIG. 5   FIG. 6

Two mutually equilateral polygons are polygons whose corresponding sides are equal; as Figs. 5 and 6.

From Figs. 3 and 4 it is seen that two polygons may be mutually equiangular without being mutually equilateral.

What similar truth may be inferred from Figs. 5 and 6?

Polygons that are mutually equiangular and equilateral may be made to coincide and are therefore equal.

166. Names of polygons. —Some polygons are used so frequently that special names have been given to them. A polygon of three sides is called a **triangle**; one of four sides, a **quadrilateral**; one of five sides, a **pentagon**; of six sides, a **hexagon**; of seven sides, a **heptagon**; of eight sides, an **octagon**; of ten sides, a **decagon**; of twelve sides, a **dodecagon**; of fifteen sides, a **pentadecagon**; of *n* sides, an **n-gon**.

Ex. 1. How does the number of vertices of a polygon compare with the number of sides?

Ex. 2. Can two triangles be mutually equilateral without being mutually equiangular? What polygons can?

Proposition XXXVI. Theorem

167. *The sum of the angles of a polygon of n sides is* $(2n - 4)$ *right angles.*

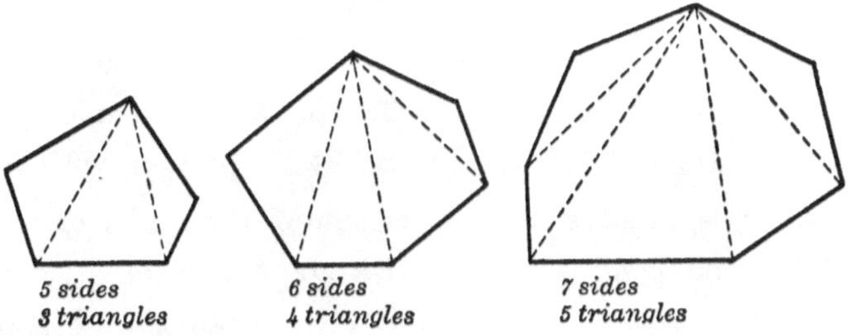

Given a polygon of n sides.

(The above polygons of 5, 6, 7 sides are used merely as particular illustrations, to aid in carrying forward the proof.)

To prove the sum of the angles of the polygon

$$= (2n - 4) \text{ rt. } \measuredangle.$$

Proof. 1. Separate the polygon into $\measuredangle$ by diagonals drawn from some one vertex.

1. Post. 1.

2. There will be $(n - 2)$ of these $\measuredangle$.

2. Each of the n sides of the polygon will be the base of a $\triangle$, except the two sides adjacent to the chosen vertex.

3. The sum of the $\measuredangle$ of each $\triangle = 2$ rt. $\measuredangle$.

3. The sum of the angles of a $\triangle = 2$ rt. $\measuredangle$. (§ 102.)

4. The sum of the $\measuredangle$ of $(n - 2) \measuredangle = (n - 2) 2$ rt. $\measuredangle$; that is, $(2n - 4)$ rt. $\measuredangle$.

4. Ax. 4.

5. But the sum of the $\measuredangle$ of the polygon $=$ sum of the $\measuredangle$ of the $\measuredangle$.

5. The whole is equal to the sum of its parts. (Ax. 7.)

6. $\therefore$ the sum of the $\measuredangle$ of the polygon $= (2n - 4)$ rt. $\measuredangle$.

6. Ax. 1.

Q.E.D.

168. Cor.   *In an equiangular polygon of n sides, each angle equals* $\dfrac{2n-4}{n}$ *rt. $\angle$s.*

EXERCISES : GROUP 15

How many right angles are there in the sum of the angles of

Ex. 1. A quadrilateral?   **Ex. 3.** A sixteen-sided polygon?

Ex. 2. A hexagon?   **Ex. 4.** A polygon with 20 sides?

How many degrees are there in the sum of the angles of

Ex. 5. A pentagon?   **Ex. 7.** A decagon?

Ex. 6. An octagon?   **Ex. 8.** A polygon of 18 sides?

State the number of degrees in each angle of an equiangular

Ex. 9. Hexagon.   **Ex. 11.** Decagon.

Ex. 10. Heptagon.   **Ex. 12.** Polygon of 16 sides.

Ex. 13.   If two angles of a quadrilateral are 73° and 106°, how many degrees are there in the sum of the other two angles of the quadrilateral?

Ex. 14.   If three of the angles of a quadrilateral are 82°, 97°, and 63°, find the other angle of the quadrilateral without measuring it.

Ex. 15.   Make up and solve a problem similar to Ex. 14 concerning a pentagon.

Ex. 16.   Prove that if two of the angles of a quadrilateral are supplementary, the other two angles must be supplementary also.

Ex. 17.   Prove that the sum of the three exterior angles, *a*, *b*, *c*, of a triangle, as indicated on the figure, is four right angles.

Ex. 18.   If one angle of a parallelogram is a right angle, prove that the figure is a rectangle.

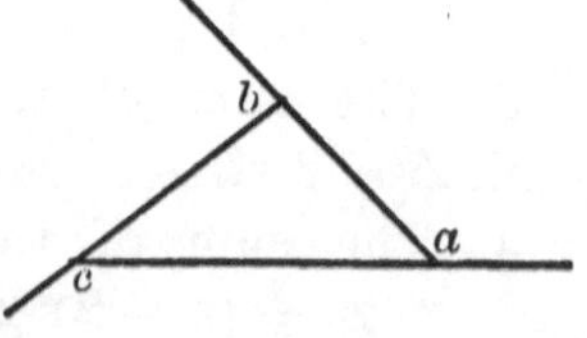

Ex. 19.   If one of the angles of an equiangular polygon contains 108°, how many sides has the polygon?

Ex. 20.   Would a quadrilateral constructed of rods hinged at the ends (*i.e.*, at the vertices of the quadrilateral) be rigid? Would a triangle so constructed be rigid? Would a pentagon?

Proposition XXXVII. Theorem

169. *If a series of parallel lines cut off equal segments on one transversal, they cut off equal segments on any other transversal.*

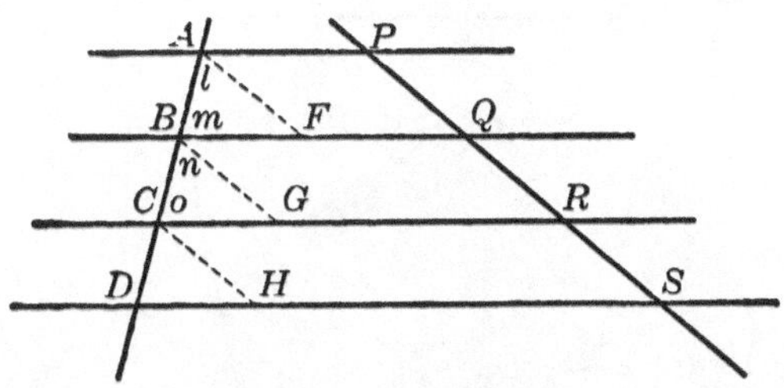

Given AP, BQ, CR, and DS parallel lines intercepting the equal parts AB, BC, and CD on the transversal AD and the parts PQ, QR, RS on the transversal PS.

To prove $PQ = QR = RS$.

Proof. 1. Through A, B, C, construct AF, BG, CH, $\parallel PS$ and meeting BQ, CR, DS, in the points F, G, H, respectively.

1. § 95.

2. Then the lines AF and BG are $\parallel$.

2. § 101.

3. Then in the $\triangle ABF$ and BCG, $AB = BC$.

3. Why?

4. Also $\angle l = \angle n$, and $\angle m = \angle o$.

4. § 97.

5. $\therefore \triangle ABF = \triangle BCG$.

5. Why?

6. $\therefore AF = BG$.

6. Why?

7. But $AF = PQ$, and $BG = QR$.

7. Parallel lines comprehended between parallel lines are equal. (§ 157.)

8. $\therefore PQ = QR$.

8. Ax. 1.

9. In like manner, it may be proved that $QR = RS$.

9. Reasons 2–8.

Q.E.D

Proposition XXXVIII.   Problem

170. *To divide a given straight line into any given number of equal parts.*

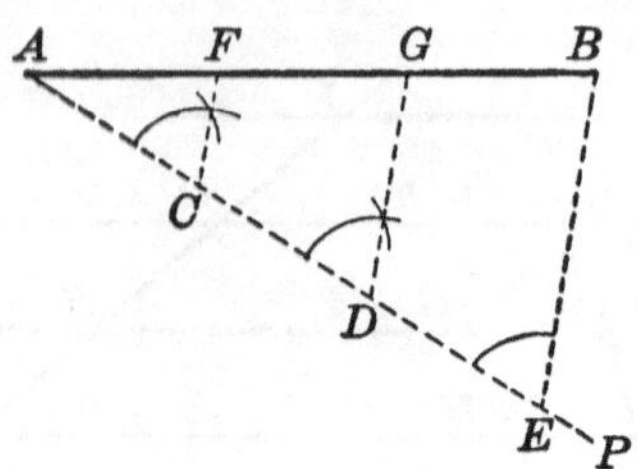

Given the line AB.

To divide AB into a given number of equal parts (as three equal parts).

Construction. 1. From A draw the line AP making a convenient angle with AB.	1. Post. 1.
2. Take AC (any line of convenient length) and apply it to AP a number of times equal to the number of parts into which AB is to be divided.	2. Post. 2.
3. From E, the end of the measure when last applied to AP, draw EB.	3. Post. 1
4. Through the other points of division on AP (viz., C and D) draw lines ‖ EB and meeting AB at F and G.	4. § 95.
Then AB is divided into the required number of parts at F and G.	
Proof. 1. $AC = CD = DE$.	1. Constr.
2. $\therefore\ AF = FG = GB$.	2. § 169. Q.E.D.

Ex. 1.   Draw a line 2 inches long and divide it into 3 equal parts.

Ex. 2.   Draw a line 3″ long and divide it into 5 equal parts.

Ex. 3.   Draw a line and then determine $\frac{2}{3}$ of the line.

Ex. 4.   Draw a line and determine $\frac{4}{5}$ of it.

Ex. 5. Draw a line and then construct a triangle whose sides shall be $\frac{2}{3}$, $\frac{3}{4}$, and $\frac{4}{5}$ of the given line.

Ex. 6. Given its perimeter, construct an equilateral triangle.

171. Proving triangles equal.—Let the student form a list of the conditions that make two triangles equal. (See §§ 79, 80, 83, 109, 110, 111, 117.)

EXERCISES: GROUP 16

EQUALITY OF TRIANGLES

Ex. 1. Given ABC any triangle, BO the bisector of $\angle ABC$, and $AD \perp BO$. **Prove** $\triangle ABO = \triangle BOD$.

Ex. 2. If, upon the sides of an angle, equal segments are laid off from the vertex, and lines are drawn from the ends of these segments to any point in the bisector of the angle, prove that the triangles formed are equal.

Ex. 3. If two sides of a triangle are produced, each its own length, through the vertex in which they meet, and the extremities of the produced parts are joined, prove that a new triangle is formed which equals the original triangle.

Ex. 4. Given $AB = DC$, and $BC = DA$. **Prove** $\triangle BAC = \triangle DAC$.

What other pair of equal triangles is there in the figure?

Ex. 5. If, at any point in the bisector of an angle, a $\perp$ is erected and produced to meet the sides of the angle, how many triangles are formed? Which of these triangles are equal? Prove your statement.

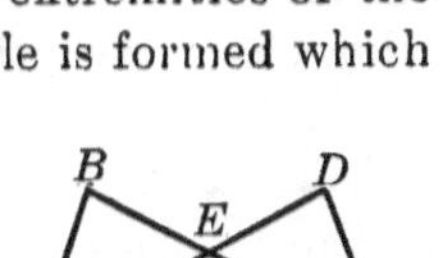

Ex. 6. If, through the midpoint of a given straight line, another line is drawn, and produced to meet the perpendiculars erected at the ends of the given line, the triangles so formed are equal.

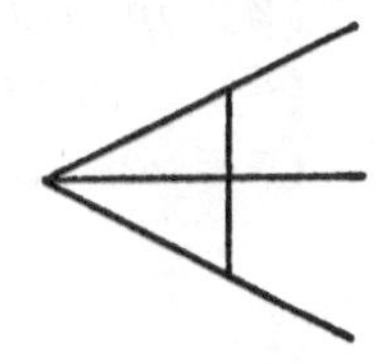

Ex. 7. If two straight lines bisect each other and their extremities are joined, how many pairs of equal triangles are formed? Prove your statement.

Ex. 8. If on the legs of an isosceles triangle equal segments are laid off from the base, and lines are drawn from the extremities of the segments to the opposite vertices, prove that two pairs of equal triangles are formed.

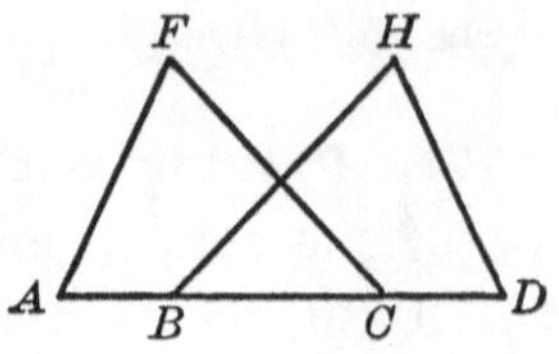

Ex. 9. On the straight line AD, $AB = CD$. Also $AF = DH$, and $CF = BH$. Prove the triangles AFC and BHD equal.

Ex. 10. Two right triangles are equal if their corresponding legs are equal.

Ex. 11. In the isosceles triangle ABC, $AB = BC$, $AQ = PC$. Prove the triangles ABP and QBC equal.

Ex. 12. The altitudes from the extremities of the base of an isosceles triangle upon the legs of the triangle divide the figure into how many pairs of equal triangles?   Prove this.

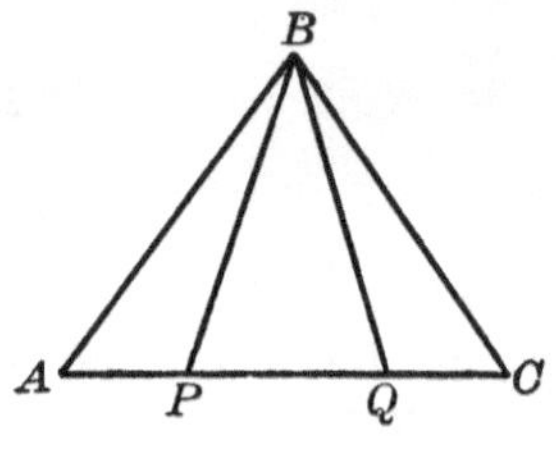

Ex. 13. In a given quadrilateral, two adjacent sides are equal and a diagonal bisects the angle between these sides. Prove that the diagonal bisects the quadrilateral.

Ex. 14. If, from the ends of the shorter base of an isosceles trapezoid, lines are drawn parallel to the legs and produced to meet the other base, prove that a pair of equal triangles is formed.

172. Proving lines equal. — Lines (segments) may be proved equal by proving that they are:

(1) *corresponding parts of equal triangles;* or
(2) *opposite equal angles in an isosceles triangle;* or
(3) *opposite sides of a parallelogram;* or
(4) *parallel lines comprehended between parallel lines.*
(See §§ 115, 155, 157.)

173. Demonstration by analysis. — It is often an advantage to use the following method in obtaining the proof of a theorem :

Assume the proposed theorem as true;
Observe what other relations among the parts of the figure must then be true;

Proceed backward thus, step by step, till the required theorem is found to depend on some known truth or truths;

Then, starting with what is known, reverse the steps taken, and thus build up a direct proof of the required theorem.

This method is called **solution by analysis.**

We shall now give an example of solution by analysis.

Observe that in the process which follows, we first write the conclusion (that is the last step of the proof) in its proper place; then, above the last step, we write the next to the last step; and so proceed backward and upward toward the first step.

Thus, in the statement given below (as the first stage of the proof), we first write $AD = DB$.

Then, if this is true, we infer that $\triangle ADC$ may equal $\triangle DBC$. Hence, we next write $\triangle ADC = \triangle DBC$ (above the step $AD = DB$).

As a means of proving $\triangle ADC = \triangle DBC$, we know that $CD = CD$ by identity. Hence, we write $CD = CD$ above the step $\triangle ADC = \triangle DBC$. Since we know that $CD = CD$ is true, we set down the reason, "Ident.," in the right-hand column.

Hence, the proof as thus far worked out will appear as follows:

Ex.   Prove that the bisector of the vertex angle of an isosceles tri-angle bisects the base.

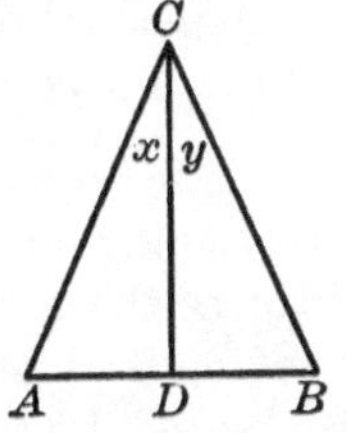

Given $\triangle ABC$ with $AC = BC$; and $\angle ACB$ bisected by CD.

To prove $AD = DB$.

Proof (FIRST STAGE)

$$CD = CD \qquad \text{Ident.}$$
$$\triangle ADC = \triangle DBC$$
$$AD = DB$$

After all the steps of the proof have been written by working backward to the first, the proof assumes the following form:

(SECOND STAGE OF THE PROOF)

Proof.
$AC = BC$	Hyp.
$\angle x = \angle y$	Hyp.
$CD = CD$	Ident.
$\therefore \triangle ADC = \triangle DBC$	
$AD = DB$	Corr. sides of $= \triangle$

We next number the steps (and reasons) in direct order 1, 2, 3, etc., filling in such reasons as were necessarily omitted in the process of working backward.   We thus obtain the

(THIRD OR FINAL STAGE OF THE PROOF)

Proof.
1.	$AC = BC$	1. Hyp.
2.	$\angle x = \angle y$	2. Hyp.
3.	$CD = CD$	3. Ident.
4.	$\triangle ADC = \triangle DBC$	4. s. $\angle$ s.
5.	$AD = DB$	5. Corr. sides of $= \triangle$

Q.E.D.

EXERCISES: GROUP 17

EQUALITY OF LINES

Ex. 1.   Given ABC any triangle, BO the bisector of $\angle ABC$, and $AD \perp BO$. **Prove** $AO = OD$.

Ex. 2.   If two sides of a triangle are produced, each its own length, through the common vertex, the line joining the extremities of the produced parts equals the third side of the triangle (*i.e.*, $DE = BA$).

Ex. 3.   If, at any point in the bisector of an angle, a perpendicular is erected to the bisector and produced to meet the sides of the angle, the perpendicular is divided into two equal parts at the given point.

Ex. 4.   If on the legs of an isosceles triangle equal segments are laid off from the base, lines drawn from the ends of these segments to the opposite vertices are equal.

Ex. 5. Given APB and RPQ straight lines, $AR \parallel QB$, and $AP = PB$. **Prove** $RP = PQ$.

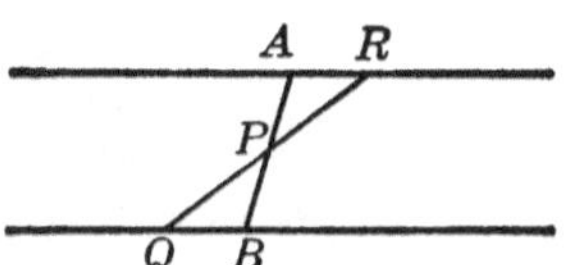

Ex. 6. Draw an angle and on its sides lay off equal segments from the vertex. Join the extremities of the segments thus formed with any point in the bisector of the angle. Prove that these two joining lines are equal.

Ex. 7. The altitudes of an isosceles triangle upon the legs are equal.

Ex. 8. The diagonals of a rectangle are equal.

Ex. 9. The medians of an isosceles triangle to the legs are equal.

Ex. 10. If two altitudes of a triangle are equal, the triangle is isosceles.

Ex. 11. The perpendiculars to a diagonal of a parallelogram from a pair of opposite vertices are equal.

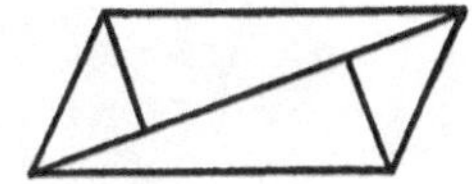

Ex. 12. If the equal sides of an isosceles triangle are produced through the vertex so that the produced parts are equal, the lines joining the extremities of the produced parts to the extremities of the base are equal.

Ex. 13. If the base of an isosceles triangle is trisected, lines drawn from the vertex to the points of trisection are equal.

Ex. 14.

In the bisectors of the equal angles of an isosceles triangle, the segments next to the base are equal ($AO = OP$).

Ex. 15.

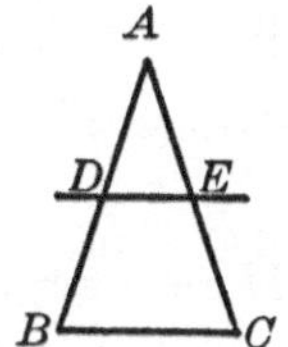

Given $\triangle ABC$, $AB = AC$, and $DE \parallel BC$.

Prove $AD = AE$.

Ex. 16.

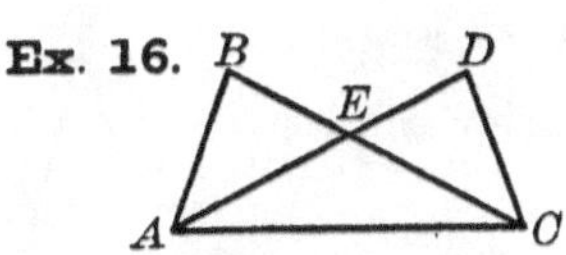

Given $AB = DC$, $BC = AD$.
Prove $AE = EC$.

Ex. 17.

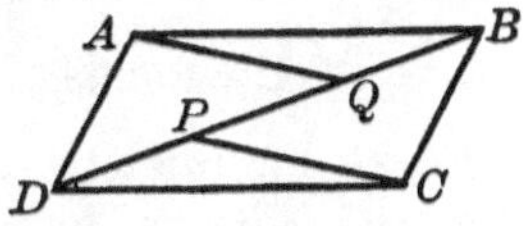

Given $ABCD$ a parallelogram and $PB = DQ$.
Prove $AQ = PC$.

174. Proving angles equal. — Among the ways of proving that two angles are equal are the following:

(1) *The given angles are corresponding parts of equal triangles; or*

(2) *they are opposite equal sides in an isosceles triangle; or*

(3) *they are vertical angles; or*

(4) *they are complements (or supplements) of equal angles; or*

(5) *by the use of the properties of parallel lines; or*

(6) *their corresponding sides are parallel, or perpendicular.*

(See §§ 66, 69, 82, 96, 97, 112, 114.)

EXERCISES: GROUP 18

Equality of Angles

Ex. 1. Given ABC any $\triangle$, BO the bisector of the $\angle ABC$, and $AD \perp BO$. **Prove** $\angle BAO = \angle BDO$.

Ex. 2. If, at any point in the bisector of an angle, a perpendicular is erected, and produced to meet the sides of the angle, the perpendicular makes equal angles with the sides of the angle.

Ex. 3. Given $AB = DC$, and $AD = BC$. **Prove** $\angle B = \angle D$.

Ex. 4. If on the legs of an isosceles triangle equal segments are laid off from the base, the lines drawn from the extremities of the segments to the opposite vertices make equal angles with the base.

Ex. 5. The altitudes upon the legs of an isosceles triangle make equal angles with the base.

Ex. 6. The diagonals of a rhombus bisect its angles.

Ex. 7. In an isosceles triangle, the exterior angles made by producing the base are equal.

Ex. 8. Given $AC = CB$, and $DE \parallel AB$. **Prove** $\angle CDE = \angle CED$.

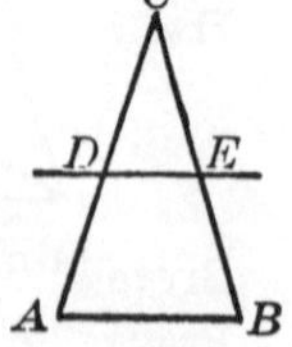

Ex. 9. Given ∠ *DCA* an exterior angle of △ *ABC*, *CE* ∥ *AB*, and ∠ *DCE* = ∠ *ECA*. **Prove** ∠ *B* = ∠ *A*.

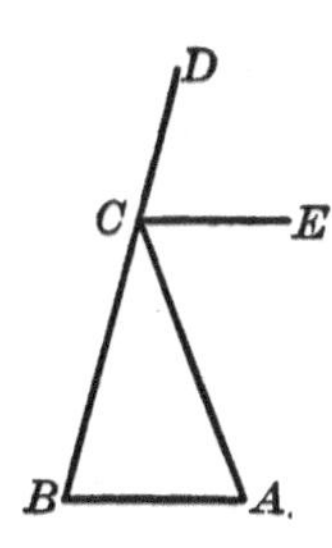

Ex. 10. Conversely, **given** ∠ *A* = ∠ *B*, and *CE* ∥ *AB*. **Prove** that *CE* bisects ∠ *DCA*.

Ex. 11. Given *BD* the bisector of the angle *ABC*, and *PR* ∥ *CB*. **Prove** that *PBR* is an isosceles △.

Let the student state this theorem in general language.

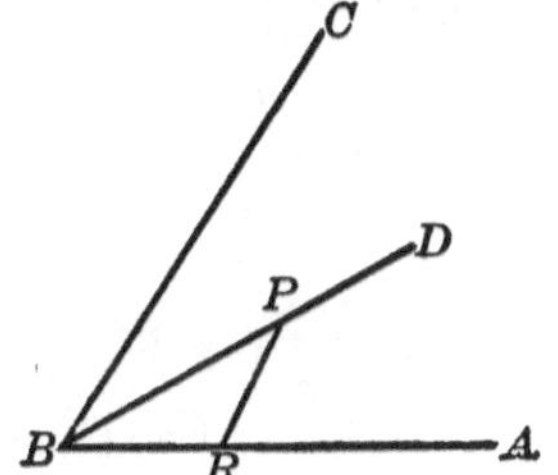

Ex. 12. Given △ *ABC*, with *AB* produced through *D*, and *AC* through *E*, *AB* = *AC*, and *BD* = *CE*. **Prove** ∠ *BCD* = ∠ *CBE*.

How many pairs of equal △ are there in the figure? Of equal lines? Of equal ∠?

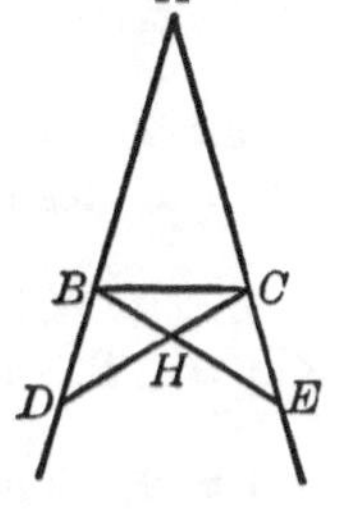

Ex. 13. A line drawn through the vertex of an angle, perpendicular to the bisector of the angle, makes equal angles with the sides of the given angle.

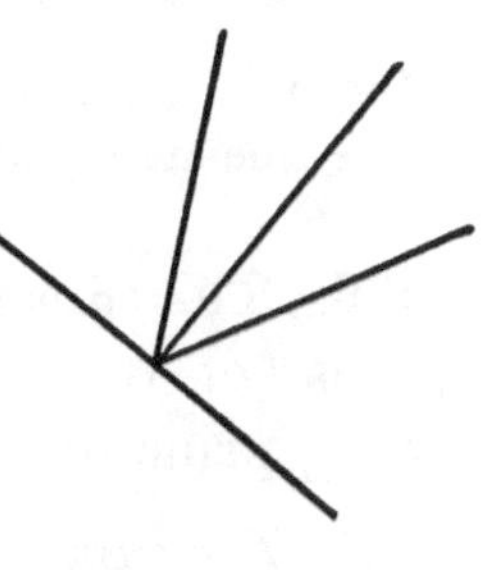

Ex. 14. If a straight line which bisects one of two vertical angles is produced, it bisects the other vertical angle also.

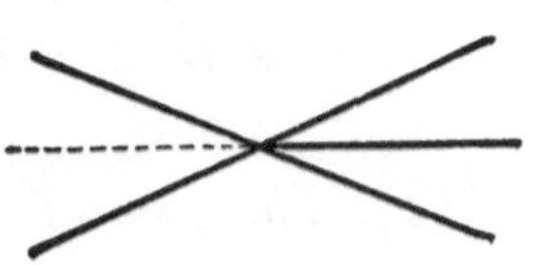

175. Proof that two lines are parallel may be obtained by showing that:

(1) *The lines are cut by a third line, making the alternate interior angles equal; or*

(2) *making the corresponding angles equal; or*

(3) *making the interior angles on the same side of the transversal supplementary; or*

(4) *that the lines are opposite sides of a parallelogram.*

(See §§ 89, 91, 94, 146.)

EXERCISES: GROUP 19

Parallel Lines

Ex. 1. If two sides of a triangle are produced, each its own length, through the common vertex, the line joining their extremities is parallel to the third side of the triangle.

Ex. 2. The bisectors of two alternate interior angles of parallel lines are parallel.

Ex. 3. Given $\angle DCA$ an exterior angle of $\triangle ABC$, $\angle A = \angle B$, and $\angle DCE = \angle ECA$. **Prove** $CE \parallel BA$.

Ex. 4. The bisectors of the opposite angles of a parallelogram are parallel.

Ex. 5. Two straight lines are parallel if two points on one line are equidistant from the other line.

176. The **proof of a numerical property of rectilinear figures** (of Book One) usually depends on one of the following principles:

(1) *The sum of the angles about a given point on the same side of a straight line passing through the point is 180°.*

(2) *The sum of the angles about a point is 360°.*

(3) *The sum of the angles of a triangle is* 180°.

(4) *The sum of the interior angles of parallel lines on the same side of a transversal is* 180°.

(5) *The sum of the interior angles of a polygon of* **n** *sides is* (2 *n* − 4) 90°.

(See §§ 67, 68, 98, 102, 167.)

EXERCISES: GROUP 20

NUMERICAL PROPERTIES

Ex. 1. If an exterior angle of a triangle is 123° and an opposite interior angle is 38°, find the other two interior angles of the triangle.

Ex. 2. Find the angle formed by the bisectors of the two acute angles of a right triangle.

Ex. 3. If two angles of a triangle are 50° and 60°, find the angle formed by their bisectors. If the two angles contain $p°$ and $q°$, find the angle formed by their bisectors.

Ex. 4. If the vertex angle of an isosceles triangle is 40°, and a perpendicular is drawn from an extremity of the base to the opposite side, find the angles of the figure.

Ex. 5. If the vertex angle of an isosceles triangle is 40°, find the angle included between the altitudes drawn from the extremities of the base to the opposite sides.

Ex. 6. How many degrees are there in each angle of an equiangular dodecagon? Of an equiangular *n*-gon?

Ex. 7. How many diagonals are there in a pentagon? In a hexagon? In a decagon? In an *n*-gon?

The methods of proving that a given angle is a right angle (or that a given line is perpendicular to another given line) or that one angle is the supplement of another, are closely related to the above methods of obtaining the numerical values of given angles.

Ex. 8. The bisectors of two supplementary adjacent angles form a right angle (are perpendicular).

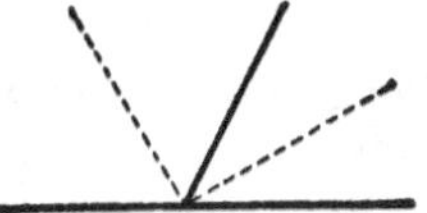

Ex. 9. The bisectors of two interior angles on the same side of a transversal of two parallel lines form a right angle.

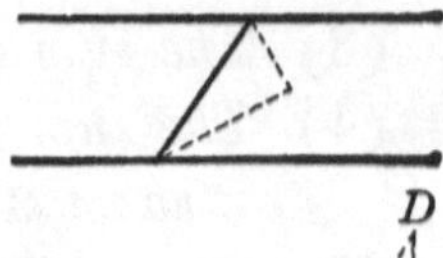

Ex. 10. If one of the legs (AB) of an isosceles triangle is produced its own length (BD), and its extremity (D) is joined to the other end of the base (C), the line last drawn (DC) is perpendicular to the base.

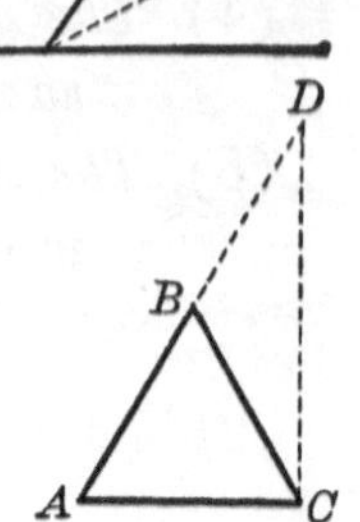

177. Algebraic method of proving theorems. — The proof of certain properties of a geometric figure is often facilitated by *using an algebraic symbol for an unknown angle or an unknown line of the figure, and using an equation or other algebraic method of solution.*

EXERCISES: GROUP 21

ALGEBRAIC METHOD

Ex. 1. Find the number of degrees in an angle which equals three times its complement.

[SUG.   See Ex. 24, p. 20.]

Ex. 2. Find the number of degrees in an angle which equals its supplement.   In an angle which equals one third of its supplement.

Ex. 3. The angular space about a point is divided into four angles which are in the ratio 1, 2, 3, 4.   Find the number of degrees in each angle.

[SUG. $x + 2x + 3x + 4x = 360°$, etc.]

Ex. 4. The angles of a triangle are in the ratio 1, 2, 3.   Find the angles.

Ex. 5. Two angles are supplementary and the greater exceeds the less by 30°.   Find the angles.

Ex. 6. If one of the angles of a parallelogram is double another of the angles, find all the angles of the parallelogram.

Ex. 7. One of the base angles of a triangle is double the other, and the exterior angle at the vertex is 105°.   Find the angles of the triangle.

Ex. 8. How many sides has a polygon in which the sum of the angles is fourteen right angles?

[SUG. $2n - 4 = 14$; find n.]

Ex. 9. How many sides has a polygon in which the sum of the angles is ten right angles? Twenty right angles? 720°?

Ex. 10. How many sides has an equiangular polygon one of whose angles is seven fourths of a right angle?

Ex. 11. If the base of any triangle is produced in both directions, the sum of the exterior angles thus formed, diminished by the vertex angle, is equal to two right angles.

[SUG. $180° - a + 180° - b - (180° - a - b) =$, etc.]

Ex. 12. The bisectors of the base angles of an isosceles triangle include an angle which is equal to the exterior angle at the base.

[SUG. To prove $a = b$, denote one of the base $\angle$ by $2x$, etc.]

Ex. 13. In an isosceles triangle, the altitude upon one of the legs makes an angle with the base which equals one half the vertex angle.

[SUG. To prove $a = \frac{1}{2}b$, show that $a = 90° - x$, $b = 180° - 2x$, etc.]

Ex. 14. If the opposite angles of a quadrilateral are equal, the figure is a parallelogram.

[SUG. $2x + 2y = 360°$, etc.]

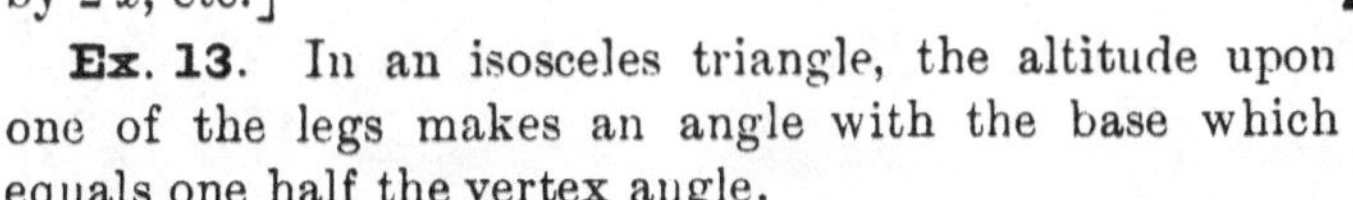

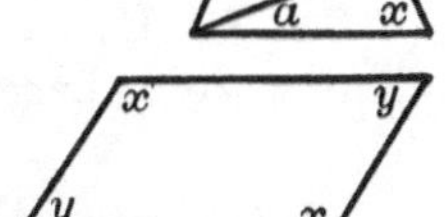

178. Use of auxiliary lines. — The demonstration of a property of a geometrical figure is frequently facilitated by drawing one or more auxiliary lines on the figure. For examples of the use of such lines, see Props. IV, V, IX, etc., of Book One.

Some of the principal auxiliary lines used on rectilinear figures are:

A line connecting two given points.

A line through a given point parallel to a given line.

A line through a given point perpendicular to a given line.

A line making a given angle with a given line.

A line produced its own length.

EXERCISES: GROUP 22

AUXILIARY LINES

Ex. 1. In the quadrilateral $ABCD$, given $AB = AD$, and $BC = CD$. **Prove** $\angle B = \angle D$.
　[SUG.　Draw AC, etc.]

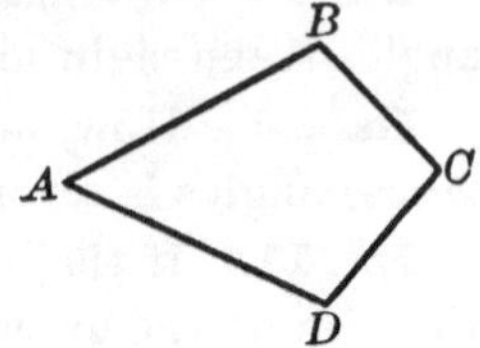

Ex. 2. Prove that the angles at the base of an isosceles trapezoid are equal.

Ex. 3. State and prove the converse of Ex. 2.

Ex. 4. **Given** $AB \parallel CD$. **Prove** $\angle b = \angle a + \angle c$.

Ex. 5. Conversely, **given** $\angle b = \angle a + \angle c$. **Prove** $AB \parallel CD$.

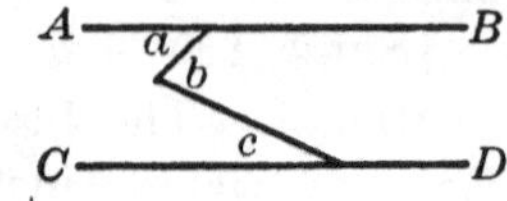

Ex. 6. The median to the hypotenuse of a right triangle is one half the hypotenuse.
　[SUG.　Draw $DF \parallel BC$. Then $AF = FC$ (§ 169), etc.]

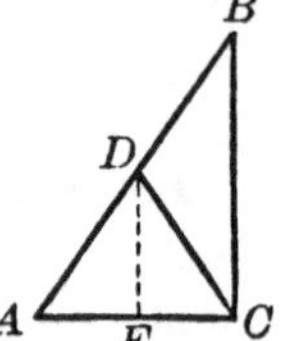

Ex. 7. If one acute angle of a right triangle is double the other, the hypotenuse is double the shorter leg.
　[SUG.　Draw the median to the hypotenuse, etc.]

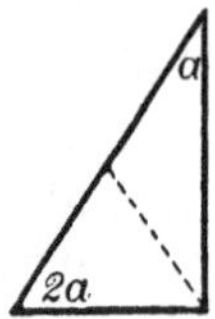

Ex. 8. In an isosceles triangle, the sum of the perpendiculars drawn from any point in the base to the legs is equal to the altitude upon one of the legs.

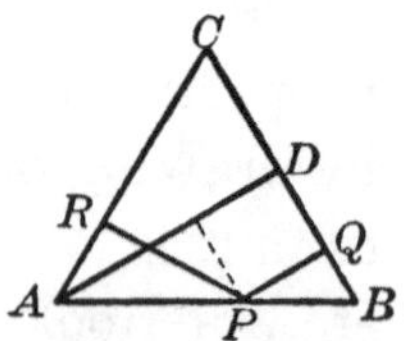

In some cases, it is useful to draw *two or more auxiliary lines.*

Ex. 9. If the opposite sides of a hexagon are equal and one pair of sides (AB and CD) are parallel, the opposite angles of the hexagon are equal.
　[SUG.　Draw AC and BD; use § 161.]

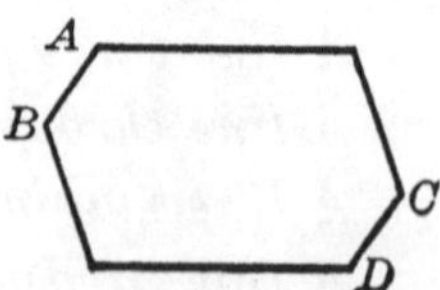

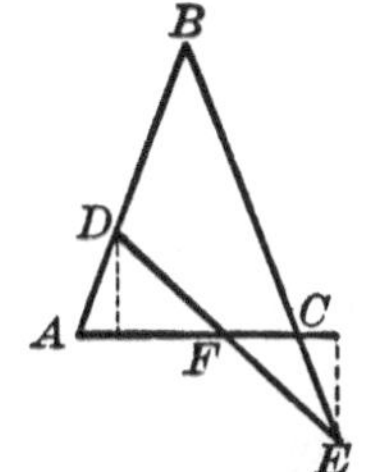

Ex. 10. Given $\triangle ABC$, $AB = BC$, BC produced to E, and $AD = CE$. **Prove** $DF = FE$.

179. Indirect demonstrations. — In Book One, three methods of indirect proof have been used:

1. The **reduction to an absurdity** (reductio ad absurdum), that is, the *proof that the negative of a given theorem leads to an absurdity.* (See Prop. X.)

2. The **method of exclusion**, that is, *showing that any statement inconsistent with the given theorem cannot be true.* This method is a special case of the preceding; the negative of a given theorem is divided into two parts which are separately shown to be impossible. (See Props. XXVI, XXIX.)

3. The **method of coincidence**, that is, *proof that a given line coincides with another line, which fulfills certain required conditions.* (See Prop. XIV.)

EXERCISES: GROUP 23

INDIRECT OR NEGATIVE DEMONSTRATIONS

Prove the following by an indirect method:

Ex. 1. Every point within an angle and not in the bisector of the angle is unequally distant from the sides of the angle.

[Sug. In the given angle, take P, any point not in the bisector of the angle. Then, if P is not unequally distant from AO and OB, it must be equally distant from them, etc.]

Ex. 2. If two straight lines are cut by a transversal, making the alternate interior angles unequal, the lines are not parallel.

Ex. 3.   The line joining the midpoints of two sides of a triangle is parallel to the third side.

[Sug.   Through one of the midpoints, draw a line ‖ to the third side.   Show that it bisects the second side and that the line joining the midpoints coincides with it.]

Ex. 4.   If, from a point P in a line AB, lines PC and PD are drawn on opposite sides of AB, making the angle APC equal to the angle BPD, PC and PD are in the same straight line.

[Sug.   From P draw PQ in the same straight line with PC, and show that PD coincides with it.]

Ex. 5.   The bisectors of two vertical angles are in the same straight line.

Ex. 6.   In the triangle ABC, D is any point in the side AB, and E is any point in the side AC.   Prove that BE and DC cannot bisect each other.

EXERCISES: GROUP 24

Theorems Proved by Various Methods

Ex. 1.   If two opposite angles of a quadrilateral are bisected by the diagonal connecting their vertices, the quadrilateral is bisected by this diagonal.

Ex. 2.   The median to the base of a scalene triangle is produced through the base, and perpendiculars are drawn from the extremities of the base to the median thus produced.   Prove that these perpendiculars are equal.

Ex. 3.   If the perpendiculars from the extremities of the base of a triangle to the other two sides are equal, (1) these perpendiculars make equal angles with the base, (2) the triangle is isosceles.

Ex. 4.   If the lines AB and CD intersect, then $AB + CD > AC + BD$.

Ex. 5.   The vertex angle of an isosceles triangle is 44°, and one of the base angles is bisected by a line produced to meet the opposite side.   Find all the angles of the figure.

Ex. 6.   Any side of a triangle is greater than the difference between the other two sides.

Ex. 7.   Perpendiculars drawn from the midpoint of the base of an isosceles triangle to the legs are equal.

Ex. 8. State and prove the converse of Ex. 7.

Ex. 9. In an isosceles triangle, an exterior angle at the base equals a right angle increased by one half the vertex angle.

Ex. 10. Prove that $\angle d = \angle a + \angle b + \angle c$ in the diagram at the right. Is this theorem true when $\angle d$ is a reflex angle?

[SUG. Draw an auxiliary line.]

Ex. 11. In the equilateral triangle ABC, BC is produced to D. Prove $BD > AD > AB$.

Ex. 12. If from a point in the bisector of an oblique angle lines are drawn parallel to and meeting the sides of the angle, the quadrilateral formed is a rhombus.

Ex. 13. If the median of a triangle is perpendicular to the base, the triangle is isosceles.

Ex. 14. Given $AB = AC$, $\angle BAC = 4\angle B$, and $DF \perp BC$. Prove $\triangle EFA$ equilateral.

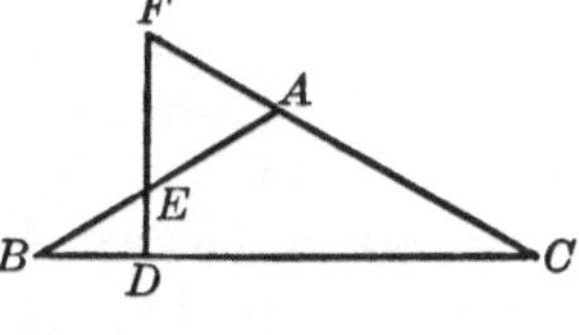

[ANALYSIS. If $\triangle FAE$ is equilateral, $\angle FEA = 60°$. $\therefore \angle DEB = 60°$. $\therefore \angle B = 30°$.

Hence, to get a direct proof, show that $\angle C = 30°$, by using $\angle BAC = 4 \angle C$.]

Ex. 15. If the diagonals of a quadrilateral bisect each other at right angles, what kind of figure is the quadrilateral? Prove this.

Ex. 16. From the point in which the altitudes drawn to the legs of an isosceles triangle intersect, a line is drawn to the vertex. Prove that this line bisects the angle at the vertex.

Ex. 17. If, from a point within an acute angle, perpendiculars are drawn to the sides of the angle, the angle formed by these perpendiculars is the supplement of the given angle.

Ex. 18. If, in the parallelogram $ABCD$, $BP = DQ$, then $AQCP$ is a parallelogram.

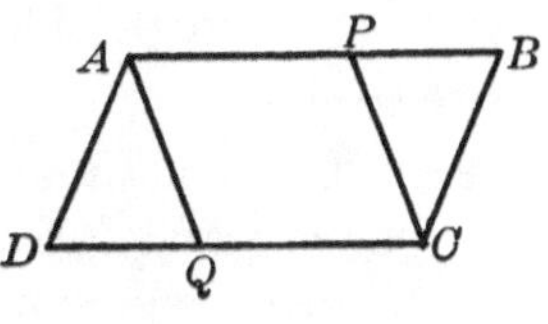

[ANALYSIS. If $AQCP$ is a $\square$, $AP =$ and $\parallel QC$. $\therefore$ begin the direct proof by showing that $AP =$ and $\parallel QC$.]

Ex. 19. If the diagonals of a parallelogram are equal, what kind of figure is the parallelogram? Prove this.

Ex. 20. If the angle A of the triangle ABC is 50° and the exterior angle BCD is 120°, which is the largest side in the triangle?

Ex. 21. Two isosceles triangles are equal if the base and an angle of one are equal to the base and the corresponding angle of the other.

Ex. 22. Two equilateral triangles are equal if an altitude of one is equal to an altitude of the other.

Ex. 23. If, from a point within a triangle, two lines are drawn to the extremities of one side of the triangle, the sum of the other two sides of the triangle is greater than the sum of the two lines thus drawn. (That is, prove $AB + BC > AP + PC.$)

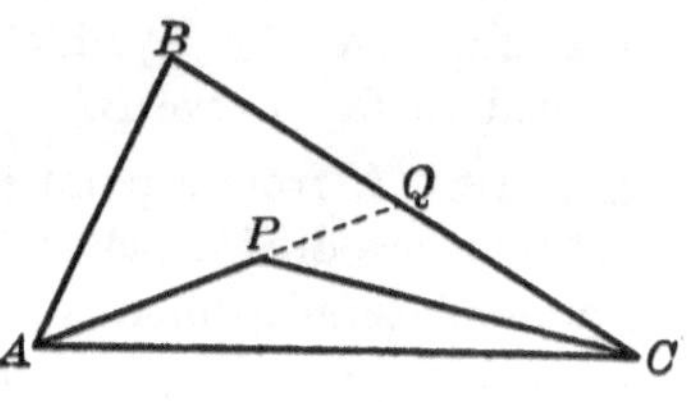

Ex. 24. On the figure of Ex. 23, prove that $\angle APC$ is greater than $\angle B$.

Ex. 25. Prove that the sum of the angles of a triangle is equal to two right angles, by drawing a line through the vertex of the triangle parallel to the base.

Ex. 26. If ABC is an equilateral triangle and $AP = BQ = CR$, then PQR is an equilateral triangle.

Ex. 27. The two base angles of a triangle are bisected, and through the point of intersection of the two bisectors a line is drawn parallel to the base. Prove that the part of this line intercepted between the two sides equals the sum of the segments of the sides included between the parallel and the base. (That is, prove $PQ = AP + QC.$)

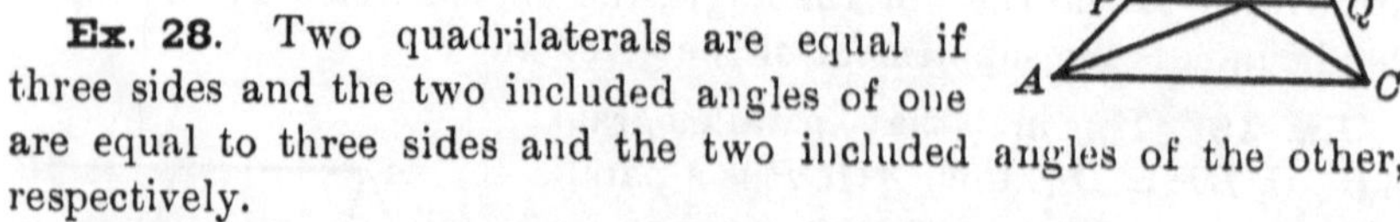

Ex. 28. Two quadrilaterals are equal if three sides and the two included angles of one are equal to three sides and the two included angles of the other, respectively.

Ex. 29. The sum of the exterior angles of a quadrilateral formed by producing the sides in succession equals four right angles. (That is, prove $\angle a + \angle b + \angle c + \angle d = 4$ rt. $\angle$s.)

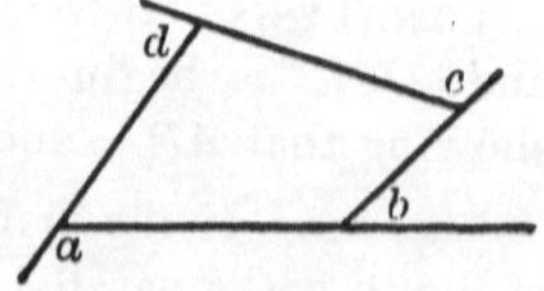

Ex. 30. The sum of the exterior angles of a pentagon is four right angles.

Ex. 31. The bisectors of the angles of a parallelogram form a rectangle.

Ex. 32. The bisectors of the angles of a rectangle form a square.

Ex. 33. If lines are drawn through the vertices of a quadrilateral parallel to the diagonals, a parallelogram is formed which is twice as large as the original quadrilateral.

Ex. 34. Lines drawn from two opposite vertices of a parallelogram to the midpoints of a pair of opposite sides trisect a diagonal of the parallelogram.

Ex. 35. On the diagonal AC of a parallelogram $ABCD$, equal parts, AP and CQ, are marked off. Prove $BPDQ$ a parallelogram. How many pairs of equal triangles does the figure contain?

Ex. 36. The opposite angles of an isosceles trapezoid are supplementary.

Ex. 37. In an isosceles trapezoid, the diagonals are equal.

EXERCISES: GROUP 25

PRACTICAL APPLICATIONS

Ex. 1. Draw a figure showing the points of the compass as used by a mariner. On this compass, how many degrees are there between N. and N. N. E.? Also between N. and E. N. E.? Between N. N. E. and S. by E.? Between any two successive compass points?

Ex. 2. When a ray of light strikes a mirror and is reflected, the angle of incidence equals the angle of reflection.

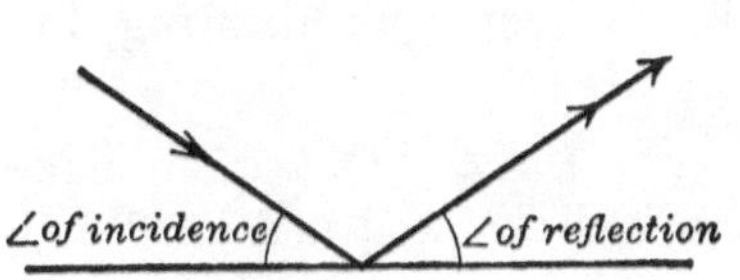

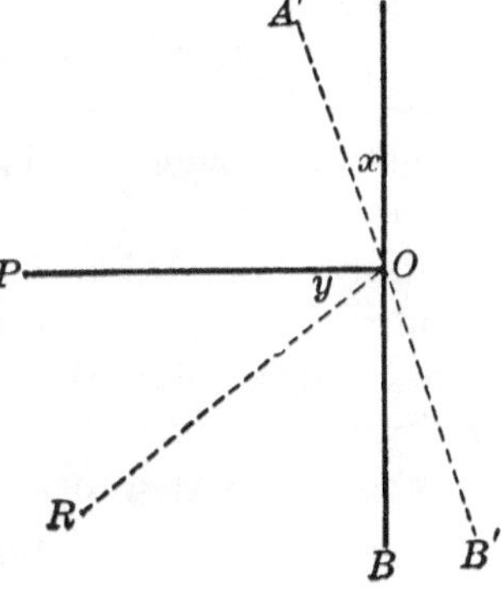

Let AB be a mirror, and PO a ray of light striking the mirror at right angles. Let the mirror be rotated about O to the position $A'B'$. The ray of light PO will then be reflected in the direction OR.

Prove $\angle y = 2 \angle x$.

Ex. 3. The diagram shows a drawing instrument called the *parallel rulers*. The dotted outline shows the rest of the instrument in another position, the part RS remaining fixed. The distance $PQ = RS$, $PR = QS$. Hence, show that PQ is parallel to RS.

In like manner, show that $P'Q'$ is parallel to RS. Hence, show that PQ is parallel to $P'Q'$.

If a line is drawn perpendicular to PQ and another line perpendicular to $P'Q'$, the perpendiculars thus drawn will be parallel to each other. (§ 101, lines perpendicular to parallel lines are parallel.)

Rods combined in these ways are instances of a kind of mechanism, called a linkage, which is of wide importance. Observe, for instance, the system of links which connects the driving wheels of a locomotive with the piston in the cylinder; also the jointed rods connecting the walking beam of a steamboat with the engine. Look up, in the Century Dictionary for instance, the words *linkage*, *cell*, and *parallel motion*.

Ex. 4. In the trusses of steel bridges, why are the beams and rods arranged so as to form as far as possible a network of triangles and not of quadrilaterals, or pentagons, for instance? (See Ex. 20, p. 86; also § 83.)

Ex. 5. Draw a map for the following survey notes to the scale of 400 ft. to the inch. In laying off the angles, draw a dotted north-and-south line through each station and then use a protractor.

Keep your drawing for later use.

Stations	Bearings	Distances
A	N. 30° E.	300 ft.
B	N.	200 ft.
C	S. 67° E.	450 ft.
D	S. 60° W.	600 ft.

Ex. 6. Obtain or make up a set of survey notes similar to those in Ex. 5 and make a drawing for them.

Ex. 7. Let DC and FC be two walls perpendicular to the plane of the paper. Let small mirrors be attached to these walls at A and B. Let $\angle C = 45°$. Let a ray of light pass through Q to A, and be reflected to B and thence to P. Prove that $\angle APB$ is a right angle.

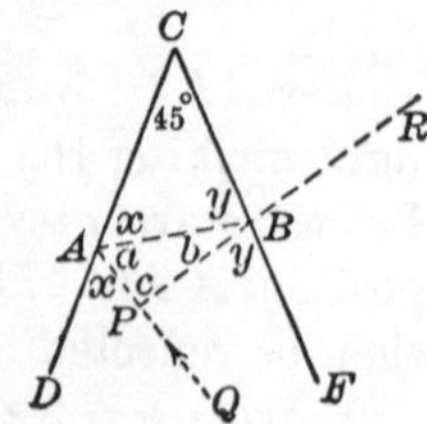

[SUG. Use the principle for the angles of incidence and reflection stated in Ex. 2.

Then in the triangle ABC, $x + y + 45° = 180°$, or $x + y = 135°$.

About the points A and B, $2x + a + 2y + b = 360°$.

$\therefore a + b = 90°$, etc.]

The preceding is the principle of an instrument called the *optical square* used by foresters in constructing right angles. A ray of light coming from R through a small hole at B above the mirror will make a right angle with the ray coming from Q through P to A.

Ex. 8. By the aid of squared paper, construct the following designs. Extend the last design to include at least five major loops.

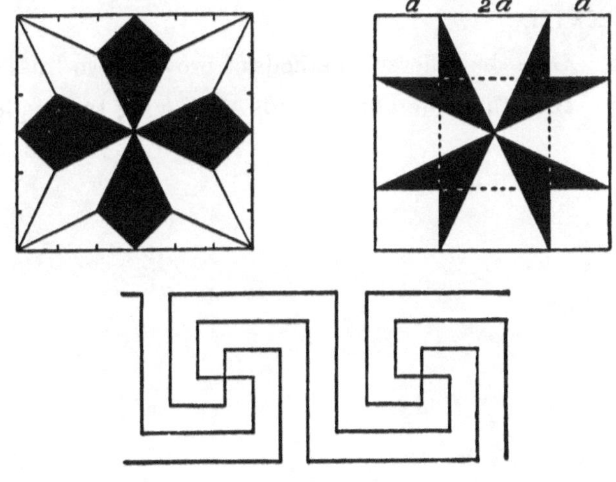

EXERCISES : GROUP 26

REVIEW WORK

Make a list of the properties of:

Ex. 1. One straight line (in connection with such points as may be related to the line, as in § 57).

Ex. 2. Two or more parallel lines (in connection with transversals and angles formed by their use).

Ex. 3. Two or more straight lines that are not parallel.

Ex. 4. Angles (independently of triangles or parallel lines).

Ex. 5. A single triangle.

Ex. 6. Two triangles.

Ex. 7. A quadrilateral.

Ex. 8. A parallelogram.

Ex. 9. A rhombus.

Ex. 10. Define as many different kinds of triangles as you can.

Ex. 11. Classify triangles according to two different methods.

Ex. 12. The three sides and the three angles of a triangle are called its six parts. Draw two triangles which have three parts of one triangle equal to three parts of the other, but which are not equal.

Ex. 13. The efficiency value of Prop. IV (p. 37) is that it enables us to determine, without effort, that two angles of the triangle are equal, if we know that the sides opposite these angles are equal. State the efficiency value of Prop. I. Also of Prop. II. Of Prop. III.

Ex. 14. State the efficiency value of Prop. V. Of Prop. XVI. Of Prop. XVIII.

Ex. 15. Give the different methods of proving two lines equal.

Ex. 16. Give the different methods of proving two angles equal.

BOOK TWO

THE CIRCLE

180. A **circle** is a closed curve all points of which lie in the same plane and are equidistant from a point in the plane called the **center**.

A circle is named by naming its center, as the circle O; or by naming two or more points on it, as the circle ACD.

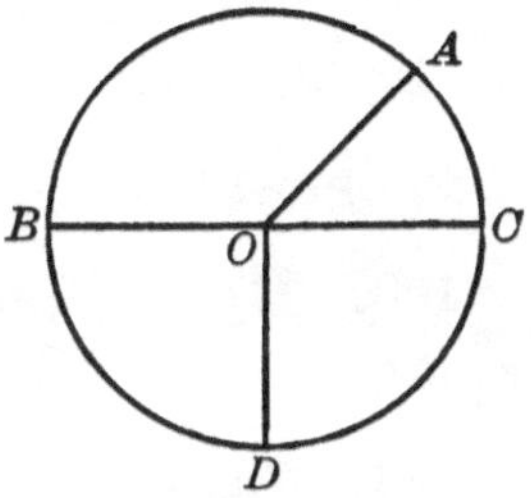

181. The **circumference** of a circle is the length of the circle.

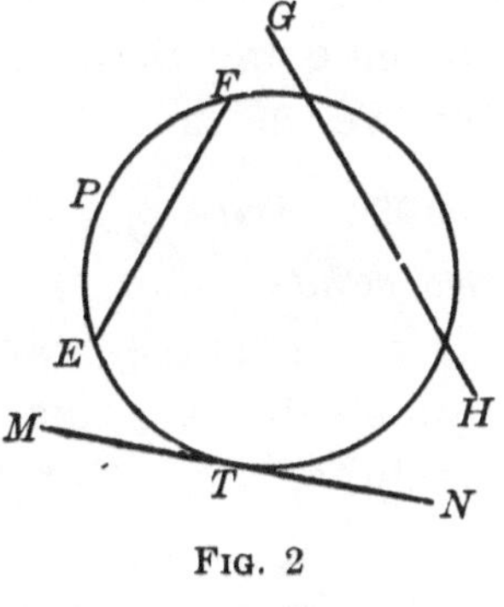

FIG. 1

182. A **radius** of a circle is a straight line drawn from the center to any point on the curve; as OA. A **diameter** is a straight line drawn through the center and terminated by the circle; as BC.

183. An **arc** is any portion of a circle; as AC. A **semicircle** is an arc equal to one half the circle; as BAC.

184. A **chord** is a straight line joining the extremities of an arc; as EF.

Every chord subtends two arcs. A **minor arc** is the smaller of two arcs subtended by a chord. A **major arc** is the larger of two arcs subtended by a chord. Thus, for the chord EF the minor arc is EPF, and the major arc is ETF.

FIG. 2

If the arc subtended by a given chord is mentioned, the minor arc is meant, unless otherwise specified.

185.   A **tangent** is a straight line which meets a circle and which, if produced, has but one point in common with the circle; as *MN* (Fig. 2).

186.   A **secant** is a straight line which cuts a circle and which, if produced, has two points in common with the circle; as *GH* (Fig. 2).

187.   A **central angle** is an angle whose vertex is at the center and whose sides are radii; as the angle *COA* (Fig. 1).

PROPERTIES OF THE CIRCLE INFERRED IMMEDIATELY

188.   *Radii of the same circle, or of equal circles, are equal.*

189.   *The diameter of a circle equals twice its radius.*

190.   *Diameters of the same circle, or of equal circles, are equal.*

191.   *If two circles are equal* (i.e., *may be made to coincide,* § 7), *their radii are equal; and conversely.*

192.   *A diameter of a circle bisects the circle.*   For, by placing the two parts of the circle so that the diameters coincide and their arcs fall on the same side of the diameter, we see that these arcs coincide.   (§ 180.)

193.   *A straight line cannot intersect a circle in more than two points.*   For, if a straight line can intersect a circle in three (or more) points, three or more equal lines (radii) can be drawn from the same point (the center) to the straight line.   But this is impossible.   (§ 141.)

Ex. Draw a diagram (composed of one circle and straight lines) which shall contain all of the geometric objects defined in §§ 180–187. Name these objects in terms of letters.

PROPOSITION I. THEOREM

194. *The diameter of a circle is greater than any other chord.*

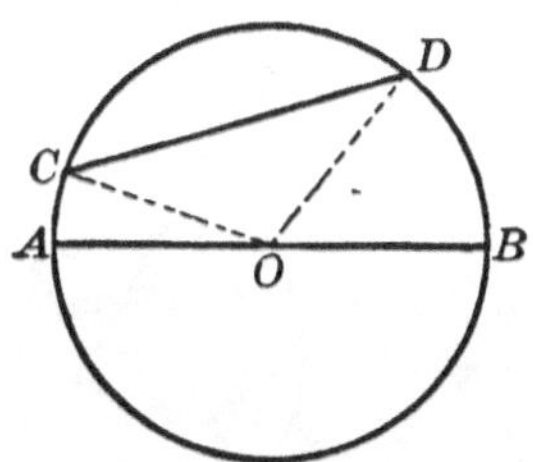

Given AB a diameter, and CD any other chord in the circle O.

To prove $AB > CD$.

Proof. 1. Draw the radii OC and OD. | 1. Post. 1.
2. Then in the $\triangle OCD$, | 2. Why?
$$OC + OD > CD.$$
3. Substituting for OC its equal OA, and for OD its equal OB, | 3. Axs. 9, 7.
$$OA + OB, \text{ or } AB, > CD.$$

Q E.D.

Ex. 1. On paper draw a circle with a radius of $1\frac{1}{2}$ in. Draw a diameter of the circle. Cut the circle out of the paper, fold it on the diameter as an axis, and show that the two parts of the circle coincide.

Ex. 2. Draw a circle with any convenient radius. Take any point, A, on the circle, and from it draw a chord which shall be 50 per cent longer than the radius.

Ex. 3. Draw a circle and in it construct a central angle of 60°. Also a central angle of 120°.

Ex. 4. Draw two circles, O and O', each with one inch as radius. In these circles construct central angles AOB and $A'O'B'$, each of 60°. Measure the chords AB and $A'B'$. How do these chords compare in length? Is each one of these chords longer or shorter than a radius of one of the circles?

Ex. 5. Make up and work an example similar to Ex. 4, using 45° as the central angle.

PROPOSITION II. THEOREM

195. *If in the same circle, or in equal circles, two angles at the center are equal, the arcs which they intercept are equal.*

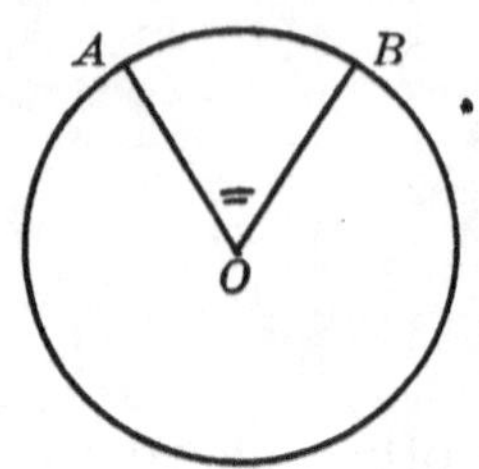 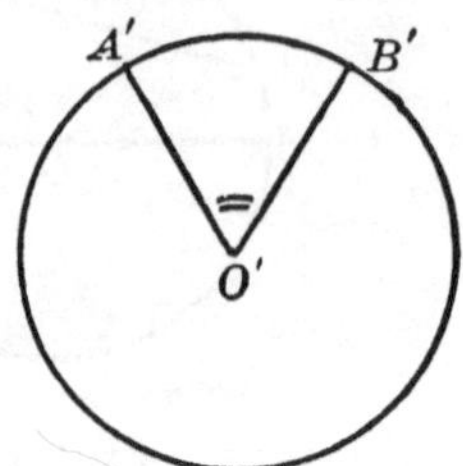

Given the equal circles O and O', and the equal central $\angle$s AOB and $A'O'B'$.

To prove $\overset{\frown}{AB} = \overset{\frown}{A'B'}$.

Proof. 1. Apply the circle O' to the circle O so that the center O' coincides with the center O, and the radius $O'A'$ with the radius OA.

    1. Geom. Ax. 2.

2. Then the radius $O'B'$ will fall on the radius OB.

    2. By hyp. $\angle O' = \angle O$.

3. $\therefore B'$ will fall on B.

    3. $OB = O'B'$, being radii of equal $\odot$.   (§ 188.)

4. Hence $\overset{\frown}{AB}$ will coincide with $\overset{\frown}{A'B'}$.

    4. All the points on the two arcs are equidistant from the center O.   (§ 180.)

5. $\therefore \overset{\frown}{AB} = \overset{\frown}{A'B'}$.

    5. Geom. Ax. 4.   Q.E.D.

Ex. 1. Draw a circle with a radius of one inch. In this circle draw two diameters in such a position with reference to each other that they shall divide the circle into 4 equal arcs.

Ex. 2. Draw a circle and divide it into 8 equal arcs.

Proposition III. Theorem (Converse of Prop. II)

196. *If in the same circle, or in equal circles, two arcs are equal, the angles which they subtend at the center are equal.*

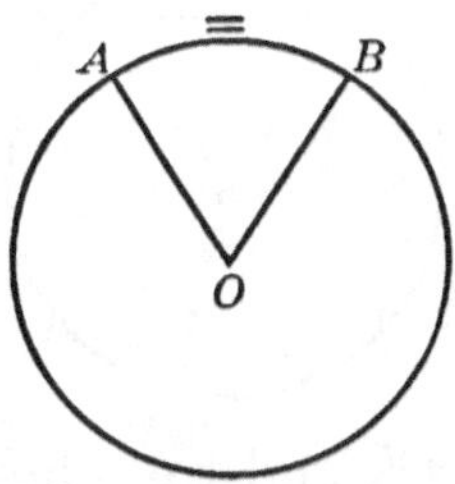 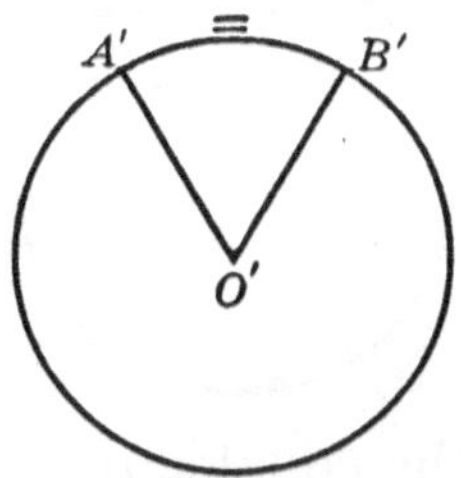

Given the equal circles O and O', and the equal arcs AB and $A'B'$ subtending the central $\angle s$ O and O'.

To prove $\angle O = \angle O'$.

Proof. 1. Apply the circle O' to the circle O so that the center O' coincides with the center O, and the point A' with the point A.

1. Geom. Ax. 2.

2. Then the point B' will fall on B.

2. $\overset{\frown}{A'B'} = \overset{\frown}{AB}$ by hyp.

3. Hence, the radius $O'A'$ will coincide with OA, and radius $O'B'$ with OB.

3. Only one straight line can be drawn connecting two points. (§ 57.)

4. Hence, $\angle O = \angle O'$.

4. Geom. Ax. 4.   Q.E.D.

197. Cor. *If in the same circle, or in equal circles, two central angles are unequal, the greater angle intercepts the greater arc;* and

Conversely, *if two arcs are unequal, the greater arc subtends the greater angle at the center.*

Ex. What is the efficiency value of Prop. II (p. 112)? Of Prop. III?

PROPOSITION IV. THEOREM

198. *If in the same circle, or in equal circles, two chords
are equal, the arcs subtended by them are equal.*

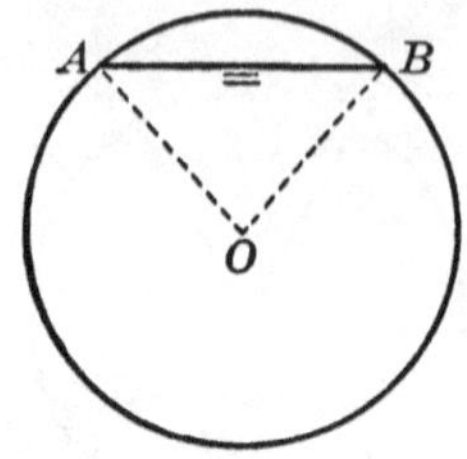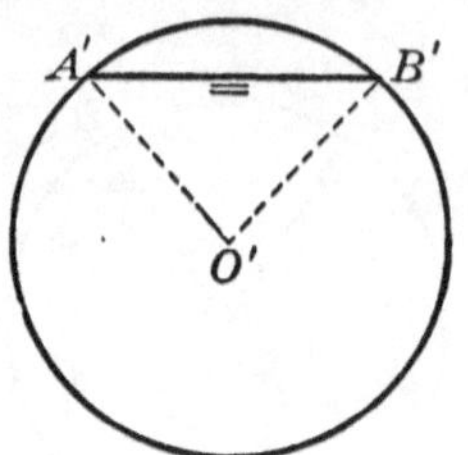

Given the equal circles O and O', and the chord $AB =$
chord $A'B'$.

To prove $\overset{\frown}{AB} = \overset{\frown}{A'B'}$.

Proof. 1. Draw the radii
OA, OB, $O'A'$, $O'B'$.

1. Post. 1.

2. Then in $\triangle AOB$ and
$A'O'B'$,
$$AB = A'B'.$$

2. Why?

3. Also $AO = A'O'$, and
$$BO = B'O'.$$

3. Why?

4. $\therefore \triangle AOB = \triangle A'O'B'$.

4. Why?

5. $\therefore \angle O = \angle O'$.

5. Why?

6. $\therefore \overset{\frown}{AB} = \overset{\frown}{A'B'}$.

6. If in the same circle, or
in equal circles, two angles at
the center are equal, the arcs
which they intercept are equal.
(§ 195.)   Q.E.D.

199. Efficiency value. — The above theorem enables us
to determine whether two arcs (in the same circle or in
equal circles) are equal, by measuring or comparing the
two chords which subtend the given arcs.

Ex. In the above figure, if chord $AB = 1$ in., chord $A'B' = 1$ in.,
and arc $AB = 1\frac{1}{4}$ in., find the length of arc $A'B'$.

PROPOSITION V. THEOREM (CONVERSE OF PROP. IV)

200. *If in the same circle, or in equal circles, two arcs are equal, the chords subtending them are equal.*

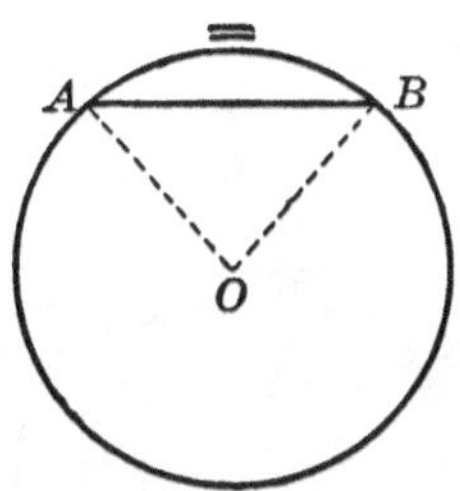 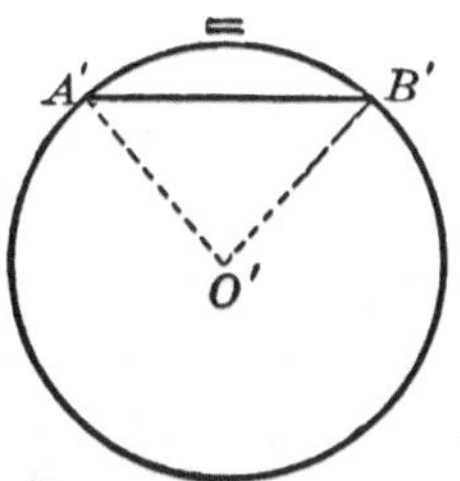

Given the equal circles O and O', and $\overset{\frown}{AB} = \overset{\frown}{A'B'}$.

To prove chord $AB =$ chord $A'B'$.

Proof. 1. Draw the radii OA, OB, $O'A'$, $O'B'$.	1. Post. 1.
2. Then in $\triangle AOB$ and $A'O'B'$, $$\angle O = \angle O'.$$	2. If in the same circle, or in equal circles, two arcs are equal, the angles which they subtend at the center are equal. (§ 196.)
3. Also $OA = O'A'$, and $OB = O'B'$.	3. Why?
4. $\therefore \triangle AOB = \triangle A'O'B'$.	4. Why?
5. $\therefore AB = A'B'$.	5. Why?　　Q.E.D.

Ex. 1. In the above figure, if arc $AB = 1\frac{1}{4}$ in., arc $A'B' = 1\frac{1}{4}$ in., and chord $AB = 1$ in., find chord $A'B'$ without measuring it.

Ex. 2. What is the efficiency value of Prop. V?

Ex. 3. Draw a circle O with a radius of one inch. In this circle construct central angles of 60° and 120°. Measure the chords which subtend these angles. Is the chord of 120° double the chord of 60°?

Ex. 4. Make up and work an example similar to Ex. 3, using 45° as one of the central angles.

PROPOSITION VI. THEOREM

201. I. *If in the same circle, or in equal circles, two minor arcs are unequal, the greater arc is subtended by the greater chord;* and

II. CONVERSELY, *if two chords are unequal, the greater chord subtends the greater minor arc.*

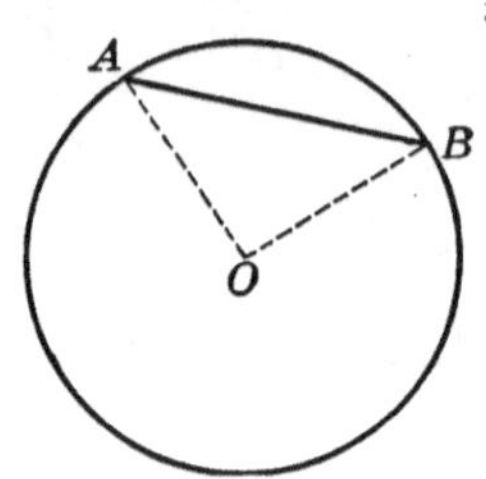 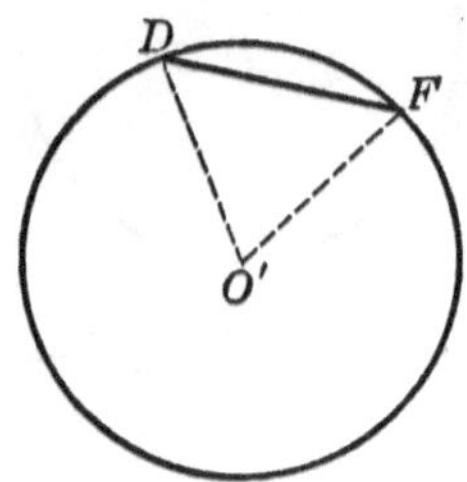

I. **Given** the equal circles O and O', and $\overarc{AB} > \overarc{DF}$.
To prove chord $AB >$ chord DF.

Proof. 1. Draw the radii OA, OB, $O'D$, $O'F$. | 1. Post. 1.

2. Then in the $\triangle AOB$ and $DO'F$, $OA = O'D$, and $OB = O'F$. | 2. § 188.

3. $\overarc{AB} > \overarc{DF}$. | 3. Hyp.

4. $\angle O > \angle O'$. | 4. § 197.

5. ∴ chord $AB >$ chord DF. | 5. § 138.

II. CONVERSELY. **Given** the equal circles O and O', and chord $AB >$ chord DF.

To prove $\overarc{AB} > \overarc{DF}$.

Proof. 1. In the $\triangle AOB$ and $DO'F$, $OA = O'D$, and $OB = O'F$. | 1. Why?

2. Also $AB > DF$. | 2. Why?

3. ∴ $\angle O$ is greater than $\angle O'$. | 3. § 139.

4. ∴ $\overarc{AB} > \overarc{DF}$. | 4. § 197.

Q.E.D.

EXERCISES: GROUP 27

Ex. 1.

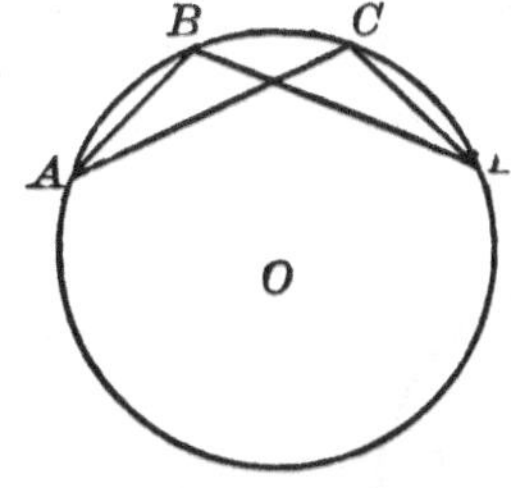

Ex. 2.

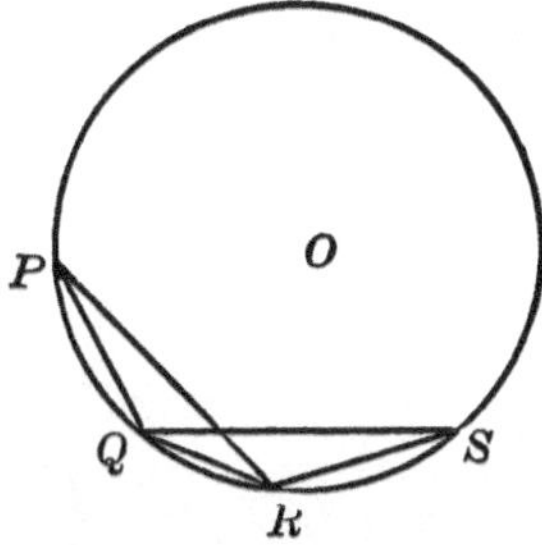

Given circle O with chord AB = chord CD.

Prove chord AC = chord BD.

Given circle O with chord PR = chord QS.

Prove $\triangle PQR = \triangle QSR$.

Ex. 3. A, B, C, and D are points taken in succession on a semicircle, and arc AC is greater than arc BD. Prove that chord $AB >$ chord CD.

Ex. 4. State the converse of the theorem in Ex. 3 and prove it.

Ex. 5. The triangle ABC is equilateral. $A1C$ and $B2C$ are arcs of circles whose centers are B and A, respectively. The arch formed by the arcs is called an equilateral Gothic arch.

Draw a straight line as base and on it construct an equilateral Gothic arch.

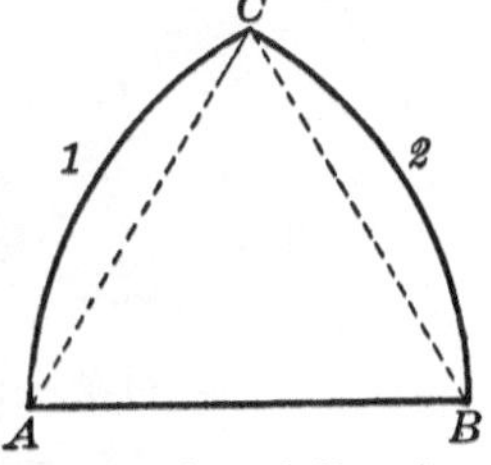

Ex. 6. By the aid of squared paper, construct the following design:

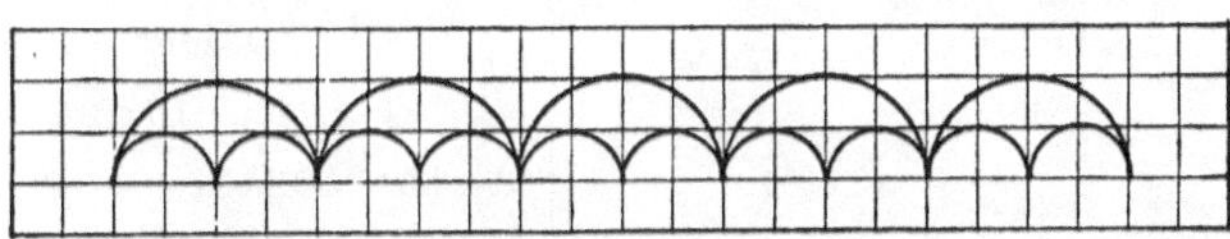

Ex. 7. Construct the following design:

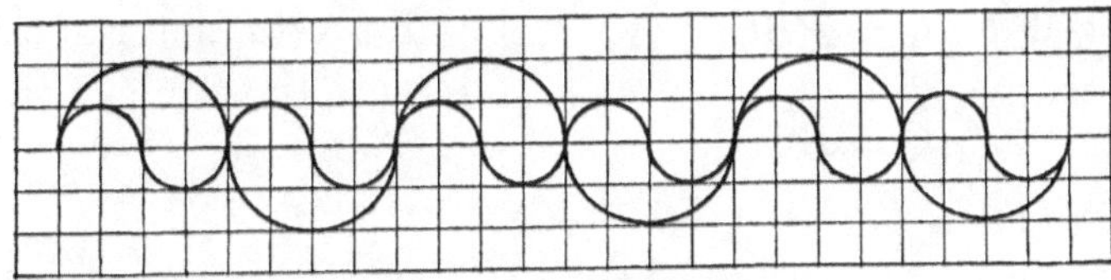

Ex. 8. If a wheel revolves 20 times per minute, through how many degrees does it revolve per second?

Proposition VII. Theorem

202. *A diameter perpendicular to a chord bisects the chord and the arcs which the chord subtends.*

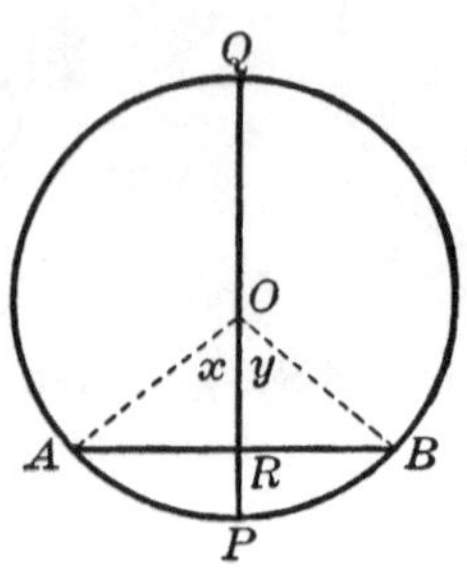

Given the circle O, and the diameter $PQ \perp$ chord AB at R.

To prove $AR = BR$, $\overset{\frown}{AP} = \overset{\frown}{BP}$, $\overset{\frown}{AQ} = \overset{\frown}{BQ}$.

Proof. 1. Draw the radii OA and OB.

2. Then in the rt. $\triangle$ OAR and OBR, $OA = OB$.

3. $OR = OR$.

4. $\therefore \triangle OAR = \triangle OBR$.

5. $\therefore AR = BR$ and $\angle x = \angle y$.

6. $\therefore \overset{\frown}{AP} = \overset{\frown}{BP}$.

7. But $\overset{\frown}{PAQ} = \overset{\frown}{PBQ}$.

8. $\therefore \overset{\frown}{AQ} = \overset{\frown}{BQ}$.

1. Post. 1.

2. Why?

3. Why?

4. Why?

5. Why?

6. If in the same circle, or in equal circles, two $\angle$ at the center are equal, the arcs which they intercept are equal. (§ 195.)

7. A diameter of a circle bisects the circle. (§ 192.)

8. Ax. 3.

Q.E.D.

203. Cor. 1. *A diameter which bisects a chord (shorter than a diameter) is perpendicular to the chord.*

204. Cor. 2. *The perpendicular bisector of a chord passes through the center of the circle, and bisects the arcs subtended by the chord.*

205. Cor. 3. *A line which fulfills any two of the following conditions fulfills the other two also :*

(1) *Is bisector of a chord ;*

(2) *Is a diameter ;*

(3) *Is perpendicular to the chord ;*

(4) *Bisects one of the arcs subtended by the chord.*

Proposition VIII. Problem

206. *To bisect a given circular arc.*

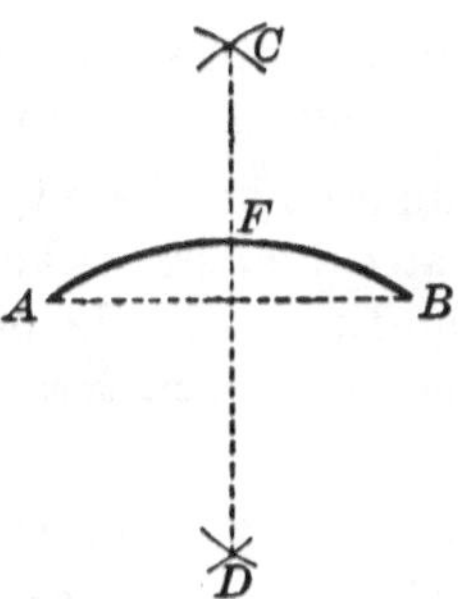

Given $\overset{\frown}{AB}$.

To bisect $\overset{\frown}{AB}$.

Construction. 1. With A and B as centers, and with convenient equal radii, describe arcs intersecting at C and D.	1. Post. 3.
2. Draw the line CD intersecting $\overset{\frown}{AB}$ at F.	2. Post. 1.
Then $\overset{\frown}{AB}$ is bisected at the point F.	
Proof. 1. Draw the chord AB.	1. Post. 1.
2. Then $CD \perp$ chord AB at its midpoint.	2. § 121.
3. ∴ CD bisects $\overset{\frown}{AB}$ at F.	3. § 204. Q.E.F

EXERCISES: GROUP 28

Ex. 1. With a radius of 1 in., construct an arc of 90°. Bisect this arc.

Ex. 2. Construct an arc of 60° having a radius of $1\frac{1}{2}$ in. Bisect this arc.

Ex. 3. Construct an arc of $22\frac{1}{2}$° with a radius of 2 in. Also an arc of 15° with the same radius.

Ex. 4. On the diagram of Prop. VIII, what is the midpoint of the arc AB? Is this also the center of arc AB?

Ex. 5. On the diagram of Ex. 1, point out the midpoint of the arc of 90°. Also the center of this arc.

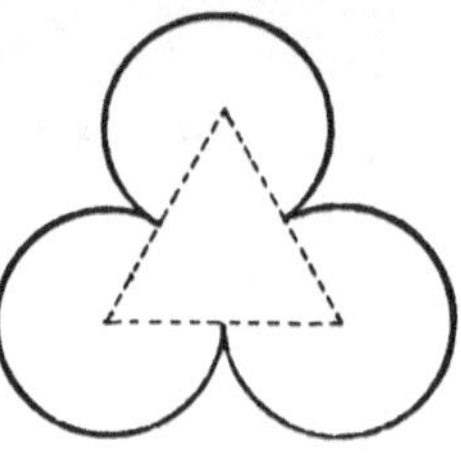

Ex. 6. Construct a trefoil.

[Sug. Construct an equilateral triangle and bisect one of its sides.]

Ex. 7. Construct a quatrefoil by first constructing a square and bisecting one of its sides.

Ex. 8. Construct a figure like the adjoining, by first constructing an equilateral triangle and bisecting its sides, and then using the midpoint of each side as a center in constructing arcs.

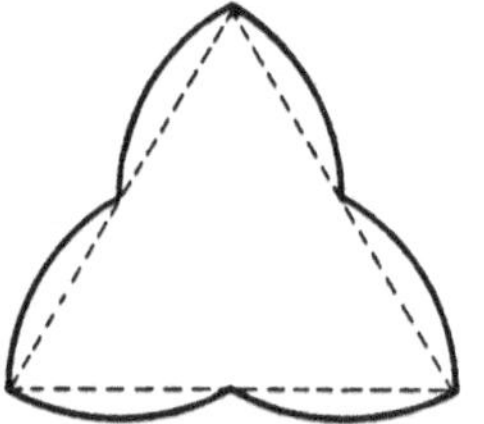

Ex. 9. By the aid of squared paper, construct the following designs for moldings. Note that some curves used are made of two arcs.

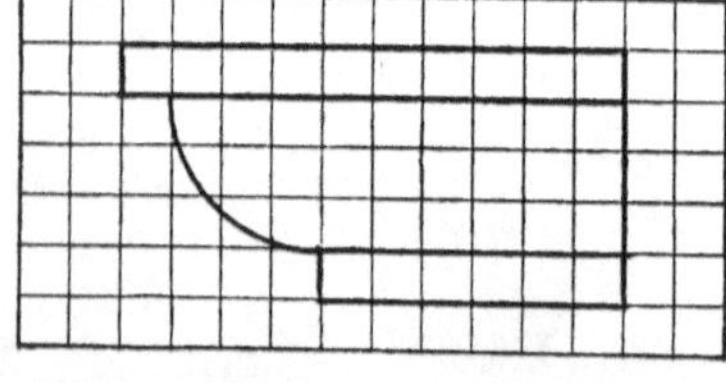

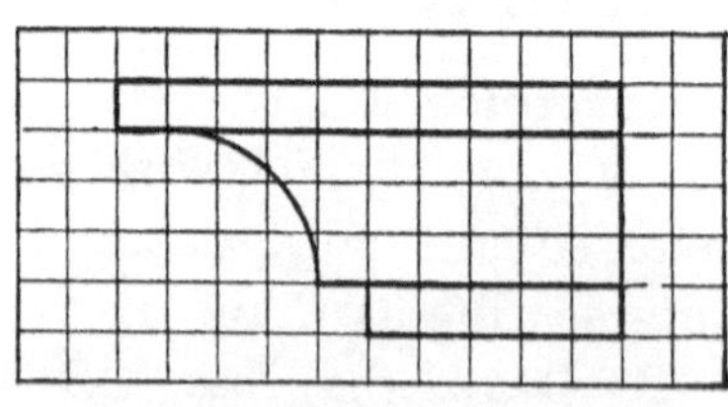

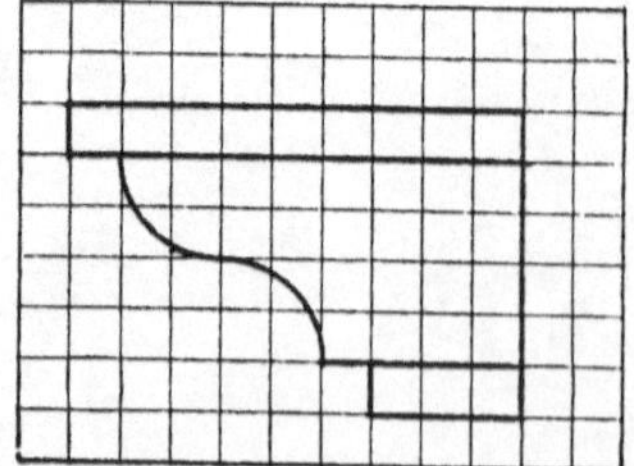

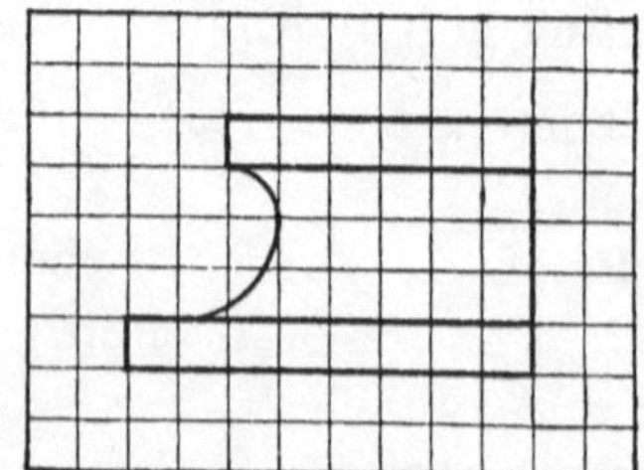

PROPOSITION IX. THEOREM

207. I. *If in the same circle, or in equal circles, two chords are equal, they are equidistant from the center;* and,

II. CONVERSELY, *if two chords are equidistant from the center, they are equal.*

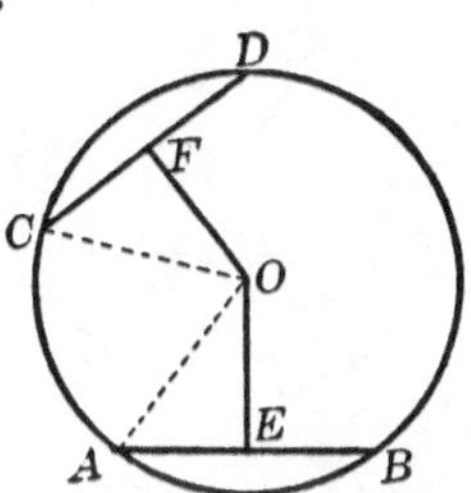

I. **Given** the circle O in which the chords AB and CD are equal, $OE \perp AB$, and $OF \perp CD$.

To prove $OE = OF$.

Proof.	
1. Draw the radii OA and OC.	1. Post. 1.
2. OE bisects AB, and OF bisects CD.	2. The diameter $\perp$ a chord bisects the chord. (§ 202.)
3. In the right $\triangle\, OAE$ and OCF, $OA = OC$.	3. Why?
4. Also $AE = CF$.	4. Ax. 5.
5. $\therefore \triangle OAE = \triangle OCF$.	5. Why?
6. $\therefore OE = OF$.	6. Why?

II. CONVERSELY. **Given** circle O, chords AB and CD, $OE \perp AB$, $OF \perp CD$, and $OE = OF$.

To prove $AB = CD$.

Proof. Let the student supply the proof.

Ex. A wheel revolves 30 times per minute. In how many seconds does a point on its circumference revolve through an arc of 90°? Through an arc of 120°?

Proposition X. Theorem

208. *If in the same circle, or in equal circles, two chords are unequal, the shorter is at the greater distance from the center.*

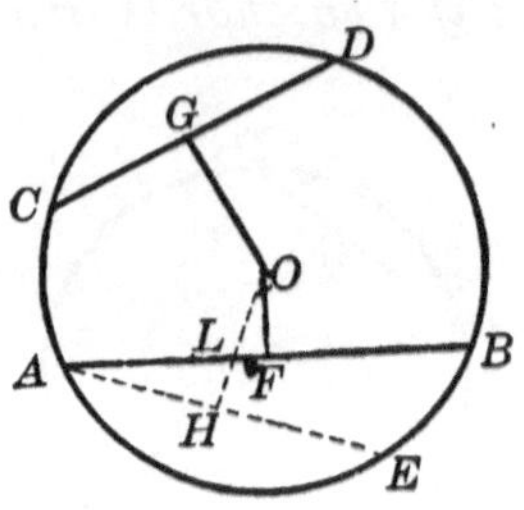

Given in the circle O the chord $CD < $ chord AB, $OF \perp AB$, $OG \perp CD$.

To prove $OG > OF$.

Proof. 1. Chord $AB >$ chord CD.	1. Hyp.
2. $\overparen{AB} > \overparen{CD}$.	2. § 201.
3. Mark off on $\overparen{AB}$ the $\overparen{AE} = \overparen{CD}$, and draw the chord AE.	3. Post. 1.
4. ∴ chord $AE =$ chord CD.	4. § 200.
5. Draw $OH \perp AE$ and intersecting AB at L.	5. § 129.
6. Then $OH = OG$.	6. § 207.
7. But $OH > OL$.	7. Ax. 8.
8. Also $OL > OF$.	8. Why ?
9. Much more then OH or its equal $OG > OF$.	9. Ineq. Ax. 4. (§ 133.) Q.E.D.

Ex. Draw a circle O, with a diameter AB. Construct an angle APB, whose sides, AP and PB, are chords. By use of the protractor measure angle P. Is this angle greater or less than a right angle?

Also on the same figure construct another angle, AQB, whose sides are chords. By use of the protractor measure this angle and compare it with angle P.

Proposition XI. Theorem

209. *If in the same circle, or in equal circles, two chords are unequally distant from the center, that one is shorter which is more remote from the center.*

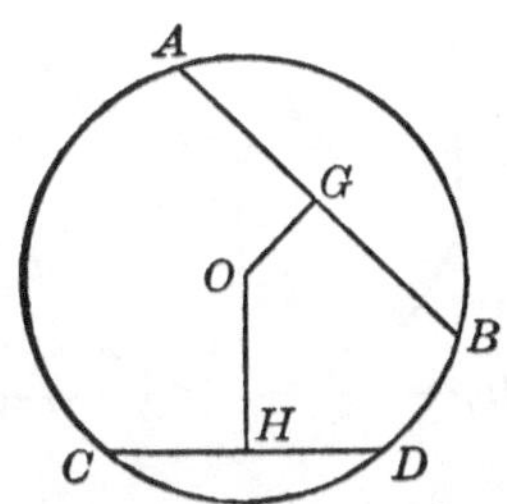

Given the chords AB and CD in the circle O, $OG \perp AB$, $OH \perp CD$, $OH > OG$.

To prove chord $CD <$ chord AB.

Proof. 1. Either $CD =$ chord AB, or $CD > AB$, or $CD < AB$.

2. But chord CD cannot $=$ chord AB.

3. Also CD cannot be greater than AB.

4. Hence, chord $CD <$ chord AB.

1. Ineq. Ax. 5. (§ 133.)

2. If it did, OH would equal OG (§ 207), which is contrary to the hypothesis.

3. If it were, OH would be less than OG (§ 208), which is contrary to the hypothesis.

4. It is neither equal to AB nor greater than AB. Q.E.D.

Ex. 1. Draw a circle O with any convenient radius. In this circle construct an acute $\angle BAC$ in which BA and AC are chords. Draw the radii OB and OC. By use of the protractor find the number of degrees in $\angle\!\!\!\angle$ A and O. How many times larger is $\angle O$ than $\angle A$?

Ex. 2. Draw the figure for the following theorem, and state the hypothesis and conclusion in terms of the letters on the figure: "If two equal chords intersect within a circle, the corresponding segments of the chords are equal."

PROPOSITION XII. THEOREM

210. *A straight line tangent to a circle is perpendicular
to the radius drawn to the point of contact.*

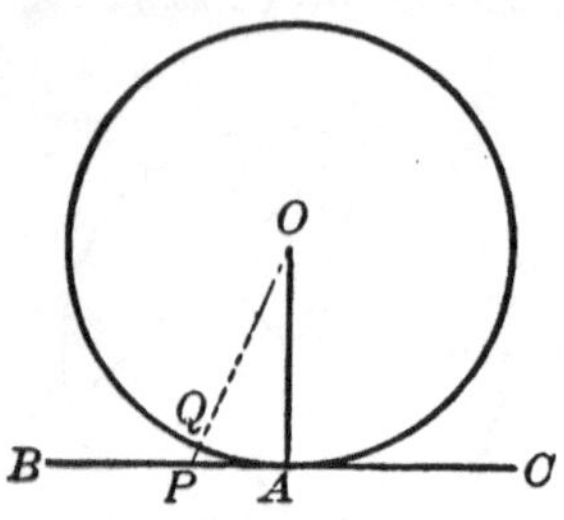

Given BC tangent to the circle O at the point A.
To prove $BC \perp OA$.

Proof. 1. Take P, any point on BC except A, and draw OP.	1. Post. 1.
2. Then P is outside the circle O.	2. A tangent to a circle can have but one point in common with the circle. (§ 185.)
3. $OP >$ radius OQ, or OA.	3. Ax. 8.
4. $\therefore$ $OA \perp BC$; that is, $BC \perp OA$.	4. § 137.

Q.E.D.

211. Cor. 1. *A straight line perpendicular to a radius
at the point where the line meets the circle is tangent to the
circle.*

212. Cor. 2. *A perpendicular to a tangent at the point
of contact passes through the center of the circle.*

213. Cor. 3. *The perpendicular drawn from the center
of a circle to a tangent passes through the point of contact.*

Ex. Construct a circle O, a radius OA, and a line $\perp OA$ at A.

EXERCISES: GROUP 29

Ex. 1. **Given** the circle O with the equal chords AB and CD intersecting at P. FH is the diameter through P. **Prove** $\angle x = \angle y$.

[Sug. From the center O, draw OR and $OS \perp$ the chords CD and AB.]

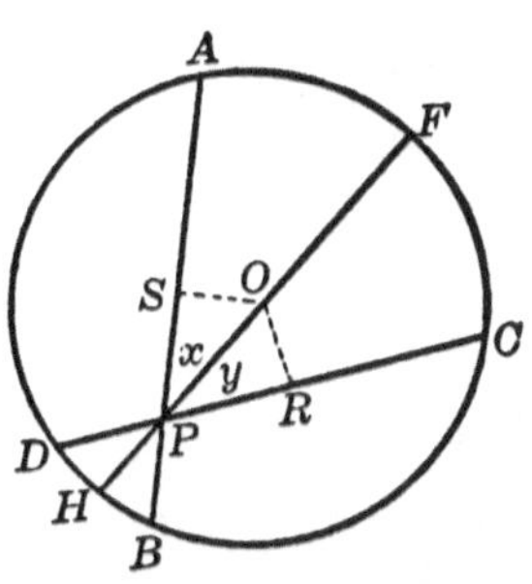

Ex. 2. On a diagram like that on p. 64, with P as a center and with a radius greater than PQ but less than PB, describe a circle. Prove that this circle intercepts equal chords on the lines AB and BC.

Ex. 3. In a given circle, is the chord of an arc of 60° twice as long as the chord of an arc of 30°? Draw a diagram and prove your statement.

Ex. 4. If the perpendiculars from the center upon two chords are equal, the arcs subtended by these chords are equal.

Ex 5. **Given** the circle O with the radii OC and OD, and AB a diameter; $\angle g = \angle h$. **Prove** chord $CD \parallel AB$.

[Sug. $\angle COD + \angle C + \angle D = 180°.$]

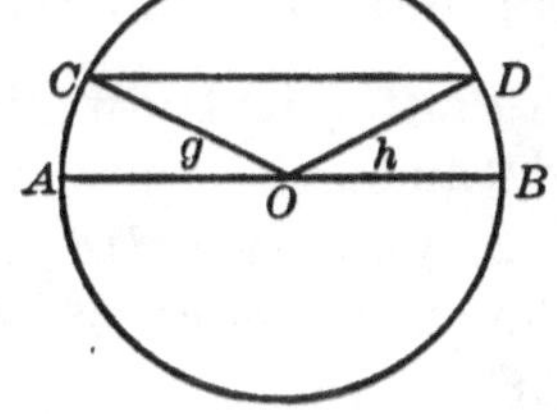

Ex. 6. In a given circle, tangents drawn at the extremities of a diameter are parallel.

Ex. 7. The line joining the center of a circle to the midpoint of a chord is perpendicular to the chord.

Ex. 8. By the aid of squared paper, construct the following arcs of spirals. (Note that Fig. 1 is composed of semicircles and Fig. 2 of quadrants. See § 228.)

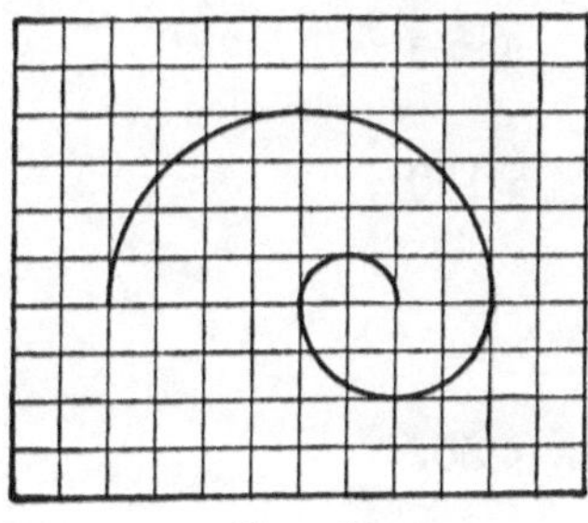

Fig. 1

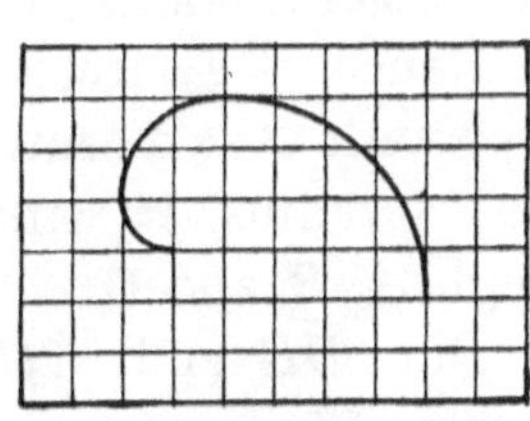

Fig. 2

Proposition XIII. Theorem

214. *Through three points, not lying in a straight line, one circle, and only one, can be drawn.*

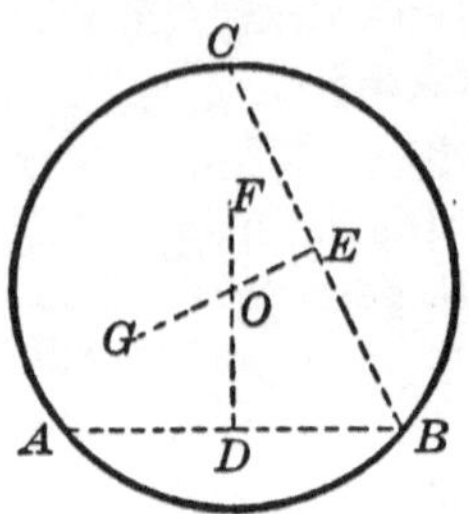

Given *A*, *B*, and *C* any three points not in the same straight line.

To prove that one circle, and only one, can be drawn through *A*, *B*, and *C*.

Proof. 1. Draw the lines *AB* and *BC*.

1. Post. 1.

2. Construct *DF* and *EG*, the ⊥ bisectors of *AB* and *BC*.

2. § 128.

3. *DF* and *EG* must intersect at some point *O*.

3. Lines ⊥ non-parallel lines are not ‖. (§ 101.)

4. Point *O* is equidistant from *A* and *B*.

4. § 120.

5. Also *O* is equidistant from *B* and *C*.

5. Why?

6. Hence, *O* is equidistant from the three points *A*, *B*, *C*.

6. Ax. 1.

7. Hence, if a circle is described with *O* as a center and *OA* as a radius, it will pass through *A*, *B*, and *C*.

7. § 180.

8. But *DF* and *EG* can intersect at but one point.

8. § 55.

9. Also between O and B only one straight line can be drawn.

9. § 57.

10. Hence, only one circle can be drawn through A, B, and C.

10. With one center and one radius, only one circle can be drawn. Q.E.D.

215. Efficiency value. — The above theorem enables us to shrink or to economize a circle into three points; or to expand any three points into a circle.

Ex. 1. How many circles can be passed through four given points in a plane, each circle passing through three, and only three, of the given points?

Ex. 2. Through two given points how many circles can be drawn? Draw three of these circles.

Ex. 3. Draw two circles so that they can have a common chord.

PROPOSITION XIV. THEOREM

216. *When two tangents to the same circle intersect each other, the distances from their point of intersection to their points of contact are equal.*

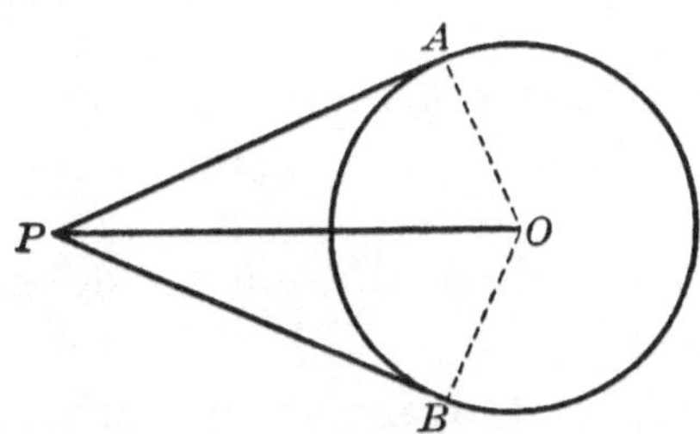

Given PA and PB tangent to the circle O at the points A and B respectively.

To prove $PA = PB$.

Proof. Let the student supply the proof.

217. The **line of centers** of two circles is the line joining their centers; as OO' (Fig. 1).

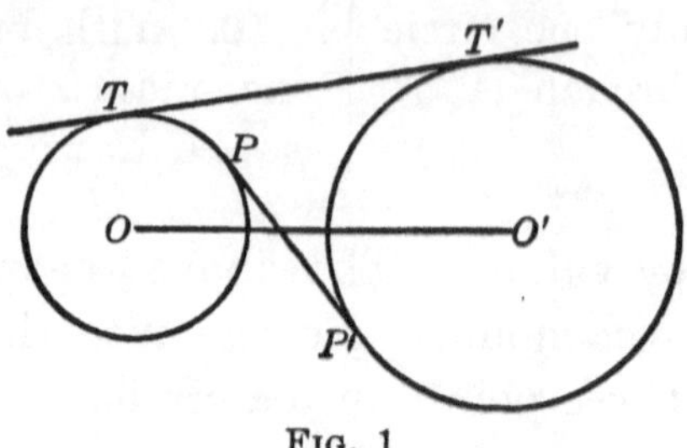

Fig. 1

218. Two circles tangent to each other are circles which are tangent to the same straight line at the same point. They are *tangent externally* or *internally* according as one circle lies entirely without or entirely within the other. See Figs. 2 and 3.

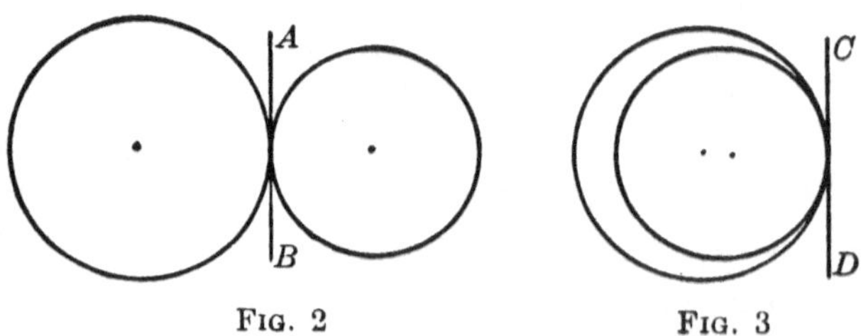

Fig. 2　　　　Fig. 3

219. Concentric circles are circles which have the same center.　Let the student draw a pair of concentric circles.

220. Two circles which do not meet may have four common tangents.

A **common internal tangent** of two circles is a tangent which cuts their line of centers; as PP' (Fig. 1) or AB (Fig. 2).

A **common external tangent** of two circles is a tangent which does not cut their line of centers; as TT' (Fig. 1) or CD (Fig. 3).

PROPOSITION XV. THEOREM

221. *When two circles intersect each other, the straight line through their centers is the perpendicular bisector of their common chord.*

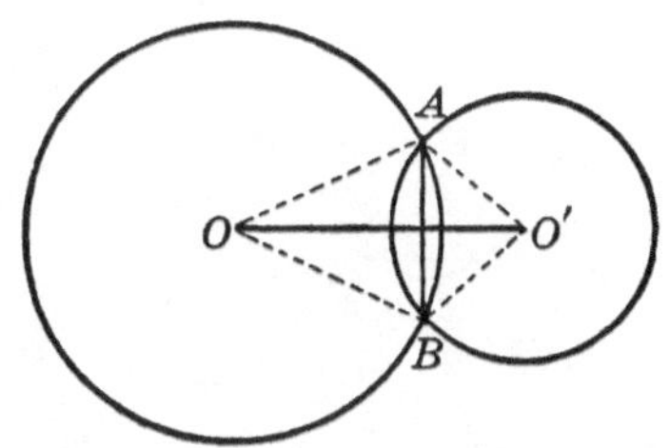

Given the circles O and O', intersecting at the points A and B.

To prove that OO' is the $\perp$ bisector of the chord AB.

Proof. 1. Draw the radii OA, OB, $O'A$, $O'B$.	1. Post. 1.
2. Then $OA = OB$, and $O'A = O'B$.	2. Why?
3. Hence, O and O' are two points equidistant from A and B, and OO' is the $\perp$ bisector of AB.	3. Why?
	Q.E.D.

Ex. 1. Draw two intersecting circles and show that the line of centers is less than the sum of the radii of the two circles.

Draw two circles in which the line of centers

Ex. 2. Equals the sum of the radii.

Ex. 3. Is greater than the sum of the radii.

Ex. 4. Is less than the sum of the radii.

Ex. 5. Is less than the sum, but greater than the difference of the radii.

Ex. 6. Can two circles which are tangent to each other have a common chord?

Ex. 7. Can two circles which are tangent to each other have a common secant?

Ex. 8. Draw two circles which can have neither a common chord nor a common tangent.

222. A **polygon inscribed in a circle** is a polygon all of whose vertices lie in the circle; as *ABCDE* (Fig. 1).

A **circle circumscribed about a polygon** is a circle which passes through every vertex of the polygon.

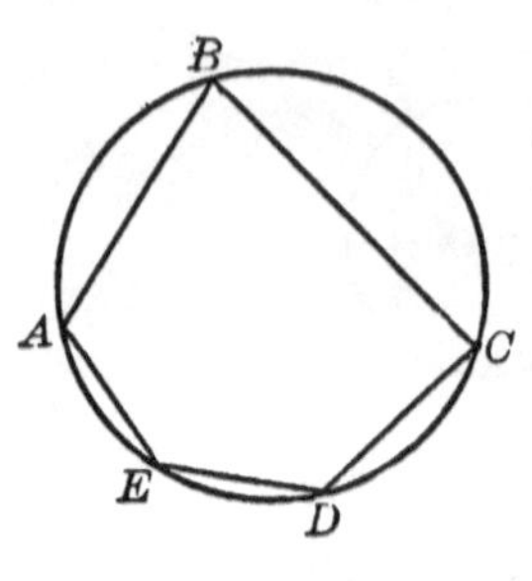

FIG. 1

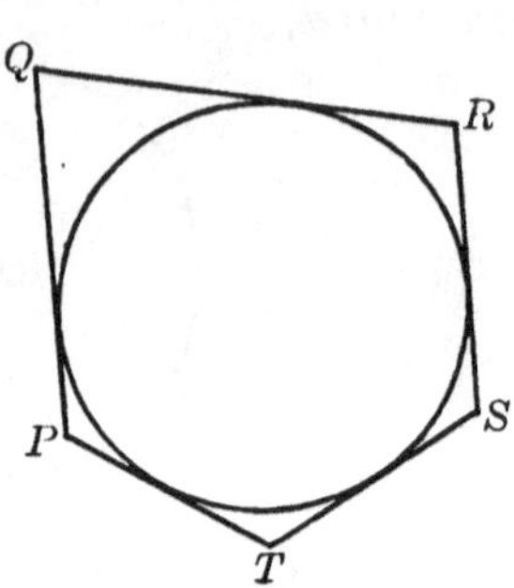

FIG. 2

223. A **polygon circumscribed about a circle** is a polygon all of whose sides are tangent to the circle; as *PQRST* (Fig. 2).

A **circle inscribed in a polygon** is a circle to which all the sides of the polygon are tangent.

How many common internal tangents and how many common external tangents have two circles

Ex. 1.   If they touch externally?

Ex. 2.   If they touch internally?

Ex. 3.   If they intersect?

Ex. 4.   If one circle lies wholly inside the other?

Ex. 5.   If one circle lies wholly outside the other?

EXERCISES : GROUP 30

Ex. 1.   *PA* and *PB* are tangents to a circle drawn from the point *P*. *O* is the center of the circle. Prove that *PO* is the perpendicular bisector of the chord *AB*.

Ex. 2.   If two tangents to a circle include an angle of 60° at their point of intersection, the chord joining the points of contact forms, with the tangents, an equilateral triangle.

Ex. 3. Given RA, RQ, and QB tangents of the circle O. Prove $RQ = RA + QB$.

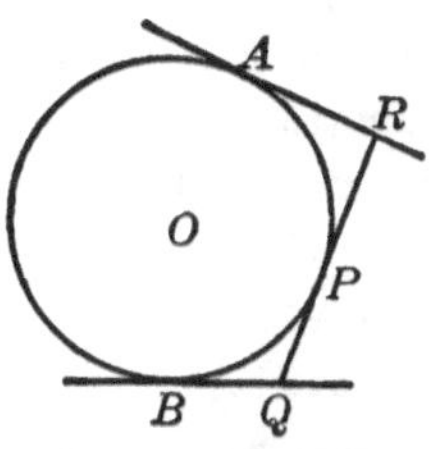

Ex. 4. If a quadrilateral is circumscribed about a circle, show that the sum of one pair of opposite sides equals the sum of the other pair.

Ex. 5. If a hexagon is circumscribed about a circle, show that the sum of three alternate sides equals the sum of the other three sides.

Ex. 6. If a polygon of $2\,n$ sides is circumscribed about a circle, the sum of n alternate sides equals the sum of the other n sides.

Ex. 7. A parallelogram circumscribed about a circle is equilateral.

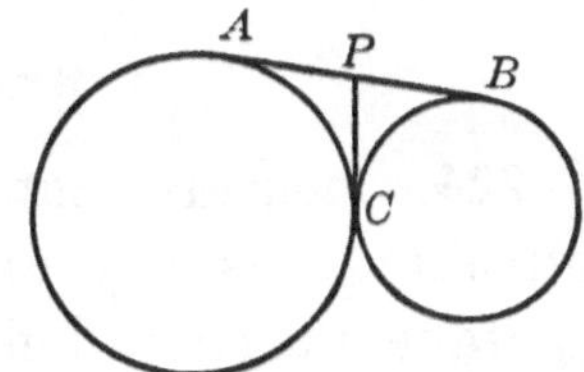

Ex. 8. If two circles are tangent externally, the common internal tangent bisects the common external tangent. (That is, prove $PA = PB$.)

Ex. 9. If two circles are tangent (either externally or internally), tangents drawn to them from any point in the common tangent are equal.

Ex. 10. Two circles whose centers are O and O' are tangent internally at P. The line PAB is drawn intersecting the circles at A and B. Prove that OA and $O'B$ are parallel.

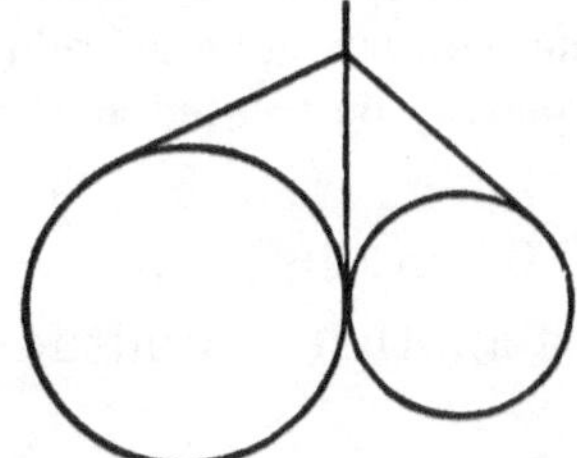

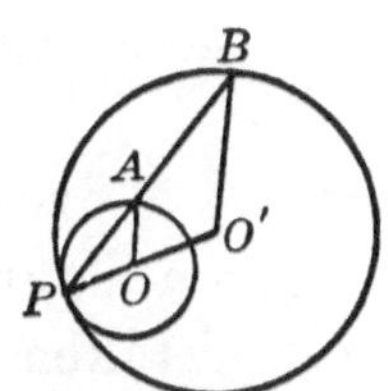

Ex. 11. By the aid of squared paper, construct the following designs:

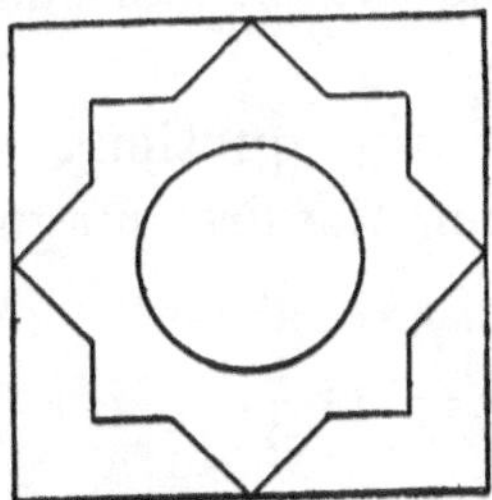

Ex. 12. Two straight street railway tracks, AB and CD, if produced, would meet at the point P. They are, however, connected by the track AFC, which is the arc of a circle to which AB is tangent at A and CD at C. If $PA = 160$ yd., how long is PC? Show how to find the center of the arc AFC.

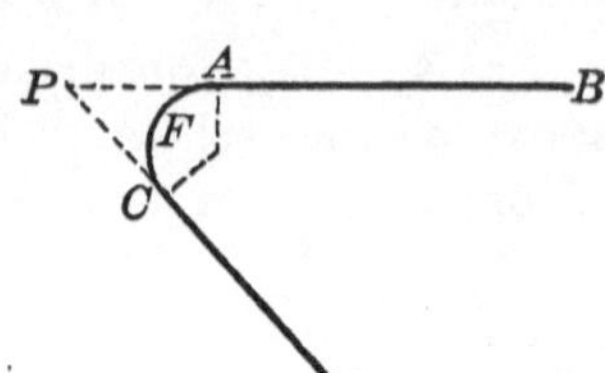

Ex. 13. Two straight street railway tracks, if produced, would meet at right angles. These tracks are to be connected by the arc of a circle whose radius is 150 yd. Using the scale 1 inch = 100 yd., draw a diagram showing the straight tracks and the connecting curve.

MEASUREMENT: RATIO

224. Measurement. — For many purposes, the most advantageous way of dealing with a given magnitude is to take a certain definite part of the magnitude as a unit, and then determine the number of times this unit must be taken in order to make up the given magnitude. Ease and precision in dealing with magnitudes are thus obtained.

Geometric magnitudes thus far have been treated as wholes, the object being simply to determine whether two given magnitudes are equal, or unequal, or to determine some similar general relation. Hereafter geometric magnitudes will frequently be treated as if composed of units.

To measure a given magnitude is to find how many times the given magnitude contains another magnitude of the same kind taken as a unit.

225. The **numerical measure** of a magnitude is the number which expresses how many times the unit of measure is contained in the given magnitude.

The **ratio** of two magnitudes is the quotient, or indicated quotient, obtained by dividing the first magnitude by the second.

Thus the ratio of 3 ft. to 1 ft. 4 in. is $\dfrac{36 \text{ in.}}{16 \text{ in.}}$ or $\dfrac{9}{4}$.

226. The **efficiency value** of ratio is illustrated by the fact that several indicated quotients, when taken together, may be simplified by cancellation before a final determination of their value is made.

227. *Two magnitudes of the same kind have the same ratio as their numerical measures.*

Also it follows from the properties of fractions that *equimultiples of two quantities have the same ratio as the quantities themselves.*

228. A **degree of arc** is $\frac{1}{360}$ part of a circle. (See § 20.)

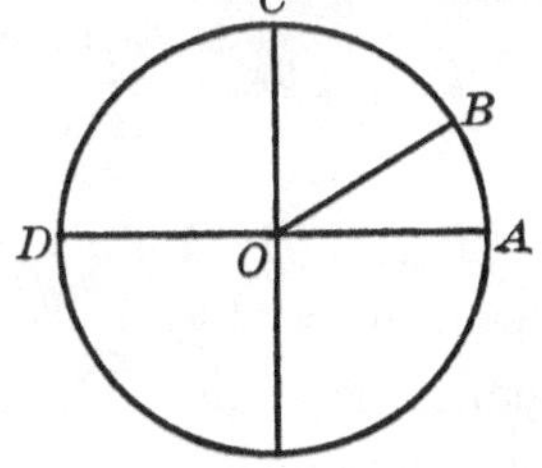

Hence, if the central angle AOB contains 30 degrees of angle, the intercepted arc AB contains 30 degrees of arc.

A **quadrant** is one fourth of a circle; as AC. Hence, a quadrant contains 90 degrees of arc.

Also a semicircle contains two quadrants, or 180 degrees of arc.

Ex. 1. With a radius of $\frac{3}{4}$ in., draw a circle and divide it into four equal arcs.

Ex. 2. With a radius of 1 in., draw a circle and divide it into eight equal arcs. How many degrees are there in each of these arcs?

Ex. 3. Draw a circle and divide it into six equal arcs. Into twelve equal arcs. How many degrees are in each of these arcs?

Ex. 4. Is 1° of angle always of the same size wherever found?

Ex. 5. Is 1° of the arc in Ex. 1 of the same size as 1° of the arc in Ex. 2?

Ex. 6. Draw two circles of such a size that 1° of arc in one of them shall equal 1° of arc in the other. Draw another circle in which 1° of arc is smaller than in the two circles first drawn.

PROPOSITION XVI. THEOREM

229. *In the same circle, or in equal circles, two central angles have the same ratio as their intercepted arcs.*

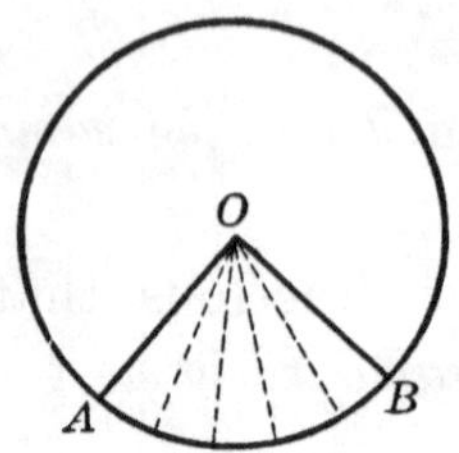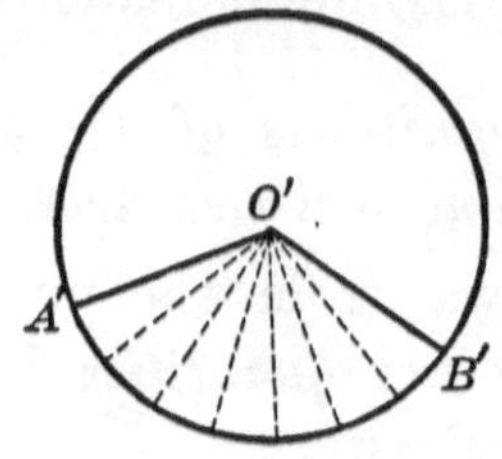

Given the equal $\odot$ O and O', with the central $\angle AOB$ and $A'O'B'$ intercepting the arcs AB and $A'B'$.

To prove $\dfrac{\angle AOB}{\angle A'O'B'} = \dfrac{\overset{\frown}{AB}}{\overset{\frown}{A'B'}}.$

Proof. 1. Let arc PQ (from a circle $= O$ and O') be an arc contained in $\overset{\frown}{AB}$ an exact number of times, as m times, and in $\overset{\frown}{A'B'}$ n times.

Then $\dfrac{\overset{\frown}{AB}}{\overset{\frown}{A'B'}} = \dfrac{m\,\overset{\frown}{PQ}}{n\,\overset{\frown}{PQ}} = \dfrac{m}{n}.$

1. Two magnitudes have the same ratio as their numerical measures.   (§ 227.)

2. From O and O' draw radii to the several points of division of arcs AB and $A'B'$.

2. Post. 1.

3. Then $\angle AOB$ will be divided into m, and $\angle A'O'B'$ into n small angles, all equal.

3. If in the same circle, or in equal circles, two arcs are equal, the $\angle$ which they subtend at the center are equal. (§ 196.)

4. $\dfrac{\angle AOB}{\angle A'O'B'} = \dfrac{m\angle R}{n\angle R} = \dfrac{m}{n}.$

4. § 227.

5. $\therefore \dfrac{\angle AOB}{\angle A'O'B'} = \dfrac{\overset{\frown}{AB}}{\overset{\frown}{A'B'}}.$

5. Ax. 1.

Q.E.D.

If in the above proof the two arcs AB and $A'B'$ should be found to have no common unit of measure, like arc PQ, the above theorem may still be proved true by a method of proof called the *method of limits*, which is beyond the scope of this book.

230. COR. *The number of angular degrees in a central angle is the same as the number of circular degrees in the intercepted arc; that is, a central angle is measured by its intercepted arc.*

231. Symbol for measurement; properties. — The expression $\angle AOB \overset{m}{=} \overset{\frown}{AB}$ is read, " The angle AOB is measured by the arc AB." Another form of statement is the following : "The number of degrees in angle AOB equals the numerical measure of arc AB."

Hence, the above expression is a form of equality, and the properties of equals, as stated in Axs. 2, 3, 4, 5 (p. 22) and others, apply here also.

Ex. 1. What is the ratio of a quadrant to a semicircle ?

Ex. 2. What is the ratio of an angle of an equilateral triangle to one of the acute angles of an isosceles right triangle ?

Ex. 3. Draw two circles so that the center of each circle is on the circumference of the other.

Ex. 4. Draw three circles so that the center of each is on the circumference of the other two.

[SUG. First draw an equilateral triangle.]

Ex. 5. Draw three circles each of which shall be tangent to the other two.

. **Ex. 6.** Draw two concentric circles and a line which is a tangent to one of these circles and a chord of the other.

Ex. 7. Draw two concentric circles and a line which is a secant of one and a chord of the other.

232. A **segment** of a circle is a figure composed of an arc of a circle and its chord; as ABC.

233. An **inscribed angle** is an angle whose vertex is in the circle and whose sides are chords; as the angle PRQ.

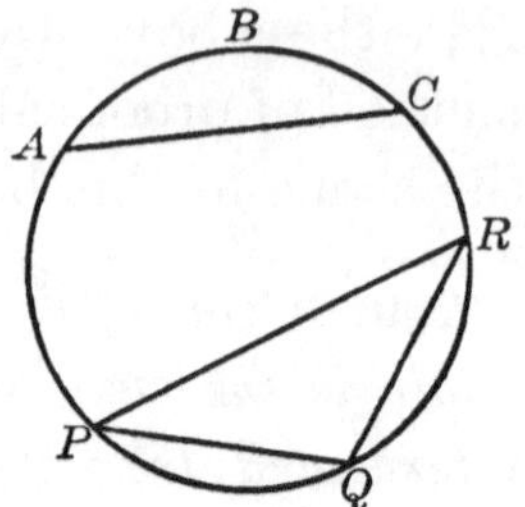

234. An **angle inscribed in a segment** is an angle whose vertex is in the arc of the segment and whose sides are chords drawn from the vertex to the extremities of the arc. Thus $\angle PQR$ is inscribed in segment PQR.

Ex. On the above diagram draw the chords AR and PC intersecting in T. Name all the inscribed angles on the figure. Is $\angle ATP$ an inscribed angle?

PROPOSITION XVII. THEOREM

235. *An angle inscribed in a circle is measured by one half its intercepted arc.*

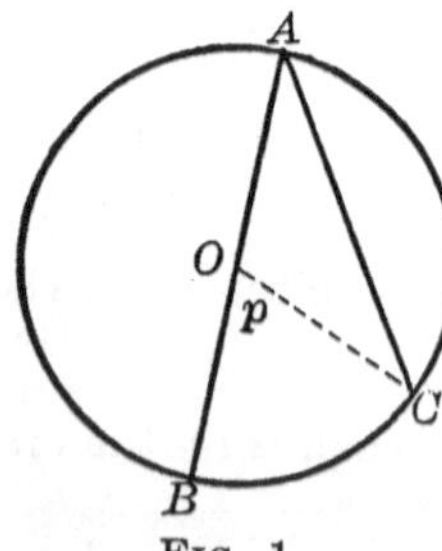

FIG. 1

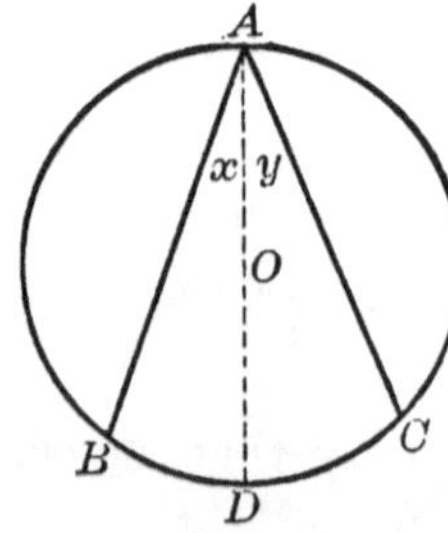

FIG. 2

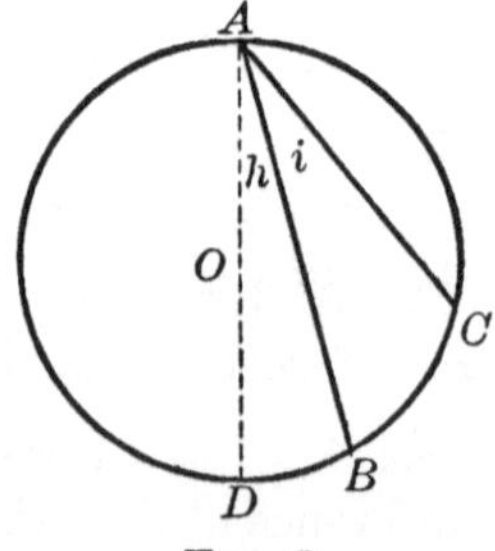

FIG. 3

CASE I. *When the center of the circle lies in one side of the inscribed angle.*

Given $\angle BAC$ (Fig. 1) inscribed in the circle O, and AB passing through the center O.

To prove $\angle BAC \stackrel{m}{=} \tfrac{1}{2}\widehat{BC}.$

Proof. 1. Draw radius OC.
        1. Post. 1.

2. Then in $\triangle\, OAC$,
       $OA = OC$.
        2. Why?

3. $\therefore \angle A = \angle C$.
        3. Why?

4. But $\angle p = \angle A + \angle C$.
        4. Why?

5. $\therefore \angle p = 2 \angle A$.
        5. Ax. 9.

6. But $\angle p \overset{m}{=} \overset{\frown}{BC}$.
        6. A central $\angle$ is measured by its intercepted arc. (§ 230.)

7. $\therefore \angle A \overset{m}{=} \tfrac{1}{2} \overset{\frown}{BC}$.
        7. Ax. 5.

CASE II. *When the center of the circle lies within the inscribed angle.*

Given the inscribed $\angle BAC$ (Fig. 2), with the center of the circle O lying within the angle.

To prove that $\angle BAC \overset{m}{=} \tfrac{1}{2} \overset{\frown}{BC}$.

Proof. 1. Draw the diameter AD.
        1. Post. 1.

2. Then $\angle BAD \overset{m}{=} \tfrac{1}{2} \overset{\frown}{BD}$.
        2. Case I.

3. Also $\angle DAC \overset{m}{=} \tfrac{1}{2} \overset{\frown}{DC}$.
        3. Why?

4. $\therefore \angle BAC \overset{m}{=} \tfrac{1}{2} \overset{\frown}{BC}$.
        4. Ax. 2.

CASE III. *When the center of the circle is outside the inscribed angle.*

Given the inscribed $\angle BAC$ (Fig. 3) with the center O outside the angle.

To prove that $\angle BAC \overset{m}{=} \tfrac{1}{2} \overset{\frown}{BC}$.

Proof. Let the student supply the proof.

236. Efficiency value. — By use of the above theorem, if the number of degrees in the intercepted arc is known, the number of degrees in the inscribed angle can be determined immediately.

Thus, if the arc BC (Fig. 3) contains 48°, the angle BAC contains 24°. Also, if it is known that the angle BAC contains, say 27°, the arc must contain 54°.

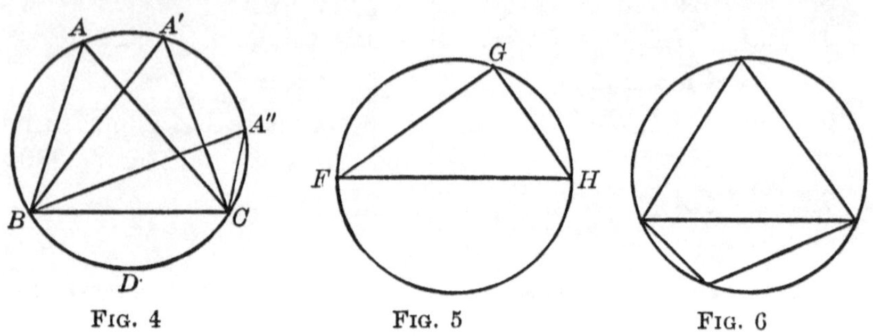

FIG. 4   FIG. 5   FIG. 6

237. Cor. 1. *All angles inscribed in the same segment, or in equal segments, are equal.*

Thus $\angle A$, A', A'' (Fig. 4) are all equal, for each of them is measured by one half the arc BDC.

238. Cor. 2. *An angle inscribed in a semicircle is a right angle*, for it is measured by one half a semicircle.

Thus FH (Fig. 5) is a diameter. ∴ $\angle FGH$ is a right angle.

239. Cor. 3. *An angle inscribed in a segment whose arc is greater than a semicircle is an acute angle. An angle inscribed in a segment whose arc is less than a semicircle is an obtuse angle.*

EXERCISES: GROUP 31

Ex. 1. If in Fig. 1 (p. 136) $\angle A$ contains 23°, how many degrees are there in $\overset{\frown}{BC}$? In $\overset{\frown}{AC}$?

Ex. 2. If in Fig. 1 $\overset{\frown}{AC} = \frac{1}{3}$ of the circle, how many degrees are there in $\angle BOC$? In $\angle BAC$?

Ex. 3. If in Fig. 3 $\overset{\frown}{AC} = 2\,\overset{\frown}{BC}$, and $\overset{\frown}{BC} = 2\,\overset{\frown}{DB}$, find $\angle DAC$. Also $\angle DAB$.

Ex. 4. Prove that each pair of opposite angles in an inscribed quadrilateral are supplementary.

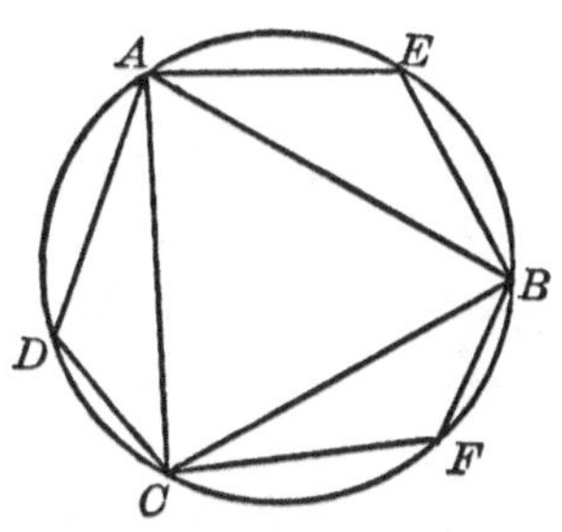

Ex. 5. ABC is an inscribed equilateral triangle. $\angle E, F, D$ are inscribed in the segments AEB, BFC, and CDA, respectively. Find the number of degrees in the sum of the $\angle E, F, D$.

Ex. 6. $PQRS$ is a quadrilateral inscribed in the circle O. $\overset{\frown}{PQ}=62°$, $\overset{\frown}{QR}=43°$, and the major arc $RS = 212°$. Find all the angles of the figure. Draw the radius OQ and then find all the new angles formed on the figure.

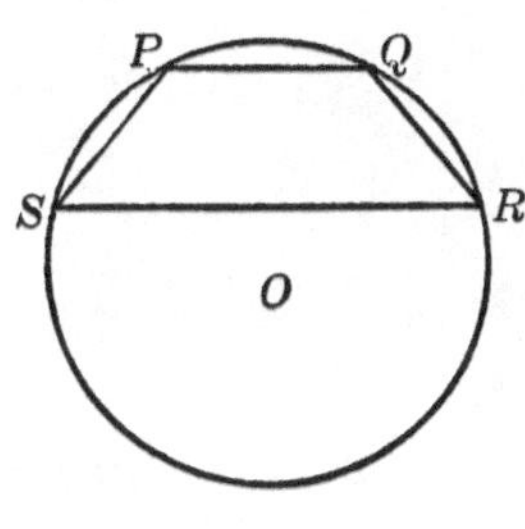

Ex. 7. Draw a circle containing an inscribed square. In each of the segments whose chords are the sides of the square, inscribe an angle. Find the number of degrees in the sum of these inscribed angles.

Ex. 8. AB is the diameter of a circle, and P is any point on the circle. AP is produced to the point L so that PL equals AP. Draw PB and prove that BL is equal to the diameter of the circle.

If the angle A contains 22°, how many degrees are there in each angle of the figure?

Ex. 9. ABC is an isosceles triangle inscribed in a circle. The vertex angle B is 30°, and D is the midpoint in the arc BC. If the line AD is drawn, how many degrees are there in the angle DAB?

Ex. 10. Circumscribe a circle about a given right triangle by bisecting only one side of the right triangle.

Ex. 11. Given the hypotenuse and an acute angle, construct a right triangle.

[Sug. Construct a semicircle whose diameter is the given hypotenuse.]

Ex. 12. Given the hypotenuse and one leg of a right triangle, construct the right triangle.

Ex. 13. Construct a segment of a circle which shall contain an inscribed angle of 120°. Of 60°. Of 90°.

Proposition XVIII. Theorem

240. *An angle formed by two chords intersecting each other within a circle is measured by one half the sum of the arc intercepted between its sides and the arc intercepted between the sides of its vertical angle.*

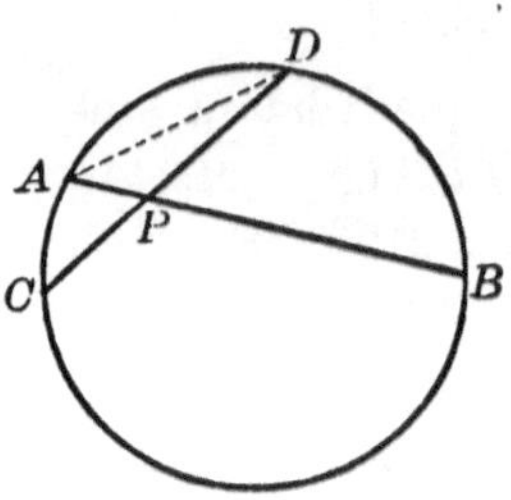

Given the chords AB and CD in the $\odot$ $ADBC$, intersecting within the circumference at the point P.

To prove that $\angle DPB$ is measured by $\frac{1}{2}$ $(\overset{\frown}{DB} + \overset{\frown}{AC})$.

Proof. 1. Draw the chord AD.	1. Post. 1.
2. In $\triangle ADP$, $\quad \angle DPB = \angle A + \angle D.$	2. Why ?
3. But $\angle A \overset{m}{=\!=} \frac{1}{2} \overset{\frown}{DB}.$	3. An angle inscribed in a circle is measured by one half its intercepted arc. (§ 235.)
4. $\qquad \angle D \overset{m}{=\!=} \frac{1}{2} \overset{\frown}{AC}.$	4. Why ?
5. $\quad \angle DPB \overset{m}{=\!=} \frac{1}{2}(\overset{\frown}{DB} + \overset{\frown}{AC}).$	5. Ax. 2.

Q.E.D.

Ex. 1.   In the above figure, if arc DB contains 94° and arc AC contains 38°, how many degrees are there in $\angle APC$? In $\angle APD$?

Ex. 2.   If arc $AD = 52°$ and $\angle APD = 124°$, find arc CB.

Ex. 3.   If in Fig. 1 (p. 136) arc AC contains 112°, how many degrees are there in the $\angle A$?

Proposition XIX. Theorem

241. *An angle formed by a tangent and a chord through the point of contact is measured by one half the intercepted arc.*

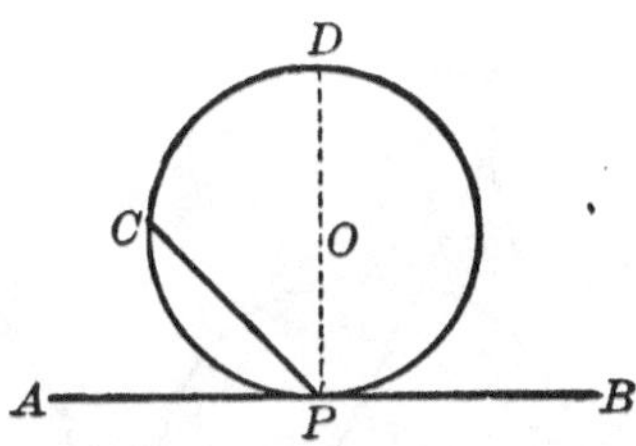

Given AB a tangent to the circle O at the point P; PC a chord.

To prove $\angle APC \overset{m}{=} \frac{1}{2}\ \overset{\frown}{PC}$.

Proof. 1. Draw the diameter PD.	1. Post. 1.
2. $\angle APD$ is a rt. $\angle$.	2. § 210.
3. $\qquad \angle APD \overset{m}{=} \frac{1}{2}\ \overset{\frown}{PCD}$.	3. For a semicircle contains 180° of arc. (§ 228.)
4. But $\quad \angle CPD \overset{m}{=} \frac{1}{2}\ \overset{\frown}{CD}$.	4. Why?
5. Hence, $\angle APC \overset{m}{=} \frac{1}{2}\ \overset{\frown}{PC}$.	5. Ax. 3.

Q.E.D.

Ex. 1. In the above figure, if arc PC contains 94°, how many degrees are there in $\angle APC$?

Ex. 2. If arc $CD = 80°$, find all the angles on the figure.

Ex. 3. If arc PDC exceeds arc PC by 128°, how many degrees are in each angle of the figure?

Ex. 4. Draw a figure for the following theorem, letter the figure and state the hypothesis and conclusion in terms of the lettered diagram (but give no proof of the theorem): "If from the point in which the bisector of an inscribed angle meets the circle, a chord is drawn parallel to one side of the angle, the chord thus drawn equals the other side of the angle."

PROPOSITION XX.　THEOREM

242. *If two lines which intersect each other in a point outside of a circle both meet the circle, the angle which they form is measured by one half the difference of the intercepted arcs.*

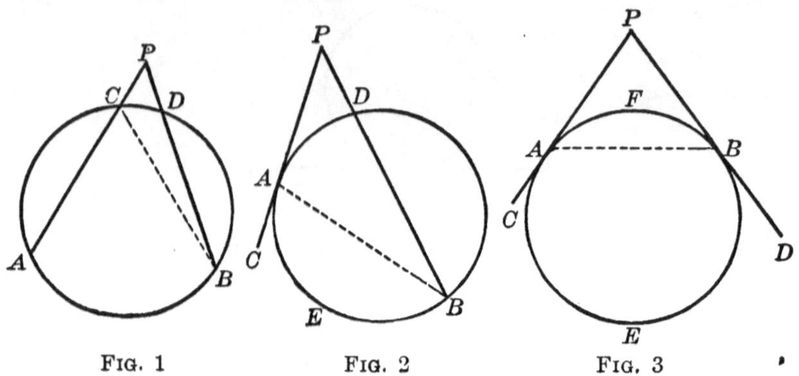

FIG. 1　　　　FIG. 2　　　　FIG. 3

I. Given the $\odot$ $ACDB$ (Fig. 1), and the $\angle APB$ formed by the secants PA and PB, meeting at the point P outside the circle, and intersecting the circle at C and D, respectively.

To prove that $\angle P$ is measured by $\frac{1}{2}(\widehat{AB} - \widehat{CD})$.

Proof. 1.　Draw the chord CB.	1.　Post. 1.
2.　Then $\angle ACB = \angle P + \angle B$.	2.　Why ?
3.　　　　$\therefore \angle P = \angle ACB - \angle B$.	3.　Ax. 3.
4.　But $\angle ACB \overset{m}{=\!=} \frac{1}{2}\widehat{AB}$.	4.　Why ?
5.　Also　$\angle B \overset{m}{=\!=} \frac{1}{2}\widehat{CD}$.	5.　Why ?
6.　　　　$\therefore \angle P \overset{m}{=\!=} \frac{1}{2}(\widehat{AB} - \widehat{CD})$.	6.　Ax. 9.

II. Given the $\odot$ ADB (Fig. 2), and $\angle CPB$ formed by the tangent PC touching the circle at A and the secant PB intersecting the circle at D.

To prove that $\angle P$ is measured by $\frac{1}{2}(\widehat{AB} - \widehat{AD})$.

Proof.　Let the student supply the proof.

III. **Given** $\angle APB$ (Fig. 3) formed by the tangents PC and PD touching the circle at A and B, respectively.

To prove that $\angle P$ is measured by $\frac{1}{2}$ $(\overarc{AEB} - \overarc{AFB})$.

Proof. Let the student supply the proof.

243. Efficiency value. — By means of Props. XVII–XX, angles formed by chords, secants, or tangents (or combinations of these) are all reduced to central angles and hence may readily be compared.

Ex. 1. If in Fig. 1 (p. 142) $\overarc{CD} = 34°$ and $\overarc{AB} = 108°$, draw AD and find all the angles of the figure.

Ex. 2. If in Fig. 3 (p. 142) angle $P = 80°$, find arcs AFB and AEB.

PROPOSITION XXI.   THEOREM

244. *Two parallel chords of a circle intercept equal arcs.*

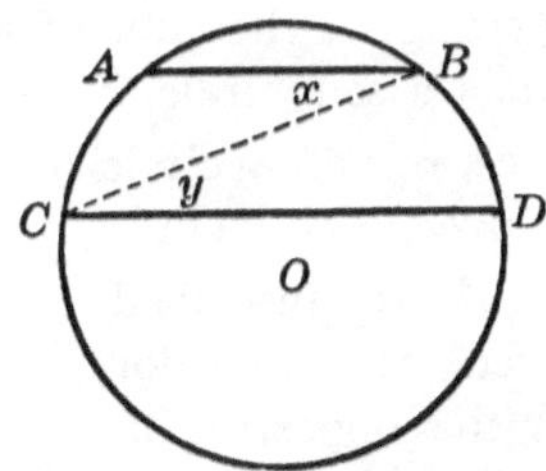

Given the parallel chords AB and CD in the circle O.

To prove $\overarc{AC} = \overarc{BD}$.

Proof. 1. Draw CB.		1. Post. 1.
2. Then $\angle x = \angle y$.		2. Why ?
3. But $\angle x \overset{m}{=} \frac{1}{2} \overarc{AC}$.		3. Why ?
4. Also $\angle y \overset{m}{=} \frac{1}{2} \overarc{BD}$.		4. Why ?
5. $\therefore \frac{1}{2} \overarc{AC} = \frac{1}{2} \overarc{BD}$.		5. Ax. 1.
6. $\therefore \overarc{AC} = \overarc{BD}$.		6. Why ?

Q.E.D.

245. Cor. 1. *If a secant and a tangent to a given circle are parallel, they intercept equal arcs on the circle.*

246. Cor. 2. *If two tangents to a given circle are parallel, they intercept equal arcs on the circle.*

EXERCISES: GROUP 32

Ex. 1. What new methods of proving two lines equal have been found in Book Two?

Ex. 2. What new methods of proving two angles equal? Of proving two angles supplementary? Of proving an angle a right angle?

Ex. 3. What methods of proving two arcs equal?

Ex. 4. A chord forms equal angles with the tangents at its extremities.

Ex. 5. If an isosceles triangle is inscribed in a circle, the tangent at its vertex makes equal angles with two of its sides and is parallel to the third side. Is the converse of this theorem true?

Ex. 6. If two chords in a circle intersect within the circle at right angles, the sum of a pair of alternate arcs equals a semicircle.

Ex. 7. Given O the center of a circle and AC a tangent. **Prove** $\angle BAC = \frac{1}{2} \angle O$.

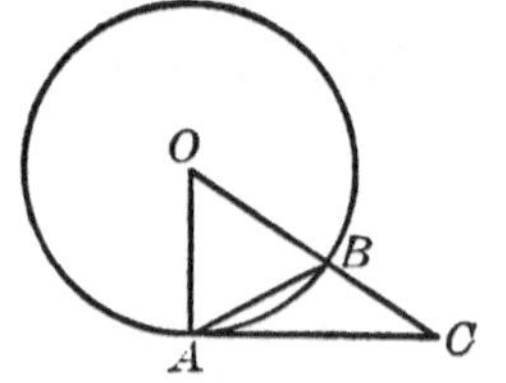

Ex. 8. If one side of an inscribed quadrilateral is produced, the exterior angle so formed equals the opposite interior angle of the quadrilateral.

Ex. 9. If AB and CD are two intersecting diameters in the circle O, prove $ADBC$ a rectangle.

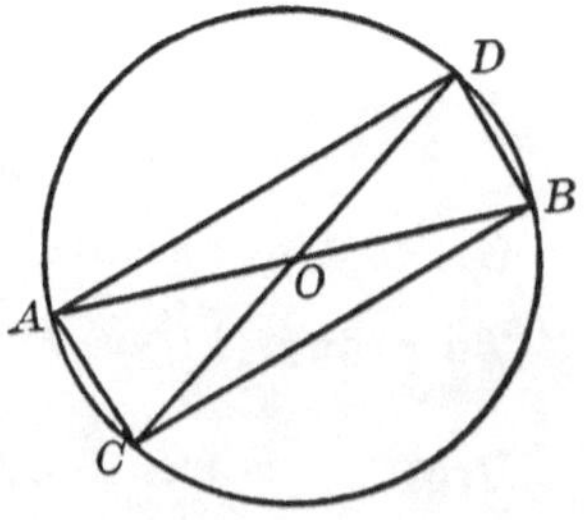

Ex. 10. A parallelogram inscribed in a circle is a rectangle.

Ex. 11. A circle is circumscribed about the triangle ABC, and P is the midpoint of the arc AB. Prove that the angle ABP equals one half the angle C.

Ex. 12. If A, B, C, D, and E are points taken in succession on a circle, and the arcs AB, BC, CD, and DE are equal, prove that the angles ABC, BCD, and CDE are equal.

Ex. 13. An inscribed angle formed by a diameter and a chord has its intercepted arc bisected by a radius which is parallel to the chord.

Ex. 14. Two secants, PAB and PCD, intersect the circle $ABDC$. Prove that the triangles PBC and PAD are mutually equiangular.

Ex. 15. Given AC a tangent and $AB \parallel CE$. Prove $\triangle ACD$ and ABE mutually equiangular.

Ex. 16. A straight line is drawn cutting two equal ⊚ and ∥ to their line of centers. Prove that the chords intercepted in the two ⊚ are equal.

Ex. 17. Given ABC an inscribed triangle, $AE \perp BC$, and $CD \perp AB$. Prove arc $BD =$ arc BE.

Ex. 18. Tangents through the vertices of an inscribed rectangle form a rhombus or a square.

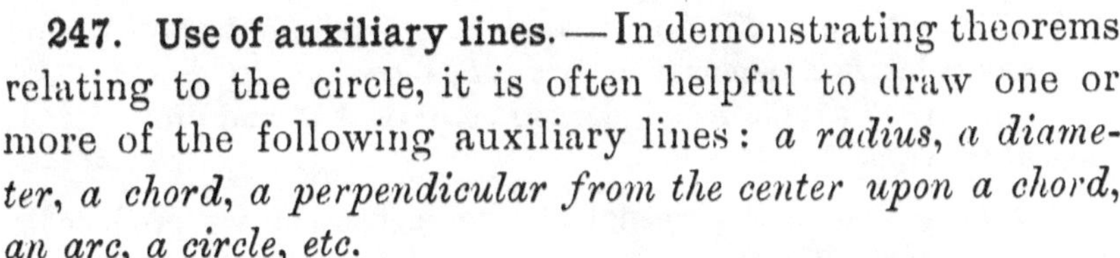

247. Use of auxiliary lines. — In demonstrating theorems relating to the circle, it is often helpful to draw one or more of the following auxiliary lines: *a radius, a diameter, a chord, a perpendicular from the center upon a chord, an arc, a circle, etc.*

EXERCISES: GROUP 33

AUXILIARY LINES

Ex. 1. Given circle O, $\overset{\frown}{AB} = \overset{\frown}{BC}$, $BM \perp OA$, and $BN \perp OC$. Prove $BM = BN$.

Ex. 2. If from any point on a circle a chord and a tangent are drawn, the perpendiculars drawn to them from the midpoint of the arc subtended by the chord are equal.

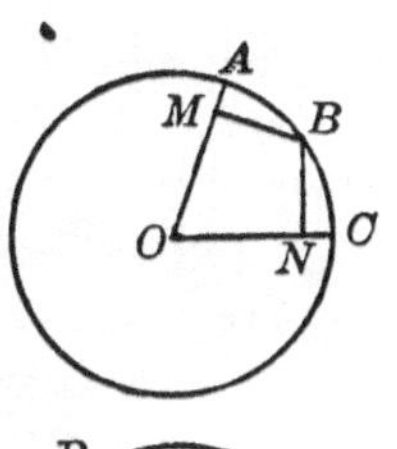

Ex. 3. Given O the center of a circle, and $OD \perp$ chord AC. Prove $\angle AOD = \angle B$.

Ex. 4. From the extremity of a diameter, chords are drawn making equal angles with the diameter. Prove that these chords are equal.

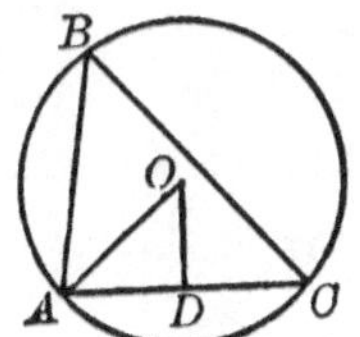

[SUG. Draw ⊥s from the center to the chords.]

Is the converse of this theorem true?

Ex. 5. If through any point within a circle equal chords are drawn, show that the line drawn from the center to the point of intersection of the chords bisects their angle of intersection.

Ex. 6. Tangents PA and PB are drawn to a circle whose center is O. Prove that angle P equals twice angle OAB.

Ex. 7. If in a circle two equal chords intersect, the segments of one chord equal the segments of the other chord.

Ex. 8. The chord AB equals the chord CD in a given circle, and the chords, if produced, intersect at the point P. Prove secant $PA =$ secant PC.

[SUG. Draw the chord AC.]

Ex. 9. If a quadrilateral is circumscribed about a circle, the angles at the center subtended by a pair of opposite sides are supplementary.

[SUG. Draw radii to the points of contact and show that there are four pairs of equal ∡ at the center.]

Ex. 10. If an equilateral triangle ABC is inscribed in a circle and any point P is taken in the arc AB, show that $PC = PA + PB$.

[SUG. On PC take PM equal to PA, draw AM, and prove ▵ PAB and MAC equal.]

Ex. 11. Two radii perpendicular to each other are produced to intersect a tangent, and from the points of intersection other tangents are drawn to the circle. Prove that the tangents last drawn are parallel.

[SUG. Draw radii to the three points of contact.]

Ex. 12. A straight line intersects two concentric circles. Show that the segments of the line intercepted between the circles are equal.

[SUG. Prove $AB = CD$.]

Ex. 13. PA and PB are equal lines drawn from an external point P to the circle O. Prove that PO bisects $\angle APB$.

[SUG. Produce PA and PB to form the secants PC and PD.

Prove $\qquad \angle x = \angle y.$

$\qquad \therefore \ \overset{\frown}{AC} = \overset{\frown}{BD}.$

$\qquad \therefore \ \triangle ORP = \triangle OSP,$ etc.]

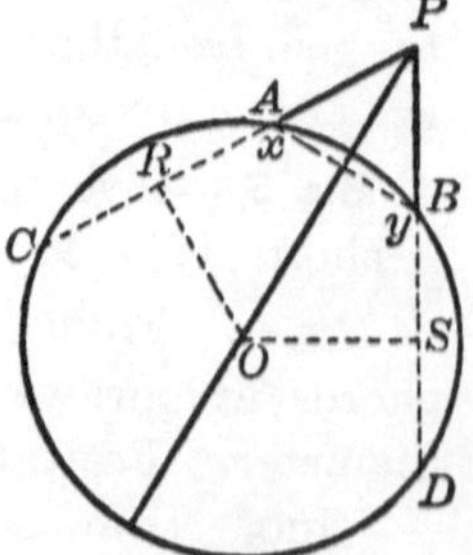

Ex. 14. A common tangent is drawn to two circles which are exterior to each other. Show that the chords drawn from the points of tangency to the points where the line of centers, produced through the center of the larger circle, cuts the smaller circle and meets the larger circle, are parallel.

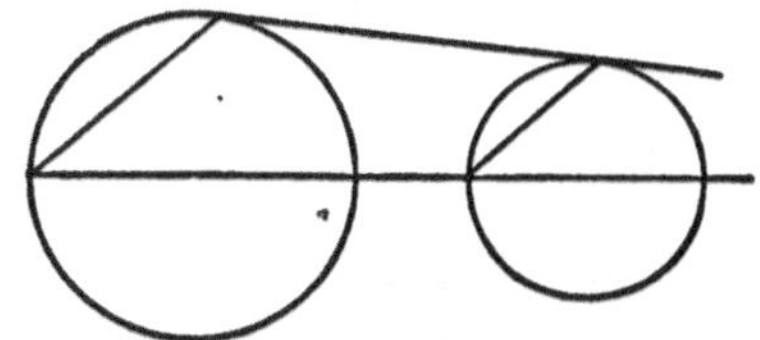

Ex. 15. A circle is described on the radius of another circle as a diameter, and a chord of the larger circle is drawn from the point of contact of the two circles. Prove that this chord is bisected by the smaller circle.

[Sug. If the chord is bisected, a ⊥ from the center of the larger circle to the chord will also bisect the chord.]

Ex. 16. Two circles are tangent externally at the point P. Through P any two lines APB and CPD are drawn, terminated by the circles. Show that the chords AC and BD are parallel.

[Sug. Draw the common tangent at P. If AC and BD are ‖, what ∠ must be equal?]

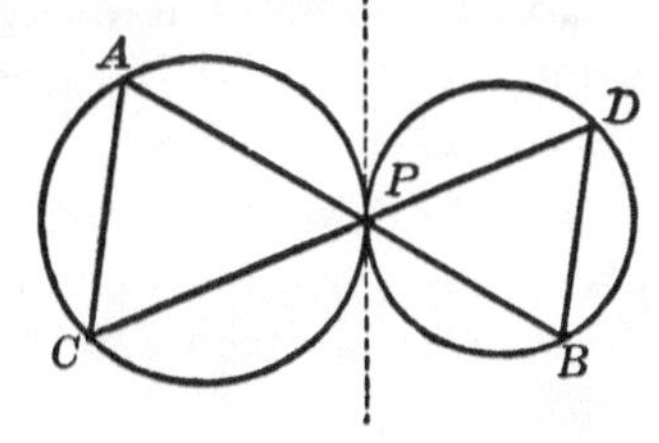

Ex. 17. Two circles intersect at the points P and Q. Lines APB and CQD are drawn, terminated by the circles. Show that AC and BD are parallel.

Ex. 18. If a square is constructed on the hypotenuse of a right triangle, a line drawn from the point where the diagonals of the square intersect to the vertex of the right angle bisects the right angle.

[Sug. Describe a circle on the hypotenuse of the right triangle as a diameter.]

Ex. 19. If two circles are tangent externally at P, and a common tangent touches them at A and B, respectively, the angle APB is a right angle.

Ex. 20. If in the triangle ABC the two altitudes BD and AE are drawn, the angle ABD equals the angle AED.

[Sug. Describe a semicircle on AB as a diameter.]

Ex. 21. Two circles intersect at P and Q. PA and PB are diameters. Prove that QA and QB form a straight line.

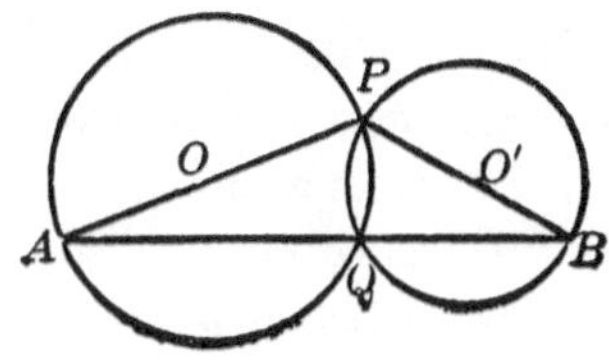

Ex. 22.   Two equal circles intersect at P and Q; through P, a line is drawn terminated by the circles at A and B. Show that QA equals QB.

[Sug.   ∡ A and B are measured by what arcs?]

Ex. 23.   What is meant by the expression, "the inscribed $\angle ABC$ is measured by $\frac{1}{2}$ arc AC"?

248.   A **maximum** is the greatest of a class of magnitudes satisfying certain given conditions, and a **minimum** is the least.

Of the chords in a given circle, which is the maximum?

EXERCISES: GROUP 34

Maxima and Minima

Ex. 1.   Of the chords drawn through a given point within a circle, determine which is the greatest, and also which is the least.

Ex. 2.   Find the shortest line, and also the longest line, that can be drawn from a given external point to a circle.

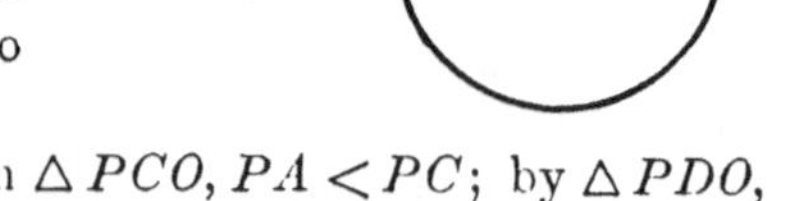

[Sug. O being the center, prove in $\triangle PCO$, $PA < PC$; by $\triangle PDO$, $PB > PD$.]

Ex. 3.   Find the shortest line, and also the longest line, that can be drawn to a circle from a point within the circle.

[Sug. O being the center, prove, by use of $\triangle OPC$, $PB < PC$.]

Ex. 4.   If two circles intersect, show that, of lines drawn through a point of intersection and terminated by the circles, that line is a maximum which is parallel to the line of centers.

[Sug.   Prove $RS < OO'$. $\therefore CPD < APB$.]

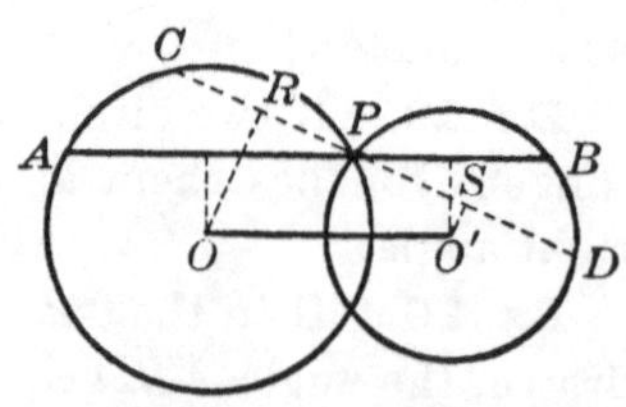

Ex. 5.   Given $AB \perp OB$ in circle O. **Prove** $\angle OAB$ the maximum of all ∡ having their vertices on the circle and their sides passing through O and B, respectively.

[Sug.   Draw a circle on OA as a diameter.]

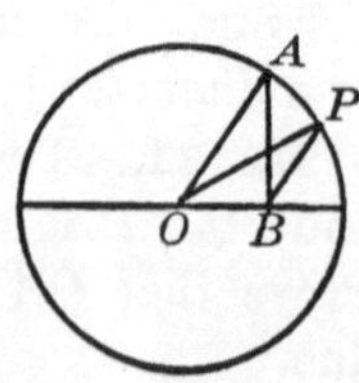
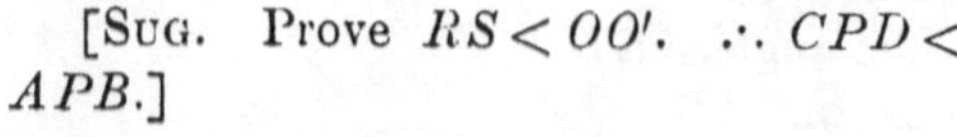
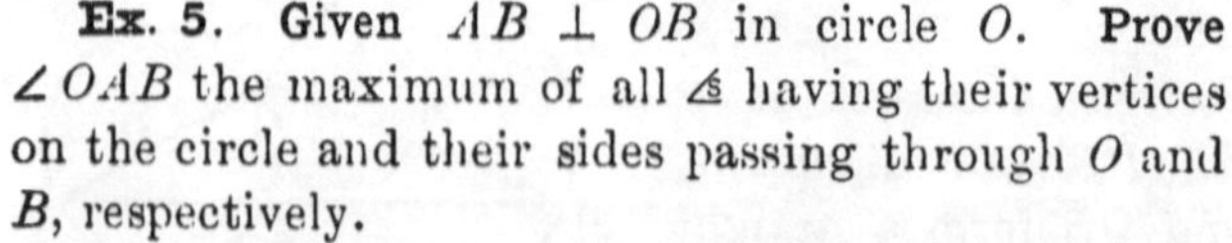

EXERCISES: GROUP 35

DEMONSTRATIONS BY INDIRECT METHODS

Prove the following by an indirect method (see § 179, p. 101) :

Ex. 1. A segment of a circle which contains a right angle is a semicircle.

Ex. 2. If a rectangle is inscribed in a circle, its diagonals are diameters.

Ex. 3. Prove the second part of Prop. VI by an indirect method.

Ex. 4. A line joining the midpoints of two parallel chords passes through the center.

[SUG. Draw a ⊥ to each chord from the center and show that these ⊥s are in the same line.]

Ex. 5. If the opposite angles of a quadrilateral are supplementary, a circle can be circumscribed about the quadrilateral.

[SUG. Pass a circle through three vertices of the quadrilateral; if it does not pass through the remaining vertex, etc.]

249. **A geometrical constant** is a geometrical magnitude which may vary in some respect, as in position, but remains constant in size.

Thus the angles inscribed in a given semicircle vary in position but are all of the same size; viz., a right angle. (See § 238.)

EXERCISES: GROUP 36

DETERMINATION OF CONSTANTS AND LOCI

Ex. 1. AB and AC are tangents to a circle. P is any point on the circle outside the triangle ABC. As P moves, prove that the sum of the $\angle A$ and $\angle BPC$ is constant.

Ex. 2. In the figure of Ex. 3, p. 131, if AR and BQ are produced to meet at T, show that the perimeter of the triangle TRQ equals the sum of TA and TB; and hence that the perimeter of triangle TRQ is constant, no matter how P may vary in position between A and B.

Ex. 3. Show on the same figure that, if O is the center, $\angle ROQ$ is constant as P varies in position.

Ex. 4. Two circles intersect in the points A and B. From any point P on one circle lines PAC and PBD are drawn, terminated by the other circle. Show that the chord CD is constant.

[Sug. Draw BC and prove $\angle CBD$ a constant.]

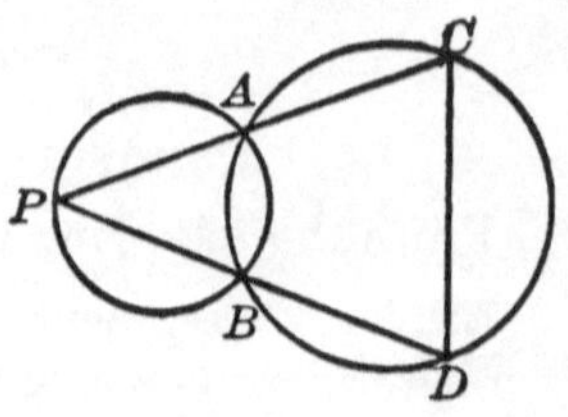

Ex. 5. Given $OA \perp OB$, and CD a line of given length moving so that D is always in OA and C in OB, and P the midpoint of CD. Prove that OP is constant in length.   (See Ex. 6, p. 100.)

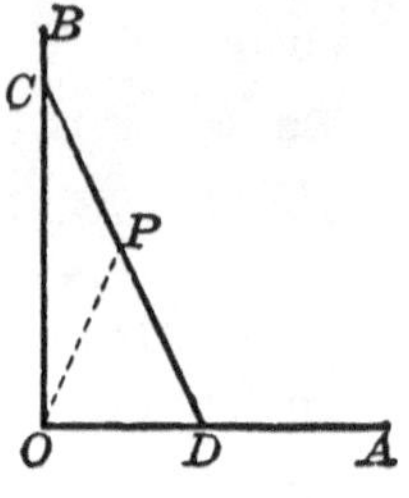

The determination of loci is often facilitated by showing that some given magnitude is a constant.

Ex. 6. Find the locus of a point moving so that it is at a given distance a from a given circle whose radius is r.

Ex. 7. Find the locus of the midpoints of the radii of a given circle.

Ex. 8. Find the locus of the midpoints of all chords of a given length drawn in a given circle.

Ex. 9. Find the locus of the vertices of all right triangles having a given hypotenuse as base.

Ex. 10. Find the locus of the midpoints of all the chords drawn from a given point on a given circle.

[Sug. Draw a line from the center to the given point, and perpendiculars from the center upon the chords.]

Ex. 11. In Ex. 5 find the locus of P.

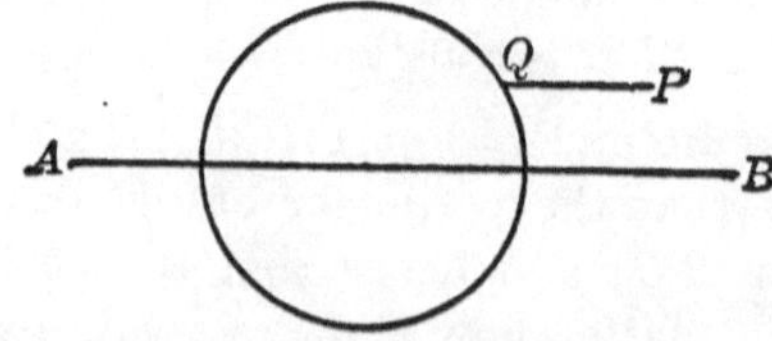

Ex. 12. QP is a line of given length and moves so that Q is always in a given circle, and QP is always parallel to a fixed line. Find the locus of P.

EXERCISES: GROUP 37

THEOREMS PROVED BY VARIOUS METHODS

Ex. 1. The line which bisects the angle formed by a tangent and a chord bisects the intercepted arc also.

Ex. 2. An inscribed trapezoid is isosceles.

Ex. 3. Given TA and TB tangents, arc $AB = 80°$, arc $BD = 95°$, and arc $DC = 150°$; find all the angles of the figure.

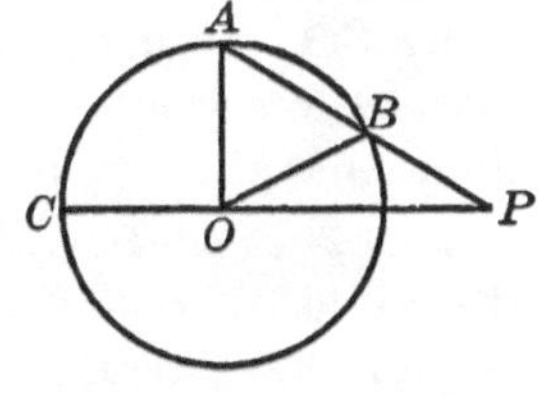

Ex. 4. If two tangents to a circle are parallel, the line joining their points of contact is a diameter. (Use § 246.)

Ex. 5. A rectangle circumscribed about a circle is a square. [SUG. Use the preceding theorem.]

Ex. 6. Given O the center of a circle, PBA and POC secants, and $BP =$ the radius. Prove $\angle AOC = 3 \angle P$.

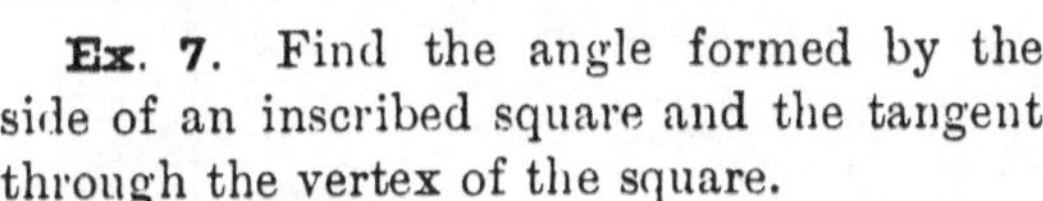

Ex. 7. Find the angle formed by the side of an inscribed square and the tangent through the vertex of the square.

Ex. 8. From an external point a secant is drawn through the center of a circle, and also two other secants making equal angles with the first secant. Show that the secants last drawn are equal.

Ex. 9. ABC is a triangle, and on the side AB the point P is taken and on BC the point Q, so that angle BPQ equals angle C. Show that a circle may be circumscribed about the quadrilateral $APQC$.

Ex. 10. Two circles are tangent to each other externally, and a line is drawn through the point of contact and is terminated by the circles. Show that the radii from the extremities of this line are parallel.

Ex. 11. If a circle is described on the leg of an isosceles triangle as diameter, the circle will bisect the base of the triangle.

Ex. 12. The chord of an arc is parallel to the tangent at the midpoint of the arc.

Ex. 13. If a triangle is inscribed in a circle, the sum of the angles inscribed in the segments exterior to the triangle is four right angles.

Ex. 14. Find the theorem for an inscribed quadrilateral, corresponding to Ex. 13.

Ex. 15. Find the locus of the centers of all circles passing through two given points.

Ex. 16. If two unequal chords intersect in a circle, the greater chord makes the less angle with the diameter through the point of intersection of the chords.

State also the converse of this theorem. Is the converse true?

Ex. 17. The sum of the legs of a right triangle equals the sum of the hypotenuse and the diameter of the inscribed circle.

Ex. 18. The sides AB, BC, and AC of a triangle touch the inscribed circle at the points P, Q, and R. Show that angle PQR and one half angle A are complementary.

[Sug. Draw radii from the center O to P and R. Then $\angle PQR = \angle POA$, etc.]

Ex. 19. From the point in which the bisector of an inscribed angle meets the circle, a chord is drawn parallel to one side of the angle. Show that this chord equals the other side of the angle.

Ex. 20. Given AB a diameter, $AP =$ the radius, AD and PC tangents. **Prove** $\triangle CED$ equilateral.

[Sug. Draw OC and CA; then in rt. $\triangle OCP$, $CA = $ radius, $\angle P = 30°$, etc.]

Ex. 21. Perpendiculars are drawn from the extremities of a diameter upon a tangent. Show that the points in which the perpendiculars intersect the tangent are equidistant from the center.

EXERCISES: GROUP 38

PRACTICAL APPLICATIONS

Ex. 1. Given a fragment of a broken wheel, show how to find the radius of the wheel.

Ex. 2. Show how to find the diameter of a given circle by applying a rectangular sheet of paper to the circle. By more than one application, show how to find the center of the circle.

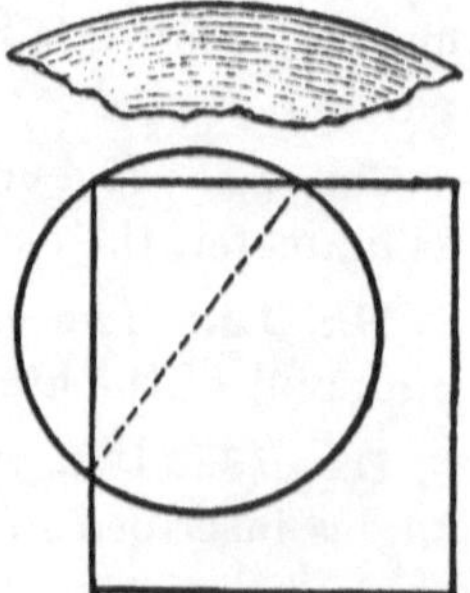

Ex. 3. Show how a pattern maker, by the use of a carpenter's square, can determine whether the cavity made in the edge of a board or piece of metal is a semicircle.

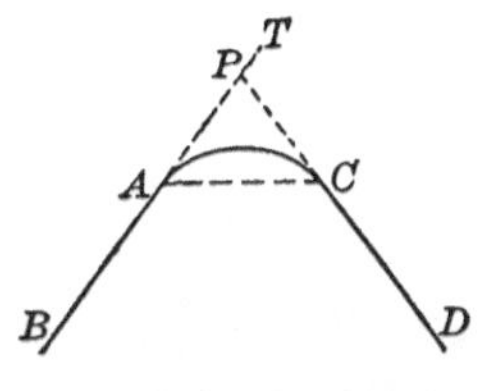

Ex. 4. The curve in a railroad track is usually an arc of a circle tangent to each straight track which it joins. If two straight tracks AB and CD are joined by a circular curve tangent to both of them, and P is the point where AB and CD would meet if extended, prove $\angle TPD = 2 \angle TAC$.

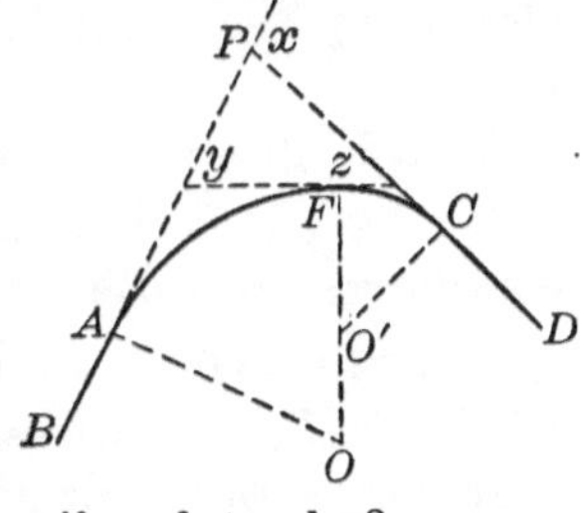

Ex. 5. Let AB and CD be two straight railroad tracks connected by an arc AF of a circle whose center is O, and an arc FC whose center is O', the arcs having a common tangent at F. Prove that the angle of intersection (x) of the two straight tracks, if produced, equals the sum of the central angles of the two tracks which are arcs of circles.

[Sug. $x = y + z$. Use Ex. 4.]

A curve like AFC composed of two or more arcs of different radii is called a *compound curve*. Can you suggest why a compound curve should be used in connecting railroad tracks?

Ex. 6. If the two arcs which compose a compound curve lie on opposite sides of their common tangent, the compound curve is called a *reverse curve*. Thus on the diagram, BCD is a reverse curve connecting the straight roads AB and DE.

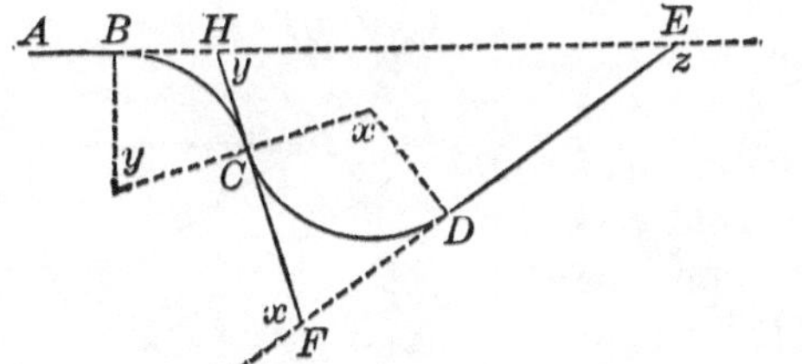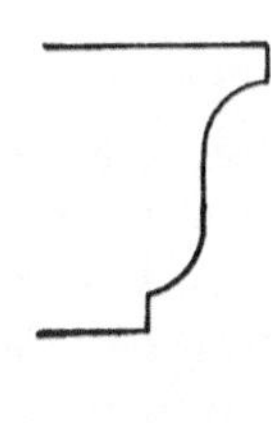

Discover the relation between the angles x, y, z.

[Sug. Use triangle HFE, where HCF is a tangent to the arcs BC and CD.]

Reverse curves are much used in architecture and ornamental work.

Ex. 7. What is a railroad frog? If a curved track crosses a straight track, show that the angle of the frog (x) equals the central angle of the curved track (o).

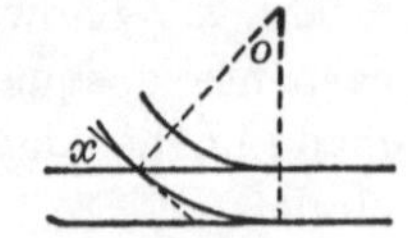

Ex. 8. Prove that the latitude of a place on the earth's surface equals the elevation of the pole. (That is, on the diagram, prove $\angle QEA = \angle PAO$.)

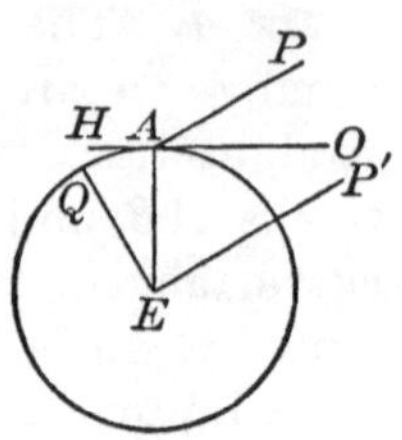

If at a given place the elevation of the north pole of the sky is 41° 30′, what is the latitude of the place?

Ex. 9. Given the sun's declination (*i.e.* distance north or south of the celestial equator), show how to determine the latitude of a place by measuring the zenith distance of the sun. Also by measuring the altitude of the sun above the horizon.

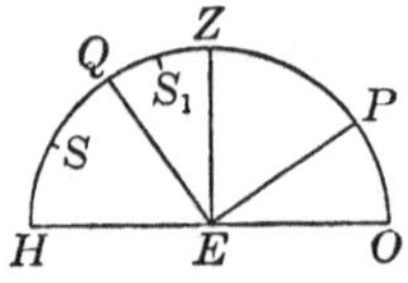

That is, given QS and ZS (or SH), find QZ.

Ex. 10. How was Peary aided by the principles of Exs. 8 and 9 in determining whether he had arrived at the North Pole?

Ex. 11. If on April 6 (the day of the year on which Peary was at the North Pole) the sun was 6° 7′ north of the celestial equator, how high above the horizon should the sun have been, as observed by Peary? At what hour of the day was this?

Ex. 12. The diagram shows an instrument called the *angle meter*. This may be used for measuring either horizontal or vertical angles.

O is the center of the arc BC and MM' is a fixed mirror. For instance, to measure the altitude of the sun the instrument is held vertically, so that a ray SO from the sun when reflected from the mirror passes into the eye (A) in a horizontal direction.

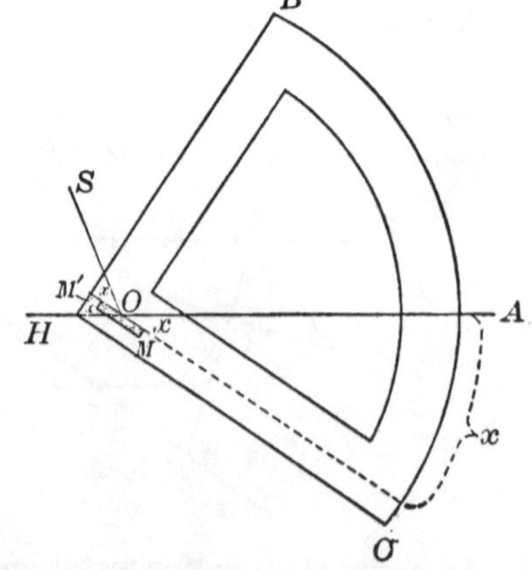

Show that the elevation of the sun above the horizon $= 2 \angle x$. The rim BC is graduated so that the angle x can be read on it.

Proposition XXII. Problem

250. *At a given point in a straight line, to erect a perpendicular to that line.*

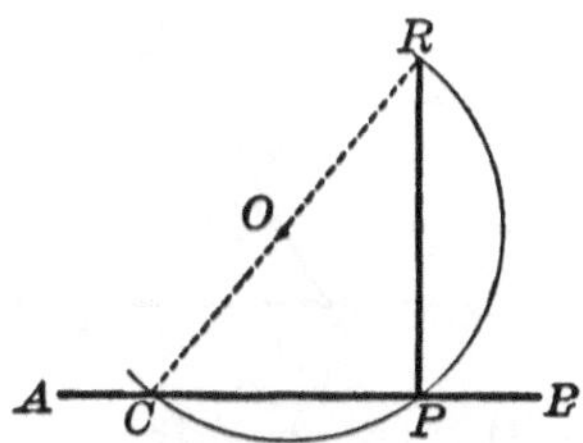

Given the point P in the line AB.

To construct a $\perp$ to line AB at P.

Construction. 1. Take any convenient point O outside the line AB, and with OP as a radius describe a circle intersecting AB at C.	1. Post. 3.
2. Draw CO and produce CO to meet the circle at R.	2. Posts. 1 and 2.
3. Draw RP. Then RP is the $\perp$ required.	3. Post. 1.
Proof. Let the student supply the proof.	Q.E.F.

251. Efficiency value. — The above method of erecting a perpendicular to a given line is particularly useful when the point at which the perpendicular is to be drawn is at or near the end of the given line.

Ex. 1. Draw a line 2 inches long, and on it as a side construct a square, making use of the method of § 250 when constructing one line perpendicular to another.

Ex. 2. Using the method of § 250, construct a rectangle 2.5 inches long and 1.5 inches wide.

Proposition XXIII.   Problem

252. *To construct a triangle, given the three sides.*

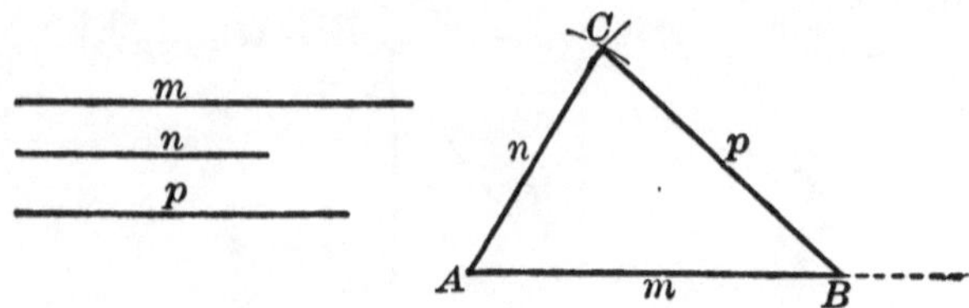

Given m, n, and p, the three sides of a triangle.

To construct the triangle.

Let the student supply the solution.

Proposition XXIV.   Problem

253. *To construct a triangle, given two sides and the included angle.*

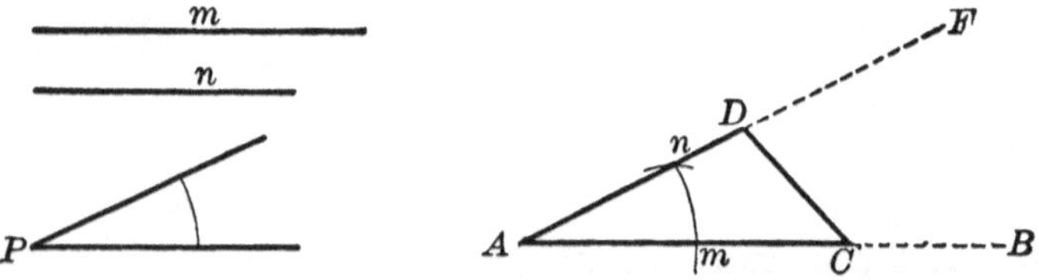

Given m and n two sides of a triangle and P the angle included by them.

To construct the triangle.

Let the student supply the solution.

Ex. 1. Construct a triangle in which two of the sides are 1 in. and $1\frac{1}{2}$ in., and the included angle is 135°.

Ex. 2. Construct an isosceles triangle in which the base shall be $1\frac{1}{2}$ in. and the altitude 2 in.

Ex. 3. Construct the complement of half a given obtuse angle.

Ex. 4. Construct the supplement of twice a given acute angle.

Ex. 5. How can the figure on p. 88 be constructed with the fewest adjustments of the compasses?

Ex. 6. Draw a line (segment) and mark off three fifths of it.

Ex. 7. From a given point on a given circle, how many equal chords can be drawn?

Ex. 8. Through a given point within a given circle, how many equal chords can be drawn?

Ex. 9. From a given point external to a given circle, how many equal secants can be drawn?

Ex. 10. In Prop. XXIII, is it possible to construct the triangle if the sum of two of the given sides is less than the third side? If one side is less than the difference of the other two sides? Draw figures to illustrate your answers.

PROPOSITION XXV. PROBLEM

254. *To construct a triangle, given two angles and the included side.*

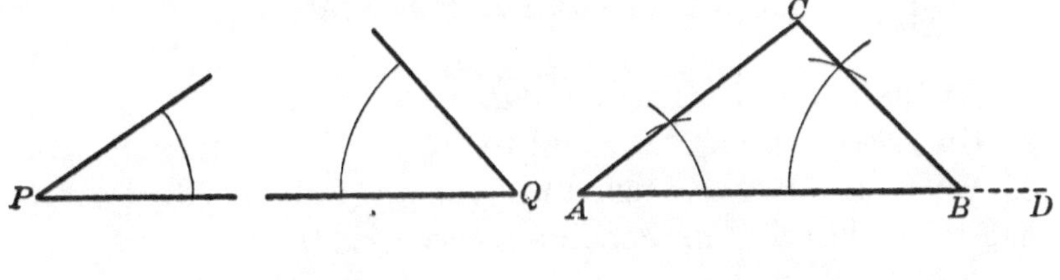

Given the $\angle s$ P and Q and the included side m.

To construct the triangle.

Let the student supply the solution.

Ex. 1. Construct a triangle in which two of the angles are 30° and 45°, and the included side is $1\frac{3}{4}$ in.

Ex. 2. Construct the complement of half a given angle.

Ex. 3. Construct an angle of 120°; of 150°; of $112\frac{1}{2}$°.

Ex. 4. Trisect a given right angle.

Ex. 5. In Prop. XXV, is it possible to construct the figure if the two given angles are supplementary? Is it possible, if their sum is greater than two right angles? Draw figures to illustrate your answers.

Proposition XXVI. Problem

255. *To construct a triangle, given two sides and an angle opposite one of them.*

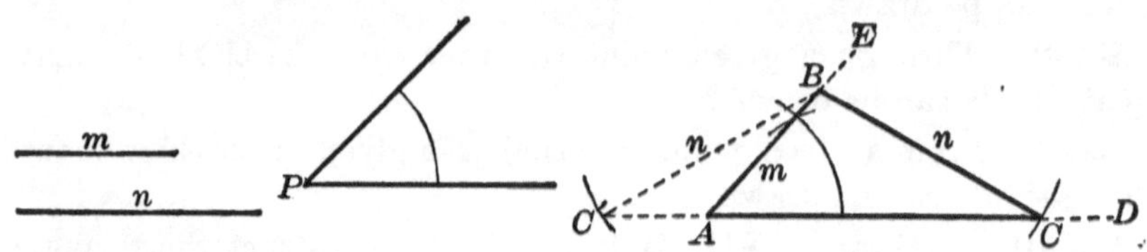

Given m and n two sides of a $\triangle$ and $\angle P$ opposite n.

To construct the triangle.

Construction. Several cases occur, according to the relative size of the given sides and the size of the given angle.

Case I. *When $n > m$ (and $\angle P$ is acute).*

1. At the point A construct $\angle DAE = \angle P$.	1. § 86.
2. On AE mark off AB equal to m.	2. Post. 2.
3. With B as a center and with a radius equal to n, describe an arc intersecting AD at C and C'.	3. Post. 3.
4. Draw BC and BC'.	4. Post. 1.
5. Two $\triangle$, ABC and ABC', are obtained, containing the sides m and n; but only one of the $\triangle$, $\triangle ABC$, contains $\angle P$.	5. Hyp.

Hence, ABC is the $\triangle$ required.

Case II. *When $n = m$ (and $\angle P$ is acute).*

Make the same construction as in Case I.

The arc drawn intersects the line AD in the points A and C.

Hence, an isosceles $\triangle ABC$ is obtained, which is the triangle required.

CASE III. *When $n < m$ (and $\angle P$ is acute).*

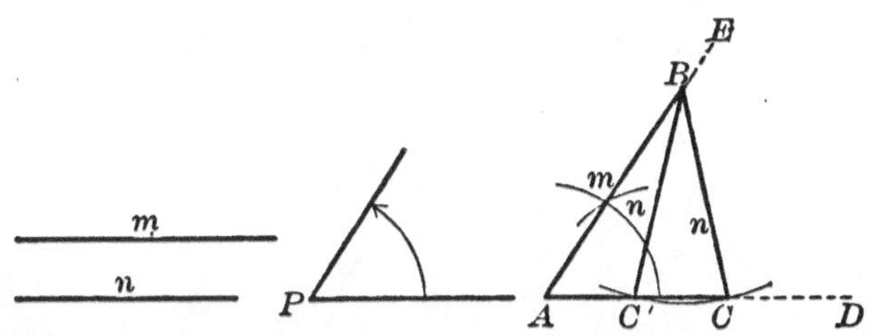

Make the construction in the same way as in Case I.

Two △, ABC and ABC', are obtained, each of which contains the sides m and n and an angle equal to $\angle P$ opposite the side n.

∴ △ ABC and ABC' are the triangles required.   Q.E.F.

Discussion. In Case I, if $\angle P$ is a right $\angle$, let the student construct the figure and show that there are two △ answering the given conditions. If $\angle P$ is an obtuse angle, let him construct the figure and show that there is but one answer.

In Case II, if $\angle P$ is right, or obtuse, what results are obtained?

In Case III, if $\angle P$ is acute and $n =$ the $\perp$ from B to AD, how many answers are there? Also, if $n <$ this $\perp$, how many?

If $\angle P$ is right, or obtuse, what result is obtained?

Ex. 1. Construct a triangle in which two of the sides are 1 in. and $1\frac{1}{2}$ in., and the angle opposite the latter side is 45°.

Ex. 2. Construct a triangle in which two of the sides are $1\frac{1}{2}$ in. and $1\frac{1}{4}$ in., and the angle opposite the latter side is 45°.

Ex. 3. Construct a triangle in which two of the sides are $1\frac{1}{2}$ in. and $\frac{3}{4}$ in., and the angle opposite the latter side is 30°.

Ex. 4. Make up the data and construct a triangle in which a given angle is acute and there are two solutions. No solution.

PROPOSITION XXVII. PROBLEM

256. *To circumscribe a circle about a given triangle.*

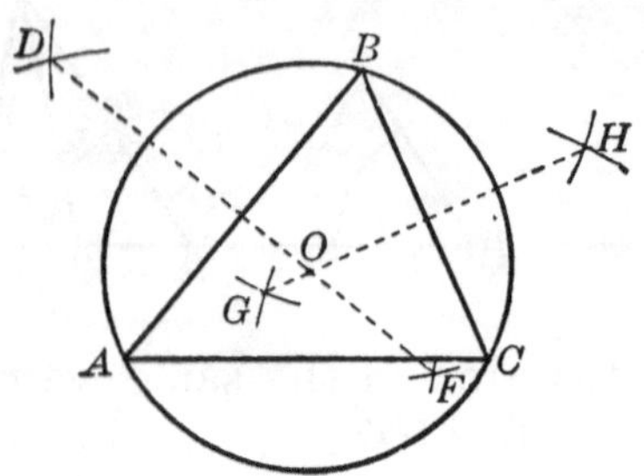

Given the $\triangle ABC$.

To circumscribe a circle about the $\triangle ABC$.

Let the student supply the solution.   (See § 214, p. 126.)

257. COR.   *The perpendicular bisectors of the sides of a triangle intersect in a common point.*

258. The **circumcenter** of a triangle is the point where the perpendicular bisectors of the three sides of the triangle intersect.

Ex. 1.   Draw an obtuse triangle and circumscribe a circle about it.

Ex. 2.   Draw any triangle, and then construct its three altitudes. (If the work is done correctly, it will be found that the three altitudes intersect in a common point.)

Ex. 3.   The line ABP points from the eye of the observer to the top of a tree. ACB is a semicircle ruled like a protractor, with its diameter applied to AP. C is the point where a plumb line from B intersects the outside circle.

Show that $\angle ACB$ is a right $\angle$. Hence, that AC is a horizontal line. Hence, that $\angle PAC$, the angle of elevation of P, is measured by $\frac{1}{2}$ arc BC.

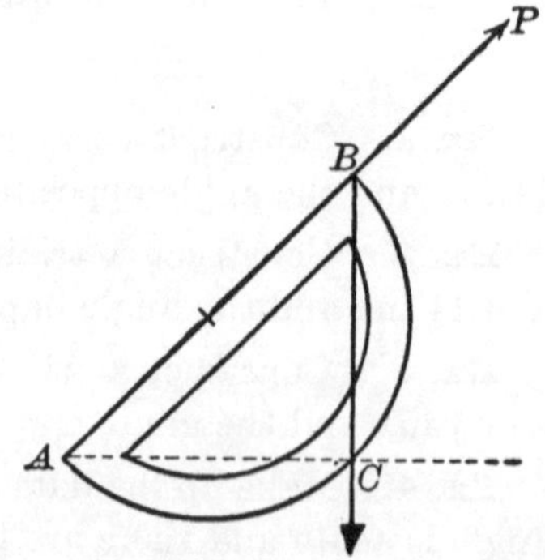

Proposition XXVIII. Problem

259. *To inscribe a circle in a given triangle.*

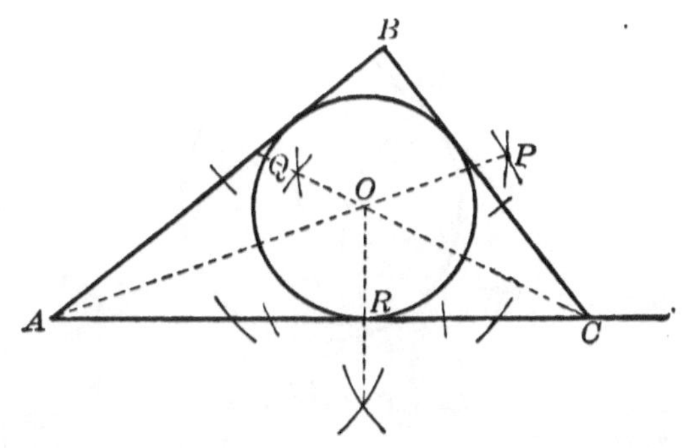

Given $\triangle ABC$.

To inscribe a circle in $\triangle ABC$.

Construction.   1. Bisect $\angle BAC$ by line AP, and $\angle BCA$ by line QC.

    2. Then AP and CQ intersect in some point O.

    3. From O, construct $OR \perp AC$.

    4. With O as a center and OR as a radius, describe a circle. This will be the circle required.

    1. § 84.

    2. § 99.

    3. § 129.

    4. Post. 3.

Proof.   Let the student supply the proof.   Q E.F.

260. Cor.   *The bisectors of the angles of a triangle intersect in a common point.*

261. The **incenter** of a triangle is the point where the bisectors of the three angles of the triangle intersect.

    Ex. 1.   Construct a right triangle and in it inscribe a circle.

    Ex. 2.   Construct an obtuse triangle and in it inscribe a circle.

    Ex. 3.   Construct a triangle whose incenter and circumcenter are the same point.

PROPOSITION XXIX.   PROBLEM

262. *At a given point on a circle, to construct a tangent to the circle.*

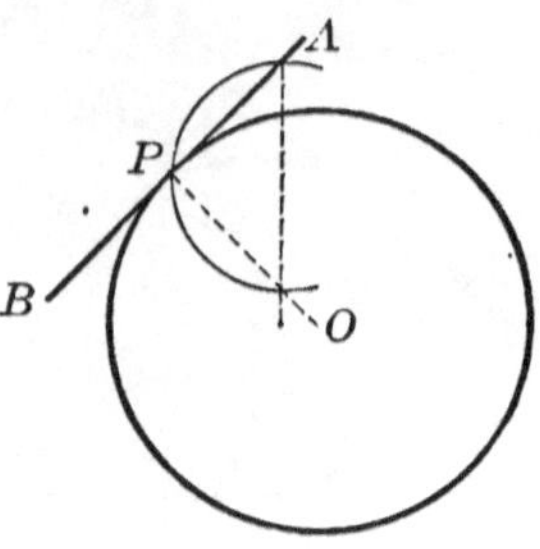

Given P any point on the circle O.

To construct a tangent to the circle through the point P.

Construction.   1. Draw the radius OP.   1. Post. 1.
2. At the point P construct the line AB 2. § 250.
$\perp OP$.

Then AB is the tangent required.

Proof.   Let the student supply the proof.

Q.E.F.

263. An **escribed circle** is a circle tangent to one side of a triangle and to the other two sides produced.   Thus the circle O is an escribed circle of the $\triangle ABC$.

A center of an escribed circle, as O, is called an **excenter** of the triangle.

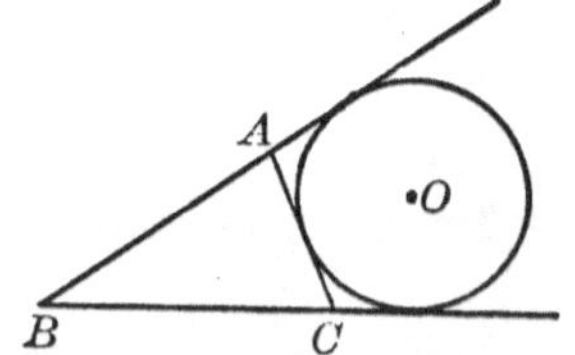

Ex. 1.   Draw a triangle and all of its escribed circles.

Ex. 2.   Construct the following designs:

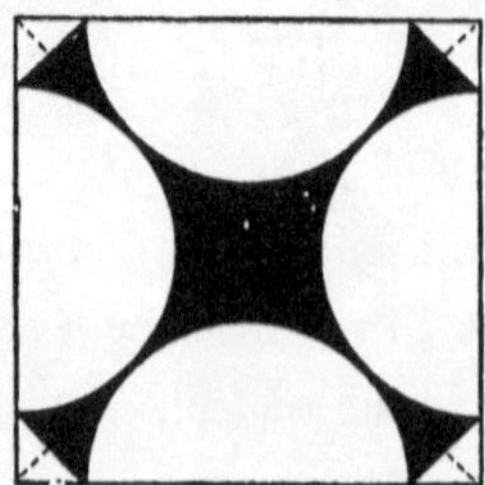

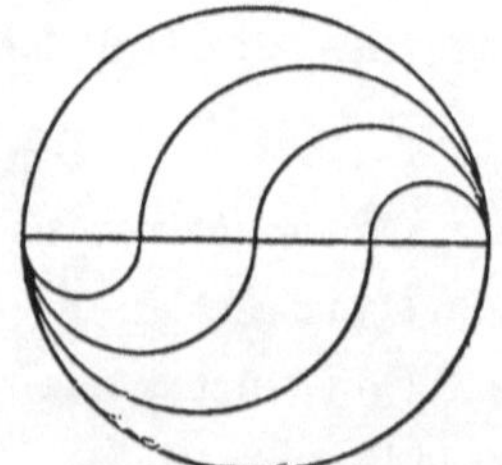

PROPOSITION XXX. PROBLEM

264. *Through a given point outside a given circle, to construct tangents to the circle.*

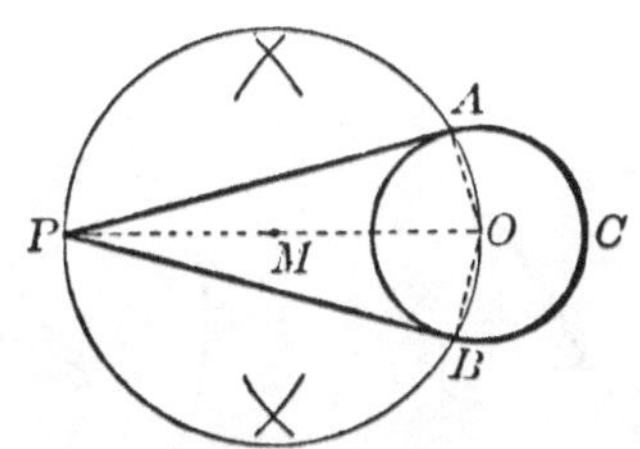

Given P any point outside the circle O.

To construct through P tangents to the circle O.

Construction. 1. Draw the line PO.	1. Post. 1.
2. Bisect the line PO at the point M.	2. § 128.
3. With M as a center and MP as a radius, describe a circle intersecting the given circle at the points A and B.	3. Post. 3
4. Draw PA and PB.	4. Post. 1
Then PA and PB are the tangents required.	
Proof. 1. $\angle PAO$ is inscribed in a semicircle.	1. Constr.
2. $\therefore$ $\angle PAO$ is a right angle.	2. Why?
3. $\therefore$ PA is tangent to the circle O.	3. Why?
4. In like manner, it may be proved that PB is tangent to the circle O.	4. Reasons 1–3.
	Q.E.F.

Ex. 1. In the diagram of Prop. XXVII (p. 160), how many line segments occur? Name them. How many circular segments? Name them, inserting additional letters on the diagram when necessary.

Ex. 2. Two equal chords of a given circle are produced till they meet. The angle formed by the extended chords is 18°, and the smaller arc intercepted by them is $\frac{1}{15}$ of the circle. Find each angle of the quadrilateral formed by joining the ends of the two chords.

PROPOSITION XXXI. PROBLEM

265. *On a given straight line as a base, to construct a circular segment in which a given angle can be inscribed.*

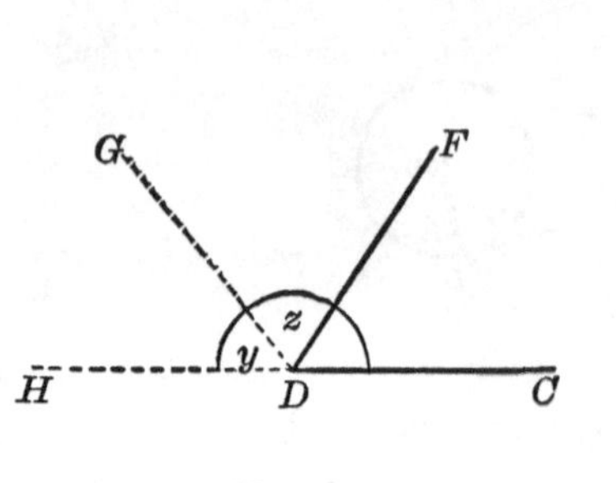

FIG. 1

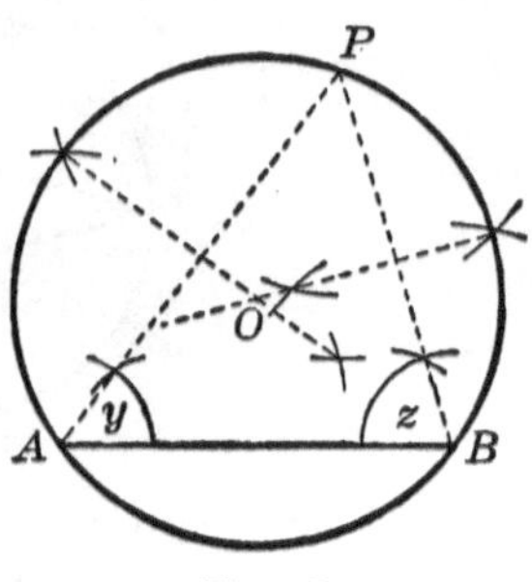

FIG. 2

Given the straight line AB and $\angle CDF$.

To construct on AB a segment of a circle in which $\angle CDF$ can be inscribed.

Construction. 1. Produce CD to H, and from D draw DG, dividing $\angle HDF$ into two convenient angles y and z.	1. Post. 1.
2. From A draw line AP making $\angle BAP = \angle y$.	2. § 86.
3. From B draw line PB making $\angle PBA = \angle z$.	3. § 86.
4. Then PA and PB intersect at some point P.	4. § 99.
5. About $\triangle APB$ circumscribe a circle.	5. § 256.
Then APB is the segment required.	
Proof. 1. $\angle P$ is sup. of $\angle y + \angle z$ (Fig. 2).	1. § 102.
2. But $\angle CDF$ is sup. of $\angle y + \angle z$ (Fig. 1).	2. § 32.
3. $\therefore \angle P = \angle CDF$.	3. § 66. Q.E.F.

266. Analysis of construction problems.—The method of analysis (see § 173) is of especial value in the solution of construction problems. In general, to investigate the solution of a problem by this method:

Draw a figure in which the required construction is assumed as made;

Draw auxiliary lines, if necessary;

Observe the relations between the parts of this figure, in order to discover a known relation on which the required construction depends;

Having discovered the required relation, construct another figure by the direct use of this relation.

Ex. Through a given point within a circle, draw a chord which shall be bisected by the given point.

ANALYSIS. Let A be the given point within the given circle O, and let PQ be a chord bisected at the point A. A bisected chord suggests a line OA joining the point of bisection with the center O, and that (§ 203) $OA \perp PQ$.

SYNTHESIS, or DIRECT SOLUTION. Taking another figure containing the data of the problem, connect the point A with the center of the circle by the line OA.

Through A draw a line $\perp OA$ (§ 250), and meeting the circles at the points P and Q. PQ is the chord required.

EXERCISES: GROUP 39

CONSTRUCTION OF STRAIGHT LINES

Ex. 1. Draw a line parallel to a given line, and tangent to a given circle.

[SUG. Suppose the required line drawn; then the radius to the point of tangency, if produced, is $\perp$ given line, etc.]

Ex. 2. Draw a line perpendicular to a given line, and tangent to a given circle.

Ex. 3. From two points on a circle, draw two equal and parallel chords.

Ex. 4.   Through a given point draw a line which shall make a given angle with a given line.

Ex. 5.   Through a given point draw a line which shall make equal angles with the sides of a given angle.

[SUG.   The bisector of the given $\angle$ will be $\perp$ the required line, etc.]

Ex. 6.   Through a given point between two given parallel lines, draw a line of given length with its extremities in the two parallel lines.

Ex. 7.   Through a given point A within a circle, draw a chord equal to a given line.

Ex. 8.   From a given point on a circle, draw a chord at a given distance from the center.

Ex. 9.   Through a given point on a circle, draw a chord which shall be bisected by another given chord.

[SUG.   Draw the radius to the given point and on it as a diameter describe a circle, etc.   When is the solution impossible?]

267. Construction of points and of loci. — In constructing a **point** to meet certain given conditions, it is often helpful to *construct the locus of a point answering one of the given conditions and observe in what point or points it meets a given line, or meets another locus answering another given condition.*

EXERCISES: GROUP 40

CONSTRUCTION OF POINTS AND LOCI

Ex. 1.   Find a point P in a given line AB equidistant from two given points C and D.

[SUG.   Construct the locus of all points equidistant from C and D, and observe where it intersects the given line AB.]

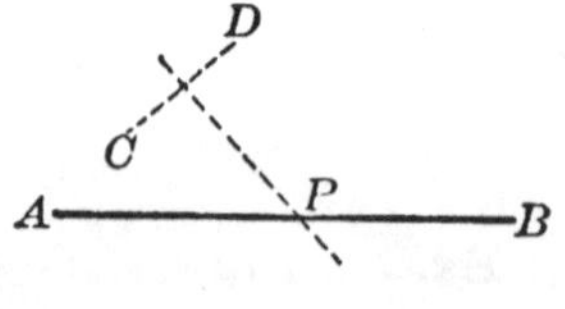

Ex. 2.   Find a point P on a given circle, which is equidistant from two given points, C and D.

Ex. 3.   Find a point P in a given line, which is equidistant from two given intersecting lines.

Ex. 4.   Find a point in a given line, which is at a given distance, d, from a given point.

Ex. 5. Find a point which is at a given distance, a, from a given point, A, and at another distance, b, from another given point, B. Discuss the limitations of this problem.

Ex. 6. Find a point equidistant from two given points, and at a given distance from a given straight line.

[SUG. Draw the locus of all points equidistant from the two given points, and also the locus of all points at the given distance from the given straight line, etc.]

Ex. 7. Find a point equidistant from two given points, and at a given distance from another given point.

Ex. 8. Find a point equidistant from two given points, and also from two given intersecting lines.

On the other hand, the **determination of certain loci** *is equivalent to the construction of all points which satisfy one or more given conditions.*

Ex. 9. Find the locus of the center of a circle, which touches a given line at a given point.

[SUG. Construct a number of circles touching the given line at the given point and observe the relation of their centers.]

Ex. 10. Find the locus of the center of a circle, with a given radius, r, which passes through a given fixed point.

Ex. 11. Find the locus of the center of a circle, touching two given intersecting lines.

Ex. 12. Find the locus of the center of a circle, touching two given parallel lines.

Ex. 13. Find the locus of the center of a circle of given radius, r, which touches a given straight line.

Ex. 14. Find the locus of the center of a circle of given radius, r, which touches a given circle.

EXERCISES: GROUP 41

CONSTRUCTION OF RECTILINEAR FIGURES

Construct:

Ex. 1. An equilateral triangle, given the altitude.

Ex. 2. An isosceles triangle, given the base and the altitude.

Ex. 3.   An isosceles triangle, given the base and an angle at the base.

Ex. 4.   An isosceles triangle, given the vertex angle and the altitude.

Ex. 5.   A right triangle, given a leg and the acute angle adjacent.

Ex. 6.   A right triangle, given a leg and the acute angle opposite.

Ex. 7.   A triangle, given the altitude and the sides including the vertex angle.

[Sug.   Through the foot of the altitude draw a line ⊥ altitude and of indefinite length.]

Ex. 8.   A triangle, given two sides and the altitude upon one of them.

Ex. 9.   A rhombus, given one angle and the diagonal passing through the vertex of the given angle.

Ex. 10.   A parallelogram, given a side, the altitude upon that side, and an angle.

Ex. 11.   A parallelogram, given the diagonals and an angle included by them.

Ex. 12.   A quadrilateral, given the sides and one angle.

268. Use of auxiliary lines in constructing rectilinear figures. — In constructing polygons, auxiliary lines are frequently of service.   Thus it is often of especial value to *construct, first, either the inscribed or the circumscribed circle, and afterward the required triangle or quadrilateral.*

Ex.   Construct an isosceles triangle, given the base, b, and the radius, r, of the inscribed circle.

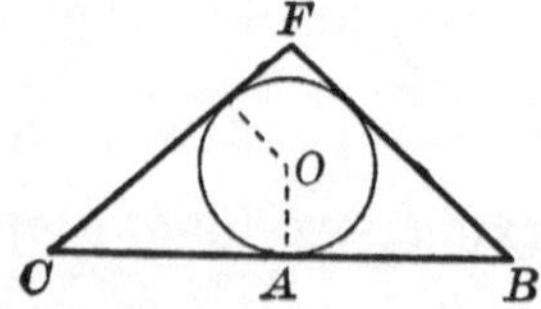

CONSTRUCTION.   Draw a circle O with radius equal to r.   Draw a tangent at any point A.   On this tangent mark off AB and AC each equal $\frac{1}{2}b$.   From B and C draw tangents BF and CF to the circle. Then BCF is the required triangle.

EXERCISES: GROUP 42
CONSTRUCTIONS; AUXILIARY LINES

Construct:

Ex. 1. An isosceles triangle, given the base and the radius of the circumscribed circle.

Ex. 2. A right triangle, given the radius of the circumscribed circle and one leg.

Ex. 3. A right triangle, given the radius of the circumscribed circle and an acute angle.

Ex. 4. A right triangle, given the radius of the inscribed circle and an acute angle.

[SUG. Draw the inscribed circle and at its center construct an angle equal to the supplement of the given angle.]

Ex. 5. A triangle, given the base, the altitude, and the vertex angle.

[SUG. On the given base construct a segment which shall contain the given vertex angle. See § 265.]

Ex. 6. A triangle, given the base, the median to the base, and the vertex angle.

Ex. 7. A triangle, given one side, an adjacent angle, and the radius of the inscribed circle. (See Ex. 4.)

Ex. 8. A triangle, given one side, an adjacent angle, and the radius of the circumscribed circle.

The use of *auxiliary straight lines* may be illustrated as follows:

Ex. 9. Construct a triangle, given the perimeter and two angles.

ANALYSIS. Suppose the required triangle ABC already constructed. Let $\angle ABC$ and ACB be the given angles. Produce BC to D and E, making $DB = AB$ and $CE = AC$. 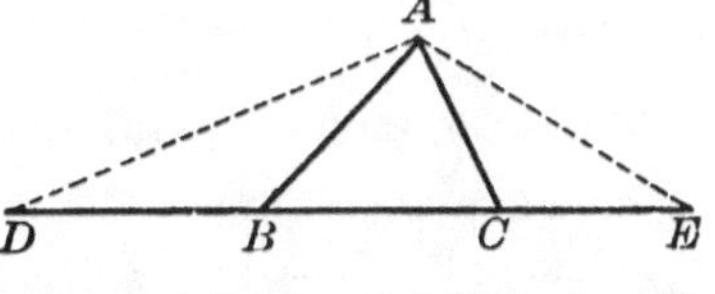
Then $DE =$ given perimeter. Also $\angle D = \angle DAB$. $\therefore \angle ABC = 2 \angle D$. Similarly $\angle ACB = 2 \angle E$. Hence,

CONSTRUCTION. Take DE the given perimeter. At D construct an angle $= \frac{1}{2}$ of one given angle. At E construct an angle $= \frac{1}{2}$ of the other given angle. Produce the sides of these angles to meet at A. Construct $\angle DAB = \angle D$ and $\angle CAE = \angle E$. Then $\triangle ABC$ is the required triangle, etc.

Construct:

Ex. 10. An isosceles triangle, given the perimeter and the altitude.

[Sug. Bisect the perimeter and construct the altitude $\perp$ to it at its midpoint.]

Ex. 11. An isosceles triangle, given the perimeter and the vertex angle.

[Sug. If the vertex $\angle$ is known, the base $\&$ may be obtained.]

Ex. 12. A right triangle, given an acute angle and the sum of the legs.

[Sug. Given AB the sum of the legs, construct $\angle A = 45°$, etc.]

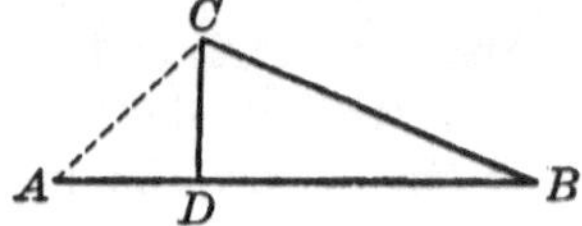

Ex. 13. A right triangle, given an acute angle and the difference of the legs.

Ex. 14. A right triangle, given the hypotenuse and the sum of the legs.

Ex. 15. A right triangle, given an acute angle and the sum of the hypotenuse and one leg.

Ex. 16. A triangle, given an angle, a side, and the sum of the other two sides.

Ex. 17. A triangle, given an angle A, the sum of the sides AB and BC, and the altitude upon AB.

269. Reduction of problems. — In many cases a problem may be solved *by reducing the problem to a problem already solved.* (This is a special kind of analysis.)

Ex. Construct a parallelogram, given the diagonals and one side.

Analysis. Suppose the $\square$ $ABCF$ to be the required $\square$ already constructed. Let AF be the given side. If the diagonals are given, half of each diagonal is given (§ 159). Hence, in the $\triangle AOF$ the three sides are given. Hence, the required problem reduces to the problem of constructing a triangle whose three sides are given (§ 252). Hence,

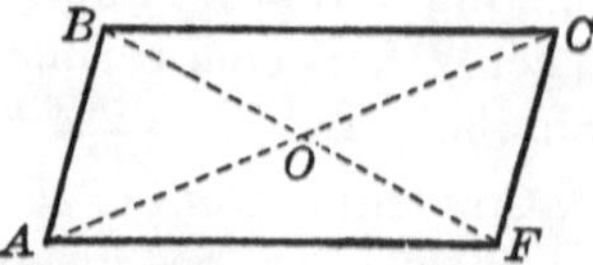

Construction. Let the student supply the direct construction.

EXERCISES: GROUP 43

REDUCTION OF CONSTRUCTION PROBLEMS

Construct:

Ex. 1. A right triangle, given the altitude upon the hypotenuse and the median upon the same.

Ex. 2. A rectangle, given the perimeter and a diagonal (see Ex. 14, p. 170).

Ex. 3. A rectangle, given the perimeter and an angle made by the diagonals.

Ex. 4. A triangle, given the three angles and the radius of the circumscribed circle.

[SUG. The sides of the △ are the chords of the segments of the ⊙ containing the given ∠.]

Ex. 5. A triangle, given two sides and the median to the third side.

Ex. 6. An isosceles trapezoid, given the bases and an angle.

Ex. 7. An isosceles trapezoid, given the bases and a diagonal.

Ex. 8. A trapezoid, given the four sides.

Ex. 9. A trapezoid, given the bases and the two diagonals.
[SUG. Reduce to § 252 by producing the lower base.)

270. Construction of circles. —The construction of a required circle is frequently a good illustration of the preceding method of reducing one construction problem to another. For the construction of a circle frequently *reduces to the problem of finding a point (the center of the circle) which answers given conditions.* (See § 267.)

Ex. Construct a circle which shall touch two given intersecting lines and have its center in another given line.

This problem is equivalent to the problem of finding a point which shall be in a given line and be equidistant from two other given lines. (See Ex. 3, p. 166.)

In some cases, however, the construction of a required circle must be made by an independent method.

EXERCISES: GROUP 44

CONSTRUCTION OF CIRCLES

Construct a circle with given radius r,

Ex. 1. Which passes through a given point and touches a given line.

Ex. 2. Which has its center in a given line and touches another given line.

Ex. 3. Which passes through two given points.

Construct a circle

Ex. 4. Which touches two given parallel lines and passes through a given point.

Ex. 5. Which passes through two given points and has its center on a given line.

Ex. 6. Which touches three given lines, two of which are parallel.

Ex. 7. Which passes through a given point A and touches a given line BC at a given point B.

[SUG. Draw AB and at B construct a $\perp$ to BC.]

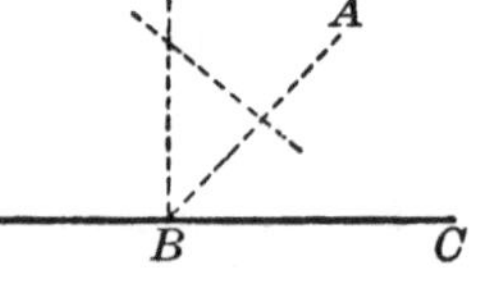

Ex. 8. Which touches a given line and also touches a given circle at a given point A.

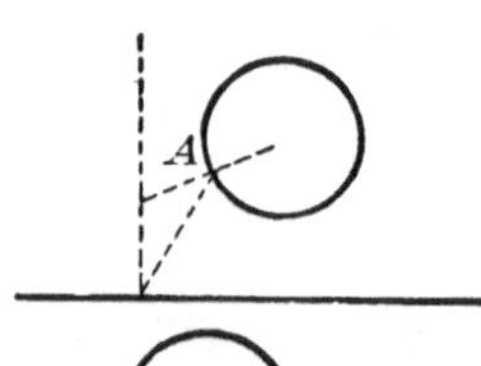

Ex 9. Which touches a given line AB at a given point A and touches a given circle.

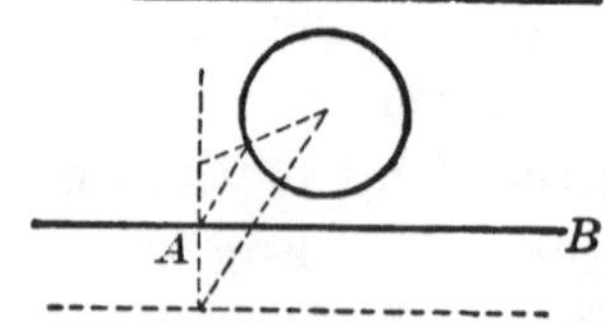

EXERCISES : GROUP 45

PROBLEMS SOLVED BY VARIOUS METHODS

Ex. 1. Through a given point, draw a line which shall cut two given intersecting lines so as to form an isosceles triangle.

Ex. 2. Construct an isosceles triangle, given the altitude and one leg.

Ex. 3. On a given circle, find a point equidistant from two given intersecting lines.

Ex. 4. Draw a circle which shall touch two given intersecting lines, one of them at a given point.

Ex. 5. Draw a line which shall be terminated by the sides of a given angle, shall equal a given line, and be parallel to another given line.

Ex. 6. Construct a triangle, given one side, an adjacent angle, and the difference of the other two sides.

Ex. 7. Find a point in a given circle at a given distance from a given point.

Ex. 8. Construct a parallelogram, given a side, an angle, and a diagonal.

Ex. 9. Through a given point within an angle, draw a straight line terminated by the sides of the angle and bisected by the given point.

[SUG. Draw a line from the vertex of the angle to the given point and produce it its own length through the point.]

Ex. 10. Construct a triangle, given the vertex angle and the segments of the base made by the altitude. (Use § 265.)

Ex. 11. Construct an isosceles triangle, given the angle at the vertex and the base.

Ex. 12. Draw a circle with given radius which shall touch a given circle at a given point.

Ex. 13. Construct a right triangle, given the hypotenuse and the altitude upon the hypotenuse.

Ex. 14. Construct a triangle, given the base and the altitudes upon the other two sides.

[SUG. Construct a semicircle on the given base as a diameter.]

Ex. 15. Construct a triangle, given the altitude and the angles at the extremities of the base.

Ex. 16. In a given circle draw a chord equal to a given line and parallel to another given line.

[SUG. Find the distance of the given chord from the center, by constructing a right triangle of which the hypotenuse and one leg are given.]

Ex. 17. Construct a triangle, given an angle, the bisector of that angle, and the altitude from another vertex.

Ex. 18. Find the locus of the points of contact of tangents drawn from a given point to a series of circles having a given center. (Use §§ 211 and 238.)

Ex. 19. Given a line AB and two points C and D on the same side of AB. Find a point P in AB, such that $\angle APC = \angle BPD$.

[Sug. Draw a $\perp$ from C to AB and produce it its own length, etc.]

Ex. 20. Given a line AB and two points C and D on the same side of AB. Find a point P in AB, such that $CP + PD$ shall be a minimum.

Ex. 21. To construct a common external tangent to two given circles.

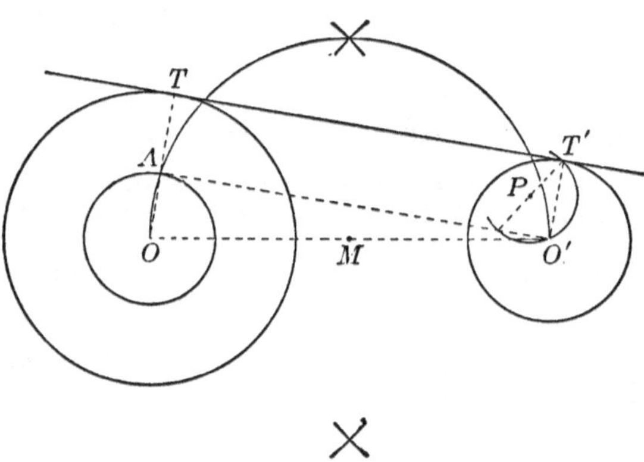

Ex. 22. To construct a common internal tangent to two given circles.

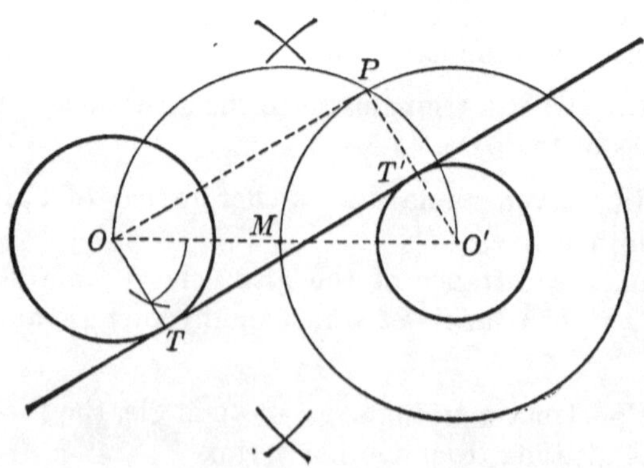

EXERCISES: GROUP 46

PRACTICAL APPLICATIONS

Ex. 1. Show how to find the center of a given circle by use of a carpenter's square.

Ex. 2. Show how to bisect a given angle by the use of a carpenter's square.

Ex. 3. By use of squared paper, divide a line $1\frac{1}{2}$ inches long into 5 equal parts. Into 7 equal parts. Into 3 equal parts. Can you make this division on paper ruled in only one direction?

Ex. 4. Make up and work an example similar to Ex. 3.

Ex. 5. To extend a straight line AB beyond an obstacle, as a building, we may proceed as follows:

At B measure off an angle $ABC = 60°$. Produce CB to D,

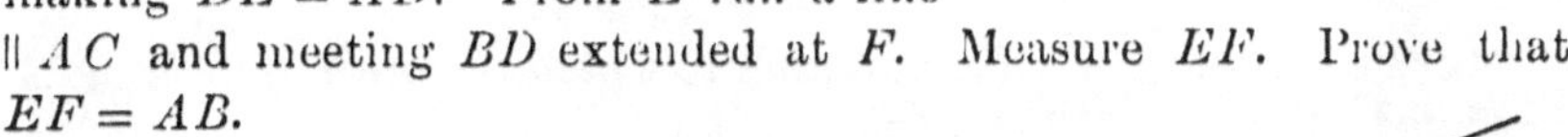

etc. Let the pupil complete the construction and prove that his method is correct.

Ex. 6. To find the distance between two points A and B, one of which (B) is inaccessible, we may proceed as follows:

Extend BA to C. Measure a convenient line AD and extend AD to E, making $DE = AD$. From E run a line

$\parallel AC$ and meeting BD extended at F. Measure EF. Prove that $EF = AB$.

Ex. 7. If two streets meet, as in the diagram, show how a curve of given radius r may be made to take the place of the angle A and be tangent with the curb of the two streets.

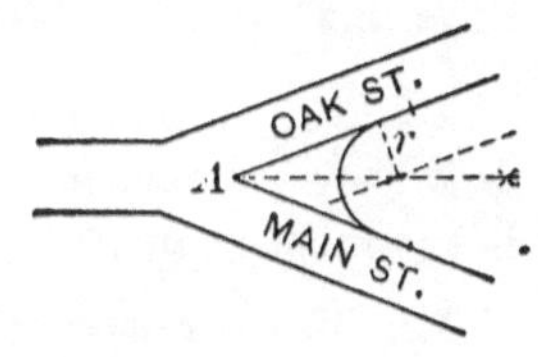

Ex. 8. Draw an easement cornice (AB) tangent to the rake cornice BC, and passing through a required point A. (The same construction is used in laying out the easements of stair rails, etc.) (Use Ex. 7, p. 172.)

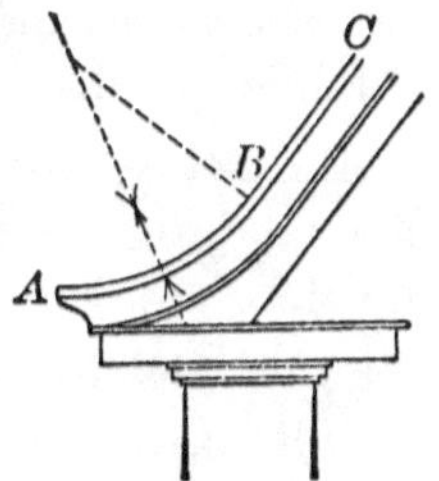

Ex. 9. A *segmental arch* is a compound curve composed of the arcs of three circles. The method of constructing a segmental arch is as follows: Let AB be the span and CD the altitude of the required arch. Complete the rectangle $GADC$. Draw the diagonal AC. Bisect the angles GAC and GCA. Let the bisectors meet at E. Draw EH perpendicular to AC, meeting AB at N and CD produced at H. Make DK equal to DN. Then show that N is the center and NA the radius, H the center and HE the radius, and K the center and KB the radius for the arcs composing the arch. (See Hanstein's *Constructive Drawing*.)

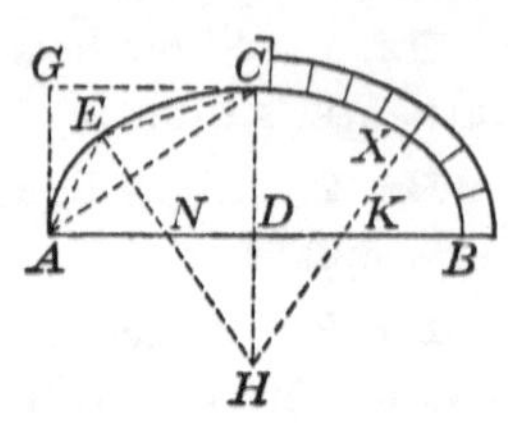

[Sug. At E draw a line perpendicular to EH. Then $\angle NEA = \angle NAE$. (Complements of equal angles are equal), etc.]

Ex. 10. What is called a *Persian arch* may be constructed as follows: Let AB be the span and CD the altitude of the required arch. Draw the isosceles triangle ADB. Divide AD into three equal parts at H and G. Construct $HK \perp AG$ at H, and meeting AB produced at K. Produce KG to meet EF which has been drawn through $D \parallel AB$. With K as a center and KA as a radius, and E as a center and EG as a radius, describe arcs meeting at G. Prove that these arcs have a common tangent at G, and therefore form a compound curve. (See Hanstein's *Constructive Drawing*.)

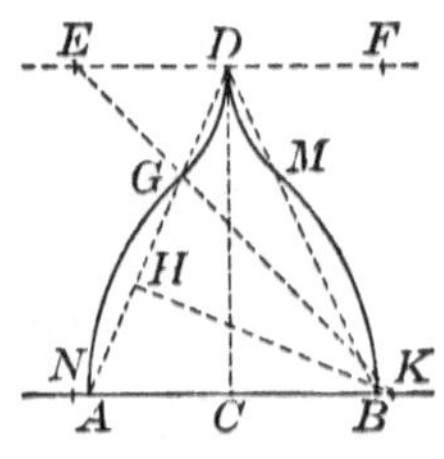

Ex. 11. Construct a Persian arch in which the arc $DG = $ arc NG. [Sug. Bisect line AD, instead of trisecting it.]

Ex. 12. Construct Persian arches in which the chords NG and DG have various ratios, and decide which of these arches you think is the most beautiful.

Ex. 13. Construct segmental arches of various shapes and decide which of these you think is the most beautiful.

Ex. 14. Construct the adjoining ornamental design by first constructing the trefoil involved and locating the center of the equilateral triangle used in constructing the trefoil. (See Ex. 6, p. 120.)

Ex. 15. Inscribe a trefoil in a given equilateral triangle.

[SUG. Bisect the angles of the triangle and inscribe a circle in each of the three triangles thus formed.]

Ex. 16. The instrument $ABCD$ is used as a means of quickly finding the center of a circular disc or end of a cylindrical roller.

The edge $AB =$ edge AC.

Also the edge AD bisects the angle BAC.

Prove that AD must pass through the center O when the points B and C are on the circle. (See Ex. 13, p. 146.)

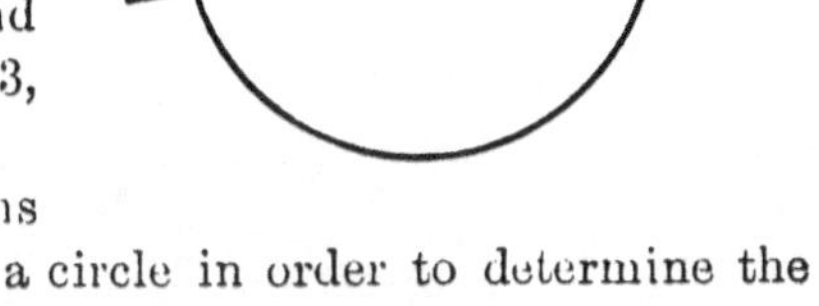

In how many different positions must the instrument be applied to a circle in order to determine the center of the circle?

EXERCISES: GROUP 47

REVIEW EXERCISES

Make a list of the properties of

Ex. 1. Arcs of a circle.	**Ex. 4.** Central angles.
Ex. 2. Chords.	**Ex. 5.** Inscribed angles.
Ex. 3. Diameters.	**Ex. 6.** Tangents.

Ex. 7. How many points determine a circle? How many determine a straight line? Two parallel lines? An angle?

Ex. 8. How many inscribed circles can a given triangle have? How many circumscribed circles? How many escribed circles?

Ex. 9. What is the difference between an incenter and a circumcenter?

Ex. 10 When is an inscribed angle a right angle? An acute angle? An obtuse angle?

State the efficiency value of

Ex. 11. Prop IX.	**Ex. 15.** Prop. XVIII.
Ex. 12. Prop. XII.	**Ex. 16.** Prop. XX.
Ex. 13. Prop. XIV.	**Ex. 17.** Prop. XXI.
Ex. 14. Prop. XVI.	**Ex. 18.** Prop. XXII.

Ex. 19. Explain the meaning of the following: $\angle ABC \stackrel{m}{=\!=} \overset{\frown}{AC}$.

BOOK THREE

PROPORTION; SIMILAR POLYGONS

THEORY OF PROPORTION

271. **Ratio** has been defined, and its use briefly indicated, in §§ 225, 226 (pp. 132, 133).

272. A **proportion** is a statement that two ratios are equal.

Ex. 1. $\frac{12}{18} = \frac{2}{3}$. Thus, when a fraction is reduced to its lowest terms, a proportion is formed.

Ex. 2. $\frac{a}{b} = \frac{c}{d}$, or $a : b = c : d$.

The last example is read " the ratio of a to b equals the ratio of c to d," or " a is to b as c is to d."

273. The **terms of a proportion** are the four quantities used in the proportion. In a proportion,
the **antecedents** are the *first* and *third* terms ;
the **consequents** are the *second* and *fourth* terms;
the **extremes** are the *first* and *last* terms;
the **means** are the *second* and *third* terms.

274. A **fourth proportional** is the fourth term of a proportion in which the first three terms are three given numbers taken in order.

Thus, in $2 : 3 = 10 : x$, x is the fourth proportional to 2, 3, and 10.
In $a : b = c : d$, what is the fourth proportional?

275. A **third proportional** is the fourth term of a proportion in which the first three terms are two given numbers, the second of these being used twice as a mean.

Thus, in $2 : 6 = 6 : y$, y is the third proportional to 2 and 6.
In $a : b = b : c$, what is the third proportional?

276. A **mean proportional** is a term in a proportion used twice as a mean between two given numbers.

Thus, in $4 : 6 = 6 : 9$, 6 is the mean proportional between 4 and 9.
In $a : b = b : c$, what is the mean proportional?

277. A **continued proportion** is a statement of the equality of two or more ratios, in which each consequent and the next antecedent are the same.

Thus $a : b = b : c = c : d = d : e$ is a continued proportion.

USEFUL PROPERTIES OF PROPORTIONS

278. Property I. *In any proportion, the product of the extremes is equal to the product of the means.*

Given the proportion $a : b = c : d$.

To prove $ad = bc$.

Proof. 1. $\dfrac{a}{b} = \dfrac{c}{d}.$ 1. Hyp.

2. Multiplying each member by bd, $ad = bc.$ 2. Ax. 4.

Q.E.D.

279. Cor. *The mean proportional between two quantities is equal to the square root of their product.*

For, if $a : b = b : c$, then $b^2 = ac$ (§ 278);

or $b = \sqrt{ac}.$ (Ax. 6.)

280. The **efficiency value** of §§ 278 and 279 is that these principles enable us to convert any given proportion into an equation, and often enable us to find the value of an unknown term in the proportion by solving the equation.

Ex. Find the value of x in the proportion $3 : 5 = x : 25$.
Using § 278, we obtain $5 x = 3 \times 25$.
Hence, $\qquad\qquad\qquad x = 15.$ *Ans.*

Ex. 1.   Construct a proportion in which the mean proportional is x, the third proportional is a, and the other term is 5.

Find the value of x

Ex. 2.   In $4 : 8 = x : 20$.

Ex. 3.   In $2 : 6 = 5 : x$.

Ex. 4.   In $a : p = q : x$.

Ex. 5.   In $x : 6 = .6 : 1.5$.

Ex. 6.   In $.06 : 2 x - 1 = 3 : 4$.

Ex. 7.   In $x : 4 b = 9 b : 3 b$.

Ex. 8.   In $.05 : 3.2 = 1.5 : x$.

Ex. 9.   Find the fourth proportional to 2, 3, and 6.   Also to 3, $\frac{1}{2}$, $\frac{3}{2}$.

[Sug.   Denote the required fourth proportional by x.]

Ex. 10.   Find the mean proportional between 3 and 6.   Between .4 and .016.

Ex. 11.   Find the third proportional to 3 and 5.   To 4.5 and .5.

Ex. 12.   Find the mean proportional between $3 p$ and $27 p^3$.

Ex. 13.   Find the mean proportional between $a + b$ and $a - b$.

281. Property II.   *If the product of two quantities is equal to the product of two other quantities, one pair may be made the extremes and the other pair the means of a proportion.*

Given $\qquad ad = bc.$

To prove $a : b = c : d.$

Proof. 1. $ad = bc.$ $\qquad\qquad$ 1. Hyp.

2. Dividing each member $\qquad$ 2. Ax. 5.

by bd, $\qquad\qquad \dfrac{a}{b} = \dfrac{c}{d}.$

Or $\qquad\qquad a : b = c : d.$ $\qquad\qquad\qquad$ Q.E.D.

282. COR. 1. *If the antecedents of a proportion are equal, the consequents are equal.*

Thus, if $a : x = a : y$, then $x = y$.
Let the student supply the proof.

283. COR. 2. *If three terms of one proportion are equal to the corresponding three terms of another proportion, the fourth terms of the two proportions are equal.*

Thus, if $a : b = c : x$, and $a : b = c : y$, then $x = y$.
Let the student supply the proof.

Ex. 1.   Write $ab = pq$ as a proportion in eight different ways.

Ex. 2.   Write $x(x + 1) = 6$ as a proportion in which x is the first term.   Write $x^2 = 15$ as a proportion in which 3 is the first term.

Ex. 3.   Write $3x = 4y$ as a proportion in which x and y are the first two terms.

Find the value of $x : y$ if

Ex. 4. $5x = 7y$ (see Ex. 3).   **Ex. 6.** $ax + bx = py + qy$.

Ex. 5. $ax = by$.   **Ex. 7.** $ax - by = cx - dy$.

284. Property III. *If four quantities are in proportion, they are in proportion by* **alternation**; *that is, the first term is to the third as the second is to the fourth.*

Given the proportion $a : b = c : d$.

To prove $a : c = b : d$.

Proof. 1. $a : b = c : d$.   1. Hyp.
2. $\therefore ad = bc$.   2. § 278.
3. $\therefore a : c = b : d$.   3. § 281.   Q.E.D.

285. Property IV. *If four quantities are in proportion, they are in proportion by* **inversion**; *that is, the second term is to the first as the fourth is to the third.*

Given the proportion $a : b = c : d$.

To prove $b : a = d : c$.

Proof.   Let the student supply the proof.

Ex. 1. Transform $x : a = b : c$ so that a shall be the third term.

Ex. 2. Transform the proportion of **Ex. 1** so that c shall be the third term.

Ex. 3. So that x shall be the last term.

Ex. 4. Write $x = \dfrac{ab}{c}$ as a proportion in which x is the last term.

Do the same with $x = \dfrac{ab}{2\,c}$.

Ex. 5. Write $x^2 = 3$ as a proportion in which x is a mean proportional. Do the same with $x = \sqrt{a^2 - b^2}$.

286. Property V. *If four quantities are in proportion, they are in proportion by* **composition**; *that is, the sum of the first two terms is to the second term as the sum of the last two terms is to the last term.*

Given the proportion $a : b = c : d$.

To prove $a + b : b = c + d : d$.

Proof. 1.　　　$\dfrac{a}{b} = \dfrac{c}{d}$.　　　　　1. Hyp.

2. Adding one to each member of the　　2. Ax. 2.

equality,　　　$\dfrac{a}{b} + 1 = \dfrac{c}{d} + 1$,

or　　　　　$\dfrac{a + b}{b} = \dfrac{c + d}{d}$.

That is, $a + b : b = c + d : d$.

Let the student show also that $a + b : a = c + d : c$.　　Q.E.D.

By use of composition, transform

Ex. 1. $12 : 3 = 8 : 2$.

Ex. 2. $2\,x - 5 : 5 = 3\,x - 7 : 7$.

Ex. 3. $\sqrt{x + 3} - 5 : 5 = \sqrt{2\,x - 1} - 7 : 7$.

Ex. 4. What is the efficiency value of composition when applied to certain proportions?

Ex. 5. Make up and solve an example similar to **Ex. 2**. To **Ex. 3**.

287. Property VI. *If four quantities are in proportion, they are in proportion by* **division**; *that is, the difference of the first two is to the second as the difference of the last two is to the last.*

Given the proportion $a : b = c : d$.

To prove $a - b : b = c - d : d$.

Proof. Let the student supply the proof.

By use of division, transform

Ex. 1. $12 : 3 = 8 : 2$.

Ex. 2. $2x + 5 : 5 = 3x + 7 : 7$.

Ex. 3. $7x + \sqrt{3x - 5} : \sqrt{3x - 5} = 4x + \sqrt{2x + 1} : \sqrt{2x + 1}$.

Ex. 4. What is the efficiency value of division when applied to certain proportions?

Ex. 5. Make up an example similar to Ex. 2.   To Ex. 3.

Ex. 6. Transform $3x + 2y : 2y = 10 : 2$ so that only one term in the result shall contain y.

288. Property VII. *If four quantities are in proportion, they are in proportion by* **composition and division**; *that is, the sum of the first two is to their difference as the sum of the last two is to their difference.*

Given the proportion $a : b = c : d$.

To prove $a + b : a - b = c + d : c - d$.

Proof. 1.	$a : b = c : d.$	1. Hyp.
2. By composition,	$\dfrac{a + b}{b} = \dfrac{c + d}{d}.$	2. § 286.
3. Also by division,	$\dfrac{a - b}{b} = \dfrac{c - d}{d}.$	3. § 287.
4. Hence,	$\dfrac{a + b}{a - b} = \dfrac{c + d}{c - d}.$	4. Ax. 5.
That is,	$a + b : a - b = c + d : c - d.$	Q.E.D.

Apply composition and division to

Ex. 1. $3x + 2y : 3x - 2y = 10 : 2.$

Ex. 2. $\dfrac{\sqrt{x+7}+\sqrt{5}}{\sqrt{x+7}-\sqrt{5}} = \dfrac{2x+1}{2x-1}.$

Ex. 3.   What is the efficiency value of composition and division as applied to certain proportions?

Ex. 4.   Make up and solve an example similar to Ex. 2.

289. Property VIII.   *In a series of equal ratios, the sum of all the antecedents is to the sum of all the consequents as any one antecedent is to its consequent.*

Given $a : b = c : d = e : f.$

To prove $a + c + e : b + d + f = a : b.$

Proof.		
1. $\quad\quad ab = ab.$	1.	Ident.
2. $a : b = c : d \;\therefore\; bc = ad.$	2.	Hyp. § 278.
3. $a : b = e : f \;\therefore\; be = af.$	3.	Hyp. § 278.
4. Adding, $\quad b(a + c + e) = a(b + d + f).$	4.	Ax. 2.
5. Hence, $a + c + e : b + d + f = a : b.$	5.	§ 281.

Q.E.D.

By use of § 289, transform

Ex. 1. $4 : 1 = 12 : 3 = 8 : 2.$

Ex. 2. $\dfrac{x+1}{y+3} = \dfrac{p+3}{q-2} = \dfrac{2-p}{5-q}.$

Ex. 3.   Find the value of $\dfrac{x}{y}$ if $\dfrac{x-a-2}{y-b-5} = \dfrac{a}{b} = \dfrac{2}{5}.$

290. Property IX.   *The products of the corresponding terms of two or more proportions are in proportion.*

Given $a : b = c : d, \; e : f = g : h,$ and $j : k = l : m.$

To prove $aej : bfk = cgl : dhm.$

Proof.		
1. $\quad \dfrac{a}{b} = \dfrac{c}{d}, \; \dfrac{e}{f} = \dfrac{g}{h}, \; \dfrac{j}{k} = \dfrac{l}{m}.$	1.	Hyp.
2. $\quad\quad \dfrac{aej}{bfk} = \dfrac{cgl}{dhm},$	2.	Ax. 4.
or $\quad\quad aej : bfk = cgl : dhm.$		

Q.E.D.

Ex. 1.   If $x : y = 10 : 5$ and $p : q = 3 : 7$, find the value of $px : qy$.

Ex. 2.   If $p : q = 1 : 5$ and $p : \dfrac{1}{q} = 4 : 5$, find the value of p.

291. Property X.   *Like powers or like roots of the terms of a proportion are in proportion.*

Given the proportion $a : b = c : d$.

To prove $a^n : b^n = c^n : d^n$, and $a^{\frac{1}{n}} : b^{\frac{1}{n}} = c^{\frac{1}{n}} : d^{\frac{1}{n}}$.

Proof.   1. $$\frac{a}{b} = \frac{c}{d}.$$ $\qquad$ 1. Hyp.

2. Raising both members to the nth power, $\qquad$ 2. Ax. 6.
$$\frac{a^n}{b^n} = \frac{c^n}{d^n},$$
or $$a^n : b^n = c^n : d^n.$$

3. In like manner, $\quad a^{\frac{1}{n}} : b^{\frac{1}{n}} = c^{\frac{1}{n}} : d^{\frac{1}{n}}.$ $\qquad$ 3. Ax. 6.

Q.E.D.

Ex. 1.   If $x : y = 2 : 3$, find the value of $x^3 : y^3$.

Ex. 2.   If $\sqrt[3]{a} : \sqrt[3]{b} = 2 : 5$, find the value of $a : b$.

Ex. 3.   If $\sqrt{x} : 2 = \sqrt{y} : 7$, find the value of $x : y$.

Ex. 4.   If $\sqrt{x} : \sqrt{x+1} = 3 : 5$, find the value of x.

Ex. 5.   If $\sqrt{y} : \sqrt{6} = \sqrt{y+5} : \sqrt{10}$, find the value of y.

Ex. 6.   State some of the efficiency values in the principle of § 291.

292. General principle. — Sometimes the two terms in a ratio have a common unit of measure (see § 226); sometimes they do not. Thus, in the ratio $\dfrac{1 \text{ ft. } 5 \text{ in.}}{1 \text{ yd.}}$, a unit of measure common to the antecedent and the consequent is 1 inch. But the terms of the ratio $\dfrac{5 \text{ in.}}{\sqrt{2} \text{ in.}}$ have no common unit of measure.

However, by the method of limits it may be shown that *if two ratios, in each of which the terms have a common unit of measure, are equal, under like circumstances two ratios whose terms have no common unit of measure (that is, are incommensurable) are equal.* For instance, see § 229 (p. 135).

Ex. 1. Find the fourth proportional to a, $2\,a$, $3\,x$.

Ex. 2. Find the third proportional to $a + b$ and $a - b$.

Ex. 3. Find the value of x in the proportion, $4 : 5 = x : 15$.

Ex. 4. Find a short method of determining whether a given proportion is true or not. Use this method to determine whether the following proportions are true: (1) $4 : 6 = 3 : 9$. (2) $5\,a : 2\,a = 15 : 6$.

Ex. 5. Transform the proportion $x + 1 : x - 1 = 7 : 5$ by composition and division, and afterwards find the value of x.

Ex. 6. Given $bx : y = bp : q$. **Prove** $x : y = p : q$.

Ex. 7. PW is a lever and F a fulcrum. The lengths of the arms of the lever are denoted by L and l.

$W =$ weight to be lifted (expressed in pounds).

$P =$ no. lb. of force applied at P, which will raise the weight W.

Then $P \times L = l \times W$.

Express this formula as a proportion.

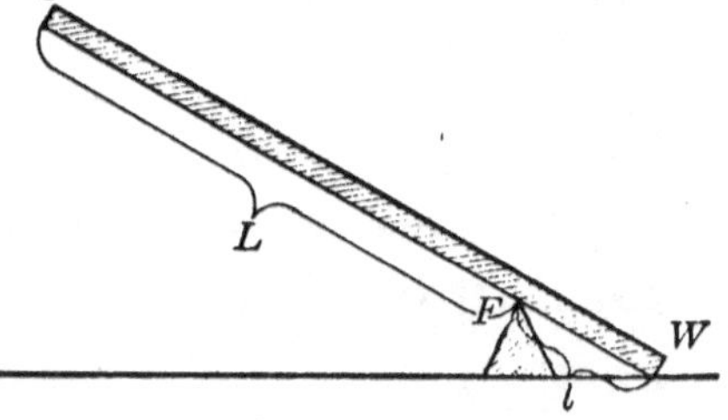

Ex. 8. In Ex. 7, if $W = 200$ lb., $l = 1$ ft., $L = 5$ ft., find P.

Ex. 9. What is the efficiency value of the law of the lever stated in Ex. 7?

Ex. 10. Make up and work an example similar to Ex. 8.

Simplify the following proportions as far as you can by use of the properties of proportions:

Ex. 11. $\dfrac{2\,x^2}{6 + 2\sqrt{1 + x}} = \dfrac{4\,x^2}{8 - 4\sqrt{1 - x}}.$

Ex. 12. $\dfrac{x^3 - 3\,x^2 + 5\,x - 7}{x^3 - 3\,x^2 - 5\,x + 7} = \dfrac{2\,x^3 + 4\,x^2 - 3\,x + 4}{2\,x^3 + 4\,x^2 + 3\,x - 4}.$

Ex. 13. $\dfrac{\sqrt{x + 2}}{\sqrt{x - 2}} = \dfrac{\sqrt{3\,x + 5}}{\sqrt{3\,x - 8}}.$

Proposition I. Theorem

293. *A straight line parallel to the base of a triangle divides the other two sides proportionally.*

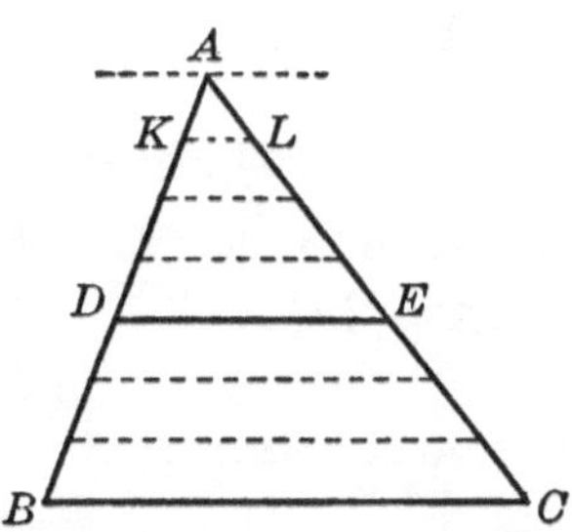

Given the triangle ABC and the line $DE \parallel$ base BC and intersecting the sides AB and AC in the points D and E, respectively.

To prove $\dfrac{AD}{DB} = \dfrac{AE}{EC}$.

Proof. 1. Take any common unit of measure of AD and DB, as AK, and let it be contained in AD m times and in DB n times.	1. § 227.
Then $\dfrac{AD}{DB} = \dfrac{m(AK)}{n(AK)} = \dfrac{m}{n}$.	
2. Through A and the points of division of AD and DB draw lines $\parallel BC$ and meeting AC.	2. § 95.
3. These lines will divide AE into m parts, and EC into n parts, all equal.	3. § 169.
4. Hence, $\dfrac{AE}{EC} = \dfrac{m(AL)}{n(AL)} = \dfrac{m}{n}$.	4. Why?
5. Hence, $\dfrac{AD}{DB} = \dfrac{AE}{EC}$.	5. Ax. 1.

Q.E.D.

294. Cor. 1. By composition (§ 286),
$$AD + DB : AD = AE + EC : AE.$$

Or $AB : AD = AC : AE.$

In like manner, $AB : DB = AC : EC.$

In general language, *if a line parallel to the base cuts the sides of a triangle, a side is to a segment of that side as the other side is to the corresponding segment of the second side.*

As a matter of convenience in making references, the principle stated in § 293 will be regarded as covering also the properties stated in § 294.

295. Cor. 2.   On the adjoining diagram,

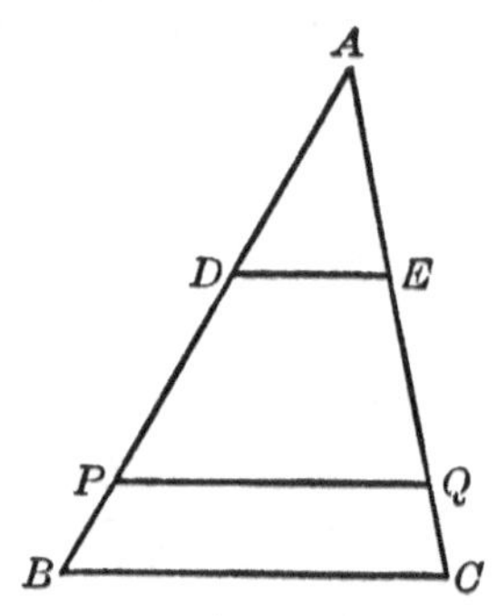

$$\frac{PB}{QC} = \frac{AP}{AQ};$$

also $$\frac{DP}{EQ} = \frac{AP}{AQ};$$

$$\therefore \frac{PB}{QC} = \frac{DP}{EQ}.$$

Hence, *if two lines are cut by a number of parallels, the corresponding segments are proportional.*

296. Cor. 3.   *A line drawn through the midpoint of one side of a triangle and parallel to the base, bisects the remaining side; and a line drawn through the midpoint of one leg of a trapezoid parallel to the base, bisects the other leg.*

If the diagram of Prop. I were so constructed that

Ex. 1. $AD = 12$, $DB = 8$, and $AC = 15$, find AE and $EC.$

Ex. 2. $AE = 2\,DB$, $AD = 5$, and $EC = 10$, find $DB.$

Ex. 3. $AD = a$, $DB = b$, $EC = c$, find $AE.$

Ex. 4.   If, on the diagram for § 295, $AD = 5\frac{3}{5}$, $DP = 6$, $PB = 2\frac{2}{5}$, $AC = 12$, find AE, EQ, $QC.$

PROPOSITION II. PROBLEM

297. *To construct the fourth proportional to three given straight lines.*

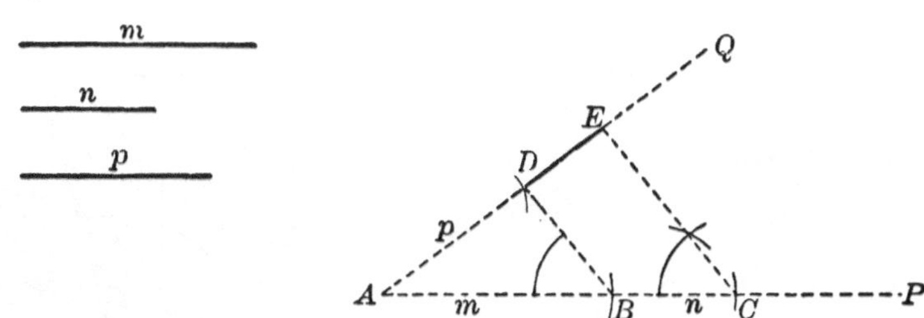

Given the lines m, n, p.

To construct a fourth proportional to m, n, and p.

Construction.   1. Draw two lines AP and AQ, making a convenient angle A.   1. Post. 1.

2. On AP mark off $AB = m$, $BC = n$; on AQ, $AD = p$.   2. Post. 2.

3. Draw DB.   3. Post. 1.

4. Through C draw $CE \parallel DB$ and meeting AQ at E.   4. § 95.

Then DE is the fourth proportional required.

Proof.   1. $AB : BC = AD : DE$.   1. § 293.

2. Hence, $m : n = p : DE$.   2. Ax. 9.

Q.E.F.

Ex. 1.   Construct a fourth proportional to three lines, $\frac{3}{4}$ in., 1 in., and $1\frac{1}{2}$ in. long.

Ex. 2.   Construct a third proportional to two lines, 2 in. and $1\frac{1}{2}$ in. long.

Ex. 3.   Construct a third proportional to any two given lines, a and b.

Ex. 4.   Given three lines a, b, c; and $a : b = c + x : c - x$; construct the line x.

[SUG.   Apply § 288 to the given proportion.]

Proposition III. Problem

298. *To divide a given straight line into parts proportional to two given straight lines.*

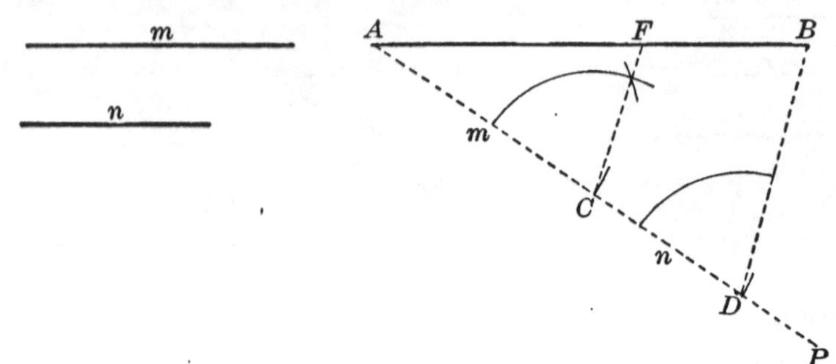

Given the lines AB, m, and n.

To divide AB into parts proportional to m and n.

Construction. 1. Draw the line AP, making any convenient angle with AB.

1. Post. 1.

2. On AP mark off $AC = m$, and $CD = n$. Draw DB.

2. Post. 2.

3. Through C draw $CF \parallel DB$ and meeting AB at F.

3. § 95.

Then AF and FB are the required parts of AB.

Proof. 1. $AF : FB = AC : CD$.

1. Why ?

2. Hence, $AF : FB = m : n$.

2. Why ?   Q.E.F.

Ex. 1. Draw a line 2 in. long and divide it into two parts which shall be in the ratio of 5 to 3.

Ex. 2. Draw any two lines and denote them by a and b.

Then draw a line $1\frac{1}{4}$ in. long and divide it into parts which shall be in the ratio of a to b.

Ex. 3. Divide a given straight line into parts which shall be proportional to three other given straight lines, denoted by m, n. p.

Ex. 4. Draw a line of convenient length and divide it into parts proportional to 2, 3, and 4.

PROPOSITION IV. THEOREM

299. *If a straight line divides two sides of a triangle proportionally, it is parallel to the third side.*

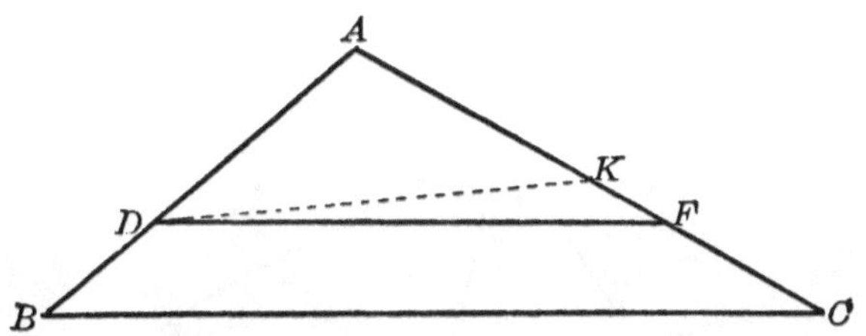

Given the $\triangle ABC$ and the line DF intersecting AB and AC so that $AB : AD = AC : AF$.

To prove $DF \parallel BC$.

Proof. 1. Through D draw the line $DK \parallel BC$ and meeting AC at K.	1. § 95.
2. Then, $AB : AD = AC : AK$.	2. § 293.
3. But $AB : AD = AC : AF$.	3. Hyp.
4. $\therefore AK = AF$.	4. § 283
5. Hence, the point K falls on F, and the line DK coincides with the line DF.	5. § 57.
6. But then, $DK \parallel BC$.	6. Constr.
7. $\therefore DF \parallel BC$.	7. DF coincides with DK which $\parallel BC$. Q.E.D.

300. Cor. *The line which joins the midpoints of two sides of a triangle is parallel to the third side.*

If the diagram of Prop. IV were so constructed that

Ex. 1. $AD = 12$, $DB = 4$, $AF = 15$, and $FC = 5$, would $DF \parallel BC$?

Ex. 2. $AB = 20$, $AD = 16$, $AC = 25$, and $AF = 18$, would $DF \parallel BC$?

Ex. 3. $AD = 3\ DB$, and $AF = 3\ FC$, would $DF \parallel BC$?

Proposition V. Theorem

301. *The bisector of an angle of a triangle divides the opposite side into segments proportional to the adjacent sides.*

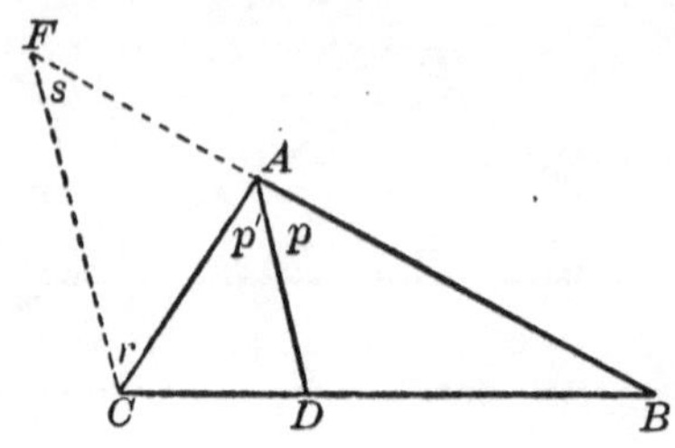

Given the $\triangle ABC$, with the line AD bisecting the $\angle BAC$ and meeting BC at D.

To prove $CD : DB = AC : AB$.

Proof.   1. Draw the line $CF \parallel AD$, and meeting BA produced at F.   1. § 95

2. Then, $CD : DB = FA : AB$.   2. § 293.

3.   But $\angle r = \angle p'$.   3. § 96.

4. $\angle s = \angle p$.   4. § 97.

5.   Also $\angle p' = \angle p$.   5. Hyp.

6. $\therefore \angle r = \angle s$.   6. Why?

7. $\therefore \triangle ACF$ is isosceles, and   7. Why?
            $AC = AF$.

8. $\therefore CD : DB = AC : AB$.   8. Ax. 9.   Q.E.D.

If the diagram of Prop. V were so constructed that

Ex. 1. $AC = 5$, $AB = 10$, and $CD = 4$, find DB.

Ex. 2. $AC = 2.4$, $AB = 5.6$, and $DB = 3.5$, find CD.

Ex. 3. $AB = 16$, $AC = 12$, and $BC = 14$, find CD and DB.
[Sug.   Let $DC = x$, $DB = 14 - x$, etc.]

Ex. 4. $AB = 22$, $AC = 11$, and $CB = 21$, find CD and DB.
[Sug.   Solve orally by separating 21 into two parts which are as $1 : 2$.]

Ex. 5.   Solve similarly, if $AC = 7$, $AB = 21$, and $CB = 20$.

Ex. 6.   Also, if $AC = 6$, $AB = 9$, and $CB = 10$.

SIMILAR POLYGONS

302. Similar polygons are polygons having their corresponding angles equal and their corresponding sides proportional.

Thus, if the figures $ABCDE$ and $A'B'C'D'E'$ are similar, the angles A, B, C, etc., must equal the angles A', B', C', etc., respectively; also $AB:A'B' = BC:B'C' = CD:C'D'$, etc.

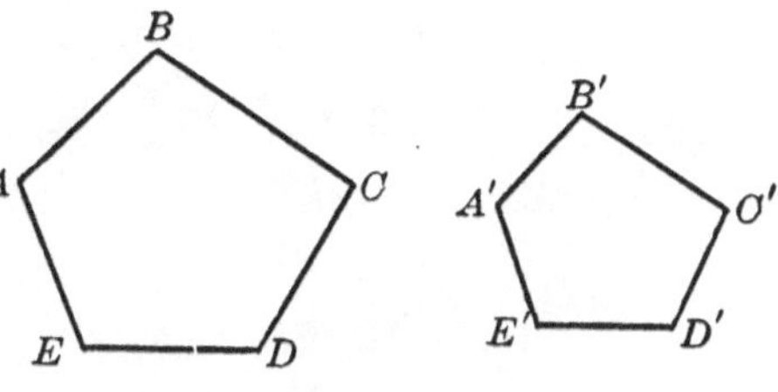

Hence, it is constantly to be borne in mind that similarity in shape or form of rectilinear figures involves two distinct properties:

1. *The corresponding angles are equal.*

2. *The corresponding sides are proportional.*

It should also be clearly realized that one of these properties may be true of two figures, and not the other.

Thus, in the rectangle A and the rhomboid B, the corresponding sides are proportional but the corresponding angles are not equal.

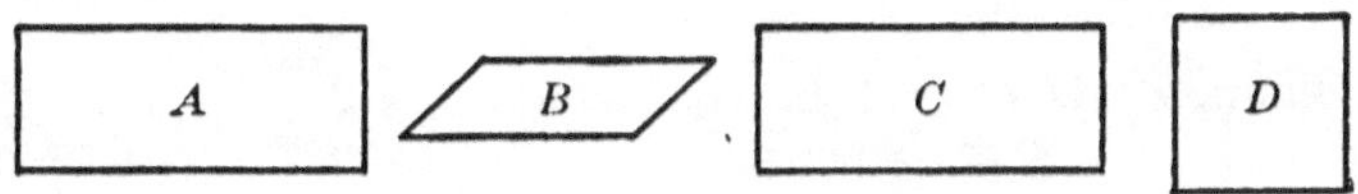

Also, in the rectangle C and the square D, the corresponding angles are equal but the corresponding sides are not proportional.

However, it will be found that, in the case of *triangles*, if one of the two properties is true, the other must be true also.

303. The **ratio of similitude** in two similar figures is the ratio of any two corresponding sides in those figures.

Ex. 1. Are any two squares similar?

Ex. 2. *A* and *B* are rectangles. Are they similar? 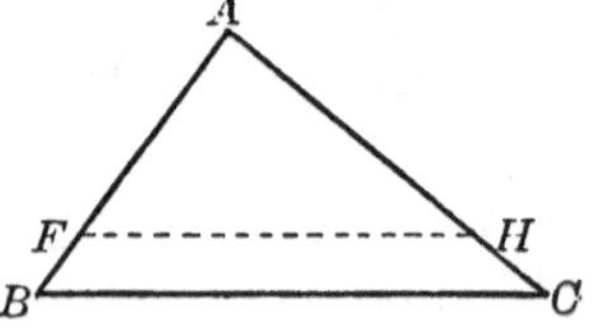

Ex. 3. If, in the similar pentagons of § 302, $AB = 30$, $BC = 47$, $CD = 36$, $ED = 33$, $AE = 24$, and $A'B' = 21$, find the other sides of the second pentagon.

Ex. 4. Make up a problem similar to Ex. 2, and answer it.

Proposition VI. Theorem.

304. *If the angles of two triangles are respectively equal to each other, the triangles are similar.*

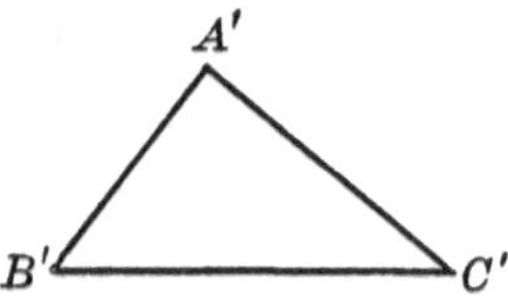

Given the $\triangle$ ABC and $A'B'C'$ with $\angle A = \angle A'$, $\angle B = \angle B'$, and $\angle C = \angle C'$.

To prove the $\triangle$ ABC and $A'B'C'$ similar.

Proof. 1. Place $\triangle A'B'C'$ upon $\triangle ABC$ so that $\angle A'$ shall coincide with its equal, $\angle A$, and $B'C'$ shall take the position FH.

2. Then, $\angle AFH = \angle B$.

3. $\therefore FH \parallel BC$.

4. $\therefore AB : AF = AC : AH$.

5. Hence, $AB : A'B' = AC : A'C'$.

6. In like manner, by placing $\triangle A'B'C'$ upon $\triangle ABC$ so that $\angle B'$ shall coincide with its equal $\angle B$, it may be proved that $AB : A'B' = BC : B'C'$.

7. Hence, $\dfrac{AB}{A'B'} = \dfrac{AC}{A'C'} = \dfrac{BC}{B'C'}$.

8. Hence, $\triangle$ ABC and $A'B'C'$ are similar.

1. Geom. Ax. 2.

2. Hyp.

3. Why?

4. § 293.

5. Ax. 9.

6. Reasons 1–5 above.

7. Ax. 1.

8. § 302.

Q.E.D.

305. COR. 1. *If two triangles have two angles of one equal to two angles of the other, the triangles are similar;* also,

If two right triangles have an acute angle of one equal to an acute angle of the other, the triangles are similar.

306. COR. 2. *If two triangles are each similar to the same triangle, they are similar to each other.*

307. The **efficiency value** of the principles arrived at in §§ 304–306 is that by them the labor of proving two triangles similar is reduced to that of proving two angles of one triangle equal to two angles of the other; or, in the case of two right triangles, of proving only one pair of angles equal.

308. **Symbol.** — It is often convenient to use the symbol ∼, as a substitute for the words " is similar to."

Ex. 1. Are two rhombuses ever similar? Are two rhomboids always similar?

Ex. 2. Construct two similar rectangles in which the ratio of similitude is $2 : 3$.

Ex. 3. $ABCD$ is a quadrilateral inscribed in a circle. The sides AB and DC are produced to meet at E, and the chords AC and BD are drawn. Prove that the triangles ACE and BDE are similar.

Can you point out another pair of similar triangles on the figure?

Ex. 4. The three sides of a given triangle are 8, 10, and 12 inches, respectively. If a line 9 inches long, parallel to the longest side, is terminated by the other two sides, find the segments into which it divides them.

Ex. 5. Draw a figure for the following theorem and state the hypothesis and conclusion in terms of the lettered diagram (but give no proof) : " The perpendiculars drawn from the vertices of a triangle to the opposite sides are the bisectors of the angles of the triangle formed by joining the feet of the perpendiculars."

Ex. 6. Write out a list of the theorems used in proving the theorem that if the opposite sides of a quadrilateral are equal, the figure is a parallelogram.

Proposition VII. Theorem

309. *If the corresponding sides of two triangles are proportional, the triangles are similar.*

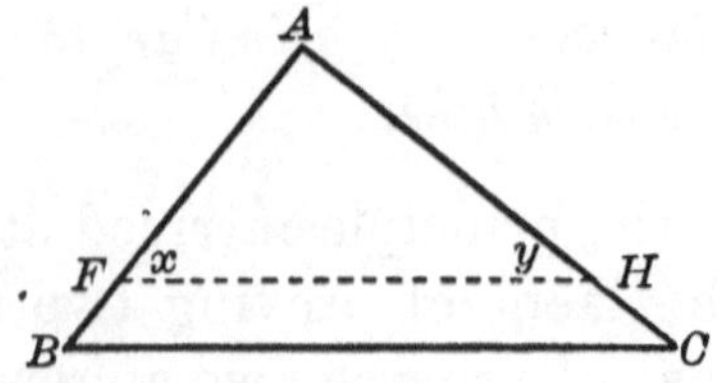 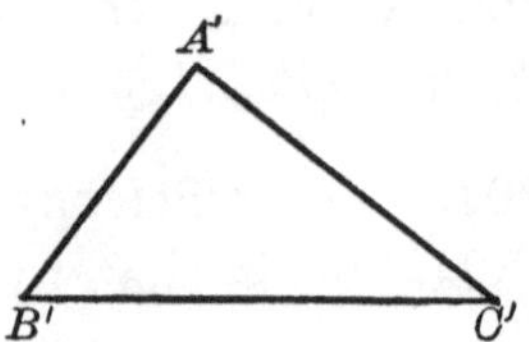

Given the $\triangle$ ABC and $A'B'C'$, in which $AB : A'B' = AC : A'C' = BC : B'C'$.

To prove $\triangle ABC \sim \triangle A'B'C'$.

Proof. 1. On AB mark off AF equal to $A'B'$, and on AC take $AH = A'C'$. Draw FH.	1. Post. 2.
2. Then $AB : AF = AC : AH$.	2. Hyp.
3. $\therefore FH \parallel BC$.	3. § 299.
4. $\therefore \angle x = \angle B$, and $\angle y = \angle C$.	4. Why?
5. $\therefore \triangle AFH \sim \triangle ABC$.	5. § 304.
6. Hence, $AB : AF = BC : FH$.	6. § 302.
7. That is, $AB : A'B' = BC : FH$.	7. Ax. 9.
8. But $AB : A'B' = BC : B'C'$.	8. Hyp.
9. $\therefore FH = B'C'$.	9. § 283.
10. Hence, $\triangle AFH = \triangle A'B'C'$.	10. § 83.
11. $\therefore \triangle ABC \sim \triangle A'B'C'$.	11. Ax. 9. Q.E.D.

Ex. 1. In $\triangle ABC$, $AB = 9$, $AC = 12$, $BC = 15$; also in $\triangle A'B'C'$, $A'B' = 6$, $A'C' = 9$, $B'C' = 10$. Are the two triangles similar?

Ex. 2. In proving Prop. VII, why cannot $\triangle A'B'C'$ be applied to $\triangle ABC$ as in the proof of Prop. VI?

Ex. 3. The bases of two isosceles $\triangle$ are 6 in. and 4 in., and their legs are 12 in. and 8 in., respectively. Are the $\triangle$ similar?

Ex. 4. Make up an example similar to Ex. 1. To Ex. 3.

EXERCISES: GROUP 48

Ex. 1. **Given** AB a diameter of the circle O; AB produced to C and $PC \perp AC$; AP a line intersecting the circle in Q. **Prove** $\triangle APC \sim \triangle AQB$.

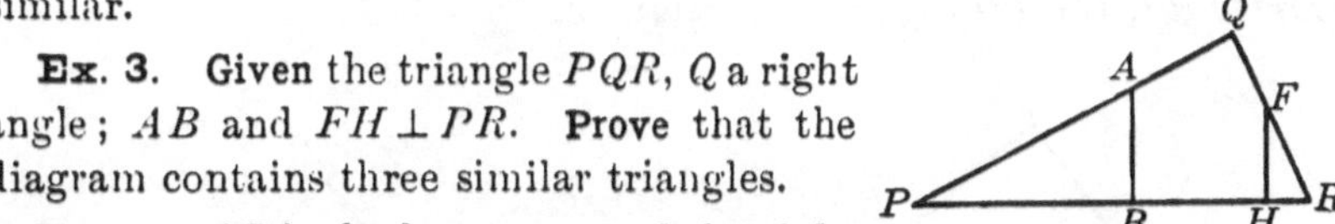

Ex. 2. Draw a triangle and a line parallel to one of its sides and meeting the other two sides produced. Prove that the two triangles thus formed are similar.

Ex. 3. **Given** the triangle PQR, Q a right angle; AB and $FH \perp PR$. **Prove** that the diagram contains three similar triangles.

Ex. 4. AB is the hypotenuse of the right triangle ABC. At A and B perpendiculars to AB are erected to meet BC and AC produced at P and Q respectively. Prove $\triangle PAC \sim \triangle BCQ$.

Ex. 5. $ABCD$ is a parallelogram. P is any point on the side CD; AP produced meets the side BC produced at Q. Prove that the figure contains three similar triangles.

Ex. 6. In a given circle draw two chords AB and CD intersecting at F. Draw lines joining the extremities of the chords. How many pairs of similar triangles does the figure contain? Give proof.

Ex. 7. From a given point outside a circle two secants are drawn to the circle. Lines are drawn connecting the points where the secants cut the circle. Prove that two pairs of similar triangles are thus formed.

Ex. 8. The line which joins the midpoints of two sides of a triangle is equal to one half the third side. (Use § 300.)

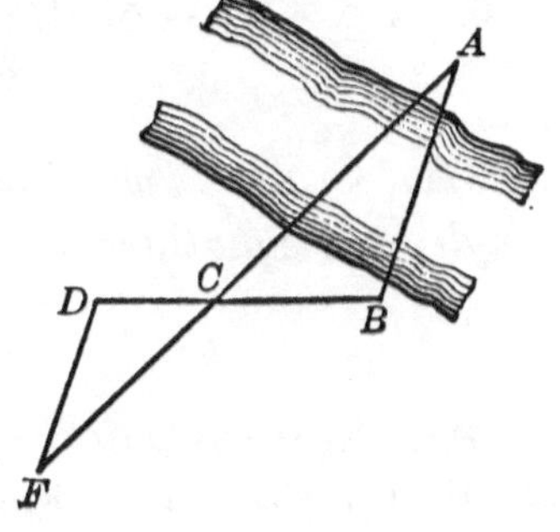

Ex. 9. To determine the distance AB across a stream, construct any convenient line BD, and $DF \parallel BA$. Determine the point C where FA crosses DB.

Then prove $\triangle FDC \sim \triangle CAB$.

If $CB = 240$ yd., $DC = 160$ yd., and $DF = 248$ yd., compute AB.

State the efficiency value of similar triangles which is illustrated by the preceding problem.

Ex. 10. Extend the non-parallel sides of a trapezoid until they meet.   Then prove that the two triangles thus formed are similar.

Proposition VIII.   Theorem

310. *If two triangles have an angle of one equal to an angle of the other, and the sides including these angles proportional, the triangles are similar.*

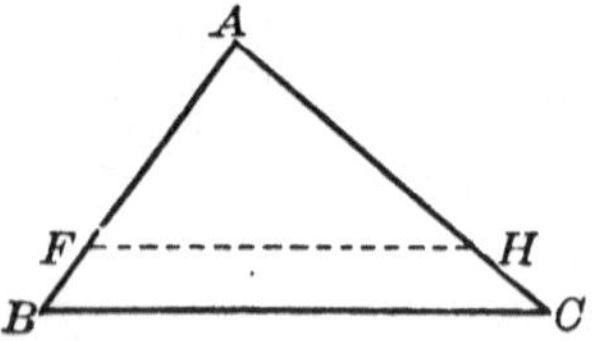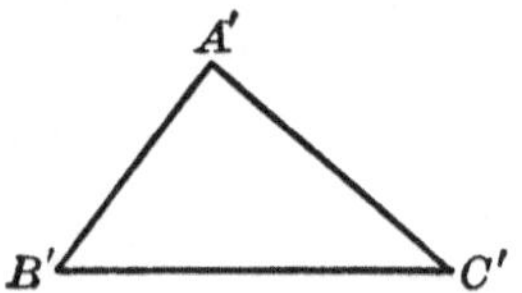

Given the $\triangle ABC$ and $A'B'C'$, in which $\angle A = \angle A'$ and $AB : A'B' = AC : A'C'$.

To prove $\triangle ABC \sim \triangle A'B'C'$.

Proof.   1.   Place $\triangle A'B'C'$ upon $\triangle ABC$ so that $\angle A'$ shall coincide with its equal, $\angle A$, and $B'C'$ take the position FH.

   2.   Then $AB : AF = AC : AH$.

   3.   Hence, $FH \parallel BC$.

   4. $\therefore \angle AFH = \angle B$, and $\angle AHF = \angle C$.

   5. $\therefore \triangle ABC \sim \triangle AFH$.

   6. $\therefore \triangle ABC \sim \triangle A'B'C'$.

1.	Geom. Ax. 2.
2.	Hyp.
3.	Why?
4.	Why?
5.	Why?
6.	Why?

Q.E.D.

311. **Cor.**   *Two isosceles triangles in which the vertex angles are equal are similar.*

Ex.   In the $\triangle ABC$, $AB = 6$, $AC = 8$, $BC = 10$; in the similar $\triangle A'B'C'$, $A'B' = 4.2$.   Find $A'C'$ and $B'C'$.

EXERCISES: GROUP 49

Ex. 1. Given $\triangle ABC$ with $AF = \frac{1}{3} AB$ and $AH = \frac{1}{3} AC$. **Prove** $\triangle AFH \sim \triangle ABC$.

[Sug. If $AF = \frac{1}{3} AB$, then $\dfrac{AF}{AB} = \dfrac{1}{3}$ (Ax. 5), etc.]

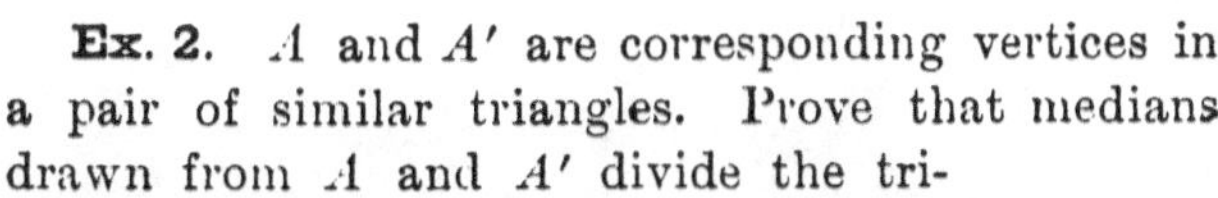

Ex. 2. A and A' are corresponding vertices in a pair of similar triangles. **Prove** that medians drawn from A and A' divide the triangles into two pairs of similar triangles.

Ex. 3. Given FH and $CD \perp$ straight line AB; $FQ \parallel CP$. **Prove** $\triangle QFH \sim \triangle CPD$.

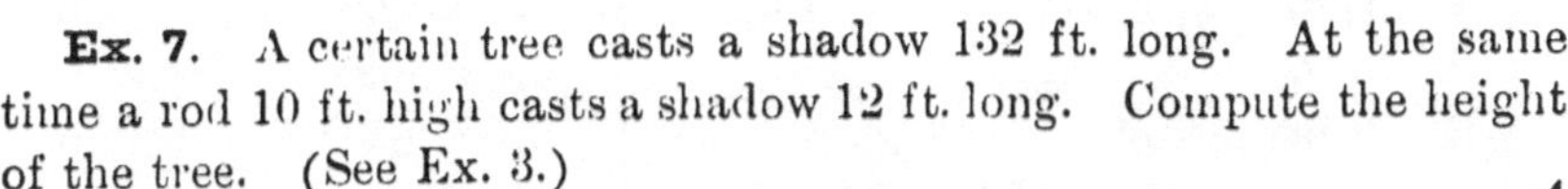

Ex. 4. Given P any point within the $\triangle ABC$; A', B', C', midpoints of PA, PB, and PC, respectively. **Prove** $\triangle A'B'C' \sim \triangle ABC$.

Ex. 5. State and prove the theorem similar to that of Ex. 4 when P is a point outside of the triangle ABC.

Ex. 6. Prove the theorem of Ex. 4 when P is a point on one of the sides of $\triangle ABC$.

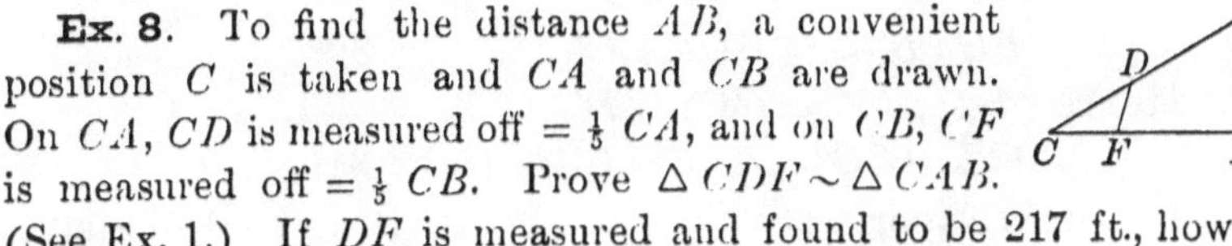

Ex. 7. A certain tree casts a shadow 132 ft. long. At the same time a rod 10 ft. high casts a shadow 12 ft. long. Compute the height of the tree. (See Ex. 3.)

Ex. 8. To find the distance AB, a convenient position C is taken and CA and CB are drawn. On CA, CD is measured off $= \frac{1}{5} CA$, and on CB, CF is measured off $= \frac{1}{5} CB$. **Prove** $\triangle CDF \sim \triangle CAB$. (See Ex. 1.) If DF is measured and found to be 217 ft., how long is AB?

Ex. 9. In a triangle ABC, the bisectors of the angles B and C meet the sides opposite these angles in Q and R, respectively. If AQ, QC, AR, and RB are 9, 15, 8, and 10 inches, respectively, find BC.

Ex. 10. If one of two similar triangles is isosceles, prove that the other is isosceles also.

PROPOSITION IX. THEOREM

312. *If two polygons are similar, they can be decomposed into the same number of triangles similar, each to each, and similarly placed.*

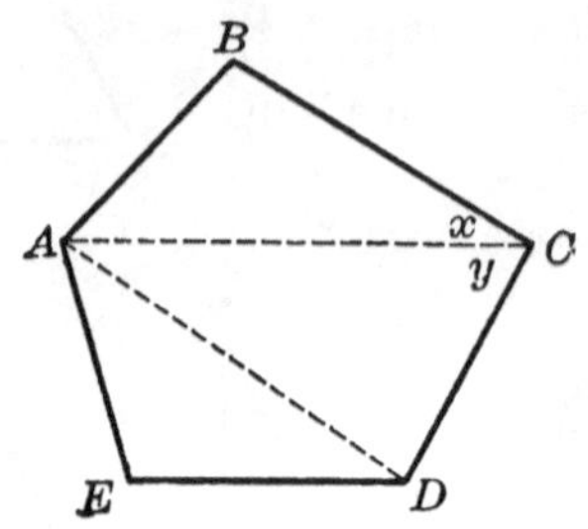
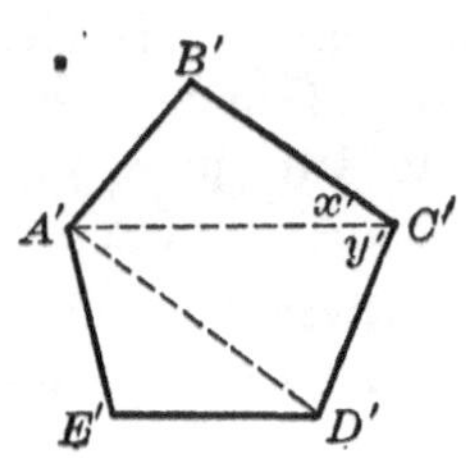

Given the similar polygons $ABCDE$ and $A'B'C'D'E'$, divided into triangles by the diagonals AC, AD, and $A'C'$, $A'D'$, drawn from the corresponding vertices A and A'.

To prove that $\triangle ABC$, ACD, ADE are similar to the $\triangle A'B'C'$, $A'C'D'$, $A'D'E'$, respectively.

Proof.		
1.	$\angle B = \angle B'$.	1. § 302.
2. Also	$AB : A'B' = BC : B'C'$.	2. § 302.
3.	$\therefore \triangle ABC \sim \triangle A'B'C'$.	3. § 310.
4. Again	$\angle BCD = \angle B'C'D'$.	4. § 302.
5. Also	$\angle x = \angle x'$.	5. § 302.
6. Subtracting,	$\angle y = \angle y'$.	6. Why ?
7. But	$BC : B'C' = CD : C'D'$.	7. § 302.
8. And	$BC : B'C' = AC : A'C'$.	8. § 302.
9. Hence,	$AC : A'C' = CD : C'D'$.	9. Ax. 1.
10.	$\therefore \triangle ACD \sim \triangle A'C'D'$.	10. § 310.
11. In like manner,		11. Reasons 1–3 above.
	$\triangle ADE \sim \triangle A'D'E'$.	Q.E.D.

Ex. Construct two rectangles whose bases are 8 and 10, and altitudes 4 and 5, respectively. Show that the rectangles are similar according to § 302. Draw a pair of corresponding diagonals and show by § 310 that the corresponding $\triangle$ formed are similar.

PROPOSITION X. THEOREM (CONVERSE OF PROP. IX)

313. *If two polygons are composed of the same number of triangles, similar, each to each, and similarly placed, the polygons are similar.*

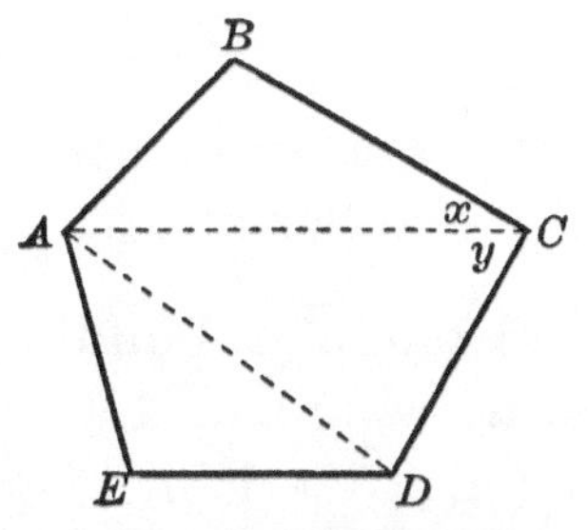
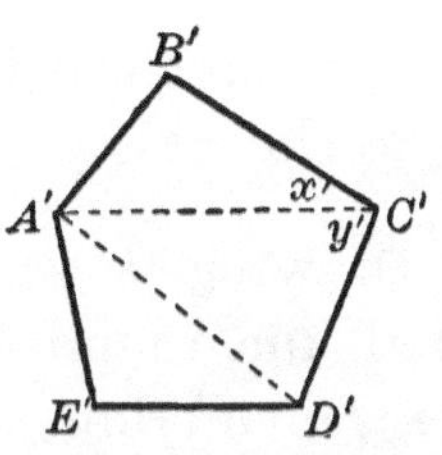

Given the two polygons $ABCDE$ and $A'B'C'D'E'$, in which the $\triangle ABC$, ACD, ADE are similar, respectively, to the $\triangle A'B'C'$, $A'C'D'$, $A'D'E'$, and are similarly placed.

To prove $ABCDE \sim A'B'C'D'E'$.

Proof.

1. $\angle B = \angle B'$.   1. Corr. $\angle$ of similar $\triangle$ are $=$. (§ 302.)

2. Also $\angle x = \angle x'$.   2. Why?

3. And $\angle y = \angle y'$.   3. Why?

4. Adding, $\angle BCD = \angle B'C'D'$.   4. Why?

5. Likewise,
$\angle CDE = \angle C'D'E'$,
$\angle BAE = \angle B'A'E'$, etc.   5. Reasons 1–4.

6. Also $\dfrac{AB}{A'B'} = \dfrac{BC}{B'C'}$.   6. Corr. sides of similar $\triangle$ are proportional. (§ 302.)

7. $\dfrac{BC}{B'C'} = \dfrac{AC}{A'C'}$, and $\dfrac{CD}{C'D'} = \dfrac{AC}{A'C'}$.   7. Why?

8. Hence, $\dfrac{BC}{B'C'} = \dfrac{CD}{C'D'}$.   8. Why?

9. So, $\dfrac{CD}{C'D'} = \dfrac{DE}{D'E'} = \dfrac{AE}{A'E'}$.   9. Reasons 6–8.

10. $\therefore ABCDE \sim A'B'C'D'E'$.   10. § 302.   Q.E.D

314. Abbreviated form of statement. — It is often convenient to write a series of equal ratios, like those used in the preceding proof, as follows:

$$\frac{AB}{A'B'} = \frac{BC}{B'C'} = \left(\frac{AC}{A'C'}\right) = \frac{CD}{C'D'} = \left(\frac{AD}{A'D'}\right) = \frac{DE}{D'E'} = \frac{AE}{A'E'},$$

in which we inclose in parenthesis a ratio that is used merely to show the equality of two other ratios.

315. Drawing to scale. — A rectangular building lot is measured and found to be 50 ft. wide and 150 ft. deep. The diagram P represents this lot, a line 1 in. long on the diagram standing for a line 100 ft. long on the lot. This method of drawing is called drawing to scale.

Drawing to scale is making a drawing of an object so that every line on the drawing is a given fractional part (or multiple) of the corresponding line on the object.

Thus, if the scale of the drawing is $\frac{1}{10}$, each line on the drawing equals $\frac{1}{10}$ of the corresponding line on the object.

Maps and architects' drawings of buildings are familiar examples of drawings to scale.

The scale of a drawing should always be indicated on the drawing. The following shows a convenient method of indicating the scale of a drawing.

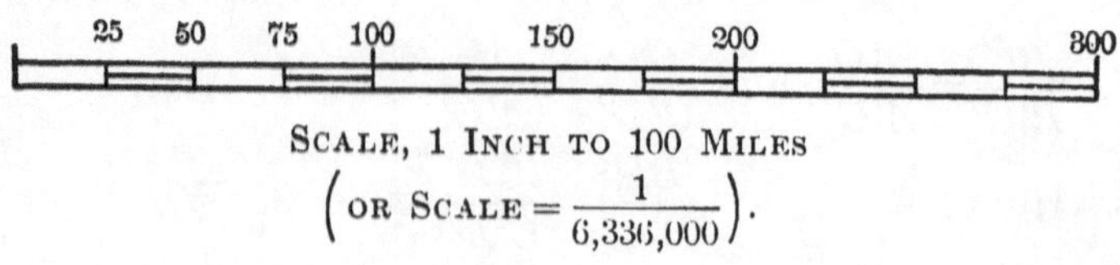

SCALE, 1 INCH TO 100 MILES

$$\left(\text{or Scale} = \frac{1}{6,336,000}\right).$$

Ex. 1. Construct a drawing scale 3 inches long, similar to the one just given, but to the scale of 1 inch to 20 ft. Of 1 in. to 1 yd. Of 1 in. to 40 miles.

Ex. 2. Using a scale of $\frac{1}{12}$, draw a line to represent 18 in. To represent 30 in. To represent 2 yd.

Ex. 3. Using a scale of $\frac{1}{12}$, construct a drawing to represent a rectangle 30 in. long and 15 in. wide.

Ex. 4. The adjoining diagram represents the plan of a cellar. The scale of the diagram is $\frac{1}{240}$. Find the perimeter of the cellar in feet.

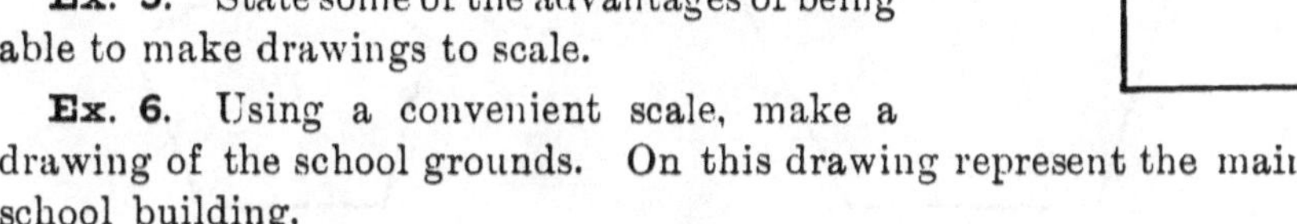

Ex. 5. State some of the advantages of being able to make drawings to scale.

Ex. 6. Using a convenient scale, make a drawing of the school grounds. On this drawing represent the main school building.

PROPOSITION XI. THEOREM

316. *The corresponding altitudes of two similar triangles have the same ratio as any two corresponding sides.*

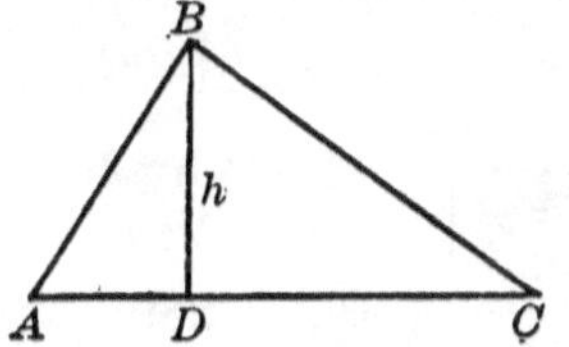
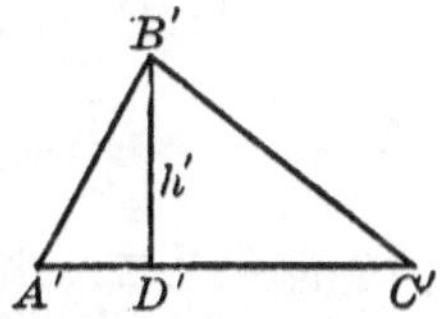

Given the similar $\triangle ABC$, $A'B'C'$, and h, h', any two corresponding altitudes in these $\triangle$.

To prove $\dfrac{h}{h'} = \dfrac{AB}{A'B'} = \dfrac{BC}{B'C'} = \dfrac{AC}{A'C'}$.

Proof. 1. In the rt. $\triangle ABD$ and $A'B'D'$, $\angle A = \angle A'$.　　1. Why?

2. $\therefore \triangle ABD \sim \triangle A'B'D'$.　　2. Why?

3. $\therefore \quad \dfrac{h}{h'} = \dfrac{AB}{A'B'}$.　　3. Why?

4. But $\dfrac{AB}{A'B'} = \dfrac{BC}{B'C'} = \dfrac{AC}{A'C'}$.　　4. Why?

5. Hence, $\dfrac{h}{h'} = \dfrac{AB}{A'B'} = \dfrac{BC}{B'C'} = \dfrac{AC}{A'C'}$.　　5. Why?

Q.E.D.

Proposition XII. Theorem

317. *The perimeters of two similar polygons are in the same ratio as any two corresponding sides.*

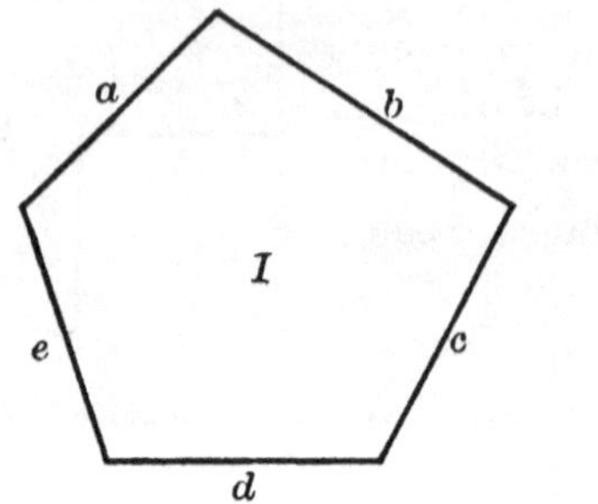
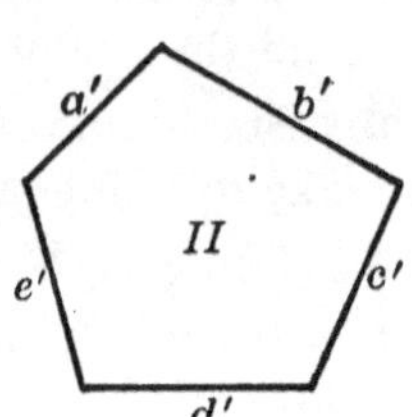

Given the similar polygons I and II with the sides a, b, c, etc., of I corresponding to the sides a', b', c', etc., of II; the perimeter of I being denoted by P, and that of II by P'.

To prove $P : P' = a : a'$.

Proof. 1. $$\frac{a}{a'} = \frac{b}{b'} = \frac{c}{c'} = \frac{d}{d'} = \frac{e}{e'}.$$ 1. Why?

2. Hence, $$\frac{a+b+c+d+e}{a'+b'+c'+d'+e'} = \frac{a}{a'}.$$ 2. § 289.

Or $$\frac{P}{P'} = \frac{a}{a'}.$$

Q.E.D.

318. Cor. *In two similar polygons, any two corresponding lines are to each other as any other two corresponding lines; and the perimeters are to each other as any two corresponding lines.*

Ex. 1. If the perimeter of a given field is 210 rods and a side of this field is to a corresponding side of a similar field as $3 : 2$, find the perimeter of the second field.

Ex. 2. One farm is twice as large, in length and width, as another farm. How many times longer is the fencing inclosing the first farm than that inclosing the second?

EXERCISES: GROUP 50

Ex. 1. Prove that any two given squares are similar to each other.

Ex. 2. On a given map, two places A and B are represented as $2\frac{3}{4}$ inches apart. How many miles is it from A to B if the scale of the map is 50 miles to the inch?

Ex. 3. How many miles apart are A and B (Ex. 2) if the scale of the map is $\dfrac{1}{1,000,000}$?

Ex. 4. Prove in full (without using § 318) that the perimeters of two similar polygons are to each other as any two corresponding diagonals.

Ex. 5. To find the distance AB, take a convenient point C and measure AC and CB. Produce AC to F, making $CF = \frac{1}{3}AC$. Also produce BC to D, making $CD = \frac{1}{3}CB$. Prove $\triangle CDF \sim \triangle ACB$.

If DF is measured and found to be 136 yd., how long is AB?

Ex. 6. On the diagram of Ex. 4, p. 199, let A' be any point on PA, $A'B' \parallel AB$, and $B'C' \parallel BC$. Prove $A'C' \parallel AC$.

Ex. 7. AB and CD are two rods fastened together at O, and each able to rotate about O. If $BO = 1\frac{1}{3}AO$ and $DO = 1\frac{1}{3}CO$, prove that in every position of the rods $BD = 1\frac{1}{3}AC$.

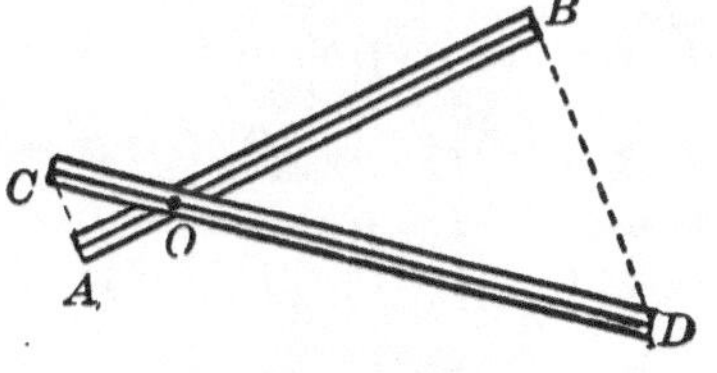

Ex. 8. If, on the diagram of Prop. XI, $AC = 18$, $A'C' = 12$, and $BD = 15$, find $B'D'$.

Ex. 9. Two sides of a triangle are 8 and 12 and the altitude on the third side is 6. In a similar triangle the side corresponding to 8 is 10. In the second triangle compute one of the other two sides and the altitude corresponding to the altitude 6.

Ex. 10. In the triangle ABC, AM bisects the angle BAC, CM is perpendicular to AM and when produced meets AB in K. D is the midpoint of BC. Prove $DM \parallel BK$. If $AB = 7$, $BC = 5.5$, and $AC = 4.6$, find the length of BK and of DM.

Ex. 11. Using a convenient scale, make a drawing to represent the outline of the schoolroom floor. On this drawing can you represent the teacher's desk? The other desks in the room?

PROPOSITION XIII. THEOREM

319. *If, in a right triangle, a perpendicular is drawn from the vertex of the right angle to the hypotenuse,*

I. *The two triangles thus formed are similar to each other and to the original triangle;*

II. *The perpendicular is the mean proportional between the segments of the hypotenuse;*

III. *Each leg of the given right triangle is a mean proportional between the hypotenuse and the segment adjacent to that leg.*

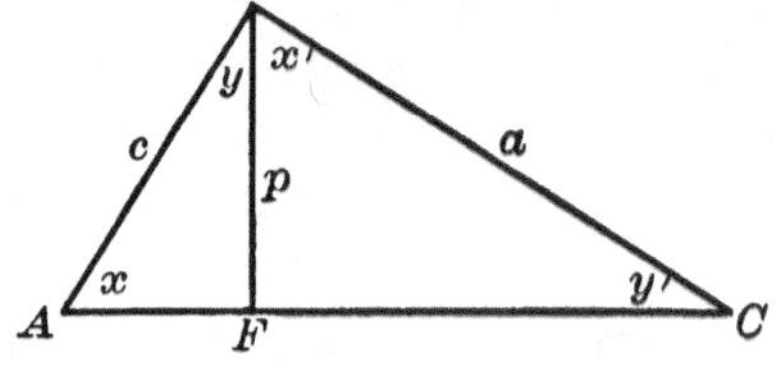

Given the right $\triangle ABC$ and BF the perpendicular from B to the hypotenuse AC.

To prove I. $\triangle ABF \sim \triangle BFC \sim \triangle ABC$.
II. $AF : p = p : FC$.
III. $AC : c = c : AF$, and $AC : a = a : FC$.

Proof. I. 1. In the rt. $\triangle ABF$ and ABC, $\angle x = \angle x$.	1. Ident.
2. $\therefore$ $\triangle ABF \sim \triangle ABC$.	2. § 305.
3. In the rt. $\triangle BFC$ and ABC, $\angle y' = \angle y'$.	3. Why ?
4. $\therefore \triangle BFC \sim \triangle ABC$.	4. Why ?
5. $\therefore \triangle ABF \sim \triangle BFC \sim \triangle ABC$.	5. § 306.
II. 1. In the $\triangle ABF$ and BFC, $AF : p = p : FC$.	1. § 302.
III. 1. In the $\triangle ABC$ and ABF, $AC : c = c : AF$.	1. Why ?
2. In the $\triangle ABC$ and BFC, $AC : a = a : FC$.	2. Why ?

Q.E.D.

320. Cor. *The perpendicular to the diameter from any point on a circle is a mean proportional be-* 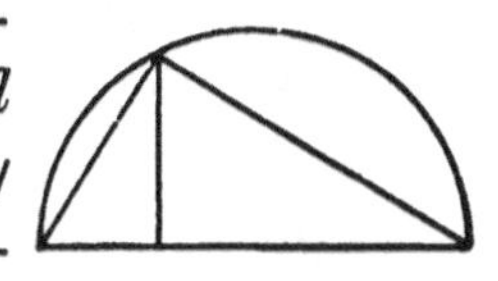 *tween the segments of the diameter; and the chord joining the point to an extremity of the diameter is a mean proportional be-tween the diameter and the segment of the diameter adjacent to the chord.*

On the diagram of Prop. XIII,

Ex. 1. If $AF = 4$ and $FC = 9$, find BF. Find AB and BC.

Ex. 2. If $BC = 1.2$ and $AC = 1.6$, find FC, AF, and BF.

Ex. 3. If $AF = .08$ and $BF = .16$, find BC.

Proposition XIV. Problem

321. *To construct the mean proportional between two given straight lines.*

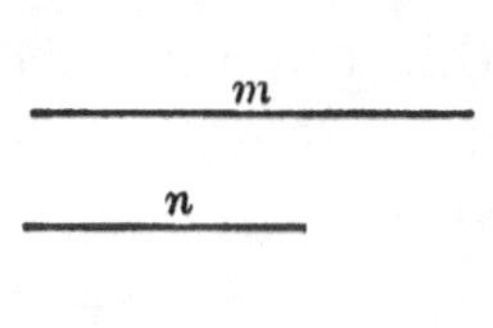

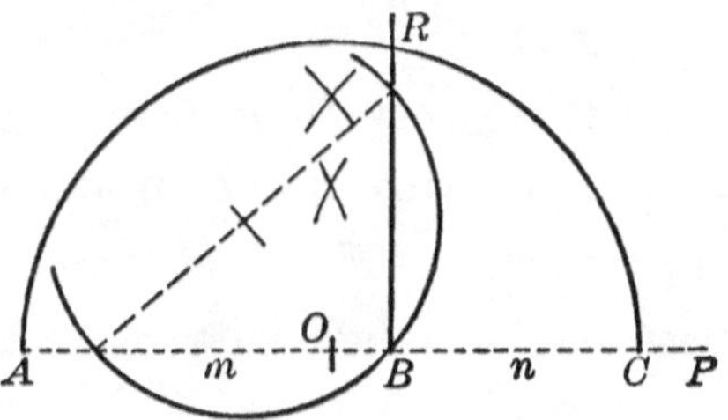

Given the lines m and n.

To construct the mean proportional between m and n.

Construction. 1. Draw a line AP and on it mark off $AB = m$ and $BC = n$.   1. Posts. 1 and 2.

2. Bisect AC at O.   2. § 128.

3. With O as a center and AO as a radius, describe the semicircle ARC.   3. Post. 3.

4. At B erect $BR \perp AC$, meeting ARC at R.   4. § 250.
BR is the mean proportional required.

Proof. 1. $AB : BR = BR : BC$.   1. § 320.

2. Substituting m for AB, and n for BC,   2. Ax. 9.
$$m : BR = BR : n.$$

Q.E.F.

Ex. 1. Construct the mean proportional between two lines 1 in. and 2 in. long, respectively. Also between lines of $\frac{3}{4}$ and $1\frac{1}{4}$ in.

Ex. 2. Taking any line as 1, construct a line equal to $\sqrt{2}$. Also $\sqrt{6}$.

Ex. 3. Construct a line $\sqrt{5}$ inches long.

Proposition XV. Theorem

322. *The product of the segments of a chord that passes through a fixed point within a circle is the same for all directions of the chord.*

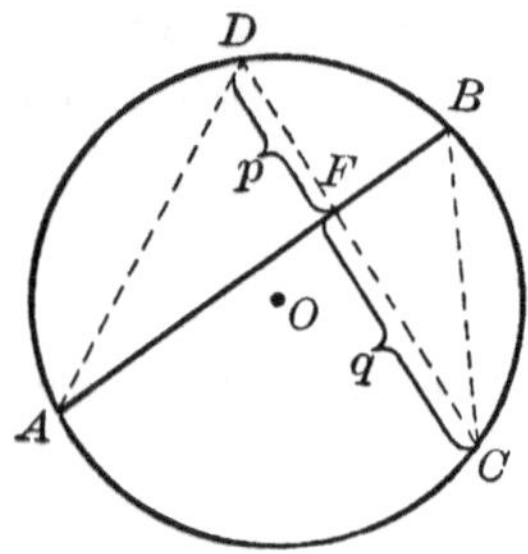

Given the circle O, F any point within the circle, AB a chord passing through F in any direction.

To prove that $AF \times FB$ always equals the same quantity.

Proof. 1. Through F draw the chord DC and denote DF by p and FC by q. Draw also DA and BC.

  2. Then, in the $\triangle ADF$ and FBC,
$$\angle D = \angle B.$$

  3. Also $\angle A = \angle C.$

  4. $\therefore \triangle ADF \sim \triangle FBC.$

  5. $\therefore AF : q = p : FB.$

  6. Hence, $AF \times FB = p \times q.$

  7. But p and q are constants.

  8. Hence, in whatever direction AB is drawn through F, $AF \times FB =$ a constant.

1. Post. 1.

2. § 237.

3. Why ?

4. Why ?

5. Why ?

6. Why ?

7. Position of DC is fixed.

8. $p \times q$ is a constant since p and q are.

Q.E.D.

323. Cor. *If two chords in a circle intersect, the product of the segments of one chord is equal to the product of the segments of the other chord.*

If the diagram of Prop. XV were so constructed that

Ex. 1. $AF = 12$, $FB = 8$, and $FC = 16$, find DF.

Ex. 2. $AF = 2 FB$, $FC = 9$, and $DF = 8$, find AF and FB.

Ex. 3. $FC = 6$, $DF = 4$, and $AB = 11$, find AF and FB.
[Sug.   Let $AF = x$, etc.]

Ex. 4. $AF = a$, $FB = b$, and $DF = c$, find FC.

Ex. 5. $FC = p$, $DF = q$, and $AB = r$, find AF.
How do you interpret the $\pm$ sign in your answer?

Proposition XVI.   Theorem

324. *If, through a point outside a given circle, a tangent and a secant are drawn to the circle, the length of the tangent is the mean proportional between the whole secant and its external segment.*

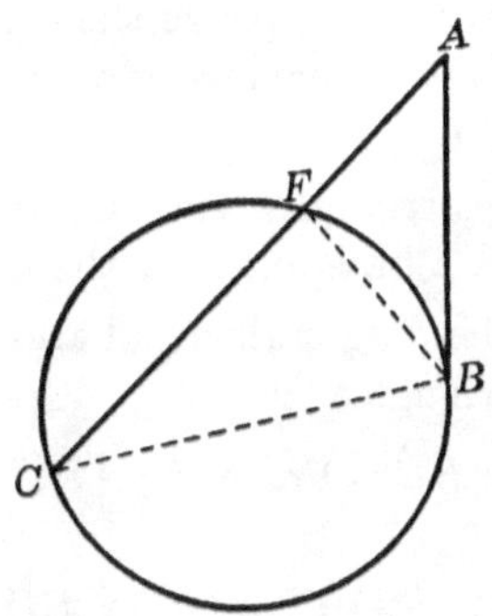

Given AB, a tangent, and AC, a secant, to the circle BCF, and AF, the external segment of the secant.

To prove $AC : AB = AB : AF$.

Proof.   Let the student supply the proof.

325. Cor. *If, from a given point without a circle, a secant is drawn, the product of the secant and its external segment is constant, in whatever direction the secant is drawn.*

For the product of each secant thus drawn and its external segment equals the square of the tangent, which is constant. •

If the diagram of Prop. XVI were so constructed that

Ex. 1. $AC = 9$ and $AF = 4$, find AB.

Ex. 2. $AC = 4\,AF$ and $AB = 12$, find AC.

Ex. 3. $AC = .64$ and $AB = .32$, find AF.

Ex. 4. O is the center, radius $= 15$, and $AO = 21$, find $AC \times AF$.

EXERCISES: GROUP 51

Similar Triangles

Let the student make a list of all the conditions that make two triangles similar.   (See §§ 304, 305, 306, etc.)

Ex. 1.   Given $AD \perp BC$, and $BF \perp AC$. Prove △ ADC and BFC similar.

Ex. 2.   In the figure of Ex. 1, prove the △ AOF and BFC similar. What other triangle on this figure is similar to $\triangle BFC$?

Ex. 3.   Two isosceles triangles are similar if a base angle of one equals a base angle of the other.

Ex. 4.   Prove that the diagonals and bases of a trapezoid together form a pair of similar triangles.

Ex. 5.   Given $\overset{\frown}{AC} = \overset{\frown}{BC}$. Prove △ APC and AFC similar.

Ex. 6. AB is the diameter of a circle, BD is a tangent, and AD intersects the circle at E. Prove the triangles ABE and ADB similar.

Ex. 7. BC is a chord in a circle, AQ is the diameter perpendicular to BC and meeting it at N; AP is any chord intersecting BC in M. Prove the △ AMN and APQ similar.

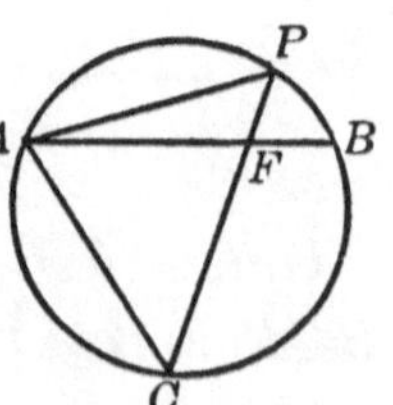

Ex. 8. The triangle ABC is inscribed in a circle; the bisector of the angle A meets BC in D and the circle in P. Prove the triangles BAD and APC similar.

Ex. 9. Prove that two rectangles are similar if two adjacent sides of one are proportional to the corresponding sides of the other.

Ex. 10. Two circles intersect in the points A and B. AC and AD are each a tangent in one circle and a chord in the other. Prove the △ ABC and ABD similar.

[SUG. Prove $\angle BAD = \angle ACB$, etc.]

326. Proof that lines are proportional.—In order to prove that certain lines are proportional, or have proportional relations, it is usually best to *show that the given lines are corresponding sides of similar triangles.*

In order to find the required pair of triangles, it is a help to mark the four lines (which are to form the required proportion) in some special way, as by brackets or colored crayon or pencil, and then to select the two triangles which contain these four lines as sides.

Sometimes, however, other methods of proof are used (as the theorems of §§ 322 and 324); but these, if investigated, are usually found to be the method of similar triangles in disguise.

EXERCISES: GROUP 52

PROPORTIONAL LINES

Ex. 1. On the figure of Ex. 1, p. 210, prove $AD \times BC = BF \times AC$, and $BC \times OD = BO \times FC$.

Ex. 2. On the figure of Ex. 5, p. 210, prove $CP : CA = CA : CF$. (Hence, as P moves, the product of what two lines is constant?)

Ex. 3. The diagonals of a trapezoid divide each other into proportional segments.

Ex. 4. In the isosceles triangle ABC, $AB = AC$; on the side AB the point P is taken so that PC equals the base. Prove $AB \times PB = \overline{BC}^2$.

Ex. 5. In a triangle the median to the base bisects all lines parallel to the base and terminated by the sides.

Ex. 6. If PQ is any line through F, the midpoint of the line AB, and AP and BQ are perpendicular to PQ, show that the ratio $PF:FQ$ is constant.

Ex. 7. The triangle ABC is inscribed in a circle. F is the midpoint of the arc AC, and BF intersects the line AC in E. Prove $AB:BC = AE:EC$. (Use § 301.)

Ex. 8. If two circles intersect, the common chord, if produced, bisects the common tangent. (Use § 324.)

Ex. 9. If two circles intersect, tangents drawn to the two circles from any point in the common chord produced are equal.

Ex. 10. Given AD, PT, and $BC \parallel$; prove $PQ = RT$.

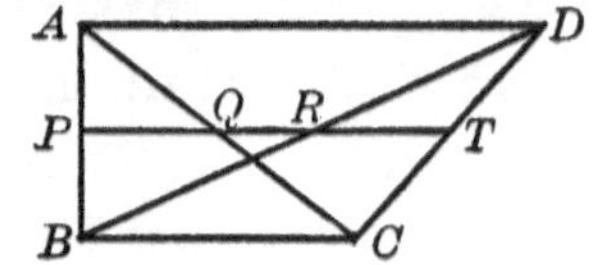

[SUG. Show that $\dfrac{PQ}{BC} = \dfrac{RT}{BC}$, by showing them equal to a common ratio.]

Ex. 11. Lines are drawn from a point O within the triangle, to the vertices of the triangle ABC. From B', any point in OB, $B'A'$ is drawn parallel to BA and meeting OA in A', and $B'C'$ is drawn parallel to BC and meeting OC in C'. Prove $A'B':AB = B'C':BC$, and the triangles ABC and $A'B'C'$ similar.

Ex. 12. Given $ABCD$ a $\square$, and P any point in BC produced. **Prove** $\overline{AR}^2 = RQ \times RP$.

[SUG. Compare the similar △ ABR and RQD; also the similar △ ARD and RBP.]

EXERCISES: GROUP 53

AUXILIARY LINES

Ex. 1. Prove that lines joining the midpoints of the sides of a quadrilateral taken in order form a parallelogram.

[SUG. Draw the diagonals of the quadrilateral and use § 300.]

Ex. 2. Lines joining the midpoints of the sides of a rectangle in order form a rhombus.

Ex. 3. Lines joining the midpoints of the sides of a rhombus in order form a rectangle.

Ex. 4. The common tangent of two circles divides the line of centers into segments which have the same ratio as the diameters of the circles.

[SUG. Draw radii to the points of contact.]

Ex. 5. AB and AC are the legs of an isosceles triangle and BF is an altitude. Prove that $2\,AC \times FC = \overline{BC}^2$.

Ex. 6. ABC is an inscribed isosceles triangle of which AB and AC are the legs. AD is a chord meeting BC in E. Prove that $\overline{AB}^2 = AD \times AE$.

Ex. 7. The line joining the midpoints of the legs of a trapezoid is parallel to the bases and equal to half their sum.

Ex. 8. Two circles touch at the point T. PTP' and QTQ' are lines drawn meeting the circles in P, Q and P', Q' respectively. Prove the triangles PTQ and $P'TQ'$ similar.

[Sug. Draw the common tangent at T.]

Ex. 9. Two circles touch at the point T, and through T three lines are drawn meeting the circles in P, Q, R and P', Q', R', respectively. Prove the triangles PQR and $P'Q'R'$ similar.

Ex. 10. If A is the midpoint of CD, an arc of a circle, and AP is any chord intersecting the chord CD in Q, prove that $AP \times AQ$ is a constant.

Ex. 11. In an inscribed quadrilateral, the product of the diagonals is equal to the sum of the products of the opposite sides.

[Sug. Draw BF so that $\angle CBF = \angle ABD$ and use similar triangles.]

EXERCISES: GROUP 54

Theorems Proved by Various Methods

Ex. 1. In the figure on p. 206, show that $AB \times BF = BC \times AF$.

Ex. 2. In the same figure, if $FC = 3\,AF$, show that $\overline{AB}^2 : \overline{BC}^2 = 1 : 3$.

Ex. 3. AB is the diameter of a circle and PB is a tangent. If AP meets the circle in the point Q, prove that $AP \times AQ = \overline{AB}^2$.

Ex. 4. In similar triangles, corresponding medians have the same ratio as corresponding sides.

Ex. 5. A diameter AB is produced to the point C; CP is perpendicular to AC; PB produced meets the circle at Q. Prove the triangles AQB and PCB similar.

Ex. 6. If PA and PB are chords in a circle, and CD is a line parallel to the tangent at P and meeting PA and PB at C and D, the triangles PAB and PCD are similar.

Ex. 7. Given AB a diameter and AD and BC tangents, AC and DB intersecting at a point F on the circle. **Prove** AB a mean proportional between the lines AD and BC.

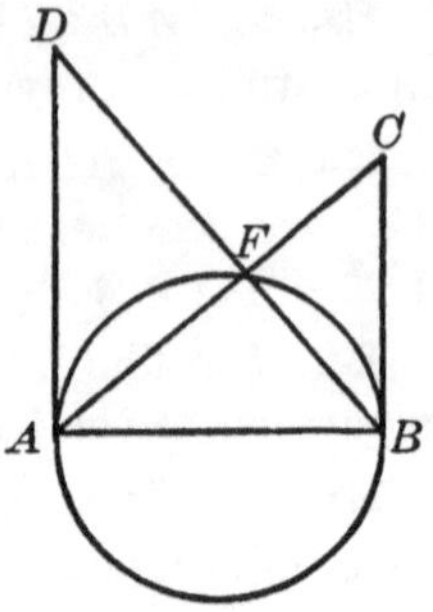

Ex. 8. A line drawn through the intersection of the diagonals of a trapezoid parallel to the bases and terminated by the legs is bisected by the diagonals.

[Sug. See Ex. 10, p. 212.]

Ex 9. If a chord is bisected by another chord, each segment of the first chord is a mean proportional between the segments of the second chord.

Ex. 10. If two circles are tangent externally, and a line is drawn through the point of contact and terminated by the circles, the chords intercepted in the two circles are to each other as the radii.

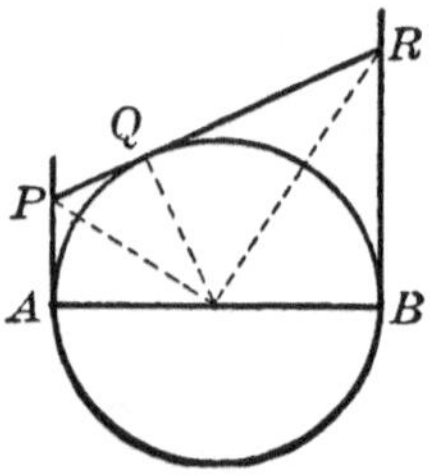

Ex. 11. Find the locus of the midpoints of lines in a triangle parallel to the base and terminated by the sides.

Ex. 12. Given AB the diameter, AP, PQR, BR, tangents. **Prove** $PQ \times QR$ a constant ($=$ radius squared).

Ex. 13. O is the center of a circle and A is any point within the circle; OA is produced to B, so that $OA \times OB$ equals the radius squared. If P is any point in the circle, the angles OPA and OBP are equal. (Use § 310.)

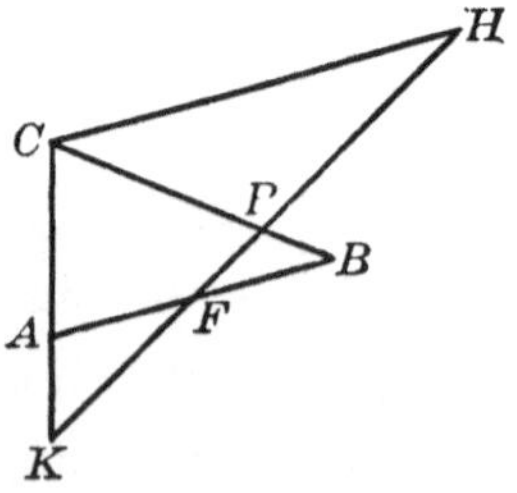

Ex. 14. Given $AF = FB$, and $CH \parallel AB$. **Prove** $HP : FP = HK : FK$.

[Sug. $HP : FP = CH : FB$, etc.]

EXERCISES: GROUP 55

Given three lines a, b, c,

Ex. 1. Construct $x = \dfrac{ab}{c}$; also $x = \dfrac{ab}{2c}$.

Ex. 2. Construct $x = \sqrt{a^2 - b^2}$, i.e., $\sqrt{(a + b)(a - b)}$.

Ex. 3. Construct $x = \sqrt{3\,ab}$, i.e., $\sqrt{(3\,a)b}$.

Ex. 4. Given a line denoted by 1, construct $\sqrt{3}$; also $\frac{1}{2}\sqrt{5}$.

Ex. 5. Divide a line into three parts proportional to 2, $\frac{1}{2}$, $\frac{2}{3}$.

Ex. 6. Divide one side of a triangle into segments proportional to the other two sides.

Ex. 7. Divide a line into segments in the ratio $1 : \sqrt{2}$.

Ex. 8. Given a point P in the side AB of a triangle ABC; draw a line from P to AC produced so that the line drawn may be bisected by BC.

[Sug. Suppose the required line, PQR, drawn meeting BC in Q and AC in R. From P draw $PL \parallel AC$ and meeting BC in L. Compare the $\triangle PLQ$ and QRC.]

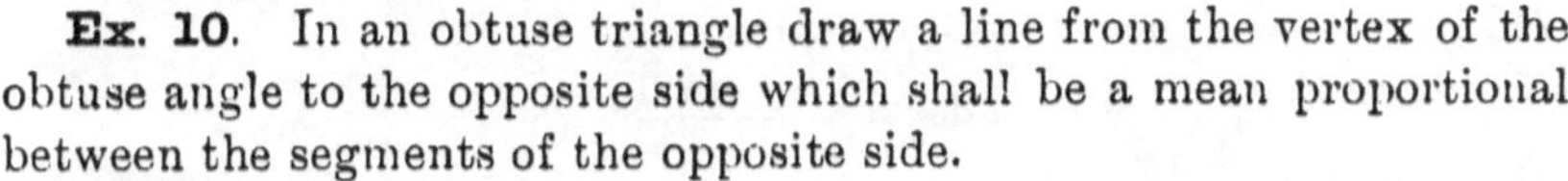

Ex. 9. Through a given point P in the arc subtended by the chord AB, draw a chord which shall be bisected by AB.

[Sug. Suppose the required chord drawn, viz., PRQ. Join the center O with P and Q. What kind of angle is OQP, etc. ?]

Ex. 10. In an obtuse triangle draw a line from the vertex of the obtuse angle to the opposite side which shall be a mean proportional between the segments of the opposite side.

[Sug. Circumscribe a circle about the triangle and reduce the problem to the conditions of Ex. 9.]

Ex. 11. Find a point P in the arc subtended by the chord AB such that chord $PA :$ chord $PB = 2 : 3$.

[Sug. Suppose the required construction made, and also the chord AB divided in the ratio $2 : 3$ at the point Q. How do the angles APQ and QPB compare ?]

Ex. 12. Given the perimeter, construct a triangle similar to a given triangle.

Ex. 13. Given the altitude of a triangle, construct a triangle similar to a given triangle.

Ex. 14. In a given circle inscribe a triangle similar to a given triangle.

Ex. 15. About a given circle circumscribe a triangle similar to a given triangle.

Ex. 16. By drawing a line parallel to one of the sides of a given rectangle, divide the rectangle into two similar rectangles.

Ex. 17. Inscribe a square in a given triangle.

[SUG. If ABC is the given triangle, suppose
$DGFE$ the required inscribed square. Join
BE and produce it to meet $AH \parallel BC$. Prove
$AH = AK$, etc.]

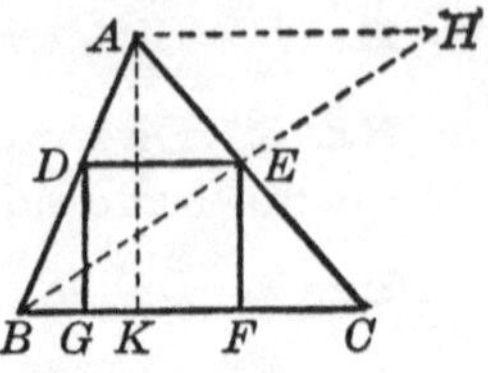

327. Algebraic analysis of problems. — *The conditions of
a problem may often be stated as an algebraic equation. By
solving the equation, the length of a desired line in terms of
known lines may be obtained, and the problem may be solved
by constructing the algebraic expression thus obtained.*

Ex. Find a point P in
the line AB, such that $\overline{AP}^2$
$= 3\,\overline{BP}^2$.

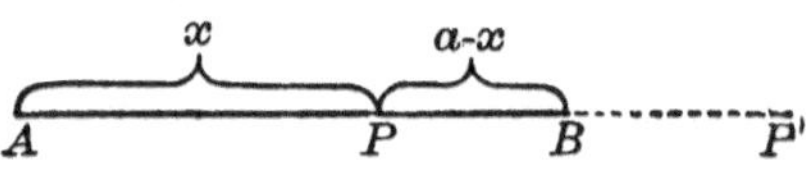

ANALYSIS AND CONSTRUCTION. Denote AB by a, AP by x, and
PB by $a - x$. Then $x^2 = 3(a - x)^2$.

$\therefore 2\,x^2 - 6\,ax = -3\,a^2$, and $x = \dfrac{3\,a \pm a\sqrt{3}}{2}$.

Construct $a\,\sqrt{3}$; whence construct $\dfrac{3\,a - a\sqrt{3}}{2}$. Lay off the line obtained, as AP, on AB. This gives the point P of internal division.
Similarly, the construction of $\dfrac{3\,a + a\sqrt{3}}{2}$ gives P', the point of external
division.

EXERCISES: GROUP 56

PROBLEMS SOLVED BY ALGEBRAIC ANALYSIS

Ex. 1. Find a point P in a given line AB, such that $\overline{AP}^2 = 2\,\overline{BP}^2$.

Ex. 2. Construct a right triangle, given one leg
a, and the projection, $2\,a$, of the other leg on the
hypotenuse.

[SUG. Denote the projection of a on the hypotenuse by x. Then $a^2 = x(x + 2\,a)$, etc.]

Ex. 3. Inscribe a square in a given semicircle.

Ex. 4. From a given line cut off a part which shall be a mean
proportional between the remainder of the line and another given line.

EXERCISES: GROUP 57

Ex. 1. Construct two lines, given their sum (a line AB) and their ratio ($m:n$).

Ex. 2. Construct two lines, given their difference and their ratio.

Ex. 3. Divide a trapezoid into two similar trapezoids by drawing a line parallel to the bases of the trapezoid.

[Sug. Suppose the figure drawn, and compare the ratio of the bases in the two trapezoids formed.]

Ex. 4. Construct a mean proportional between two given lines by use of § 324.

Ex. 5. Construct a circle which shall pass through two given points and touch a given line.

Ex. 6. From a given point draw a secant to a circle so that the external segment shall equal half the secant.

[Sug. Draw a tangent to the $\odot$ and use the algebraic method.]

Ex. 7. From a given external point P, draw a secant meeting a circle in A and B so that $PA : AB = m : n$.

[Sug. Draw a tangent to the circle from the point P and denote its length by t. Denote PA by mx and AB by nx. Then $m(m+n)x^2 = t^2$, or $t : mx = mx : \dfrac{mt}{m+n}$, etc.]

Ex. 8. Through a given point P draw a straight line so that the parts of it included between that point and perpendiculars drawn to the line from two other given points, shall be in a given ratio.

[Sug. Join the last two points, and divide the line between them in the given ratio.]

Ex. 9. Construct a straight line so that the perpendiculars on it from three given points shall be in a given ratio.

[Sug. Let P, Q, R be the given points and $m:n:p$ the given ratio. Divide PQ in the ratio $m:n$ and QR in the ratio $n:p$, etc.]

Ex. 10. Upon a given straight line construct a polygon similar to a given polygon and similarly placed.

Ex. 11. Upon a given line as hypotenuse, construct a right triangle in which the bisector of the right angle shall divide the hypotenuse into parts having a given ratio.

EXERCISES: GROUP 58

PRACTICAL APPLICATIONS

Ex. 1. In case the sun is not shining and shadows cannot be used, the height of an object, such as a tree or a steeple, can often be determined by a method indicated in the drawing. What distances must be measured and why, to determine the height of the tree?

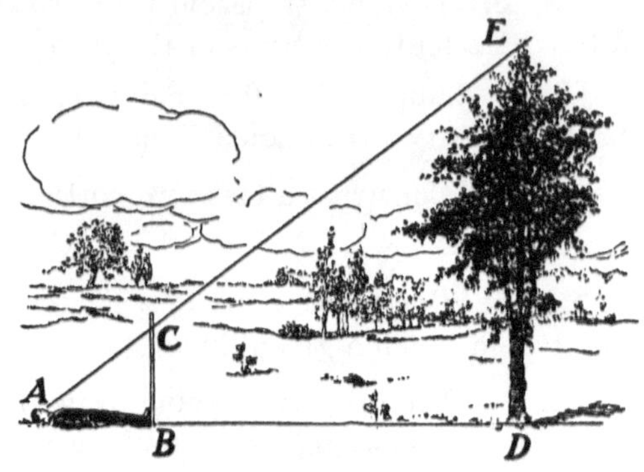

Ex. 2. Show how to find the height of a tree by placing a mirror in a horizontal position on the ground and standing so as to see the reflection of the top of the tree in the mirror. If the observer's eye is $5\frac{1}{2}$ ft. from the ground, the observer stands 6 ft. from the mirror, and the mirror is 120 ft. from the tree, how high is the tree?

Ex. 3. Foresters often determine the height of a tree by an instrument called Faustman's Height Measurer. The principle on which this instrument is constructed is shown in the diagram.

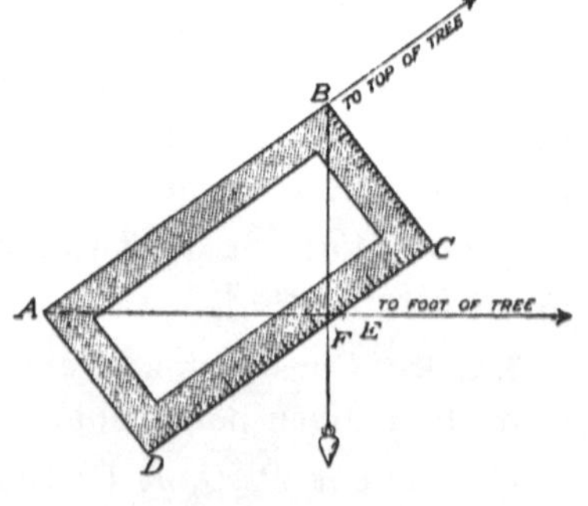

If the distance from A to the foot of the tree is 150 ft., $BC = 6$ inches, and $CF = 4\frac{1}{2}$ inches, find the height of the tree.

Ex. 4. The distance from A to B in Ex. 5, p. 205, might have been determined by a graphical method as follows: Measure AC, CB, and angle ACB. On paper make a drawing of the triangle ACB to a convenient scale. On this drawing measure the line which represents AB and hence determine the length of AB.

By use of this method, we are saved the labor of marking out and measuring the lines CD, CF, and DF.

Apply this method to the measurement of two objects in your neighborhood which are separated by an impassable barrier.

In like manner, show how the distance between two objects, only one of which is accessible, may be determined.

Ex. 5. Show how to find, by use of the graphical method, the distance between two places both of which are inaccessible.

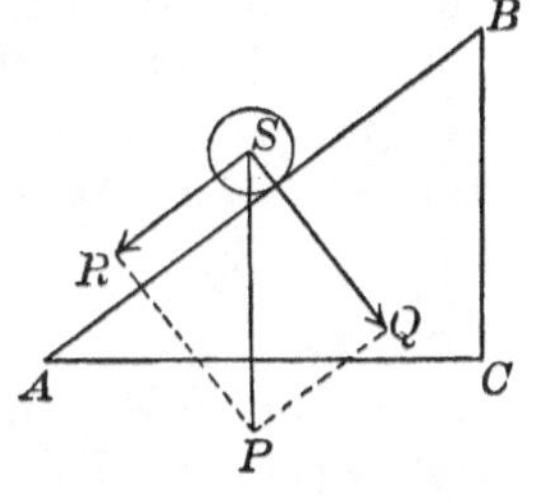

Ex. 6. The strongest beam which can be cut from a given round log is found as follows: Take AB, a diameter of the log, and trisect it at C and D. Draw CE and $DF \perp AB$ and meeting the circumference at E and F respectively. Draw AF, FB, BE, and AE.

Prove $AFBE$ a rectangle. Also that $FB : AF = 1 : \sqrt{2}$, or approximately as $5 : 7$.

[Sug. FB is a mean proportional between DB and AB. Therefore $\overline{FB}^2 = \frac{1}{3}\overline{AB}^2$. (§ 320.) In like manner, $\overline{FA}^2 = \frac{2}{3}\overline{AB}^2$, etc.]

Ex 7. A sphere S weighing 100 lb. rests on the inclined plane AB. AC contains 8 units of length, BC 6 units. A force which prevents S from rolling down the plane would be equivalent to a lifting force of how many pounds exerted on S and parallel with AB?

[Sug. Resolve the weight of S (represented by SP) into two forces, one perpendicular to AB and the other parallel to AB. Prove the triangles ACB and SPR similar, and obtain $AB : BC = SP : SR$, or $10 : 6 = 100$ lb. $: SR$.]

The principle involved in this example is of great practical importance. Thus in many machines useful results are often obtained by representing a force by the diagonal of a rectangle (or parallelogram), and separating this force into two component forces represented by the sides of the rectangle (or parallelogram), only one of these components being effective. This principle makes possible the action of the propeller of an aëroplane or steamboat, of the best water wheels and windmills, and indeed of all turbine wheels. It also determines the lifting power of the planes of an aëroplane.

Ex. 8. A wagon weighing 1800 lb. stands on the side of a hill which has a rise of 18 ft. for every 100 ft. taken horizontally. What force must a horse exert to keep such a wagon from running down hill, friction being neglected?

Ex. 9. Make up and work an example similar to Ex. 8.

Ex. 10. Show how the diameter of the earth may be determined by the following method: Drive three stakes into a level piece of ground (or into a shallow piece of water) in line, each two successive stakes being a mile apart, and let each stake project the same distance above the ground (or water). By use of a leveling instrument, determine the amount by which the middle stake projects above a horizontal line connecting the tops of the end stakes. This distance will be found to be 8 in.

[SUG. Use § 320. An arc a mile long on the earth's surface may be taken as equal to its chord. Then from the diagram of § 320 we obtain the following proportion,

the diameter of the earth : 1 mi. $= 1$ mi.: 8 in.]

Ex. 11. Also show that the distance that the middle stake projects above the horizontal line connecting the top of the two end stakes varies as the square of the distance between the end stakes. Thus, if the two end stakes were placed three times as far apart as in Ex. 10 (that is, 6 mi. apart instead of 2 mi.), the bulge of the earth between them would be 3^2, or 9, times what it was originally.

Hence, determine the projection of the middle stake (or bulge of the earth) when the end stakes are 4 mi. apart. When they are 8 mi. 16 mi. 32 mi.

Ex. 12. At the seashore an observer whose eye was 10 ft. above sea level observed a distant steamboat whose hull was hidden for a height of 12 ft. above water level by the bulge of the earth. About how far off was the steamboat?

Ex. 13. A seaman in a lookout 42 ft. above water level could barely see with a glass the topsail of a distant ship, and estimated this topsail to be 45 ft. above sea level. Estimate the distance of the observed vessel from the seaman.

Ex. 14. In the triangle OAB, A is a right angle, and OA is 1. By a method which is beyond the scope of this book, the length of AB is computed and found to be .839+. Using this fact, find RQ in the second triangle.

Ex. 15. By use of the table on the following page, find RQ if angle P is 10°. 20°. 70°. 80°.

Tables giving the other sides of all possible right triangles when one side is unity have been computed, and when used as in Exs. 14 and 15, form the basis of the subject of trigonometry. By use of this science, after measuring the length of a single line a few miles long on the earth's surface, we can determine the distances and relative positions of other places thousands of miles away, without measuring any intervening lines. By use of these results as a basis, the distance of the moon is determined as approximately 240,000 miles; of the sun as 92,800,000 miles; and of the nearest fixed star as 20,000,000,000,000 miles.

Angle O	AB	OB
10°	.176	1.015
20°	.364	1.064
30°	.577	1.155
40°	.839	1.305
50°	1.192	1.556
60°	1.732	2.000
70°	2.747	2.924
80°	5.671	5.759

A knowledge of these distances has led to important improvements in methods of navigation and has thus facilitated travel and commerce and increased their benefits for us all.

Ex. 16. On the diagram, given AB 6000 ft. long, and the angles as indicated; compute the length of CD, by use of the table given in Ex. 15.

Ex. 17. To the diagram in Ex. 16 annex another triangle CFD, giving it angles which are multiples of 10°, and compute the length of CF.

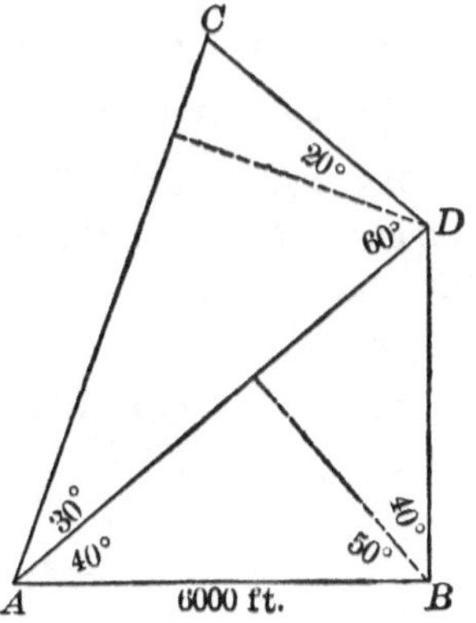

EXERCISES: GROUP 59

REVIEW QUESTIONS

Ex. 1. Write a proportion which contains a third proportional.

Ex. 2. Write a proportion in which a given number is used twice as a term.

Ex. 3. Write a proportion which can be simplified by the use of composition and division.

Ex. 4. What is the difference between a ratio and a proportion? Show this by an example.

Ex. 5.   Are two mutually equiangular polygons necessarily similar? Draw two polygons which illustrate your answer.

Ex. 6.   Are two polygons whose corresponding sides are proportional necessarily similar?   Draw two polygons which illustrate your answer.

Give a list of the properties proved in Book Three concerning

Ex. 7.   Chords in a circle.   **Ex. 9.**   Polygons.

Ex. 8.   Secants and tangents.   **Ex. 10.** Triangles.

Ex. 11.   In making a drawing of an object, what is meant by a scale of $\frac{1}{50}$?   By a scale of 1 in. to 100 ft.?

Ex. 12.   On the diagram on page 206, how many lines must be measured in order to determine the others?   Illustrate your answer numerically (*i.e.*, express in numbers the lengths of the fewest possible lines and then determine the remaining lines).

Ex. 13.   What is the efficiency value of Prop. V?   Of Prop. XII?

Ex. 14.   On the diagram of Prop. XV, how many of the line-segments AF, FB, DF, FC, AB, CD, must be measured in order to determine the others?   What, then, is the efficiency value of this theorem?

Ex. 15.   Make up and answer an example similar to Ex. 14 concerning Prop. XVI.

BOOK FOUR

AREAS OF POLYGONS

328. A **unit of surface** is a square whose side is a unit of length; as a square inch, a square yard, or a square centimeter.

329. The **area of a surface** is the number of units of surface which the given surface contains.

330. Efficiency principle. — It is important for the student to grasp firmly the fact that *area* means not merely a vague largeness of surface, but that it is a *number*. Being a number, it can be resolved into factors; it may be determined as a product of simpler numbers; and may be handled with ease and precision in various ways. (See Ex. 1, p. 7.)

EXERCISES: GROUP 60

Ex. 1. Draw a rectangle 6 inches long and 4 inches wide, and divide the rectangle into inch squares by drawing lines parallel to the sides. Obtain the area of the rectangle by counting the number of small squares composing the figure. Do you know of any shorter way of getting the area of the rectangle than this?

Ex. 2. Obtain the area of the triangle ABC by counting the number of small squares composing it (piece together the parts of the squares). Do you know of any shorter way of getting the area of the triangle ABC?

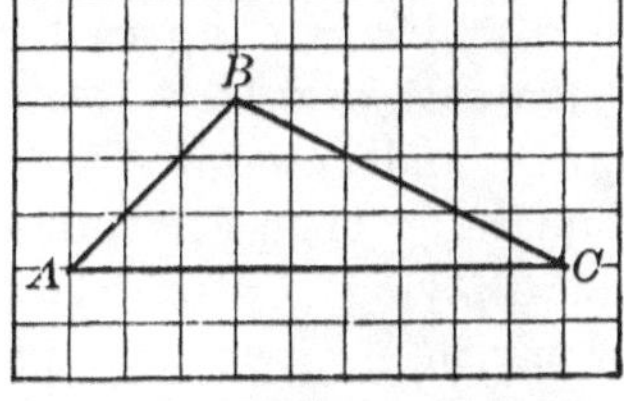

On squared paper, locate the triangle or quadrilateral whose vertices are as follows (p. 224), and determine the area of each figure.

Each pair of numbers inclosed in a parenthesis represents a point

Thus in (4, 3) the first number, 4, represents a distance of four spaces to the right of the vertical line YY' (see diagram of Ex. 4) and the number 3, a distance of three spaces above the horizontal line XX'. If the first number in a parenthesis is negative, the number represents a distance to the left of the line YY'; and if the second number is negative, it represents a distance below the line XX'.

Ex. 3.   (1, 1), (1, 5), (3, 3).

Ex. 4.   (4, 3), (4, − 1), (− 2, 3), (− 2, − 1).

Ex. 5.   (0, 0), (4, 4), (6, 0), (10, 4).

Ex. 6.   (0, 4), (− 3, 1), (6, 1).

Ex. 7.   (4, 5), (8, 1), (−1, 5), (− 3, 1).

Ex. 8.   (2, 3), (5, 0), (2, −6), (− 1, 0).

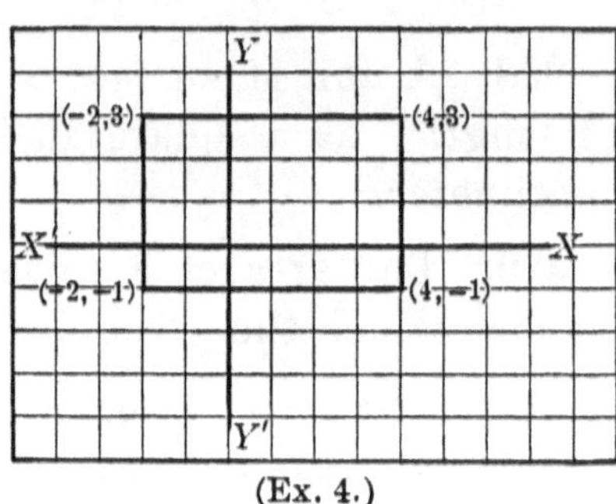

(Ex. 4.)

Ex. 9.   (1, 0), (4, 3), (7, − 3), (4, − 6).

Ex. 10.   (2, 6), (10, 2), (4, − 4), (− 2, 2).

Ex. 11.   On squared paper, construct a square each side of which is $2\frac{1}{2}$ linear spaces, as on the adjoining diagram. Determine the number of small squares composing it (that is, its area) by counting the small squares. Then determine the area by multiplying $2\frac{1}{2}$ by $2\frac{1}{2}$. Compare the amount of work in the two methods of determining the area of the square.

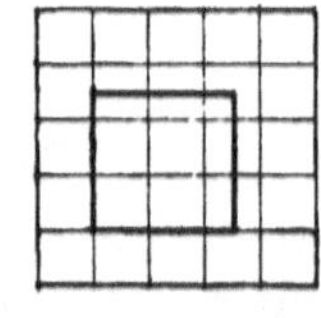

Ex. 12.   On squared paper, construct a square each side of which is 3.5 and determine the area of the square.

Ex. 13.   Treat in like manner a square each side of which is $2\frac{1}{4}$. $3\frac{3}{4}$.

Ex. 14.   On squared paper, construct a square each side of which is $\sqrt{8}$, as in the adjoining diagram, and determine its area by counting the small squares. Then determine the area of the square by multiplying $\sqrt{8}$ by $\sqrt{8}$. Compare the amount of work in the two methods.

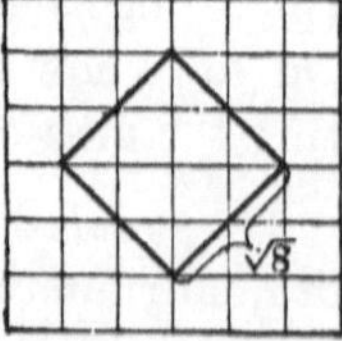

Ex. 15.   Treat in like manner a square whose side is $\sqrt{32}$. $\sqrt{18}$.

Ex. 16.   Also a rectangle whose sides are $\sqrt{8} \times \sqrt{2}$. $\sqrt{18} \times \sqrt{8}$.

Ex. 17. In Ex. 2, what is the area represented by the triangle *ABC*, if each linear space on the squared paper represents 1 yard? If it represents 1 mile?   10 miles?

331. Fundamental principle of areas. —The preceding examples illustrate the fact that the *area of a rectangle equals the product of the number of units of length in the base by the number in the altitude.*   Some of the examples also illustrate the fact that this is true when the numbers involved are fractional or irrational, as well as when they are integers.   We shall now treat the matter of areas from another point of view, for the sake of special advantages thus obtained.

332. Equivalent plane figures are plane figures having equal areas.

Construct a square whose side is 3 in.; also a right triangle whose legs are 6 in. and 3 in.   The area of each of these figures is 9 sq. in.

Hence, the two figures are equivalent; but they are not congruent (or equal) figures, since they are not of the same shape.

Construct two triangles which are equivalent but not congruent.

In dealing with plane figures, it is often convenient to use the word "equal," or the sign =, and let the neighboring words determine whether congruence or equivalence is meant.

Similarly, when we say "bill of a bird" or "a five-dollar bill," we let the words next to the word "bill" determine what kind of bill is meant.

333. Certain abbreviations are often used when speaking of areas.   Thus, instead of "area of a rectangle," for example, it is often convenient to say simply "rectangle."   Similarly, instead of "the number of linear units in the base," we may say "the base."   In like manner, for "product of the number of linear units in the base by the number of linear units in the altitude," a common abbreviation is "product of the base by the altitude."

Proposition I. Theorem

334. *If two rectangles have the same altitude, they are to each other as their bases.*

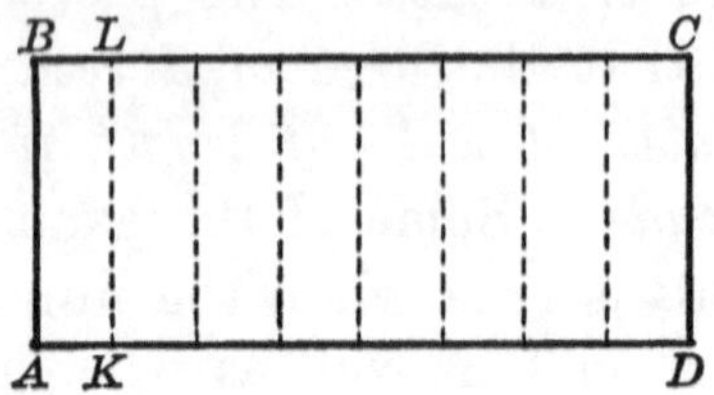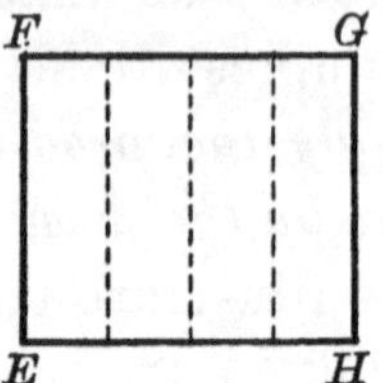

Given the rectangles $ABCD$ and $EFGH$, having their altitudes AB and EF equal.

To prove $ABCD : EFGH = AD : EH$.

Proof. 1. Take some common unit of measure of AD and EH, as AK, and let it be contained in AD m times and in EH n times ;

then $$\dfrac{AD}{EH} = \dfrac{m(AK)}{n(AK)} = \dfrac{m}{n}.$$

1. § 227.

2. Through the points of division of the bases of the two rectangles draw lines $\perp$ the bases.

2. § 85.

3. These lines will divide $ABCD$ into m, and $EFGH$ into n small rectangles, all equal.

3. §§ 92, 149, 165.

4. Hence, $$\dfrac{ABCD}{EFGH} = \dfrac{m(ABLK)}{n(ABLK)} = \dfrac{m}{n}.$$

4. Why ?

5. $$\therefore \dfrac{ABCD}{EFGH} = \dfrac{AD}{EH}.$$

5. Why ?

Q.E.D.

If in the above proof the two lines AD and EH should be found to have no common unit of measure, like AK, the above theorem may still be proved true by a method of proof called the *method of limits*, which is beyond the scope of this book.

335. Cor. *If two rectangles have equal bases, they are 'o each other as their altitudes.*

Proposition II. Theorem

336. *The areas of any two rectangles are to each other as the products of their bases and their altitudes.*

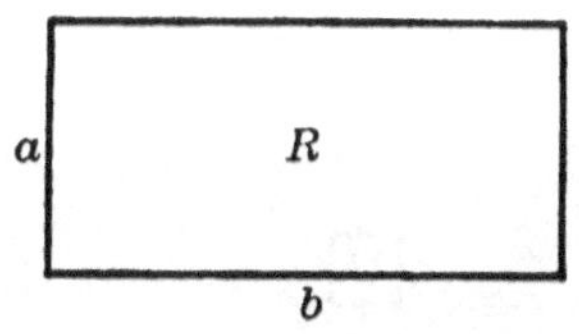
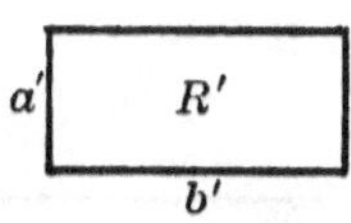
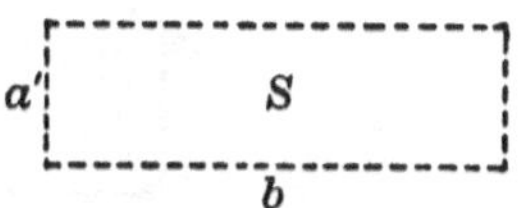

Given the rectangles R and R', having the bases b and b', and the altitudes a and a', respectively.

To prove $\dfrac{R}{R'} = \dfrac{ab}{a'b'}$.

Proof. 1.   Construct a rectangle, S, having its base equal to that of R, and its altitude equal to that of R'.

1.   § 85, Post. 2.

2.   Then $\dfrac{R}{S} = \dfrac{a}{a'}$.

2.   § 335.

3.   Also $\dfrac{S}{R'} = \dfrac{b}{b'}$.

3.   § 334.

4.   Hence, $\dfrac{R}{R'} = \dfrac{ab}{a'b'}$.

4.   Ax. 4.

Q.E.D.

Ex. 1.   Find the ratio of the area of a rectangle whose dimensions are 12 × 8 in. to that of one whose dimensions are 9 × 2 in.

Ex. 2.   How many bricks, each 8 × 5 in., will it take to cover a pavement 60 × 9 ft.?

Ex. 3.   Find the ratio of the areas of two rectangles, one of which is 1.2 ft. by 4.2 ft., and the other 1.68 ft. by 10.24 ft.

Ex. 4.   The ratio of the areas of two rectangles is 2 to 5. The base of the first rectangle is $3\frac{2}{3}$ feet, and the altitude is $5\frac{1}{2}$ feet. If the altitude of the second rectangle is $6\frac{2}{3}$ feet, find its base.

Proposition III. Theorem

337. *The area of a rectangle is equal to the product of its base and its altitude.*

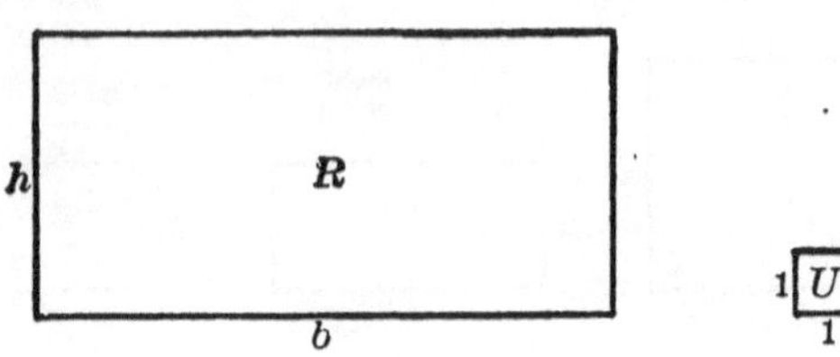

Given the rectangle R, with a base containing b, and an altitude containing h units of linear measure.

To prove area of $R = bh$.

Proof. 1. Let U be a square each side of which contains 1 linear unit; then U is the unit of surface.	1. § 328.
2. $\therefore \dfrac{R}{U} = \dfrac{bh}{1 \times 1} = bh.$	2. § 336.
3. But $\dfrac{R}{U}$ is the area of R.	3. § 329.
4. Hence, area of $R = bh$.	4. Ax. 1. Q.E.D.

338. Efficiency value. — By use of this theorem, the problem of finding the area of a rectangle is reduced to the simpler problem of measuring the two linear dimensions of the rectangle and taking their product. Hence, the statement in the theorem of § 337 may be taken as the definition of the area of a rectangle, if the teacher so desires.

Ex. 1. Find the area of a rectangle whose base is $8\frac{3}{4}$ yd. and whose altitude is $2\frac{1}{2}$ yd.

Ex. 2. The area of a given rectangle is 54.95 sq. rd. and the altitude is 3.14 rd. Find the base of the rectangle.

Ex. 3. The perimeter of a given square is 1 ft. Find the area of the square in square inches.

PROPOSITION IV. THEOREM

339. *The area of a parallelogram is equal to the product of its base and its altitude.*

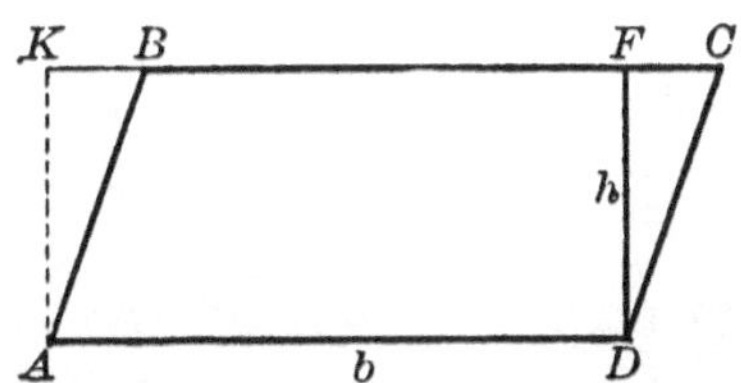

Given the $\square$ *ABCD* with the base *AD* (denoted by b) and the altitude *DF* (denoted by h).

To prove area of $ABCD = bh$.

Proof. 1. From *A* draw *AK* ∥ *DF*, and meeting *CB* produced at *K*.	1. § 95, Post. 2.
2. Then, $AK \perp CK$.	2. § 100.
3. ∴ *AKFD* is a rectangle with base b and altitude h.	3. § 149.
4. In the rt. △ *AKB* and *DFC*, $AB = DC$.	4. Why?
5. And $AK = DF$.	5. Why?
6. Hence, △ $AKB = △ DFC$.	6. Why?
7. Subtract each of these equal △ in turn from the figure *AKCD*; then, $\square ABCD = $ rectangle *AKFD*.	7. Why?
8. But area of rectangle *AKFD* $= bh$.	8. Why?
9. ∴ area of $\square ABCD = bh$.	9. Why? Q.E.D.

340. Cor. 1. *Parallelograms which have equal bases and equal altitudes are equivalent.*

341. Cor. 2. *Parallelograms which have equal bases are to each other as their altitudes;*

Parallelograms which have equal altitudes are to each other as their bases.

342. Cor. 3. *Any two parallelograms are to each other as the products of their bases and altitudes.*

Ex. 1. The base of a parallelogram is 1 ft. 8 in. and the altitude is 1 ft. Find the area of the parallelogram in square inches.

Ex. 2. The area of a parallelogram is 255.78 sq. ft. and the base is 12.6 ft. Find the altitude.

Proposition V. Theorem

343. *The area of a triangle is equal to half the product of its base and its altitude.*

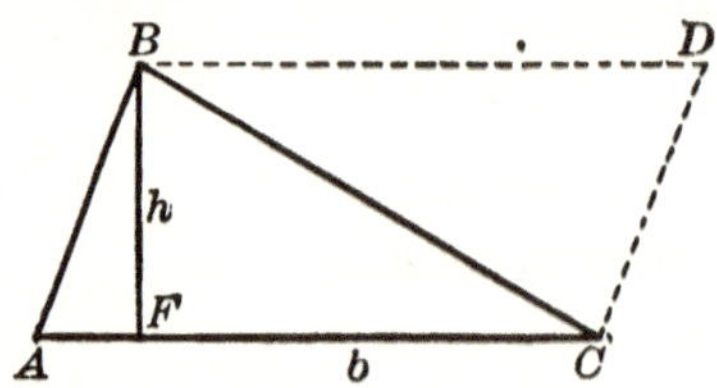

Given the $\triangle ABC$ with the base AC (denoted by b), and the altitude FB (denoted by h).

To prove area of $\triangle ABC = \frac{1}{2} bh$.

Proof. 1. Draw $BD \parallel AC$, and $CD \parallel AB$.   1. § 95.

2. Then $ABDC$ is a parallelogram and BC is one of its diagonals.   2. § 146.

3. $\therefore \square ABDC = 2 \triangle ABC$.   3. § 156.

4. But   area $ABDC = bh$.   4. Why?

5. Hence, $2 \triangle ABC = bh$.   5. Ax. 1.

6. $\therefore$ area of $\triangle ABC = \frac{1}{2} bh$.   6. Ax. 5.

                                                      Q.E.D.

344. Cor. 1. *Triangles which have equal bases and equal altitudes (or which have equal bases in the same straight line and their vertices in a line parallel to the base) are equivalent.*

345. Cor. 2. *Triangles which have equal bases are to each other as their altitudes ;*

Triangles which have equal altitudes are to each other as their bases.

346. Cor. 3. *Any two triangles are to each other as the products of their bases and altitudes.*

347. Cor. 4. *A parallelogram is equivalent to twice a triangle having the same base and altitude.*

Ex. 1. Find the area of a triangle whose base is 17.06 in. and whose altitude is 8.9 in.

Ex. 2. The area of a given triangle is 180 sq. in. and the base is 1 ft. 3 in. Find the altitude in feet and inches.

Proposition VI. Theorem

348. *The area of a rhombus is equal to half the product of the diagonals of the rhombus.*

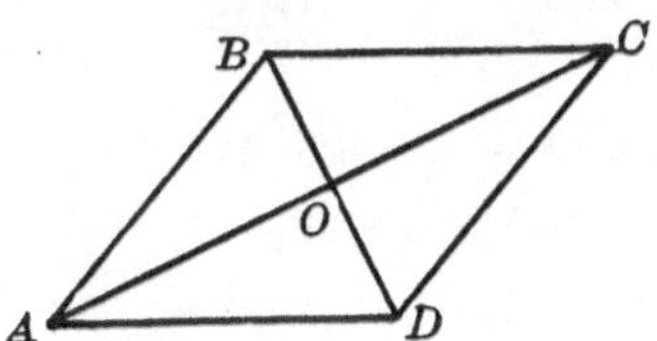

Given the rhombus $ABCD$ with the diagonals AC and BD.

To prove area of $ABCD = \frac{1}{2} AC \times BD$.

Proof.		
1.	$AB = BC.$	1. § 148.
2.	$AD = DC.$	2. Why?
3.	$\therefore BD \perp AC.$	3. § 121.
4.	Area of $\triangle ABC = \frac{1}{2} AC \times BO.$	4. § 343.
5.	Area of $\triangle ADC = \frac{1}{2} AC \times OD.$	5. Why?
6.	$\therefore \triangle ABC + \triangle ADC = \frac{1}{2} AC(BO + OD).$	6. Why?
7.	$\therefore$ Area of $ABCD = \frac{1}{2} AC \times BD.$	7. Ax. 7.

Q.E.D.

349. Cor. *If the diagonals of a quadrilateral are perpendicular to each other, the area of the quadrilateral is equal to half the product of the diagonals.*

Ex. 1. The diagonals of a rhombus are 1 yd. and 1 ft. Find the area of the rhombus in square feet.

Ex. 2. The area of a given rhombus is 256 sq. in. and one diagonal is double the other. Find the diagonals.

EXERCISES: GROUP 61

Ex. 1. D is the midpoint of the base AC of the triangle ABC. The altitude of the triangle is 10 in. and the base is 14 in. Construct the figure and find the area of the triangle ABD, and of the triangle DBC.

Ex. 2. **Given** PTR a straight line; $PT = TR$. **Prove** the $\triangle PQT$ and TQR equal in area.

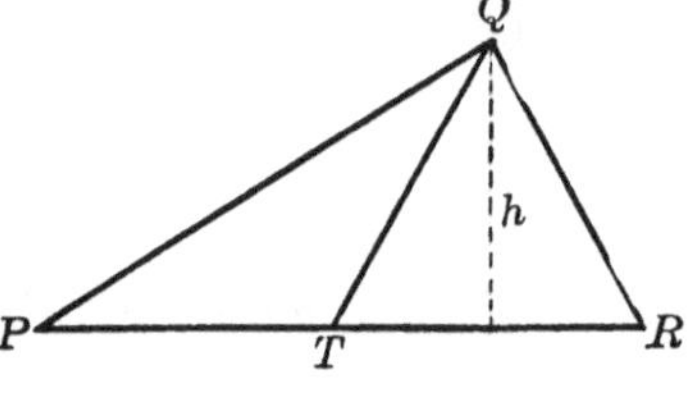

Ex. 3. Prove that the diagonals of a parallelogram divide the parallelogram into four equivalent triangles.

Ex. 4. If the area of a triangle is 96 sq. in. and its altitude is 1 ft., find the base in feet and inches.

Ex. 5. The base of a given triangle is 14.4 ft. and the altitude is 3.2 ft. Find the side of a square whose area is equivalent to that of the given triangle.

Ex. 6. Why is a square whose side is some unit of length (as 1 ft. or 1 in.) a more convenient unit of area than an equilateral triangle whose side is a unit of length?

Ex. 7. Find the area of each of the following cellar floors by dividing them into rectangles.

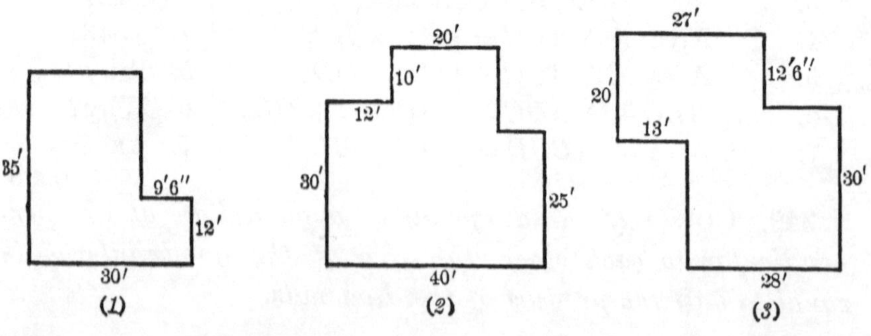

Proposition VII.   Theorem

350. *The area of a trapezoid is equal to the product of its altitude and half the sum of its parallel sides.*

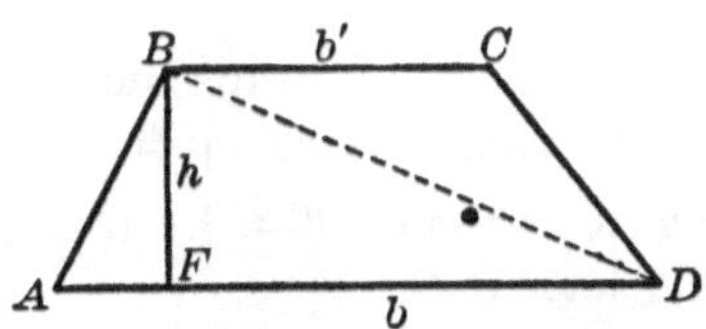

Given the trapezoid $ABCD$ with the bases AD and BC (denoted by b and b'), and the altitude FB (denoted by h).

To prove area of $ABCD = \frac{1}{2} h (b + b')$.

Proof. 1. Draw the diagonal BD.	1. Post. 1.
2. $ABCD = \triangle ABD + \triangle BCD$.	2. Ax. 7.
3. h is the altitude of both $\triangle ABD$ and $\triangle BCD$.	3. § 158.
4. Area of $\triangle ABD = \frac{1}{2} bh$.	4. Why?
5. Area of $\triangle BCD = \frac{1}{2} b'h$.	5. Why?
6. $\therefore \triangle ABD + \triangle BCD = \frac{1}{2} h(b+b')$.	6. Ax. 2.
7. $\therefore$ Area of $ABCD = \frac{1}{2} h(b+b')$.	7. Ax. 1. Q.E.D.

351. The area of a polygon of four or more sides can usually be found in one of several ways; as:

By dividing the polygon into triangles and taking the sum of the areas of the triangles; or,

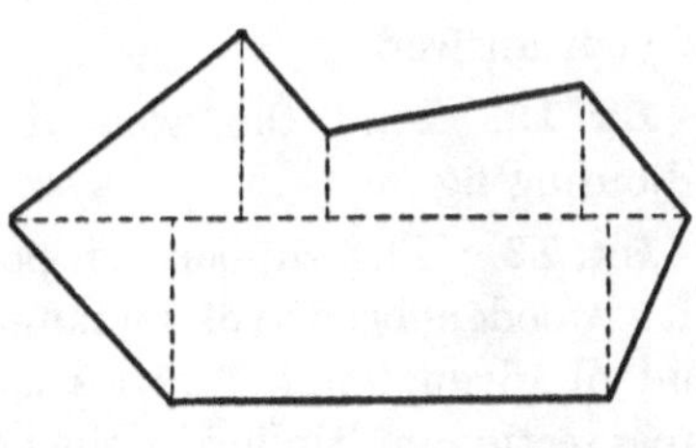

By drawing the longest diagonal of the polygon and drawing perpendiculars to this diagonal from the vertices which it does not meet, and obtaining the sum of the areas of the triangles, rectangles, and trapezoids thus formed.

EXERCISES: GROUP 62

Ex. 1. The bases of a trapezoid are 3 ft. 6 in. and 2 ft. 8 in., and the altitude is 2 ft. 2 in. Find its area in square inches.

Ex. 2. If the area of a trapezoid is 135, and its bases are 12 and 18, find its altitude.

Ex. 3. Find the altitude of a trapezoid in which the bases are 1.4 ft. and 2.5 ft. and the area is 4.368 sq. ft.

Ex. 4. By solving the formula $K = \frac{1}{2} h (b + b')$, find the value of b in terms of the other letters.

Ex. 5. The cross section of a railroad cutting is a trapezoid, the width at the bottom being 12.4′, the width at the top 32.4′, and the depth 7.5′. Find the area of the cross section.

Ex. 6. The measurement of the area of a parallelogram reduces to the measurement of what two straight lines?

Ex. 7. The measurement of the area of a triangle reduces to the measurement of what lines?

Ex. 8. The measurement of the area of a trapezoid reduces to the measurement of what lines?

Ex. 9. The perimeters of two triangles are 12 in. and 3 in. respectively, and each of the triangles has a base of 1 in. Is it possible for these triangles to have the same area? Draw a rough sketch to illustrate your answer.

Ex. 10. Make up and work a similar example concerning two parallelograms.

Ex. 11. Can two squares with different perimeters have the same area? Give a numerical illustration of your answer.

Ex. 12. Find the area of the adjoining figure.

Ex. 13. The supporting power of a wooden beam (of rectangular cross section and of given length) varies as the area of the cross section multiplied by the height of the beam. If the cross section of a given beam is 4″ × 8″, compare the supporting power of the beam when it rests on the narrow edge (4″) with its supporting power when it rests on its wide edge (8″).

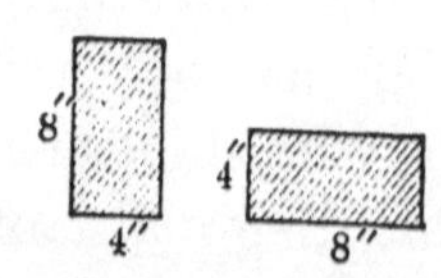

Ex. 14. The diagonal PR of the parallelogram $PQRS$ is produced to the point T. Prove that the triangles PQT and PST are equal in area.

Ex. 15. On squared paper, locate the polygon whose vertices are $(0, 0)$, $(3, 6)$, $(7, 2)$, $(10, 8)$, $(12, 0)$, $(8, -4)$, $(4, -4)$, and determine its area.

What is this area, if one linear space on the squared paper represents 10 ft.?

PROPOSITION VIII. THEOREM

352. *The areas of two similar triangles are to each other as the squares of any two corresponding sides.*

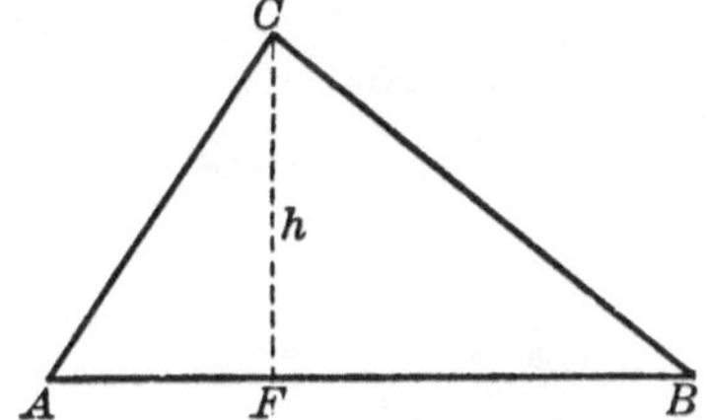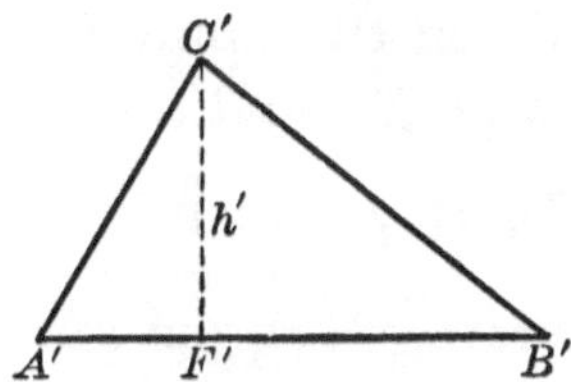

Given the similar $\triangle\ ABC$ and $A'B'C'$ with AB and $A'B'$ corresponding sides.

To prove $\dfrac{\triangle ABC}{\triangle A'B'C'} = \dfrac{\overline{AB}^2}{\overline{A'B'}^2}.$

Proof. 1. Draw the corresponding altitudes h and h'.   1. § 129.

2. $\dfrac{\triangle ABC}{\triangle A'B'C'} = \dfrac{AB \times h}{A'B' \times h'} = \dfrac{AB}{A'B'} \times \dfrac{h}{h'}.$ 2. § 346.

3. But $\dfrac{h}{h'} = \dfrac{AB}{A'B'}.$ 3. § 316.

4. Substituting $\dfrac{AB}{A'B'}$ for its equal $\dfrac{h}{h'}$,   4. Ax. 9.

$$\dfrac{\triangle ABC}{\triangle A'B'C'} = \dfrac{AB}{A'B'} \times \dfrac{AB}{A'B'} = \dfrac{\overline{AB}^2}{\overline{A'B'}^2}.$$

                                Q.E.D.

Ex. If a pair of corresponding sides of two similar triangles are 4 ft. and 5 ft., find the ratio of the areas of the triangles.

PROPOSITION IX. THEOREM

353. *The areas of two similar polygons are to each other as the squares of any two corresponding sides.*

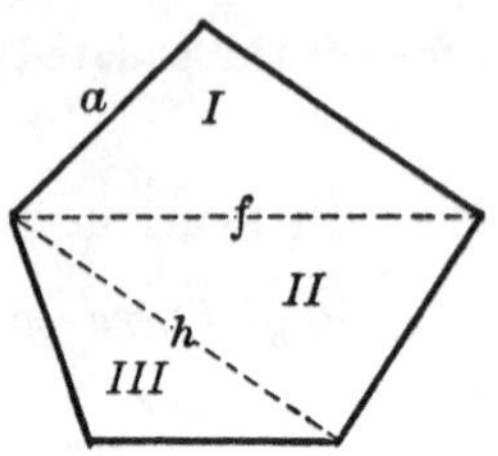
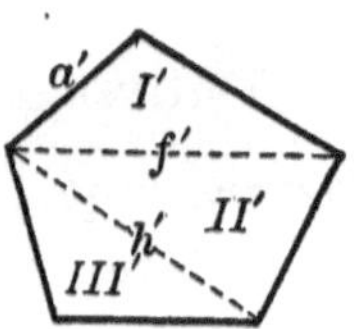

Given two similar polygons with their areas denoted by K and K', and a and a' any pair of corresponding sides.

To prove $K : K' = a^2 : a'^2$.

Proof. 1. From any pair of corresponding vertices, draw the corresponding diagonals f and f', and h and h'. — 1. Post. 1.

2. These diagonals will divide the polygons into pairs of similar triangles, denoted by I, I'; II, II'; and III, III', respectively. — 2. § 312.

3. But $\dfrac{I}{I'} = \dfrac{a^2}{a'^2}$. — 3. § 352.

4. Then $\dfrac{I}{I'} = \left(\dfrac{f^2}{f'^2}\right) = \dfrac{II}{II'} = \left(\dfrac{h^2}{h'^2}\right) = \dfrac{III}{III'}$. — 4. § 352, Ax. 1.

5. $\therefore \dfrac{I}{I'} = \dfrac{II}{II'} = \dfrac{III}{III'}$. — 5. Ax. 1.

6. Hence, $\dfrac{I + II + III}{I' + II' + III'} = \dfrac{I}{I'} = \dfrac{a^2}{a'^2}$. — 6. § 289, Ax. 1.

7. $\therefore \dfrac{K}{K'} = \dfrac{a^2}{a'^2}$. — 7. Ax. 7.

Q.E.D.

354. COR. *The areas of two similar polygons are to each other as the squares of their perimeters, or of any two of their corresponding lines.*

Proposition X. Theorem

355. *The square on the hypotenuse of a right triangle is equivalent to the sum of the squares on the other two sides.*

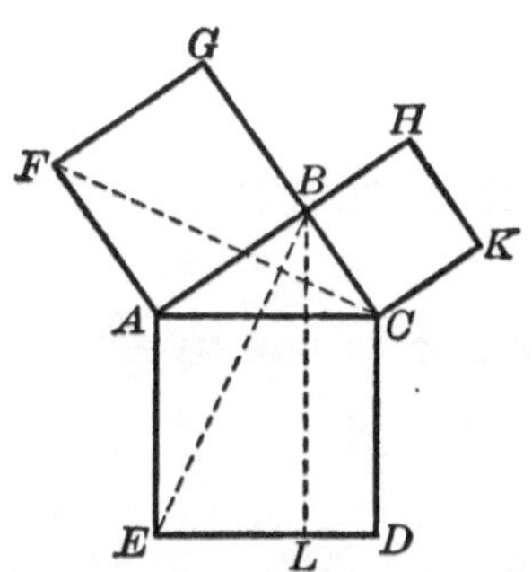

Given AD the square on AC the hypotenuse of the rt. $\triangle ABC$, and BF and BK the squares on the legs BA and BC, respectively.

To prove $AD = BF + BK$ (or $\overline{AC}^2 = \overline{AB}^2 + \overline{BC}^2$).

Proof. 1. Through B draw $BL \parallel AE$ and meeting ED at L. Draw BE and FC.	1. § 95, Post. 1.
2. $\angle s\ ABC$ and ABG are rt. $\angle s$.	2. Why?
3. $\therefore GBC$ is a straight line.	3. Why?
4. In $\triangle s\ BAE$ and FAC, $AB = AF$, $AE = AC$.	4. Why?
5. $\angle BAC = \angle BAC$.	5. Why?
6. $\angle CAE = \angle FAB$.	6. Why?
7. $\therefore \angle BAE = \angle FAC$.	7. Ax. 2.
8. $\therefore \triangle BAE = \triangle FAC$, and $2\triangle BAE = 2\triangle FAC$.	8. Why?
9. Rectangle AL and $\triangle BAE$ have the base, AE, and the altitude, EL.	9. § 158.
10. $\therefore$ Rectangle $AL = 2\triangle BAE$.	10. § 347.
11. So, square $BF = 2\triangle FAC$.	11. §§ 158, 347.
12. $\therefore$ Rectangle $AL =$ square BF.	12. Ax. 1.
13. In like manner, $LC = BK$.	13. Reasons 1–12.
14. $\therefore\ AL + LC$, or $AD = BF + BK$.	14. Axs. 2, 7. **Q.E.D.**

If the teacher prefers, the following proof of Prop. X may be used:

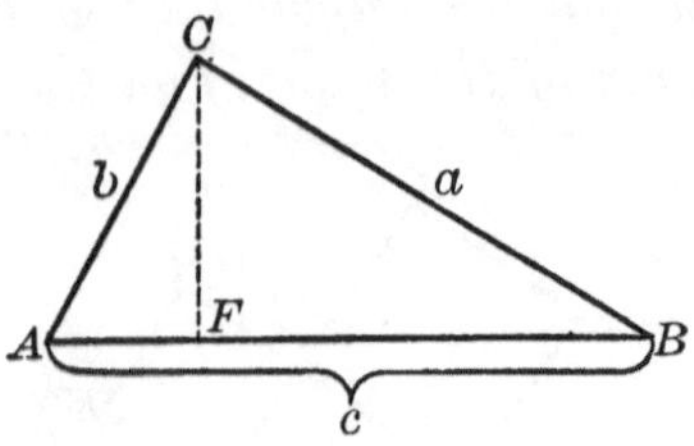

Given the rt. $\triangle ABC$ with the hypotenuse AB denoted by c, and the legs by a and b.

To prove $c^2 = a^2 + b^2$.

Proof. 1. Draw $CF \perp AB$.	1. § 129.
2. Then $c : a = a : BF$.	2. § 319.
3. $\therefore BF \times c = a^2$.	3. § 278.
4. Also $c : b = b : AF$.	4. Why ?
5. $AF \times c = b^2$.	5. Why ?
6. $BF \times c + AF \times c = a^2 + b^2$.	6. Ax. 2.
Or $(BF + AF)c = a^2 + b^2$.	
7. But $BF + AF = c$.	7. Why ?
8. $\therefore c^2 = a^2 + b^2$.	8. Ax. 9.

Q.E.D.

356. Cor. *The square on either leg of a right triangle is equivalent to the square on the hypotenuse diminished by the square on the other leg.*

Ex. 1. Find the hypotenuse of a right triangle in which the legs are 12 in. and 5 in.

Ex. 2. A certain ladder is 17 ft. long and is placed with its foot 8 ft. from the bottom of a building. How far up the side of the building will the top of the ladder reach?

Ex. 3. Find the area of a rectangle whose diagonal is 20 in. and one of whose sides is 16 in.

Ex. 4. Find the area of a square whose diagonal is 10 in.

Ex. 5. Find the altitude of an equilateral triangle whose side is 24 in.

Ex. 6. Two sides of a parallelogram are 20 ft. and 10 ft., and the angle between them is 60°. Find the area of the parallelogram.

Ex. 7. Two sides of a triangle are 24 in. and 18 in., and the angle between them is 45°. Find the area of the triangle.

Ex. 8. Find the area of a rectangle whose diagonal is b, and one of whose sides is a.

Ex. 9. Two poles are 20 ft. and 38 ft. high, respectively. The distance between the poles is 60 ft. Find the distance between their tops.

EXERCISES: GROUP 63

THEOREMS CONCERNING AREAS

Ex. 1. Any straight line drawn through the point of intersection of the diagonals of a parallelogram divides the parallelogram into two equivalent parts.

Ex. 2. If, in the triangle ABC, D and F are the midpoints of the sides AB and AC, respectively, the area of ADF equals one fourth the area of ABC. (Use § 352.)

Ex. 3. If the midpoints of two adjacent sides of a parallelogram are joined, the area of the triangle so formed equals one eighth the area of the parallelogram.

Ex. 4. If, in the triangle ABC, D and F are the midpoints of the sides AB and AC, respectively, the triangles ADC and AFB are equivalent.

Ex. 5. In a right triangle show, by obtaining expressions for the area of the figure, that the product of the legs equals the product of the hypotenuse by the altitude upon the hypotenuse.

Ex. 6. If two triangles are equivalent, and the altitude of one is three times the altitude of the other, find the ratio of their bases.

Ex. 7. If two isosceles triangles have their legs equal, and if half of the base of one is equal to the altitude of the other, the triangles are equivalent.

Ex. 8. The area of an isosceles right triangle equals one fourth of the square on the hypotenuse of the right triangle.

[SUG. Denote the hypotenuse by h and a leg by x. Then show that $\frac{1}{2} x^2 = \frac{1}{4} h^2$.]

Ex. 9. The line joining the midpoints of the parallel sides of a trapezoid divides the trapezoid into two equivalent parts.

Ex. 10. Given AOC and BOD **straight lines and** $OB = OD$. **Prove the** $\triangle\,ABC$ **and** ADC **equivalent.**

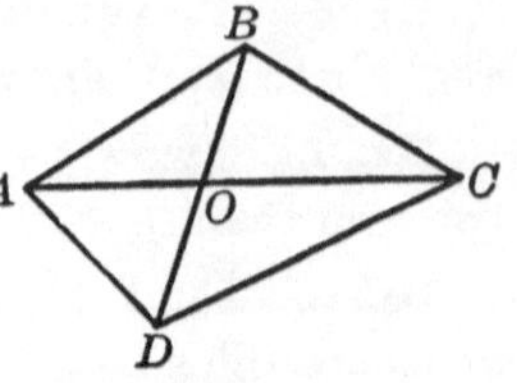

Ex. 11. Given QR and TS **passing through** P, any point on the diagonal AC of a $\square$, $QR \parallel AD$, and $TS \parallel AB$. **Prove the** $\boxed{s}\,QBTP$ and $PRDS$ **equivalent.**

Ex. 12. The lines joining the midpoint of one diagonal of a quadrilateral to the vertices not joined by the diagonal divide the quadrilateral into two equivalent parts.

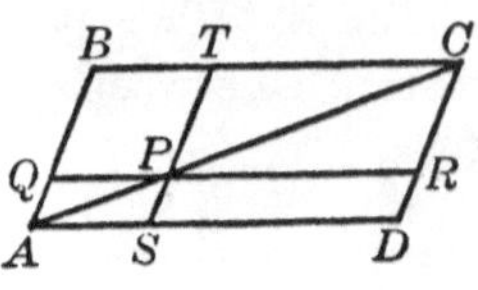

EXERCISES: GROUP 64

NUMERICAL PROPERTIES OF LINES (OR AREAS)

Ex. 1. If AD is the altitude of the triangle ABC, $\overline{AB}^2 - \overline{AC}^2 = \overline{BD}^2 - \overline{DC}^2$.

Ex. 2. If the diagonals of a quadrilateral are perpendicular to each other, the sum of the squares of one pair of opposite sides equals the sum of the squares of the other pair of sides.

Ex. 3. The square of the altitude of an equilateral triangle is three fourths the square of one side.

Ex. 4. If AB is the hypotenuse of a right triangle, and the leg BC is bisected at K, $\overline{AB}^2 - \overline{AK}^2 = 3\,\overline{CK}^2$.

Ex. 5. PQ is a line parallel to the hypotenuse AB of a right triangle ABC, and meeting AC in P and BC in Q. Prove $\overline{AQ}^2 + \overline{BP}^2 = \overline{AB}^2 + \overline{PQ}^2$.

Ex. 6. In the right triangle ABC, BE and CF bisect the legs AC and AB in the points E and F. Prove $4\,\overline{BE}^2 + 4\,\overline{CF}^2 = 5\,\overline{BC}^2$.

Ex. 7. Prove geometrically that $(a + b)^2 = a^2 + b^2 + 2\,ab$.

Ex. 8. Similarly, prove $(a - b)^2 = a^2 + b^2 - 2\,ab$.

Ex. 9. Similarly, prove $(a + b)(a - b) = a^2 - b^2$.

Ex. 10. Two beams of the same length and material have cross sections which are $2'' \times 4''$ and $3'' \times 8''$, respectively. Find the ratio of the greatest supporting power of the two beams.

Ex. 11. On a given map, a certain country occupies an area of $12\frac{3}{4}$ sq. in. If the scale of the map is 1 inch to 50 miles, find the area of the country in square miles.

EXERCISES: GROUP 65

USE OF AUXILIARY LINES

Ex. 1. **Given** $ABCD$ a $\square$ and P any point inside $ABCD$. **Prove** $\triangle PAD + \triangle PBC = \triangle PAB + \triangle PCD$.

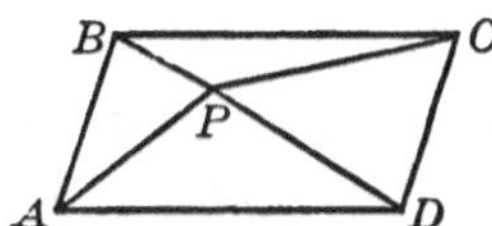

Ex. 2. **Given** $ABCD$ a rectangle. **Prove** $\overline{PA}^2 + \overline{PC}^2 = \overline{PB}^2 + \overline{PD}^2$.

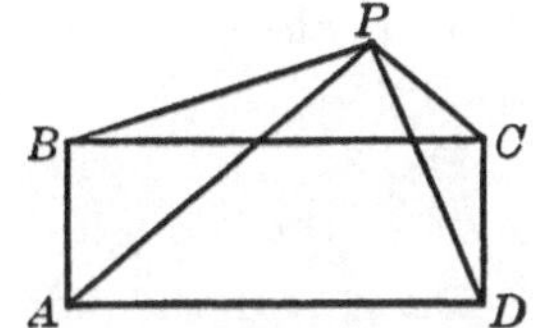

Ex. 3. The area of a triangle is equal to one half the product of its perimeter by the radius of the inscribed circle.

[SUG. If the $\triangle$ is ABC and O is the center of the inscribed circle, draw OA, OB, OC and find the sum of the areas of the $\triangle$ AOC, AOB, BOC.]

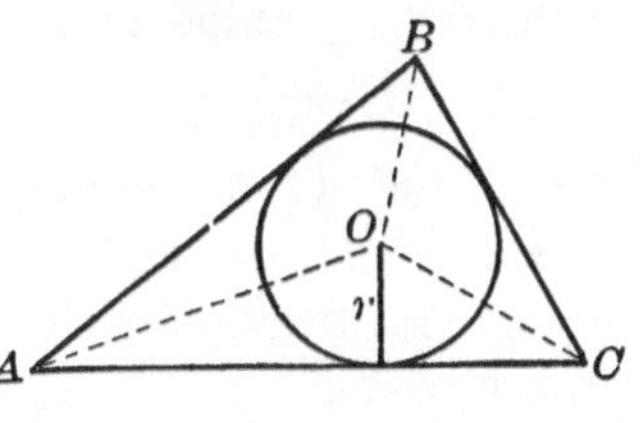

Ex. 4. If the extremities of one leg of a trapezoid are joined to the midpoint of the other leg, the middle one of the three triangles thus formed is equivalent to half the trapezoid.

Ex. 5. The area of a trapezoid is equal to the product of one leg by the perpendicular on that leg from the midpoint of the other leg.

Ex. 6. **Given** the chords AB and CD perpendicular to each other and intersecting at O. **Prove** $\overline{OA}^2 + \overline{OB}^2 + \overline{OC}^2 + \overline{OD}^2 = (\text{diameter})^2$.

[SUG. Draw the diameter BE and the chords AC, BD, DE. Prove $AC = ED$, etc.]

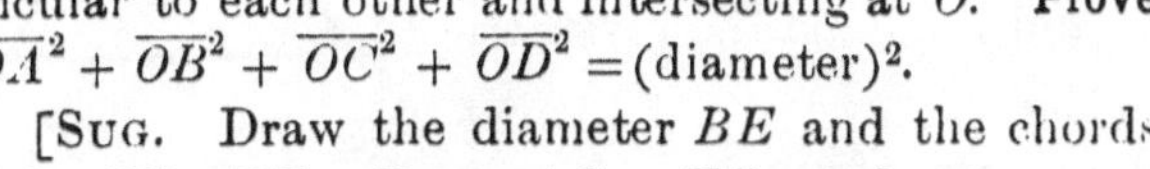

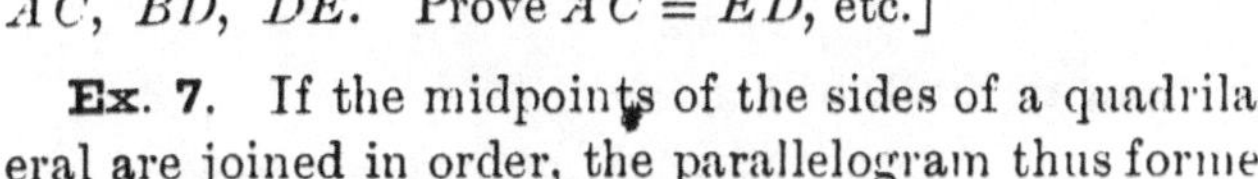

Ex. 7. If the midpoints of the sides of a quadrilateral are joined in order, the parallelogram thus formed is equivalent to one half the quadrilateral.

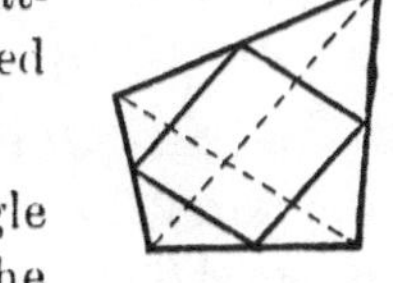

Ex. 8. A quadrilateral is equivalent to a triangle two of whose sides are equal to the diagonals of the quadrilateral, the angle included by these sides being equal to one of the angles formed by the intersection of the diagonals.

EXERCISES: GROUP 66

THEOREMS PROVED BY VARIOUS METHODS

Ex. 1. If through the midpoint of one leg of a trapezoid a line is drawn parallel to the other leg to meet one base and the other base produced, the parallelogram so formed is equivalent to the trapezoid.

Ex. 2. If the midpoints of two sides of a triangle are joined to any point in the base, the quadrilateral so formed is equivalent to half the triangle.

Ex. 3. If P is any point on AC, the diagonal of a parallelogram $ABCD$, the triangles APB and APD are equivalent.

Ex. 4. If the side of an equilateral triangle is denoted by a, the area of the triangle equals $\dfrac{a^2\sqrt{3}}{4}$.

Ex. 5. Find the ratio of the areas of two equilateral triangles, if the altitude of one equals the side of the other.

Ex. 6. If perpendiculars are drawn from any point within an equilateral triangle to the three sides, their sum is equal to the altitude of the triangle.

Ex. 7. If, in the quadrilateral $ABCD$, the triangles ABC and ADC are equivalent, the diagonal AC bisects the diagonal BD.

Ex. 8. If two triangles have two sides of one equal to two sides of the other, and the included angles supplementary, the triangles are equivalent.

Ex. 9. If two triangles have an angle of one equal to an angle of the other, the areas of the triangles are to each other as the products of the sides including the equal angles.

[SUG. Let ABC and ADF be the given triangles.

Then it is required to prove that $\dfrac{\triangle ADF}{\triangle ABC} = \dfrac{AD \times AF}{AB \times AC}$.

Draw BF, and compare each of the given $\triangle$ with ABF.]

Ex. 10. P is any point in the side BC of the parallelogram $ABCD$ and DP produced meets AB produced in Q. Show that the triangles BPA and CPQ are equivalent.

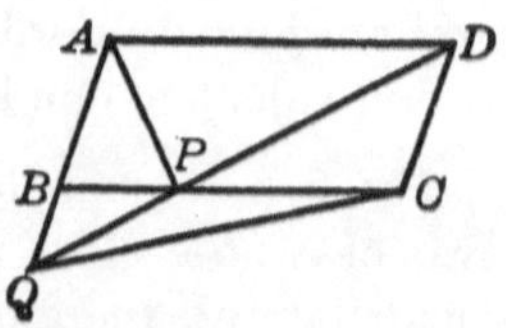

EXERCISES : GROUP 67

PROBLEMS IN CONSTRUCTING AREAS

Ex. 1. Construct a square equivalent to the sum of two given squares.

Ex. 2. Construct a square equivalent to the difference of two given squares.

[SUG. A side of the larger of the two given squares may be taken as the hypotenuse of a right triangle of which a side of the other given square is one leg.]

Ex. 3. Construct a square having twice the area of a given square.

Ex. 4. Construct a square having three times the area of a given square.

Ex. 5. Construct a square equivalent to the sum of three given squares.

Ex. 6. Transform a given triangle into an equivalent isosceles triangle having the same base.

Ex. 7. Transform a given triangle into an equivalent triangle having the same base, but having a given angle adjacent to the base.

Ex. 8. Transform a triangle into an equivalent triangle with the same base, but having another given side.

Ex. 9. Transform a parallelogram into an equivalent parallelogram having the same base, but containing a given angle.

Ex. 10. Construct a triangle similar to a given triangle and containing twice the area.

How is the construction changed to construct a similar triangle containing five times the area?

Ex. 11. Bisect the area of a given triangle by a line parallel to the base.

Ex. 12. Bisect a parallelogram by a line perpendicular to the base.

Ex. 13. Through any given point draw a line bisecting the area of a given parallelogram.

Ex. 14. Construct a square equivalent to a given parallelogram.

[SUG. If b denotes the base and h the altitude of the given parallelogram, and x denotes a side of the required square; then $x^2 = bh$, etc.]

EXERCISES: GROUP 68

PRACTICAL APPLICATIONS

Ex. 1. Find the ratio between the supporting power of a $2'' \times 6''$ beam when placed on a $6''$ side and the supporting power of the same beam when placed on a $2''$ side. Treat similarly a beam $a'' \times b''$.

Ex. 2. How many beams, each $1\frac{1}{2}'' \times 6''$, must be placed on their wide edges to equal in supporting power one beam of the same size when placed on its narrow edge?

Ex. 3. Given a log 12 in. in diameter, find the ratio of the strength of a beam cut from it by the method described in Ex. 6, p. 219, to the strength of a square beam cut from the same log.

Ex. 4. Find the ratio of the strength of a beam cut from the same log by the method of Ex. 6, p. 219, to the strength of a beam cut so that its width equals $\frac{1}{4}$ the diameter of the log.

Ex. 5. When an irregular area like $ABCD$ is calculated by means of equidistant offsets (like AB, DC and the lines $\parallel$ to them in diagram), the following rule is used.

To the half sum of the initial and final offsets add the sum of all the intermediate offsets, and multiply the sum by the common distance between the offsets.

Prove this rule.

Ex. 6. Show how the rule of Ex. 5 could be used to calculate an area whose entire boundary is an irregular curved line.

Ex. 7. Surveyors often determine the area of a piece of land, as of $ABCD$, by taking an auxiliary line as NS, measuring the perpendicular distances from A, B, C, D, E to NS, and the intercepts on NS between these perpendiculars, and combining the areas of the various trapezoids (or triangles) formed. Supply probable numbers for the lengths of lines on the diagram, and compute the area of $ABCDE$.

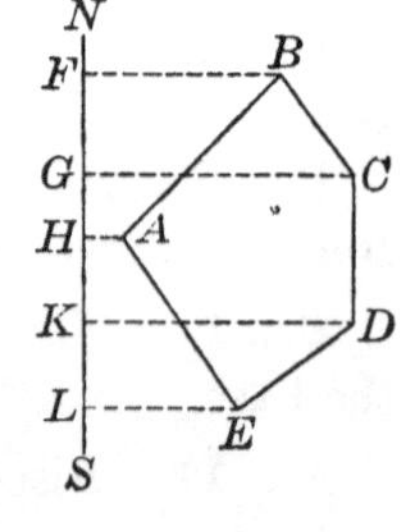

Ex. 8. Frequently (as in the case where the center of the curve cannot be seen from the curve) a railroad curve is laid out by constructing a series of equidistant offsets perpendicular to the tangent of the curve.

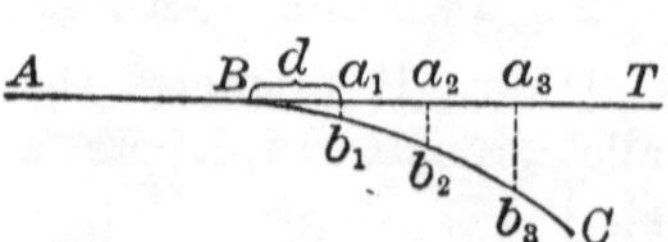

Thus, if ABT is a straight track and BC is a curve to be laid out tangent to AB at B, mark off Ba_1, a_1a_2, a_2a_3, all $= d$, and construct the $\perp$ offsets a_1b_1, a_2b_2, a_3b_3 by using the formula $a_nb_n = r - \sqrt{r^2 - n^2d^2}$ where r is the radius of the curve. Prove that this formula is correct.

Ex. 9. A steamboat is traveling at the rate of 12 mi. an hour, and a boy walks across her deck at right angles to her line of motion at the rate of 3 mi. an hour. Draw a diagram to show the direction of the boy's resultant motion. From this, determine the speed at which he is going.

Ex. 10. Make up and work a similar example concerning a mail bag thrown from a train.

Ex. 11. Also concerning a breeze blowing into a window of a moving trolley car.

Ex. 12. Two forces, one of 300 lb., the other of 400 lb., act at right angles on the same body. Find their resultant.

Ex. 13. Make up and work an example similar to Ex. 12.

Ex. 14. A river is flowing at a rate of 4.25 mi. per hour, and a man is rowing at right angles with the current at a rate of 3.75 mi. per hour. What is the resultant velocity of the man?

Ex. 15. If a star has a velocity of 15 mi. a second toward the earth and a velocity of 20 mi. a second at right angles with a line drawn from the star to the earth, find the velocity of the star in its own path.

Ex. 16. Using the fact that a triangle whose sides are 3, 4, and 5 units of length is a right triangle, show how, by stretching a 100-ft. tape, to construct a right angle as accurately as possible. (Among the ancient Egyptians a class of workmen existed called rope stretchers, whose business it was to construct right angles in this general way.)

Ex. 17. It is customary for carpenters to express the pitch of a roof as the quotient obtained by dividing the height (BD) of the peak above the span (AC) by the span.

Thus, if $AC = 2\,BD$, the pitch is $\frac{1}{2}$; if $AC = 3\,BD$, the pitch is $\frac{1}{3}$, etc.

If the pitch of a given roof is $\frac{1}{3}$ and the span is 20 ft., compute the length of the rafters, projections at the eaves being neglected. Also show how, if the rafters are 8 in. by 2 in., by use of the carpenter's square the bevel lines at B may be cut. Also those at A.

EXERCISES: GROUP 69

Review Questions

Ex. 1. Construct two triangles which are equivalent but not congruent.

Ex. 2. Construct two rectangles which are equivalent but not congruent.

Give a list of the properties proved in Book IV concerning

Ex. 3.	Triangles.	**Ex. 6.**	The rhombus.
Ex. 4.	Rectangles.	**Ex. 7.**	The trapezoid.
Ex. 5.	Parallelograms.	**Ex. 8.**	Similar polygons.

Ex. 9. In geometry, the expression "the product of the base by the altitude" is an abbreviation for what? In general, "the product of two lines" is an abbreviation for what?

Ex. 10. "The area of a rectangle divided by the base" is an abbreviation for what?

Ex. 11. How many sides of a right triangle is it necessary to measure in order to determine all of the sides of the right triangle? What, then, is the efficiency value of Prop. X?

Ex. 12. State the efficiency value of Prop. IV. Of Prop. V.

Ex. 13. State the efficiency value of Prop. VII. Of Prop. VIII.

Ex. 14. Prop. X is sometimes called the Pythagorean Theorem. Find out and state why it has this name.

Ex. 15. In order to find the area of a quadrilateral whose sides taken in order are a, b, c, and d, the ancient Egyptians used the formula $\left(\dfrac{a+c}{2}\right)\left(\dfrac{b+d}{2}\right)$. State for what classes of quadrilaterals this formula will give the correct area. When the formula is incorrect does it give an area which is too large or too small?

BOOK FIVE

REGULAR POLYGONS; MEASUREMENT OF THE CIRCLE

357. A **regular polygon** is a polygon that is both equilateral and equiangular.

358. Efficiency principle. — Many of the properties of regular polygons are best obtained by the aid of circles. On the other hand, certain important properties of circles are derived to the best advantage by the use of regular polygons.

PROPOSITION I. THEOREM

359. *An equilateral polygon inscribed in a circle is a regular polygon.*

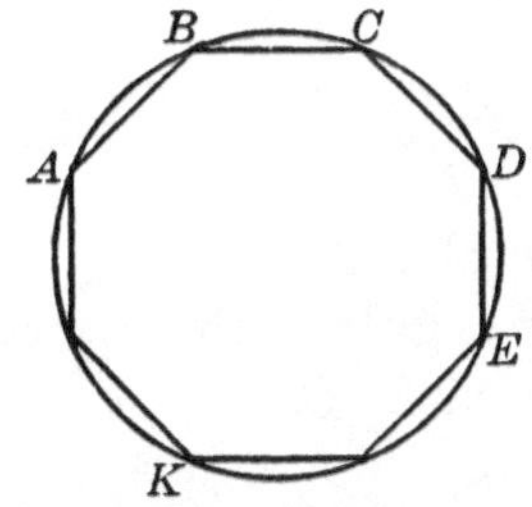

Given $ABC \ldots K$ an inscribed polygon, with its sides AB, BC, CD, etc., equal.

To prove that $ABC \ldots K$ is a regular polygon.

Proof.	
1. $\overset{\frown}{AB} = \overset{\frown}{BC} = \overset{\frown}{CD}$, etc.	1. § 198.
2. $\therefore \overset{\frown}{ABC} = \overset{\frown}{BCD} = \overset{\frown}{CDE}$, etc.	2. Ax. 2.
3. $\therefore \angle ABC = \angle BCD = \angle CDE$, etc.	3. § 237.
4. Hence, polygon $ABC \cdots K$ is regular.	4. § 357. Q.E.D.

247

PROPOSITION II. PROBLEM

360. *To inscribe a square in a given circle.*

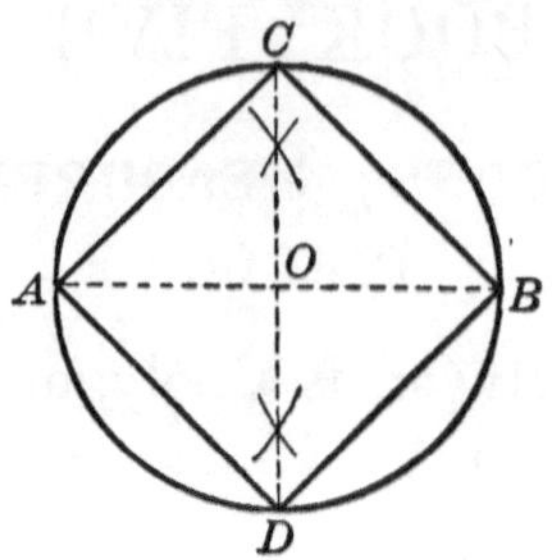

Given the circle O.

To inscribe a square in the circle O.

Construction. 1. Draw any diameter, AB, of the circle O.	1. Post. 1.
2. At O construct the line $CD \perp AB$ and meeting the circle at the points C and D.	2. § 85.
3. Draw the chords AC, CB, BD, DA. Then $ACBD$ is the square required.	3. Post. 1.
Proof. 1.	1. § 63.
$\quad \angle AOC = \angle COB = \angle BOD = \angle DOA.$	
2. $\overset{\frown}{AC} = \overset{\frown}{CB} = \overset{\frown}{BD} = \overset{\frown}{DA}.$	2. § 195.
3. $\therefore$ chord $AC =$ chord CB, etc.	3. § 200.
4. Hence, $ACBD$ is regular; that is, is a square inscribed in the circle O.	4. §§ 359, 150.
	Q.E.F

361. COR. *By bisecting the arcs AC, CB, BD, etc., and drawing chords, a regular octagon may be inscribed in the circle; by repeating the process, regular polygons of 16, 32, 64, . . . and 2^n sides may be inscribed, where n is a positive integer greater than 1.*

Ex. In the shortest way, find the ratio of the areas of two squares whose diagonals are 9 in. and 24 in., respectively. (Use § 354.)

Proposition III. Problem

362. *To inscribe a regular hexagon in a given circle.*

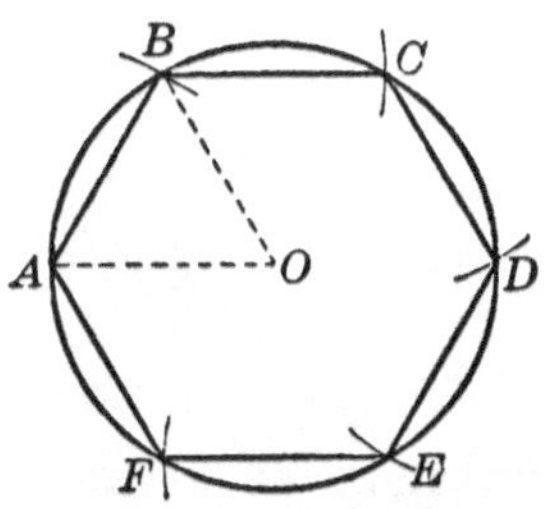

Given the circle O.

To inscribe a regular hexagon in the circle O.

Construction and Proof.

1. Draw any radius OA.	1. Post. 1.
2. With A as a center and AO as a radius, describe an arc intersecting the circle in B.	2. Post. 3.
3. Draw BO.	3. Post. 1.
4. Then $\triangle ABO$ is equilateral.	4. Ax. 1, § 73.
5. ∴ $\angle O = 60°$.	5. § 106.
6. Hence, $\overset{\frown}{AB} = 60°$, or $\frac{1}{6}$ of the circle.	6. § 230.
7. With B as a center and a radius $= AB$, describe an arc intersecting the circle in C.	7. Post. 3.
8. Then $\overset{\frown}{BC} = \overset{\frown}{AB} = 60°$.	8. § 198.
9. In like manner, construct arcs CD, DE, EF, and FA, each $= 60°$, and draw their chords.	9. Reasons 7–8, Post. 1.
10. Then $ABCDEF$ is a regular hexagon inscribed in the circle O.	10. § 359.

Q.E.F.

363. Cor. 1. *The side of a regular inscribed hexagon equals the radius of a circle.*

364. Cor. 2.   *By joining the alternate vertices of a regular inscribed hexagon, an equilateral triangle can be inscribed in a given circle.*

365. Cor. 3.   *By bisecting the arcs AB, BC, CD, etc. and drawing chords, a regular polygon of 12 sides can be inscribed in a given circle; by repeating the process, regular polygons of 24, 48, ... 3×2^n sides can be inscribed.*

366. A regular pentagon or decagon can be inscribed in a circle by the use of the ruler and compasses, but the consideration of these cases lies beyond the scope of this book.

A regular polygon of seven, nine, or eleven sides cannot be inscribed in a circle by the use of the ruler and compasses.

Proposition IV.   Theorem

367.   *A circle may be circumscribed about any regular polygon, and a circle may also be inscribed in it.*

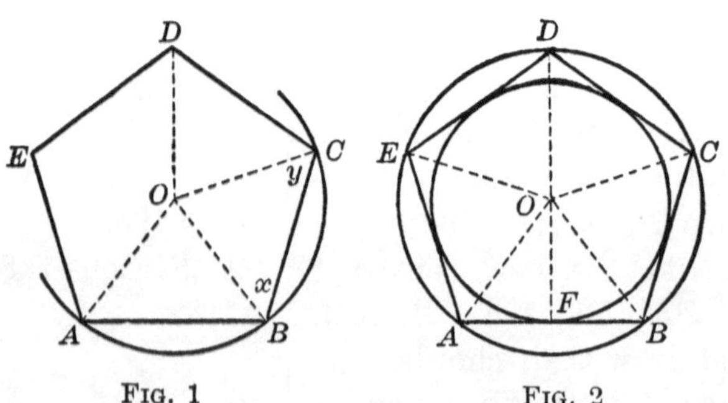

Fig. 1   Fig. 2

Given the regular polygon $ABCDE$.

To prove that a ⊙ may be circumscribed about, or inscribed in, $ABCDE$.

Proof. I. 1. Through A, B, and C (Fig. 1), any three successive vertices of the polygon $ABCDE$, construct a circle, with center O.

1. § 214.

2. Draw the radii OA, OB, OC. Also draw OD.

2. Post. 1.

3. Then, in $\triangle OBC$, $OB = OC$.

3. Why?

4. $\therefore \angle x = \angle y$.

4. Why?

5.   But $\angle ABC = \angle BCD$.

5. § 357.

6.   Hence, $\angle OBA = \angle OCD$.

6. Ax. 3.

7. Hence, in the $\triangle OAB$ and OCD,

                $OB = OC$.

7. Why?

8. $AB = CD$.

8. Why?

9. $\angle OBA = \angle OCD$.

9. Step. 6.

10. $\therefore \triangle ABO = \triangle OCD$.

10. Why?

11. $\therefore OD = OA$.

11. Why?

12. Hence, the circle which passes through the vertices A, B, and C will pass through D also.

12. § 180.

13. In like manner, it may be proved that this circle will pass through the vertex E.

13. Reasons 2–12.

14. Hence, a circle will be circumscribed about the polygon $ABCDE$.

14. § 222.

II. 1. The sides AB, BC, CD, etc. (Fig. 2), of the given polygon are chords in the circumscribed circle.

1. § 184.

2. Construct $OF \perp AB$.

2. § 129.

3. With O as a center and OF as a radius, describe a circle.

3. Post. 3.

4. This circle will touch all the sides of the given polygon.

4. § 207.

5. Hence, a circle will be inscribed in the polygon $ABCDE$.

5. § 223.

Q.E.D.

Ex. 1. How many degrees in each angle of a regular pentagon?

Ex. 2. Prove that the diagonals of a regular pentagon are equal.

EXERCISES: GROUP 70

In a circle whose radius is one inch, inscribe

Ex. 1. A square.   **Ex. 3.** A regular octagon.

Ex. 2. A regular hexagon.   **Ex. 4.** An equilateral triangle.

Ex. 5. On a given line as a side, construct a regular hexagon.

Ex. 6. In a circle whose radius is $1\frac{1}{2}''$, inscribe a regular polygon of 12 sides.

Ex. 7. In a circle whose radius is 3 inches, inscribe a square. Find the length of a side of the square. Also find the area of the square.

Ex. 8. In a given circle, the side of an inscribed square is 1.5 in. Find the radius of the circle.

Ex. 9. A log is 14 inches in diameter. Find a side of the largest square piece of lumber that can be cut from the log.

Ex. 10. The diagonals of a regular quadrilateral are perpendicular to each other.

Ex. 11. A square inscribed in a circle is greater than any other inscribed rectangle.

[Sug. Let the inscribed square and any inscribed rectangle with which it is compared have the same diagonal. Show that this diagonal is a diameter, etc.]

Ex. 12. A cooper, in fitting a head to a barrel, adjusts a pair of compasses till, when applied six times in succession in the chine, they will exactly complete the circumference. He then takes the distance between the points of the compasses as the radius of the head of the barrel. Why is this?

368. The **center of a regular polygon** is the common center of the inscribed and circumscribed circles; as the point O in Fig. 2, p. 250.

369. The **radius of a regular polygon** is the radius of the circumscribed circle; as OA in Fig. 2, p. 250.

370. The **apothem** of a regular polygon is the radius of the inscribed circle; as OF in Fig. 2.

371. The **angle at the center of a regular polygon** is the angle between two radii drawn to the extremities of any side; as the angle AOB.

372. Cor. *The angle at the center of a regular polygon is equal to four right angles divided by the number of sides.*

Hence, if n denotes the number of sides in the polygon, the *angle at the center of a regular polygon equals* $\dfrac{4 \ rt. \ \angle}{n}$.

EXERCISES: GROUP 71

Find the number of degrees in the central angle of

Ex. 1. A regular pentagon.

Ex. 2. A regular hexagon.

Ex. 3. A square.

In a circle whose radius is 10 in., find the apothem and area of

Ex. 4. The inscribed square.

Ex. 5. The regular inscribed hexagon.

In a circle whose radius is b, find the apothem and area of

Ex. 6. The regular inscribed hexagon.

Ex. 7. The inscribed square.

Ex. 8. In a given circle, a side of the inscribed square is 8 in. Find the apothem of this square.

Ex. 9. Prove that in any circle the apothem of the regular inscribed triangle equals half the radius.

[**Sug.** Produce the apothem OD to meet the circle at F. Then use § 121.]

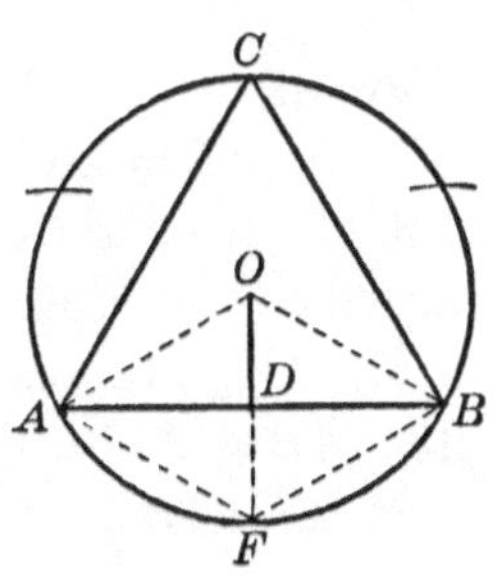

Ex. 10. Find the apothem and area of an equilateral triangle whose side is 6 in.

Ex. 11. Find the radius of an equilateral triangle whose side is $4\sqrt{3}$.

Ex. 12. Diagonals drawn from a vertex of a regular polygon of n sides divide the angle at the vertex into $n - 2$ equal parts.

Ex. 13. Using a scale of 1 in. to 20 ft., construct a drawing to represent a regular hexagonal flower bed each side of which is 15 ft. Also find the area of the flower bed.

Proposition V. Theorem

373. *If a circle is divided into any number of equal parts,*

I. *The chords joining the successive points of division form a regular polygon inscribed in the circle; and*

II. *The tangents drawn at the points of division form a regular polygon circumscribed about the circle.*

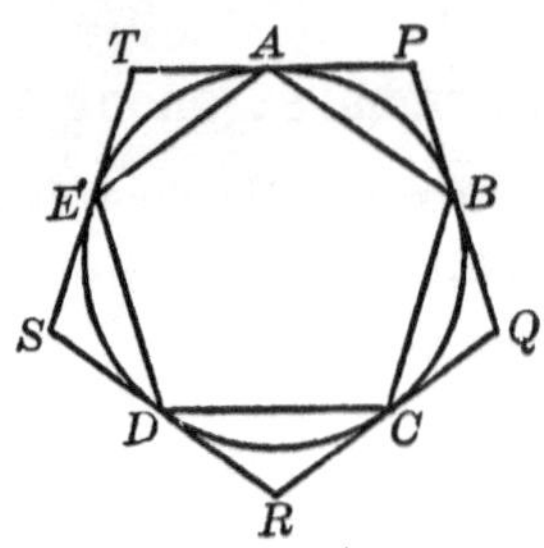

Given the circle ABC divided into the equal arcs AB, BC, CD, etc., the chords AB, BC, etc., and PQ, QR, etc., lines tangent to the circle at B, C, etc.

To prove $ABCDE$ a regular inscribed polygon, and $PQRST$ a regular circumscribed polygon.

Proof. I. 1. $\overset{\frown}{AB} = \overset{\frown}{BC} = \overset{\frown}{CD}$, etc.	1. Why?
2. $\therefore AB = BC = CD$, etc.	2. Why?
3. Hence, $ABCDE$ is a regular inscribed polygon.	3. §§ 359, 222.
II. 1. In the $\triangle APB, BQC, CRD,$ etc., $AB = BC = CD$, etc.	1. Why?
2. $\angle PAB = \angle PBA = \angle QBC$ $= \angle QCB$, etc.	2. § 241.
3. $AP = PB;$ also $BQ = QC$, etc.	3. § 115.
4. $\triangle APB = \triangle BQC = \triangle CRD$, etc.	4. § 80.
5. $\therefore \angle P = \angle Q = \angle R$, etc.	5. Why?
6. $AP = PB = BQ = QC = CR$, etc.	6. Ax. 1.
7. $\therefore PQ = QR = RS$, etc.	7. Ax. 4.
8. $\therefore PQRST$ is a regular circumscribed polygon.	8. §§ 357, 223.

Q.E.D.

374. COR. 1. *If the vertices of a regular inscribed polygon are joined with the midpoints of the arcs subtended by the sides of the polygon, the joining lines will form a regular inscribed polygon of double the number of sides.*

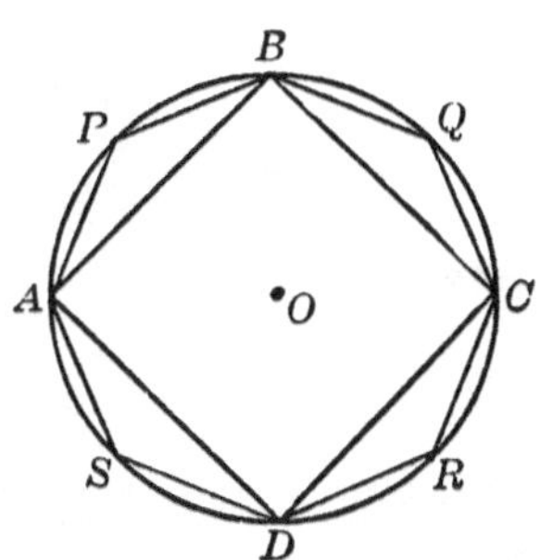

375. COR. 2. *If, at the midpoints of the arcs joining the adjacent points of contact of the sides of a regular circumscribed polygon, tangents are drawn, a regular circumscribed polygon of double the number of sides will be formed.*

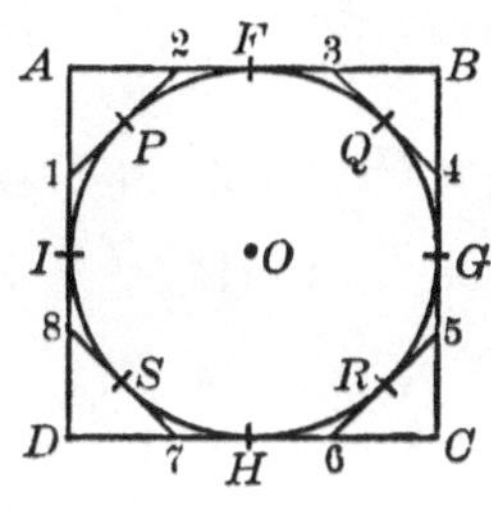

EXERCISES: GROUP 72

About a circle whose radius is one inch, circumscribe

Ex. 1. An equilateral triangle. **Ex. 3.** A regular hexagon.

Ex. 2. A square. **Ex. 4.** A regular octagon.

For a circle whose radius is 10 in., find the area of

Ex. 5. The circumscribed square.

Ex. 6. The inscribed and circumscribed regular triangles.

Ex. 7. Prove that in a given circle the area of the inscribed regular hexagon is double the area of the inscribed regular triangle.

Ex. 8. In any circle, find the ratio of the area of the inscribed square to that of the circumscribed square.

Ex. 9. Find the ratio of the area of the inscribed regular hexagon to that of the area of the circumscribed regular hexagon.

Ex. 10. Construct a six-pointed star (called a hexagram).

Ex. 11. By the aid of squared paper, construct the adjacent design, which shows one of the ways in which a mosaic or pavement may be formed out of regular polygons.

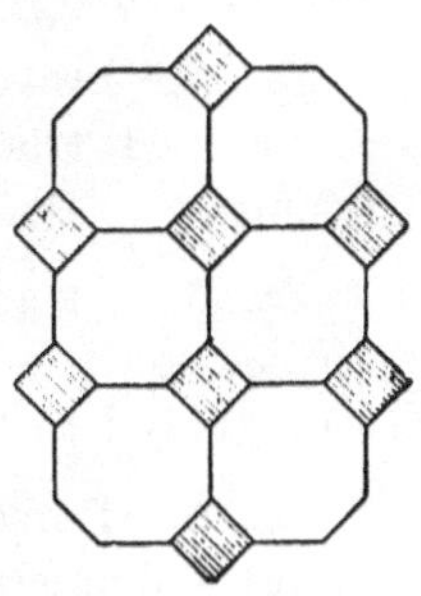

Proposition VI.   Theorem

376. *Two regular polygons of the same number of sides are similar.*

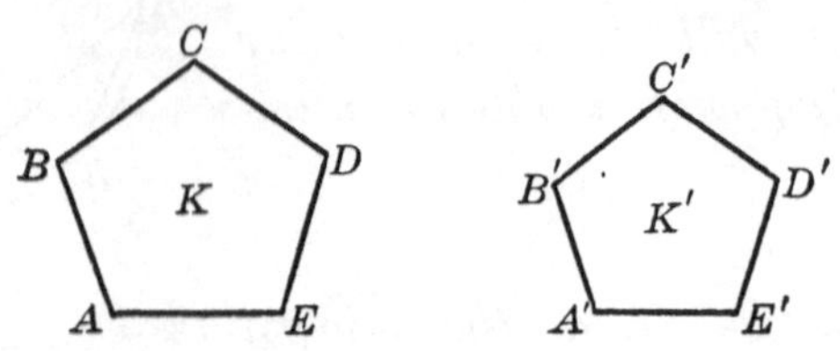

Given K and K' two regular polygons, each of n sides.

To prove K and K' similar.

Proof. 1. Each $\angle$ of $K = \dfrac{2n-4}{n}$ rt. $\angle$s.	1. § 168.
2. Each $\angle$ of $K' = \dfrac{2n-4}{n}$ rt. $\angle$s.	2. Why?
3. Hence, K and K' are mutually equiangular.	3. Ax. 1.
4. Also $\quad AB = BC = CD$, etc.	4. Why?
5. And $\quad A'B' = B'C' = C'D'$, etc.	5. Why?
6. Hence, $\dfrac{AB}{A'B'} = \dfrac{BC}{B'C'} = \dfrac{CD}{C'D'}$, etc.	6. Ax. 5.
7. $\therefore K$ and K' are similar.	7. § 302.

Q.E.D.

Ex. 1.   For a circle whose radius is 8 inches, find the area of the circumscribed regular hexagon. .

Ex. 2.   Prove that in a given circle the side of a regular circumscribed triangle is double the side of the regular inscribed triangle.

Ex. 3.   In any circle prove that the ratio of the area of the inscribed equilateral triangle to the area of the circumscribed equilateral triangle is 1 to 4.

Ex. 4.   Prove that the altitude of an inscribed equilateral triangle is to the diameter of the circumscribed circle as 3 is to 4.

PROPOSITION VII. THEOREM

377. *The perimeters of regular polygons of the same number of sides are to each other as the radii of the circumscribed circles, or as the radii of the inscribed circles.*

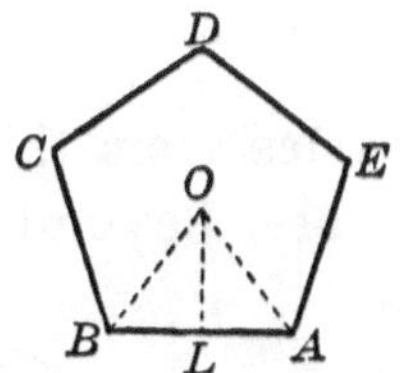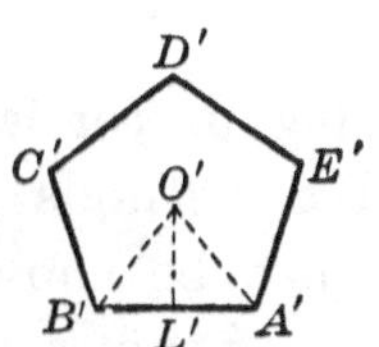

Given AC and $A'C'$ two regular polygons, each of n sides, with centers O and O', with apothems OL and $O'L'$, and with perimeters denoted by p and p', respectively.

To prove $\dfrac{p}{p'} = \dfrac{OA}{O'A'} = \dfrac{OL}{O'L'}$.

Proof. 1. Polygon $AC \sim$ polygon $A'C'$.	1. § 376.
2. $\therefore p : p' = AB : A'B'$.	2. § 317.
3. $\angle BOA = \dfrac{4 \text{ rt. } \angle}{n} = \angle B'O'A'$.	3. § 372, Ax. 1.
4. $OA = OB$, and $O'A' = O'B'$.	4. § 188.
5. $\triangle OAB \sim \triangle O'A'B'$.	5. § 311.
6. $AB : A'B' = OA : O'A' = OL : O'L'$.	6. §§ 302, 316.
7. $p : p' = OA : O'A' = OL : O'L'$.	7. Ax. 1. Q.E.D.

378. Cor. *The areas of regular polygons of the same number of sides are to each other as the squares of the radii of the inscribed, or circumscribed, circles.*

Ex. 1. If the sides of two regular octagons are 3 in. and 6 in., respectively, find the ratio of the perimeters of the octagons. Also the ratio of their areas.

Ex. 2. Find the ratio of the areas of two regular hexagons whose sides are $1\frac{1}{2}$ in. and $2\frac{1}{4}$ in. Also find the ratio of their perimeters. Of their apothems.

Ex. 3. The sides of two regular polygons of the same number of sides are 2.4 in. and 3.6 in. The area of the first polygon is 184.3ʸ sq. in. Find the area of the second polygon.

Ex. 4. Two logs are 12 in. and 15 in., respectively, in diameter. Find the ratio between the area of the cross section of the largest square beam that can be cut from the first log and that cut from the second log. Also of octagonal beams thus cut.

379. Deriving properties of circles from those of regular polygons. — By methods which are beyond the scope of this book, it may be shown that, if the number of sides of a regular inscribed or regular circumscribed polygon is repeatedly doubled, the polygons remaining regular, the perimeter of each of these polygons approaches nearer and nearer to the length of the circle: and also the area of each of these polygons ap-

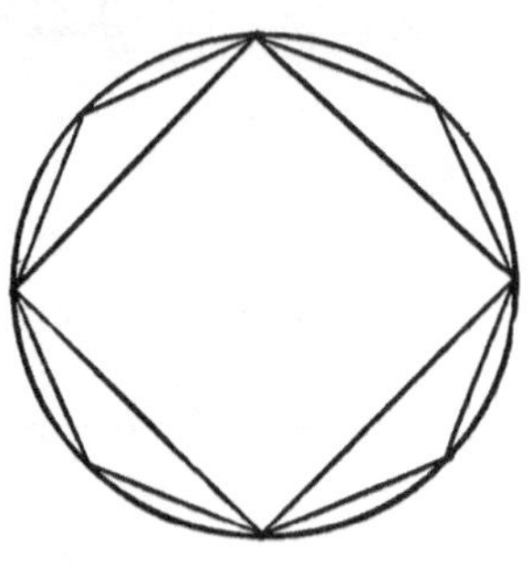

proaches nearer and nearer to the area of the circle.

Hence, we employ the following principle (the proof of which lies beyond the scope of this book) as a means of deriving the properties of circles from those of regular polygons:

Any property of regular polygons which does not depend on the number of the sides of the polygon is true also of circles.

Ex. 1. In a circle whose radius is 10, find the side of the inscribed regular triangle.

Ex. 2. In a circle whose radius is r, show that a side of the regular inscribed triangle is $r\sqrt{3}$.

Ex. 3. In a circle whose radius is 10 in., find the difference between the perimeters of the regular inscribed hexagon and triangle. If the radius of the circle were increased to 20 in., by use of proportion find what the perimeters would become, and then find their difference.

Proposition VIII. Theorem

380. *The circumferences of two circles are to each other as the radii.*

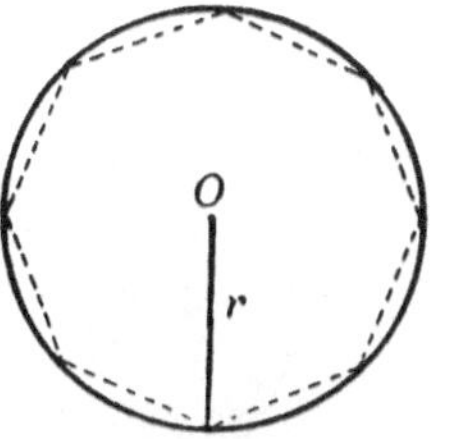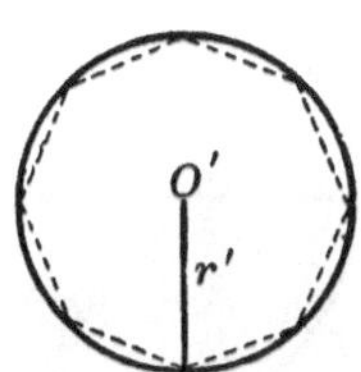

Given the circles O and O' with circumferences denoted by c and c', and radii by r and r', respectively.

To prove $c : c' = r : r'$.

Proof. 1. In the given circles, let regular polygons of the same number of sides be inscribed, and denote their perimeters by p and p'.

    1. § 361.

2. $p : p' = r : r'$.

    2. § 377.

3. Hence, $c : c' = r : r'$.

    3. § 379.

        Q.E.D.

381. Cor. *The circumferences of two circles are to each other as their diameters.* For, denote the circumferences by c and c'. Then

$$\frac{c}{c'} = \frac{r}{r'}\,(\S\,380) = \frac{2\,r}{2\,r'}\,(\S\,227) = \frac{d}{d'}\,(\S\,189).$$

Ex. 1. If the diameter of the earth is approximately 8000 miles and that of the moon is 2000 miles, find the ratio of the lengths of the equators of the two globes.

Ex. 2. In a circle whose radius is 6 in., find the difference between the areas of the inscribed regular hexagon and triangle. Also the difference between the areas of the inscribed square and equilateral triangle.

Ex. 3. On a line $1\frac{1}{4}$ in. long as a chord, construct a segment of a circle which shall contain an angle of 45°. Also a segment containing an angle of 60°. Of 120°.

Proposition IX. Theorem

382. *The ratio of the circumference of any circle to its diameter is constant.*

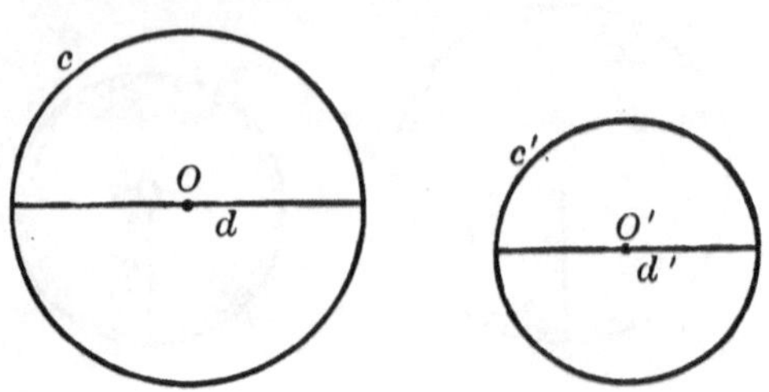

Given the circle O with its circumference denoted by c and its diameter by d.

To prove that the value of $\dfrac{c}{d}$ is always the same, no matter what the size of the given circle.

Proof. 1. Construct another circle O' to be used as a standard of reference, and denote its circumference by c' and its diameter by d'.

1. Post. 3.

2. $\dfrac{c}{c'} = \dfrac{d}{d'}.$

2. § 381.

3. $\therefore \dfrac{c}{d} = \dfrac{c'}{d'}.$

3. § 284.

4. Hence, $\dfrac{c}{d}$ has the same value as $\dfrac{c'}{d'}$ in the standard circle; that is, $\dfrac{c}{d}$ is constant.

4. § 249.

Q.E.D.

383. Formulas for the circumference. — If we denote the constant $\dfrac{c}{d}$ by the symbol π, $\dfrac{c}{d} = \pi$; hence, $c = \pi d$.

Also, since $d = 2\,r$, $c = \pi(2\,r) = 2\,\pi r$.

384. Numerical value of π. — By means of methods which are beyond the scope of this book, it is found that, when expressed as a number, $\pi = 3.141592^{+}$. A convenient approximation to this value is $\pi = \tfrac{22}{7}$.

385. Formula for length of arc of a circle. —

$$\frac{\text{arc}}{\text{circumference}} = \frac{\text{central} \angle}{360°} (\S\ 229) \therefore \text{arc} = \frac{\text{central} \angle}{360°} \times 2\,\pi r.$$

$$\therefore \text{arc} = \frac{\text{central} \angle}{180°} \times \pi r.$$

EXERCISES : GROUP 73

Using $\pi = \frac{22}{7}$, find the circumference of the circle in which

Ex. 1. $r = 1\frac{1}{4}$ in.   **Ex. 3.** $r = 1\frac{3}{4}$ ft.   **Ex. 5.** $d = 3.25$ ft.

Ex. 2. $d = 21$ in.   **Ex. 4.** $d = 2\frac{1}{2}$ yd.   **Ex. 6.** $r = .0158$ in.

Ex. 7. To how many decimal places is $\frac{22}{7}$ a correct value for π?

Find the radius and diameter of the circle in which the circumference is

Ex. 8.   88 in.   **Ex. 10.** $\frac{22}{21}$ in.

Ex. 9.   13.2 in.   **Ex. 11.** $18\,\pi$.

Ex. 12.   The diameters of two wheels are 22 in. and 33 in., respectively.   Find the ratio of their circumferences.

Ex. 13.   The circumferences of two hot-air pipes are 25 in. and 35 in., respectively.   Find the ratio of the diameters of the pipes.

In a circle whose diameter is 14 in., find the length of an arc of
Ex. 14. 60°.   **Ex. 15.** 75°.   **Ex. 16.** 117°.   **Ex. 17.** 22° 45′.

Ex. 18.   A wheel with 6 cogs is geared to a wheel with 48 cogs. How many revolutions will the smaller wheel make while the larger wheel revolves once?

Ex. 19.   In a circle whose radius is 21 in., a certain arc is 33 in. long.   How many degrees are there in this arc?

Ex. 20.   How many degrees are there in an arc 5.5 ft. long, if the radius of the circle is 14 ft.?

Ex. 21.   How many degrees in an arc 25 ft. long, if the radius of the circle is 10 ft.?

Ex. 22.   If the radius of a circle is multiplied by 3, by what number is the circumference multiplied?

Ex. 23.   In a circle whose radius is $1\frac{1}{2}$ in., construct a segment which shall contain an angle of 45°.   Of 60°.

Ex. 24.   Draw two circles whose radii are 1 and $1\frac{1}{2}$ in., respectively, and in each circle construct a segment containing an angle of 120°.

Proposition X.   Theorem

386. *The area of a regular polygon is equal to half the product of its perimeter and its apothem.*

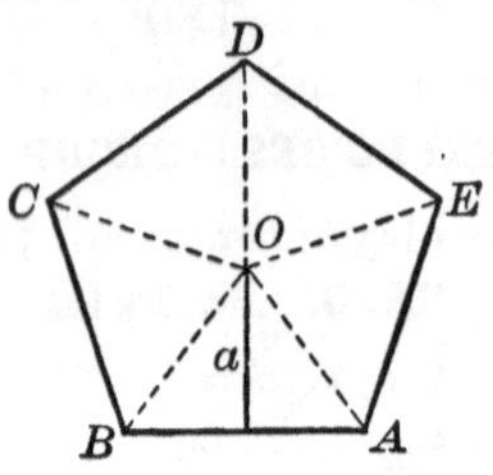

Given the regular polygon $ABCDE$ with area denoted by K, perimeter by p, and apothem by a.

To prove $K = \frac{1}{2} ap$.

Proof. 1. Draw the radii OA, OB, OC, etc., dividing the polygon into as many △ as the polygon has sides. | 1. Post. 1.

2. All of these △ have the same altitude, a. | 2. § 188.

3. Area of each $\triangle = \frac{1}{2}$ product of its base by a. | 3. § 343.

4. Hence, sum of areas of △ $= \frac{1}{2}$ (sum of bases of △) $\times a = \frac{1}{2} ap$. | 4. Axs. 2, 7.

5. $\therefore K = \frac{1}{2} ap$. | 5. Ax. 9.   Q.E.D.

387.   A **sector** of a circle is the figure formed by two radii and the arc intercepted by them.

388. Similar sectors are sectors in different circles which have equal angles at the center.

389. Similar segments are segments in different circles whose arcs subtend equal angles at the center.

Ex. In a given circle construct a segment which is greater than the sector with the same arc.

Proposition XI. Theorem

390. *The area of a circle is equal to half the product of its circumference and its radius.*

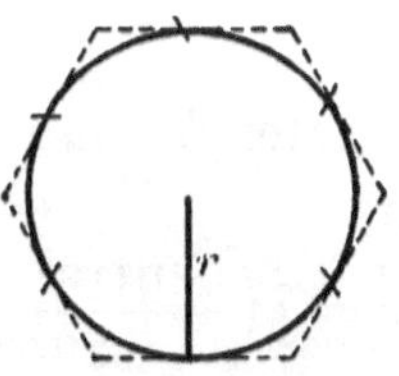

Given a $\odot$ with circumference denoted by c, radius by r, and area by K.

To prove $K = \frac{1}{2}\, rc$.

Proof. 1. Circumscribe a regular polygon about the given circle, and denote its perimeter by p, and its area by K'.	1. §§ 362, 373.
2. The apothem of the circumscribed regular polygon is the radius of the given circle, or r.	2. § 370.
3. $K' = \frac{1}{2}\, rp$.	3. § 386.
4. $\therefore K = \frac{1}{2}\, rc$.	4. § 379. Q.E.D.

391. Formulas for the area of a circle. — Substituting for c its value $2\,\pi r$ (§ 383),

$$K = \tfrac{1}{2}(2\,\pi r)\, r, \text{ or } K = \pi r^2.$$

Again, $r = \frac{1}{2}\, d$. $\therefore K = \frac{1}{4}\,\pi d^2$.

392. Cor. 1. *The area of a circle is equal to the square of the radius, multiplied by π; or to one fourth the square of the diameter, multiplied by π.*

393. Cor. 2. *The areas of two circles are to each other as the squares of their radii, or as the squares of their diameters.* The reason for this is as follows:

Denoting the areas of any two circles by K and K', their radii by r and r', and their diameters by d and d', respectively,

$$\frac{K}{K'} = \frac{\pi r^2}{\pi r'^2} = \frac{r^2}{r'^2}; \quad \text{also} \quad \frac{K}{K'} = \frac{\frac{1}{4}\pi d^2}{\frac{1}{4}\pi d'^2} = \frac{d^2}{d'^2}.$$

394. The **area of a sector** *is equal to one half the product of its radius by its arc.*

Hence, area of sector $= \frac{1}{2}\left(\dfrac{\text{central } \angle}{180°} \times \pi r\right) r.$ (§ 385.)

Or area of sector $= \dfrac{\text{central } \angle}{360°} \times \pi r^2.$

395. Cor. 3. *Similar sectors are to each other as the squares of their radii.*

EXERCISES: GROUP 74

Using $\pi = \frac{22}{7}$, find the area of a circle in which

Ex. 1. $r = 14$ in.   **Ex. 3.** $r = .014$ ft.   **Ex. 5.** $d = 2\frac{3}{4}$ in.

Ex. 2. $d = 21$ in.   **Ex. 4.** $d = .28$ in.   **Ex. 6.** $r = 1\frac{1}{2}$ in.

Ex. 7. $r = a$ ft.   **Ex. 8.** $d = \frac{1}{4}a$ ft.

Find the area of the circle in which the circumference is

Ex. 9. 176 ft.   **Ex. 10.** 1.32 in.   **Ex. 11.** $2\frac{2}{11}$ in.   **Ex. 12.** $36\,\pi$.

Ex. 13. The circumference of a hot-air pipe is 22.5 in. Find the area of a cross section of the pipe.

Ex. 14. If the radius of one circle is 10 times as great as the radius of another, find the ratio of the areas of the circles. Also of their circumferences. Of their diameters.

Ex. 15. Assuming that the amount of water flowing through a pipe is proportional to the area of the cross section, a 2-in. pipe will discharge how many times as much water in a given time as a 1-in. pipe?

Ex. 16. The side of a square inscribed in a given circle is 6 in. Find the area of the circle.

Find the radius of a circle of which the area is

Ex. 17. 1386. **Ex. 18.** $16\,\pi b^2$. **Ex. 19.** $400\,\pi$.   **Ex. 20.** 100 sq. ft.

Ex. 21. In a circle whose radius is 14 in., find the area of a sector of 60°. Of 80°. Of 21°.

Find the area of a circle

Ex. 22. Whose radius is b ft.; $\frac{1}{2}b$ ft.; $2b$ ft.

Ex. 23. Whose radius is $\frac{1}{2}R$; $2R$; $R\sqrt{3}$.

Ex. 24. Whose diameter is $\frac{1}{2}R$; $R\sqrt{2}$; $\frac{1}{2}R\sqrt{2}$.

Ex. 25. In heating a house by a hot-air furnace, the area of the cross section of the cold-air box should equal the sum of the areas of the pipes conducting hot air from the furnace. If a given furnace has three hot-air pipes, each 6″ in diameter, and one pipe 8″ in diameter, and the width of the cold-air box is 15″, how deep should the box be?

Ex. 26. What is the most convenient way of determining the diameter of a hot-air pipe if you have no callipers and the ends of the pipe are not accessible?

Ex. 27. A belt runs over two wheels one of which has a diameter of 3 ft. and the other of 6 in. If the first wheel is making 120 revolutions per minute, how many is the second wheel making. How many revolutions per minute must the first wheel make in order that the second may make 300 revolutions in the same time?

Assuming (what is not strictly true, owing to friction against the sides of the pipe, etc.) that the rate of flow through a cylindrical pipe is proportional to its area of cross section :

Ex. 28. If a $1\frac{1}{2}$-in. pipe is replaced by a 1-in. pipe, how much is the flow of water decreased?

Ex. 29. A 3-in. pipe is to be replaced by one which will deliver not less than twice as much water per minute. Find, to the nearest quarter of an inch, the diameter of the new pipe.

Ex. 30. A city of 40,000 people is barely supplied with water by 12-in. mains from the reservoirs. If these mains are torn out, and 18 in. mains substituted, what future population of the city is allowed for?

Ex. 31. The weight which a round (cylindrical) bar of metal will sustain suspended from its end is proportional to the area of the cross section of the bar. A steel bar 1 in. in diameter will hold up 50,000 lb. What load would be sustained by a bar of the same material $\frac{3}{4}$ in. in diameter? What would be the diameter of a cylindrical bar which is to sustain 150,000 lb.?

MAXIMA AND MINIMA

PROPOSITION XII. THEOREM

396. *Of all triangles which have two sides equal, that triangle in which these sides include a right angle is the maximum.*

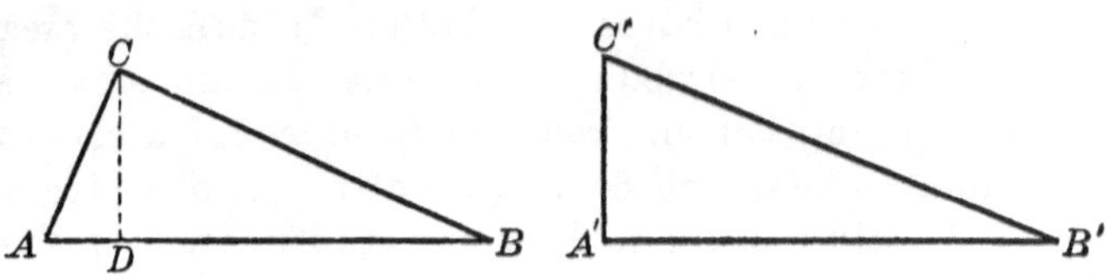

Given the $\triangle\, ABC$ and $A'B'C'$ in which $AB = A'B'$, $CA = C'A'$, $\angle A'$ is a rt. $\angle$, and $\angle A$ an oblique $\angle$.

To prove $\triangle\, A'B'C > \triangle\, ABC$.

Proof. 1. Construct $CD \perp AB$.	1. § 129.
2. Then $\qquad CD < CA$.	2. Why ?
3. $\qquad\qquad \therefore CD < C'A'$.	3. Ax. 9.
4. $\qquad\qquad AB = A'B'$.	4. Hyp.
5. $\therefore$ area $\triangle\, ABC :$ area $\triangle\, A'B'C'$ $\qquad\qquad = CD : C'A'$.	5. § 345.
6. $\qquad \triangle\, A'B'C' > \triangle\, ABC$.	6. For $C'A' > CD$.

Q.E.D.

397. Maximum plane figure of given perimeter. — By methods which are beyond the scope of this book, it may be shown that, for regular polygons having a given perimeter, the greater the number of sides, the greater the area; and hence that, *of all plane figures having a given perimeter, the circle is the maximum.*

EXERCISES: GROUP 75

Ex. 1. Find the minimum line that can be drawn having an end in each of two given parallel lines.

Ex. 2. Find the length of the largest stick that can be placed on a rectangular table 12 × 5 ft., and not have an end projecting over a side of the table.

Ex. 3. A grazier has a movable and flexible fence, $\frac{1}{2}$ mile long, with which he incloses his sheep when grazing. Find the difference between the amount of ground inclosed when the fence is arranged in the form of a square and of a circle.

Ex. 4. Find the area of a triangle in which two of the sides are 6 and 12 in., and the included angle is 90°. Find the area of another triangle having two sides of 6 and 12 in., and the included angle 60°.

Ex. 5. How long is the fence about a garden 60 × 40 ft.? How many square feet are there in the area of the garden? Find also the length of fence and area of a garden 50 ft. square.

Ex. 6. Find the area of an equilateral triangle, a square, a hexagon, and a circle, in each of which the perimeter is 1 ft.

Ex. 7. Find the perimeter of an equilateral triangle, a square, and a circle, in each of which the area is 24 sq. in.

SYMMETRY

398. Symmetry of polygons. — Many of the properties of regular figures can be obtained in a simple and expeditious way by the use of the ideas of symmetry.

The principles of symmetry are also useful in treating of such properties of physical bodies as their centers of gravity.

399. An **axis of symmetry** is a line such that, if part of a figure is folded over upon the line as an axis, the part folded over will coincide with the rest of the figure.

EXERCISES: GROUP 76

Ex. 1. How many axes of symmetry has an isosceles triangle? An equilateral triangle?

Ex. 2. How many has a square? A regular pentagon?

Ex. 3. How many has a regular hexagon?

Ex. 4. How many has a regular heptagon? A regular octagon? A regular polygon of n sides? A circle?

Ex. 5. Which capital letters have an axis of symmetry?

400. A **center of symmetry** for a polygon is a point such that any line drawn through the point and terminated by the perimeter is bisected by the point.

EXERCISES: GROUP 77

Ex. 1. Has an equilateral triangle a center of symmetry? Has a square?

Ex. 2. Has a regular pentagon a center of symmetry? Has a regular hexagon?

Ex. 3. In general, which regular polygons have a center of symmetry, and which do not?

Ex. 4. Has a circle a center of symmetry?

Ex. 5. Which is the most symmetrical figure studied thus far?

Ex. 6. A rhombus has how many axes of symmetry? Has it a center of symmetry?

Ex. 7. What axis of symmetry has a quadrilateral which has two pairs of equal adjacent sides?   Has such a figure a center of symmetry?

Ex. 8. Prove that a parallelogram is symmetrical with respect to the point of intersection of its diagonals.

Ex. 9. A segment of a circle is symmetrical with respect to what axis?

Ex. 10. Has a trapezium a center of symmetry? An axis of symmetry?

Ex. 11. How many axes of symmetry have two equal circles taken as one figure? Have they a center of symmetry?

Ex. 12. What axis of symmetry have any two circles?

Ex. 13. Which capital letters have a center of symmetry? Small letters?

EXERCISES: GROUP 78

THEOREMS

Ex. 1. If $ABCDE$ is a regular pentagon, the triangles ABK and ABC are similar.

Ex. 2. In the same figure, $BC = KC$.

Ex. 3. Show that the area of a regular inscribed triangle is $\dfrac{3\sqrt{3}\, r^2}{4}$.

Ex. 4. In a circle whose radius is r, find the difference between the area of an inscribed square and that of an inscribed equilateral triangle.

Ex. 5. In a circle whose radius is r, prove that the side of the inscribed regular octagon is $r\sqrt{2 - \sqrt{2}}$.

Ex. 6. In a circle whose radius is r, prove that the side of an inscribed regular polygon of twelve sides is $r\sqrt{2 - \sqrt{3}}$.

Ex. 7. From a log whose diameter is a inches a rectangular beam is to be cut so as to have a cross section of the greatest possible area. Find a side of the beam.

Ex. 8. The diagonals joining the alternate vertices of a regular hexagon form another regular hexagon. Find also the ratio of the areas of the two hexagons.

Ex. 9. If squares are erected on the sides of a regular hexagon, the lines joining their exterior vertices form a regular dodecagon. Find also the area of this dodecagon in terms of b, a side of the hexagon.

Ex. 10. The area of a circle equals four times the area of a circle described on its radius as a diameter.

Ex. 11. The area of a circular ring equals the area of a circle whose diameter is the chord of the outer circle tangent to the inner circle.

Ex. 12. Given $AaBbC$, AcB, BdC, semicircles; prove that the sum of the two crescents $AcBa$ and $BdCb$ equals the area of the right triangle ABC.

Ex. 13. An equiangular polygon inscribed in a circle is regular if the number of its sides is odd.

[Sug. In the figure of Prop. V, p. 254, arc $AEDC = $ arc $EDCB$. $\therefore$ arc $AE = $ arc BC, $\therefore$ side $AE = $ side BC, etc.]

Ex. 14. An equiangular polygon circumscribed about a circle is regular.

[Sug. Draw radii from the points of contact, and lines from the vertices of the polygon to the center.]

Ex. 15. An equilateral polygon circumscribed about a circle is regular if the number of its sides is odd.

[Sug. See figure of Prop. V, p. 254. Prove $AT = BQ$. Draw radii and prove $\angle T = \angle Q$, etc.]

EXERCISES : GROUP 79

PROBLEMS

Ex. 1. Construct a circumference equal in length to the sum of two given circumferences.

Ex. 2. Construct a circumference equal in length to the difference of two given circumferences.

Ex. 3. Construct a circle whose area is equal to the sum of the areas of two given circles.

Ex. 4. Construct a circle whose area is equal to the difference of the areas of two given circles.

Ex. 5. It is desired to plant 8 trees so that they shall be equidistant from a given point, and also so that each two successive trees shall be 20 ft. apart. Draw a diagram to some definite scale, showing the relative position of the trees.

Ex. 6. Bisect the area of a given circle by drawing another circle concentric with the given one.

Ex. 7. Inscribe a circle in a given sector.

Ex. 8. Inscribe a square in a given segment.

Ex. 9. In a given equilateral triangle, inscribe three equal circles, each of which touches the other two circles and a side of the triangle.

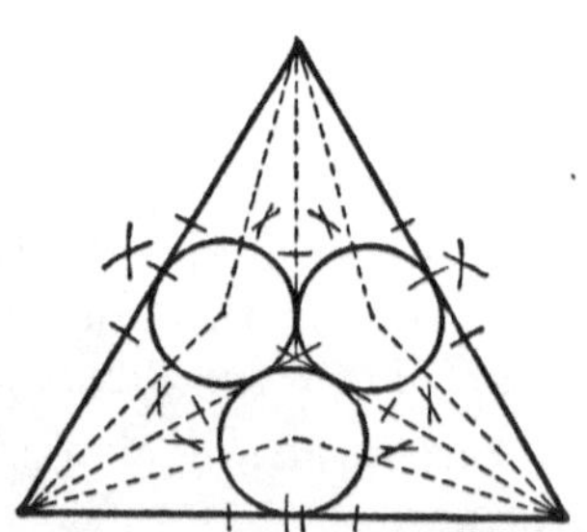

Ex. 10. In a given circle, inscribe three equal circles which shall touch each other and the given circle.

Ex. 11. Inscribe a regular octagon in a given square.

Ex. 12. Construct a circle whose area shall be equal to the area of a given semicircle.

EXERCISES : GROUP 80

PRACTICAL APPLICATIONS

Ex. 1. A half-mile running track is to have equal semicircular ends and parallel straight sides. The extreme length of the rectangle together with the semicircular ends is to be 1000 ft. Find the width of the rectangle.

[Sug. Denote the length of the radius of the semicircular ends by x and that of one of the parallel side straight tracks by y, and obtain a pair of simultaneous equations.]

Ex. 2. If, in laying a track, a rail 10 ft. long is bent through an arc of 5° 10′, what is the radius of the curve?

Ex. 3. A given revolving wheel is liable to fly to pieces if the speed of its outer rim exceeds 5000 ft. per minute. If the diameter of the wheel is 27 in., how many revolutions can the wheel safely make per minute?

Ex. 4. Construct a circular basket by the method indicated by the adjoining diagram. Thus, after drawing two concentric circles, locate the vertices of 1, 2, 3, etc. of the regular hexagon inscribed in the smaller circle. Draw the straight lines as indicated. Cut out the notches $A1B$, $C2D$, $E3F$, etc. Fold up the parts of the outer circular ring which are left, so that B coincides with A, D with C, etc.

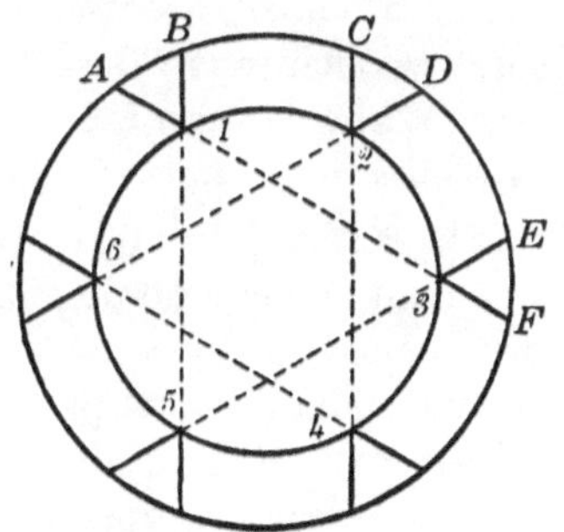

Ex. 5. If the center of symmetry of a flat, homogeneous object is the center of mass, find the center of mass of a square. Of a rectangle. Regular hexagon. Circle.

Ex. 6. If a box has a square end, subject to the same pressure at all points, at what single point on the end must a supporting pressure be applied?

Ex. 7. The cross section of a cylinder is a circle. The weight-supporting strength of a horizontal solid cylindrical beam of given material and length varies as the area of the cross section times its radius.

Compare the weight-supporting power of two solid horizontal iron cylindrical beams of the same length and quality of iron, the radii being 3 in. and 6 in. respectively. (Point out and use the short way of getting the desired result.)

Ex. 8. The cross section of a hollow cylinder (*i.e.* of a tube) is a circular ring. Denote the outside radius of the tube by R and the inside radius by r. Then it may be shown that the weight-supporting power of a hollow cylindrical tube of given length and material varies as the area of the cross section (*i.e.* of the ring) times

$$\frac{R^2 + r^2}{R}.$$

If $R = 4$ in. and $r = 3$ in., compare the weight-supporting power of the tube with that of a solid cylindrical beam of the same length and the same cross-sectional area.

In general, a cylindrical tube is stronger than a solid cylindrical beam of the same length and containing the same amount of material.

Hence, in a framework, as in that of an airship where the maximum strength must be obtained from a given amount of material, the metallic rods and posts are all tubular. In like manner, bamboo rods, since they are hollow, are used in an aëroplane instead of solid wooden rods wherever possible. For the same reason, the bones of flying birds, and many bones in men and animals, are hollow and not solid.

Ex. 9. Adjoining is a picture of the drawing instrument called a 60-degree triangle. By use of this instrument (or by constructing equilateral triangles and constructing lines parallel to their sides) form several sheets of paper ruled similarly to squared paper except that the lines on them intersect at angles of 60° instead of 90°, thus:

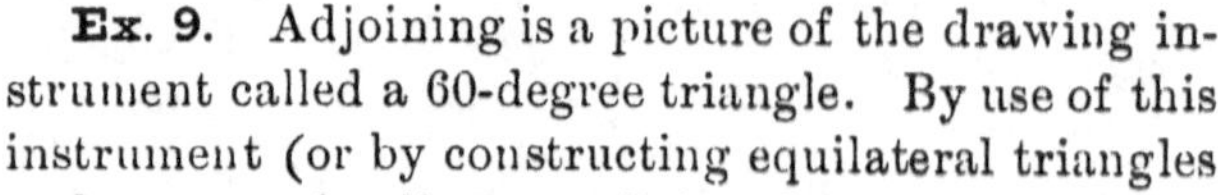

Ex. 10. By the aid of paper ruled as in Ex. 9, construct the following designs, which illustrate the way in which a mosaic or pavement may be formed of regular polygons.

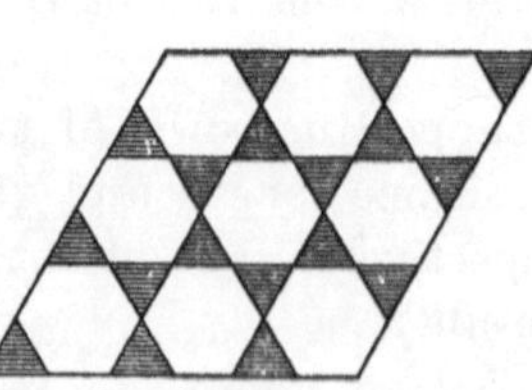
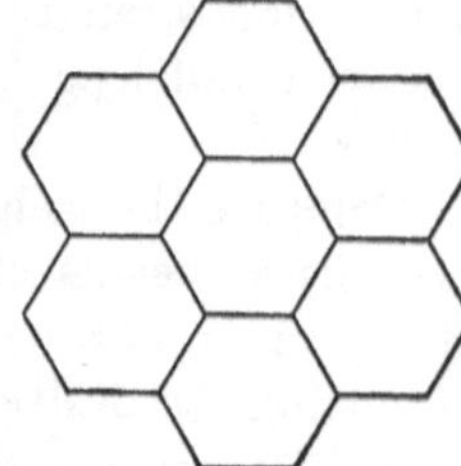

Ex. 11. To construct a square which shall be approximately equivalent to a given circle O, divide the radius OA into four equal

parts, produce each end of two perpendicular diameters a distance equal to one fourth of the radius, and connect the extremities of the lines thus formed. Show that taking the square thus formed as equivalent to the circle is the same as taking $\pi = 3\frac{1}{8}$. Also find the per cent of error in taking this square as equivalent to the circle.

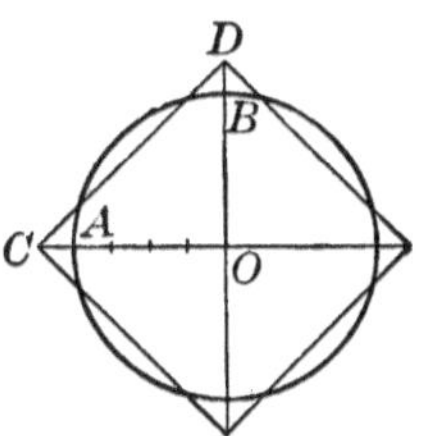

Ex. 12. A short way to construct a regular inscribed pentagon and also a five-pointed star (or pentagram) is as follows: Draw a circle O and two diameters AB and CD at right angles. Bisect the radius OB at F, and with F as a center and FC as a radius describe an arc cutting AO at H. Then CH is the length of a side of the regular inscribed pentagon. By joining the alternate vertices of this pentagon, the pentagram (or 5-pointed star) may be formed.

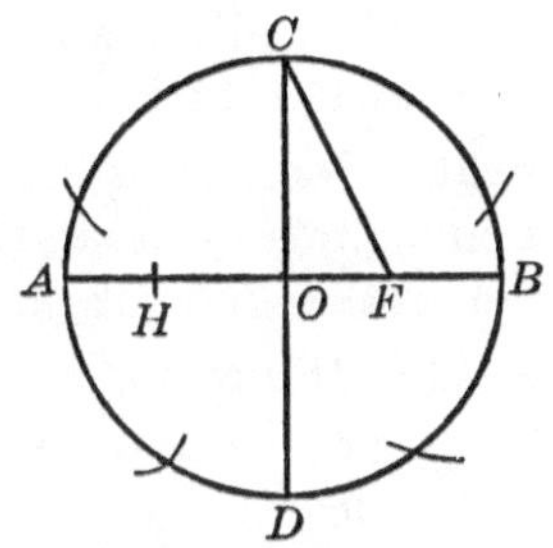

Ex. 13. Construct a square. Take each vertex of the square as a center and one half a side of the square as a radius and outside of the square describe arcs which meet. Erase the square and you have a quatrefoil. By drawing other circles and arcs of circles, elaborate the quatrefoil into an ornamental design. (See the figure for Ex. 14, p. 176.)

Ex. 14. In like manner, construct a cinquefoil by use of a regular pentagon, and develop it into an ornamental design.

Ex. 15. Treat a regular hexagon in the same way.

EXERCISES: GROUP 81

REVIEW OF BOOK V

Ex. 1. Construct a regular polygon of three sides and on it mark its center, radius, and apothem.

Ex. 2. The measurement of the area of a circle can be reduced to the measurement of the length of what single straight line? Can it be reduced to the measurement of any other single straight line? To the measurement of a single curved line?

Ex. 3. What is the efficiency value of Prop. XI?

Ex. 4. Of Prop. IX? Of Prop. X?

Ex. 5. State some of the ways in which circles aid in dealing with regular polygons.

Ex. 6. State some of the ways in which regular polygons aid in dealing with circles.

Ex. 7. When are two regular polygons similar?

Ex. 8. The circumferences of two circles are c and c', respectively. In terms of c and c', give the ratio of the diameters of these circles. Of their radii. Of their areas.

Ex. 9. How does the side of a regular inscribed hexagon compare with the radius in length? How does the apothem of the inscribed equilateral triangle compare with the radius of the circle?

Ex. 10. Name five different regular polygons which you can inscribe in a circle by use of the ruler and compasses. Name five which you cannot thus inscribe in a circle.

Ex. 11. If a and a' are the sides of two regular polygons of the same number of sides, give the ratio of the perimeters of the polygons. Of their radii. Of their apothems. Of their areas.

Give a list of the properties proved or stated in Book V concerning

Ex. 12. A single regular polygon.

Ex. 13. Two regular polygons of the same number of sides.

Ex. 14. A single circle.

Ex. 15. Two or more circles taken together.

Ex. 16. Give an account of the history of the successive approximations which have been made to the value of π. (See p. 281.)

HISTORY OF GEOMETRY

401. Origin of geometry as a science. — The beginnings of geometry as a science are found in Egypt, dating back at least three thousand years before Christ. Herodotus says that geometry, as known in Egypt, grew out of the need of remeasuring pieces of land which had been in part washed away by the Nile floods, in order to make an equitable readjustment of the taxes on the land.

The substance of the Egyptian geometry is found in an old papyrus roll, now in the British Museum. This roll is, in effect, a mathematical treatise written by a scribe named Ahmes at least as early as 1700 B.C., and is, the writer states, a copy of a work dating, say, 3000 B.C.

402. Epochs in the development of geometry. — From Egypt a knowledge of geometry was transferred to Greece, whence it spread to other countries. Hence, we have the following principal epochs in the development of geometry:

1. **Egyptian:** 3000 B.C.–1500 B.C.
2. **Greek:** 600 B.C.–100 B.C.
3. **Hindu:** 500 A.D.–1100 A.D.
4. **Arab:** 800 A.D.–1200 A.D.
5. **European:** 1200 A.D.–

In the year 1120 A.D., Athelard, an English monk, visited Cordova, in Spain, in the disguise of a Mohammedan student, and procured a copy of Euclid in the Arabic language. This book he brought back to central Europe, where it was translated into Latin and became the basis of all geometric study in Europe till the year 1533, when, owing to the capture of Constantinople by the Turks, copies of the works of the Greek mathematicians in the original Greek were scattered through Europe,

HISTORY OF GEOMETRICAL METHODS

403. Rhetorical methods. — By "rhetorical methods" in the presentation of geometric truths, is meant the use of definitions, axioms, theorems, geometric figures, the representation of geometric magnitudes by the use of letters, the arrangement of material in Books, etc. The **Egyptians** had none of these, their geometric knowledge being recorded only in the shape of the solutions of certain numerical examples, from which the rules used must be inferred.

Thales (Greece, 600 B.C.) first made an enunciation of an abstract property of a geometric figure. He had a crude idea of the geometric theorem.

Pythagoras (Italy, 525 B.C.) introduced formal definitions into geometry, though some of those used by him were not very accurate. For instance, his definition of a point is "unity having position." Pythagoras also arranged the leading propositions known to him in something like logical order.

Hippocrates (Athens, 420 B.C.) was the first systematically to denote a point by a capital letter, and a segment of a line by two capital letters (as the line AB), as is done at present. He also wrote the first textbook on geometry.

Plato (Athens, 380 B.C.) made definitions, axioms, and postulates the beginning and basis of geometry.

To **Euclid** (Alexandria, 280 B.C.) is due the division of geometry into Books, the formal enunciation of theorems, the particular enunciation, the formal construction, proof, and conclusion, in presenting a proposition. He also introduced the use of the corollary.

Using these methods of presenting geometric truths, Euclid wrote a textbook of geometry in thirteen books, which was the standard textbook on this subject for nearly two thousand years.

The use of the symbols $\triangle$, $\square$, $\parallel$, etc., in geometric proofs originated in the United States in recent years.

404. Logical methods. — The **Egyptians** used no formal methods of proof. They probably obtained their few crude geometric processes as the result of experiment.

The **Hindus** also used no formal proof. One of their writers on geometry merely states a theorem, draws a figure, and says " Behold ! "

The use of logical methods of geometric proof is due to the **Greeks**. The early Greek geometricians used *experimental methods* at times, in order to obtain geometric truths. For instance, they determined that the angles at the base of an isosceles triangle are equal, by folding half of the triangle over on the altitude as an axis and observing that the angles mentioned coincided as a fact, but without showing that they *must* coincide.

Pythagoras (525 B.C.) was the first to establish geometric truths by systematic *deduction*, but his methods were sometimes faulty. For instance, he believed that the converse of a proposition is necessarily true.

Hippocrates (420 B.C.) used correct and *rigorous deduction* in geometric proofs. He also introduced specific varieties of such deduction, such as the method of *reducing* one proposition to another (§ 269) and the *reductio ad absurdum* (§ 179).

The methods of deduction used by the Greeks, however, were defective in their lack of generality. For instance, it was often thought necessary to have a separate proof of a theorem for each different kind of figure to which the theorem applied. Thus, the theorem that the sum of the angles of a triangle equals two right angles was proved,

(1) for the equilateral triangle by use of the regular hexagon ;

(2) for the right triangle by the use of a rectangle;

(3) for a scalene triangle by dividing the scalene triangle into two right triangles.

The Greeks appeared to fear that a general proof might be vitiated if it were applied to a figure in any way special or peculiar.

Plato (380 B.C.) introduced the method of proof by *analysis*, that is, by taking a proposition as true and working from it back to known truths.   (See § 173.)

To **Eudoxus** (380 B.C.) is virtually due proof by the method of *limits*, though his method, known as the method of exhaustions, is crude and cumbersome.

Apollonius (Alexandria, 225 B.C.) used *projections*, *transversals*, etc., which, in modern times, have developed into the subject of projective geometry.

405. Mechanical methods. — The **Greeks**, in demonstrating a geometrical theorem, usually drew the figure employed in a bed of sand.   This method had certain advantages, but was not adapted to demonstration before a large audience.

At the time when geometry was being developed in Greece, the interest in the subject was very general.   There was scarcely a town but had its lectures on the subject.   The news of the discovery of a new theorem spread from town to town, and the theorem was redemonstrated in the sand of each marketplace.

The Greek treatises, however, were written on vellum or papyrus by the use of the reed, or calamus, and ink.

In **Roman times**, and in the **Middle Ages**, geometrical figures were drawn in wax smeared on wooden boards, called tablets.   They were drawn by the use of the stylus, a metal stick which was pointed at one end for making marks and broad at the other end for erasing marks. These wax tablets were still in use in Shakespeare's time. (See *Hamlet*, Act I, Sc. 5, l. 107.)   The blackboard and crayon are **modern** inventions, their use having developed within the last one hundred years.

The **Greeks** invented many kinds of drawing instruments for tracing various curves. It was due to the influence of Plato (380 B.C.) that, in constructing geometric figures, the use of only the ruler and compasses is permitted.

HISTORY OF GEOMETRIC TRUTHS; PLANE GEOMETRY

406. Rectilinear figures.— The **Egyptians** measured the area of any four-sided field by multiplying half the sum of one pair of opposite sides by half the sum of the other pair; which was equivalent to using the formula,

$$\text{area} = \frac{a+c}{2} \times \frac{b+d}{2}.$$

This, of course, gives a correct result for the rectangle and the square, but gives too great a result for other quadrilaterals, as the trapezoid. Joseph, of the Book of Genesis, in buying the fields of the Egyptians for Pharoah in time of famine by the use of this formula in many cases paid for a larger field than he obtained.

The Egyptians had a special fondness for geometrical constructions, probably growing out of their work as temple builders. A class of workers existed among them called "rope-stretchers," whose business was the marking out of the foundations of buildings. These men knew how to bisect an angle and also to construct a right angle. The latter was probably done by a method essentially the same as forming a right triangle whose sides are three, four, and five units of length. Ahmes, in his treatise, has various constructions of the isosceles trapezoid from different data.

Thales (600 B.C.) enunciated the following theorems :

If two straight lines intersect, the opposite or vertical angles are equal ;

The angles at the base of an isosceles triangle are equal;

Two triangles are equal if two sides and the included angle of one are equal to two sides and the included angle of the other;

The sum of the angles of a triangle equals two right angles ;

Two mutually equiangular triangles are similar.

Thales used the last of these theorems to measure the height of the great pyramid ; he measured the length of the shadow cast by the pyramid and also measured the length of the shadow of a post of known height at the same time and made a proportion between these quantities.

Pythagoras (525 B.C.) and his followers discovered correct formulas for the areas of the principal rectilinear figures, and also discovered the theorems that the areas of similar polygons are as the squares of their corresponding sides, and that the square on the hypotenuse of a right triangle equals the sum of the squares on the other two sides. The latter is called the Pythagorean theorem. They also discovered how to construct a square equivalent to a given parallelogram, and to divide a given line in mean and extreme ratio.

To **Eudoxus** (380 B.C.) we owe the general theory of proportion in geometry, and the treatment of incommensurable quantities by the method of exhaustions. By the use of these, he obtained such theorems as that the areas of two circles are to each other as the squares of their radii, or of their diameters.

In the writings of **Hero** (Alexandria, 125 B.C.) we first find the formula for the area of a triangle in terms of its sides, $K = \sqrt{s(s-a)(s-b)(s-c)}$. Hero also was the first to place land-surveying on a scientific basis.

It is a curious fact that Hero, at the same time, gives an incorrect formula for the area of a triangle, viz. $K = \frac{1}{2}a(b+c)$, this formula being apparently derived from Egyptian sources.

The **Romans**, although they excelled in engineering, apparently did not appreciate the value of the Greek geometry. Even after they became acquainted with it, they continued to use antiquated and inaccurate formulas for areas, some being of obscure origin. Thus, they used the Egyptian formula for the area of a quadrilateral, $K = \dfrac{a+b}{2} \times \dfrac{c+d}{2}$. They determined the area of an equilateral triangle whose side is a, by different formulas, all incorrect, as $K = \dfrac{13\,a^2}{30}$, $K = \frac{1}{3}(a^2 + a)$, and $K = \frac{1}{2}a^2$.

407. The circle. — **Thales** enunciated the theorem that every diameter bisects a circle, and proved the theorem that an angle inscribed in a semicircle is a right angle.

To **Hippocrates** (420 B.C.) is due the discovery of nearly all the other principal properties of the circle given in this book.

The **Egyptians** regarded the area of the circle as equivalent to $\frac{64}{81}$ of the diameter squared, making $\pi = 3.1604$.

The **Jews** and the **Babylonians** treated π as equal to 3.

Archimedes (Sicily, 250 B.C.), by the use of inscribed and circumscribed regular polygons, showed that the true value of π lies between $3\frac{1}{7}$ and $3\frac{10}{71}$; that is, between 3.14285 and 3.1408.

The **Hindu** writers assign various values to π, as 3, $3\frac{1}{8}$, $\sqrt{10}$, and **Aryabhatta** (530 A.D.) gives the correct approximation, 3.1416. The Hindus used the formula $\sqrt{2 - \sqrt{4 - \overline{AB}^2}}$ in computing the numerical value of π.

Within recent times, the value of π has been computed to 707 decimal places.

The use of the symbol π for the ratio of the circumference of a circle to the diameter was established in mathematics by **Euler** (Germany, 1750).

METHODS OF NUMERICAL COMPUTATIONS

408. Cancellation. — In numerical work in geometry, as elsewhere, the labor of computations may frequently be economized. Those methods of abbreviating work, which are particularly serviceable in the ordinary numerical applications of geometry, may be briefly indicated, as follows:

To simplify numerical work by cancellation, *group together as a whole all the numerical processes of a given problem, and make all possible cancellations, before proceeding to a final numerical reduction.*

Ex. Find the ratio of the area of a rectangle, whose base and altitude are 42 and 24 inches, to the area of a trapezoid, whose bases are 21 and 35 and altitude 12 inches.

By §§ 337, 350

$$\frac{\text{area of rectangle}}{\text{area of trapezoid}} = \frac{42 \times 24}{6(21 + 35)} = \frac{42 \times 24}{6 \times 56} = 3, \textit{Ratio.}$$

409. Use of radicals and of π. — Where radicals enter in the course of the solution of a numerical problem, it frequently saves labor *not to extract the root of the radical till the final answer is to be obtained.*

Ex. 1. Find the area of a circle circumscribed about a square whose side is 8.

The diagonal of the square must be $8\sqrt{2}$ (§ 355).

∴ the radius of $\odot = 4\sqrt{2}$.

∴ by § 391, area of $\odot = \pi(4\sqrt{2})^2 = 32\,\pi = 100.6, \textit{Area.}$

Similarly in the use of π, it frequently saves labor *not to substitute its numerical value for π till late in the process of solution.*

Ex. 2.   Find the radius of a circle whose area is equal to the sum of the areas of two circles whose radii are 6 and 8 inches, respectively.

Denote the radius of the required circle by x.

Then, by § 391,
$$\pi x^2 = 36\,\pi + 64\,\pi.$$
$$\therefore\ \pi x^2 = 100\,\pi.$$
$$\therefore\ x^2 = 100,$$
$$\therefore\ x = 10,\ \textit{Radius.}$$

410. Use of x, y, etc., as symbols for unknown quantities. — In some cases *a numerical computation is greatly facilitated by the use of a specific symbol for an unknown quantity.*

Ex.   In a triangle whose sides are 12, 18, and 25, find the segments of the side 25 made by the bisector of the angle opposite.

Denote the required segments of side 25 by x and $25 - x$.

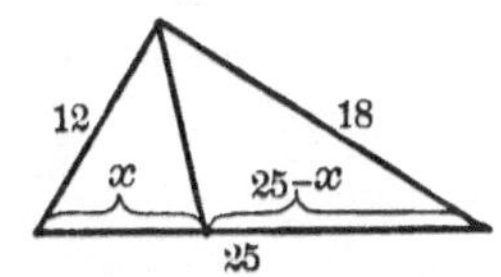

Then $12 : 18 = x : 25 - x$ (§ 301).

$\therefore\ 18\,x = 12(25 - x)$ (§ 278).

$\therefore\ x = 10$ ⎫

And $25 - x = 15$ ⎬ *Segments.*

411. Limitations of numerical computations. — Owing to the limitations of human eyesight and of the instruments used in making measurements, no measurement can be accurate beyond the fifth or sixth figure; and in ordinary work, such as is done by a carpenter, measurements are not accurate beyond the third figure. As all numerical applications of geometry are based on practical measurements, *it is not necessary to carry arithmetical work beyond the fifth or sixth significant digit.*

Other methods of facilitating numerical computations, as by the **use of logarithms** or the *slide rule,* are beyond the scope of this book.

REVIEW EXERCISES

EXERCISES: GROUP 82

LINES

Ex. 1. A tree 90 ft. high is broken off 40 ft. from the ground. How far from the foot of the tree will the top strike?

Ex. 2. Find the diagonals of a rectangle whose sides are 5 and 12.

Ex. 3. If the base of an isosceles triangle is 8 and a leg is 5, find the altitude.

Ex. 4. One side of a rhombus is 17 and one diagonal is 30. Find the other diagonal.

Ex. 5. In a circle whose radius is 5, find the length of the longest and shortest chords through a point at a distance 3 from the center.

Ex. 6. In a circle whose radius is 25 in., find the distance from the center to a chord 48 in. long.

Ex. 7. If a chord 12 in. long is 5 in. from the center of a circle, how far from the center of the same circle is a chord 10 in. long?

Ex. 8. A ladder 40 ft. long reaches a window 20 ft. high on one side of a street and, if turned on its foot, reaches a window 30 ft. high on the other side. How wide is the street?

Ex. 9. If one leg of a right triangle is 10 and the hypotenuse is twice the other leg, find the hypotenuse.

Ex. 10. Find the altitude of an equilateral triangle whose side is 6.

Ex. 11. Find the side of an equilateral triangle whose altitude is 8.

Ex. 12. Find the side of a square whose diagonal is 15.

Ex. 13. One leg of a right triangle is 3, and the sum of the hypotenuse and the other leg is 9. Find the sides.

Ex. 14. The radii of two circles are 1 in. and 6 in., and their centers are 13 in. apart. Find the length of the common external tangent.

Ex. 15. The sides of a triangle are 12, 18, and 20. Find the segments of the side 20, made by the bisector of the angle opposite.

Ex. 16. If the legs of a right triangle are 6 and 8, find the hypotenuse, the altitude on the hypotenuse, and the segments of the hypotenuse made by the altitude.

Ex. 17.   Two sides of a triangle are 17 and 16, and the altitude on the third side is 15.   Find the third side.

Ex. 18.   The hypotenuse of a right triangle is 10, and the altitude on the hypotenuse is 4.   Find the segments of the hypotenuse and the legs.

Ex. 19.   A bicycle wheel 28 in. in diameter makes, in an afternoon, 3000 revolutions.   How many miles does the bicycle travel?

Ex. 20.   What is the diameter of a wheel which makes 1400 revolutions in going 8800 yd.?

Ex. 21.   If the diameter of a circle is 20, find the length of an arc of 60°.   Also of 83°.

Ex. 22.   If the length of an arc is 14 and the radius is 6, find the number of degrees in the arc.

Ex. 23.   If the arc of a quadrant is 1 ft. in length, find the diameter.

Ex. 24.   Two concentric circles are 88 in. and 132 in. in length, respectively.   Find the width of the circular ring between them.

Ex. 25.   If the year is taken as $365\frac{1}{4}$ da., and the earth's orbit is taken as a circle whose radius is 93,250,000 mi., find the velocity of the earth in its orbit per second.

Find the radius and circumference of a circle circumscribed about

Ex. 26.   A square whose side is 5.

Ex. 27.   A rectangle whose sides are 12 and 5.

Ex. 28.   Find the central angle of a sector whose perimeter equals one half the circumference.

Ex. 29.   Find the radius of a circle whose circumference equals the perimeter of a square whose diagonal is 10.

Ex. 30.   Two intersecting chords of a circle are 11 in. and 14 in. and the segments of the first chord are 8 in. and 3 in.   Find the segments of the second chord.

Ex. 31.   In a circle whose radius is 12 in., a chord 16 in. long is passed through a point 9 in. from the center.   Find the segments of the chord.

Ex. 32.   Two secants drawn from a point to a circle are 24 in. and 27 in. long.   If the external segment of the first is 6 in., find the external segment of the second.

Ex. 33.   From a given point a secant, whose external and internal segments are 9 and 16, is drawn to a circle.   Find the length of the tangent drawn from the same point to the circle.

Ex. 34. From a given point a tangent 24 in. long is drawn to a circle whose radius is 18 in.   Find the distance of the point from the center.

Ex. 35. If a diameter 60 in. long is divided into 5 equal parts by chords perpendicular to it, find the length of the chords.

Ex. 36. If the greatest distance at which a mountain 3 miles high is visible at sea is 150 miles, what is the diameter of the earth?

Ex. 37. If the earth is a sphere of radius 4000 mi., how far will the light of a lighthouse 100 ft. high be visible at sea?

Ex. 38. In a triangle whose base is 14 and altitude 12, a line is drawn parallel to the base and at a distance 2 from the base.   Find the length of the line thus drawn.

Ex. 39. The upper and lower bases of a trapezoid are 12 and 20 and the altitude is 8.   If the legs are produced till they meet, find the altitude of each of the two triangles thus formed.

Ex. 40. If the upper and lower bases of a trapezoid are b_1 and b, and the altitude is h, find the altitude of each of the triangles formed by producing the legs.

Ex. 41. If the sides of a triangle are 6, 7, and 8, compute the length of the altitude on 8.

Ex. 42. Also the length of the median on the same side.

Ex. 43. Also the length of the bisector of the angle opposite the side 8.

Ex. 44. Find the three medians, the three bisectors, and the three altitudes of a triangle whose sides are 13, 14, 15.

EXERCISES: GROUP 83

AREAS

Ex. 1. Find to three decimal places the area in acres of a triangular field whose base is 300 ft. and altitude 200 ft.

Ex. 2. Find the area of a triangle whose sides are 10, 17, and 21.

Ex. 3. Find the area in acres of a triangular field each of whose sides is 10 chains.

Find the area of

Ex 4. An isosceles triangle whose base is 16, and each of whose legs is 34.

Ex. 5. An equilateral triangle whose altitude is 8.

Ex. 6. An isosceles right triangle whose hypotenuse is 12.

Ex. 7. A right triangle in which the hypotenuse is 41 and one leg is 9.

Ex. 8. The area of an equilateral triangle is $4\sqrt{3}$. Find a side.

Ex. 9. Find the number of boards, each 4 yd. long and 6 in. wide, which are necessary to cover a floor 48×24 ft.

Ex. 10. How many persons can stand in a room 15×9 ft., if each person requires 27×18 in.?

Ex. 11. The baseball diamond is a square each side of which is 90 ft. What fraction of an acre is its area?

Ex. 12. Find the area of a rhombus one of whose sides is 17, and one of whose diagonals is 30.

Ex. 13. The bases of an isosceles trapezoid are 20 and 36 and the legs are 17. Find the area.

Ex. 14. The base of a triangle is 20 and the altitude 18. Find the length of a line parallel to the base which cuts off a trapezoid whose area is 80 sq. ft.

[SUG. Denote the altitude of the trapezoid by $18 - x$ and find its upper base by similar triangles.]

Ex. 15. The perimeter of a polygon, circumscribed about a circle whose radius is 20, is 340. Find the area of the polygon.

Ex. 16. The area of a rectangle is 144 and the base is three times the altitude. Find the dimensions.

Ex. 17. Find a side of a regular hexagon whose area is 200 sq. in.

Ex. 18. Find the area of a circle whose circumference is p.

Ex. 19. Find the radius of a circle whose area equals the sum of the areas of two circles whose radii are 9 in. and 40 in.

Ex. 20. Find the radius of a circle whose area equals the sum of the areas of three circles whose radii are 20, 28, 29.

Ex. 21. In a circle of radius 50, find the area of a sector of 80°.

Ex. 22. Also of a segment of 60°; of a segment of 300°; of a segment of 240°.

Ex. 23. In a circle whose radius is 7, the area of a sector is 45 sq. ft. Find the number of degrees in its angle.

Ex. 24. In a circle whose radius is 10, find the sum of the segments formed by an inscribed square.

Ex. 25. A circular mill-pond, $\frac{1}{2}$ mi. in diameter, contains a circular island, 100 yd. in diameter. Find the water surface of the pond in acres.

Ex. 26. Two tangents to a circle, whose radius is 15, include an angle of 60°. Find the area included between the tangents and the radii to the points of contact.

Ex. 27. Find the length of the tether by which a cow must be tied, in order that she may graze over exactly one acre.

Ex. 28. Three equal circles touch each other externally. Show that the area included between them is $R^2\left(\sqrt{3}-\dfrac{\pi}{2}\right)$.

Ex. 29. In a triangle whose base is 24 in. and altitude is 18 in., the altitude is bisected by a line parallel to the base. Find the area of the triangle cut off.

Ex. 30. In the triangle of Ex. 29, what part of the altitude must be cut off in order that the area of the triangle may be bisected?

Ex. 31. In a circle whose diameter is 30 in., what are the diameters of concentric circles which divide the area into three equivalent parts?

EXERCISES: GROUP 84

GENERAL NUMERICAL EXERCISES IN PLANE GEOMETRY

Ex. 1. The leg of an isosceles triangle is 10 and the base is 16. Find the altitude and the area.

Ex. 2. Find the area of a triangle whose sides are 25, 39, 40. Also find the radius of a circle equivalent to this triangle.

Ex. 3. Find the area of a regular hexagon inscribed in a circle whose radius is 2.

Ex. 4. The sides of a triangle are 7, 8, and 9 inches. Find the sides of a similar triangle of four times the area. Also, of twice the area.

Ex. 5. If the sides of a triangle are 12, 16, and 21, what are the segments of the side 21 made by the bisector of the angle opposite?

Ex. 6. The sides of a quadrilateral in order are 5, 5, 4, 3, and the first two of these sides contain an angle of 60°. Find the area.

Ex. 7. Find the diameter of a wheel which, in a mile, makes 480 revolutions.

Ex. 8. The area of a trapezoid is 112 and the two bases are 12 and 16. Find the altitude.

Find the radius of a circle equivalent to

Ex. 9. A square whose side is 10.

Ex. 10. An equilateral triangle whose side is 12.

Ex. 11. A trapezoid whose bases are 16 and 18 and altitude 9.

Ex. 12. A circle, a square, and an equilateral triangle each have a perimeter of 12 yd. Find the area of each figure.

Ex. 13. In a circle whose area is 400, the area of a sector is 125. Find the angle of the sector.

Ex. 14. How many acres are included within a half-mile running track, if the track is in the shape of a rectangle twice as long as it is wide?

Ex. 15. In a square whose side is 6 in., find the area of the inscribed and of the circumscribed circles.

Ex. 16. One leg of a right triangle is 12, and the difference between the hypotenuse and the other leg is 8. Find the area.

Ex. 17. Find the area of an isosceles right triangle whose hypotenuse is 20 ft.

Ex. 18. In a circle whose diameter is 20, a chord is passed through a point at a distance 6 from the center, perpendicular to the diameter through that point. Find the length of this chord, and of the chords drawn from its extremities to the ends of the diameter.

Ex. 19. If three arcs, each of 60° and having 10 for a radius, are each concave to the other two arcs, find the area included by them.

Ex. 20. A square piece of land and a circular piece each contain 1 acre. How many more feet of fence does one require than the other?

Ex. 21. If the base of a triangle is doubled and the altitude remains unchanged, how is the area affected? If the altitude is doubled and the base remains unchanged? If both the base and the altitude are doubled?

Ex. 22. Find the side of an equilateral triangle equivalent to a circle whose diameter is 10.

Ex. 23. The area of a rhombus is 156 sq. in. and one side is 1 ft. 1 in. Find the diagonals.

EXERCISES: GROUP 85

Exercises Involving the Metric System

Ex. 1. Find the area of a triangle of which the base is 16 dm. and the altitude 80 cm.

Ex. 2. Find the area of a triangle whose sides are 6 m., 70 dm., 800 cm.

Ex. 3. Find the area in square meters of a circle whose radius is 14 dm.

Ex. 4. If the hypotenuse of a right triangle is 17 dm. and one leg is 150 cm., find the other leg and the area.

Ex. 5. If the circumference of a circle is 1 m., find the area of the circle in square decimeters.

Ex. 6. Find the area in hectares, and also in acres, of a circle whose radius is 100 m.

Ex. 7. If the diagonal of a rectangle is 35 dm. and one side is 800 mm., find the area in square meters, and also in square inches.

Ex. 8. Find the area of a trapezoid whose bases are 600 cm., and 2 m., and whose altitude is 80 dm.

Ex. 9. If a rectangular field is 700 dm. long and 200 m. wide, find its area in hectares and in acres.

Ex. 10. In a given circle two chords, whose lengths are 15 dm. and 13 dm., intersect. If the segments of the first chord are 12 dm. and 3 dm., find the segments of the second chord.

Ex. 11. Find in decimeters the radius of a circle equivalent to a square whose side is 1 ft. 6 in.

Ex. 12. Find in feet the diameter of a wheel which, in going 10 kilometers, makes 5000 revolutions.

EXERCISES: GROUP 86

Review Exercises in Plane Geometry

Ex. 1. If the bisectors of two adjacent angles are perpendicular to each other, the angles are supplementary.

Ex. 2. If a diagonal of a quadrilateral bisects two of its angles, the diagonal bisects the quadrilateral.

Ex. 3. Through a given point draw a secant at a given distance from the center of a given circle.

Ex. 4. The bisectors of one angle of a triangle and of an exterior angle at another vertex form an angle which is equal to one half the third angle of the triangle.

Ex. 5. The side of a square is 18 in. Find the circumference of the inscribed and circumscribed circles.

Ex. 6. The quadrilateral $ADBC$ is inscribed in a circle. The diagonals AB and DC intersect in the point F. Arc $AD = 112°$, arc $AC = 108°$, $\angle AFC = 74°$. Find all the other angles of the figure.

Ex. 7. Find the locus of the center of a circle which touches two given equal circles.

Ex. 8. The line joining the midpoints of two radii is perpendicular to the line bisecting their angle.

Ex. 9. If a quadrilateral is inscribed in a circle and its diagonals are drawn, how many pairs of similar triangles are formed?

Ex. 10. A rectangular piece of cardboard is $12'' \times 14''$. From this is cut an isosceles trapezoid with bases of $14''$ and $8''$ and sides of $5''$; and also a square with sides of $8''$. What per cent of the board is wasted? Draw to scale a diagram illustrating this problem.

Ex. 11. Draw a square $ABCD$. On the diagonal AC take the point E so that $AE = AB$ and draw through E a perpendicular to AE cutting BC in F. Prove $BF = EC$.

Ex. 12. In a circle whose radius is 12 cm., find the length of the tangent drawn from a point at a distance 240 mm. from the center.

Ex. 13. If two non-adjacent sides of a regular pentagon are produced, find the angle of their intersection.

Ex. 14. In the parallelogram $ABCD$, points are taken on the diagonals such that $AP = BQ = CR = DS$. Show that $PQRS$ is a parallelogram.

Ex. 15. A chord 6 in. long is at the distance 4 in. from the center of a circle. In the same circle, find the distance from the center of a chord 8 in. long.

Ex. 16. If B is a point on a circle whose center is O, PA a tangent at any point P, meeting OB produced at A, and PD perpendicular to OB, then PB bisects the angle APD.

Ex. 17. Construct a parallelogram, given a side, an angle, and a diagonal.

Ex. 18. Find in inches the sides of an isosceles right triangle whose area is 1 sq. yd.

Ex. 19. Find the locus of the vertices of all triangles on a given base and having a given area.

Ex. 20. If, on the sides AC and BC of the triangle ABC, the squares AD and BF are constructed, AF and DB are equal.

Ex. 21. Prove that in a quadrilateral the angle between the bisectors of two adjacent angles is one half the sum of the other two angles.

Ex. 22. Let A and B be two fixed points on a circle, and P and Q the extremities of a variable diameter of the same circle. Find the locus of the point of intersection of the straight lines AP and BQ.

Ex. 23. Find the area of a circle in which the length of an arc of $22\frac{1}{2}°$ is $\dfrac{3\,\pi}{2}$ ft.

Ex. 24. The sum of the areas of two circles is 20 sq. yd., and the difference of their areas is 15 sq. yd. Find their radii.

Ex. 25. In a given square, inscribe a square having a given side.

Ex. 26. If perpendiculars are drawn to a given line from the vertices of a parallelogram, the sum of the perpendiculars from two opposite vertices equals the sum of the other two perpendiculars.

Ex. 27. Two equal circles overlap in such a way that the center of each circle lies upon the other circle. In terms of π and r, find an expression for the area common to the two circles.

Ex. 28. A given circle has an area of 80 sq. ft. In this circle, find the length of an arc of 80°.

Ex. 29. The area of a given triangle is K and the sides of the triangle are a, b, c. In terms of a, b, and c, find the radius of the circle inscribed in the triangle.

Ex. 30. In a triangle ABC, a point P is taken on AC so that the ratio of AP to PC is $\frac{2}{3}$. Through P lines are drawn parallel to AB and BC within the triangle. What is the ratio of the area of the resulting parallelogram to the area of the triangle ABC?

Ex. 31. In a square $ABCD$, E is the midpoint of CD. Construct and describe the locus of P, the midpoint of a line drawn parallel to BE and terminated by the sides of the square.

Ex. 32. If E is the intersection of the diagonals AC and BD of a quadrilateral, and the triangle ADE is equivalent to the $\triangle BEC$, then the lines AB and CD are parallel.

Ex. 33. A 2-in. steam pipe conveying steam from the boiler to the radiators in a school building is found to supply only two thirds the needed amount of steam. If available sizes of pipe are each an exact number of inches in diameter, what is the diameter of the smallest pipe that will convey the needed amount?

APPENDIX

This appendix contains the propositions which, over and above those already given in the body of the book, are called for by the Report of the Committee of Fifteen of the National Education Association on Geometry Syllabus. Hence the book, with the appendix, precisely covers the specifications of the Committee of Fifteen and therefore exactly meets the requirements in plane geometry of the College Entrance Examination Board.

PROPOSITION I.   PROBLEM

412. *Upon a given straight line to construct a triangle similar to a given triangle.*

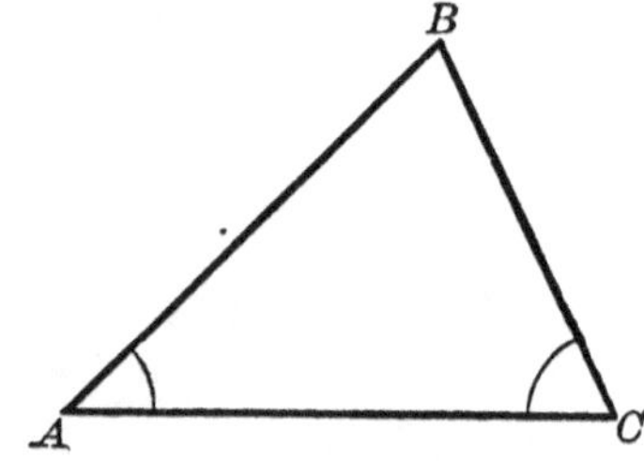

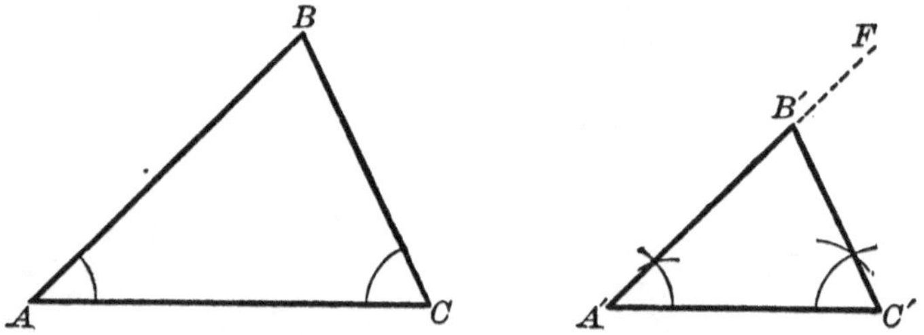

METHOD I.

Given $\triangle ABC$ and the line $A'C'$.

To construct on $A'C'$ a $\triangle$ similar to ABC.

Construction and proof. 1. At A' construct $\angle FA'C' = \angle A$.

  2. At C' construct $\angle A'C'B' = \angle C$.

  3. Produce $A'F$ and $C'B'$ to meet at B'. Then $A'B'C'$ is the triangle required.

  4. For $\triangle A'B'C' \sim \triangle ABC$.

  1. § 86.

  2. § 86.

  3. Post. 2.

  4. Why ?

Q.E.F.

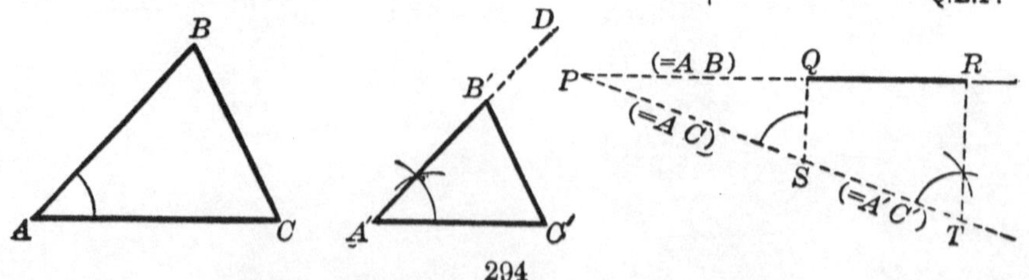

294 "

Method II.

Given $\triangle ABC$ and the line $A'C'$.

To construct on $A'C'$ a $\triangle$ similar to ABC.

Construction and proof. 1. At A' construct $\angle DA'C' = \angle A$.	1. § 86.
2. Construct QR, the fourth proportional to AC, $A'C'$, and AB.	2. § 297.
3. On $A'D$ mark off $A'B' = QR$ and draw $B'C'$.	3. Post. 2.
Then $\triangle A'B'C'$ is the triangle required.	
4. For $\triangle A'B'C' \sim \triangle ABC$.	4. Why?

Q.E.F.

PROPOSITION II.   PROBLEM

413. *Upon a given straight line to construct a polygon similar to a given polygon and similarly placed.*

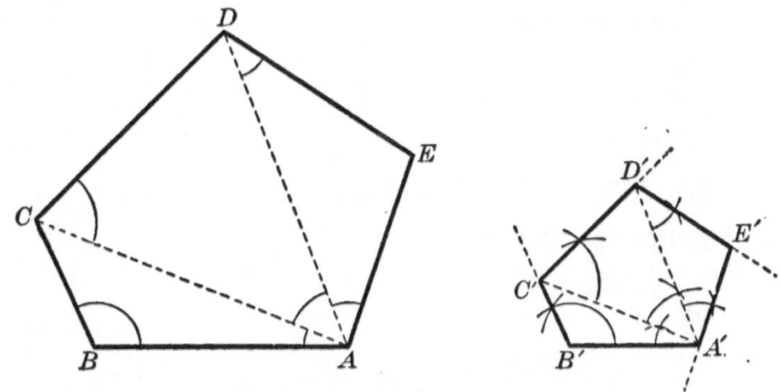

Given the polygon $ABCDE$ and the line $A'B'$.

To construct on $A'B'$ a polygon similar to $ABCDE$ and similarly placed.

Construction and proof. 1. On $A'B'$ construct $\triangle A'B'C'$ similar to $\triangle ABC$ and similarly placed.	1. § 412.

Let the pupil complete the construction and give the proof.

PROPOSITION III.   THEOREM

414. *If two right triangles have two sides of one proportional to the corresponding two sides of the other, the triangles are similar.*

CASE I.   *When the given proportional sides are the legs of the two triangles.*

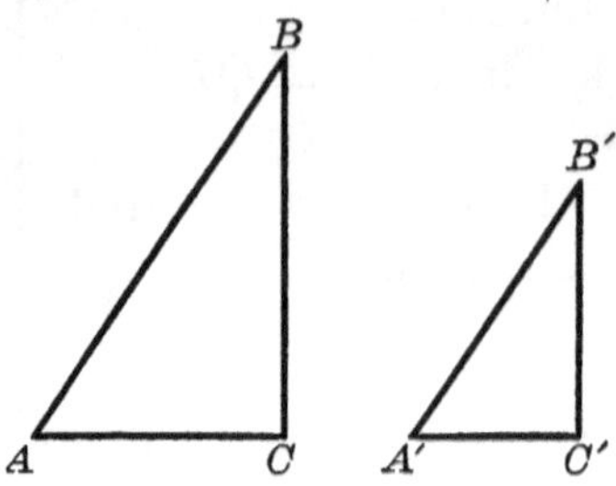

Given $\triangle$ ABC and $A'B'C'$, C and C'' right $\angle\!\!\!\angle$, and $AC : A'C' = BC : B'C'$.

To prove $\triangle ABC \sim \triangle A'B'C'$.

Proof. 1. $\angle C = \angle C''$. | 1. Why ?
2. $AC : A'C' = BC : B'C'$. | 2. Why ?
3. $\therefore \triangle ABC \sim \triangle A'B'C'$. | 3. Why ?

CASE II.   *When the proportional sides in each triangle are the hypotenuse and a leg.*

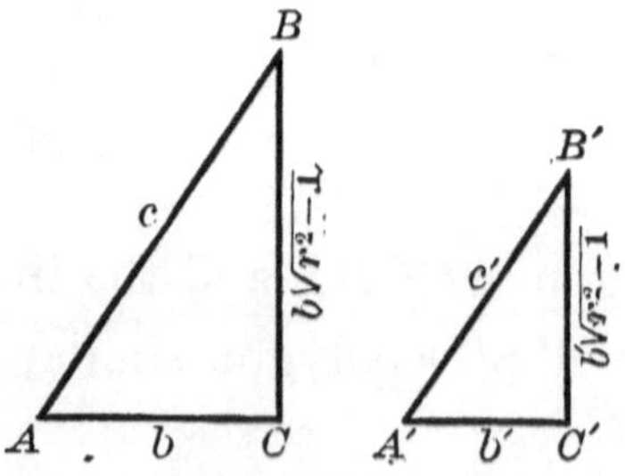

Given $\triangle$ ABC and $A'B'C'$, C and C'' right $\angle\!\!\!\angle$, and $AB : A'B' = AC : A'C'$.

To prove $\triangle ABC \sim \triangle A'B'C'$.

Proof. 1. Let $\dfrac{c}{b} = r$. Hence $c = br$. | 1. Ax. 4.

2. $\overline{BC}^2 = c^2 - b^2$. | 2. § 356.

3. $\therefore \overline{BC}^2 = b^2 r^2 - b^2 = b^2(r^2 - 1)$. | 3. Ax. 9.

4. $\therefore BC = b\sqrt{r^2 - 1}$. | 4. Ax. 6.

5. In like manner, $B'C' = b'\sqrt{r^2 - 1}$. | 5. Reasons 1–4.

6. $\therefore \dfrac{BC}{B'C'} = \dfrac{b\sqrt{r^2 - 1}}{b'\sqrt{r^2 - 1}} = \dfrac{b}{b'} = \dfrac{AC}{A'C'}$. | 6. Ax. 9, § 227.

7. $\therefore \dfrac{AB}{A'B'} = \dfrac{AC}{A'C'} = \dfrac{BC}{B'C'}$. | 7. Hyp., Ax. 1.

8. $\therefore \triangle ABC \sim \triangle A'B'C'$. | 8. Why ?

Q.E.D.

415. The **projection of a point** upon a line is the foot of the perpendicular drawn from the point to the line.

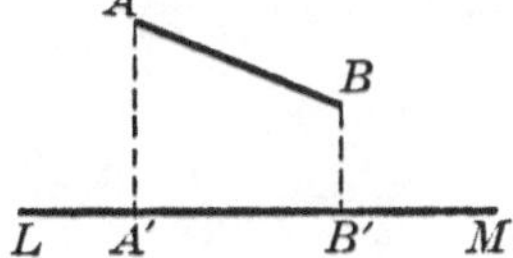 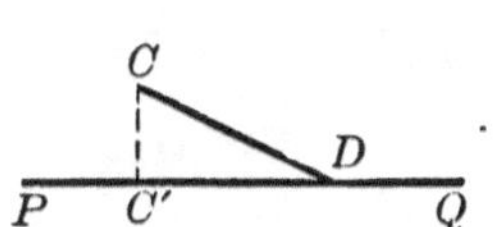

Thus if AA' is perpendicular to LM, A' is the projection of the point A on the line LM.

416. The **projection of a line** upon another given line is that part of the second line which is included between perpendiculars drawn from the extremities of the first line upon the second line. Thus, the projection of AB on LM is $A'B'$; of CD on PQ, is $C'D$.

Ex. 1. A line 10 in. long makes an angle of 45° with a second line; find the projection of the first line on the second.

Ex. 2. Find the same, if the angle is 60°.

Ex. 3. If the side of an equilateral triangle is a, find its projection on the base.

Proposition IV. Theorem

417. *In any obtuse triangle, the square of the side opposite the obtuse angle is equal to the sum of the squares of the
other two sides, increased by twice the product of one of those
sides by the projection of the other side upon it.*

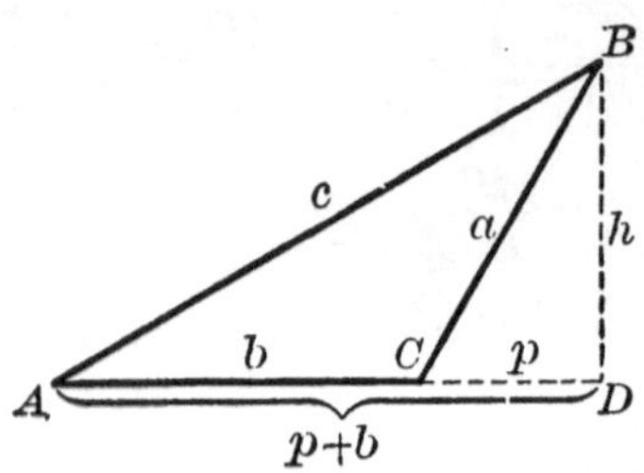

Given $\triangle ABC$ with $\angle ACB$ an obtuse angle, and CD
(or p) the projection of CB on AC produced.

To prove $c^2 = a^2 + b^2 + 2\,bp.$

Proof.   1. In the rt. $\triangle ABD,$ 1. § 355.
$$c^2 = h^2 + (p + b)^2,$$
or $$c^2 = h^2 + p^2 + b^2 + 2\,bp \quad . \quad (1)$$

2. In rt. $\triangle CBD,$ $h^2 + p^2 = a^2$.   .   (2)   2. Why?

3. Substituting from (2) in (1),   3. Why?
$$c^2 = a^2 + b^2 + 2\,bp.$$

                                           Q.E.D.

Ex. 1. If, in a diagram lettered like the above figure, $BC = 10,$
$AC = 2,$ and $\angle BCA = 120°,$ find $AB.$

Ex. 2. If, in the diagram of Prop. IV,
$AB = 20,$ $BC = 14,$ and $AC = 12,$ find $CD.$

Ex. 3. In the $\triangle ABC,$ AC is produced
to $D,$ and $CD = \frac{1}{3} AC.$ If BC is produced
through C to some point F so as to make
$\triangle CDF$ similar to $\triangle ABC,$ CF must be what
fractional part of BC?

Ex. 4. Show how PQ may be determined
by use of the method of Ex. 3.

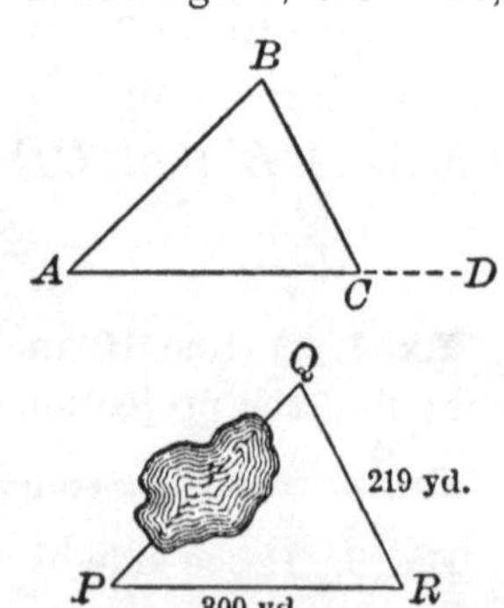

Proposition V. Theorem

418. *In any oblique triangle, the square of a side opposite an acute angle is equal to the sum of the squares of the other two sides, diminished by twice the product of one of those sides by the projection of the other side upon it.*

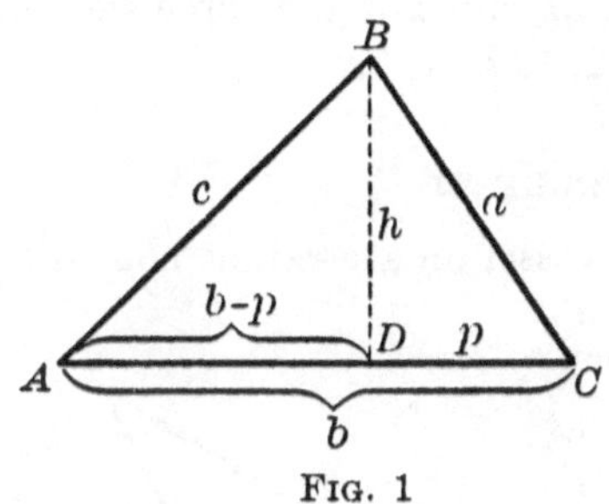

Fig. 1

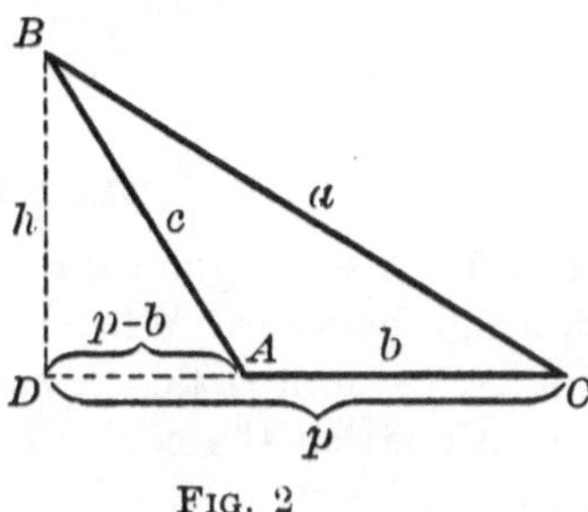

Fig. 2

Given $\triangle ABC$ (Fig. 1), $\angle C$ an acute angle, and DC (or p) the projection of BC on CA.

To prove $c^2 = a^2 + b^2 - 2\,bp$.

Proof.   1. In the rt. $\triangle ABD$,
$$c^2 = h^2 + (b - p)^2,$$
or
$$c^2 = h^2 + b^2 + p^2 - 2\,bp. \qquad (1)$$
    2. In the rt. $\triangle BDC$, $h^2 + p^2 = a^2$. $\qquad (2)$
    3. Substituting from (2) in (1),
$$c^2 = a^2 + b^2 - 2\,bp.$$
    4. Similarly in Fig. 2, from $\triangle ABD$,
$$c^2 = h^2 + (p - b)^2,$$
whence $c^2 = a^2 + b^2 - 2\,bp.$

1. Why?

2. Why?
3. Why?

4. Reasons 1–3.

Q.E.D.

419. Cor. *If the square on one side of a triangle equals the sum of the squares on the other two sides, the angle opposite the first side is a right angle;* for it cannot be acute (§ 418), or obtuse (§ 417).

Ex. 1. If, in a diagram lettered like Fig. 1, $BC = 10$, $AC = 12$, and $\angle C = 60°$, find AB.

Ex. 2. If the square on one side of a triangle is greater than the sum of the squares on the other two sides, will the angle opposite the first side be acute or obtuse?

Ex. 3. If the square on one side of a triangle is less than the sum of the squares on the other two sides, will the angle opposite the first side be acute or obtuse?

Ex. 4. Is a triangle acute, obtuse, or right, if the three sides are 5, 12, 14? If they are 5, 11, 12? 5, 12, 13? 4, 5, 6?

EXERCISES: GROUP 87

Ex. 1. A sea captain is sailing his vessel on a straight course CD past a lighthouse P. When at a certain point, A, he notices that $\angle PAB = 27°$. He continues on the course CD till, at a point B, he finds $\angle PBD$ is double $\angle PAB$, or is 54°. If he knows from the rate of the ship that the distance $AB = 3\frac{1}{4}$ mi., how far is it from B to P?

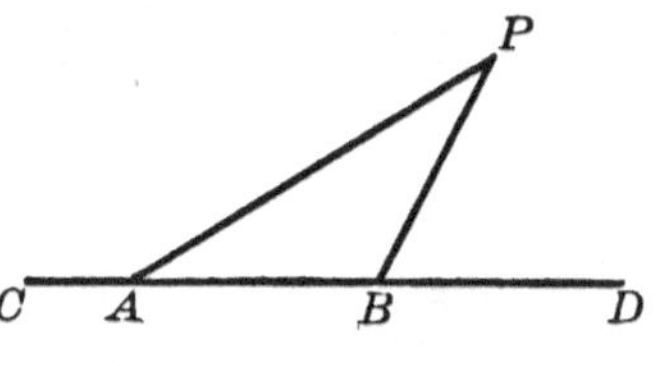

Ex. 2. If in Ex. 1, $\angle PAB = 30°$, $\angle PBD = 60°$, and $AB = 3\frac{1}{4}$ mi., find the length of AP.

Ex. 3. R and S are points separated by a stream, and an observer is at S. Show how he can determine the distance from R to S by means of the principle used in Ex. 1.

Ex. 4. In any isosceles triangle, the square of one of the legs equals the square on a line drawn from the vertex to any point of the base plus the product of the segments of the base.

Ex. 5. If C is the vertex of an isosceles triangle ABC, and D is a point in the base produced, then $\overline{CD}^2 = \overline{CB}^2 + AD \times BD$.

Ex. 6. Upon a given line as hypotenuse construct a right triangle one leg of which shall be a mean proportional between the other leg and the hypotenuse.

Ex. 7. $ABCD$ is a parallelogram in which $AB = 10$ ft., $BC = 20$ ft., and $\angle BAD = 45°$. Find the length of the diagonals AC and BD.

Ex. 8. If a, b, and c are the sides of a triangle in which $\angle B < 90°$, and m is the projection of a on c produced, state in general language the meaning of the formula $b^2 = a^2 + c^2 + 2\,cm$.

PROPOSITION VI. THEOREM

420. *Tangents to a circle at the mid-points of the arcs sub-tended by the sides of a regular inscribed polygon form a regular circumscribed polygon whose sides are parallel to the corresponding sides of the inscribed polygon.*

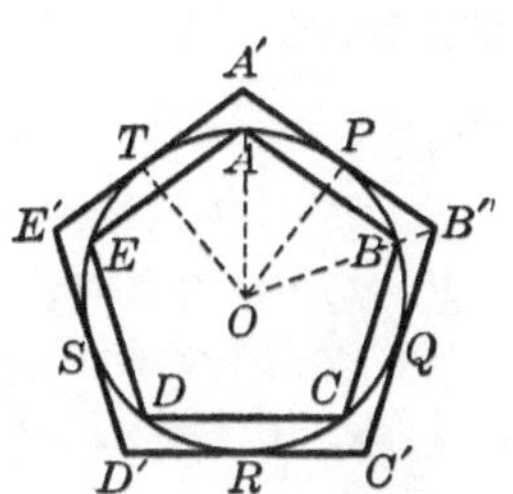

Given the regular polygon $ABCDE$ inscribed in the $\odot$ ACD; P, Q, R, etc., the mid-points of the arcs AB, BC, CD, etc.; and $A'B', B'C', C'D'$, etc., tangents to the circle at P, Q, R, etc.

To prove $A'B'C'D'E'$ a regular polygon with its sides ‖ corresponding sides of the polygon $ABCDE$.

Proof : 1. $\overset{\frown}{AB} = \overset{\frown}{BC} = \overset{\frown}{CD}$, etc.		1. § 198.
2. $\therefore \overset{\frown}{AP} = \overset{\frown}{PB} = \overset{\frown}{BQ} = \overset{\frown}{QC}$, etc.		2. Ax. 5.
3. $\therefore \overset{\frown}{PQ} = \overset{\frown}{QR} = \overset{\frown}{RS}$, etc.		3. Ax. 4.
4. $\therefore A'B'C'D'E'$ is a regular polygon.		4. § 373.
5. $\therefore AB \perp OP.$		5. § 205 (2, 4).
6. $A'B' \perp OP.$		6. Why ?
7. $AB \parallel A'B'.$		7. Why ?
8. In like manner, each pair of corresponding sides in the two polygons are parallel.		8. Reasons 5–7.

Q.E.D.

Ex. Draw a circle with radius $= 1$ in. and in the circle inscribe a square $ABCD$. Bisect the arcs AB, BC, CD, DA at the points P, Q, R, S, respectively. At these points construct tangents to the circle. Draw the chords AP, PB, BQ, etc. Compute the perimeter of the octagon thus formed. (Use § 320.)

421. Cor. *Corresponding radii of an inscribed and a circumscribed regular polygon, whose sides are parallel, coincide in direction.* Thus, in the figure on p. 302, $\angle POA$ and POA' each $= \dfrac{2 \text{ rt. } \angle}{n}$ (§ 372). $\therefore$ OA and OA' coincide in direction.

Proposition VII. Problem

422. *Given a circle, p the perimeter of a regular inscribed polygon and P the perimeter of a regular circumscribed polygon, each of the polygons having n sides, to find p' and P', the perimeters of the regular inscribed and circumscribed polygons each of $2\,n$ sides, in terms of p and P.*

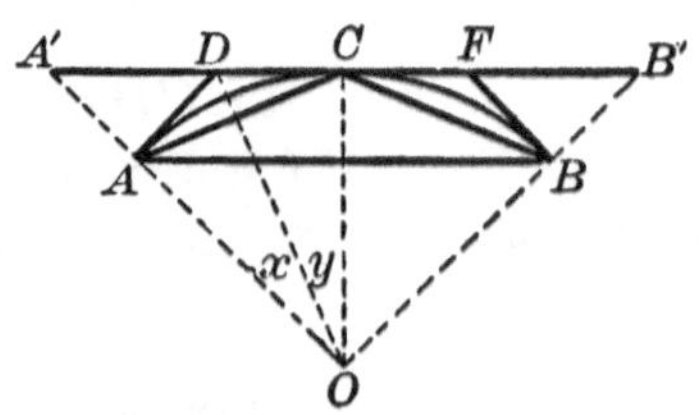

Given the circle O, AB a side of a regular inscribed polygon, and $A'B'$ a side of a regular circumscribed polygon (each of n sides), formed as in § 420; AC a side of a regular inscribed polygon, and DF a side of a regular circumscribed polygon (each of $2\,n$ sides), formed as in §§ 374, 375; the perimeters of the four polygons denoted by p, P, p', P', in order.

To find p' and P' in terms of p and P.

Solution. 1. $\dfrac{P}{p} = \dfrac{OA'}{OC}$.	1. §§ 376, 318.
2. $AD = DC$, $AO = CO$, $DO = DO$.	2. Why?
3. $\triangle ADO = \triangle DCO$.	3. Why?
4. $\angle x = \angle y$.	4. Why?
5. In $\triangle A'CO$, $\dfrac{OA'}{OC} = \dfrac{A'D}{DC}$.	5. § 301.

6. $\therefore$ from 1 and 5, $\dfrac{P}{p} = \dfrac{A'D}{DC}.$ | 6. Ax. 1.

7. $\therefore \dfrac{P+p}{p} = \dfrac{A'D + DC}{DC} = \dfrac{A'C}{DC}$ | 7. § 286, Ax. 7, 9.

$$= \frac{\frac{1}{2} A'B'}{\frac{1}{2} DF} = \frac{A'B'}{DF} = \frac{P}{n} \div \frac{P'}{2\,n} = \frac{2\,P}{P'}.$$

8. Hence, $P + p : p = 2\,P : P'$, whence | 8. Ax. 1, § 278, Ax. 5.

$$P = \frac{2\,Pp}{P + p}. \qquad \ldots \ldots \ldots \quad (1)$$

9. $\angle DAC = \angle CAB,$ | 9. §§ 235, 241.
$\angle DCA = \angle CBA.$

10. $\therefore \triangle ACB \sim \triangle ADC.$ | 10. Why?

11. $AB : AC = AC : DC.$ | 11. Why?

12. Whence | 12. Why?

$$\overline{AC}^2 = AB \times \tfrac{1}{2} DF, \text{ or } \left(\frac{p'}{2\,n}\right)^2 = \frac{p}{n} \times \frac{P'}{4\,n}.$$

13. Whence $p'^2 = pP'$, and $p' = \sqrt{pP'}.$ (2) | 13. Why?

Q.E.F.

423. Principle. — It may be proved by methods which are beyond the scope of this book that *a circumference* (that is, the length of a circle) *is greater than the perimeter of an inscribed and less than the perimeter of a circumscribed polygon.*

This principle is sometimes taken as a definition of a circumference.

Ex. 1. How shall a mile of wire fence be stretched so as to contain the maximum area?

Ex. 2. Find the area in acres included by a mile of wire fence if it is stretched as a square, a regular hexagon, and a circle, respectively.

Ex. 3. Given PQ parallel to AC, and PR parallel to AB, prove $\triangle QAR$ a mean proportional between $\triangle BQP$ and $\triangle PRC$.

Proposition VIII. Problem

424. *To compute approximately the numerical value of π.*

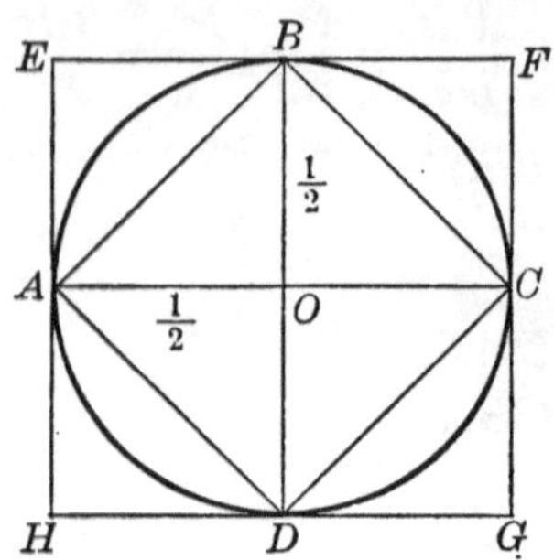

Given a circle O whose diameter is 1, and whose circumference is denoted by c.

To compute c approximately and hence find the approximate numerical value of π.

Solution. 1. In the circle O, inscribe the square $ABCD$, and circumscribe the square $EFGH$, and denote the perimeters of the two squares by p and P respectively.

1. §§ 360, 373.

2. $AB = \sqrt{(\tfrac{1}{2})^2 + (\tfrac{1}{2})^2} = \tfrac{1}{2}\sqrt{2}.$

   $\therefore p = 2\sqrt{2} = 2.82843^+.$

2. § 355.

3. $EF = AC = 1. \quad \therefore P = 4.$

3. § 157.

4. Denoting the perimeters of the regular inscribed and circumscribed octagons by p_8 and P_8 respectively,

4. § 422.

$$P_8 = \frac{2\,Pp}{P+p} = 3.31371^+,$$

and $\quad p_8 = \sqrt{pP_8} = 3.06147^+.$

5. Similarly, $P_{16} = \dfrac{2\,P_8 p_8}{P_8 + p_8} = 3.18260^+,$

5. § 422.

and $\quad p_{16} = \sqrt{p_8 P_{16}} = 3.12145^+.$

6. Proceeding in like manner we obtain the following table:

6. § 422.

Number of Sides	Perimeter of Circumscribed Polygon	Perimeter of Inscribed Polygon
4	4	2.82843
8	3.31371	3.06147
16	3.18260	3.12145
32	3.15172	3.13655
64	3.14412	3.14033
128	3.14222	3.14128
256	3.14175	3.14151
512	3.14163	3.14157

7. The result given in the last line in the table shows that the length of the circumference of the circle O, that is of c, lies between 3.14163[+] and 3.14157[+]. Hence the approximate numerical value of π, when carried out to four decimal places, is 3.1416.

7. § 423.

Q.E.F.

Proposition IX. Problem

425. *To construct a square equivalent to a given rectangle.*

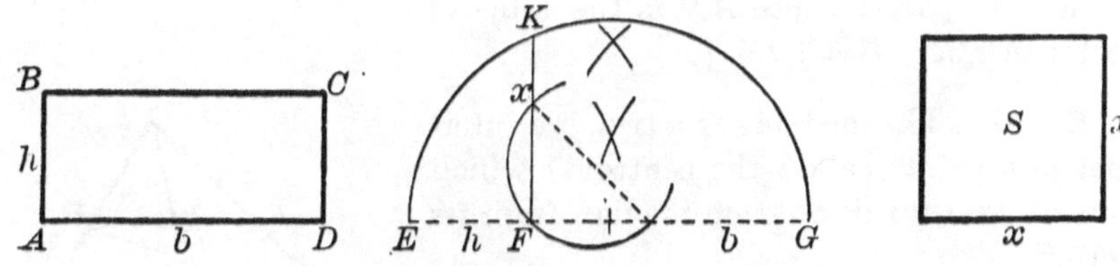

Given the rectangle $ABCD$ with the base b, and the altitude h.

To construct a square equivalent to $ABCD$.

Let the pupil supply the construction and proof.

EXERCISES: GROUP 88

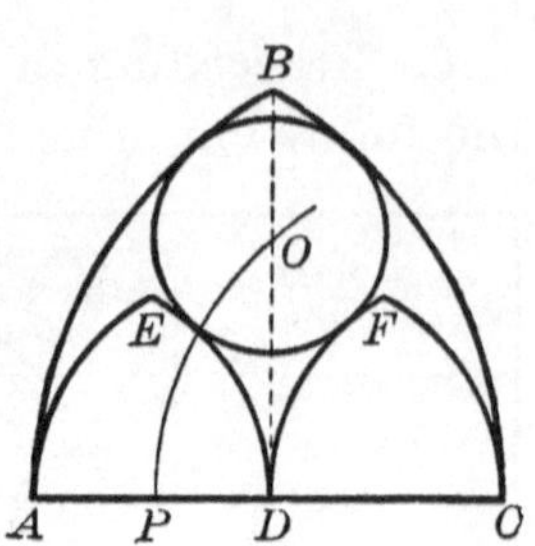

Ex. 1. D is the mid-point of the straight line AC. ABC, AED, and DFC are equilateral arches (see Ex. 5, p. 117). Construct a circle tangent to the four arcs AB, BC, ED, DF. (This geometric figure is the basis of various ornamental designs in Gothic windows in architecture.)

[SUG. Determine the center of the required circle by the method of intersection of loci (see p. 167). Thus find the locus of the centers of all circles tangent to the arcs AB and BC. Also find the locus of the centers of all circles tangent to the arcs AB and DF, etc.]

Ex. 2. In the diagram of Ex. 1, the figure as a whole is symmetrical with respect to what axis? Is the figure symmetrical with respect to a center? Point out four subordinate parts of the figure which have axis symmetry. Also one part which has symmetry with respect to a center.

Ex. 3. Transform a given rectangle into an equivalent rectangle with a given base.

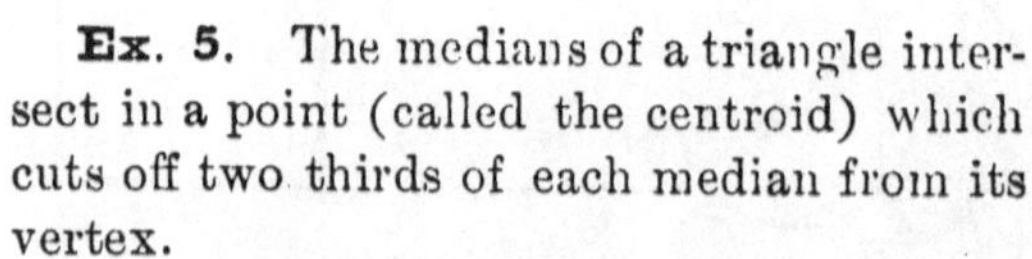

Ex. 4. The three altitudes of a triangle meet in a point (called the orthocenter).

[SUG. Through each vertex of the given $\triangle ABC$, draw a line $\parallel$ the side opposite. Prove PA and AR each $= BC$ by use of § 155; hence AD is the $\perp$ bisector of PR. Use § 257.]

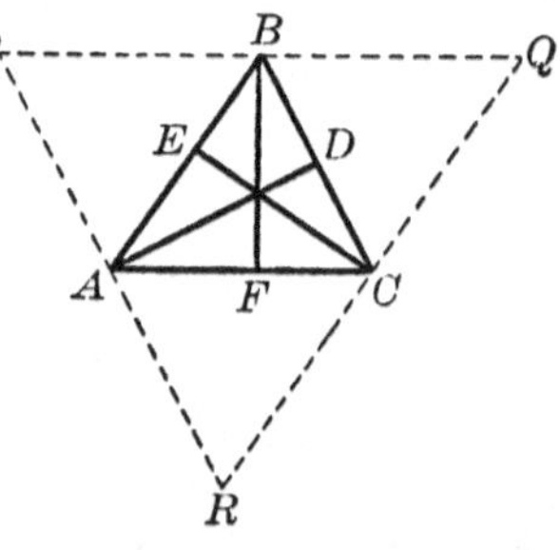

Ex. 5. The medians of a triangle intersect in a point (called the centroid) which cuts off two thirds of each median from its vertex.

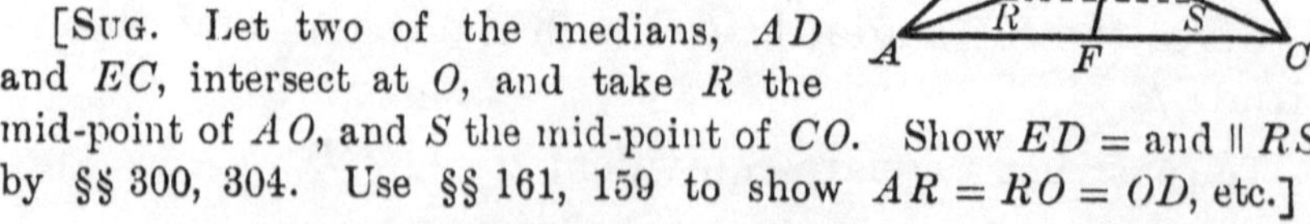

[SUG. Let two of the medians, AD and EC, intersect at O, and take R the mid-point of AO, and S the mid-point of CO. Show $ED =$ and $\parallel RS$ by §§ 300, 304. Use §§ 161, 159 to show $AR = RO = OD$, etc.]

Ex. 6. If the center of symmetry of a flat, homogeneous object is the center of mass, find the center of mass of a square; of a rectangle; regular hexagon; circle.

Ex. 7. It is evident that if the median of a triangle (BM) is placed on a knife-edge the triangle will balance (for if PP' is $\parallel AC$, the pull on P is balanced by the pull on P'). Hence, find the center of mass for any triangle. For a regular pentagon.

It is useful to be able to determine the center of mass of an object by geometry, or by any other means, since a knowledge of the center of mass of a body often enables us to treat the body in a simple way, for example, as if the body were concentrated at a single point.

Ex. 8. If a box has a triangular end, subject to the same pressure at all points, at what single point on the end must a supporting pressure be applied?

Ex. 9. If two triangles have their corresponding sides parallel, they are similar.

Ex. 10. If two triangles have their corresponding sides perpendicular, they are similar.

Ex. 11. If three or more lines pass through the same point and intersect two parallel lines, they intercept proportional segments on the parallel lines; that is, on the diagram,
$$\frac{AB}{A'B'} = \frac{BC}{B'C'} = \frac{CD}{C'D'}.$$

Ex. 12. If, in any triangle, a median is drawn to one side, the sum of the squares of the other two sides is equal to twice the square of half the given side, increased by twice the square of the median upon that side; that is, on the diagram, if AM is a median to BC,

prove $b^2 + c^2 = \dfrac{a^2}{2} + 2\,m^2.$

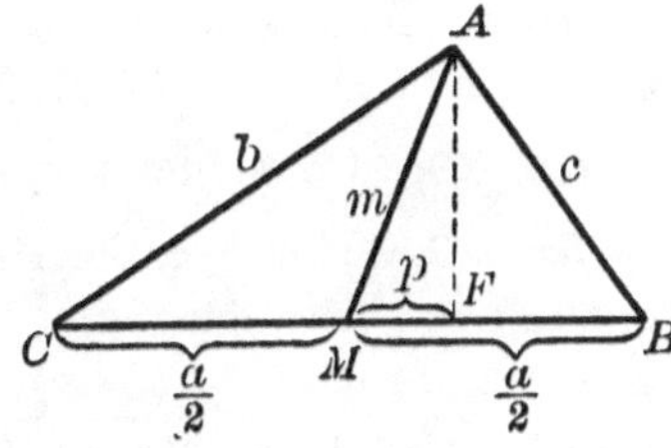

Show also that $m = \frac{1}{2}\sqrt{2(b^2 + c^2) - a^2}.$

[Sug. Apply § 418 to $\triangle ABM$, and § 417 to $\triangle AMC$.]

Ex. 13. In a parallelogram the sum of the squares of the sides equals the sum of the squares of the diagonals.

Ex. 14. The square of the bisector of an angle of a triangle is equal to the product of the sides forming the angle, diminished by the product of the segments of the third side formed by the bisector; that is, on the diagram show that $t^2 = ab - mn$.

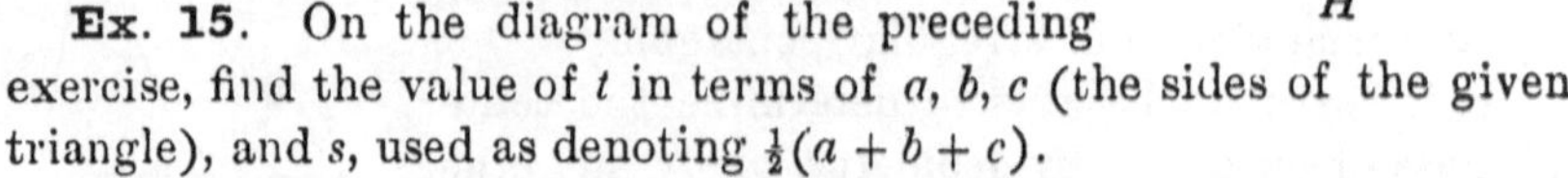

[SUG. Prove $\triangle AFC \sim \triangle HCB$, and hence that $b : t = x + t : a$. Use §§ 278, 322.]

Ex. 15. On the diagram of the preceding exercise, find the value of t in terms of a, b, c (the sides of the given triangle), and s, used as denoting $\frac{1}{2}(a + b + c)$.

[SUG. This amounts to finding the value of m and n in terms of a, b, c. By § 301, $n : m = a : b$. Hence, $m + n : m = b + a : b$ (§ 286), or $c : m = b + a : b$, etc.]

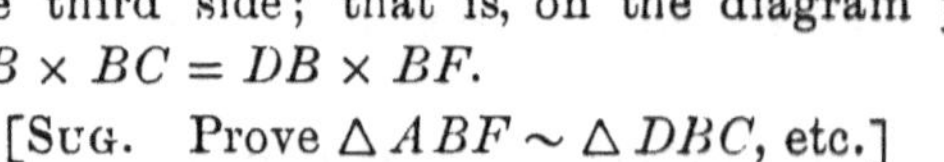

Ex. 16. In any triangle, the product of any two sides is equal to the product of the diameter of the circumscribed circle by the altitude upon the third side; that is, on the diagram prove $AB \times BC = DB \times BF$.

[SUG. Prove $\triangle ABF \sim \triangle DBC$, etc.]

Ex. 17. Divide a given straight line into parts proportional to a number of given lines.

Ex. 18. Divide a given straight line in extreme and mean ratio; that is, so that the whole line is to the larger part as the larger part is to the smaller part. Thus, on the diagram, divide AB so that $AB : AP = AP : PB$.

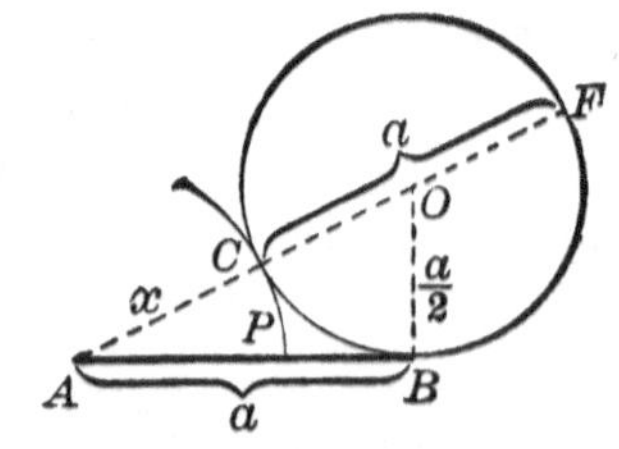

[SUG. At B erect the $\perp OB = \frac{1}{2} AB$ and draw the circle O with the radius OB. Use §§ 211, 324, 287, etc.]

Ex. 19. Construct a square equivalent to a given triangle.

Ex. 20. If a, b, c, denote the sides of a triangle opposite the angles A, B, C, respectively, and $s = \frac{1}{2}(a + b + c)$, the area of the triangle $= \sqrt{s(s - a)(s - b)(s - c)}$.

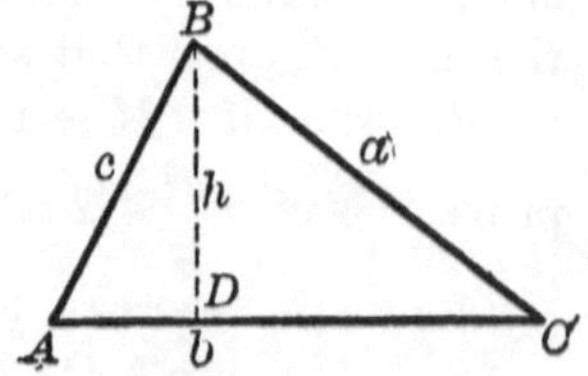

[SUG. By § 418,
$$a^2 = b^2 + c^2 - 2 b \times AD.$$
Hence, $$AD = \frac{b^2 + c^2 - a^2}{2 b}.$$

But, by § 356, $\qquad h^2 = c^2 - \overline{AD}^2 = (c + AD)(c - AD).$

$$\therefore h^2 = \left(\frac{2\,bc + b^2 + c^2 - a^2}{2\,b}\right)\left(\frac{2\,bc - b^2 - c^2 + a^2}{2\,b}\right), \text{ etc.]}$$

Ex. 21. Construct a triangle equivalent to a given pentagon ; that is, on the diagram, construct $\triangle FCG$ equivalent to $ABCDE$.

Ex. 22. Construct a triangle equivalent to a given hexagon.

Ex. 23. Construct a square equivalent to a given pentagon.

Ex. 24. Construct a square which shall have a given ratio to a given square.

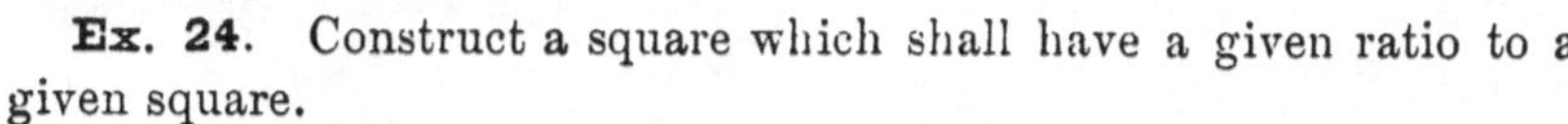

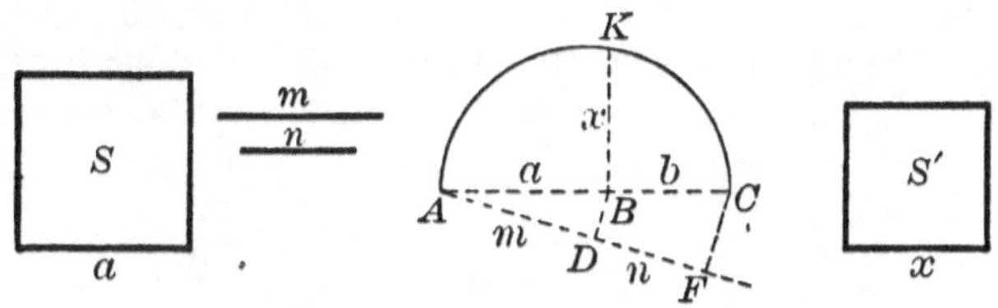

[Sug. Given the square S, construct the diagram as indicated and obtain S', which is to S as $n : m$. Then, by use of §§ 320, 293, prove that $\dfrac{S}{S'} = \dfrac{a^2}{x^2} = \dfrac{a^2}{ab} = \dfrac{a}{b} = \dfrac{m}{n}.$]

Ex. 25. Construct a square which shall be to a given square as $3 : 2$.

Ex. 26. Inscribe a regular decagon in a given circle.

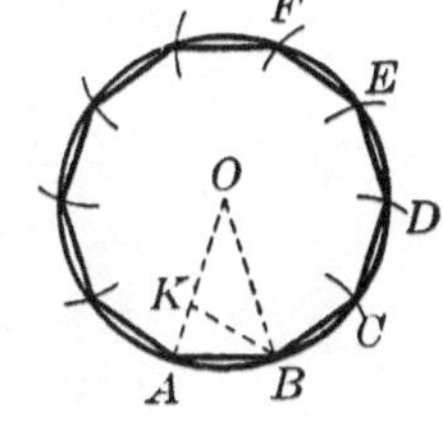

[Sug. Divide the radius OA at K so that $OA : OK = OK : KA$ (see Ex. 18, p. 308). Insert the chord $AB = OK$. Prove $\triangle AOB \sim \triangle AKB$ by § 310. Hence, $AB = KB = KO$, and $\angle A = \angle AKB = 2 \angle O = \angle OBA. \quad \therefore \angle O = 36°$, etc.]

Ex. 27. Construct a five-pointed star (called a pentagram).

Ex. 28. Construct a six-pointed star.

Ex. 29. By what per cent does 3.1416, the approximate value of π, differ from 3.141592, a closer approximation to the value of π?

Ex. 30. By what per cent does $\frac{22}{7}$ differ from 3.1416 ?

Ex. 31. *HG* is a straight line, and *HA = AD = DC = CG*.
ABC is an equilateral arch. *H* is the center of the arc *ED*, and *G*
of *DF*. Construct a circle which
shall be tangent to the arcs *AB*,
BC, *ED*, and *FD*. (This diagram, with the dotted lines
omitted, is the basis of ornamental designs in Gothic windows in architecture.)

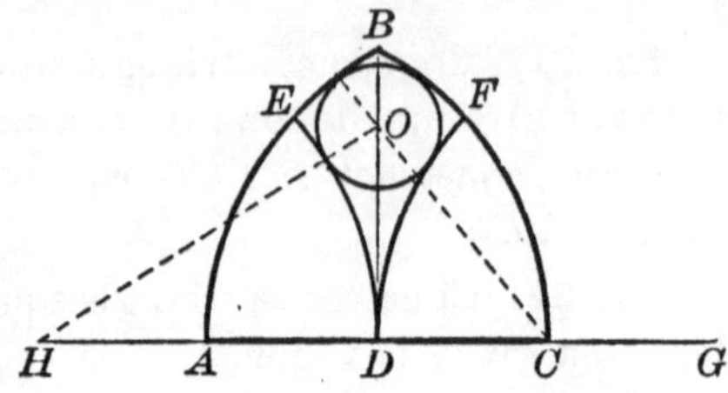

[Sug. Denote *AC* by *s* and
the radius of the required circle by *r*. Then in the right $\triangle HOD$,
$\overline{OD}^2 = (s + r)^2 - s^2$. Also in $\triangle ODC$, $\overline{OD}^2 = (s - r)^2 - (\tfrac{1}{2}s)^2$. Hence,
find $r = \dfrac{3s}{16}$, and $HO = \dfrac{19s}{16}$.]

Ex. 32. Discuss with reference to both axis and center symmetry
the diagram of Ex. 28 and also different parts of this diagram.

FORMULAS OF PLANE GEOMETRY

SYMBOLS

a, b, c = sides of triangle ABC.
$s = \frac{1}{2}(a + b + c)$.
h_c = altitude on side c.
m_c = median on side c.
t_c = bisector of angle opposite side c.
p = perimeter.
r = radius of a circle.

d = diameter of a circle, or diagonal of a square.
c = circumference of a circle.
π = $\frac{22}{7}$ approx. (or 3.1416—).
K = area.
b = base of a triangle.
h = altitude of a triangle.
b_1 and b_2 = bases of a trapezoid.

a = apothem of a regular polygon.

LENGTHS OF LINES

1. **In a right triangle,** C being the right angle,
$$c^2 = a^2 + b^2.$$
§ 355.

2. **In an equilateral triangle,** $h = \dfrac{b}{2}\sqrt{3}$.

3. **In a square,** $\qquad d = b\sqrt{2}$.

4. $h_c = \dfrac{2}{c}\sqrt{s(s - a)(s - b)(s - c)}$.

5. $m_c = \frac{1}{2}\sqrt{2(a^2 + b^2) - c^2}$.
6. $t_c = \dfrac{2}{a + b}\sqrt{abs(s - c)}$.

7. **In similar polygons,** $\quad p : p' = a : a'$. § 317.
8. **In circles,** $\qquad c : c' = r : r' = d : d'$. §§ 380, 381.
9. $\qquad\qquad c = 2\pi r$, or $c = \pi d$. § 383.
10. $\qquad\qquad$ An arc $= \dfrac{\text{central angle}}{180°} \times \pi r$. § 385.

AREAS OF PLANE FIGURES

1. **In a rectangle,** $\qquad K = bh$. § 337.
2. **In a square,** $\qquad K = b^2$. § 337.
3. **In a parallelogram,** $\quad K = bh$. § 339.
4. **In a triangle,** $\qquad K = \frac{1}{2}bh$. § 343.
5. **In a triangle,** $\qquad K = \sqrt{s(s - a)(s - b)(s - c)}$.
6. **In an equilateral triangle,** $K = \dfrac{b^2\sqrt{3}}{4}$.

7. In a **trapezoid**, $\qquad K = \frac{1}{2} h (b_1 + b_2)$. $\qquad$ § 350.

8. In a **regular polygon**, $\quad K = \frac{1}{2} ap$. $\qquad$ § 386.

9. In a **circle**, $\quad K = \pi r^2$ or $K = \frac{1}{4} \pi d^2$. $\qquad$ § 391.

10. In a **sector** of a circle, $\quad K = \frac{1}{2} r \times$ arc, $\qquad$ § 394.

$$\text{or } K = \frac{\text{central } \angle}{360°} \times \pi r^2. \qquad \text{§ 394.}$$

11. In a **segment** of a circle, $K =$ sector $\pm \triangle$ formed by the chord and radii of the segment.

12. In any two **similar plane figures**,

$$K : K' = a^2 : a'^2; \qquad \text{§ 353.}$$

$$\text{also } a : a' = \sqrt{K} : \sqrt{K'}. \qquad \text{§ 353, Ax. 6.}$$

13. In two circles, $\qquad K : K' = r^2 : r'^2 = d^2 : d'^2 = c^2 : c'^2$. $\qquad$ § 393.

$$r : r' = d : d' = c : c' = \sqrt{K} : \sqrt{K'}. \qquad \text{§ 381, Ax. 6.}$$

SUMMARY OF THE METRIC SYSTEM

TABLE FOR LENGTH

10 millimeter (mm.)	= 1 centimeter (cm.)
10 cm.	= 1 decimeter (dm.)
10 dm.	= 1 meter (m.)
10 m.	= 1 Dekameter (Dm.)
10 Dm.	= 1 Hektometer (Hm.)
10 Hm.	= 1 Kilometer (Km.)
10 Km.	= 1 Myriameter (Mm.)

Similar tables are used for the unit of weight, the *gram;* for the unit of capacity, the *liter;* for the unit of land measure, the *are;* and for the unit of wood measure, the *stere.*

TABLE FOR SQUARE MEASURE

100 sq. mm.	= 1 sq. cm.
100 sq. cm.	= 1 sq. dm., etc.

TABLE FOR CUBIC MEASURE

1000 cu. mm.	= 1 cu. cm.
1000 cu. cm.	= 1 cu. dm., etc.

A *liter* = 1 cu. dm.

A *gram* = weight of 1 cu. cm. of water at 39.2° Fahrenheit,

An *are* = 100 sq. m.

A *stere* = 1 cu. m.

EQUIVALENTS

1 meter	= 39.37 inches
1 liter	= 1.057 liquid quarts
	or .9581 dry quarts
1 kilogram	= 2.2046 pounds avoirdupois
1 hektare	= 2.471 acres
1 square meter	= 1550 − square inches

INDEX

KEY TO PLANE GEOMETRY

PAGE 11

17. He first sets out two of the trees in position and then sights through them and places the other trees in line with the two already set out.

22. Straight, I; curved, C, O, Q, S, U; broken, $A, E, F, H, K, L, M, N, T, V, W, X, Y, Z$; mixed, B, D, G, J, P, R.

PAGE 18

3. 47°; 137°.

4. 32° 41′; 27° 36′ 17″; 122° 41′; 117° 36′ 17″.

5. Construct a right angle having the same vertex as the given angle and a side in common with this angle, and including the given angle as a part of itself.
   To construct the supplement, produce a side of the given angle through the vertex.

6. Obtuse.

8. 60°; 90°; 150°.

7. 6°.

9. 135°; 22° 30′; 7° 30′.

10. 10 min.; 8⅓ min.; 40 min.; 2 hr.; 1 hr. 40 min.; 8 hr.

11. 810°.

PAGE 19

12. ⅛.

13. 30°; 90°; 22½°; 15°; 1⅞°.

14. 1 lb.; ⅔ lb.; 1½ lb.; 2¼ lb.; $\frac{1}{16}$ lb.; 6 lb.

15. Acute; obtuse; right.

19. Reflex; acute.

18. Obtuse; acute.

20. Right; obtuse; acute.

21. Right angle, for, denote the given angle by x. Then $(180° - x) - (90° - x) = 90°$.

22. (a) $r = t$. (b) $r = t$. (c) $t > r$, for s and r are acute. $\therefore t$ is obtuse. (d) $r > t$, for s is acute and $\therefore r$ is obtuse.

23. (a) $m > p$. (b) $m = p$. (c) $m < p$. (d) Denote the comp. of m by x. Then $x + m = 90°$, $x + p = 180°$. $\therefore p - m = 90°$. $\therefore p = m + 90°$. $\therefore p > m$.

3

PAGE 20

24. $x = 2(90° - x)$. $\therefore x = 60°$.   *Ans.*

25. $x = \frac{1}{4}(180° - x)$. $\therefore x = 45°$.   *Ans.*

26. $x = \frac{4}{5}(180° - x)$. $\therefore x = 80°$.   *Ans.*

27. (1) $x = 90° - x + 12°$. $\therefore x = 51°$.   *Ans.*

    (2) $x = 180° - x + 15\frac{1}{2}°$. $\therefore x = 97° \, 45'$.   *Ans.*

28. $90° - x + 180° - x = 126°$. $\therefore x = 72°$.   *Ans.*

29. $180° - x = 4(90° - x)$. $\therefore x = 60°$.   *Ans.*

PAGE 21

2. Yes, by placing the edge of the ruler on the pipe in a direction parallel to the length of the pipe.   No.

3. No.

4. Place the straight edge on the surface in various directions. In all positions every point of the straight edge should be in contact with the surface of the tennis court.

5. Yes.

PAGE 24

1. Ax. 7.   **2.** 140°; 210°; Ax. 7.

3.
$$\begin{array}{r} 7 = 7 \\ -2 = -2 \\ \hline 5 = 5 \end{array}$$

4. (1)
$$\begin{array}{r} 5 = 5 \\ \times 2 = \times 2 \\ \hline 10 = 10 \end{array}$$

    (2) $12 = 12$.   Dividing each of these by 3, $4 = 4$.

5. $8 = 8$. $\therefore \sqrt[3]{8} = \sqrt[3]{8}$, or $2 = 2$.

6. Ax. 4.

PAGE 25

7. Ax. 2.

8. Use the diagram of Ex. 7. Thus, if $LN = MO$, then $LM = NO$ (Ax. 3).

11. Ax. 1.   **12.** Ax. 2.   **13.** Ax. 9.

14. Through two points only one straight line can be passed; and a right angle is half of a straight angle.

PAGE 28

1. Three.

2. Six.

3. In Ex. 1 each point helps to locate two lines; in Ex. 2, each point helps to locate three lines. Hence, a point in the latter case does $1\frac{1}{2}$ times as much work, or is $1\frac{1}{2}$ times as efficient as in the former case.

5. $140.°$ 6. $r = 43°$, etc.

8. $\angle ABP = 40°$; $\angle PBQ = 50°$; $\angle QBC = 40°$.

9. $\angle COD = 180° - 142° = 38°$. $\angle COB = 120° - 38° = 82°$.

Ans.

10.

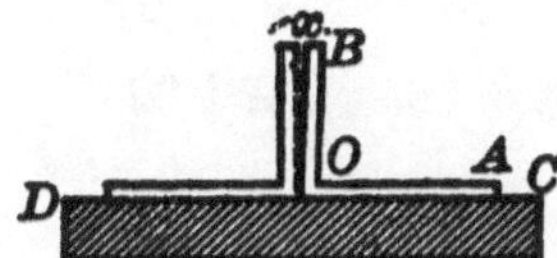

Place AO, one of the inside edges of the square, in contact with the straight edge CD. Then repeat the act, placing O at the same point on CD, with OA pointed in the opposite direction from the first position.

By § 23, the sum of two right angles must be a straight angle.

PAGE 30

2. Any two of the angles which are not vertical.

3. $157°$ (§ 69).

4. $s = p = 153° - 107° = 46°$. *Ans.*

5. $t = q = 138°$ (see Ex. 9, p. 28).

6. $4r = 180° - 24°$. $\therefore r = x = 39°$. *Ans.*

PAGE 32

2. $72°$; $104°$.

3. Add the complement to $90°$; subtract $90°$ from the supplement.

4. $150°$; $12° \, 30'$.

5. As the sides of a triangle; two ∥ lines, one through each point, and a third line through the two given points; etc.

6. 12 in.   7. No.   8. No.

10. Denote the angle of the square by y. Then
$2(y + e) = 2y + x$. $\therefore 2e = x$. $\therefore e = \frac{1}{2}x$.

PAGE 33

1. $EF = 18$; $\angle E = 70°$; $\angle F = 50°$.

PAGE 35

1. $DE = 24$; $EF = 27$; $\angle E = 55°$.
1. (Group 9). Use § 79.
2. § 79.   3. § 79.   4. § 79.
5. Prove $\triangle DCF = \triangle ACB$ by § 79. 217 yd.
6. § 80.

PAGE 36

7. § 80.   8. § 80.
9. $\angle ABO = \angle CBO$ by § 66. Use § 80.
10. Use § 80. 137 yd.

PAGE 37

1. By the principle proved in § 82, $\angle C = \angle A = 67°$.

PAGE 39

1. $\angle BAC = \angle BCA$ (§ 82). $\therefore p = r$ (§ 66).
   Then prove $\triangle DAB = \triangle BCF$ by § 79.
2. Use § 82 twice and Ax. 3.
3. § 83.   4. § 83.
5. Draw AC and use § 83.

PAGE 41

2. Construct a right angle and bisect it. Also through the vertex
   draw a line $\perp$ the bisector.

PAGE 50

2. No, for $d = 110°$, and hence d and f are not supplementary.
   Use § 99.
1. (Group 11). $\angle MOQ = \angle POL$ (§ 69). $PO = OQ$ (Hyp.).
   $\angle MQO = \angle OPL$ (§ 96). $\therefore \triangle POL = \triangle OMQ$ (§ 80).
2. $\angle A = \angle C$ (§ 82); $\angle D = \angle C$ (§ 96), etc.
3. Prove $\triangle ABP = \triangle PCD$ by § 80, etc.
4. $x = p$ (§ 69); $y = q$ (§ 69); $x = y$ (Ax. 1). $\therefore AB \parallel CD$ (§ 89).
5. $\angle ABC = \angle BCD$ (Ax. 2), etc.

PAGE 51

6. $y = m$ (§ 82). $x = y$ (§ 97); $l = m$ (§ 97), etc.

7. Prove $\triangle ABD = \triangle BFC$ by § 79, etc.

8. $\angle B = \angle C$ (§ 82). Then use § 96 twice and Ax. 1.

9. $\angle CBE = 115°$ (Ax. 7). $\therefore \angle ABE = 65°$ (§ 32).
   $\therefore BE \parallel CD$ (§ 91).

10. $\angle B = \angle i$ (step 6, p. 43), etc.

PAGE 53

1. 62°.   3. 60°.   5. No.

2. 53° 45′.   4. 45°.

PAGE 54

6. 138°.   8. 71°.   10. 78°; 78°; 24°.

7. 142°; 115°; 103°.   9. 80°.

11. Construct an equilateral triangle and bisect one of its angles. Bisect an angle of 30°.

12. Construct the supplement of 60°. 75° = 45° + 30°.

13. 150° = 90° + 60°. 195° = 180° + 15°.

15. Construct an equilateral triangle and a perpendicular to the base through an extremity of the base.

16. See Ex. 12.

17. Construct an angle of 45° at each end of the 2-in. line.

19. Corr. $\angle$ are = (§ 107). $\angle$ are not equal.

20. Through the vertex of the acute angle construct a $\perp$ to one side of the angle.

21. Produce one side of the angle through the vertex.

PAGE 57

1. Use § 114.   3. $\angle B$ (§ 114).

2. § 114.   4. § 114.

5. $\angle OAQ = \angle OBP$ (§ 114).
   $\angle AOQ = \angle BOP$ (§ 69).
   $\angle AOB = \angle POQ$ (§ 69).
   $\angle AQO = \angle OQC = \angle APC = \angle APB$ (§ 63).

6. See Ex. 1, p. 39.

PAGE 60

1. Use § 117. $PQ = PR$ (corr. sides of $= \triangle$).

PAGE 61

1. Use § 110.

PAGE 63

4. The locus is a straight line, parallel to the top of the level track and 1 ft. above it.

5. The locus is a straight line $\perp$ the line joining the two given points at the midpoint of this line.

6. Last sentence of § 123.

PAGE 69

1. Ineq. Ax. 2.

2. (1)
$$\begin{array}{r} 7 > 5 \\ + 3 + 3 \\ \hline 10 > 8 \end{array}$$
(2)
$$\begin{array}{r} 7 > 5 \\ - 2 - 2 \\ \hline 5 > 3 \end{array}$$
(3)
$$\begin{array}{r} 7 > 5 \\ 5 > 3 \\ \hline 12 > 8 \end{array}$$

3. (1) See Ex. 1.   (2) $10 > 8$.   Ill. of Ineq. Ax. 3,
$$\therefore 5 > 4$$
$$\begin{array}{r} 10 = 10 \\ - 6 > - 2 \\ \hline 4 < 8 \end{array}$$

4. $9 > 7 > 3.$ $\therefore 9 > 3.$ 5. § 134.

PAGE 72

1. Four; five. Three points will not determine a pair of parallel lines, for two pairs might be passed through the three points; thus through the points A, B, C the $\parallel$ lines 12 and 34 might be passed, also the parallel lines 56 and 78.

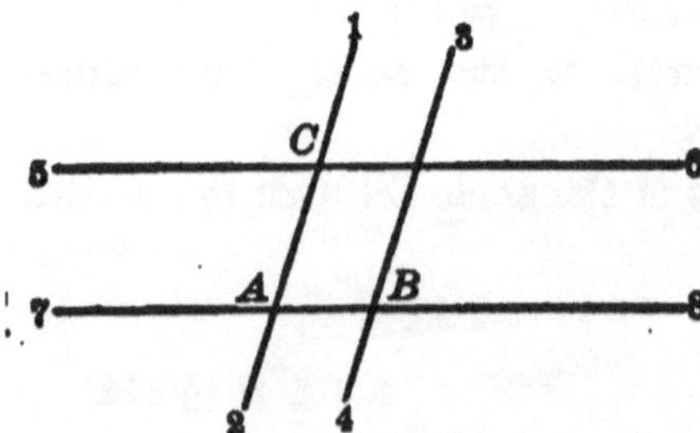

2. No.

PAGE 74

1. Hence, $\angle APB$ is obtuse. Use § 138.

2. $AB + BF > AF$ (§ 78). Also $FC + CD > FD$ (§ 78). $AD = AD$ (Ident.). Adding by Ineq. Ax. 1, $AB + BC + CD + DA > AF + FD + AD.$

3. $BD + DF > DF$ (§ 78). To each of these unequals add $AD + FC$ (Ineq. Ax. 1).

4. Use ▲ ABD and ADC, and § 138.

5. Use ▲ ABD and DBC, and § 139.

PAGE 76

2. Yes; no.

3. ∠ of a square are rt. ∠; ∠ of a rhombus are oblique. Have same number of sides; sides are equal; opposite sides are parallel.

4. 48 in.

5. Rhombus, rhomboid, parallelogram, quadrilateral.

6. Have same number of sides; opposite sides are parallel.

7. Two ▲; isosceles.

9. Construct a rectangle and a rhomboid whose corresponding sides are equal.

PAGE 77

1. $\angle r = \angle s$ and $\angle q = \angle p$ (corr. ∠ of = ▲).
$\therefore \ \angle BAD = \angle BCD$ (Ax. 2).

2. Produce BC to F and DC to H.
Then $\angle BAD = \angle HCF$ (§ 112), $\angle BCD = \angle HCF$ (§ 69).
$\therefore \ \angle BAD = \angle BCD$ (Ax. 1).

PAGE 78

1. Four, viz.: AFD and BFC; AFB and DFC; ABD and CBD; ABC and ADC.

2. $180° - p° - q°$.   3. $90° - 2x°$.

7.

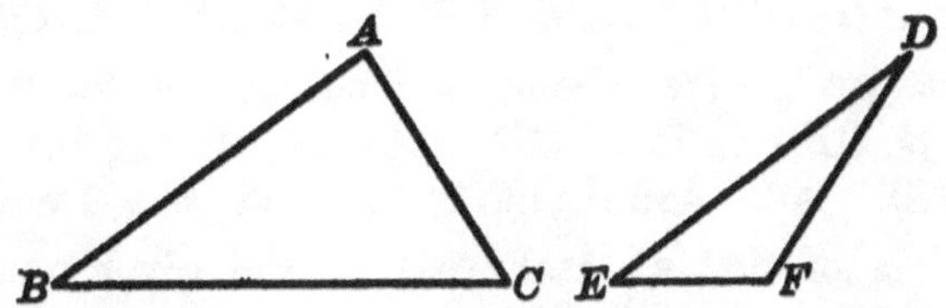

Construct the triangles ABC and DEF in which $\angle B = \angle E$, $AB = DE$, and $AC = DF$. See text-book, p. 159.

PAGE 79

1. Geom. Ax. 2, Post. 1 (§ 46), § 82 (twice), Ax. 2 (§ 41), Ax. 7 (§ 41), § 79.

PAGE 80

1. Use § 98.   **2.** 43°; 137°.

3. Denote the given angles by x and $3x$.
Then $x + 3x = 180°$ (§ 98). $\therefore x = 45°$; $3x = 135°$. *Ans.*

4. $a°$; $180° - a°$.

5. AC, longest; AB, shortest (§ 135).

PAGE 81

1. § 159.

2. No. (1) Converse of § 69, viz.: if two angles are equal, they are vertical. (2) Converse of § 112, viz.: if two angles are equal, their corresponding sides are parallel.

3. If we know that the diagonals of a quadrilateral bisect each other, by § 162, we at once know without effort that the given quadrilateral is a parallelogram.

PAGE 82

1. $AD \parallel BC$ (§ 92). Then use § 161. AB is 312 yd. (§ 155).

2. $BH = CF$ (Ax. 2). Then prove $\triangle ABH = \triangle DFC$ by § 79.

3. In $\triangle DPC$ and AQB, $DC = AB$ (§ 155), $DP = BQ$ (Hyp.), $\angle PDC = \angle QBA$ (§ 96). Use § 79.

4. Prove $\triangle RAB = \triangle DCS$ by § 79. Also $\triangle RAD = \triangle BCS$ by § 79, etc. Use § 160.

5. In $\triangle AOP$ and QOC, $AO = OC$ (§ 159), $\angle PAO = \angle QCO$ (§ 96), $\angle AOP = \angle QOC$ (§ 69), etc.

PAGE 83

8. Prove both AD and $HF \parallel$ and $= BC$ by §§ 146, 101, 155, and Ax. 1.

9. Use figure, p. 81 (text-book). Then $AB + BC > AC$ (§ 78). $BC + CD > BD$ (§ 78). $CD + AD > AC$ (§ 78). $AD + AB > BD$ (§ 78). Add, and divide by 2 (Ineq. Axs. 1 and 2).

12. Construct $\angle$ of 45° at each end of the given diagonal. Use §§ 102, 115, 92.

13. Construct the $\perp$ bisector of one diagonal (§ 128), and on it from the point of intersection mark off parts $= \frac{1}{2}$ the other diagonal.

PAGE 84

2. No. All polygons except triangles.

PAGE 86

1. 4.	**6.** 1080°.	**11.** 144°.
2. 8.	**7.** 1440°.	**12.** $157\frac{1}{2}°$.
3. 28.	**8.** 2880°.	**13.** 181°.
4. 36.	**9.** 120°.	**14.** 118°.
5. 540°.	**10.** $128\frac{4}{7}°$.	

16. Denote the angles of the quadrilateral by a, b, c, d. Let $a + b$ = 180°. Then $a + b + c + d$ = 360° (§ 167). $\therefore$ $c + d$ = 180° (Ax. 3).

17. Complete the figure thus:

$$A + a = 180° \text{ (§ 64)}$$
$$B + b = 180° \text{ (§ 64)}$$
$$C + c = 180° \text{ (§ 64)}$$

$$\therefore A + B + C + a + b + c = 540°.$$

(Ax. 2).

But $A + B + C$ = 180° (§ 102). $\therefore$ $a + b + c$ = 360° (Ax. 3).

18. Denote the angles of the $\square$ in order by a, b, c, d. If a = 90°, then b = 90° (§ 98), $c = d$ = 90° (§ 155).

19. $\left(\dfrac{2n - 4}{n}\right)$ 90 = 108, whence $180n - 360 = 108n$; $72n = 360$. $\therefore$ $n = 5$. *Ans.*

20. No; yes; no.

PAGE 89

6. Divide the given perimeter into 3 equal parts by § 170.

1. (Group 16). Use § 80.

2. Use figure, p. 64 (text-book). Thus,
Given $\angle ABC$, $BQ = BR$, BP the bisector of $\angle ABC$.
To prove $\triangle BQP = \triangle BRP$.
Proof. Use § 79.

3. Use § 79. Use figure of Ex. 2, p. 92.

4. § 83. Also $\triangle BAE = \triangle EDC$. For $\angle BAC = \angle DCA$ (corr. $\angle$ of = $\triangle$). $\angle DAC = \angle BCA$ (same reason). $\therefore$ $\angle BAE = \angle DCE$ (Ax. 3). $AB = DC$ (Hyp.). $\angle B = \angle D$ (corr. $\angle$ of = $\triangle$). $\therefore$ $\triangle BAE = \triangle DEC$ (§ 80).

5. Use § 80.

6.

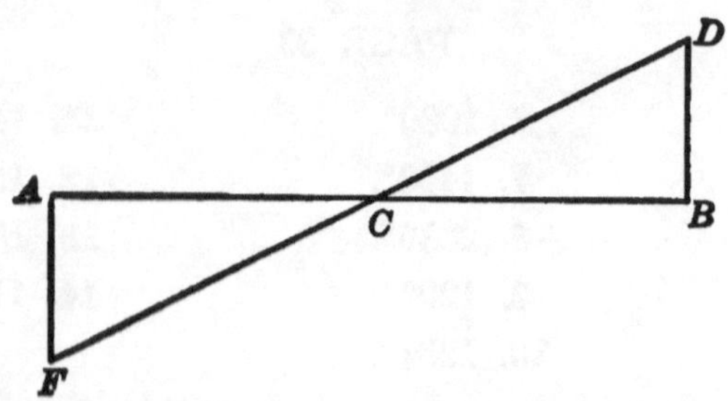

Given *ACB* and *FCD* straight lines; *AC* = *CB*; *AF* and *BD* ⊥ *AB*.
To prove △ *ACF* = △ *CDB*.
Proof.   *AC* = *CB*   (Hyp.);   ∠ *ACF* = ∠ *DCB*   (§ 69);   ∠ *A*
= ∠ *B* (§ 63).   ∴ △ *ACF* = ∠ *CDB* (§ 80).

7. Use figure, p. 78, (text-book).   Thus,
   Given line *AC* intersecting the line *BD* at the point *F*, and *AF*
   = *FC*, *BF* = *FD*.
   To prove △ *BFC* = △ *AFD*, and △ *BFA* = △ *CFD*.
   Proof.   Use § 79.

PAGE 90

8.

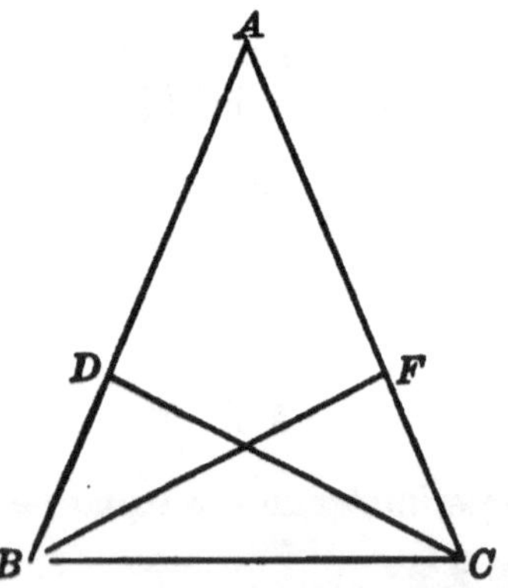

Given △ *ABC*, *AB* = *AC*, and *BD* = *FC*.
To prove △ *DBC* = △ *FBC*, and △ *ADC* = △ *AFB*.
Proof.   In ▲ *DBC* and *FBC*, *BC* = *BC* (Ident.), *DB* = *FC*
(Hyp.), ∠ *DBC* = ∠ *FCB* (§ 82).   ∴ △ *DBC* = △ *FBC* (§ 79).
Also in ▲ *ABF* and *ADC*, ∠*A* = ∠*A* (Ident.), *AB* = *AC* (Hyp.),
DB = *FC* (Hyp.).   ∴ *AD* = *AF* (Ax. 3).   ∴ △ *ABF* = △ *ADC*
(§ 79).

9. *AC* = *BD* (Ax. 2).   Use § 83.

10. The angles included by the legs are = (§ 63).   ∴ The ▲ are
    = (§ 79).

11. $AP = QC$ (Ax. 3).   Use § 79.

12. Two pairs.   Thus, using the figure of Ex. 8,
Given the $\triangle ABC$, $AB = AC$, $CD \perp AB$, $BF \perp AC$.
To prove $\triangle DBC = \triangle BFC$, and $\triangle ABF = \triangle ADC$.
Proof.   In $\triangle DBC$ and BFC, $BC = BC$ (Ident.), $\angle DBC = \angle FCB$ (§ 82). $\therefore \triangle DBC = \triangle BFC$ (§ 110).   Also in $\triangle ADC$ and ABF, $AB = AC$ (Hyp.), $\angle A = \angle A$ (Ident.). $\therefore \triangle ADC = \triangle ABF$ (§ 110).

13.

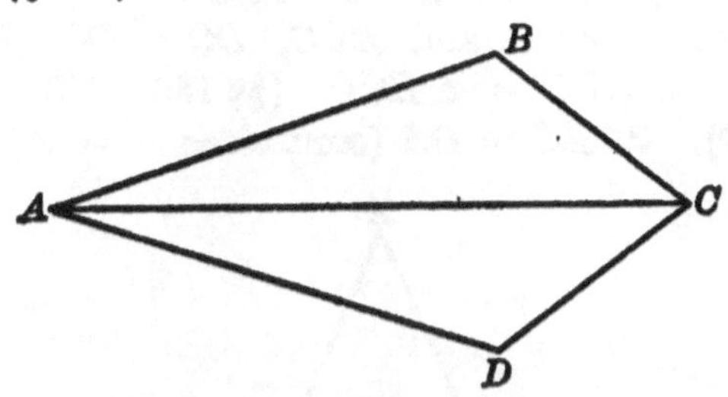

Given the quadrilateral $ABCD$, $AB = AD$, and $\angle BAC = \angle DAC$.
To prove $\triangle BAC = \triangle DAC$.
Proof.   Use § 79.

14.

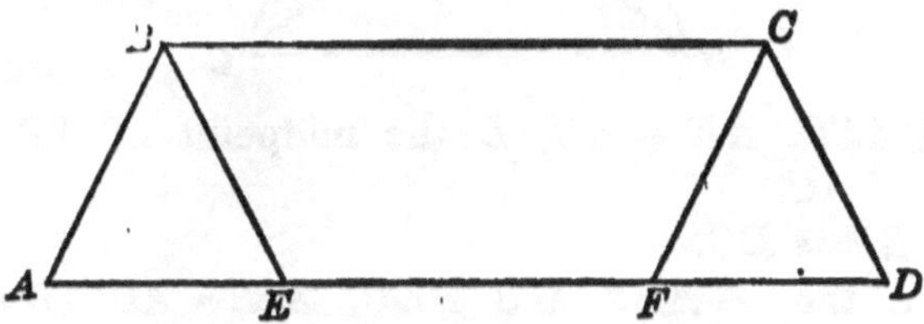

Given $BC \parallel AD$, $AB = CD$. $BE \parallel CD$, $CF \parallel AB$.
To prove $\triangle ABE = \triangle CFD$.
Proof.   In $\triangle ABE$ and CFD, $AB = CF$, $BE = CD$ (§ 155). $\angle ABE = \angle FCD$ (§ 112). $\therefore \triangle ABE = \triangle FCD$ (§ 79).

PAGE 92

1. See Ex. 1, p. 89.

2. See Ex. 3, p. 89.

3. See Ex. 5, p. 89.

4. See Ex. 8, p. 90.

PAGE 93

5. See Ex. 1, p. 50.

6. Use § 79.

7. See Ex. 12, p. 90.

8.

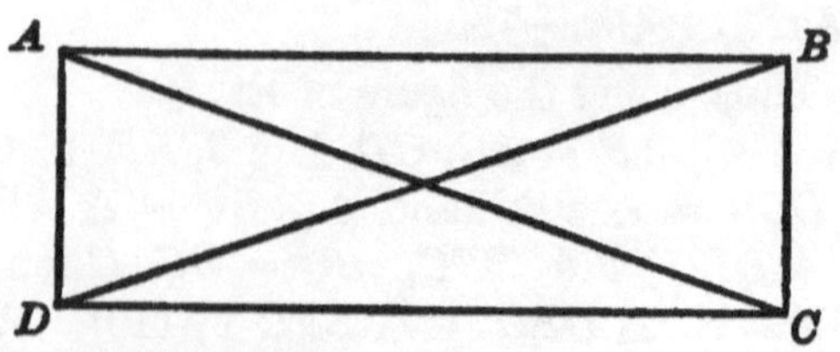

Given the rectangle $ABCD$.

To prove the diagonals AC and BD equal.

Proof. In the ▲ ADC and BDC, $DC = DC$ (Ident.), $AD = BC$ (§ 155), $\angle ADC = \angle BCD$ (§§ 149, 63). ∴ $\triangle ADC = \triangle DBC$ (§ 79). ∴ $AC = DB$ (corr. sides of = ▲).

9.

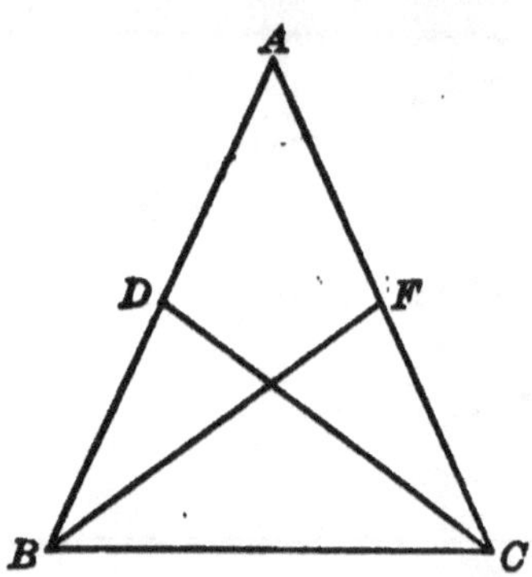

Given $\triangle ABC$, $AB = AC$, D the midpoint of AB, and F the midpoint of AC.

To prove $BF = DC$.

Proof. In the ▲ ABF and ADC, $AB = AC$ (Hyp.). $AF = AD$ (Ax. 5.) $\angle A = \angle A$ (Ident.). ∴ $\triangle ABF = \triangle ADC$ (§ 79). ∴ $BF = DC$.

10. Use the figure of Ex. 8, p. 90.

Given the $\triangle ABC$, $CD \perp AB$, and $BF \perp AC$; and $CD = BF$.

To prove $AB = AC$.

Proof. In the ▲ CDB and BFC, $BC = BC$ (Ident.), $DC = FB$ (Hyp.). ∴ $\triangle DBC = \triangle FBC$ (§ 117). ∴ $\angle DBC = \angle FCB$ (corr. ⊿ of = ▲). ∴ $AB = AC$ (§ 115).

11. **Given** $ABCD$ a ▱, BD a diagonal, AF and $CH \perp DB$.

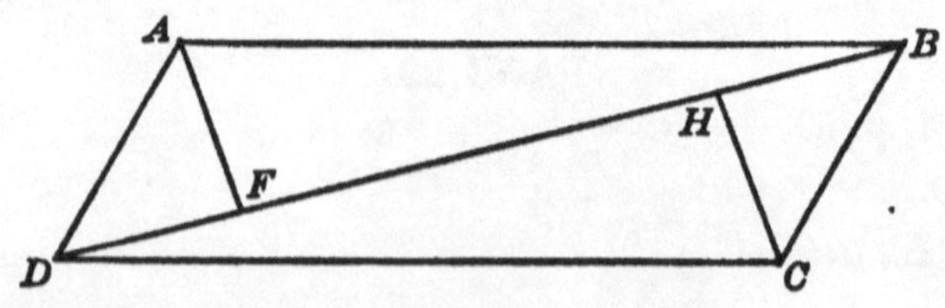

To prove *AF = HC.*

Proof. In the ▲ *AFB* and *DHC, AB = DC* (§ 155), ∠ *ABF =* ∠ *CDH* (§ 96).   ∴ △ *AFB* = △ *DCB* (§ 110), etc.

12. Use § 79.   **13.** Use §§ 82, 79.

14. Put the letter *B* at the vertex.   Then ∠ *BAP* = ∠ *BPA*   (§ 82). ∴ ∠ *OAP* = ∠ *OPA* (Ax. 5).   ∴ *OA = OP* (§ 115).

15. ∠ *B* = ∠ *C*   (§ 82).   ∠ *ADE* = ∠ *B* (§ 97).   ∠ *AED* = ∠ *C* (§ 97).   ∴ ∠ *AED* = ∠ *ADE* (Ax. 1).   ∴ *AD = AE* (§ 115).

16. △ *BAC* = △ *DAC* (Ex. 4, p. 89).   ∴ ∠ *DAC* = ∠ *BCA* (corr. ∠ of = ▲).   ∴ *AE = EC* (§ 115).

17. Use ▲ *ADQ* and *PBC* and § 79.

PAGE 94

1. See Ex. 1, p. 89.   **4.** See Ex. 8. p. 90.

2. See Ex. 5, p. 89.   **5.** See Ex. 12, p. 90.

3. See Ex. 4, p. 89.

6.

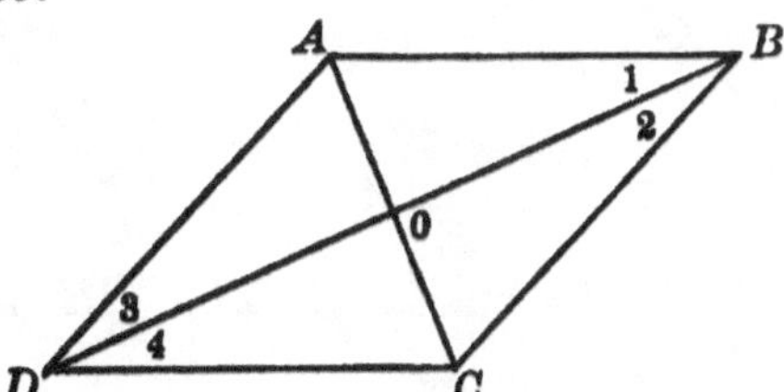

Given *ABCD* a ▱ in which *AB = BC = CD = DA.*

To prove   ∠ *ADB* = ∠ *CDB,* and   ∠ *ABD* = ∠ *CBD;*   also ∠ *DAC* = ∠ *BAC,* and ∠ *DCA* = ∠ *BCA.*

Proof.   ∠ 1 = ∠ 4 (§ 96).   But in △ *ABD, AB = AD* (Hyp.). ∴ ∠ 1 = ∠ 3 (§ 82).   ∴ ∠ 3 = ∠ 4 (Ax. 1), etc.   Or, the theorem may be proved by the use of ▲.

7. See Ex. 1, p. 39.   **8.** See Ex. 15, p. 93.

PAGE 95

9. ∠ *DCE* = ∠ *ECA* (Hyp.).   ∠ *A* = ∠ *ECA* (§ 79).   ∠ *B* = ∠ *DCE* (§ 97).   ∠ *A* = ∠ *B* (Ax. 1).

10. ∠ *DCE* = ∠ *B* (§ 97).   ∠ *A* = ∠ *ECA* (§ 96).   But ∠ *A* = ∠ *B* (Hyp.).   ∴ ∠ *DCE* = ∠ *ECA* (Ax. 1).

11. ∠ *CBD* = ∠ *BPR* (§ 96).   ∠ *PBR* = ∠ *CBD* (Hyp.).   ∴ ∠ *BPR* = ∠ *PBR* (Ax. 1).   ∴ *BR = PR* (§ 115).

If from any point in the bisector of an angle a line is drawn parallel to one side of the angle, and meeting the other side, the triangle thus formed is isosceles.

12. $\angle ABC = \angle ACB$ (§ 82). $\therefore$ $\angle DBC = \angle ECB$ (§ 66). $\therefore$ $\triangle DBC = \triangle BCE$ (§ 79), etc.

13. Use § 66 (complements of equal $\angle$ are equal).

14. Denote the small $\angle$ to the left of the vertex by 1, 2; those to the right by 3, 4. Then $\angle 1 = \angle 4$ (§ 69); $\angle 2 = \angle 3$ (§ 69). But $\angle 3 = \angle 4$ (Hyp.). $\therefore$ $\angle 1 = \angle 2$ (Ax. 1).

PAGE 96

1. Use figure of Ex. 2, p. 92 (text-book.) Show $\triangle DCE = \triangle BCA$ (§79). $\therefore$ $\angle E = \angle B$ (corr. $\angle$ of $=$ $\triangle$). $\therefore$ $DE \parallel BA$ (§ 89).

2. § 96, Ax. 5, § 89.

3. $\angle DCA = \angle A + \angle B$ (§ 103). $\therefore$ $2 \angle DCE = 2 \angle B$ (Ax. 9). $\therefore$ $\angle DCE = \angle B$ (Ax. 5). $\therefore$ $CE \parallel AB$ (§ 91).

4.

Given the $\square ABCD$, AF bisects $\angle DAB$, CH bisects $\angle DCB$.
To prove $AF \parallel HC$.
Proof. $\angle DAB = \angle DCB$ (§ 155); $\angle 2 = \angle 3$ (Ax. 5). But $\angle 3 = \angle 5$ (§ 96); $\angle 2 = \angle 5$ (Ax. 1). $\therefore$ $AF \parallel CH$ (§ 91).

5. Use the figure of Ex. 8, p. 93.
Given the lines AB and DC, AD and $BC \perp DC$, $AD = BC$.
To prove $AB \parallel DC$.
Proof. $AD \parallel BC$ (§ 92), $AD = BC$ (Hyp.). $DABC$ is a $\square$ (§ 161).

PAGE 97

1. 57°; 85°.

2. 135°.

3. $125°$; $180° - \dfrac{p° + q°}{2}$.

4. 70°; 20°; 50°.

5. 140°.

6. § 168. $\dfrac{(12 - 2) 180°}{12}$, or 150°.

7. 5; 9; 35; $\dfrac{n(n - 3)}{2}$. In general, in a polygon of n sides the number of diagonals $= {}_nC_2 - n = \dfrac{n(n - 1)}{2} - n = \dfrac{n^2 - n - 2n}{2} = \dfrac{n(n - 3)}{2}$. Or we may reason thus: from each vertex $n - 3$

diagonals may be drawn. $\therefore$ from n vertices $n(n-3)$ diagonals are drawn; but each of these is used twice. The number of distinct diagonals is $\dfrac{n(n-3)}{2}$.

8. Denote the supplementary adj. $\measuredangle$ by $2 \angle a$ and $2 \angle b$. Then $2 \angle a + 2 \angle b = 180°$ (§ 68). $\therefore$ $\angle a + \angle b = 90°$ (Ax. 5).

PAGE 98

9. Denote the $\parallel$ lines by AB and CD, the transversal by PQ, the bisectors by PR and QR. Then $\angle BPQ + PQD = 2$ rt. $\measuredangle$. (§ 98). $\therefore$ $\angle RPQ + \angle PQR = 1$ rt. $\angle$ (Ax. 5). .... (1) But $\angle R + \angle RPQ + \angle PQR = 2$ rt. $\measuredangle$ (§ 102) ... (2) Subtract (1) from (2), $\angle R = 1$ rt. $\angle$ (Ax. 3).

10. $\angle BCA = \angle A$ (§ 82), $\angle BCD = \angle D$ (§ 82). $\therefore$ $2 \angle A + 2 \angle D = 180°$ (§ 102). $\therefore$ $\angle A + \angle D = 90°$, or $\angle BCA + \angle BCD = 90°$ (Ax. 9).

1. Let x be the complement. $\therefore$ $3x =$ the $\angle$. $\therefore$ $3x + x = 90°$. $\therefore$ $x = 22\frac{1}{2}°$, $3x = 67\frac{1}{2}°$. *Ans.*

2. 90°; 45°.   **3.** 36°; 72°; 108°; 144°.   **4.** 30°; 60°; 90°.

5. Let $x =$ the less $\angle$. Then $x + 30° =$ the greater $\angle$. $\therefore$ $x + x + 30° = 180°$. $\therefore$ $x = 75°$; $x + 30° = 105°$. *Ans.*

6. $x + 2x + x + 2x = 360°$, etc.; 60°; 120°. *Ans.*

7. The vertex $\angle = 180° - 105° = 75°$. Hence, $x + 2x + 75° = 180°$, etc. 35°; 70°; 75°. *Ans.*

PAGE 99

8. 9.   **9.** 7; 12; 6.

10. Denote the number of sides by n. Then $\dfrac{2n-4}{n} = \dfrac{7}{4}$ (§ 168). $\therefore$ $n = 16$. *Ans.*

11. The exterior $\measuredangle$ at the base are $180° - a$ and $180° - b$. The vertex $\angle$ of the $\triangle$ is $180° - (a + b)$ (§ 102). $180° - a + 180° - b - (180° - a - b) = 180° - a + 180° - b - 180° + a + b = 180°$.

12. The exterior $\angle$ of the small $\triangle$ on the base (to the right) is $b + x$. $\therefore$ $a + x = b + x$ (§ 103). $\therefore$ $a = b$ (Ax. 3).

13. In the original $\triangle$ the $\measuredangle$ are b, x, x. $\therefore$ $b + x + x = 180°$ (§ 102). $\therefore$ $\angle b = 180° - 2x$. $\therefore$ $\frac{1}{2}b = 90° - x$ (Ax. 5). But $a = 90° - x$ (§ 106). $\therefore$ $a = \frac{1}{2}b$ (Ax. 1).

14. $x + y = 180°$ (Ax. 5).   ∴ each pair of opposite sides in the figure is || (§ 94), etc.

<h2 style="text-align:center">PAGE 100</h2>

1. Use § 83.

2. Use the figure of Ex. 14, p. 90 (omitting line BE). Draw CF || AB. Then $BA = FC$ (§ 157). But $BA = CD$ (Hyp.). ∴ $CF = CD$ (Ax. 1). ∴ $\angle CFD = \angle D$ (§ 82). But $\angle A = \angle CFD$ (§ 97). ∴ $\angle A = \angle D$ (Ax. 1).

3. If the angles which the legs of a trapezoid make with a base of the trapezoid are equal, the trapezoid is isosceles.

Draw the same auxiliary line as in the preceding Ex. and reverse the process of proof.

Exs. 2 and 3 may also be proved by drawing ⊥s from the extremities of the upper base to the lower base and using §§ 92, 157, 117, 111.

4. Draw a line through the vertex of $\angle b$ parallel with AB and use §§ 101, 96, and Ax. 2.

5. Draw the same auxiliary line as in Ex. 4.

6. Then prove $\triangle ADF = \triangle FDC$ by §§ 100, 63, 79.

7. Use the figure of Ex. 6 (text-book).

Let $\angle A = 2 \angle B$. Draw the median DC as an auxiliary line. Then $DA = DC$ (Ex. 6). ∴ $\angle DCA = \angle A$ (§ 82). Also $DB = DC$ (Ex. 6). ∴ $\angle DCB = \angle B$. Adding, $\angle A + \angle B = \angle DCA + \angle DCB = 90°$ (Ax. 2). ∴ $3 \angle B = 90°$, or $2 \angle B = 60°$. ∴ $\angle DCA = 60°$ (Ax. 1). ∴ $\angle ADC = 60°$ (§ 102). ∴ $AC = AD$ (§ 115) $= \frac{1}{2}AB$ (Hyp.).

8. From P draw $PT \perp AD$. ∴ PT || BC (§ 92), $\angle APT = \angle B$ (§ 97). ∴ $\triangle ARP = \triangle ATP$ (§ 110). ∴ $PR = AT$. But $PQ = TD$ (§ 157). Use Ax. 2.

9. Denote the vertex between A and C by F, and the other vertex by H. Draw AC and BD. Then $ABDC$ is a ▱ (§ 161). ∴ $AC = BD$ (§ 155). ∴ $\triangle AFC = \triangle BHD$ (§ 83). ∴ $\angle F = \angle H$. Also $\angle ABD = \angle ACD$ (§ 155). $\angle HBD = \angle ACF$ (corr. ∠ of = ▵). Adding, $\angle HBA = \angle FCD$ (Ax. 2), etc.

<h2 style="text-align:center">PAGE 101</h2>

10. Draw $DX \perp AC$, meeting AC in the point X, and draw $EY \perp AC$, and meeting AC produced at Y. Prove $\triangle ADX = \triangle CEY$ (§ 110). ∴ $\triangle DXF = \triangle FYE$ (§ 111), etc.

2. For if the two lines are parallel, the alt. int. $\angle$ are $=$ (§ 96), which is contrary to the hypothesis. Hence the two given lines are not ‖.

PAGE 102

4. *CPQ* is a straight line (Constr.). ∴ $\angle BPQ = \angle CPA$ (§ 69). But $\angle BPD = \angle CPA$ (Hyp.) ∴ $\angle BPQ = \angle BPD$ (Ax. 1). ∴ *PQ* coincides with *PD*. ∴ *PD* is in the same straight line with *CP* (for it coincides with *PQ*, which is in the same straight line with *CP*).

5. Produce the bisector of one of the vertical $\angle$ and show that the bisector of the other vertical $\angle$ coincides with the produced line (use the same method of proof as in Ex. 4).

6. Let *BE* and *DC* intersect at the point *F*. If *DC* and *BE* bisect each other show $\triangle BFD = \triangle FEC$ (§ 79). ∴ $\angle FBD = \angle FEC$ (corr. $\angle$ of $=$ $\triangle$). ∴ $DB \parallel EC$ (§ 89), which is impossible, since *AB* and *AC* meet in the point *A*. ∴ *BE* and *DC* cannot bisect each other.

1. (Group 24). Use the figure of Ex. 13, p. 90. Let $\angle BAC = \angle DAC$, and $\angle BCA = \angle DCA$; prove $\triangle ABC = \triangle ADC$. Use § 80.

2.

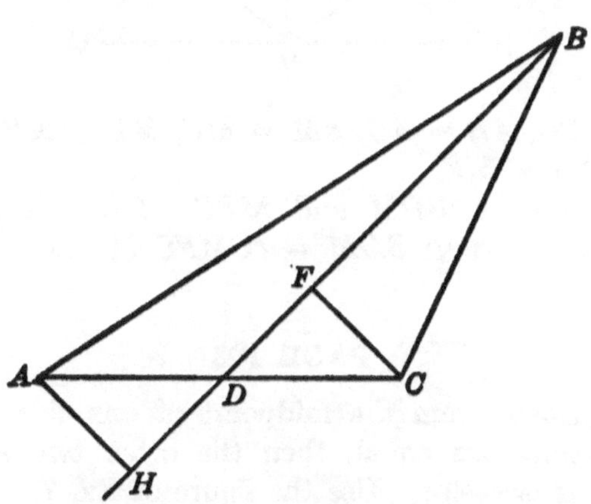

Given the $\triangle ABC$, the median *BH*, *AH* and *FC* $\perp$ *BH*.
To prove $AH = FC$.
Proof. In the $\triangle$ *AHD* and *DFC*, $AD = DC$ (Hyp.). $\angle ADH = \angle FDC$ (§ 69). $\angle AHD = \angle CFD$ (§ 63). ∴ $\triangle AHD = \triangle DFC$ (§ 110). ∴ $AH = FC$ (corr. sides of $=$ $\triangle$).

3. Use the figure of Ex. 8, p. 90. Let *ABC* be the given $\triangle$, *CD* $\perp$ *AB*, *BF* $\perp$ *AC*; prove $\triangle DBC = \triangle BFC$ (§ 117), etc.

4. Denote the point of intersection by F. Then $AF + FC > AC$ (§ 78), $FD + FB > DB$ (§ 78). Add, etc.

5. 68°; 34°; 102°; etc.

6.

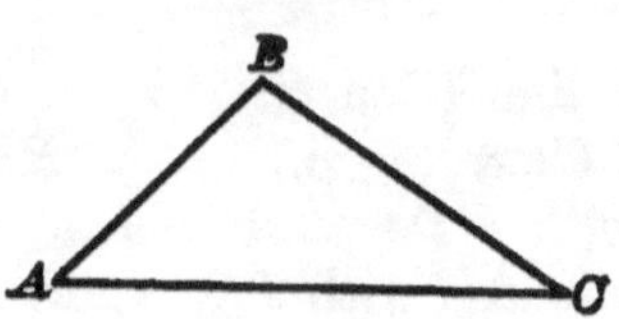

Given AB any side of the $\triangle ABC$, and $AC > BC$.

To prove $AB > AC - BC$.

Proof. $AB + BC > AC$ (§ 78). Subtracting BC from each member of the inequality, $AB > AC - BC$ (Ineq. Ax. 1, § 133).

7.

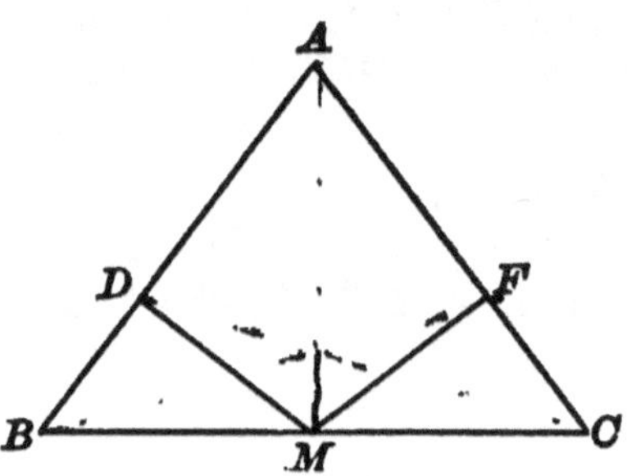

Given $\triangle ABC$, $AB = AC$, $BM = MC$, $MD \perp AB$, $MF \perp AC$.

To prove $DM = MF$.

Proof. In the $\triangle BDM$ and MFC, $\angle B = \angle C$ (§ 82). $BM = MC$ (Hyp.). $\therefore \triangle BDM = \triangle MFC$ (§ 110). $\therefore DM = MF$, etc.

PAGE 103

8. If the $\perp$s drawn from the midpoint of one side of a $\triangle$ to the other two sides are equal, then the other two sides are equal, and the $\triangle$ is isosceles. Use the figure of Ex. 7. **Prove** $\triangle BDM = \triangle MFC$ (§ 117). $\therefore \angle B = \angle C$. $\therefore AB = AC$ (§ 115).

9. Denote the vertex $\angle$ by $2x$. Then each base $\angle = 90° - x$ (§ 102). Hence an ext. $\angle$ at the base $= 2x + 90° - x$ (§ 103), etc.

10. Draw an auxiliary line from the vertex of $\angle a$ to the vertex of $\angle d$, and produce this line through vertex of $\angle d$. Use § 103 (twice) and add (Ax. 2).

11. $AC + CD > AD$ (§ 78), or $BC + CD > AD$ (Ax. 9). Also $\angle ACD$ is 120° (§ 103). ∴ $\angle ACD > \angle D$ (§ 105). ∴ $AD > AC$ (§ 135), or $AD > AB$ (Ax. 9).

12.

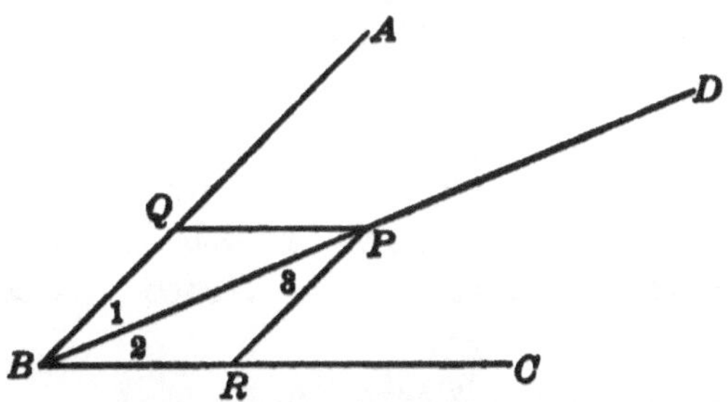

Given BD the bisector of the $\angle ABC$, $PQ \parallel BC$, $PR \parallel AB$.
To prove $PQBR$ a rhombus.
Proof. $\angle 1 = \angle 2$ (Hyp.), $\angle 1 = \angle 3$ (§ 96). ∴ $\angle 2 = \angle 3$ (Ax. 1). ∴ $BR = PR$ (§ 115). But $BQ = PR$ and $QP = BR$ (§ 155). ∴ $PR = BR = BQ = QP$ (Ax. 1).

13. Use the figure of p. 37 (text-book).
Given $\triangle ABC$, $BD \perp AC$, $AD = DC$.
To prove $AB = BC$.
Proof. Show $\triangle ADB = \triangle BDC$ by § 79, etc. Or use § 120.

14. $\angle B = \angle C$ (§ 82). ∴ $2 \angle C + 4 \angle C = 180°$ (§ 102). ∴ $6 \angle C = 180°$. ∴ $\angle C = 30°$ (Ax. 5). ∴ $\angle BED = 60°$ (§ 102). ∴ $\angle EAF = \angle B + \angle C = 2 \angle C = 60°$ (§ 103). ∴ $\angle EFA = 60°$ (§ 102).

15. Use the figure of Ex. 6, p. 94.
Given the quadrilateral $ABCD$, in which the diagonals AC and BD intersect at rt. $\angle$ in the point O, $AO = OC$, and $BO = OD$.
To prove $ABCD$ a rhombus.
Proof. In the $\triangle AOB$ and BOC, $AO = OC$ (Hyp.), $BO = BO$ (Ident.), $\angle BOA = \angle BOC$ (§ 63). ∴ $\triangle AOB = \triangle BOC$ (§ 79). ∴ $AB = BC$ (corr. $\angle$ of = $\triangle$). In like manner it can be proved that $BC = CD = AD$. Hence $ABCD$ is a $\square$ (§ 160), and a rhombus (§ 148). If the diagonals of the given figure are equal the figure may be shown to be a square.

16. Use the figure of Ex. 8, p. 90. Let DC and BF intersect at the point O and draw OA. Prove $\triangle DBC = \triangle BFC$ (§ 110). ∴ $\angle OBC = \angle OCB$. ∴ $BO = OC$ (§ 115). Hence prove $\triangle BOA = \triangle AOC$ (§ 83), etc.

17. See figure, p. 64 (text-book). Let $PQ \perp AB$, $PR \perp BC$. Then, in the quadrilateral $PQBR$, $\angle PQB + \angle QBR + \angle BRP + \angle$

$RPQ = 4$ rt. $\angle$ (§ 167).   But $\angle PQR + \angle PRB = 2$ rt. $\angle$ (Hyp.) Subtract, etc.

18. $AP \parallel QC$ (Hyp. and § 146), $AB = DC$ (§ 155). $\therefore AP = QC$ (Ax. 3). $\therefore APCQ$ is a $\square$ (§ 161).

19. Use figure of Ex. 8, p. 93.   Prove $\triangle ADB = \triangle ACD$ (§ 83). $\therefore \angle BAD = \angle CDA$ (corr. $\angle$ of $=$ $\triangle$).   But $\angle BAD + \angle CDA = 2$ rt. $\angle$ (§ 98). $\therefore 2 \angle BAD = 2$ rt. $\angle$ (Ax. 9). $\therefore \angle BAD = 1$ rt. $\angle$.   In like manner it may be shown that the other $\angle$ of $ABCD$ are rt. $\angle$.   Hence $ABCD$ is a rectangle (§ 149).

PAGE 104

20. AC.   For $\angle BCA = 60°$ (§ 64). $\therefore \angle B = 70°$ (§ 102).   Use § 135.

21.

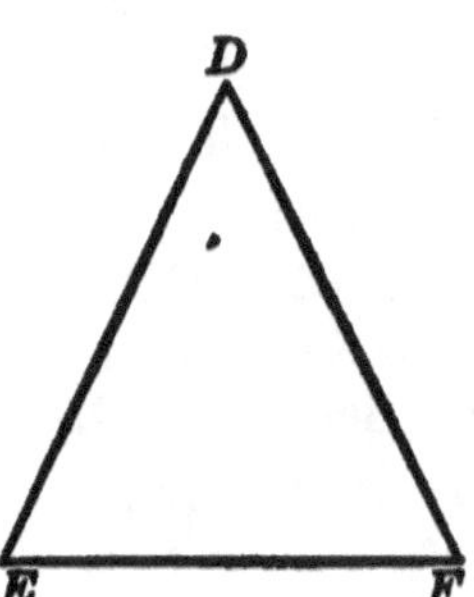

Two cases arise according as the given $\angle$ is a base $\angle$ or a vertex $\angle$.
I. Given $\triangle$ ABC and DEF, $BC = EF$, $AB = AC$, $DE = DF$, $\angle B = \angle E$.
To prove $\triangle ABC = \triangle DEF$.
Proof. $\angle C = \angle B$ (§ 82), $\angle F = \angle E$ (§ 82).   But $\angle B = \angle E$ (Hyp.). $\therefore \angle C = \angle F$ (Ax. 1).   Hence, prove $\triangle ABC = \triangle DEF$ (§ 80).
II. Given ABC and DEF isosceles $\triangle$ in which the base $BC =$ the base EF and $\angle A = \angle D$.
To prove $\triangle ABC = \triangle DEF$.
Proof. Show that $\angle B = \frac{1}{2}(180° - \angle A)$ (§ 102).   Also, $\angle E = (180° - D)$ (§ 102). $\therefore \angle B = \angle E$ (Ax. 1), etc.   Use § 80.

22. Use §§ 111, 102, 115, etc.

23. Produce AP to meet BC at Q.
Then $AB + BQ > AP + PQ$ (§ 78); $PQ + QC > PC$ (§ 78).
$\therefore AB + BQ + PQ + QC > AP + PQ + PC$ (Ineq. Ax. 1).
$\therefore AB + BQ + QC > AP + PC$ (Ineq. Ax. 1), etc.

24. $\angle APC > \angle PQC > \angle B$ (§ 87). ∴ $\angle APC > \angle B$ (§ 133, Ineq. Ax. 4).

25.

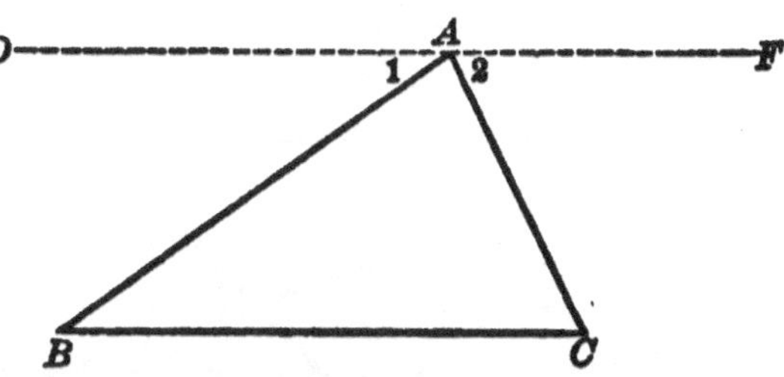

Given the $\triangle ABC$.

To prove $\angle B + \angle BAC + \angle C = 2$ rt. $\angle$.

Proof. Draw DF through $A \parallel BC$. Then $\angle 1 + \angle BAC + \angle 2 = 2$ rt. $\angle$ (§ 68). But $\angle 1 = \angle B$, $\angle 2 = \angle C$ (§ 96). Substituting, $\angle B + \angle BAC + \angle C = 2$ rt. $\angle$ (Ax. 9).

26. $AC = BC$ (Hyp.), $RC = BQ$ (Hyp.), $AR = QC$ (Ax. 3). $\angle A = \angle C$ (§ 82). ∴ $\triangle APR = \triangle QRC$ (§ 79). ∴ $PR = QR$. In like manner show $PR = PQ$, etc.

27. Denote the point of intersection of the bisectors by R. Then show the $\triangle APR$ to be isosceles (§ 96, Ax. 1, § 115). ∴ $AP = PR$. In like manner show that $\triangle RQC$ is isosceles and $RQ = QC$. Use Ax. 2.

28. Use superposition. Or, draw a pair of corresponding diagonals and use § 79, Ax. 3, and § 79 again.

29. See Ex. 17, p. 86.

PAGE 105

30. See Ex. 17, p. 86.

31. Use Ex. 9, p. 98, and § 92.

32. Use Ex. 31. Then show that the sides of the rectangle are equal.

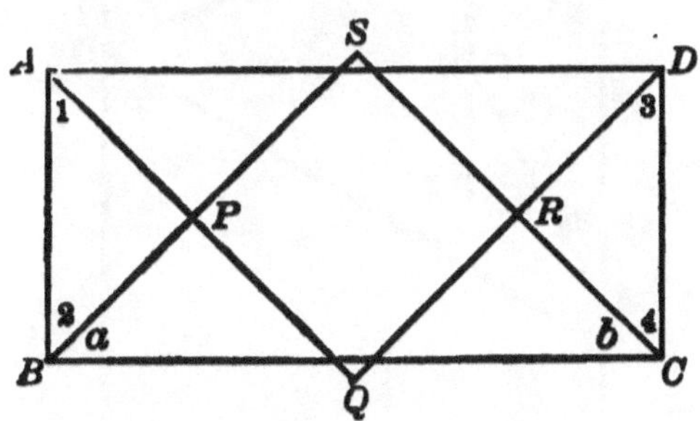

Thus, on the figure, $\angle 1 = \angle 2 = \angle 3 = \angle 4$ (each $= \frac{1}{2}$ a rt. $\angle$). $AB = CD$ (§ 155). ∴ $\triangle ABP = \triangle CRD$ (§ 119).

∴ *BP* = *RC* (corr. sides of = △).   But ∠ *a* = ∠ *b* (each = ½ a rt. ∠).   ∴ *BS* = *CS* (§ 115).   ∴ *PS* = *SR* (Ax. 3).

33. §§ 101, 155, 83.

34.

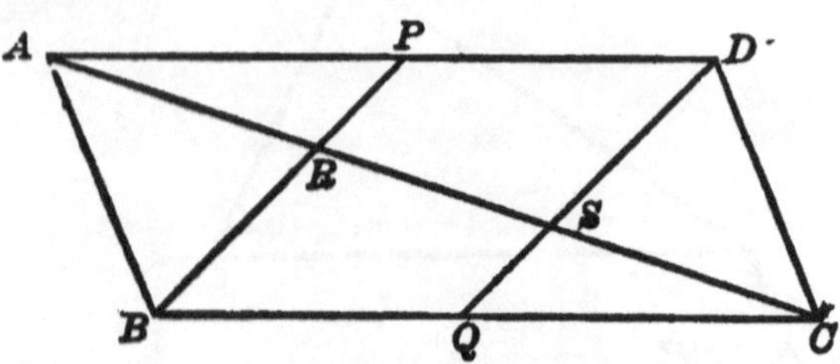

Given *ABCD* a ▱, *AP* = *PD*, *BQ* = *QC*.

To prove *AR* = *RS* = *SC*.

Proof.   *PD* = *BQ* (Ax. 5).   ∴ *PDQB* is a ▱ (§ 161).   In △ *ADS*, *AR* = *RS* (§ 169).   Also in △ *CRB*, *RS* = *SC* (§ 169).   ∴ *AR* = *RS* = *SC* (Ax. 1).

35. △ *ABP* = △ *CQD* (§ 79).   ∴ ∠ *BPQ* = ∠ *DQP* (§ 66).   ∴ *BP* ‖ *QD* (§ 89).   Use § 161.   Six.

36. Use Ex. 2, p. 100, and § 98.

37. Use Ex. 2, p. 100, and § 79.

1. 22½°; 67½°; 146¼°; 11¼°.

2. By the law of reflection, ∠ *POA'* = ∠ *ROB'*;   or, 90° − *x* = ∠ *POB* − *y* + ∠ *BOB'*.   ∴ 90° − *x* = 90° − *y* + *x*.   ∴ *y* = 2*x*.

PAGE 106

3. See Ex. 8, p. 83.

5.

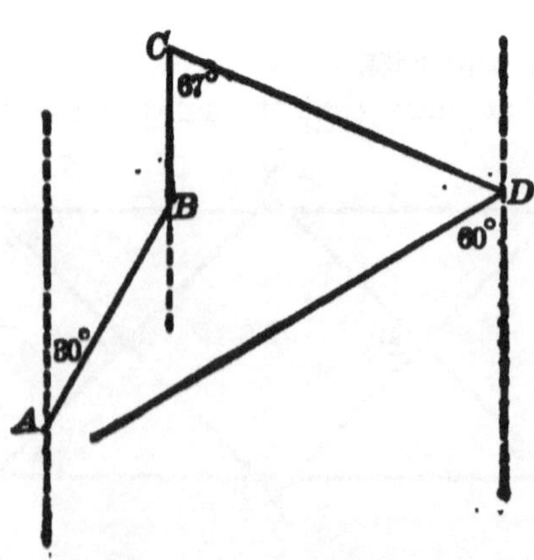

7. But *a* + *b* + *c* = 180° (§ 102).   ∴ *c* = 90° (Ax. 3).

PAGE 107

1. §§ 57, 59.
2. §§ 15, 96, 97, 98, 100, 101, 157, 158, 169.
3. §§ 55, 56, 58, 69, 99.
4. §§ 60, 61, 63, 64, 65, 66, 67, 68, 69, 112, 113, 114, 126.
5. §§ 70, 78, 87, 102, 103, 104, 105, 134, 135.
6. §§ 79, 80, 83, 107, 109, 110, 111, 117, 138, 139.
7. §§ 142, 160, 161, 162.
8. §§ 146, 155, 156, 159, 167.
9. § 148, also see Ex. 6, p. 82.

PAGE 108

10. See §§ 73, 74.   11. See §§ 73, 74.
12. Make the three angles of one $\triangle$ = the corresponding angles of the other, but the corresponding sides unequal.
13. When two straight lines intersect after one of the angles of intersection has been measured, Prop. I enables us to determine the other angles without the labor of measuring them, etc.
15. § 172.   16. § 174.

PAGE 113

1. Prop. II enables us to determine without effort the equality of two arcs in a circle or equal circles, when the central angles which these arcs subtend are equal, etc.

PAGE 114

1. 1¼ in.

PAGE 115

1. 1 in.
2. Prop. V enables us to determine without effort the equality of two chords in a circle or equal circles, when the arcs subtended by these chords are known to be equal.
3. No.

PAGE 117

1. $\therefore$ $\overparen{AB} = \overparen{CD}$ (§ 198). To each of these add $\overparen{BC}$, etc.
2. $\therefore$ $\overparen{PR} = \overparen{QS}$ (§ 198). $\therefore$ $\overparen{PQ} = \overparen{RS}$ (Ax. 3). $\therefore$ Chord $PQ =$ chord RS (§ 200), etc.

3. $\overset{\frown}{AC} > \overset{\frown}{BD}$ (Hyp.). Subtract $\overset{\frown}{BC}$ from each. $\therefore \overset{\frown}{AB} > \overset{\frown}{CD}$ (Ineq. Ax. 1). $\therefore$ chord $AB >$ chord CD (§ 201).

4. If A, B, C, and D are four points taken in succession on a semi-circle, and chord $AB >$ chord CD, then $\overset{\frown}{AC} > \overset{\frown}{BD}$.

For $\overset{\frown}{AB} > \overset{\frown}{CD}$ (§ 201). Add $\overset{\frown}{BC}$ to each, etc.

8. 120°.

PAGE 120

3. Construct an arc of 45° and bisect it.

4. The point F; no.

PAGE 121

1. $\frac{1}{2}$ sec.; $\frac{3}{4}$ sec.

PAGE 125

1. Then $SO = OR$ (§ 207). Prove $\triangle SPO = \triangle OPR$ by § 117.

2. Use § 207.   **3.** No. Use § 78.

4. Use the figure of p. 121 (text-book). Chord $AB =$ chord CD (§ 207). $\therefore \overset{\frown}{AB} = \overset{\frown}{CD}$ (§ 198).

5. $\angle C + \angle D$ is suppl. $\angle COD$ (§ 102);
$\angle g + \angle h$ is suppl. $\angle COD$ (§ 68);
$\therefore \angle C + \angle D = \angle g + \angle h$ (§ 66). $\therefore 2 \angle D = 2 \angle h$ (Ax. 9), etc.

6. The tangents are $\perp$ the diameter (§ 210), and $\therefore$ $\parallel$ (§ 92).

7. Use § 121.

PAGE 127

1. 4.   **2.** An infinite number.   **3.** The circles intersect.

PAGE 129

1. Use § 78.   **2.** $\odot$ touching externally.

3. One $\odot$ outside the other.

4. Intersecting $\odot$ or one $\odot$ within the other.

5. Intersecting $\odot$.   **6.** No.   **7.** Yes.

8. One circle is wholly within the other.

PAGE 130

1. One internal, two external.   **3.** Two external.

2. One external.   **4.** None.

5. Two internal and two external.

1. (Group 30). Use the figure, p. 127 (text-book). Draw AB. $PA = PB$ (§ 216), $OA = OB$ (§ 188), $PO \perp AB$ (§ 121).

2. Use figure 3, p. 142 (text-book). $PA = PB$ (§ 216). $\therefore \angle PAB = \angle PBA$ (§ 82). $\therefore \angle PAB = \frac{1}{2}(180° - 60°) = 60°$ (§ 102), etc.

PAGE 131

3. $RP = RA$ (§ 216), $PQ = QB$ (§ 216). $\therefore RP + PQ = RA + QB$ (Ax. 2).

4.

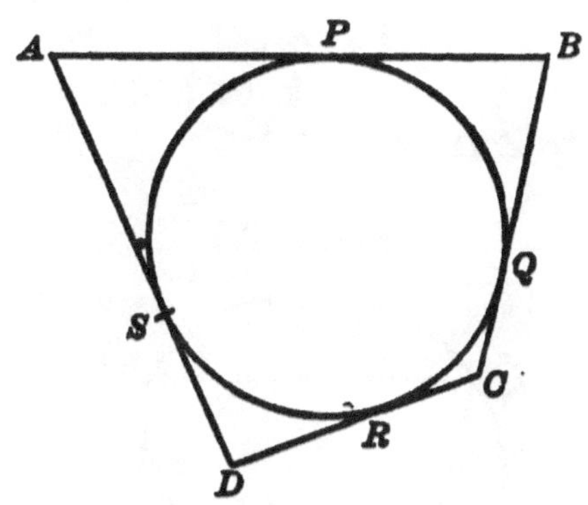

On the figure,
$$\left.\begin{array}{l} PA = SA, \\ PB = QB, \\ RD = SD, \\ RC = QC. \end{array}\right\} \text{(§ 216).}$$
Adding, $AB + CD = AD + BC$ (Ax. 2).

5 Use the method of Ex. 4.   6. Use the method of Ex. 4.

7. In the figure of Ex. 4, if $ABCD$ becomes a $\square$, $AB = DC$, and $BC = AD$ (§ 155). $\therefore AB + AB = AD + AD$ (Ex. 4 and Ax. 9). $\therefore 2AB = 2AD$. $\therefore AB = AD$ (Ax. 5), etc.

8. $AP = PC$ (§ 216), $PB = PC$ (§ 216). $\therefore AP = PB$ (Ax. 1).

9. Use same method of proof as in Ex. 8.

10. $OA = OP$ (§ 188). $\therefore \angle OAP = \angle OPA$ (§ 82). Also $O'B = O'P$ (§ 188). $\therefore \angle O'BP = \angle O'PB$ (§ 82). $\therefore \angle OAP = \angle O'BP$ (Ax. 1). $\therefore OA \parallel O'B$ (§ 91).

PAGE 132

12. PC is 160 yd. (§ 216). Erect $\perp$ to AB and CD at A and C. Use § 212.

PAGE 133

4. Yes.   5. No.

PAGE 135

1. ⅓.   **2.** ⅔⅓ or ⅘.

3. Take a given line as a radius, and the ends of the line as a center in turn.

4. Use each vertex of the △ as a center and a side as the radius.

5. Use each vertex of an equilateral △ as a center and one half the side of the △ as a radius.

PAGE 138

1. 46°; 134°.   **2.** 60°; 30°.

3. ∠ DAC = 25½°; ∠ DAB = 12½°.

PAGE 139

4.

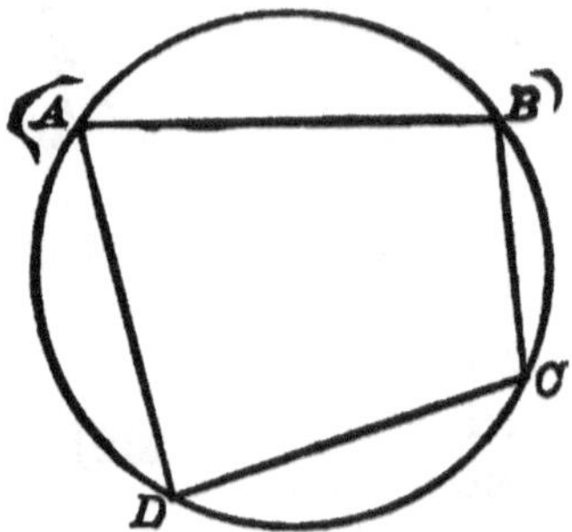

On the figure, $\angle B \stackrel{m}{=} \frac{1}{2} \widehat{ADC}$ (§ 235).   Also $\angle D \stackrel{m}{=} \frac{1}{2} \widehat{ABC}$ (§ 235).
Adding, $\angle B + \angle D \stackrel{m}{=} \frac{1}{2}$ the circle $ABCD$ (Ax. 2).   ∴ $\angle B + \angle D = 180°$, etc.

5. 360°.   **6.** $\angle S = 52\frac{1}{2}°$, etc.   **7.** 540°.

8. $\angle APB = 90°$ (§ 238).   Prove $\triangle APB = \triangle PBC$ (§ 79).

9. $37\frac{1}{2}°$.   **10.** Use § 238.

11. Then at one end of the diameter construct an angle equal to the given acute angle, etc. Or at one end of the hypotenuse construct an ∠ = the given acute ∠ (§ 86). From the other end of the hypotenuse draw a ⊥ to the other side of the acute ∠ (§ 129), etc.

12. On the given hypotenuse as a diameter construct a semicircle (§ 128, Post. 3). With one end of the given hypotenuse as a center and the given leg as a radius, describe an arc intersecting the semicircle. From the point of intersection draw lines to the extremities of the given hypotenuse. Use § 238.

13. Construct a circle and in it draw a chord smaller than the radius. At one end of the chord construct an angle of 120° (twice 60°), etc.

PAGE 140

1. 66°; 114°.

2. $124° = \frac{1}{2}(52° + \overset{\frown}{CB})$. ∴ 196°. *Ans.*

3. 34°.

PAGE 141

1. 47°.

2. $\angle CPD = 40°$; $\angle CPA = 50°$, etc.

3. $\overset{\frown}{PDC} - (360° - \overset{\frown}{PDC}) = 128°$. ∴ $\overset{\frown}{PDC} = 244°$, etc.

PAGE 143

1. $\angle P = 37°$, etc.

2. Denote the $\overset{\frown}{AFC}$ by x. Then $80° = \frac{1}{2}(360° - x - x)$. ∴ $x = 100°$.

PAGE 144

1. §§ 200, 202, 207, 216.

2. (1) §§ 196, 237, 241, 242; (2) See Ex. 4, p. 139; (3) §§ 210, 238.

3. §§ 195, 198, 202, 235, 244.

4. Use figure 3, p. 142 (text-book). $\angle PAB \overset{m}{=\!=} \frac{1}{2} \overset{\frown}{AFB}$ (§ 241). Also $\angle PBA \overset{m}{=\!=} \frac{1}{2} \overset{\frown}{AFB}$. ∴ $\angle PAB = \angle PBA$ (Ax. 1).

5.

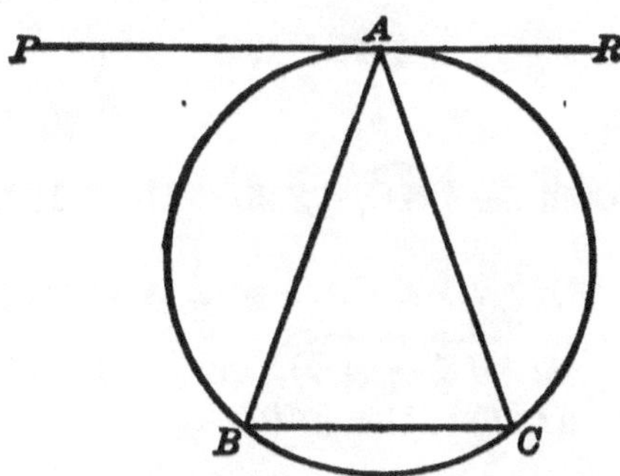

Let ABC be an inscribed $\triangle$ in which $AB = AC$, and let PR be tangent to the $\odot$ at A. Then $\overset{\frown}{AB} = \overset{\frown}{AC}$ (§ 198). $\angle PAB = \angle RAC$ (measured by $=$ arcs, § 241). But $\angle ABC \overset{m}{=\!=}$

$\frac{1}{2}\widehat{AC}$ (§ 235).   ∴ ∠ ABC = ∠ RAC (Ax. 1).   ∴ $PR \parallel BC$ (§ 89).   The converse is true.

6. On the figure, p. 140 (text-book), if ∠ DPB should be made a rt. ∠, ∠ $DPB \stackrel{m}{=} \frac{1}{2}(\widehat{DB} + \widehat{AC})$ (§ 240).   ∴ $\frac{1}{2}(\widehat{DB} + \widehat{AC}) =$ 90°.   ∴ $\widehat{DB} + \widehat{AC} = 180°$ (Ax. 4).

7. ∠ $BAC \stackrel{m}{=} \frac{1}{2}\widehat{AB}$ (§ 241).   But ∠ $AOB \stackrel{m}{=} \widehat{AB}$.   ∴ $\frac{1}{2}$ ∠ $AOB \stackrel{m}{=} \frac{1}{2}\widehat{AB}$ (Ax. 5).   ∴ ∠ $BAC = \frac{1}{2}$ ∠ AOB (Ax. 1).

8. On the figure to Ex. 4, p. 139, produce DC through C to F. Then ∠ BCF is supplement of ∠ BCD (§ 32).   But ∠ DAB is supplement of ∠ BCD (Ex. 4, p. 139).   ∴ ∠ A = ∠ BCF (§ 66).

9. Use § 238.

10. Use the figure of Ex. 18, p. 145, as given in the Key (omitting the circumscribed rhombus).   Then chord $AD \parallel$ chord BC. $\widehat{AB} = \widehat{DC}$ (§ 244).   In like manner $\widehat{BC} = \widehat{AD}$.   Adding, $\widehat{ABC} = \widehat{ADC}$.   ∴ $\widehat{ABC}$ = semicircle.   ∴ ∠ B = rt. ∠ (§ 238). In like manner ∡ A, C, D are rt. ∡, etc.

11. Use § 235.

12. Then $\widehat{ABC} = \widehat{BCD} = \widehat{CDE}$, etc.   (Ax. 4).   ∴ ∠ ABC = ∠ BCD = ∠ CDE, etc. (§ 237).

PAGE 145

13. §§ 97, 230, 235.

14. ∠ B = ∠ D (each $\stackrel{m}{=} \frac{1}{2}\widehat{AC}$, § 235).   Use § 107.

15. $\widehat{AD} = \widehat{BE}$ (§ 244).   ∴ ∠ CAD = ∠ AED (§§ 241, 235, Ax. 1). Also, ∠ $C \stackrel{m}{=} \frac{1}{2}(\widehat{ABE} - \widehat{AD})$, or $\frac{1}{2}\widehat{AB}$ (§ 242).   ∴ ∠ C = ∠ AEB (§ 235, Ax. 1).   Use § 107.

16. Draw ⊥ from the centers of the circles to the cutting line. These ⊥ are $\parallel$ (§ 92), and ∴ = (§ 157).   Then use § 207.

17. ∠ BAE = ∠ BCD (§ 114).   ∴ $\widehat{BD} = \widehat{BE}$, since they measure equal ∡.

18.

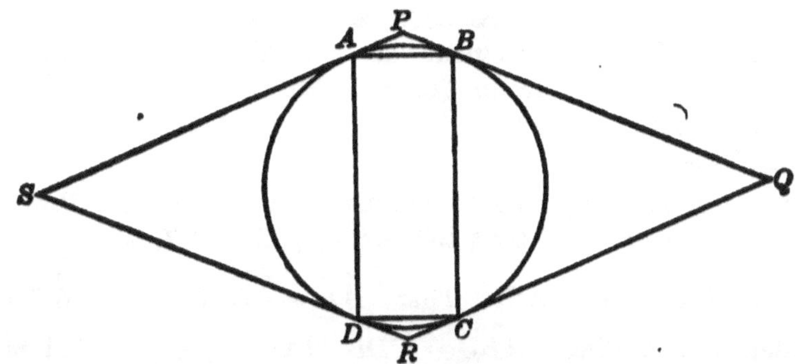

In the figure $AB \parallel CD$ (Hyp.). $\therefore \overset{\frown}{BC} = \overset{\frown}{AD}$ (§ 244). $\therefore \angle SAD = \angle SDA = \angle QBC = \angle QCB$ (§ 241). Chord $BC =$ chord AD (§ 155). $\therefore \triangle SAD = \triangle QBC$ (§ 80). $\therefore BQ = SA$ (corr. sides of $= \triangle$).

But $AP = BP$ (§ 216). Adding, $SP = PQ$ (Ax. 2). In like manner, $PQ = QR = RS$, etc. Use § 160.

1. Draw OB. Then $\angle AOB = \angle BOC$ (§ 196). $\therefore \triangle AOB = \triangle BOC$ (§ 110), etc.

2.

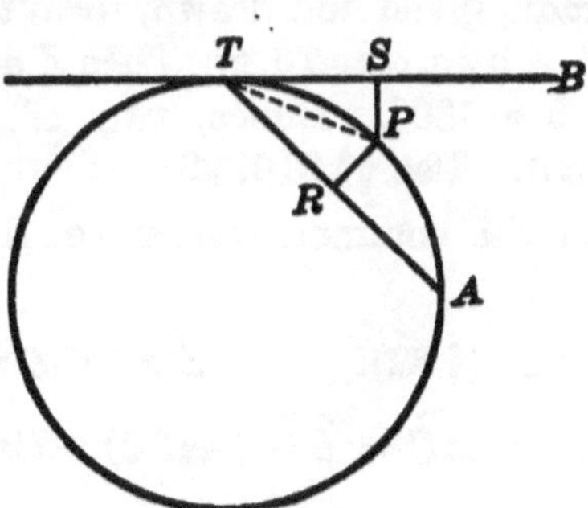

On the figure, $\overset{\frown}{PT} = \overset{\frown}{AP}$ (Hyp.). Draw PT. Then $\angle ATP = \angle PTS$ ($\overset{m}{=} \frac{1}{2}$ of equal arcs AP and TP, §§ 235, 241). $\therefore \triangle RPT = \triangle STP$ (§ 110), etc.

3. Produce OD to meet the circle at F. Then $\overset{\frown}{AF} = \frac{1}{2}\overset{\frown}{AC}$ (§ 202). $\therefore \angle ABC \overset{m}{=} \overset{\frown}{AF}$ (§ 235). But $\angle AOF \overset{m}{=} \overset{\frown}{AF}$ (§ 230), etc.

4. §§ 110, 207. The converse is true.

PAGE 146

5. Draw a line from the center to the point of intersection. Use §§ 204, 117.

6. Use the figure, p. 127 (text-book) and draw AB.
Then $\angle APO$ = complement of $\angle AOP$ (§§ 210, 102). Also $AB \perp OP$ (Ex. 1, Group 30, p. 130). ∴ $\angle OAB$ is complement $\angle AOP$ (§ 102). ∴ $\angle OAB = \angle APO$ (§ 66). But $\angle APB = 2 \angle APO$, etc.

7. Draw the auxiliary lines as indicated in the figure. Prove the two △ formed, equal by § 198, Ax. 3, §§ 200, 237, 80.

8. Draw the chord AC. Then $\overset{\frown}{AB} = \overset{\frown}{CD}$ (§ 198). $\overset{\frown}{BD} = \overset{\frown}{BD}$ (Ident.). Adding, $\overset{\frown}{ABD} = \overset{\frown}{CDB}$ (Ax. 2). ∴ $\angle A = \angle C$ (measured by equal arcs, § 235). ∴ $PA = AC$ (§ 115).

9. On the diagram, p. 127 (text-book), prove $\angle POA = \angle POB$. Denote the equal △ at the center of the diagram for Ex. 9 by a, a; b, b; c, c; d, d. Then $2a + 2b + 2c + 2d = 360°$ (§ 67). ∴ $a + b + c + d = 180°$ (Ax. 5), etc.

10. $\angle APM = 60°$ (§ 235, for $\overset{\frown}{AC} = 120°$). ∴ $\triangle PAM$ is equilateral (§ 102). ∴ $PA = AM$. But $AB = AC$ (Hyp.). ∴ $\angle PAB = \angle MAC$ (each $60° - \angle BAM$). Use § 80, etc.

11. Show that the radii, given and drawn, form two pairs of equal △, and denote these △ by a, a and b, b. Then $\angle a + \angle b = 90°$ (Hyp.). ∴ $2 \angle a + 2 \angle b = 180°$. Hence, two of these radii form a straight line. (§ 65). Use §§ 210, 92.

12. Draw ∴ ⊥ from the common center to AD. Use ⌐ 202 and Ax. 3.

13. $\angle PAB = \angle PBA$ (§ 82). ∴ $\angle x = \angle y$ (§ 66). ∴ $\overset{\frown}{BDC} = \overset{\frown}{ACD}$ (§ 235). ∴ $\overset{\frown}{AC} = \overset{\frown}{BD}$ (Ax. 3). Use §§ 200, 207, etc.

PAGE 147

14.

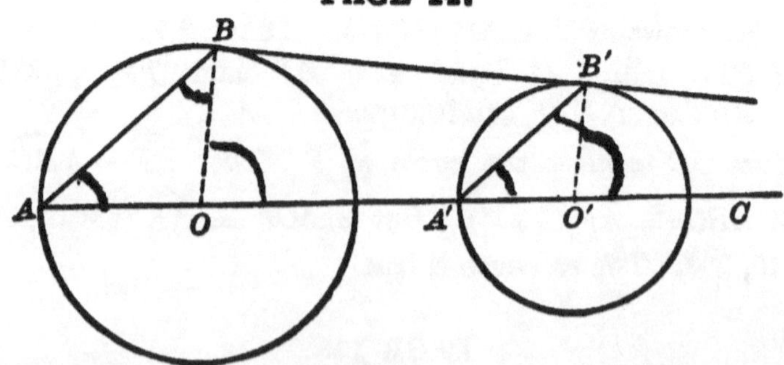

Draw radii OB and $O'B'$ from the centers O and O' to the point of tangency B and B'.

∴ *OB* and *O'B'* are ⊥ *BB'* (§ 210).   ∴ *OB* ∥ *O'B'* (§ 92). ∠ *BOA'* = ∠ *B'O'C*   (§ 97).   But   ∠ *A* = ∠ *ABO*   (§ 82). ∴ ∠ *BOA'* = 2 ∠ *A* (§103). Similarly, ∠ *B'O'C* = 2 ∠ *B'A'O'*. ∴ 2 ∠ *A* = 2 ∠ *B'A'O'* (Ax. 1).   ∴ ∠ *A* = ∠ *B'A'O'* (Ax. 5). ∴ *AB* ∥ *A'B'* (§ 97).

15. §§ 238, 202.

16. Denote the tangent by *RS*.   ∠ *D* = ∠ *SPB* = ∠ *APR* = ∠ *C* (§§ 235, 241, 69, Ax. 1).   Use § 89.

17. Draw the common chord.   Use Ex. 4, p. 139, §§ 64, 66, 94.

18. The circle will pass through both the center of the square and the vertex of the rt. △ (§ 238 used conversely).   Use §§ 198, 235.

19. Through *P* draw a common tangent intersecting *AB* in *R*. Then (Ex. 8, p. 131), *RA* = *RP* = *RB*.   ∴ describe a ⊙ with *R* as center and *RA* as radius.   Use § 238.

20. Use § 238 conversely and § 237.

21. Draw the auxiliary line *PQ*.   Then ∠ *PQA* = 1 rt. ∠ = ∠ *PQB* (§ 238).   ∴ *AQB* is a straight line (§ 65).

PAGE 148

22.

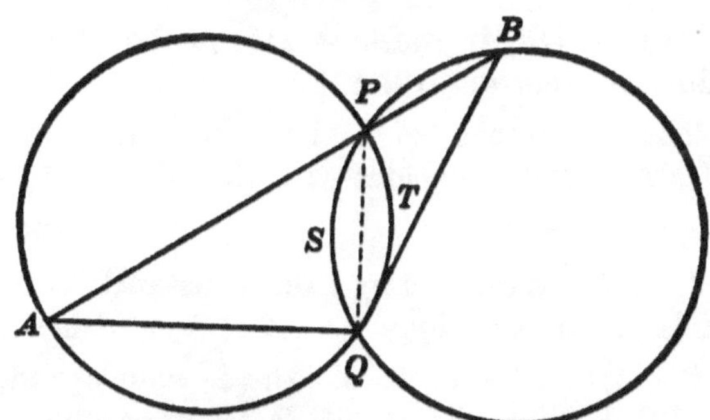

Draw the common chord *PQ*. Then $\overset{\frown}{PSQ}$ = $\overset{\frown}{PTQ}$ (§ 198). ∴ ∠ *B* = ∠ *A* (measured by ½ equal arcs, *PSQ* and *PTQ*, § 235).   ∴ *QA* = *QB* (§ 115).

23. The number of angular degrees in the inscribed ∠ *ABC* is one half the number of degrees of arc in $\overset{\frown}{AC}$.

1. The diameter through the given point is greatest chord (§ 194). The chord ⊥ this diameter is least.   For draw any other chord through the point and a ⊥ to this chord from the center.   Use §§ 136, 209.

2. $PO - CO < PC$ (Ex. 6, group 24, p. 102). $\therefore PA < PC$ (Ax. 9). Also $PO + OD > PD$ (§ 78). $PB > PD$ (Ax. 9).

3. $OC < OP + PC$ (§ 78), $OP + PB < OP + PC$ (Ax. 9). $\therefore PB < PC$ (Ineq. Ax. 1). Also $OD + OP > PD$ (§ 78). $\therefore AP > PD$ (Ax. 9).

4. From O' draw a line $\parallel CD$ to meet OR in T. Then $O'T \perp OR$ (§ 100). $\therefore OO' > O'T$ (§ 135). But $O'T = RS$ (§ 157). $\therefore OO' > RS$ (Ax. 9). $\therefore AB > CD$ (§ 202, Ax. 2, Ineq. Ax. 2).

5. This circle will pass through the point B (§ 238 used conversely). Let this $\odot$ cut OP at point R. $\therefore \angle OAB = \angle ORB$ (§ 237). But $\angle ORB > \angle P$ (§ 87), etc.

PAGE 149

1. For if it is not, on the chord opposite the rt. $\angle$, as a diameter, describe a semicircle. Either this semicircle will cut the sides of the given $\angle$, or one of the sides produced cuts the semicircle. In either case use § 87.

2. If they are not diameters, the $\angle$ of the rectangles are not right $\angle$ (§ 239), etc.

3. If $\overset{\frown}{AB}$ is not $> \overset{\frown}{DF}$, it must $= \overset{\frown}{DF}$, or be less than $\overset{\frown}{DF}$, etc. (See method of proof in § 135.)

4. For the longer $\perp$ must be $\perp$ the other chord (§ 100) and bisect it (§ 202). $\therefore$ it coincides with the other $\perp$ (§ 93), etc.

5. Use § 87 and Ex. 4, p. 139.

1. (Group 36). $\angle P$ is measured by $\frac{1}{2}\overset{\frown}{BC}$ (constant). $\therefore \angle P$ is constant. But $\angle A$ is constant by hyp. $\therefore \angle P + \angle A$ is constant.

2. $RQ = AR + QB$. To each of these equals add $TR + TQ$. $\therefore RQ + TR + TQ = TA + TB$ (a constant sum).

3. See Ex. 9, p. 146. $\angle AOR = \angle POR$. $\angle BOQ = \angle POQ$. Adding, $\angle AOR + \angle BOQ = \angle POR + \angle POQ = \angle ROQ$. $\therefore \angle ROQ = \frac{1}{2} \angle AOB$. But $\angle AOB$ is constant. $\therefore \angle ROQ$ is constant.

PAGE 150

4. $\angle CBD = \angle P + \angle PCB$ (§ 103). $\angle P$ is measured by $\frac{1}{2}\overset{\frown}{AB}$ (in its circle). $\angle PCB$ is measured by $\frac{1}{2}\overset{\frown}{AB}$ (in its circle), etc.

5. CD is constant (Hyp.). $OP = \frac{1}{2} CD$ (Ex. 6, p. 100). $\therefore OP$ is constant.

6. In order to give a convenient formal proof of this and the remaining exs. in this group it is best to give the following

LEMMA. The locus of a point moving so as to be always at a given distance from a given fixed point is a circle whose center is the given point and whose radius is the given distance.

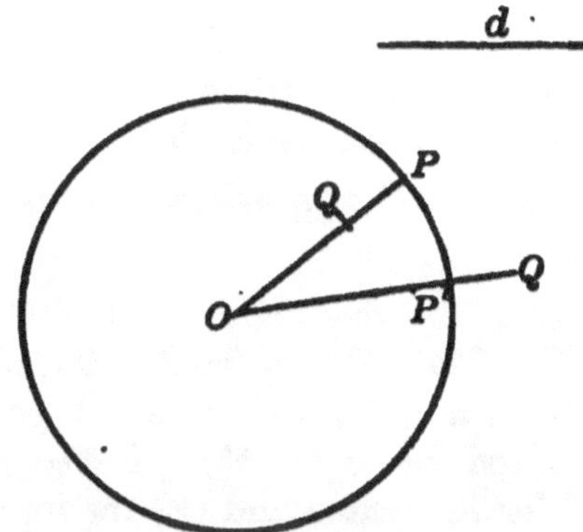

Given the point O, the line (segment) d, and the circle PP' whose center is O and radius $= d$.

To prove PP' the locus of the point moving so as always to be at distance d from O.

Proof. Let P be any point on the given circle. Then $PO = d$ (§ 188). Hence, every point on the given circle is at the given distance from O. Again, let Q be any point not on the given circle. Draw OQ. Then either OQ intersects the given circle at some point P', or on being produced OQ meets it at P. In the first case $OQ > OP'$, i.e., $OQ > d$ (Ax. 8). In the second case $OQ < OP$; that is, $OQ < d$ (Ax. 8). Hence, every point not on the given circle is not at the distance d from O. Hence, the circle PP' is the required locus (§ 123).

To prove Ex. 6, the moving point is at the distance $r + a$ or $r - a$ from the center of the given circle (Hyp.). Hence, its locus is the two circles whose common center is the center of the given circle and whose radii are $r + a$ and $r - a$ respectively (Lemma). In case $a > r$ the second part of the answer disappears.

7. The moving point is always at a distance $\frac{1}{2}r$ from the center of the given circle (Hyp.); hence, its locus is the circle whose center is the center of the given circle and whose radius $= \frac{1}{2}$ radius of given circle (Lemma of Ex. 6).

8. The midpoints of all the given chords are equidistant from the center of the given circle (§§ 203, 207). Hence the locus of the moving point is a circle whose center, etc. (Lemma of Ex. 6).

9. Draw a line from the vertex of one of the right △ to the mid-point of the given hypotenuse. The line thus drawn = ½ the hypotenuse (Ex. 6, p. 100). Hence, the locus of the vertex of the given right ∠ is the circle having the given hypotenuse for is its diameter (Lemma of Ex. 6).

10. Ex. 10 reduces to Ex. 9 (§ 203). Hence the locus is the circle having for its diameter that radius of the original circle which is drawn to the given point on the circle.

11. The circle whose center is O and radius = $\frac{1}{2}CD$ (see Ex. 6, p. 100 and Lemma of Ex. 6).

12. Let O be the center of the given circle. On OB lay off $OC = QP$. Draw OQ amd CP. Then C is a fixed point, since QP is a constant. Also $OQPC$ is a $\square$ (§ 161); in every position of P, $CP = OQ$ = radius of given circle (§ 155). Hence the locus of P is a circle having C for its center and OQ for its radius (Lemma of Ex. 6).

PAGE 151

1. See figure of Ex. 2, p. 145. Let TB be a tangent, TA a chord, $\angle ATP = \angle PTB$, and prove $\overset{\frown}{TP} = \overset{\frown}{PA}$. Use §§ 235 and 241.

2. §§ 244, 200.

3. $\overset{\frown}{AC} = 35°$; $\angle T = 100°$; $\angle TAB = \angle TBA = 40°$; $\angle TBC = 57\frac{1}{2}°$. $\angle BAD = 47\frac{1}{2}° = \angle BCD$; $\angle S = 30°$; $\angle ABC = \angle ADC = 17\frac{1}{2}°$. If AD and BC intersect at O, $\angle BOD = \angle AOC = 65°$. $\angle BOA = \angle COD = 115°$.

4. By · § 246, the $\parallel$ tangents bisect the circle at their points of tangency. Hence, the line joining the points of contact is a diameter (§ 192).

5. Use Ex. 7, p. 131.

6. $OB = BP$ (Hyp.). $\therefore \angle ABO = 2 \angle P$ (§§ 103, 82, Ax. 9). But $\angle A = \angle OBA$ (§ 82). $\angle AOC = \angle A + \angle P$ (§ 103) $= 2 \angle P + \angle P = 3 \angle P$.

7. By § 198 each side of the square subtends an arc of 90°. $\therefore$ required $\angle = 45°$ (§ 241).

8. Draw ⊥ from the center upon the given secants. The two rt. △ thus formed are = (§ 110). $\therefore$ chords are = (§ 207). Add equal semichords to equal corresponding sides of △.

9. Use Ex. 5, p. 149, §§ 64, 167.

10. Draw the line of centers. Prove that this passes through the point of contact of the two circles. Then use §§ 69, 82, Ax. 1, § 89.

11.

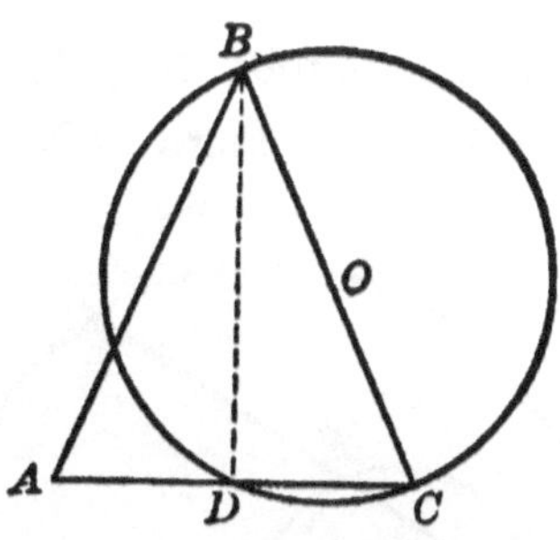

Let ABC be a triangle in which $AB = BC$ and O a circle having BC for its diameter and intersecting AC in D. Then BDC is a right $\angle$ (§ 238). $\therefore \triangle ABD = \triangle DBC$ (§ 117). $\therefore AD = DC$.

12. Draw a line from one end of the chord to the midpoint of the arc. Use §§ 235, 241, Ax. 1, § 89.

13.

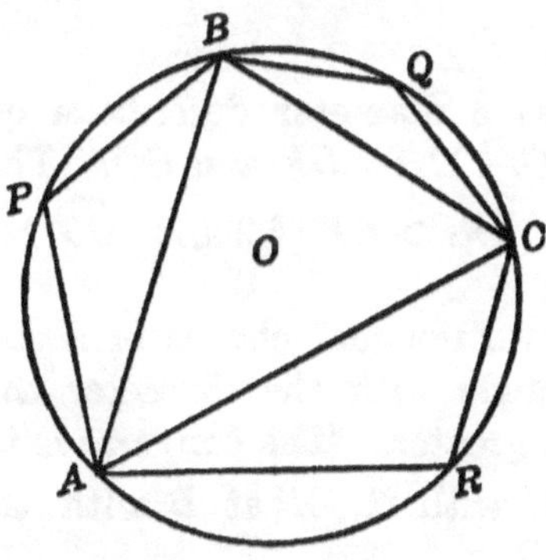

Given the circle O with the inscribed $\triangle ABC$, P any point on $\overarc{AB}$, Q on $\overarc{BC}$, R on $\overarc{AC}$.

To prove $\angle APB + \angle BQC + \angle ARC = 4$ rt. $\angle$.

Proof. $\angle APB \overset{m}{=} \tfrac{1}{2} (\overarc{BQC} + \overarc{ARC})$ (§ 235). $\angle ARC \overset{m}{=} \tfrac{1}{2} (\overarc{BQC} + \overarc{APB})$ (§ 235). $\angle BQC \overset{m}{=} \tfrac{1}{2} (\overarc{ARC} + \overarc{APB})$ (§ 235).

Adding, $\angle APB + \angle ARC + \angle BQC \overset{m}{=} \tfrac{1}{2} (2\,\overarc{BQC} + 2\,\overarc{ARC} + 2\,\overarc{APB})$, or by $\overarc{BQC} + \overarc{ARC} + \overarc{APB}$; that is, by the circle. Hence, the sum of the $\angle$ named $= 4$ rt. $\angle$.

PAGE 152

14. Sum = 6 rt. ∠. Method of proof is the same as that used in Ex. 13.

15. The ⊥ bisector of the line joining the points (§§ 188, 122).

16. Given circle O, chord AB > chord CD, and E their point of intersection.

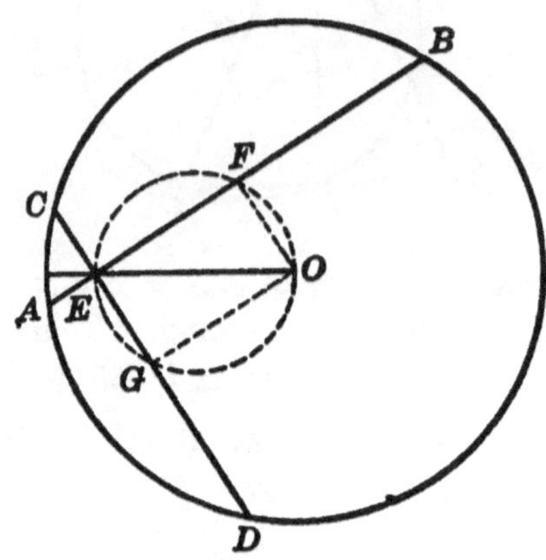

To prove ∠ OED > ∠ OEB.

Proof. On OE as a diameter describe a circle intersecting AB at F and CG at G. Draw OF and OG. Then △ OFE and OGE are rt. ∠ (§ 238). $OG > OF$ (§ 208). $\overparen{OG} > \overparen{OF}$ (§ 201). ∠ OEG > ∠ OEF (§ 235).

Converse. Of two unequal chords in a circle, the chord which makes the less angle with the diameter through their point of intersection is the greater. The converse is true.

17. Given rt. △ ABC with rt. ∠ at B with the inscribed circle O whose radius is OQ.

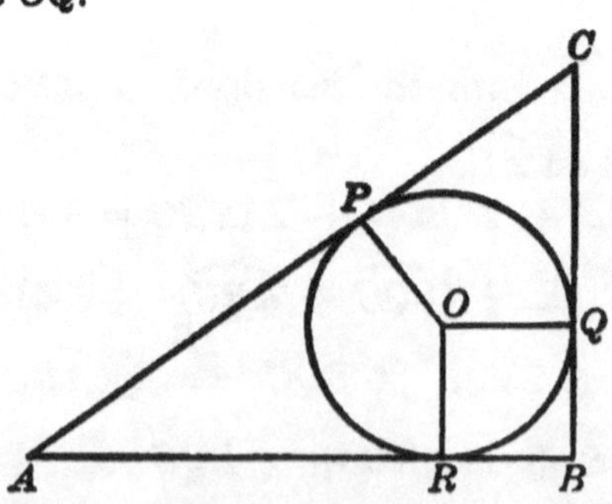

To prove that leg AB + leg BC = AC + 2 OQ.

Proof. Let P, Q, R, be the points of contact, and draw OP,

$OR, OQ.$ $AR = AP$ (§ 216), $CQ = CP$ (§ 216) (1). $\triangle\, OQB$ and ORB are rt. $\triangle$ (§ 210), $\angle B = $ rt. $\angle$ (Hyp.). $\therefore OR \parallel QB$ and $RB \parallel OQ$ (§ 92). $\therefore QB = OR$ and $RB = OQ$ (§ 155) (2).   Adding (1) and (2), $AB + BC = AC + 2\,OQ$ (Ax. 2).

18.

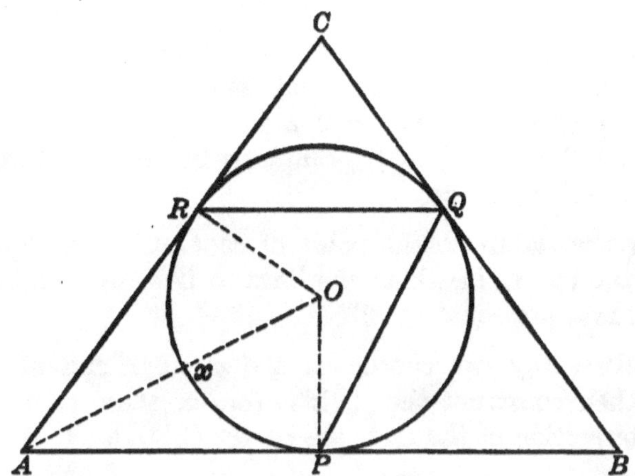

Draw also line OA intersecting the circle at x.   Then $\angle POx = \angle ROx$ (§ 216, and corr. $\triangle$ in $=$ $\triangle$). $\therefore \overset{\frown}{Px} = \overset{\frown}{Rx}$ (§ 195). $\angle POx \overset{m}{=\!=} \overset{\frown}{Px}$ (§ 230). $\angle PQR \overset{m}{=\!=} \tfrac{1}{2} \overset{\frown}{RP}$ or $\overset{\frown}{Px}$ (§ 235). $\therefore \angle PQR = \angle POx$ (Ax. 1).   But $\angle POA$ is complement of $\angle PAO$ (§ 102). $\angle PAO = \tfrac{1}{2} \angle RAP$ (§ 216). $\therefore \angle PQR$ is complement of $\tfrac{1}{2} \angle RAP$ (Ax. 9).

19.

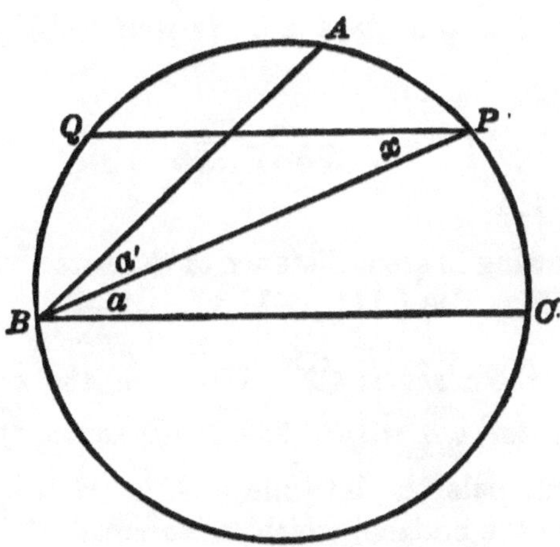

Given PB the bisector of the inscribed $\angle ABC$. PQ a chord $\parallel$ BC.

To prove $AB = PQ$.

Proof. $\angle x = \angle a$ (§ 96). $\angle a = \angle a'$ (Hyp.). $\therefore \angle x = \angle a'$ (Ax. 1). $\overset{\frown}{BQ} = \overset{\frown}{AP}$ (§ 235). Add AQ to each arc. $\therefore \overset{\frown}{AQB} = \overset{\frown}{QAP}$ (Ax. 2). $\therefore$ chord $AB =$ chord PQ (§ 200).

20. Draw OC and AC. Then, in the $\triangle\, OCP$, $CA =$ radius (Ex. 6, p. 100). $\therefore \triangle OCA$ is equilateral. But $\angle CAO = \angle P + \angle PCA$ (§ 103), or $60° = 2\,\angle P$ (§ 82, Ax. 9). $\therefore 30° = \angle P$. $\therefore \angle AEP = 60°$ (§ 106). Similarly by use of $\triangle BOC$, $\angle B = 30°$. $\therefore \angle CDE = 60°$, etc.

21. Draw the radius to the point of contact. Use § 169 and prove that the rt. $\triangle$, in which the lines to be proved equal are the hypotenuses, are equal (§ 79).

1. Construct any two chords of the circular rim of the fragment and then construct the $\perp$ bisectors of these chords. The point of intersection of the $\perp$s is the center (§ 204).

2. See diagram. Use § 238.

PAGE 153

3. Use § 238.

4. $\angle TPC = \angle PAC + \angle PCA$ (§ 103). But $PA = PC$ (§ 216), etc.

5. Prove $\angle y = \angle O$, and $\angle z = \angle FO'C$.

6. In $\triangle\, FEH$, $z = y + 180° - x$ (§ 103). $\therefore x - y + z = 180°$. *Ans.*

PAGE 154

7. Use §§ 210, 114.

8. $AP \parallel EP'$, owing to great distance of the sun. $\therefore AP$ (if produced) $\perp QE$ (§ 100). Use § 114. $41° 30'$. *Ans.*

9. Latitude of the place is $\overset{\frown}{QZ}$. Hence, if the sun is north of the celestial equator, $\overset{\frown}{QZ} = \overset{\frown}{QS_1} + \overset{\frown}{S_1Z}$. If south, $\overset{\frown}{QZ} = \overset{\frown}{SZ} - \overset{\frown}{QS}$.

10. At the north pole the latitude $= 90°$. Hence, $QS_1 =$ sun's elevation above the horizon, which must equal the sun's declination.

11. $6° 7'$. At any hour of the day.

12. From the diagram, $\angle HOS = x + x = 2x$.

PAGE 157

3. $112\frac{1}{2}° = 90° + 22\frac{1}{2}°.$

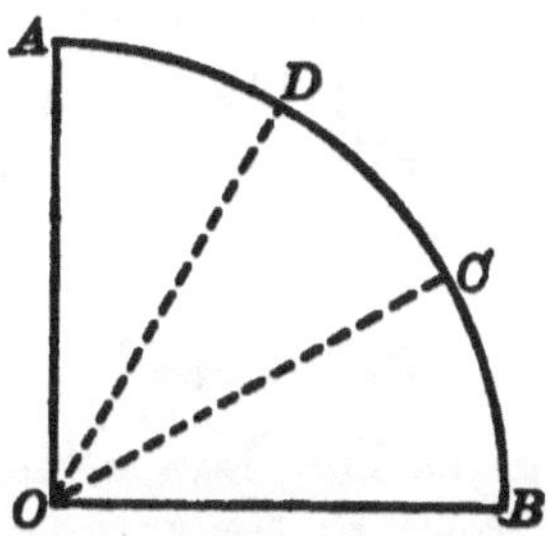

Let AOB be the given rt. $\angle$, and $\overset{\frown}{AB}$ a quadrant with O as a center. With OA as a radius and A and B as centers, describe arcs intersecting AB in D and C. Draw OD and OC. $\angle AOB$ will be trisected by OD and OC. For $\angle DOB = 60°$ (angle of an equilateral $\triangle$ if chord DB is drawn). $\therefore \angle AOD = 30°$, etc.

5. No.

PAGE 159

4. (1) In diagram on p. 159 make $\angle A = 60°$, $m = 2$ in., $n = 1\frac{3}{4}$ in.
(2) On diagram p. 159, make $\angle A = 60°$, $m = 2$ in., $n = 1$ in.

PAGE 160

3. Use § 238. Hence, since BC is a vertical line AC is $\perp$ to it and $\therefore$ horizontal.

PAGE 161

3. Construct an equilateral triangle.

PAGE 162

1. Bisect the exterior angles of the triangle.

2. In first diagram, let A, B, C, D be the vertices of the square, and O the midpoint of AB. A $\perp$ from O to AC is the radius of the semicircle.

PAGE 163

2. 81°; 81°; 99°; 99°.

PAGE 165

1. From the center of the given circle draw a $\perp$ the given line (§ 129). At the points where this $\perp$ intersects the given circle draw tangents to the circle (§ 262). Use §§ 210, 92.

2. From the center of the given circle draw a line || the given line (§ 95). At the points where the line drawn meets ·the given circle, draw tangents to the circle (§ 262). Use §§ 210, 100.

3. Draw the chord connecting the two given points. Draw the radius ⊥ this chord (§ 129). Through the two given points draw lines || this radius. Use §§ 202, 100, 155, 207.

PAGE 166

4. At any point in the given line draw a line which makes an angle with the given line equal to the given ∠ (§ 86). Through the given point draw a line || last line drawn (§ 95).

6. Take any point on one of the given || lines as a center, and with a radius equal to the given line-segment describe an arc intersecting the other || line. Connect this point of intersection with the center of the arc. Through the given point draw a line || last line drawn. Use § 157. (Two solutions in general.)

7. Let O be the center of the given circle. With any point P on the given circle as a center and the given line as a radius describe an arc intersecting the given circle at Q. Draw the chord PQ. With O as a center and the distance of PQ from O as a radius describe a circle. From A draw a tangent to this last circle (§ 264). This tangent produced is the chord required. Use §§ 188, 207. (Two solutions in general.)

8. Draw a concentric circle with the given distance as radius. Use § 264, etc.

9.

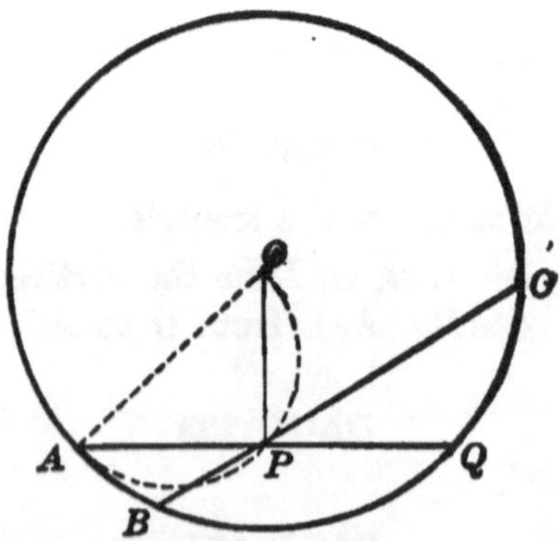

Let O be the given circle, A the given point, and BC the given chord. It is required to draw a chord from A to be bisected by BC.

Draw the radius OA. On OA as a diameter describe the semi-circle intersecting BC at P (§ 128). Draw AP and produce it to meet the given circle at Q. Then AQ is the chord required.
For $\angle APO$ is a rt. $\angle$ (§ 238). $\therefore AP = PQ$ (§ 202).
There is no solution when the circle drawn (APO) does not intersect the given chord (BC).

1. (Group 40.) That is, draw the $\perp$ bisector of the line CD (§ 128). Use § 120.

2. Draw the $\perp$ bisector of CD. See Ex. 1. The $\perp$ bisector will meet the circle in two, one, or no points, according to circumstances

3. Draw the bisectors of the $\angle$ made by the given intersecting lines (§ 84). Use § 125. (Two solutions in general.)

4. With the given point as a center and d as a radius describe an arc intersecting the given line (Post. 3). (Two solutions in general.)

PAGE 167

5. Construct a circle with radius a, and another with radius b, having A and B for their respective centers. In general the two circles will intersect in two points and there will be two solutions. When $a + b = $ line AB, the circles touch and there is one solution. When $a + b < AB$, the circles do not meet and there is no solution.

6. That is, draw the $\perp$ bisector of the line connecting the two given points (§ 128). Also draw two lines $\parallel$ the given line, at the given distance from it (§§ 85, 95). (Two solutions.)

7. § 128, Post. 3.   8. §§ 128, 84.

9. A line $\perp$ the given line at the given point (§ 210).

10. The moving point is always at the distance r from the given point (§ 188). Hence, the locus is the circle having the given fixed point for its center and r for its radius. (See Ex. 6, p. 150, Lemma.)

11. The moving point is equidistant from the two given lines (§§ 210, 188). Hence, the locus is the bisectors of the $\angle$ made by the given intersecting lines (§ 127).

12. The moving point is equidistant from the given $\parallel$ lines (§§ 210, 188). Hence, the locus is a line $\parallel$ the given lines and midway between them.

13. The moving point is always at the distance r from the given line (§§ 210, 188). Hence, the locus is two lines $\parallel$ the given line and at the distance r from it.

14. See Ex. 6, p. 150.

1. Construct any equilateral $\triangle$. Bisect one of its $\measuredangle$ (§ 84). Cut off a part of the bisector from the vertex, equal to the given altitude. At the end of the altitude remote from the vertex of the $\angle$, erect a $\perp$ (§ 85), etc.

2. Bisect the base (§ 128). Erect a $\perp$ at midpoint of the base = given altitude (§ 85), etc.

PAGE 168

3. At each end of the base and on the same side of the base construct an $\angle$ = the given $\angle$ (§ 86).

4. Bisect the given vertex $\angle$ (§ 84), make the bisector = given altitude, etc.

5. At one end of the given leg construct an $\angle$ = given acute $\angle$ (§ 86). At the other end of the leg erect a $\perp$ (§ 85), etc.

6. Construct the complement of the given acute $\angle$, and use Ex. 5.

7. Then with the other end of the altitude as a center, describe arcs with the given sides as radii, etc.

8. Draw a line $\parallel$ one of the given sides and at a distance = the given altitude (§§ 85, 95). With one end of the side thus used as a center, describe an arc with the other side as a radius, etc.

9. Bisect the given $\angle$ (§ 84) and from the vertex mark off on the bisector a part = the given diagonal. At the other end of the diagonal draw lines $\parallel$ the sides of the given $\angle$ (§ 95). Use §§ 96, 115, etc.

10. At the end of the given altitude construct an $\angle$ = complement of the given $\angle$. At the other end of the altitude erect a $\perp$ to the altitude, etc.

11. Bisect the given diagonals and construct a $\triangle$ with the semi-diagonals as sides and the included $\angle$ = the given $\angle$ (§ 253), etc.

12. Use §§ 253, 252.

PAGE 169

1. Draw the circumscribed $\odot$. In this insert a chord = the given base. Construct the $\perp$ bisector of the base (§ 128), etc.

2. Draw the circumscribed $\odot$. Insert a chord in this circle = given leg. Draw the diameter from one end of this chord, etc. Use § 238.

3. Draw the circumscribed $\odot$ and a diameter in this $\odot$. At one end of this diameter construct an $\angle$ = the given acute $\angle$ (§ 86), etc. Use § 238.

4.

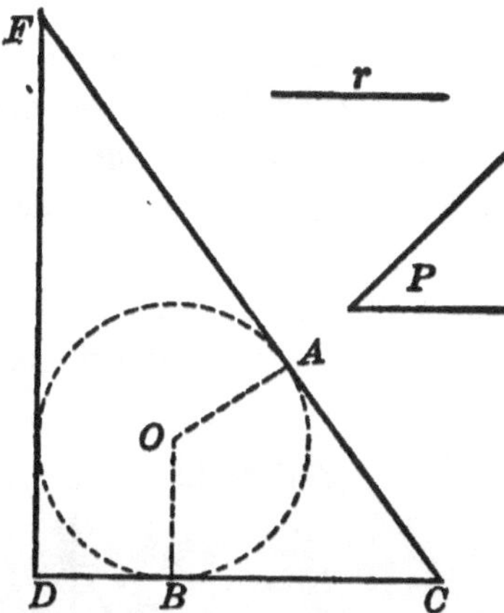

Then, at the ends of the radii of this central ∠ (*A* and *B*) draw tangents to the given circle, meeting at *C*.

Draw *DF* tangent circle and ‖ *OB* (Ex. 1, p. 165) meeting *CA* produced at *F* and *CB* produced at *D*. Then △ *DFC* is the △ required. For *OB* ⊥ *DC* (§ 210). ∴ *FD* ⊥ *DC* (§ 100), etc.

5. Also draw a line ‖ given base at a distance = given altitude (§§ 85, 95). From the points where this ‖ line intersects the circle draw lines to the extremities of the base. (Two solutions in general.)

6. On the given base construct a segment containing the given ∠ (§ 265). With the midpoint of the base as a center and with a radius = given median describe an arc intersecting the circle. From the points of intersection draw lines to the extremities of the given base. (Two solutions in general.)

7.

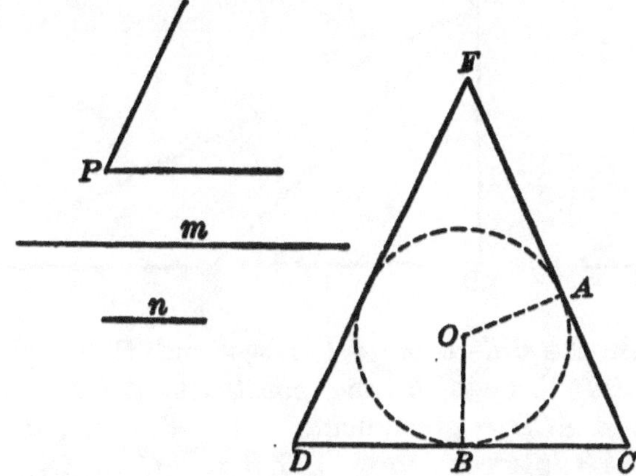

Let *m* be the given side, *P* the given ∠, and *n* the radius of the inscribed ⊙.

Draw the inscribed ⊙. At O construct $\angle AOB$ supplement of P. At A and B draw tangents to the circle O intersecting at C (§ 262). On CB produced mark off $CD = m$. From D draw DF tangent to circle O (§ 264) and meeting AC produced at F, etc.

8. Draw the circumscribed ⊙. In this circle insert a chord = the given side. At one end of this chord construct an $\angle$ = the given $\angle$, etc.

PAGE 170

10.

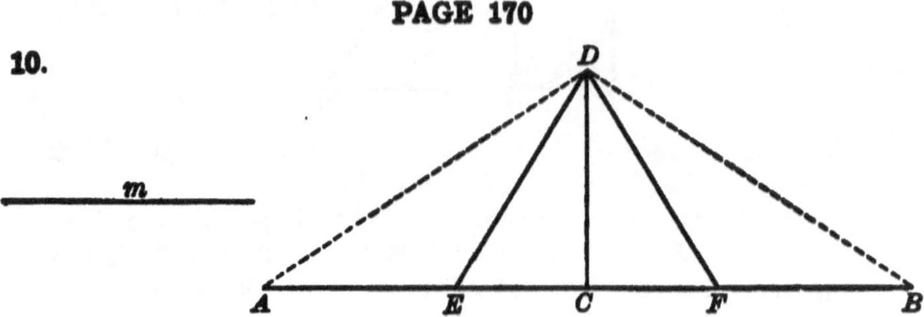

Let m be the given altitude, AB be the given perimeter. At C, its midpoint, construct $CD \perp AB$ and equal to the given altitude m. Connect AD and BD. Construct $\angle ADE = \angle A$, and $\angle FDB = \angle B$. Then EDF is $\triangle$ required. For $AE = ED$, $FB = DF$ (§ 115), etc.

11. A base $\angle = \frac{1}{2}(180° - \text{vertex } \angle)$. Then follow method of Ex. 9.

12. Also at B construct an $\angle$ = given acute $\angle$, etc.

13.

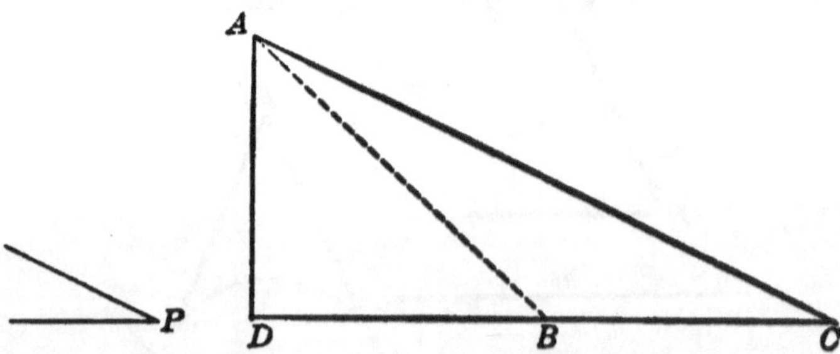

Let BC be the difference of the legs and P the given acute $\angle$. Produce BC through B and construct $\angle DBA = 45°$. At C construct $\angle ACB$ = given acute $\angle P$. From A, the point where AC and AB intersect, drop $\perp AB$ to DC (§ 129). Then ADC is the $\triangle$ required. For $\angle DAB = 45°$ (§ 106). $\therefore AD = DB$ (§ 115), etc.

14. Take a line equal to the sum of the legs and at one end of this line construct an $\angle$ of 45°. With the other end as a center, and the given hypotenuse as a radius, describe an arc cutting the indefinite side of $\angle$ 45°. From the point of intersection thus formed drop a $\perp$ to the line which is the sum of the legs, etc.

15.

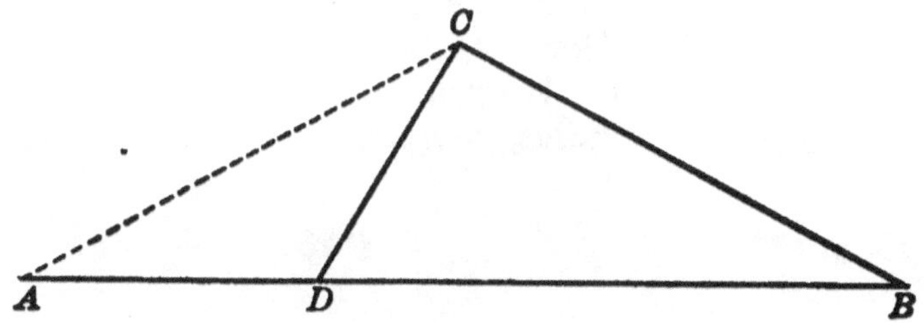

Let x be the given acute $\angle$ and AB the sum of hypot. and one leg. At B construct $\angle B = \angle x$. At A construct $\angle A = \frac{1}{2}(90° - x)$. At C, the intersection of CA and CB, construct $\angle ACD = \angle A$. Then $\triangle DCB$ is the $\triangle$ required. For $\angle CDB = 2\angle A = 90° - x$ (§ 103), etc.

16. At an end of the line $=$ sum of two sides construct an angle $= \frac{1}{2}$ the given $\angle$. With the other end as a center and the given side as a radius describe an arc, etc.

17.

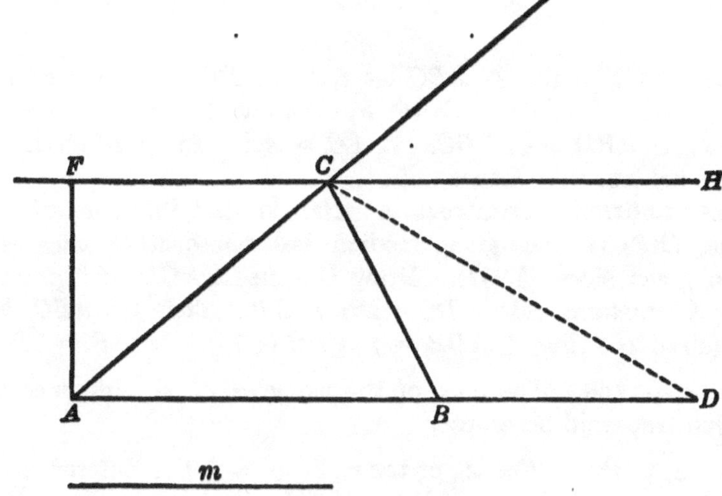

Let AD be the sum of the two sides; $\angle CAB =$ given $\angle$, m $=$ alt. on AB. Then at A draw $AF \perp AD$ and $= m$ (§ 85).

Through F draw $FH \parallel AD$ and intersecting AC in C (§ 95). Draw CD. At C construct $\angle BCD = \angle D$. Then $\triangle ACB$ is the $\triangle$ required, etc.

PAGE 171

1. Construct a right $\triangle$ having the given median for its hypotenuse and the given altitude for a leg (Ex. 12, p. 139). Then with that vertex of this $\triangle$ which is opposite given altitude, as a center, and the median as a radius, describe a circle (use Ex. 6, p. 100), etc.

3. Ex. 12, p. 170.   **4.** § 252.

5.

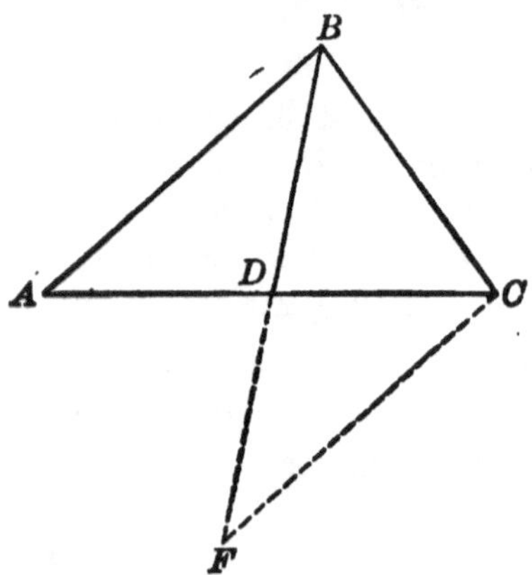

ANALYSIS. In the $\triangle ABC$ let AB and BC and the median BD be given. Produce BD to F, making $DF = DB$. Draw FC. Then $\triangle ABD = \triangle FDC$. $\therefore FC = AB$. In $\triangle BCF$ the three sides are known. Hence,

CONSTRUCTION. Construct a triangle (BCF), one of whose sides (BF) is twice given median and whose other sides are the two given sides (§ 252). Draw the median CD and produce it to A, making $AD = DC$. Draw AB. Then $\triangle ABC$ is the required $\triangle$. For $\triangle ADB = \triangle FDC$ (§ 79). $\therefore AB = CF$, etc.

6. Ex. 3, p. 168. The base of the isosceles $\triangle$ = difference of the given trapezoid bases, etc.

7. Ex. 12, p. 139. The leg of the right $\triangle = \frac{1}{2}$ the difference of the given trapezoid bases, added to the shorter base of the trapezoid, etc.

8. § 252.

9.

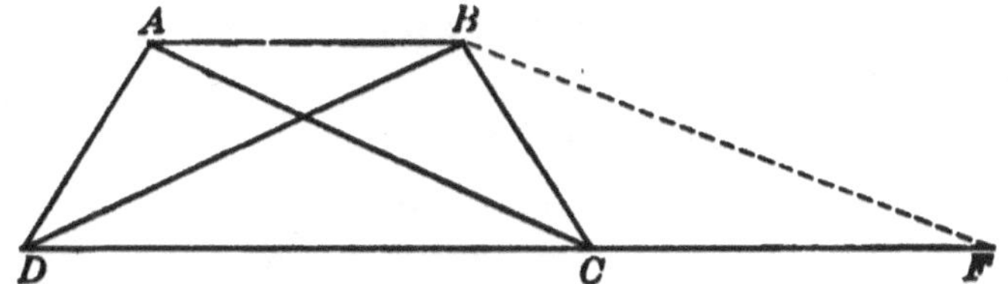

ANALYSIS. Let AB and CD be the bases of the trapezoid $ABCD$.
Produce DC to F, making $CF = AB$. Draw BF. Then $ABFC$
is a $\square$ (§ 161). $\therefore$ $BF = AC$. Hence,

CONSTRUCTION. Construct the $\triangle$ (DBF) whose base $(DF) =$
sum of bases of required trapezoid, and whose other two sides
are its diagonals (§ 252). Through the vertex B draw a line
(BA) || base and equal to one base (CF) (§ 95). Then draw
$AC \parallel BF$ and meeting DF in C. Draw BC. Then $ABCD$ is
the trapezoid required. For $AC = BF$ (§ 157).

PAGE 172

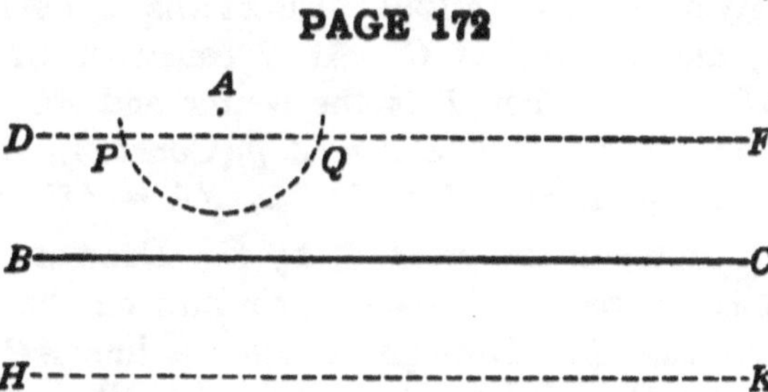

Let A be the given point, BC the given line, r the given radius.
Then construct the locus of all points at the distance r from BC,
viz., the lines DF and $HK \parallel BC$. Also construct the locus of
all points at the distance r from the point A, viz., $\overset{\frown}{PQ}$ (Ex. 6,
p. 150, Lemma). These loci may intersect in certain points
as P and Q. Then with P and Q as centers describe circles with
r as a radius. These circles will be the circles required.

2. Draw lines || the second line at the distance r, etc.

3. Find a point at distance r from each point. (See Ex. 5, p. 167.)

4. Draw a line || the given lines and midway between them. Find
a point in this last line at a distance from the given point
equal to ½ the distance between the given || lines.

5. Find a point in the given line equidistant from the two given
points. (See Ex. 1, p. 166.)

6. Bisect the △ made by the intersection of these lines. Use § 126 in the proof.

7. Also draw the ⊥ bisector of AB.

8.

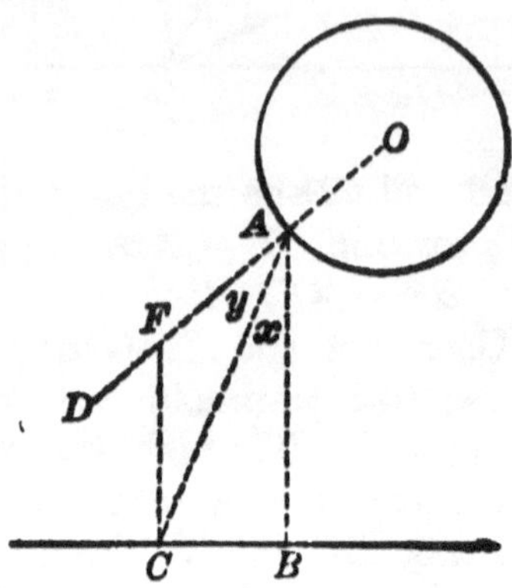

Draw the radius OA and produce it to D. Drop a ⊥ AB from A to the given line BC (§ 129). Bisect the ∠ DAB by the line AC (§ 84), meeting BC at C. At C construct CF ⊥ BC and meeting OD at F. Then F is the center and FC the radius of the required circle. For ∠ x = ∠ y (Constr.), ∠ x = ∠ FCA (§ 96). ∴ ∠ y = ∠ FCA (Ax. 1). ∴ FA = AC (§ 115), etc.

9. Denote the center of the given ⊙ by O. Draw a line CF ∥ AB at a distance = radius of given circle and on the opposite side of AB from the ⊙. Through A draw a line AC ⊥ line CF. Draw OC. At O in OC construct the ∠ COP = ∠ ACO (§ 86). Let OP meet AC produced at P and intersect the circle at D. Then P is the center of the ⊙ required and PA is its radius. For in △ PCO, ∠ PCO = ∠ O (Constr.). ∴ PC = PO (§ 115). But AC = DO (Constr.). ∴ PA = PD (Ax. 3), etc.

1. (Group 45). Bisect the △ of intersection of the two given lines (§ 84). From the given point draw ⊥ to the bisectors of these △ (§ 129).

2. See Ex. 12, p. 139.

3. Bisect the △ made by the given intersecting lines (§ 84) and produce the bisectors to meet the given circle. Use § 127.

PAGE 173

4. Bisect the △ made by the given intersecting lines (§ 84). At the given point erect a ⊥ to the line in which the point is and produce it to meet the bisectors, etc.

5.

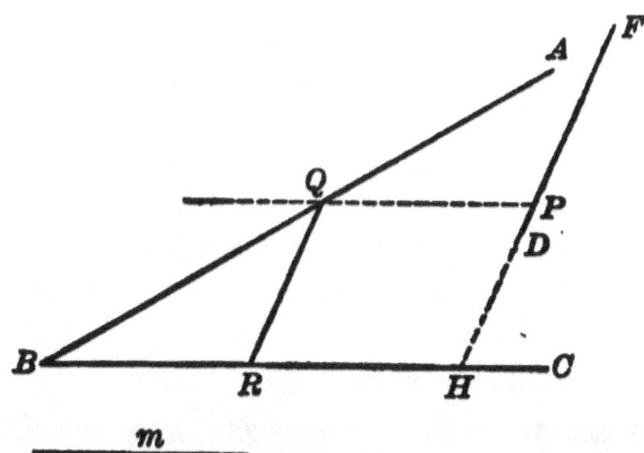

Let *ABC* be the given ∠, *m* the given line-segment, and *DF* last given line. Produce *DF* to meet *BC* in *H*. On *HF* mark off *HP* = *m*. Through *P* draw *PQ* ‖ *BC* and meeting *BA* in *Q* (§ 95); from *Q* draw *QR* ‖ *FH* and meeting *BC* at *R*. Then *QR* is the line required, etc.

6.

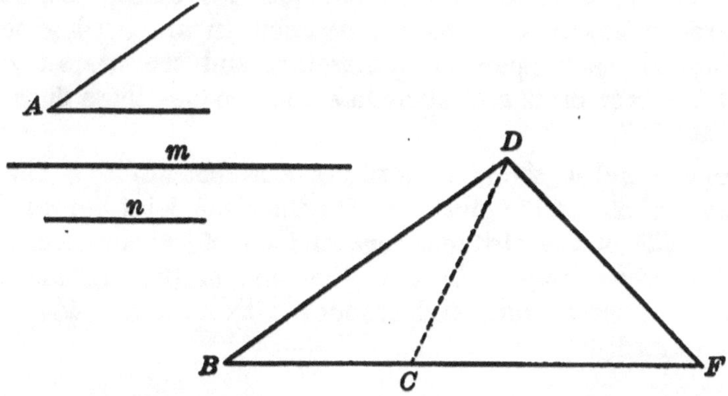

Let *m* be the given side, *A* the adjacent ∠, and *n* the difference of the other two sides. Then construct △ *BCD* having *BC* = *n*, *BD* = *m*, ∠ *B* = ∠ *A* (§ 253). Produce *BC* to *F* and at *D* in the line *CD* construct ∠ *CDF* = ∠ *DCF* (§ 86). Produce *DF* to meet *CF* at *F*. Then ∠ *BDF* is the △ required. For *CF* = *DF* (§ 115). ∴ *BF* − *DF* = *BF* − *CF* = *BC*.

7. Describe a circle with the given point as a center and the given distance as a radius.

8. Reduce to § 255.

9. Then through the extremity of the last line draw a line ‖ one side of the given ∠ and meeting the other side at the point *O*.

From O draw a line through the given point to meet the other side of the given $\angle$. The last line drawn is the line required. Use §§ 69, 96, 80.

10. Put the segments of the base together in line to form the base. On this base construct a segment of a circle which shall contain the given vertex $\angle$ (§ 265). At the point of the base which separates the given segments erect a $\perp$ (§ 85) and produce it to meet the arc of the segment, etc.

11. A base $\angle = \frac{1}{2}(180° - \text{vertex } \angle)$.

12. From the center of the given circle draw a radius to the given point on its circle. Produce this radius till the produced part $=$ the radius of the required circle. The extremity of the produced part is the center of the required circle.

13. Upon the given hypotenuse as a diameter describe a semicircle. Draw a line $\parallel$ the hypotenuse at a distance $=$ given altitude, etc. Use § 238.

14. Then, with each end of the given base as a center, and one of the given altitudes as a radius, describe an arc cutting the circle. Through each point of intersection and the nearest extremity of the base draw a straight line and produce these lines to meet. Use § 238.

15. At one end of the given altitude construct an $\angle =$ the complement of one of the given $\angle$. At the same point but on the opposite side of the altitude, construct an $\angle =$ complement of the other given angle. At the other end of the altitude construct a $\perp$ to the altitude and produce it to meet the sides of the $\angle$ so formed.

16.

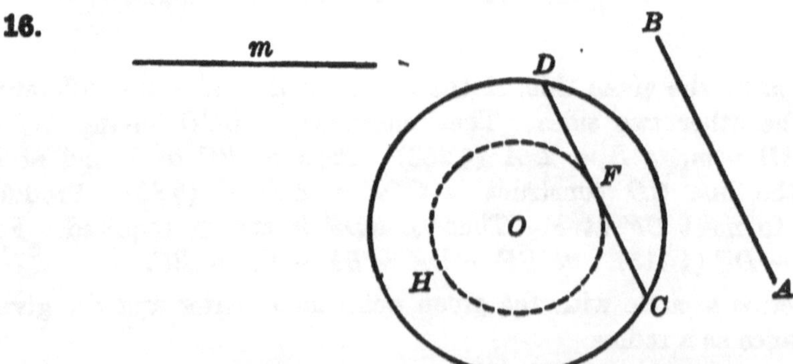

Let O be the given $\odot$, m the given line-segment, and AB the given line. Denote the radius of the given circle by R. Bisect the line *m*. Construct a rt. $\triangle$ having *R* for its hypotenuse and $\frac{1}{2}m$ for a leg (see Ex. 12, p. 139). With *O* as a center, and a radius = the other leg of this rt. $\triangle$, describe the circle *FH*. Draw *DC* $\parallel$ *FH* and tangent to circle *O* (Ex. 1, p. 165). Then *CD* is the chord required. Use §§ 210, 202, 117.

17. Construct the given $\angle$ and its bisector. Draw a line $\parallel$ one side of the $\angle$, at a distance from it = given altitude and intersecting the other side of the $\angle$. Draw a line from this point of intersection through the end of the bisector, etc.

PAGE 174

18. The locus will be a circle having as its diameter the line connecting the given point and the given center.

19.

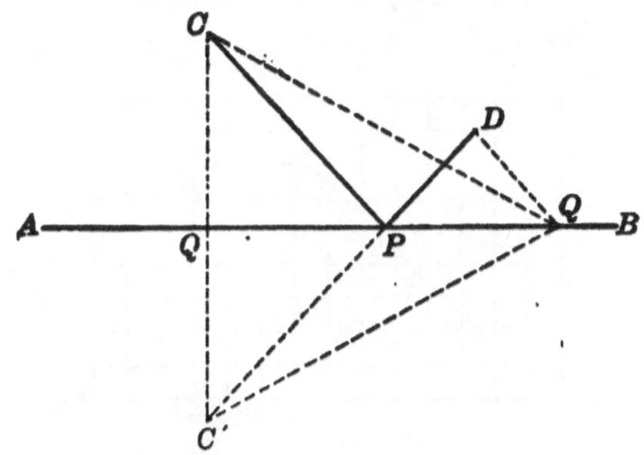

Draw $CQ \perp AB$ and produce CQ to C', making $QC' = CQ$. Draw $C'D$ cutting AB in P. Draw CP. Then P is the point required.

Proof. In $\triangle$ CPQ and $C'PQ$, $CQ = QC'$ (Constr.), $QP = QP$ (Ident.), $\triangle CQP = \triangle C'QP$ (§ 79). $\therefore \angle CPQ = \angle C'PQ$. But $\angle C'PQ = \angle DPB$ (§ 69). $\therefore \angle CPQ = \angle DPB$ (Ax. 1).

20. Use the same figure and construction as in Ex. 19. Then take any other point in AB except P as Q, and draw DQ and $C'Q$ and CQ. Then in $\triangle C'DQ$, $C'P + PD < C'Q + DQ$ (§ 78). For $C'P$ substitute its equal CP. $\therefore CP + PD < C'Q + DQ$ (Ax. 9). For $C'Q$ substitute its equal CQ. $\therefore CP + PD < CQ + DQ$ (Ax. 9).

21. Using the center of the larger $\odot$ as a center and the difference of the radii of the given circles as a radius, describe a circle. Use §§ 264, 210, 161, 98, 155, 211.

22. Same construction as in Ex. 21, except that the new radius = sum of given radii.

PAGE 175

1. Locate two diameters of the circle by use of § 238.

2.

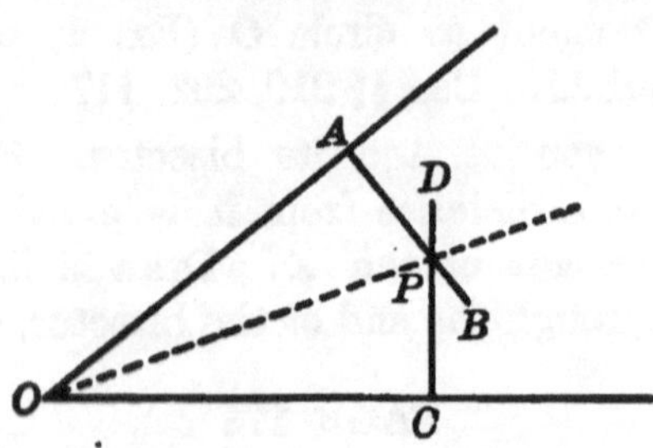

Let O be the given angle. Place the carpenter's square in the two positions, OAB and OCD, OA being equal to OC. Then OP bisects $\angle O$ (§ 117).

3.

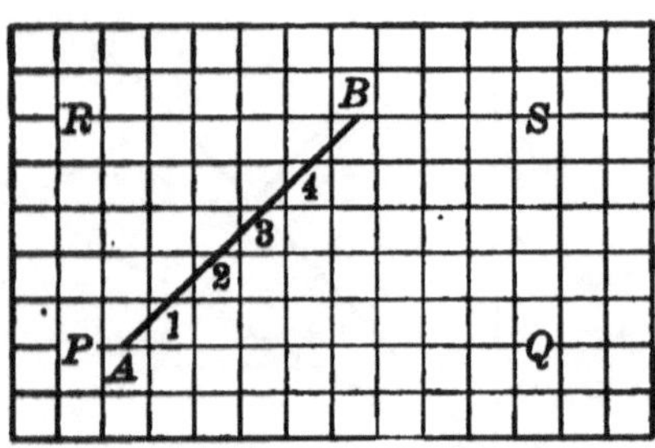

On the squared paper let the cross line RS be 5 spaces from the ‖ cross line PQ. Take A, any point on PQ, and with A as a center and a radius $= 1\frac{1}{2}$ in., describe an arc cutting RS at B. Denote the points where AB cuts the cross lines ‖ PQ, by 1, 2, 3, 4. Then AB is divided into 5 equal parts at 1, 2, 3, 4 (§ 169). The construction can be made on paper ruled in only one direction.

5. At D construct $\angle BDF = 60°$. Make $DF = BF$. Produce DF to H and construct $\angle KFH = 60°$. Then FK is an extension of AB. To prove this draw BF. In $\triangle BFD$ show $\angle FBD = \angle BFD = 60°$. ∴ BF is an extension of AB and also of KF.

6. Use §§ 96, 80.   **7.** See Ex. 12, p. 132.

PAGE 176

9. In $\triangle EAN$, $\angle EAN$ is comp. of $\angle GAE$; $\angle AEN$ is comp. of $\angle EAC$. But $\angle GAE = \angle EAC$ (Constr.). ∴ $\angle EAN = \angle AEN$ (§ 66). ∴ a circle may be described with N as a center and radius *AN*. Similarly show that *H* is equidistant from *E* and *C*. Through *E* draw *PQ* $\perp$ *EH*. Then *EP* is tangent to arcs *AE* and *EC*. $\therefore$ *AEC* is a compound curve (§ 211). Etc.

10. *KG* = *KA* (§ 120). $\therefore$ arc from *A* passes through *G*. Also in $\triangle$ *EDG*, $\angle$ *EDG* = $\angle$ *HAB*, $\angle$ *EGD* = $\angle$ *HGK*. $\therefore$ $\angle$ *EDG* = $\angle$ *EGD* (Ax. 1). $\therefore$ an arc drawn with *E* as a center and *EG* as a radius passes through *D*. Through *G* draw a line $\perp$ *EK*. This line will be a common tangent to the arcs *NG* and *GD* (§ 211). Hence, these arcs form a compound curve.

PAGE 177

1. §§ 183, 196, 197, 200, 201.

2. §§ 184, 194, 198, 201, 202, 207, 208, 209.

3. §§ 182, 192, 202.

4. §§ 195, 197, 229, 230.

5. §§ 233, 234, 235, 237, 238, 239.

6. §§ 185, 210, 211, 212, 213, 216, 218, 242.

7. Three; two; four; three if one is at the vertex, otherwise four.

8. One; one; three.

9. See §§ 258 and 261.

10. §§ 238–239.

11. If we know that in the same circle or in equal circles two chords are equal, Prop. IX enables us to determine, without effort, that the chords are equidistant from the center, and conversely.

12. If we know that a straight line is tangent to a circle, Prop. XII enables us to determine without effort that it is $\perp$ the radius drawn to the point of contact.

13. If we know the length of one of the tangents drawn from a given point to a given circle, we are enabled to determine the length of the other tangent thus drawn, without measuring it.

14. If in a circle or in two equal circles we know the relative size of two arcs intercepted by two central angles, Prop. XVI enables us to determine without effort the relative size of these angles.

18. See § 251.

19. The number of degrees of angle in $\angle$ *ABC* equals the number of degrees of arc in $\overset{\frown}{AC}$.

PAGE 180

1. $5 : x = x : a.$
2. 10.
3. 15.
4. $\dfrac{pq}{a}.$

5. 2.4
6. .54.
7. $12\,b.$
8. 96.
9. 9; $\frac{1}{4}.$

10. $3\sqrt{2}$; .08.
11. $8\frac{1}{3}$; $\frac{1}{18}.$
12. $9\,p^2.$
13. $\sqrt{a^2 - b^2}.$

PAGE 181

1. $a : p = q : b;\ b : p = q : a,$ etc.
2. $x : 3 = 2 : x + 1;\ 3 : x = x : 5.$
3. $x : y = 4 : 3.$
4. $\frac{7}{8}.$
5. $\dfrac{b}{a}.$
6. $\dfrac{p + q}{a + b}.$
7. $\dfrac{b - d}{a - c}.$

PAGE 182

1. $x : b = a : c.$
2. $a : x = c : b.$
3. $c : a = b : x.$

4. $c : a = b : x.$
$2c : a = b : x.$

5. $1 : x = x : 3.$
$a + b : x = x : a - b.$

1. (§ 286). $15 : 3 = 10 : 2.$
2. $2x : 5 = 3x : 7.$
3. $\sqrt{x + 3} : 5 = \sqrt{2x - 1} : 7.$

4. It simplifies the proportion by the cancellation of like terms.

PAGE 183

1. $9 : 3 = 6 : 2.$
2. $2x : 5 = 3x : 7.$
3. $7x : \sqrt{3x - 5} = 4x : \sqrt{2x + 1}.$

4. It simplifies the proportion by the cancellation of like terms.

6. Use § 287. $3x : 2y = 8 : 2.$

PAGE 184

1. $6x : 4y = 12 : 8.$
2. $2\sqrt{x + 7} : 2\sqrt{5} = 4x : 2.$
3. See Ex. 4, p. 183.

1. (§ 289). $24 : 6 = 4 : 1.$
2. $\dfrac{x + 6}{y + 6} = \dfrac{x + 1}{y + 3}.$
3. $\dfrac{x}{y} = \dfrac{2}{5}.$

PAGE 185

1. $\frac{6}{7}$.　　1. (§ 291). 8 : 27.　　3. 4 : 49.　　5. $\frac{14}{9}$.

2. $\frac{4}{5}$.　　2. 8 : 125.　　4. $\frac{9}{16}$.

6. (1) When we know the value of the ratio of like roots of two quantities, § 291 enables us to find the ratio of the numbers themselves.

(2) It enables us often to find the value of an unknown quantity involved in a proportion containing radicals.

PAGE 186

1. $6x$.

2. $\dfrac{(a-b)^2}{a+b}$.

3. 12.

4. Use § 278.

5. $2x : 2 = 12 : 2$; $x = 6$.

6. $\qquad bqx = bpy$ (§ 278).
$\therefore \qquad qx = py$ (Ax. 5).
$\therefore x : y = p : q$ (§ 281).

7. $P : W = l : L$.

8. 40 lb.

9. Any three of the four quantities P, W, l, L being given, it enables us to find the remaining one.

11. $\dfrac{2x^2}{4x^2} = \dfrac{6 + 2\sqrt{1+x}}{8 - 4\sqrt{1-x}}$ (§ 284); hence, $\dfrac{1}{1} = \dfrac{3 + \sqrt{1+x}}{2 - \sqrt{1-x}}$ (§ 227).

12. $\dfrac{2x^3 - 6x^2}{10x - 14} = \dfrac{4x^3 + 8x^2}{-6x + 8}$ (§ 288); hence, $\dfrac{x-3}{5x-7} = \dfrac{2x+4}{-3x+4}$ (§§ 284, 227).

13. $\dfrac{x+2}{x-2} = \dfrac{3x+5}{3x-8}$ (§ 291); $\dfrac{x}{2} = \dfrac{6x-3}{13}$ (§§ 288, 227).

PAGE 188

1. 9; 6.　　2. 5.　　3. $\dfrac{ac}{b}$.　　4. $4\frac{4}{5}$; $5\frac{1}{7}$; $2\frac{2}{35}$.

PAGE 189

3. Use the method of § 297, making $p = n$.

4. $\therefore a + b : a - b = c : x$ (§ 288). Use § 297.

PAGE 190

3. In general use the method of § 298, but on AP lay off the three lines m, n, p in succession.

PAGE 191

1. Yes.　　　　　　2. No.　　　　　　3. Yes.

PAGE 192

1. 8.　　　　　3. 6; 8.　　　　　5. 5; 15.

2. 1.5.　　　　4. 14; 7.　　　　　6. 4; 6.

PAGE 194

1. Yes.　　　　　　3. 32.9; 252; 23.1; 16.8.

2. No, for $\frac{4}{10}$ does not equal $\frac{8}{15}$.

PAGE 195

1. Yes, when they are mutually equiangular; no.

3. Use § 304.　Also let BD and CA intersect in the point O.　Then the $\triangle$ BOA and COD are similar.

4. 8 into 6 and 2; 10 into $7\frac{1}{2}$ and $2\frac{1}{2}$.

6. § 83; § 89 (twice).

PAGE 196

1. No.

2. Because it is not given that $\angle A$ and A' are equal.

3. Yes.

PAGE 197

1. Use §§ 238, 305.　　　　　2. Use §§ 96, 304.

3. $\triangle$ APB, FHR, PQR are similar (§§ 108, 305, 306).

4. § 305.

5. The $\triangle$ are ABQ, CPQ, APD.　Use § 305.

6. Draw DB and AC on the figure, p. 208 (text-book).　Two pairs.

7. See Ex. 14, p. 145.　　　　8. Use §§ 300, 97, 304, 302.

9. 372 yd.　It enables us to determine the distance from a given place to an inaccessible object.

PAGE 198

10. Use §§ 97, 305.　　　　　1. 5.6; 7.

PAGE 199

1. Similarly $\dfrac{AH}{AC} = \dfrac{1}{3}$. Use Ax. 1 and § 310.

2. Let ABC and $A'B'C'$ be the given similar $\triangle$ and BD and $B'D'$ the corresponding medians. Then in the $\triangle$ ABD and $A'B'D'$, $\angle A = \angle A'$ (§ 302). Also $AB : A'B' = AC : A'C'$ (§ 302). But $AC : A'C' = AD : A'D'$ (§ 227). $\therefore$ $AB : A'B' = AD : A'D'$ (Ax. 1). $\therefore$ the $\triangle$ ABD and $A'B'D'$ are similar (§ 310). In like manner the $\triangle$ BDC and $B'D'C'$ may be proved similar.

3. Use §§ 97, 305.

4. In $\triangle$ ABP and $A'B'P'$, $A'B' \parallel AB$ (§ 300). **Prove** $\triangle$ ABP and $A'B'P$ similar by § 305. $\therefore$ $AB : A'B' = BP : B'P$. Similarly, $BC : B'C' = BP : B'P$. $\therefore$ $AB : A'B' = BC : B'C'$, etc. Use § 309.

5. In Ex. 4, change "within" to "without." Use the same method of proof as in Ex. 4.

6. Let P fall on the side AC. **Prove** $AB \parallel A'B'$; $BC \parallel B'C'$. Also,
$$\frac{AP}{A'P} = \frac{AB}{A'B'} = \frac{BP}{B'P} = \frac{BC}{B'C'} = \frac{PC}{PC'}. \quad \therefore \frac{AP}{A'P} = \frac{PC}{PC'}, \text{ whence } \frac{AP}{PC}$$
$$= \frac{A'P}{PC'} \text{ (§ 284).} \quad \therefore \frac{AP + PC}{PC} = \frac{A'P + PC'}{PC'} \text{ (§ 286).} \quad \text{Or;} \frac{AC}{PC}$$
$$= \frac{A'C'}{PC'}. \quad \text{Hence, } \frac{AC}{A'C'} = \frac{PC}{PC'} = \frac{BC}{B'C'}. \quad \text{Use § 309.}$$

7. 110 ft.

8. 1085 ft.

9. By § 301, $8 + 10 : BC = 9 : 15$. $\therefore$ $BC = 30$. *Ans.*

10. Let ABC and $A'B'C'$ be the two similar triangles. Let $AB = BC$. Then $AB : BC = A'B' : B'C'$ (§ 302). $\therefore$ $A'B' = B'C'$ (§§ 284, 282).

PAGE 203

2. Lengths of lines drawn are $1\frac{1}{2}$ in.; $2\frac{1}{2}$ in.; 6 in.

3. $2\frac{1}{2}$ in. by $1\frac{1}{2}$ in.

4. 100 ft.

5. Facilitates (1) a more ready comparison of parts; (2) discussion of changes; (3) sending information to a distance.

PAGE 204

1. 140 rd.

2. Twice.

PAGE 205

1. Divide the squares into triangles and use §§ 310, 313.

2. $137\frac{1}{2}$ miles.

3. Distance $= 1,000,000 \times \frac{11}{4}$ in. $= 43.40 +$ mi. *Ans.*

4. Draw a pair of corresponding diagonals denoted by h and h'. Then, by § 312, $h : h' = a : a'$. $\therefore$ $P : P' = h : h'$ (Ax. 1).

5. See Ex. 1, p. 199; 680 yd.

6. Prove $\dfrac{PA}{PA'} = \dfrac{AB}{A'B'} = \dfrac{PB}{PB'} = \dfrac{BC}{B'C'} = \dfrac{PC}{PC''}$ $\therefore$ $\dfrac{PA}{PA'} = \dfrac{PC}{PC'}$ (Ax. 1). Use § 299.

7. $\dfrac{OB}{OA} = \dfrac{11}{3} = \dfrac{OD}{OC}$ (Hyp.). Use § 310.

8. 10.

9. 15; $7\frac{1}{2}$.

10. Prove $\triangle AKM = \triangle AMC$ (§ 80). $\therefore$ $KM = MC$. $\therefore$ $DM \parallel BK$ (§ 300). $AK = AC$ (corr. sides of $= \triangle$). $\therefore$ $7 - BK = 4.6$. $\therefore$ $BK = 2.4, MD = 1.2$. *Ans.*

PAGE 207

1. 6; $2\sqrt{13}$; $3\sqrt{13}$.

2. .9; .7; $\sqrt{.63} = \frac{1}{10}\sqrt{7} = .793 +$.

3. First find $FC = .32$; then $BC = \frac{4}{25}\sqrt{5} = .357 +$.

PAGE 208

2. Construct the mean proportional between 1 and 2; between 2 and 3.

3. Construct the mean proportional between 1 in. and 5 in.

PAGE 209

1. 6.

2. 12, 6.

3. $x(11 - x) = 6 \times 4$. $\therefore$ 8, 3. *Ans.*

4. $\dfrac{ab}{c}$.

5. $AF = \dfrac{r}{2} \pm \sqrt{\dfrac{r^2}{4} - pq}$. The $\pm$ sign means that two constructions of the figure are possible according as AF is greater or less than FB.

PAGE 210

1. 6.

2. $4\overline{AF}^2 = 144.$ $\therefore AC = 24.$ *Ans.*

3. .16.

4. Let OA cut the circle in $D.$ Then $OD = 21 - 15 = 6.$ $\therefore AC \times AF = 36 \times 6 = 216$ (§ 325).

1. (Group 51.)   ▲ ADC and BFC are rt. ▲ having the acute $\angle C$ in common.   Use § 305.

2. ▲ AOF and ACD are rt. ▲ having the acute $\angle CAD$ in common.   Use §§ 305, 306.

3. Denote a base $\angle$ of each by $A.$ Then the vertex $\angle$ of each $\triangle = 180° - 2 \angle A.$ Hence the ▲ are mutually equiangular. Use § 304.

4. Use figure Ex. 10, p. 212 (text-book).   Denote the point where AC and BD intersect by $F.$ Then ▲ AFD and BFC are mutually equiangular (§ 96), and $\therefore$ similar (§ 304).

5. $\angle P$ is measured by $\frac{1}{2}$ arc AC (§ 235).   Also $\angle FAC$ by $\frac{1}{2}$ arc BC (§ 235). $\therefore$ $\angle P = \angle FAC.$ Also $\angle C = \angle C$ (Ident.). $\therefore$ ▲ APC and AFC are similar (§ 305).

6. $\angle AEB$ is a rt. $\angle$ (§ 238). $\angle ABD$ is a rt. $\angle$ (§ 210).   Use § 305.

7. $\angle APQ$ is a rt. $\angle$ (§ 238).   Use § 305.

PAGE 211

8. $\angle ABD = \angle APC$ (each $\overset{m}{=\!=} \frac{1}{2} \widehat{AC},$ § 235).   Also, $\angle BAD = \angle PAC$ (Hyp.).   Use § 305.

9. Draw a pair of corresponding diagonals in the given rectangles. Then each pair of corresponding ▲ in the two rectangles are similar (§ 310).   Hence, the rectangles are similar (§ 313).

10. In the $\odot$ $CAB,$ $\angle BAD \overset{m}{=\!=} \frac{1}{2} \widehat{AB}$ (§ 241).   Also $\angle C \overset{m}{=\!=} \frac{1}{2} \widehat{AB}$ (§ 235). $\therefore$ $\angle BAD = \angle C.$ In like manner, $\angle CAB = \angle D.$ $\therefore$ the ▲ are similar (§ 305).

1. In the similar ▲ ACD and $BFC,$ $AD : BF = AC : BC$ (§ 302). $\therefore AD \times BC = BF \times AC$ (§ 278), etc.

2. By Ex. 5, p. 210, ▲ APC and AFC are similar, etc. $CP \times CF = \overline{CA}^2$ (§ 278); CA is constant. $\therefore CP \times CF$ is constant.

3. See Ex. 4, p. 210.

4. ▲ ABC and PBC are similar by Ex. 3, p. 210, etc.

5.

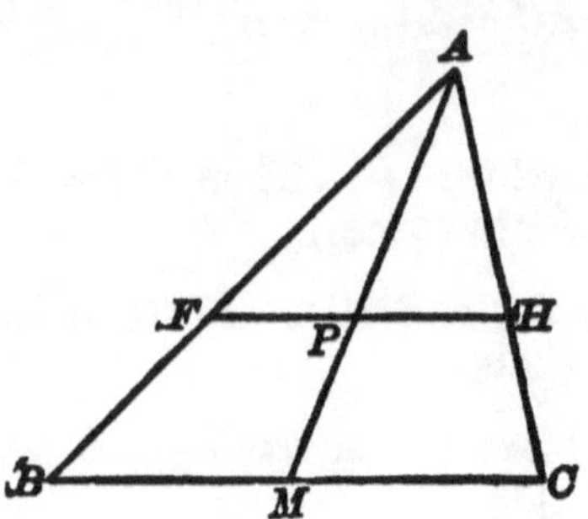

Let AM be a median of $\triangle ABC$, $FH \parallel BC$. Let FH intersect AM in P. Then by means of similar ▲ show that $\dfrac{BM}{FP} = \dfrac{AM}{AP} = \dfrac{MC}{PH}$. $\therefore FP = PH$ (§ 282).

PAGE 212

6. The ▲ APF and FQB are similar (§ 305).

$\therefore PF : FQ = AF : FB$ (§ 302). But $\dfrac{AF}{FB}$ is constant, etc.

7. $\angle ABF = \angle FBC$ (measured by ½ of equal arcs (§ 235)). $\therefore$ in the $\triangle ABC$, $AB : BC = AE : EC$ (§ 301)

9. Use § 324.

10. $\dfrac{PQ}{BC} = \dfrac{AP}{AB} = \dfrac{DT}{DC} = \dfrac{RT}{BC}$ (§§ 294, 295). Use § 282.

11.

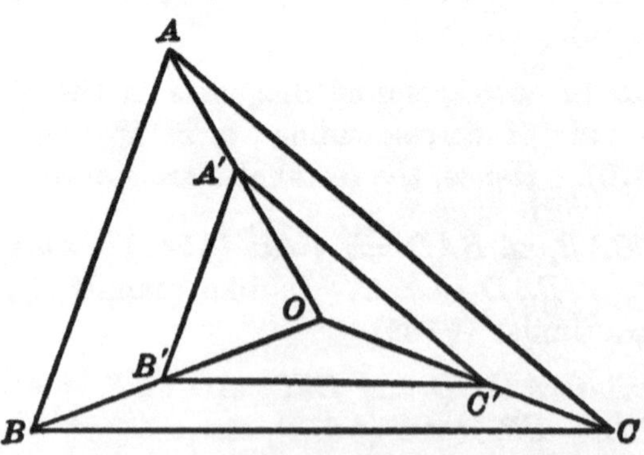

▲ ABO and $A'B'O$ are similar (§ 305). ▲ $OB'C'$ and OBC are similar (§ 305). $\therefore A'B' : AB = (OB' : OB) = B'C' : BC$ (§ 302).

But $\angle A'B'C' = \angle ABC$ (§ 112). $\therefore$ ▲ $A'B'C'$ and ABC are similar (§ 310).

12. $\dfrac{AR}{RQ} = \left(\dfrac{BR}{RD}\right) = \dfrac{RP}{AR}$ (§ 302). $\therefore \overline{AR}^2 = RQ \times RP$ (§ 278).

1. Then use §§ 101, 146.

2. Use Ex. 8, p. 93, and Ex. 1, p. 212.

3.

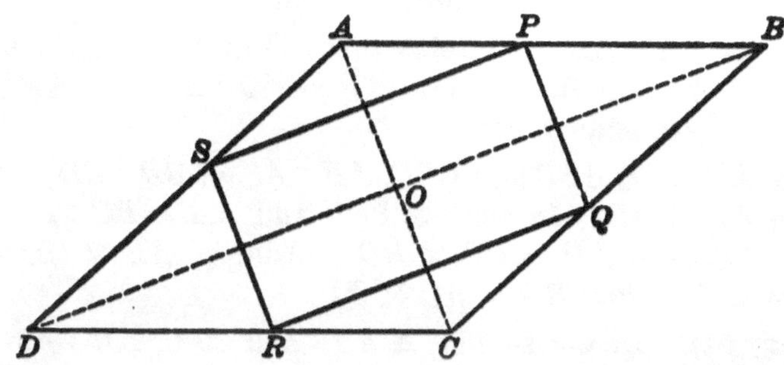

Let $ABCD$ be the given rhombus, and P, Q, R, S be the midpoints of its sides. Then $PQRS$ is a $\square$ (Ex. 1, p. 212). But $AC \perp DB$ (§ 121), $SP \parallel DB$, $PQ \parallel AC$. $\therefore \angle SPQ = \angle AOB$ (§ 112). In like manner $\angle PQR = $ a rt. $\angle = \angle QRS = \angle RSP$. $\therefore PQRS$ is a rectangle (§ 149).

4. Use § 305.

PAGE 213

5. Draw the altitude AH. Then the ▲ AHC and BFC are similar (§ 305). $\therefore AC : HC = BC : FC$ (§ 302). But $HC = \frac{1}{2} BC$ (§ 118). $\therefore AC : \frac{1}{2} BC = BC : FC$ (Ax. 9). $\therefore AC \times FC = \frac{1}{2} \overline{BC}^2$ (§ 278). Or, $2 AC \times FC = \overline{BC}^2$ (Ax. 4).

6. Draw the chord BD and prove the ▲ ABE and ABD similar (Ex. 5, p. 210).

7.

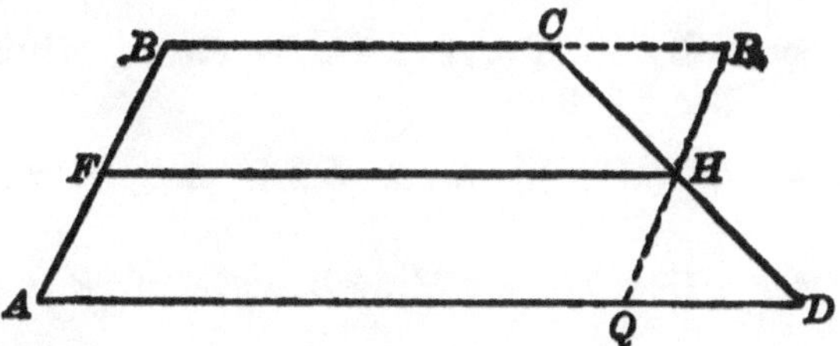

Let $ABCD$ be the trapezoid and F and H the midpoints of its legs AB and CD. Then $FH \parallel AD$ and BC, otherwise § 296 (last sentence) would be violated. Through H draw $PQ \parallel AB$ and meeting

AD in *Q* and *BC* produced at *P*.   **Prove** $\triangle CHP = \triangle HQD$ (§ 80).
$\therefore CP = QD$. $FH = AQ$ (§ 155) $= AD - QD$. $FH = BP$ (§ 155)
$= BC + PC$. $\therefore 2FH = AD + BC$, etc.

8. Denote the tangent by *RTS*.   Then $\angle P = \angle QTR = \angle STQ'$
   $= \angle P'$ (§§ 235, 241), etc.

9. Let the point *P* lie between *Q* and *R*. $\angle RQP = \angle RTP = \angle P'TR' = \angle P'Q'R'$ (§§ 235, 241), etc.

10. Draw the diameter *AR* intersecting *CD* in *F*. $\triangle AFQ$ and *ARP* are similar (§ 305). $\therefore AR : AP = AQ : AF$. $\therefore AP \times AQ = AR \times AF$ (constant), etc.

11. In the similar $\triangle ABF$ and *DBC*, $AB : AF = BD : CD$. $\therefore AB \times CD = AF \times BD$.   In sim. $\triangle BCF$ and *ABD*, $BC : FC = BD : AD$. $\therefore BC \times AD = CF \times BD$.   Adding, $AB \times CD + BC \times AD = (AF + FC) BD = AC \times BD$.

1. (Group 54).   In the similar $\triangle ABF$ and *BFC*, $AB : AF = BC : BF$, etc.

2. $\overline{AB}^2 = AC \times AF$, and $\overline{BC}^2 = AC \times FC$ (§ 319), etc.

3. Draw the chord *QB*.   Then $\triangle AQB$ and *APB* are similar (§ 305), etc.

4. See Ex. 2, p. 199.   **5.** Use §§ 69, 238, 304.   **6.** Use §§ 96, 235, 304.

PAGE 214

7. $\angle AFB$ is a rt. $\angle$ (§ 238).   **Prove** $\triangle DAB$ and *ABC* each similar to $\triangle AFB$ (§ 305), hence to each other (§ 306), etc.

9. § 323.

10. Draw the line of centers and the radii to the points of contact. **Prove** the $\triangle$ thus formed similar (§§ 69, 82, 305), etc.

11. The line joining the vertex to the midpoint of the base (See Ex. 5, p. 211).

12. Denote the center by *O*.   **Prove** $\angle POR$ a rt. $\angle$.   (For $\angle POA = \angle POQ$, etc.)   Use § 319.

13. $OA \times OB = \overline{OP}^2$ (Hyp.). $\therefore \triangle OPA$ and *OPB* are similar (§ 310).

14. By sim. $\triangle$, $HP : FP = CH : FB = CH : AF = CK : AK = HK : FK$.

1. Construct a fourth proportional to *c*, *a*, *b*; to 2 *c*, *a*, *b* (§ 297).

2. § 321.   Construct a mean proportional between $a + b$ and $a - b$.

3. § 321.   Construct a mean proportional between 3 *a* and *b*.

4. § 321; §§ 321, 128. Construct a mean proportional between 1 and 3. To construct $\frac{1}{2}\sqrt{5}$, construct a mean proportional between 1 and 5 and bisect the result.

PAGE 215

5. *I.e.*, proportional to 12, 3, 4 (§ 298).

6. § 301. That is, bisect the $\angle$ of the $\triangle$ opposite the side to be divided.

7. §§ 321, 298. That is, find a mean proportional between 1 and 2 (§ 321). Then use § 298.

8. These $\triangle$ are $=$ (§ 80). $\therefore$ to construct, draw $PL \parallel AC$ and meeting BC at L, bisect CL, etc.

9. $PQ = QR$. $\therefore OQ \perp PR$ (§ 203). $\therefore$ to construct PQ, on OP as a diameter construct a semicircle, etc. Use § 238.

10. Use § 323.

11. They are equal (§ 301). $\therefore$ divide the chord AB into line segments which shall be as $2 : 3$ (§ 298) and on AQ construct a segment of a $\odot$ which shall contain an $\angle = \frac{1}{2}\angle$ inscribed in segment APB (§ 265).

12. See Ex. 9, p. 169.   **13.** § 316.

14. Sides of required $\triangle$ = chords subtended by inscribed $\measuredangle$ = $\measuredangle$ of given $\triangle$.

15. Suppose the construction made and lines drawn from the center to the points of contact. Then $\measuredangle$ at the center = supplements of $\measuredangle$ of given $\triangle$. Hence to construct, at the center of the given $\odot$ construct adj. $\measuredangle$ = supplements of the $\measuredangle$ of the given $\triangle$. At the points where the radii which separate these $\measuredangle$ meet the circle draw tangents to the circle.

16. Draw a line bisecting two opposite sides of the rectangle. Or let $ABCD$ be the given rectangle. On AD, its lower base, describe a semicircle intersecting BC in F. Draw $FH \perp AD$. Then FH divides the rectangle as required. For $AH : HF = HF : HD$ (§ 320). Use Ex. 9, p. 211. In case the semicircle does not reach the side BC, the latter method of construction cannot be used.

PAGE 216

17. By similar $\triangle$, $AH : DE = (AB : DB) = AK : DG$. But $DE = DG$. $\therefore AH = AK$ (§ 282). Hence,

CONSTRUCTION. Draw AK the altitude of the given $\triangle$. From A draw $AH \parallel BC$ and $= AK$. Draw HB intersecting AC in E. Draw $ED \parallel BC$ and meeting AB in D. Draw DG and $EF \perp BC$, etc.

1. Use the method of the Ex. in § 327.

2. Hence, $x = -a \pm a\sqrt{2}$. Construct $a\sqrt{2}$, then $a\sqrt{2} - a$; use Ex. 12, p. 139.

3.

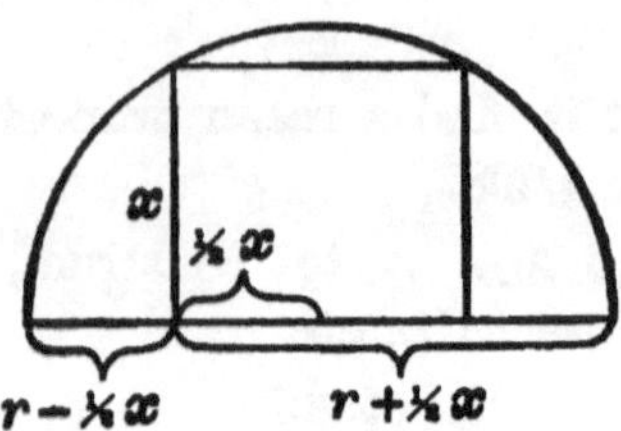

Denote a side of the required square by x. Then $r - \dfrac{1}{2}x : x = x : r$

$+ \dfrac{1}{2}x$ (§320). $\therefore x^2 = r^2 - \dfrac{1}{4}x^2$, or $x^2 = \dfrac{4r^2}{5}$, or $x = \dfrac{2}{5}\sqrt{5r^2}$. $\therefore$ to

construct x, construct a mean proportional between r and $5r$ and take $\frac{2}{5}$ of the result.

4. Denote the first given line by a, the other given line by b, and the required part by x. Then $a - x : x = x : b$.

$$\therefore x = \frac{-b \pm \sqrt{b^2 + 4ab}}{2}.$$

Hence, construct a mean proportional between b and $b + 4a$, etc.

PAGE 217

1. Divide the given line AB in the ratio of $m : n$ (§ 298).

2.
$$\underline{\hspace{4cm}}_{n} \qquad \underline{\hspace{5cm}}_{m} \qquad \underline{\hspace{3cm}}_{d}$$

Let d be the difference of the two required lines and m and n two other lines in the given ratio. Denote the smaller of the required lines by x. Then the other line required is $d + x$. Hence $m : n = d + x : x$ (Hyp.) or $m - n : n = d : x$ (§ 287). Hence construct a 4th proportional to $m - n$, n, and d, etc.

3. Use the figure of Ex. 10, p. 212 (text-book). Let $ABCD$ be the given trapezoid and PT the line $\parallel$ the base BC which divides $ABCD$ into two similar trapezoids $APTD$ and $PBCT$. Then $AD : PT = PT : BC$ (§ 302). Hence,

CONSTRUCTION. Construct the mean proportional between AD and BC (§ 321). From any point X in AB draw a line $XY \parallel AD$ and $=$ this mean proportional. Through Y draw a line $\parallel AB$ and meeting CD in T. From T draw $TP \parallel BC$, etc.

Proof. The trapezoids $APTD$ and $PBCT$ are mutually equiangular (§ 97). Let AB and CD be produced and meet at O. Then $OA : OP = (AD : PT = PT : BC) = OP : OB$. $\therefore OA - OP : OA = OP - OB : OP$. $\therefore AP : OA = BP : OP$. $\therefore AP : BP = (OA : OP) = AD : PT$, etc.

4. Let AB be the smaller given line. Produce it through B to C, making $AC =$ larger given line. Through C and B pass any convenient circle. From A draw a tangent to $\odot$ (§ 264), viz. AD. Then $\overline{AD}^2 = AB \times AC$ (§ 324).

5. Construct by drawing a line from one point A through the other, B, to meet given line at P. Find the mean proportional between PA and PB (§ 321). On the given line lay off $PC =$ this mean proportional. Through A, B, and C pass a circle (§ 256). (Another solution is obtained by laying off PC' in the opposite direction from C.)

6. Denote the external segment by x. From the given point draw a tangent $(= a)$. Then $2x : a = a : x$ (§ 324). Use § 327.

7. $m^2x^2 = \dfrac{mt^2}{m + n}$. $\therefore t : mx = mx : \dfrac{mt}{m + n}$.

Given the lines m, n, t, find $\dfrac{mt}{m + n}$ by constructing the 4th proportional to $m + n$, m, t. Find mx by § 321.

8. From the point of division so made draw a line to P. Through P draw a $\perp$ to the last line, etc. Use § 295.

9. Through the points of division on PQ and QR draw a line, etc. Use §§ 305, 302.

10.

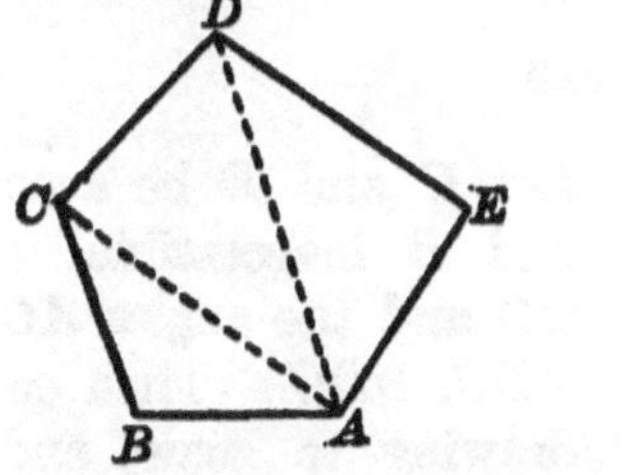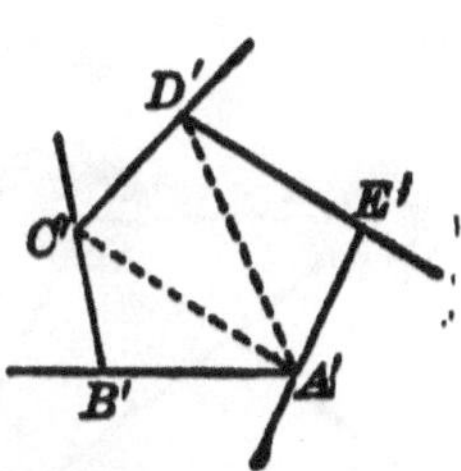

Given the polygon $ABCDE$ and the line $A'B'$.

To construct on $A'B'$ a polygon similar to $ABCDE$ and similarly placed.

CONSTRUCTION. In the given polygon, draw the diagonals AC and AD, dividing the polygon into triangles. At B', on the line $A'B'$, construct $\angle A'B'C'$ equal to $\angle B$; and at A' construct $\angle B'A'C'$ equal to $\angle BAC$ (§ 86). Produce the lines $B'C'$ and $A'C'$ to meet at C'. $\therefore \triangle ABC \sim \triangle A'B'C'$ (§ 305). Proceed in like manner, using § 305 twice again, and § 313.

11. Divide the given line into parts in the given ratio by § 295. Upon the given line as a diameter construct a circle. Use § 265. Or, construct a diameter $\perp$ given line, and a chord from end of second diameter through the point of division of the first, etc.

PAGE 218

1. AB, BC, AD, so as to be able to use the proportion $AB : BC = AD : DE.$.

2.

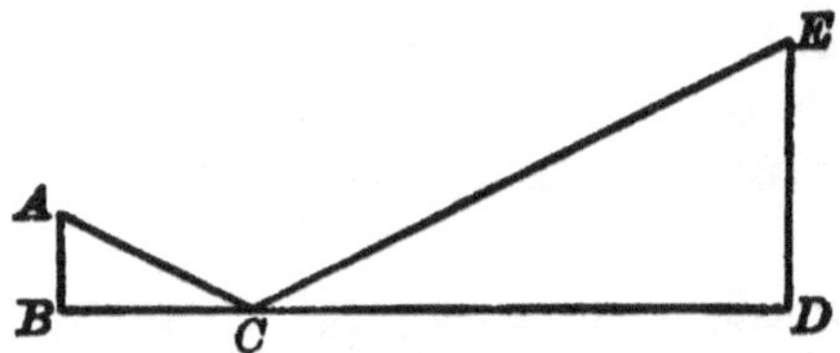

Let AB be the observer, ED the tree, and let the mirror be at C. Then $\angle ACB = \angle ECD$ (Ex. 2, p. 105). $\therefore$ the $\triangle$ are similar (§ 305). $\therefore BC : AB = CD : ED$, or $6 : 5\frac{1}{2} = 120 : ED$. $\therefore ED = 110$ ft. $Ans.$

3. $\angle FBC = \angle EAB$ (§ 114). Denote the height of the tree by x. $\therefore x : 150 = 4\frac{1}{2} : 6$. $\therefore x = 112\frac{1}{2}$ ft. $Ans.$

4. See Ex. 9, p. 197 (text-book). Construct the diagram to scale and on it measure AB, and hence, by use of a proportion, find the distance represented by AB.

PAGE 219

5.

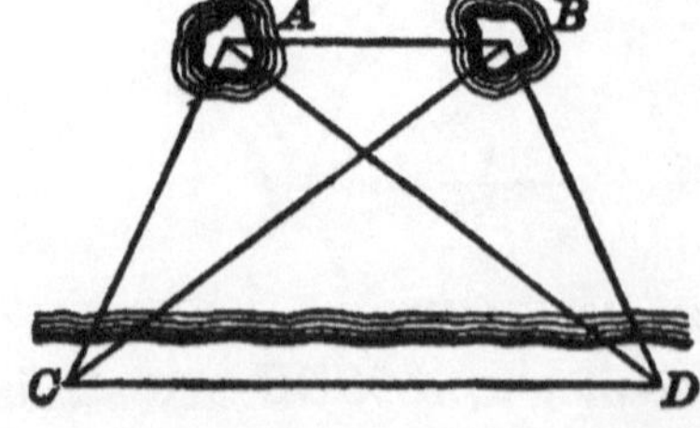

Let C and D be accessible, A and B inaccessible. Measure CD and the angles ACD, BCD, ADC, BDC. Then construct a drawing to scale, and on the drawing measure AB, and then compute the distance represented by AB.

6. $\therefore \dfrac{\overline{FB}^2}{\overline{FA}^2} = \dfrac{1}{2}.$ $\therefore \dfrac{FB}{FA} = \dfrac{1}{\sqrt{2}} = \dfrac{1}{1.41 +} = \dfrac{5}{7}$ approx.

7. $\therefore SR = 60.$ $\therefore$ 60 lb. *Ans.*

8. The diagram of Ex. 7 would need to be changed so that $BC = 18$, and $AC = 100.$ $\therefore AB = \sqrt{100^2 + 18^2} = 101.6 +$ ft. $\therefore 101.6 : 18 = 1800$ lb. $: x.$ $\therefore x = 318.8 +$ lb. *Ans.*

PAGE 220

11.

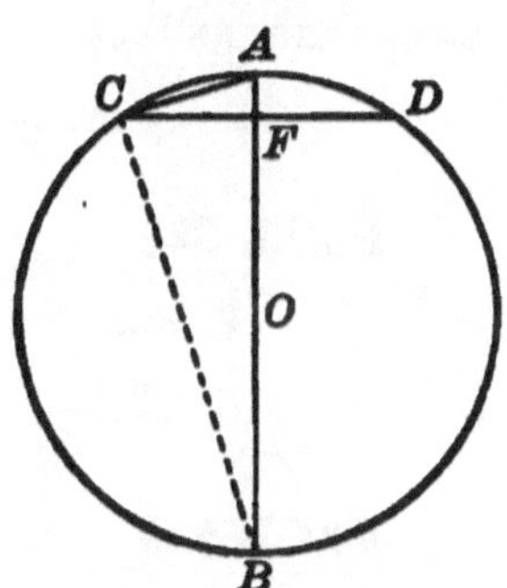

Let O be the center of the earth, and CAD be a circle through the tops of the three stakes. Then AB is $\perp$ bisector of the chord CD (§ 205). $\therefore$ by § 320, $AF : AC = AC : AB.$ $\therefore AF = \dfrac{\overline{AC}^2}{\overline{AB}} = \dfrac{4\overline{AC}^2}{4AB} = \dfrac{(2AC)^2}{4\,(\text{diam. of earth})}.$ Hence, AF varies as the square of $2AC.$ But for a small arc, $2AC$ approximately $=$ arc $CAD.$ Bulge for 4 miles $= 2^2(\tfrac{2}{3}$ ft.$) = 2\tfrac{2}{3}$ ft. *Ans.*
Similarly, $10\tfrac{2}{3}$ ft.; $42\tfrac{2}{3}$ ft.; $170\tfrac{2}{3}$ ft. *Ans.*

12. Denote the distance in miles by $x.$ Then $x^2 : 2^2 = 11 : \tfrac{2}{3}.$ $\therefore x = 8 +$ miles. *Ans.*

13. 16 mi.$+$.

14. 209.75.

15. 44; 91; 687 $-$; 1418 $-$.

PAGE 221

16. Let the $\perp$ from B meet AD at F, and that from D meet AC at $H.$ Then $AF : 6000 = 1 : 1.305.$ $\therefore AF = 4597 +.$ $BF : 6000 = 1 : 1.556.$ $\therefore BF = 3856 +.$ $3856 + : FD = 1 : .839.$ $\therefore FD = 3235 +,$ etc. $CD = 4166 +.$ *Ans.*

PAGE 222

5. Not unless the polygons have three sides.

6. Not unless the polygons have three sides.

7. §§ 320, 322.   **8.** §§ 324, 325.

9. §§ 302, 312, 313, 317, 318.

10. §§ 293, 294, 296, 299, 300, 301, 302, 304, 305, 306, 309, 310, 311, 316, 319.

11. Each line on the object is fifty times as long as the corresponding line on the drawing; 1200 times as long.

12. Two.   **14.** Three.

PAGE 224

3. 4.   **5.** 24.   **7.** 32.   **9.** 27.

4. 24.   **6.** $13\frac{1}{2}$.   **8.** 27.   **10.** 60.

PAGE 225

17. $13\frac{1}{2}$ sq. yd.; $13\frac{1}{2}$ sq. mi.; 1350 sq. mi.

PAGE 227

1. 16 : 3.   **2.** 1944.   **3.** 75 : 256.   **4.** $8\frac{1}{3}$ ft.

PAGE 228

1. $21\frac{1}{4}$ yd.   **2.** 17.5.   **3.** 9 sq. in.

PAGE 230

1. 240 sq. in.   **2.** 20.3 ft.

PAGE 231

1. 75.917 sq. in.   **2.** 2 ft.

PAGE 232

1. $1\frac{1}{2}$ sq. ft.   **2.** 16 in.; 32 in.

1. (Group 61). 35 sq. in.; 35 sq. in.

2. Area of $\triangle PQT = \frac{1}{2}PT \times h = \frac{1}{2}TR \times h =$ area $\triangle TQR$ (§ 343, Ax. 9, § 343).

3. Use §§ 159, 343, Ax. 1.   4. 1 ft. 4 in.   5. 4.8 ft.

6. In the world about us a vastly larger number of rectangles occur than of equilateral triangles; and it is easier to resolve rectangles into squares than into equilateral triangles.

7. $831\frac{1}{2}$ sq. ft.; 1360 sq. ft.; 1275 sq. ft.

PAGE 234

1. 962 sq. in.   3. 2.24 ft.   5. 168 sq. ft.

2. 9.   4. $\dfrac{2K - b'h}{h}$.   6. The base and altitude.

7. The base and altitude, or the three sides. See Formula 5, under *Areas*, p. 294.

8. The two bases and the altitude.

9. Yes.   11. No.   12. 447 sq. in.   13. $\dfrac{8^2 \times 4}{4^2 \times 8} = \dfrac{8}{4} = \dfrac{2}{1}$.

PAGE 235

14. Draw QA and $SB \perp PT$.
Prove $\triangle QAR = \triangle PBS$ (§ 110). $\therefore QA = SB$.

15. 80; 8000 sq. ft.

1. 16 : 25.

PAGE 238

1. 13 in.   2. 15 ft.

3. Other side of rectangle $= \sqrt{20^2 - 16^2} = 12$. $\therefore$ 192 sq. in. *Ans.*

4. Let x = side of square. $\therefore x^2 + x^2 = 100$. $\therefore x^2 = 50$. *Ans.*

5. Alt. $= \sqrt{24^2 - 12^2}$ in. (§ 356) $= 12\sqrt{3}$ in. $= 20.78 +$ in. *Ans.*

PAGE 239

6. By the method of Ex. 5, p. 238, find altitude of $\square = 5\sqrt{3}$.
$\therefore$ Area $= 100\sqrt{3}$ sq. ft. $= 173.2 +$ sq. ft. *Ans.*

7. Let 24 in. be the base. Denote the altitude by x. Then $x^2 + x^2 = 18^2$. $\therefore x = 9\sqrt{2}$. $\therefore$ Area $= 108\sqrt{2}$ sq. in. or $152.73 +$ sq. in. *Ans.*

8. $a\sqrt{b^2 - a^2}$.

9. Distance $= \sqrt{60^2 + 18^2}$ ft. $= 62.64$ ft. *Ans.*

1. (Group 63).

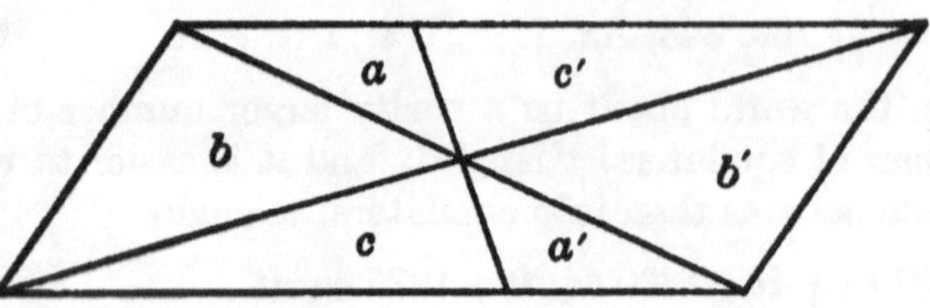

Show that $\triangle\,a = \triangle\,a'$ (§ 80), $\triangle\,b = \triangle\,b'$ (§ 79), $\triangle\,c = \triangle\,c'$ (§ 80). Add, etc.

2.

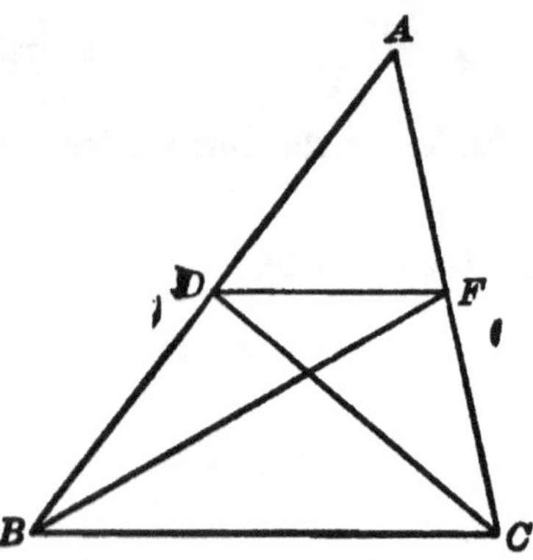

$DF \parallel BC$ (§ 300) $\therefore \triangle ABC \sim \triangle ADF$ (§ 305) $\therefore$ by § 352 $\dfrac{\triangle ABC}{\triangle ADF}$

$= \dfrac{\overline{AC}^2}{\overline{AF}^2} = \dfrac{(2\overline{AF})^2}{\overline{AF}^2} = \dfrac{4}{1}$. Or, in $\triangle ABC$, let $AB = 2AD$, $AC = 2AF$. $\dfrac{\triangle ABC}{\triangle ADC} = \dfrac{2}{1}$ (§ 345). $\dfrac{\triangle ADC}{\triangle ADF} = \dfrac{2}{1}$ (§ 345). $\therefore \dfrac{\triangle ABC}{\triangle ADF} = \dfrac{4}{1}$ (Ax. 4).

3. See Ex. 2, and § 156.

4. See figure of Ex. 2. Show that the $\triangle$ ADF, DFB, and DFC are all equal in area.

5. Use figure, p. 206 (text-book). Area of $\triangle ABC = \frac{1}{2}AB \times BC$ (§ 343) or $= \frac{1}{2}AC \times BF$ (§ 343). $\therefore \frac{1}{2}AB \times BC = \frac{1}{2}AC \times BF$ (Ax. 1). $\therefore AB \times BC = AC \times BF$ (Ax. 4).

6. $\frac{1}{2}b \times a = \frac{1}{2}b' \times 3a$ (Hyp.). $\therefore b' : b = a : 3a = 1 : 3$ (§ 281).

7. Denote one of the legs by c and half the base of the first $\triangle$ (and $\therefore$ the altitude of the second $\triangle$) by b. Then the area of each $\triangle = b\sqrt{c^2 - b^2}$ (§§ 356, 343).

9. Two trapezoids are formed whose corresponding bases and whose altitudes are equal. Thus,

$\frac{1}{2}(\frac{1}{2}b + \frac{1}{2}b')h = \frac{1}{2}(\frac{1}{2}b + \frac{1}{2}b')h$ (§ 350).

PAGE 240

10. Area of $\triangle AOB$ = area of $\triangle AOD$ (§ 344). Area of $\triangle BOC$ = area of $\triangle DOC$ (§ 344). $\therefore$ area of $\triangle ABC$ = area of $\triangle DAC$ (Ax. 2).

If one diagonal of a parallelogram bisects the other diagonal, the first diagonal divides the parallelogram into two equivalent triangles.

11. $\triangle ABC = \triangle ADC$ (1), $\triangle PTC = \triangle PRC$ (2), $\triangle AQP = \triangle ASP$ (3) (§ 156). Add (3) and (2) and subtract the result from (1) (Axs. 2, 3).

12. Let $ABCD$ be the given quadrilateral, and P the midpoint of the diagonal AC. Then $\triangle ABP = \triangle PBC$ (§ 344). Also $\triangle ADP = \triangle PDC$ (§ 344). Adding, quad. $ABPD$ = quad. $PBCD$ (Ax. 2).

1. (Group 64). See figure of Ex. 1 (Group 51), p. 210 (text-book). $\overline{AB}^2 = \overline{AD}^2 + \overline{DB}^2$ (§ 355). Also $\overline{AC}^2 = \overline{AD}^2 + \overline{CD}^2$ (§ 355). Subtract.

2. Let $ABCD$ be the given quadrilateral and let the diagonals AC and BD intersect at right $\angle$ at the point O. Then, by § 355, $\overline{AB}^2 = \overline{BO}^2 + \overline{OA}^2$, $\overline{CD}^2 = \overline{OC}^2 + \overline{OD}^2$. $\therefore \overline{AB}^2 + \overline{CD}^2 = \overline{BO}^2 + \overline{OA}^2 + \overline{OC}^2 + \overline{OD}^2$. Also $\overline{BC}^2 = \overline{BO}^2 + \overline{OC}^2$, $\overline{AD}^2 = \overline{AO}^2 + \overline{OD}^2$. $\therefore \overline{BC}^2 + \overline{AD}^2 = \overline{BO}^2 + \overline{OA}^2 + \overline{OC}^2 + \overline{OD}^2$. Use Ax. 1.

3. The altitude bisects the base (§ 117). Denote one side of the $\triangle$ by a, and the altitude by x. $\therefore a^2 = x^2 + \left(\frac{a}{2}\right)^2$ (§ 355). $\therefore x^2 = \frac{3a^2}{4}$.

4. AB is the hypotenuse. $\therefore \overline{AB}^2 = \overline{AC}^2 + (2\overline{CK})^2 = \overline{AC}^2 + 4\overline{CK}^2$. Also $\overline{AK}^2 = \overline{AC}^2 + \overline{CK}^2$ (§ 355). Subtract, etc.

5. $\overline{AQ}^2 = \overline{AC}^2 + \overline{CQ}^2$, $\overline{BP}^2 = \overline{PC}^2 + \overline{BC}^2$ (§ 355). Adding, $\overline{AQ}^2 + \overline{BP}^2 = \overline{AC}^2 + \overline{BC}^2 + \overline{PC}^2 + \overline{CQ}^2$ (Ax. 2) $= \overline{AB}^2 + \overline{PQ}^2$ (Ax. 9).

6. $\overline{BE}^2 = \overline{AB}^2 + \overline{AE}^2 = \overline{AB}^2 + \frac{1}{4}\overline{AC}^2$ (§ 355). $\overline{CF}^2 = \overline{AF}^2 + \overline{AC}^2 = \frac{1}{4}\overline{AB}^2 + \overline{AC}^2$ (§ 355). $\therefore \overline{BE}^2 + \overline{CF}^2 = \frac{5\overline{AB}^2}{4} + \frac{5\overline{AC}^2}{4}$ (Ax. 3). $4(\overline{BE}^2 + \overline{CF}^2) = 5(\overline{AB}^2 + \overline{AC}^2) = 5\overline{BC}^2$ (Ax. 9).

7.

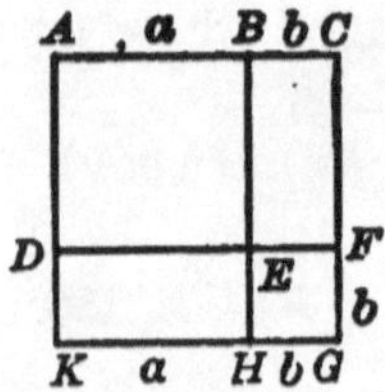

Let line AB be denoted by a, BC by b; let AG be the square on AC, and AE the square on AB. Then $EG = b^2$, and rectangles BF and EK each $= ab$. $\therefore BF = EK$. But $AG = AE + EG + 2BF$, or $(a + b)^2 = a^2 + b^2 + 2ab$.

8.

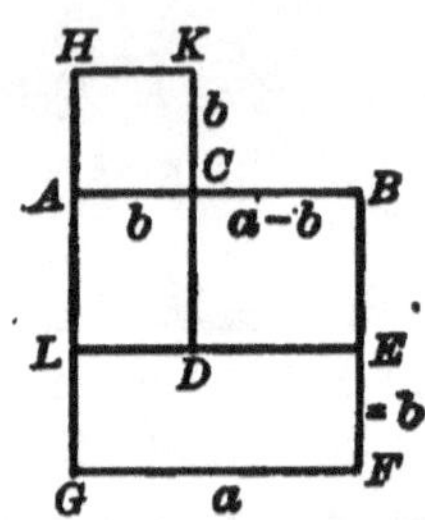

Let $AB = a$, $AC = b$. Then $BC = a - b$. Let AF be the square on AB, CE the square on CB, and AK the square on AC. Hence, the rectangles LK and GE each $= ab$. Then $BD = AF + AK - 2GE$, or $(a - b)^2 = a^2 + b^2 - 2ab$.

9.

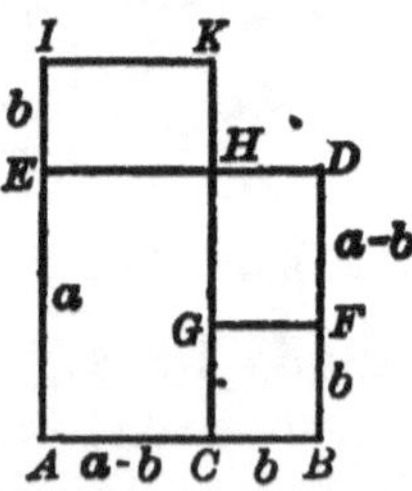

Let $AB = a$, $BC = b = IE$; then $DF = a - b$. Let AD be the square on AB, and CF the square on CB. Then the rectangle $EK = DG$ (for each $= b(a - b)$). But rectangle $AK = AD + EK - DG - CF = AD - CF$. $\therefore (a + b)(a - b) = a^2 - b^2$.

10. $1 : 6$.   **11.** $31{,}875$ sq. mi.

PAGE 241

1. Draw the altitude of the $\square$ through P and $\perp AD$, and denote it by h. Then by § 343 and Ax. 2, $\triangle PAD + \triangle PBC = \tfrac{1}{2}AD \times h = \tfrac{1}{2} \square ABCD$ (§ 339), etc.

2. Draw a $\perp$ from P to AD. Use § 355 (four times), Ax. 2, etc.

3. See method of proof in § 386.

4. Show that the top and bottom $\triangle$ together $= \frac{1}{2}$ the trapezoid, i.e. $= \frac{1}{2}h(b_1 + b_2)$.

5. See Ex. 4.

6. $\overset{\frown}{AC} + \overset{\frown}{BD} =$ semicircle (for $\frac{1}{2}$ their sum measures the rt. $\angle O$). Also $\overset{\frown}{BD} + \overset{\frown}{DE} =$ semicircle (constr.). $\therefore \overset{\frown}{AC} + \overset{\frown}{BD} = \overset{\frown}{BD} + \overset{\frown}{DE}$ (Ax. 1). $\therefore \overset{\frown}{AC} = \overset{\frown}{DE}$ (Ax. 3). $\therefore$ chord $AC =$ chord DE (§ 200). $\therefore \overline{OA}^2 + \overline{OC}^2 = (\text{chord } AC)^2 = (\text{chord } ED)^2$ (§ 355). But $\overline{OB}^2 + \overline{OD}^2 = (\text{chord } BD)^2$ (§ 355). $\therefore \overline{OA}^2 + \overline{OC}^2 + \overline{OB}^2 + \overline{OD}^2 = (\text{chord } ED)^2 + (\text{chord } DB)^2 = \overline{EB}^2$.

7. Denote the vertices of the quadrilateral by A, B, C, D, and the midpoints of AB, BC, CD, DA by 1, 2, 3, 4, respectively. Let the diagonals BD and AC intersect in O. Draw $O1$. Let 12 intersect BD in P. Then $OP = PB$ (§ 296). $\therefore \triangle O1P = \triangle 1PB$ (§ 344). Let 14 intersect AO in Q. Then similarly $\triangle O1Q = \triangle A1Q$, etc.

8.

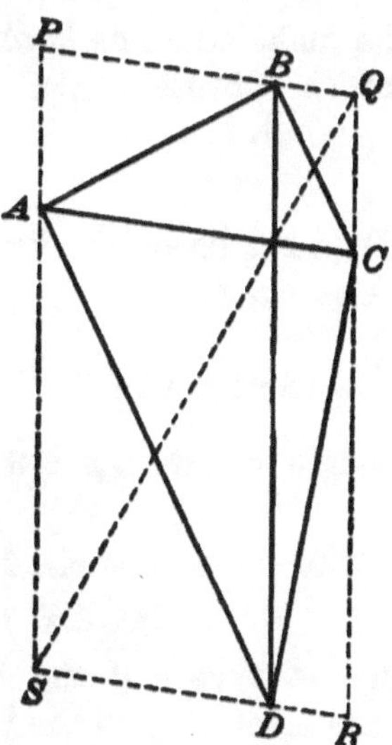

Let $ABCD$ be the given quadr. Through B draw $PQ \parallel$ the diagonal AC, through D draw $SR \parallel AC$, through C draw $QR \parallel BD$, through A draw $PS \parallel BD$. Then show $ABCD = \frac{1}{2}PQRS$. Also $\triangle SPQ = \frac{1}{2}PQRS$ (§ 156). $\therefore ABCD = \triangle PQS$. But $PQ = AC$ (§ 157), etc.

PAGE 242

1. The base of $\square$ = median of the trapezoid (§ 157). Use § 339, Ex. 7, p. 213.

2. Join the vertex with the point in base. Use two pairs of $\triangle$ equal in area. Add.

3. Draw $\perp$ from the other vertices of the $\square$, viz.: B and D, to the diagonal AC. See Ex. 11, p. 93.

4. The altitude $= \sqrt{a^2 - \dfrac{a^2}{4}} = \dfrac{a\sqrt{3}}{2}$ (§ 356), etc.

5. By Ex. 4, if the side of the second $\triangle$ is a, the side of the first $\triangle$ is $\dfrac{a\sqrt{3}}{2}$. $\therefore K : K' = \left(\dfrac{a\sqrt{3}}{2}\right)^2 : a^2\,(\S\,352) = \dfrac{3a^2}{4} : a^2 = 3 : 4$.

6. Denote side of $\triangle$ by a and draw lines from the given point to the vertices of the $\triangle$. Then area of $\triangle = \frac{1}{2}a \times$ (sum of $\perp$) (§ 343, Ax. 2). But area of $\triangle = \frac{1}{2}a \times h$ (§ 343). $\therefore \frac{1}{2}a \times$ (sum of $\perp$) $= \frac{1}{2}a \times h$ (Ax. 1). $\therefore$ sum of $\perp = h$ (Ax. 5).

7. See Ex. 10, p. 240.

8. In the $\triangle$ in which the included angle is obtuse, produce the base through the vertex of the obtuse angle, till the produced part = base, etc.

9. Use § 345, Ax. 4.

10. $\triangle QDC = \frac{1}{2}\,\square\,ABCD$ (same base CD, etc.). $\triangle ABP + \triangle PCD = \frac{1}{2}\,\square\,ABCD$, etc. Use Ax. 3.

PAGE 243

1. Construct a right triangle whose legs are the sides of the given squares.

2. Reduces to Ex. 12, p. 139.   4. See Ex. 1.

3. See Ex. 1.   5. See Ex. 1.

6. Draw a line through the vertex $\parallel$ the base. Bisect base; at the midpoint of the base erect a $\perp$ to the base, etc.

7. Draw a line through the vertex $\parallel$ to the base. At one end of the base construct an $\angle$ = given $\angle$, etc.

8. Draw a line through the vertex $\parallel$ the base. Using one end of the base as a center and the required side as a radius, describe an arc, etc.

9. See Ex. 7.

10. Let b be the base of the given $\triangle$, and x that of the required $\triangle$. $\therefore$ $b^2 : x^2 = 1 : 2$. $\therefore$ $x = b \sqrt{2}$ (see Ex. 2, p. 208).

11. Let ABC be the given triangle. Construct any square and draw its diagonal. Then divide the side BC into segments at G such that $BC : BG =$ diagonal of square : side of square. Through G draw a line $\parallel AC$, etc.

12. Draw the $\perp$ through the intersection of the diagonals. (See Ex. 1, p. 239.)

13. Draw the line through the given point and through the intersection of the diagonals. (See Ex. 1, p. 239.)

14. Use § 321.

PAGE 244

1. $\dfrac{2 \times 36}{4 \times 6} = \dfrac{3}{1}$. *Ans.* $\quad \dfrac{b''}{a''}$. *Ans.* $\qquad$ 2. 4.

3. Since $6 =$ radius of the log, a side of the square beam $= \sqrt{6^2 + 6^2}$ $= 6 \sqrt{2}$. On the diagram of Ex. 6, p. 219, $AB = 12$, $DB = 4$. $\therefore$ $FB = \sqrt{4 \times 12} = 4 \sqrt{3}$ (§ 320). $FB : AF = 1 : \sqrt{2}$, or $4\sqrt{3} : AF = 1 : \sqrt{2}$. $\therefore$ $AF = 4\sqrt{6}$. $\dfrac{(4\sqrt{6})^2 \times 4\sqrt{3}}{(6\sqrt{2})^2 \times 6\sqrt{2}} = \dfrac{8\sqrt{3}}{9\sqrt{2}}$ $= \dfrac{13.85 +}{12.72 +}$. *Ans.*

4. When the width of the beam is 3 in., by § 320 we find height of beam $= 3\sqrt{15}$. $\therefore$ Required ratio $= \dfrac{(4\sqrt{6})^2 \times 4\sqrt{3}}{(3\sqrt{15})^2 \times 3} = \dfrac{128\sqrt{3}}{135}$ $= \dfrac{221.69 +}{135}$. *Ans.*

5. Denote the offsets by $a_1, a_2, a_3, \ldots a_n$, and the common distance between them by h. Then the sum of the areas of the small trapezoids forming the figure $= \frac{1}{2}h(a_1 + a_2) + \frac{1}{2}h(a_2 + a_3) + \ldots + \frac{1}{2}h(a_{n-1} + a_n) = \frac{1}{2}h(a_1 + a_n) + h(a_2 + a_3 + \ldots + a_{n-1})$.

6. In Ex. 5, if the initial and final offsets reduce to zero the formula becomes $h(a_2 + a_3 + \ldots + a_{n-1})$. In the diagram of Ex. 6 draw the longest possible chord to the irregular curve and divide this chord into a suitable number of equal parts. At the points of division erect $\perp$ to meet the curve. Then the entire area approximately equals the sum of the $\perp$ multiplied by the common distance between them.

7. Let $FG = 100$ ft., $GK = 140$ ft., $KL = 80$ ft., $FB = 160$ ft., $GC = 220$ ft., $KD = 220$ ft., $LE = 140$ ft., $HA = HG = 50$ ft. Then area of $ABCD = \frac{100}{2}(160 + 220) + 140 \times 220 + \frac{80}{2}(220 + 140) - \frac{110}{2}(160 + 50) - \frac{170}{2}(50 + 140) = 32{,}300$ sq. ft. *Ans.*

8. Let O be the center of $\overset{\frown}{BC}$. At B erect $BO \perp AT$. Draw Ob_2. From b_2 draw $b_2H \perp OB$. Then $OH = \sqrt{r^2 - (3d)^2}$. $\therefore a_3 b_3 = BH = r - \sqrt{r^2 - (3d)^2}$. In like manner, $a_n b_n = r - \sqrt{r^2 - (nd)^2}$.

PAGE 245

9. Speed per hour $= \sqrt{12^2 + 3^2}$ mi. $= 12.36 +$ mi.

12. 500 lb.   **14.** 5.66 $+$ mi. per hour.   **15.** 25 mi. per second.

16. Use the tape to make a right triangle whose sides are 24 ft., 32 ft., 40 ft.

17.

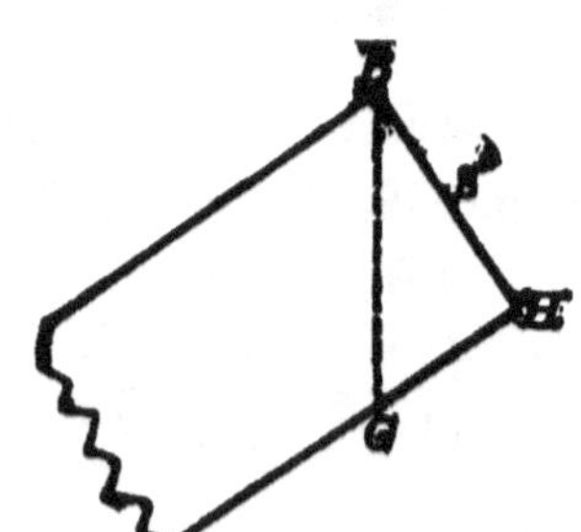

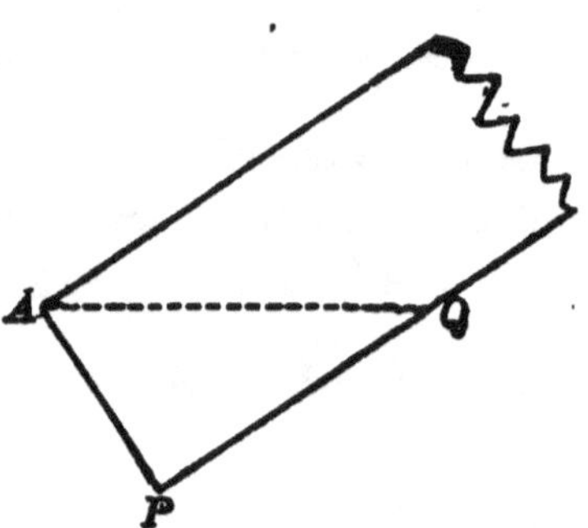

$AD = 10$ ft., $BD = 6\frac{3}{4}$ ft., $\therefore AB = 12.01 +$ ft.

At the peak, GH, the part cut off from the lower edge of the rafter, is $\frac{3}{4}$ of BH. To determine the line along which, at the lower end of the rafter, the lower edge of the rafter must be cut, $PQ = \frac{3}{4} AP$, where AP is the width of the rafter.

PAGE 246

3. §§ 343, 344, 345, 346, 352, 355, 356.

4. §§ 334, 335, 336, 337.   **7.** § 350.

5. §§ 339, 340, 341, 342, 347.   **8.** §§ 353, 354.

6. § 348.   **9.** See § 333.

10. " The number of units in the area of a rectangle divided by the number of linear units in the base."

11. When two sides of a right triangle are known, Prop. X enables us to find the third side without the labor of measuring it.

14. See p. 280.

15. Correct for square and rectangle. It gives too large a result for all other quadrilaterals.

PAGE 248

1. $9 : 64$.

PAGE 251

1. $108°$. **2.** Use § 79.

PAGE 252

7. Side of square $= \sqrt{3^2 + 3^2}$ in. $= 3\sqrt{2}$ in. $= 4.23 +$ in. Area $= 18$ sq. in. *Ans.*

8. $r^2 + r^2 = (\tfrac{3}{2})^2$. $\therefore r = 1.06 +$ in. *Ans.*

9. $7\sqrt{2}$ in. $= 9.89 +$ in. *Ans.*

10. Use § 121. **11.** Use § 345. **12.** § 363.

PAGE 253

1. $72°$. **2.** $60°$. **3.** $90°$.

4. $5\sqrt{2}$ in. $= 7.07 +$ in. *Ans.* Area $= 200$ sq. in. *Ans.*

5. Apothem $= 5\sqrt{3}$ in. $= 8.66 +$ in. *Ans.* Area $\dfrac{3\sqrt{3}}{2} \times 100$ sq. in. $= 259.8 +$ sq. in. *Ans.*

6. $\tfrac{1}{2}b\sqrt{3}$; $\dfrac{3\sqrt{3}b^2}{2}$.

7. $\tfrac{1}{2}b\sqrt{2}$; $2b^2$.

8. 4 in.

9. $\overset{\frown}{FA} = \overset{\frown}{FB}$ (§ 202) $\therefore FA = FB$ (§ 363), etc.

10. If apothem $= x, r = 2x$ (Ex. 9). $\therefore (2x)^2 - x^2 = 9$. $\therefore x = \sqrt{3}$ in. Area $= 9\sqrt{3}$ sq. in. *Ans.*

11. See Ex. 10. $r = 4$. *Ans.*

12. Circumscribe a circle about the given polygon. Use §§ 198, 235.

13. Area $= 584.56 +$ sq. ft.

PAGE 255

5. 400 sq. in.

6. 129.90 sq. in.; 519.61 sq. in.

7. Denote the radius of the circle by r. Then area of hexagon

$$= \frac{3\sqrt{3}r^2}{2} = 2\left(\frac{3\sqrt{3}r^2}{4}\right) = 2 \text{ area of triangle.}$$

8. $\dfrac{2r^2}{4r^2} = \dfrac{1}{2}$. *Ans.*   **9.** $3 : 4$.

10. On the diagram of p. 249, draw straight lines connecting the alternate vertices.

11. In each of at least two adjacent squares on the squared paper, inscribe a regular octagon (see Ex. 11, p. 270). The figure is completed by drawing lines parallel to the sides of these octagons, which lines will form sides of inscribed octagons in the other squares composing the squared paper.

PAGE 256

1. $128\sqrt{3}$ sq. in. $= 221.70 +$ sq. in.

2. Use §§ 241, 102, etc.

3. Use Ex. 2 and § 352.   **4.** See Ex. 9, p. 253.

PAGE 257

1. $1 : 2$; $1 : 4$.   **2.** $4 : 9$; $2 : 3$; $2 : 3$.

3. Use §§ 376, 353. ∴ 414.72 sq. in. *Ans.*

4. $16 : 25$; $16 : 25$.

PAGE 258

1. (§ 379). $10\sqrt{3}$.

3. $8.04 -$ in. *Ans.* The perimeters and their difference would each be doubled. $16.07 +$ in. *Ans.*

PAGE 259

1. $4 : 1$.

2. $27\sqrt{3}$ sq. in. or $46.764 +$ sq. in.; $25.236 +$ sq. in.

PAGE 261

1. 88 in.   **6.** $.0993 +$ in.   **11.** $r = 9$.

2. 66 in.   **7.** Two places.   **12.** $2 : 3$ (§ 381).

3. 11 ft.   **8.** $r = 14$ in.   **13.** $5 : 7$.

4. $7\frac{7}{8}$ yd.   **9.** $r = 2.1$ in.   **14.** $7\frac{1}{4}$ in.

5. $10\frac{1}{2}$ ft.   **10.** $r = \frac{1}{4}$ in.   **15.** $9\frac{1}{4}$ in.

16. $\frac{117}{360} \times 44$ in. $=$ 14.3 in. *Ans.*

17. $2\frac{281}{360}$ in.   18. 8.

19. Circf. $=$ 132 in. $\frac{33}{132}$ of 360° $=$ 90°. *Ans.*

20. $22\frac{1}{2}$°.   21. $152\frac{4}{11}$°.   22. 3.

PAGE 262

1. Make the arc greater than a semicircle.

PAGE 264

1. 616 sq. in.

2. 346.5 sq. in.

3. .000616 sq. ft.

4. .0616 sq. in.

5. $5\frac{211}{224}$ sq. in.

6. $7\frac{1}{14}$ sq. in.

7. $\dfrac{22a^2}{7}$ sq. ft.

8. $\dfrac{11a^2}{224}$ sq. ft.

9. 2464 sq. ft.

10. .1386 sq. in.

11. $\frac{504}{1331}$ sq. in.

12. $1018\frac{2}{7}$.

13. 40.26 sq. in.

14. 100 : 1; 10 : 1; 10 : 1.

15. 4 times (§ 393).

16. $56\frac{2}{7}$ in.

17. 21.

18. $4b$.

19. 20.

20. 5.64 $+$ sq. ft.

PAGE 265

21. $102\frac{1}{4}$ sq. in.; $136\frac{2}{3}$ sq. in.; $35\frac{11}{14}$ sq. in.

22. πb^2; $\dfrac{\pi b^2}{4}$; $4\pi b^2$.

23. $\dfrac{\pi R^2}{4}$; $4\pi R^2$; $3\pi R^2$.

24. $\dfrac{\pi R^2}{16}$; $\dfrac{\pi R^2}{2}$; $\dfrac{\pi R^2}{8}$.

25. 9.00 $+$ in.

26. Measure the circumference of the pipe and divide the result by π.

27. Circf. of the first wheel $=$ 6 times the circf. of the second. $\therefore$ 6 $\times$ 120 $=$ 720. *Ans.* 300 $\div$ 6 $=$ 50. *Ans.*

28. It becomes $\frac{9}{4}$ of what it was (since $(1\frac{1}{2})^2 : 1^2 = \frac{9}{4} : 1$).

29. $3^3 : x^3 = 1 : 2$. $\therefore x = 3\sqrt[3]{2} = 4.24 +$. $\therefore 4\frac{1}{4}$ in. *Ans.*

30. $\overline{12}^2 : \overline{18}^2 = 2^2 : 3^2 = 4 : 9$. $\therefore 40,000 \times \frac{9}{4} = 90,000$. *Ans.*

31. (1) $\frac{9}{16}$ of 50,000 lb. $=$ 28,125 lb. *Ans.*

    (2) $1 : x^3 = 50,000 : 150,000$. $\therefore x^3 = 3$. $\therefore 1.732 +$ in. *Ans.*

82 PLANE GEOMETRY

PAGE 266

1. A line $\perp$ to both the given lines (§§ 137, 100).

2. Diagonal $= \sqrt{12^2 + 5^2}$ ft. $= 13$ ft. long. *Ans.*

PAGE 267

3. Side of square $= \frac{1}{8}$ mi. $\therefore$ Area $= \frac{1}{64}$ sq. mi. $= 10$ acres. Radius of circle $= \frac{7}{88}$ mi. $\therefore$ area of circle $= \frac{7}{363}$ sq. mi. $= 12\frac{8}{11}$ acres. $\therefore$ $2\frac{8}{11}$ acres. *Ans.*

4. 36 sq. in. In the second $\triangle$, alt. $= 3\sqrt{3}$. $\therefore K = 18\sqrt{3}$ sq. in. $= 31.176 +$ sq. in.

5. 200 ft., 2400 sq. ft.; 200 ft., 2500 sq. ft.

6. $6.928 +$ sq. in.; 9 sq. in.; $10.392+$ sq. in.; $11.45 +$ sq. in.

For, by Ex. 4, p. 242, $a = 4$. $\therefore K$ of $\triangle = \dfrac{16\sqrt{3}}{4} = 6.928+$.

By § 362, K of a regular hexagon, whose side is a, $= \dfrac{6a^2\sqrt{3}}{4} = \dfrac{3a^2\sqrt{3}}{2}$. $\therefore K$ of given hexagon $= \dfrac{3 \times 2^2\sqrt{3}}{2} = 6\sqrt{3} = 10.392+$.

For method of finding area of $\odot$ see Ex. 9, p. 264.

7. $22.33+$ in.; $19.593+$ in.; $17.05+$ in. By Ex. 4, p. 242, in given $\triangle$, $\dfrac{a^2\sqrt{3}}{4} = 24$. $\therefore a = 7.43+$. Side of square $= \sqrt{24} = 4.899+$. For circle, $\pi R^2 = 24$. $\therefore R = \sqrt{\dfrac{84}{11}}$, etc.

1. (Group 76). One; three.

2. Four; five. 3. Six.

4. Seven; eight; n; an infinite number.

5. *A B D E H I M O T U V W X Y.*

PAGE 268

1. No; yes. 2. No; yes.

3. Regular polygons of an even number of sides have a center of symmetry; regular polygons of an odd number of sides do not.

4. Yes.

6. Two (the diagonals); yes.

7. One diagonal; no, except when the figure is a rhombus.

8. Draw any iine through this point and terminated by the perimeter. Show that it is bisected (§ 80).

9. Diameter $\perp$ the chord of the segment.

10. No; no.   **12.** Line of centers.

11. Two; yes.   **13.** $I\,N\,O\,X\,Z;\ o\,s\,x\,z.$

1. (Group 78).   §§ 367, 235, 304.

2. Circumscribe a circle about the given pentagon (§ 367). $\angle KBC \overset{m}{=} \frac{1}{2}\widehat{EDC},$ and $\angle BKC \overset{m}{=} \frac{1}{2}(\widehat{AE} + \widehat{BC}).$ $\therefore \angle KBC = \angle BKC,$ etc.

3. Find side of $\triangle$ is $r\sqrt{3}$ (see Ex. 9, p. 253), etc.

4. $2r^2 - \dfrac{3\sqrt{3}r^2}{4}$ or $r^2(2 - \tfrac{3}{4}\sqrt{3}).$

PAGE 269

5.

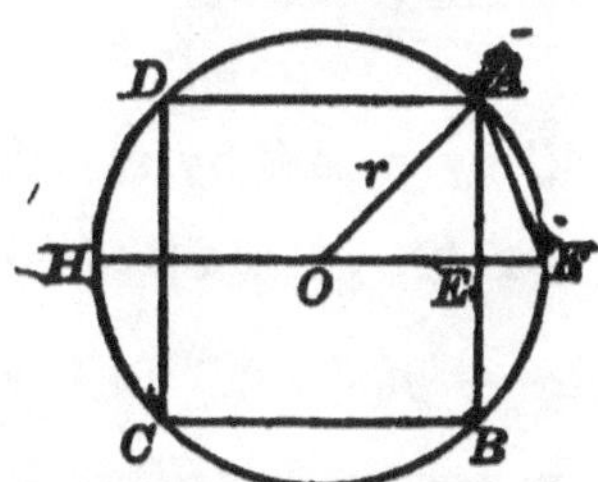

In the circle O, let $ABCD$ be an inscribed square, and F the midpoint of the arc AB. $\therefore$ chord AF = side of inscribed regular octagon (§ 361). $OE = \sqrt{r^2 - \overline{AE}^2} = \sqrt{r^2 - \dfrac{r^2}{2}} = \dfrac{r}{2}\sqrt{2}.$

$\therefore EF = r - \dfrac{r}{2}\sqrt{2}.$

Then, by § 320, $AF = \sqrt{HF \times EF} = \sqrt{2r\left(r - \dfrac{r}{2}\sqrt{2}\right)}$

$$= r\sqrt{2\left(1 - \dfrac{\sqrt{2}}{2}\right)} = r\sqrt{2 - \sqrt{2}}. \quad Ans.$$

6. Follow the method used in Ex. 5.

7. See Ex. 11, p. 252.   Side $= \sqrt{\dfrac{a^2}{4} + \dfrac{a^2}{4}} = \dfrac{1}{2}a\sqrt{2}.$ Ans.

8. $1:3.$

9. The squares formed include between them six equilateral $\triangle$ each of whose sides is b. $\therefore$ area of dodecagon $= (3\sqrt{3} + 6)b^2.$

10. § 393.

11.

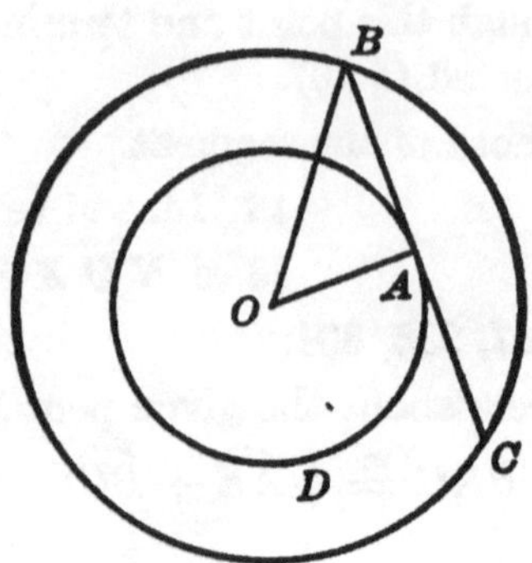

Let OAD and OBC be the two circles forming the circular ring. Denote the radius of the larger circle by R and that of the smaller circle by r. $\therefore$ area of ring $= \pi(R^2 - r^2)$. But in the right $\triangle$ OAB, $\overline{OB}^2 - \overline{OA}^2 = \overline{AB}^2$, *i.e.*, $R^2 - r^2 = \overline{AB}^2$. $\therefore$ area of ring $= \pi\overline{AB}^2$, etc.

12. Denote AB by q, BC by p, AC by r. The sum of the crescents

$$= \triangle ABC + AcB + BdC - AaBbC = \frac{1}{2}pq + \frac{\pi q^2}{8} + \frac{\pi p^2}{8} - \frac{\pi r^2}{8}$$

($\S 390$) $= \frac{1}{2}pq + \frac{\pi}{8}(q^2 + p^2 - r^2)$. But $r^2 = p^2 + q^2$ ($\S 355$).

$\therefore$ sum of crescents $= \frac{1}{2}pq = \triangle ABC$.

13. $\therefore$ in like manner side $BC =$ side $DE =$ side $AB =$ side $DC =$ side AE. (Use $\S\S 235, 357$, Ax. 3, $\S 200$.)

14. Prove the right $\triangle$ thus formed equal by $\S 216$, Ax. 5, $\S 111$.

15. Denote the center by O. Then $PT = PQ$ (Hyp.), $PA = PB$ ($\S 216$). $\therefore$ $AT = BQ$ (Ax. 3). $\therefore$ rt. $\triangle OAT =$ rt. $\triangle OBQ$ ($\S 79$). $\therefore$ $\angle T = \angle Q$ ($\S 216$, Ax. 4). Similarly, $\angle Q = \angle S = \angle P = \angle R = \angle T$.

PAGE 270

1. Denote the radii of the given circles by R and r. Then the new radius $= R + r$.

2. The new radius $= R - r$.

3. The new radius $= \sqrt{R^2 + r^2}$. See Ex. 1, p. 243.

4. New radius $= \sqrt{R^2 - r^2}$. See Ex. 2, p. 243.

5. The trees must be arranged at the vertices of a regular octagon of which each side is 20 ft. By Ex. 5, p. 269, $20 = r\sqrt{2 - \sqrt{2}}$, whence $r = 10 \sqrt{2 + 2\sqrt{2}}$. Hence, if a circle is described with a radius of one inch, and a regular octagon is inscribed in the circle, the drawing will answer the given conditions and have a scale of 1 in. to $10 \sqrt{2 + 2\sqrt{2}}$ ft.

6. Let x be the radius of the new circle. Then $\pi x^2 : \pi r^2 = 1 : 2$.
$$\therefore x = r \frac{\sqrt{2}}{2}, \text{ etc.}$$

7. Produce the radii of the given sector, and draw a tangent at the midpoint of the arc of the sector. Inscribe a $\odot$ in the $\triangle$ thus formed (§ 259).

8. Construct any square, and join the midpoint of one side of the square with a vertex which is not one of the extremities of the side taken. At the midpoint of the chord of the given segment construct an $\angle = \angle$ formed between the line drawn in the square and the side of the square whose midpoint is taken, etc.

9. Draw the bisectors of the three $\angle$ of the given $\triangle$. In each $\triangle$ thus formed inscribe a $\odot$ (§ 259).

10. Divide the given $\odot$ into three equal sectors (§ 362), and inscribe a circle in each sector (Ex. 7).

11. Draw lines from the center of the given square $\perp$ sides, and also to the vertices. Bisect the $\angle$ thus formed, etc.

12. Denote the radius of the given semicircle by R, and that of the required circle by x. Then $\pi x^2 = \frac{1}{2}\pi R^2$. $\therefore x^2 : R^2 = 1 : 2$.
$$\therefore x = \frac{\sqrt{2}R}{2}.$$

1. (Group 80). $2\pi x + 2y = 2640$, $2x + y = 1000$. Hence, $x = 280$ ft., $2x = 560$ ft. *Ans.*

PAGE 271

2. Use § 385. $\dfrac{5\frac{1}{2}°}{180°}\left(\dfrac{22r}{7}\right) = 10$. $\therefore r = 110.8 +$ ft. *Ans.*

3. Limit of speed $= 5000 \times 12$ in. per minute. Circf. of wheel $= \frac{22}{7} \times 27$ in. $\therefore$ no. rev. per min. $= 60,000$ in. $\div (\frac{22}{7} \times 27$ in.) $= 707 +$. *Ans.*

5. Point of intersection of the diagonals of the square; point of intersection of the diagonals; center of the polygon; center.

6. Center of the square.

7. Ratio $= \dfrac{\pi(3^2)3}{\pi(6^2)6} = \dfrac{27}{216} = \dfrac{1}{8}$.　*Ans.*

8. The area of the circular ring which forms the cross-section of the hollow tube $= \pi(R^2 - r^2)$. Hence, the radius of a solid cylindrical beam having an equivalent cross-section would be $\sqrt{R^2 - r^2}$. Use law of strains stated in Ex. 7. Hence, ratio $=$

$$\frac{\pi(R^2 - r^2)\left(\dfrac{R^2 + r^2}{R}\right)}{\pi(R^2 - r^2)\sqrt{R^2 - r^2}} = \frac{\pi 7 \left(\dfrac{16 + 9}{4}\right)}{\pi 7(\sqrt{7})} = \frac{25}{4\sqrt{7}} = 2.36 + .\quad Ans.$$

PAGE 272

11. If $OA = r$, $OC = \dfrac{5r}{4}$. $\therefore$ area of square $= \dfrac{25r^2}{8}$, while the area of the circle is $\dfrac{22r^2}{7}$. Hence, the approximation described in Ex. 11 consists essentially in using $\dfrac{25}{8}$ as the value of π. To obtain the per cent of error, we have $\left(\dfrac{22}{7} - \dfrac{25}{8}\right) \div \dfrac{22}{7} = \dfrac{1}{56} \times \dfrac{7}{22}$ $= .0056 + .$ Hence, a little more than $\frac{1}{2}$ per cent. *Ans.*

PAGE 273

1. See § 364.

2. Radius; diameter; circumference.

3. It reduces the measurement of the area of a circle to the measurement of a single straight line.

4. After we have computed the ratio of the circumference to the diameter in any one circle, by the aid of Prop. IX we know the value of this ratio in every other circle without the labor of any further computation.
Prop. X reduces the measurement of the area of a regular polygon to the measurement of two straight lines, viz.: one side and the apothem.

PAGE 274

5. Circles aid (1) in the construction of regular polygons. See §§ 360, 361, 362, 364, 373, etc. (2) In determining whether a given polygon is regular. See § 359. (3) In proving the properties of regular polygons. See Ex. 2 (Group 78), p. 268.

6. (1) In proving properties of a single circle and, hence, of parts of a circle. §§ 379, 390, 394. (2) In proving properties of two or more circles. §§ 380, 382, 393.

7. § 376.

8. $d : d' = c : c'$; $r : r' = c : c'$; $K : K' = c^2 : c'^2$. (Use § 291.)

9. It is equal to it; $\frac{1}{4}$.

11. The polygons are similar (§ 376). $\therefore P : P' = a : a'$ (§ 317); also $r : r' = a : a'$ (§ 318). Ratio of apothems $= a : a'$ (§ 318). $K : K = a^2 : a'^2$ (§ 353).

12. §§ 357, 359, 360, 361, 362, 363, 364, 365, 367, 368, 369, 370, 372.

13. §§ 376, 377, 378.

14. §§ 382, 383, 384, 390, 391, 392, 397.

15. §§ 379, 380, 381, 393.

PAGE 284

1. $x = \sqrt{50^2 - 40^2}$ ft. $= 30$ ft. *Ans.*

2. $\sqrt{12^2 + 5^2} = 13$. *Ans.*

3. The altitude of an isosceles $\triangle$ bisects the base (§ 110). Hence, altitude $= \sqrt{5^2 - 4^2} = 3$. *Ans.*

4. See § 121. $\sqrt{17^2 - 15^2} = 8$. Hence, the other diagonal $= 16$. *Ans.*

5. Longest chord $=$ the diameter, or 10. The diameter through the given point is $\perp$ shortest chord (§§ 208, 136). $\therefore$ half of the shortest chord (§ 202) $= \sqrt{5^2 - 3^2} = 4$. $\therefore$ shortest chord $= 8$. *Ans.*

6. Use figure p. 118 (text-book). Let $OA = 25$ in., $AB = 48$ in. Then $AR = 24$ in. (§ 202). $\therefore OR = \sqrt{25^2 - 24^2}$ in. $= 7$ in. *Ans.*

7. Use figure p. 122 (text-book). Draw OD and OB. Let $CD = 12$ in., $OG = 5$ in., $AB = 10$ in. Then $GD = 6$ (§ 202). $\therefore OD = \sqrt{6^2 + 5^2}$ in. $= \sqrt{61}$ in. Also $FB = 5$ in. (§ 202). $\therefore OF = \sqrt{61 - 25}$ in. $= 6$ in. *Ans.*

8. $\sqrt{40^2 - 20^2} + \sqrt{40^2 - 30^2} = 61.09 +$. $\therefore 61.09 +$ ft. *Ans.*

9. Denote the hypotenuse by $2x$. Then the unknown leg $= x$. $\therefore 4x^2 - x^2 = 100$. $\therefore 2x = \dfrac{20\sqrt{3}}{3} = 11.547 +$. *Ans.*

10. Alt. $= \sqrt{36 - 9} = \sqrt{27} = 5.196 +.$ *Ans.*

11. The altitude bisects the base (§ 117). Denote a side of the given $\triangle$ by $2x$. Then $4x^2 - x^2 = 8^2$ (§ 355). $\therefore 2x = \dfrac{16\sqrt{3}}{3} = 9.237 +.$ *Ans.*

12. Denote a side of the square by x. Then $x^2 + x^2 = \overline{15}^2$. $\therefore x = \dfrac{15\sqrt{2}}{2} = 10.606 +.$ *Ans.*

13. Denote the hypotenuse by x. Then $9 - x =$ the other leg. $\therefore x^2 - (9 - x)^2 = 9.$ $\therefore x = 5, 9 - x = 4.$ *Ans.*

14. See Ex. 21, p. 174. The radius of the small auxiliary $\odot$ is 6 in. $-$ 1 in. $= 5$ in. $\therefore$ length of common tangent $= \sqrt{13^2 - 5^2}$ in. $= 12$ in. *Ans.*

15. See Ex. of § 410. Hence, $12 : 18 = x : 20 - x.$ $\therefore x = 8, 20 - x = 12.$ *Ans.*

16. See the figure of § 319. Let $AB = 6$, $BC = 8$. Then $AC = \sqrt{6^2 + 8^2} = 10$. Also $AF : AB = AB : AC$. $\therefore AF : 6 = 6 : 10$. $\therefore AF = 3.6.$ *Ans.* Similarly, $BC = 6.4.$ *Ans.* Also $AF : BF = BF : FC$ or $3.6 : BF = BF : 6.4.$ $\therefore BF = 4.8.$ *Ans.*

PAGE 285

17.

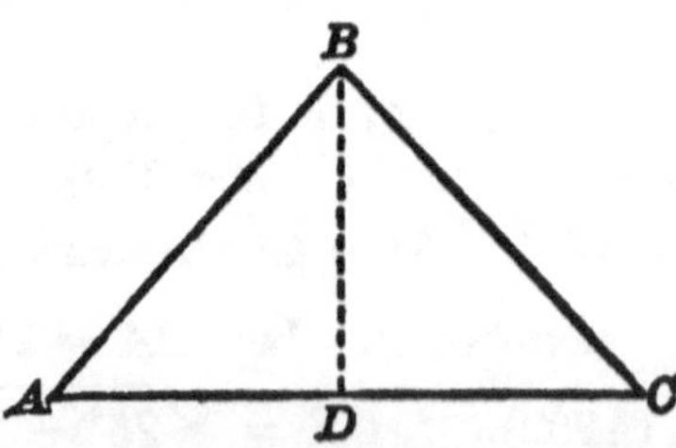

Let ABC be the triangle and BD the altitude. Then $AB = 16$, $BC = 17$, $BD = 15$, $AD = \sqrt{16^2 - 15^2} = \sqrt{31}$. Also $DC = \sqrt{17^2 - 15^2} = 8$. $\therefore AC = 13.567 +.$ *Ans.*

18. Denote the segments of the hypotenuse by x and $10 - x$. Then $x : 4 = 4 : 10 - x$ (§ 319). $\therefore x = 2, 10 - x = 8.$ The legs (by § 319) are $2\sqrt{5}$ or $4.472+$, and $4\sqrt{5}$ or $8.944+.$ *Ans.*

19. $\dfrac{22 \times 28 \times 3000}{7 \times 5280 \times 12}$ mi. $= 4\tfrac{1}{6}$ mi. *Ans.*

20. $c = \dfrac{8800}{1400}$ yd. $\quad d = \dfrac{c}{\pi} = \dfrac{8800 \times 7}{1400 \times 22}$ yd. $= 2$ yd. or 6 ft. *Ans.*

21. See § 385. $\quad 10.47 +; \; 14.49 +.$ *Ans.*

22. See § 385. Let $x =$ no. of degrees in the arc. $\quad \therefore 14 = \dfrac{x}{180°} \times \dfrac{22}{7} \times 6.$ $\quad \therefore x = 133\frac{7}{11}°.$ *Ans.*

23. See § 385. $\quad 12$ in. $= \dfrac{90°}{180°} \times \dfrac{22r}{7}.$ $\quad \therefore 2r = 15\frac{3}{11}$ in. *Ans.*

24. $2\pi R - 2\pi r = 132$ in. $- 88$ in. $\quad \therefore \dfrac{22}{7}(R - r) = 44$ in. $\quad \therefore R - r = 7$ in. *Ans.*

25. Velocity in miles per second $= \dfrac{44 \times 93,250,000}{7 \times 365\frac{1}{4} \times 24 \times 60 \times 60}$ mi. $= 18.5+$ mi.

26. The diagonal of the square $= \sqrt{5^2 + 5^2} = 5\sqrt{2}.$ Hence, the radius of the circumscribed circle $= \dfrac{5\sqrt{2}}{2} = 3.535+.$ Hence, $c = \dfrac{110\sqrt{2}}{7} = 22.223+.$ *Ans.*

27. Diagonal of the rectangle $= \sqrt{12^2 + 5^2} = 13.$ $\quad \therefore r = \frac{13}{2}.$ $\quad c = 13\pi = 40.857+.$ *Ans.*

28. Use § 385. Denote the central $\angle$ by x. Then $\dfrac{\pi x}{180°} + 2r = \pi r$ or $\dfrac{\pi x}{180°} + 2 = \pi.$ $\quad \therefore x = 65\frac{5}{11}°.$ *Ans.*

29. Denote a side of the square by x. $\quad \therefore x^2 + x^2 = 100$ (§ 355). $\quad \therefore x = 5\sqrt{2}.$ $\quad \therefore$ perimeter of square $= 20\sqrt{2}.$ $\quad \therefore 2\pi R = 20\sqrt{2}.$ $\quad \therefore R = 4.4997+.$ *Ans.*

30. $x(14 - x) = 8 \times 3$ (§ 323). $\quad \therefore x = 12$ or 2. *Ans.*

31.

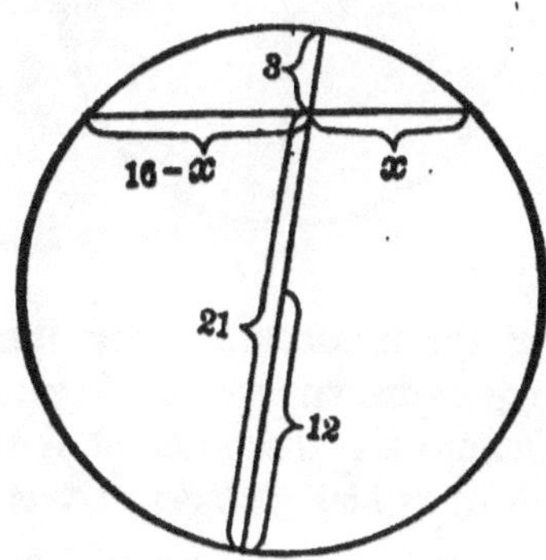

$x(16 - x) = 21 \times 3$ (§ 323). $\quad \therefore x = 9, 7.$ $\quad 16 - x = 7, 9.$ *Ans.*

32. Denote the external segment of the second secant by x. Then $27x = 6 \times 24$ (§ 325). $\therefore x = 5\frac{1}{3}$. *Ans.*

33. The entire secant $= 9 + 16$ or 25. Let $x =$ length of the tangent. $\therefore 25 \times 9 = x^2$. $\therefore x = 15$. *Ans.*

PAGE 286

34. The line drawn from the point to the center $(= x)$, the tangent, and the radius to the point of contact form a right $\triangle$. $\therefore x^2 = \overline{24}^2 + \overline{18}^2$. $\therefore x = 30$. *Ans.*

35.

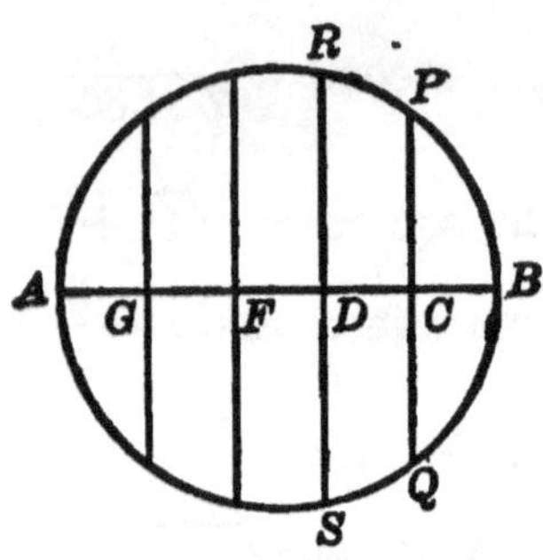

Let AB be the diameter and G, F, D, C the points of division. Then $AC = 48$, $CB = 12$. $\therefore PC = \sqrt{48 \times 12} = 24$ (§ 320), $PQ = 48$. Similarly, $RS = 24\sqrt{6}$ or $58.787 +$, etc.

36.

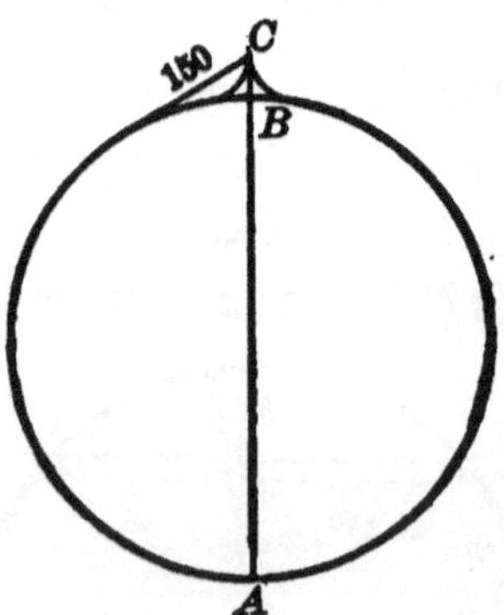

Let C be the top of the mountain. The limit of visibility is determined by the tangent drawn from the top of the mountain to the earth's surface. Denote the diameter of the earth by x. $\therefore AC = x + 3$. $\therefore 3(x + 3) = \overline{150}^2$ (§ 324). $\therefore x = 7497$ mi. *Ans.*

37. See Ex. 36. Denote the distance by x. But 100 ft. $= 0.019 +$ mi. $\therefore x^2 = 0.019\,(8000.019)$ mi. $\therefore x = 12.309 +$ mi. *Ans.*

38. The altitude of the upper $\triangle$ is 10. Hence, to find the base of the upper $\triangle$, 12 : 10 = 14 : line drawn (§ 316). $\therefore$ 11¾. *Ans.*

39.

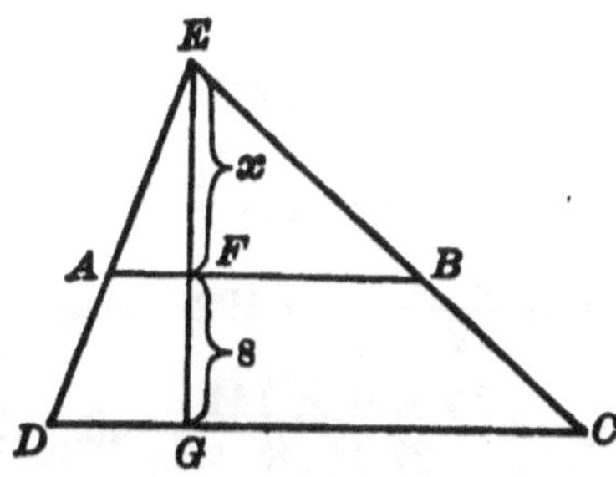

Let $ABCD$ be the trapezoid; let the legs produced meet in E, and EG be $\perp DC$. Denote EF by x. $\triangle AEB$ and DEC are similar (§ 304). $x : x + 8 = 12 : 20$ (§ 316). $\therefore x = 12.$ $\left.\begin{array}{c} x = 12. \\ x + 8 = 20. \end{array}\right\}$. *Ans.*

40. See solution of Ex. 39. $\dfrac{b_1 h}{b_2 - b_1}$, $\dfrac{b_2 h}{b_2 - b_1}$. *Ans.*

41. See formula 4 for h_c, p. 294. $\therefore \dfrac{21\sqrt{15}}{16}$ or 5.083 +. *Ans.*

42. See formula 5 for m_c, p. 294. $\therefore \frac{1}{2}\sqrt{106}$ or 5.147 +. *Ans.*

43. See formula 6 for t_c, p. 294. $\therefore \dfrac{21\sqrt{10}}{13}$ or 5.108 +. *Ans.*

44. See formulas for h_c, m_c, t_c, p. 294. The medians are $\frac{1}{2}\sqrt{673}$ or 12.971 +, $\frac{1}{2}\sqrt{592}$ or 12.165 +, $\frac{1}{2}\sqrt{505}$ or 11.236 +. The bisectors are $\dfrac{168\sqrt{5}}{29}$ or 12.953 +, $\frac{8}{5}\sqrt{65}$ or 12.093 +, $\dfrac{28\sqrt{13}}{9}$ or 11.217 +. The altitudes are 12$\frac{12}{13}$ or 12.923 +, 12, 11.2. *Ans.*

1. No. acres $= \dfrac{300 \times 200}{2 \times 43560} = 0.688+$. *Ans.*

2. Use Formula 5 (Areas), p. 294. 84. *Ans.*

3. Use Formula 5 (Areas), p. 294. 10 sq. ch. = 1 A. 203.33 + A. *Ans.*

4. Draw the altitude. Then alt. $= \sqrt{34^2 - 8^2}$, etc. 264.36+. *Ans.*

PAGE 287

5. Denote a side of the equilateral $\triangle$ by $2x$. Then $4x^2 - x^2 = 64$ (§ 355). $\therefore 2x = 9.236+$. Area $= 36.9504+$. *Ans.*

6. Denote a leg by x. $\therefore x^2 + x^2 = 144$ (§ 355). $\therefore x = 6\sqrt{2}$.

Area $= \dfrac{6\sqrt{2} \times 6\sqrt{2}}{2} = 36$. *Ans.*

7. Other leg $\sqrt{41^2 - 9^2} = 40$ (§ 356). $\therefore$ area $= 180$. *Ans.*

8. $\dfrac{b^2\sqrt{3}}{4} = 4\sqrt{3}.$ $\therefore b = 4$. *Ans.*

9. The no. of boards $= \dfrac{48 \times 24}{12 \times \frac{1}{2}} = 192$. *Ans.*

10. The no. of persons $= \dfrac{15 \times 9 \times 144}{27 \times 18} = 40$. *Ans.*

11. No. of acres $= \dfrac{90 \times 90}{43560} = 0.186-$. *Ans.*

12. See § 121. The diagonals divide the rhombus into four rt. ▲, each of which has 17 for the hypotenuse and 15 for a leg. $\therefore \frac{1}{2}$ of the other diagonal $= \sqrt{17^2 - 15^2} = 8$. $\therefore$ area $= 240$. *Ans.*

13.

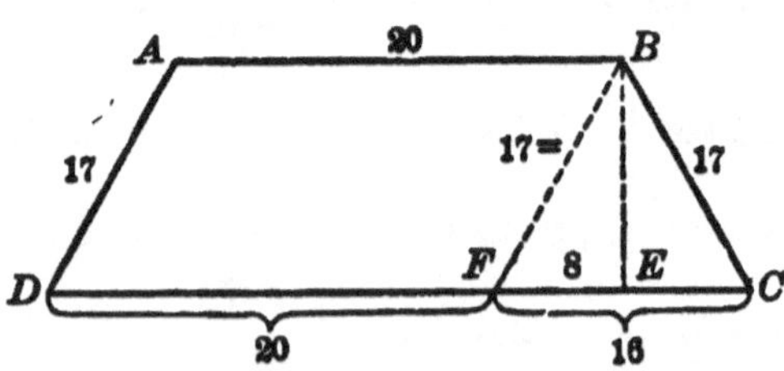

Let $ABCD$ be the trapezoid. Draw $BF \parallel AD$. $\therefore BFC$ is an isosceles $\triangle$ (§ 155). Draw its alt., BE. $\therefore BE = \sqrt{17^2 - 8^2} = 15$. $\therefore$ area $= 420$. *Ans.*

14. Denote the altitude of the upper $\triangle$ by x. $\therefore$ alt. of the trapezoid $= 18 - x$. Find, by use of similar ▲, base of upper $\triangle = \dfrac{10x}{9}$. $\therefore$ area of trapezoid $= \left(\dfrac{5x}{9} + 10\right)(18 - x) = 80$. $\therefore x = 13.42-$. $\therefore$ upper base $= 14.907+$. *Ans.*

15. Draw lines from the center of the circle to the vertices of the polygon. In all the ▲ thus formed the altitude is the same, viz.: the radius of the circle. $\therefore$ area of polygon $= \dfrac{20 \times 340}{2} = 3400$. *Ans.*

16. Denote the altitude by x. $\therefore (3x)\,x = 144$.

$\therefore x = 4\sqrt{3},$ or $6.928+$.

$3x = 12\sqrt{3},$ or $20.785+$. $\Big\}$ *Ans.*

17. Denote a side of the hexagon by x. Then $\dfrac{6x^2\sqrt{3}}{4} = 200$. $\therefore x = 8.77 +$ in. *Ans.*

18. By § 383, $c = 2\pi r$, or $p = 2\pi r$. $\therefore r = \dfrac{p}{2\pi}$. $\therefore K = \dfrac{\pi p^2}{4\pi^2} = \dfrac{p^2}{4\pi}$. (§ 390).

19. Denote the radius by x. $\therefore \pi x^2 = 81\pi + 1600\pi$. $\therefore x^2 = 1681$. $\therefore x = 41$ in. *Ans.*

20. $\pi x^2 = \pi(\overline{20}^2 + \overline{28}^2 + \overline{29}^2)$. $\therefore x = 45$. *Ans.*

21. See § 394. $K = \dfrac{80°}{360°} \times \dfrac{22 \times \overline{50}^2}{7} = 1746+$. *Ans.*

22. Area of a sector of $60° = \dfrac{60°}{360°} \times \dfrac{22 \times 2500}{7} = 1309.5238+$.

Area of an equilateral $\triangle$ of side $50 = \dfrac{\overline{50}^2\sqrt{3}}{4} = 1082.5319+$.

Area of a segment of $60° = 226.99 +$. *Ans.* Area of a segment of $300° =$ (area of the circle) $-$ (segment of $60°$) $= 7630.15 +$. *Ans.* A segment of $240°$ is cut off by the side of an inscribed equilateral $\triangle$ (segment AB). A side of $\triangle ABC$

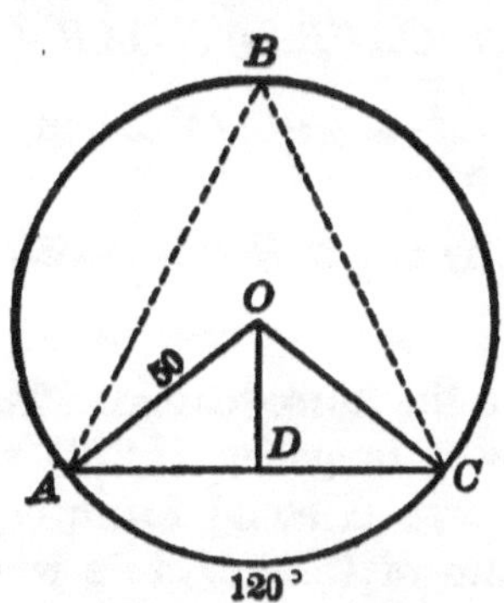

$= 50\sqrt{3} = AC$. $\therefore OD = 25$. $\therefore$ segment $ABCD =$ sector $ABCO + \triangle AOC = \tfrac{2}{3} \times \tfrac{22}{7} \times 2500 + \tfrac{1}{2} \times 50\sqrt{3} \times 25 = 6320.627+$. *Ans.*

23. See § 394. Denote the angle by x. Then $\dfrac{x^2}{360°} \times \dfrac{22}{7} \times 49 = 45$. $\therefore x = 105.2°$. *Ans.*

24. Side of inscribed square $= 10\sqrt{2}$. Sum of the segments $=$ (area of whole circle) $-$ (area of inscribed square) $= 100\pi - 200 = 114.28+$. *Ans.*

PAGE 288

25. $\frac{1}{2}$ mi. = 880 yd. $\therefore$ water area $= \dfrac{22}{4 \times 7}(\overline{880}^2 - \overline{100}^2) \times \dfrac{1}{4840}$ A.

= 124.09 + A. *Ans.*

26.

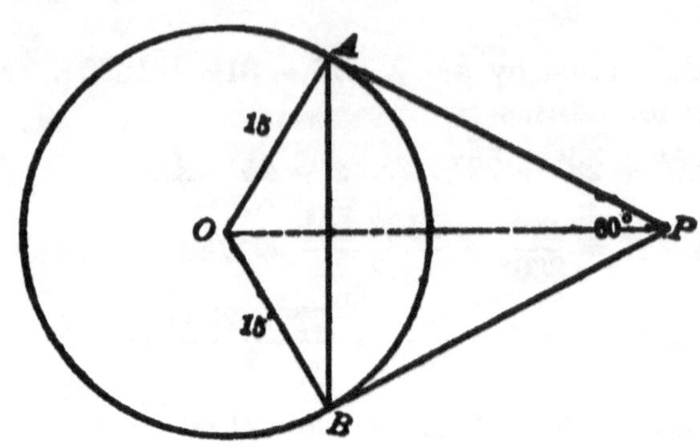

Let O be the center of the circle and PA and PB tangents. $\triangle ABP$ is isosceles ($PA = PB$, by § 216). $\therefore \angle PAB = 60° = \angle PBA$ (§ 102). $\therefore \angle OAB = 90° - 60° = 30° = \angle OBA$. $\therefore \angle AOB = 120°$. $\therefore AB$ is a side of an inscribed equilateral $\triangle$. $\therefore AB = 15\sqrt{3}$. $\therefore$ area $OAPB = \triangle OAB + \triangle ABP = \frac{1}{2} \times 15 \times \dfrac{15\sqrt{3}}{2} + \dfrac{\overline{15}^2 \times 3\sqrt{3}}{4} = 225\sqrt{3} = 389.71+$. *Ans.*

27. Denote the radius by x. $\therefore \frac{22}{7}x^2 = 43560$ sq. ft. $\therefore x = 117.7 +$ ft. *Ans.*

28. Join the centers of the three circles. The lines of centers pass through the points of tangency (§ 221) and form an equilateral $\triangle$. The included area is equal to an equilateral $\triangle$ whose side is $2r$, minus the sum of three sectors which together equal $\frac{1}{2}$ of one of the circles. $\therefore$ it $= \dfrac{(2r)^2\sqrt{3}}{4} - \dfrac{\pi r^2}{2} = r^2\left(\sqrt{3} - \dfrac{\pi}{2}\right)$.

29. The areas of the two similar $\triangle$ are to each other as the squares of any pair of corresponding altitudes (§§ 352, 316, 291). Denote the area of the entire $\triangle$ by K and of the upper by K'. $\therefore K : K' = \overline{18}^2 : 9^2 = 4 : 1$. But $K = 216$ sq. in. $\therefore K' = 54$ sq. in. *Ans.*

30. In this case K' must $= \frac{1}{2}K$. Denote the alt. of upper $\triangle$ by x. $\therefore K : \frac{1}{2}K = \overline{18}^2 : x^2$. $\therefore x = 9\sqrt{2}$ in., or $12.728-$ in. *Ans.*

31. Denote area of circle APB by $3K$. Denote area of circle ERF by K. Denote area of circle CQD by $2K$. $3K : K = \overline{30}^2 : \overline{EF}^2$

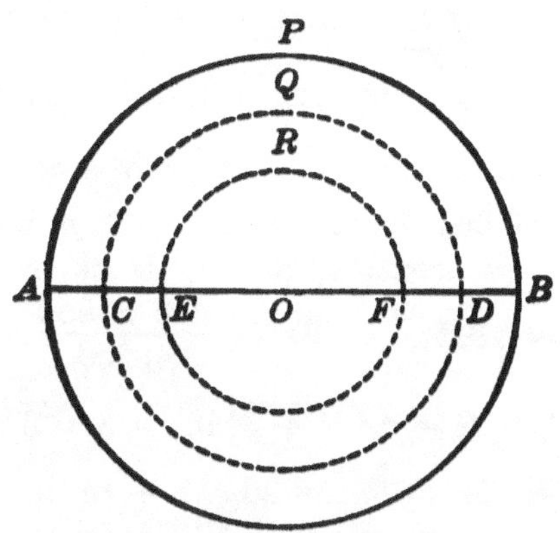

($\S$ 393). $\therefore EF = 10\sqrt{3}$ in. $= 17.320+$ in., also $3K : 2K = \overline{30}^2 : \overline{CD}^2$. $\therefore CD = 10\sqrt{6}$ in. $= 24.495-$ in. *Ans.*

1. Alt. $= \sqrt{\overline{10}^2 - 8^2} = 6$. $\therefore$ area $= 48$. *Ans.*

2. Area of $\triangle = 468$ by formula 5 (Areas), p. 294. Denote radius of the circle by x. Then $\pi x^2 = 468$. $\therefore x = 12.228 +$. *Ans.*

3. $6\sqrt{3}$, or $10.392+$.

4. 14 in.; 16 in.; 19 in.; $7\sqrt{2}$ in.; $8\sqrt{2}$ in.; $9\sqrt{2}$ in. (or $9.899+$ in., $11.313 +$ in., $12.727+$ in.). *Ans.*

5. See Ex. of $\S$ 41?. 9, 12. *Ans.*

6. By drawing the diagonal which does not cut the $\angle$ of 60°, the quadrilateral is divided into an equilateral and a rt. $\triangle$. $16.825+$. *Ans.*

7. Denote the diameter by x. Then $480 \times \pi x = 5280$ ft. $\therefore x = 3.5$ ft. *Ans.*

PAGE 289

8. $\dfrac{h}{2}(12 + 16) = 112$ ($\S$ 350). $\therefore h = 8$. *Ans.*

9. Denote the radius of the circle by x. $\therefore \pi x^2 = 100$ ($\S$ 390). $\therefore x = 5.6407+$. *Ans.*

10. $\pi x^2 = \dfrac{144\sqrt{3}}{4}$ ($\S$ 390 and Ex. 4, p. 242). $\therefore x = 4.4542-$. *Ans.*

11. $\pi x^2 = \frac{1}{2}(16 + 18)$ ($\S\S$ 390, 350). $\therefore x = 6.977+$. *Ans.*

12. For area of circle see Ex. 18, p. 287. $K = \dfrac{\overline{12}^2}{4\pi}$ sq. yd. $= 11.45+$ sq. yd. *Ans.* Area of square $= 3^2$ sq. yd. $= 9$ sq. yd. *Ans.* Area of eq. $\triangle = \dfrac{4^2\sqrt{3}}{3}$ sq. yd. $= 6.9282+$ sq. yd. *Ans.*

13. $400 : 125 = 360° : \angle$ of sector. $\therefore \angle$ of sector $= 112\tfrac{1}{2}°$. *Ans.*

14. Let $x =$ width of field included in ft. $6x =$ perimeter of running track in ft. $2x^2 =$ area included by track in sq. ft. But $6x = 2640$ ft. $\therefore x = 440$ ft. $\therefore 2x^2 = \dfrac{440 \times 880}{43560}$ A. $= 8.8+$ A. *Ans.*

15. $r = \dfrac{6 \text{ in.}}{2} = 3$ in. $R = \sqrt{3^2 + 3^2}$ in. $= 3\sqrt{2}$ in.

By § 390, $\left.\begin{array}{l}\pi r^2 = 9\pi \text{ sq. in.} = 28.285 + \text{ sq. in.} \\ \pi R^2 = 18\pi \text{ sq. in.} = 56.571 + \text{ sq. in.}\end{array}\right\}$ *Ans.*

16. Denote the other leg by x. Then $x + 8 =$ hypotenuse. $\therefore (x + 8)^2 = x^2 + \overline{12}^2$ (§ 355). $\therefore x = 5$. $\therefore$ area $= 30$. *Ans.*

17. Let $x =$ a leg of the $\triangle$. $\therefore x^2 + x^2 = \overline{20}^2$ (§ 355). $\therefore x = 10\sqrt{2}$. Area $= \tfrac{1}{2}(10\sqrt{2})^2 = 100$. *Ans.*

18. Use § 319. $16, 4\sqrt{5}, 8\sqrt{5}$ (or $16, 8.944+, 17.888+$). *Ans.*

19.

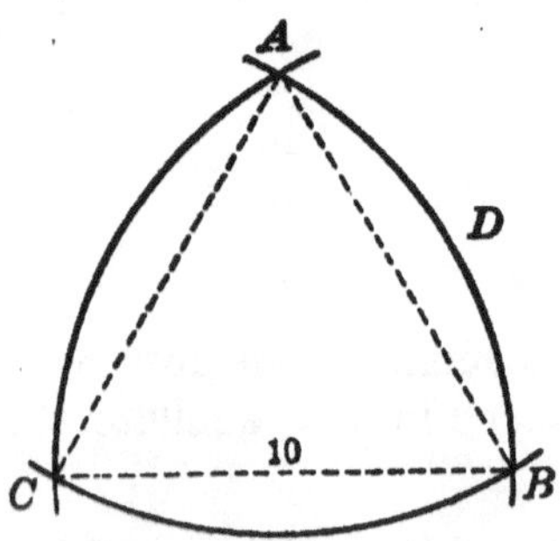

Let ABC be the given figure. Draw the chords of these arcs. These chords form an equilateral $\triangle$ whose side is 10 (§ 363). Area of $\triangle ABC = \dfrac{\overline{10}^2\sqrt{3}}{4} = 43.301+$. Area segment $ABD =$ sector $ACBD - \triangle ABC = \dfrac{\pi \overline{10}^2}{6} - 43.301 + = 9.07+$. $\therefore$ required area $= \triangle ABC + 3$ segment $ADB = 70.5403+$. *Ans.*

20. $\sqrt{43560} = 208.7 -$. $\therefore$ perimeter of square field $= 834.841+$ ft. For circle $43560 = \pi R^2$. $\therefore R = \sqrt{\dfrac{43560}{\pi}}$. $\therefore C = 2\pi\sqrt{\dfrac{43560}{\pi}} =$

$2 \sqrt{\pi} \sqrt{43560}$ ft. $= 740.016+$ ft. $\therefore$ difference $= (834.841 - 740.016 +)$ ft. $= 94.83+$ ft. *Ans.*

21. Area is doubled (§ 345); is doubled (§ 345); quadrupled (§ 346).

22. Denote the side of the $\triangle$ by x; then $\dfrac{x^2 \sqrt{3}}{4} = \dfrac{100\pi}{4}$. $\therefore x = 13.47-$. *Ans.*

23.

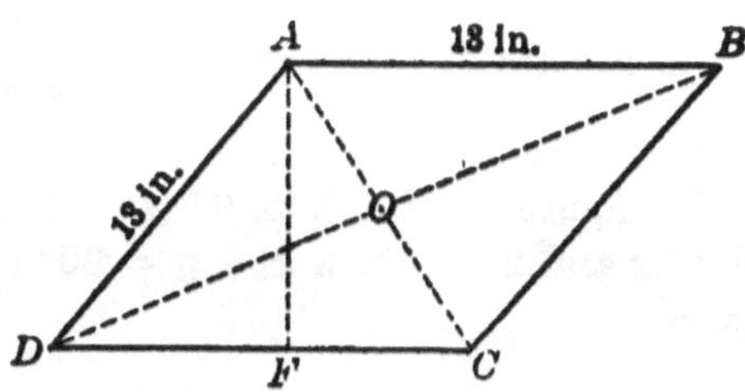

Let $ABCD$ be the given rhombus and AF its altitude. Then $AF \times 13$ in. $= 156$ sq. in. $\therefore AF = 12$ in. $\therefore DF = \sqrt{13^2 - 12^2}$ in. $= 5$ in. $\therefore FC = 13$ in. $- 5$ in. $= 8$ in. In the rt. $\triangle AFC$, $AC = \sqrt{12^2 + 8^2}$ in. $= 4\sqrt{13}$ in. $= 14.422+$ in. *Ans.* Area of rhombus $= 156$ sq. in. $= \dfrac{AC \times DB}{2} = 2\sqrt{13}$ in. $\times DB$. $\therefore DB = \dfrac{156 \text{ in.}}{2\sqrt{13}} = 6\sqrt{13}$ in. $= 21.633+$ in. *Ans.*

PAGE 290

1. Alt. $= 8$ dm. $\therefore K = 64$ sq. dm. (§ 343). *Ans.*

2. The sides are 6 m., 7 m., 8 m. $\therefore$ by Formula 5 (Areas), p. 294, $K = \frac{21}{4}\sqrt{15}$ sq. m. $= 20.333+$ sq. m. *Ans.*

3. $R = 1.4$ m. $\therefore K = \pi 1.4^2$ sq. m. $= 6.16 +$ sq. m. *Ans.*

4. The other leg $= \sqrt{17^2 - 15^2}$ dm. $= 8$ dm. $\therefore K = 60$ sq. m. *Ans.*

5. See Ex. 18, p. 287. 7.9545 $+$ sq. dm. *Ans.*

6. $K = \pi 100^2$ sq. m. $= \frac{10000}{10000}\pi$. Ha. $= \pi$. Ha. $= 3.1428 +$ Ha. *Ans.* 3.14 Ha. $= (3.14 +)(2.471 +)$A. $= 7.7659+$ A. *Ans.*

7. The side $= 8$ dm. $\therefore$ other side $= \sqrt{35^2 - 8^2}$ dm. $= 34.07 +$ dm. Area $= 2.7258 +$ sq. m. $= 4225.09 +$ sq. in. *Ans.*

8. The bases are 6 m. and 2 m., and the alt. is 8 m. $\therefore K = 32$ sq. m. *Ans.*

9. The dimensions are 70 m. and 200 m. $\therefore K = 1.4$ Ha. $= 3.459 +$ A. *Ans.*

10. 9 dm. and 4 dm. *Ans.*

11. Side of square $= 18$ in. $\therefore$ area of square $= 324$ sq. in. $\therefore \pi R^2$ $= 324$ sq. in. $\therefore R = \sqrt{\dfrac{324}{\pi}}$ in. $\therefore R$ in dm. $= \dfrac{10}{39.37}\sqrt{\dfrac{324}{\pi}}$ dm. $= 2.578 +$ dm. *Ans.*

12. Circf. of wheel in meters $= \dfrac{10000}{5000}$ m. $= 2$ m. $\therefore$ diameter of wheel $= \dfrac{2}{\pi}$ m. Diameter of wheel in feet $= \dfrac{2 \times 39.37}{\pi \times 12} = 2.087 +$ ft. *Ans.*

1. (Group 86). Use figure of Ex. 8, p. 97 (text-book). Denote the given adj. $\measuredangle$ by $2x$ and $2y$. Then $x + y = 90°$ (Hyp.). $\therefore 2x + 2y = 180°$ (Ax. 4).

2. Use § 80.

PAGE 291

3. With the center of the given $\odot$ as a center and the given distance as a radius, describe a circle. From the given point draw a tangent to this circle. (§ 264), etc.

4.

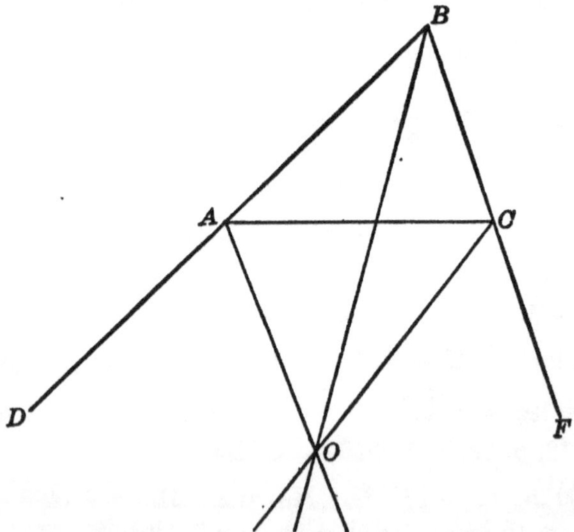

Let $\angle ABO = \angle OBC$, and $\angle ACO = \angle OCF$. It is required to show that $\angle BOC = \frac{1}{2} \angle BAC$. Let $p = \angle ABO = \angle OBC$, $q = \angle BAC$, $r = \angle BCA$, $x = \angle BOC$. Then in $\triangle BOC$, $x + p + r + \frac{1}{2} \angle ACF = 180°$ (§ 102). Also in $\triangle ABC$, $2p + q + r = 180°$ (§ 102). But $\angle ACF = 2p + q$ (§ 103). $\therefore \frac{1}{2} \angle ACF = p + \frac{1}{2}q$ (Ax. 5). By Axs. 1 and 9, $x + p + r + p + \frac{1}{2}q = 2p + q + r$. $\therefore x = \frac{1}{2}q$ (Ax. 3).

5. Radius of inscribed $\odot$ = 9 in., of circumsc. $\odot$ = 9 $\sqrt{2}$ in., etc.

6. Denote $\overset{\frown}{DB}$ by x, and $\overset{\frown}{BC}$ by y. Then $74° = \frac{1}{2}(x + 108°)$ ($\S$ 240). $\therefore$ $x = 40°$. Similarly, $106° = \frac{1}{2}(y + 112°)$. $\therefore$ $y = 100°$. $\angle ADB$ = $104°$ ($\S$ 235), etc.

7. A straight line which is the $\perp$ bisector of the line of centers. Use $\S\S$ 221, 123.

8. Use Ax. 5, $\S\S$ 82, 79, 23, 24.

9. Two pairs. See figure of $\S$ 322. (Draw chords DB and AC.) $\therefore$ $\triangle DFB$ and AFC are mutually equiangular ($\S$ 235) and similar ($\S$ 304). Likewise $\triangle DFA$ and BFC are similar.

10. Area of trapezoid = 44 sq. in. Area of square = 64 sq. in. To find per cent wasted, $\frac{80}{168}$ = .357+. $\therefore$ 35.7 + per cent. *Ans.*

11. Draw AF. $\triangle ABF = \triangle AFE$ ($\S$ 117). $\therefore$ $BF = FE$. Then prove $FE = EC$, by showing $\angle ECF = 45° = \angle EFC$ ($\S\S$ 82, 102, 114).

12. Draw the radius to the point of contact. Thus a rt. $\triangle$ is formed ($\S$ 210) whose hypotenuse is 24 cm. and one leg of which is 12 cm. $\sqrt{24^2 - \overline{12}^2}$ cm. = 20.78+ cm. *Ans.*

13. 36°. By $\S$ 168, each $\angle$ of a regular pentagon = 108°, etc.

14. Let the diagonals intersect at O. Then $OP = OR$ (Ax. 3). $OQ = OS$ (Ax. 3), etc.

15. See Ex. 7, p. 284. 3 in. *Ans.*

16. Produce PD to meet the circle at F. Then $\overset{\frown}{BF} = \overset{\frown}{BP}$ ($\S$ 202). $\angle APB \overset{m}{=} \frac{1}{2}\overset{\frown}{BP}$ ($\S$ 241), $\angle BPF \overset{m}{=} \overset{\frown}{BF}$ ($\S$ 235), etc.

17. Reduces to $\S$ 255.

PAGE 292

18. Denote a leg of the given rt. $\triangle$ by x. Then $\dfrac{x^2}{2}$ = 1296 sq. in. ($\S$ 343). $\therefore$ $x = 50.91$ + in. *Ans.*

19. Let h = altitude of the given $\triangle$. Then h is a constant ($\S$ 343). Hence, the locus is two lines $\parallel$ base of given $\triangle$ and at the distance h from this base.

20. In the $\triangle ACF$ and DCB, $DC = AC$ (sides of same square), $CF = CB$ (same reason), $\angle ACF = \angle BCD$ (each = $\angle ACB$ + 1 rt. $\angle$), etc. Use $\S$79.

21. Let $ABCD$ be the given quadrilateral and BP and PC the bisectors of the $\triangle ABC$, BCD. Denote each half of $\angle ABC$ by a, and each half of $\angle BCD$ by b. Then $2 \angle a + 2 \angle b + \angle D + \angle A = 360°$ (§ 167). Also $\angle a + \angle b + \angle P = 180°$ (§ 102). $\therefore 2 \angle a + 2 \angle b + \angle D + \angle A = 2 \angle a + 2 \angle b + 2 \angle P$, etc.

22. Let AP and QB intersect in R outside the given circle.

$$\therefore \angle R \overset{m}{=} \tfrac{1}{2}(\widehat{AQ} - \widehat{BP}) \ (§ 242).$$

$$\overset{m}{=} \tfrac{1}{2}(\widehat{AQ} + \widehat{AP} - \widehat{AP} - \widehat{BP}).$$

$$\overset{m}{=} \tfrac{1}{2}(180° - \widehat{AB}) = \text{a constant.}$$

Hence, if on the chord AB a segment of a circle is constructed which shall contain $\angle R$ (§ 265), the arc of the segment is the locus of R.

In like manner if AP and BQ intersect inside the circle it may be shown that $\angle ARB \overset{m}{=} \tfrac{1}{2}(180° + \widehat{AB})$.

23. Arc of $22\tfrac{1}{2}° = \dfrac{3\pi}{2}$; but $22\tfrac{1}{2}° = \tfrac{1}{16}(360°)$. $\therefore$ arc of $360° = 16\left(\dfrac{3\pi}{2}\right)$
$= 24\pi$.
Hence, $2\pi r = 24\pi$. $\therefore r = 12$. $\therefore \pi r^2 = 452\tfrac{2}{5}$. Hence, $452\tfrac{2}{5}$ ft. *Ans.*

24. Denote the radii of the given circles by x and y. Then $\pi x^2 + \pi y^2 = 20$ sq. yd. $\pi x^2 - \pi y^2 = 15$ sq. yd., etc. $\therefore x = 2.359 +$ yd. $y = 0.891 +$ yd. *Ans.*

25. This problem reduces to one of constructing a right $\triangle$, given the hypotenuse (viz.: a side of the required square) and the sum of the legs (viz.: a side of the given square). See Ex. 14, p. 170.

26. Draw the diagonals of the $\square$ and from their point of intersection draw a $\perp$ to same line. Then the sum of the $\perp$s from either pair of vertices of the $\square =$ twice the $\perp$ from the point of intersection of the diagonals (Ex. 7, p. 213).

27. If the centers of the two circles are joined with each other and also with the points where the two circles intersect, two equilateral triangles are formed in each of which a side is r, the radius of each circle.

Hence, sum of areas of the two $\triangle = \dfrac{r^2 \sqrt{3}}{2}$ (Ex. 4, p. 242). The remainder of the area common to the two circles is four segments of $60°$ each in a circle with radius r. Area of one segment $=$ sector of $60° -$ one of the $\triangle = \dfrac{\pi r^2}{6} - \dfrac{r^2 \sqrt{3}}{4} = \dfrac{2\pi r^2 - 3r^2 \sqrt{3}}{12}$.

Hence, area common to the two circles

$$= \frac{r^2 \sqrt{3}}{2} + \frac{4(\,^?\pi r^2 - 3r^2 \sqrt{3})}{12} = \frac{4\pi r^2 - 3r^2 \sqrt{3}}{6}. \quad \textit{Ans.}$$

28. $\pi r^2 = 80.$ $\therefore r = \sqrt{\tfrac{280}{11}}.$

Arc of $80° = (\tfrac{2}{9}) \tfrac{44}{7} \sqrt{\tfrac{280}{11}} = \tfrac{8}{63} \sqrt{280 \times 11} = 7.04+.$ *Ans.*

29. See Ex. 3, p. 241. Denote the radius of the inscribed circle by r.
$\therefore K = \tfrac{1}{2}(a + b + c)r.$

$$\therefore r = \frac{2K}{a + b + c} = \frac{2 \sqrt{s(s - a)(s - b)(s - c)}}{a + b + c},$$

where $s = \tfrac{1}{2}(a + b + c)$. (See formula 5 under areas, p. 294.)

30.

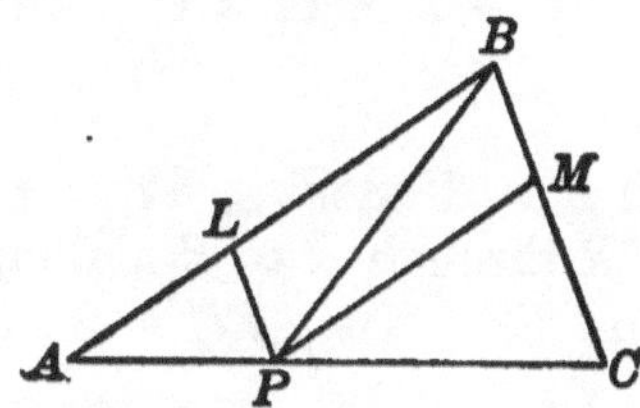

Let $PLBM$ be the resulting $\square$. $\therefore AL : LB = AP : PC = 2 : 3$
(§ 293). $\therefore \triangle ABP = \tfrac{2}{5} \triangle ABC$ (§ 345). $\therefore \triangle LBP = \tfrac{3}{5} \triangle$
$ABP = \tfrac{6}{25} \triangle ABC.$ $\square LBMP = 2 \triangle LBP = \tfrac{12}{25} \triangle ABC.$ Hence,
$12 : 25.$ *Ans.*

31. Let F be the midpoint of BE. From D draw $DH \parallel BE$ and
meeting AB at H. Let K be the midpoint of HD. Then the
locus is the broken line $CFKA$.

PAGE 293

32. Add $\triangle ECD$ to each of the equivalent $\triangle$. $\therefore$ $\triangle BCD$ and ACD
are equivalent. Since these $\triangle$ have the same base, CD, they must
have equal altitudes, etc.

33. Let x be the exact diameter in inches of the required pipe. Then
$2^2 : x^2 = 2 : 3.$ $\therefore x = \sqrt{6} = 2.76 + (§ 393).$ $\therefore 3$ in. pipe. *Ans.*

PAGE 297

1. Denote the projection by x, then by §§ 102, 355, $x^2 + x^2 = 10^2$. $\therefore x = 5\sqrt{2}$. *Ans.*

2. Use an equilateral $\triangle$ whose side is 10. The altitude bisects the base. $\therefore$ projection = 5. *Ans.*

3. $\frac{1}{2}a$. See Ex. 2.

PAGE 298

1. $2\sqrt{31}$ (or $11.135+$). For $\angle BCD = 60°$. $\therefore CD = 5$ (see Ex. 3, p. 297).

2. $\frac{4}{5}$. For $\overline{20}^2 = \overline{14}^2 + \overline{12}^2 + 2 \times 12 \times CD$, etc.

3. $\frac{1}{4}$.

4. Produce PR through R to T making $RT = \frac{1}{3}$ of 300 yd., or = 100 yd. Also produce QR through R to S making $RS = \frac{1}{3}$ of 219 yd. or = 73 yd. Measure TS. Then $PQ = 3\,TS$.

PAGE 299

1. $2\sqrt{31}$ (or $11.135+$). For $DC = 5$ (see Ex. 3, p. 297). $\therefore \overline{AB}^2 = \overline{10}^2 + \overline{12}^2 - 2 \times 12 \times 5 = 124$.

PAGE 300

2. Obtuse (see § 417).   3. Acute (see § 418).

4. Obtuse. Acute. Right. Acute.

---

1. $\angle P = 54° - 27° = 27°$. $\therefore BP = AB = 3\frac{1}{4}$ mi. *Ans.*

2. Use § 417 and find $\overline{AP}^2 = (\frac{13}{4})^2 + (\frac{13}{4})^2 + 2\,(\frac{13}{4})\frac{13}{8}$. $\therefore AP = \frac{13}{4}\sqrt{3}$ mi. = 5.629 + mi. *Ans.*

3. Through S draw a straight line, TSP, along the bank of the stream so that $\angle RTS = \frac{1}{2} \angle RSP$. Measure TS. Then $RS = TS$.

4. Denote the point taken in the base by P. Draw the altitude BQ. Then, $\overline{BC}^2 = \overline{BP}^2 + \overline{PC}^2 - 2\,PQ \times PC$ (§ 418) $= \overline{BP}^2 + (PC - 2\,PQ)PC = \overline{BP}^2 + AP \times PC$.

5.

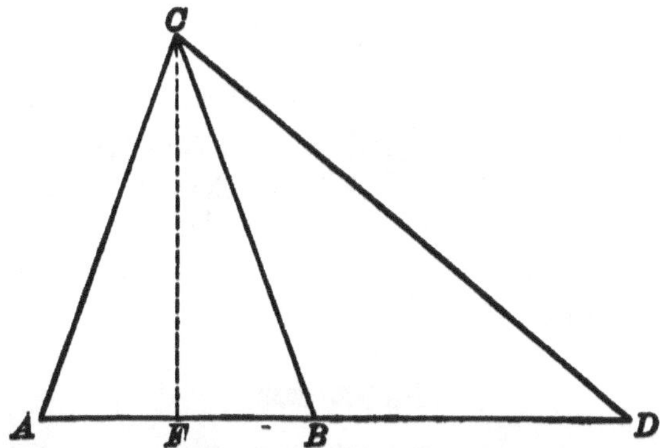

Draw $CF \perp AB$. Then $\overline{CD}^2 = \overline{BC}^2 + \overline{BD}^2 + 2\,BD \times FB$. But $AF = FB$ (§ 118). $\therefore 2\,BF = AB$. $\therefore \overline{CD}^2 = \overline{BC}^2 + \overline{BD}^2 + AB \times BD$ (Ax. 9) $= \overline{BC}^2 + BD\,(BD + AB) = \overline{BC}^2 + BD \times AD$.

6. Denote the hypotenuse by a, and the last leg by x. Then $\sqrt{a^2 - x^2}$ is the required leg, $a : \sqrt{a^2 - x^2} = \sqrt{a^2 - x^2} : x$. $\therefore a^2 - x^2 = ax$ (§ 278), etc. Use § 327.

7. By § 417, $\overline{AC}^2 = \overline{10}^2 + \overline{20}^2 + 2\,(20)\,5\sqrt{2} = 782.84+$.
$$\therefore AC = 27.97 + \text{ft.} \quad \textit{Ans.}$$

By § 418, $\overline{BD}^2 = \overline{10}^2 + \overline{20}^2 - 2\,(20)\,5\sqrt{2} = 217.16-$.
$$\therefore BD = 14.73 + \text{ft.} \quad \textit{Ans.}$$

8. Quote theorem of § 417.

PAGE 301

1.

$OL = \tfrac{1}{2}\sqrt{2}$. $\therefore LQ = 1 - \tfrac{1}{2}\sqrt{2}$. $\therefore$ by § 320
$$\overline{BQ}^2 = SQ \times LQ = 2\,(1 - \tfrac{1}{2}\sqrt{2}).$$
$\therefore BQ = .7653+$.
$\therefore$ perimeter of the inscribed octagon $= 6.1229+$ in. $\quad \textit{Ans.}$

PAGE 303

1. In the shape of a circle.　　　　**2.** $40A.$　$46.8 + A.$　$50.9 + A.$

3. $ARPQ$ is a $\square$ (Def.)　$\therefore \triangle QAR = \triangle QPR$ (§ 156).　$RC \parallel QP$, hence $\triangle PRC : \triangle QPR = RC : QP$ (§ 345).　$\triangle QPR : \triangle BQP = PR : BQ$ (§ 345).　But $\triangle BQP$ and PRC are similar (§§ 112, 304).　$\therefore RC : QP = RP : BQ$ (§ 312).　$\therefore \triangle PRC : \triangle QPR = \triangle QPR : \triangle BQP$ (Ax. 1).　But $\triangle QPR = \triangle QAR$, etc.

PAGE 306

1.

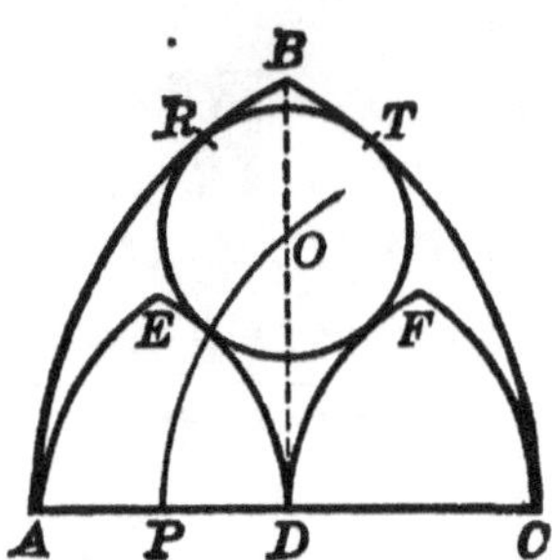

The line BD is the locus of the centers of all circles tangent to both AB and BC. For in § 221, if the points A and B come together as a point at which the two circles are tangent to each other, this point will be on OO'. Hence, in Ex. 1, if the circle O is tangent to AB and BC, $AO = AT - OT$. Also $CO = RC - RO$. $\therefore AO = CO$. $\therefore O$ is on BD (§ 120).

Also if P is the midpoint of AD, an arc described with C as a center and CP as radius is the locus of all circles tangent to both AB and DF (for every point in it is equidistant from the two arcs) (§ 188, Axs. 3, 5), etc.

2. $BD.$　No.　AED, DFC, RBT, the circle O.　The circle O.

3. Denote the base of the given rectangle by b, its altitude by h, the base of the required rectangle by b'. Then find a fourth proportional to b', b, and h (§ 297). This will be altitude of the required rectangle, etc.

PAGE 307

6. Point of intersection of the diagonals of the square.　Point of intersection of the diagonals of the rectangle.　Center of the circumscribed circle.　Center of the circle.

7. The centroid of the triangle (see Ex. 5, p. 306). Center of the circle circumscribed about the pentagon.

8. At the centroid of the triangle.　　10. Use §§ 114, 304.

9. Use §§ 112, 304.　　11. Use §§ 97, 304, etc.

13. Draw ⊥s from two opposite vertices of the parallelogram to the diagonal joining the other two vertices. Apply §§ 417, 418 to the four ▲ into which the parallelogram is divided, etc.

PAGE 308

17. Use §§ 95, 295.

19. Denote the base of the given △ by b and its altitude by h. Construct the mean proportional between b and $\frac{1}{2}h$ (§ 321). Construct a square which has this mean proportional as a side.

PAGE 309

23. Construct a △ equivalent to the given pentagon (see Ex. 21). Then use Ex. 19, p. 308.

25. In Ex. 2, change m into 2, and n into 3, etc.

27. Construct a regular pentagon (as by drawing the chords FD, DB, etc. in the diagram of Ex. 26) and draw its diagonals.

28. First construct a regular hexagon. Then draw its diagonals.

29. .00025 + %.　　30. .04 + %.

PAGE 310

31. Hence, construct a line which is a fourth proportional to 16, 19, and s. Then with H as a center and this line as a radius describe an arc intersecting BD, etc.

www.ingramcontent.com/pod-product-compliance
Lightning Source LLC
Chambersburg PA
CBHW031738180726
48283CB00005B/1571